# The World of William Clissold

## BY THE SAME AUTHOR
## ALL PUBLISHED BY HOUSE OF STRATUS

**FICTION**

ANN VERONICA
APROPOS OF DOLORES
THE AUTOCRACY OF MR PARHAM
BABES IN THE DARKLING WOOD
BEALBY
THE BROTHERS *AND* THE CROQUET PLAYER
BRYNHILD
THE BULPINGTON OF BLUP
THE DREAM
THE FIRST MEN IN THE MOON
THE FOOD OF THE GODS
THE HISTORY OF MR POLLY
THE HOLY TERROR
IN THE DAYS OF THE COMET
THE INVISIBLE MAN
THE ISLAND OF DR MOREAU
KIPPS: THE STORY OF A SIMPLE SOUL
LOVE AND MR LEWISHAM
MARRIAGE
MEANWHILE
MEN LIKE GODS
A MODERN UTOPIA
MR BRITLING SEES IT THROUGH
THE NEW MACHIAVELLI
THE PASSIONATE FRIENDS
THE SEA LADY
THE SHAPE OF THINGS TO COME
THE TIME MACHINE
TONO-BUNGAY
THE UNDYING FIRE
THE WAR IN THE AIR
THE WAR OF THE WORLDS
THE WHEELS OF CHANCE
WHEN THE SLEEPER WAKES
THE WIFE OF SIR ISAAC HARMAN
THE WONDERFUL VISIT

**NON-FICTION**

THE CONQUEST OF TIME *AND* THE HAPPY TURNING
EXPERIMENT IN AUTOBIOGRAPHY VOLUMES 1,2
H G WELLS IN LOVE
THE OPEN CONSPIRACY AND OTHER WRITINGS

# A Note before the Title Page

Novels with prefaces are like pictures with inscriptions below them; there is a confession that something was left over and had to be expressed by an addendum. But the note which is offered here is not a preface so much as a protest, and in token therefore it is put before the title page and does not figure in the list of contents. It is a protest against certain stock tricks of the book reviewer and certain prevalent vulgarities about books. They concern the treatment of opinion in works of fiction and what is called "putting people into novels".

This book, then, *The World of William Clissold*, is a novel. It is claimed to be a complete full-dress novel, that and nothing more. William Clissold is a fictitious character, and his thoughts and ideas throughout are the thoughts and ideas natural to his mental and social type. He is (to the best of his author's ability) his own self and not his author's self, in his emotional reactions, in his hard wilfulness, in his faith, in his political ideas, in his judgments. He is a specimen of modern liberalism, using liberalism in its broadest sense. He is a study of a modern type seeking modes of self-realisation. His circumstances and his views are fitted together with the utmost care to make one consistent personality. His views run very close at times – but not always – to the views his author has in his own person expressed; nevertheless, is it too much to ask that they should be treated here as his own? Naturally his point of view is like Mr Wells'. That was to be expected. How can one imagine and invent the whole interior world of an uncongenial type? Every author must write of the reactions he knows; he must be near enough to them to *feel* them sympathetically. It is unreasonable to expect the author of this book to write of the inner life of such people as the devout Mr Belloc, for example, or the aristocratic Duke of Northumberland, or the political Mr Ramsay MacDonald. He can only comment on such types from an inaccessible remoteness, attack them, admire them, state his differences from them. Their ultimate processes are inconceivable to him. There never was a character created by an imaginative author from the inside which did not contain this quite unavoidable element of self-projection. Even Hamlet is believed to be a self-projection of Shakespeare. But while this is forgiven and taken for granted in the criticism of most authors, it is made a stock grievance against the present writer. It would be a great kindness to a no doubt undeserving author if in this instance William Clissold could be treated as William Clissold, and if Mr Wells could be spared the standard charge of having changed his views afresh, and so forth and so on, because William Clissold sees many things from a different angle than did Mr Polly, George Ponderevo, Susan Ponderevo, Mr Preemby, Dr Devizes, Dr Martineau, Remington, Kipps, the artilleryman in *The War of the Worlds,* Uncle Nobby, Benham, Billy Prothero, and the many other characters who have been identified as mouthpieces and exponents of Mr Wells' scandalously varied views and attitudes. And it is a point worth considering in this period of successful personal memoirs that if the author had wanted to write a mental autobiography instead of a novel, there is no conceivable reason why he should not have done so.

Clearly he did not want to do so.

Which brings us to the second point in this intimate but necessary plea. This is not a *roman à clé*. It is a work of fiction, purely and completely. One thing which is something of an innovation has to be noted. A great number of real people are actually named in this story. It is, the author submits, impossible to get the full effect of contemporary life in which living ideas and movements play a dominant part without doing that. You cannot have a man like William Clissold going about the world of today and never meeting anybody one has ever heard of. Some of these living personages are not only mentioned but more or less described. But always under their proper names. Dr Jung is made to talk in a London flat. It is very much as he talked in a London flat. He appears because certain original ideas of his have been taken and woven into the Clissold point of view, and it was at once ungracious not to acknowledge the far-reaching suggestions that came from him and clumsy and self-important to make a footnote or a prefatory note. Shaw, again, the Shaw of the 'eighties, blows into a Kensington evening, and Keynes lunches with Clissold. These are affectionate hospitalities; they do not wound nor injure and can awaken no resentment.

With one transparent exception, the vignette of a great scientific man at home in Book One, which is partially a portrait, every character that appears in the book under a fictitious name is an entirely fictitious character. The more nearly they may approach to living instances, the more fictitious they are. They say and do things that living people are saying and doing. That is inevitable in a picture of contemporary life. If one were to write a story in which a Prime Minister had to figure during the Balfour régime, it would be necessary to have a Prime Minister rather like Lord Balfour – or everything would have to be different. If an August Personage has to descend into the narrative, it would have to be drawn to the figure of the August Personage of the period. A beggar or a policeman must be something like some beggar or policeman one actually knows. People must be more or less similar to real people up and down the scale, so long as one is writing a novel and not a fantasy. But though you made your Prime Minister as Balfouresque as possible or your Prince as princely, it would be for atmosphere and not for statement, and the last imputation that is permissible against a novelist is that he is trying to say or insinuate this or that about an individual without daring to say it plainly and directly to the proper address. Cannot this sort of imputation be checked? Cannot those who criticise books and write about books cease to pander to that favourite amusement of vulgar, half-educated, curious, but ill-informed people, the hunt for the imaginary "originals" of every fictitious character – for those who will, for example, discover in the present case that X or Y or Z, who is an advertising specialist, "sat for" the brother Dickon of this story, or that Lady Steinhart is some particular resident in Cannes or Nice – because she has a large garden? And that it is all great fun and very malicious and not for a moment to be treated as serious literature. This identification of "originals" is an old trick of the Victorian novelist and publisher; it was, I suppose, an attempt to enhance interest by that faint intimation of libel. It is really not just to the spirit and intention of a book of this type.

An inanimate instance from this book will make the matter clearer without touching upon any personal note. There is written here the most exact and detailed description of the *mas*, which is the scene of nearly the whole novel. Rooms in that house are described, bits of its garden, the view from the windows. It is possible to locate that *mas* within a few miles of Grasse; it is possible to find not one but a score of views closely similar to the view pictured so explicitly, a similar *mas* is to be found. But the actual *mas* no one will ever find, nor the precise rooms, nor the exact view. That *mas* does not exist. That view does not exist. It is the case of Mr Britling's home over again, which everyone who did not know Mr Wells' home in Essex very well, knew so surely was an exact account of Easton Glebe. The less these identifiers knew about it, the more they appreciated the photographic quality of the picture. The less they knew Mr Wells, the more certainly they recognised him in Mr Britling. Enthusiastic strangers still invade Mr Wells at times with the demand to see the place where he wept when he heard that his eldest son was killed. It is embarrassing to encounter such intrusive sympathy for an entirely imaginary loss. And matters become complicated when "originals" volunteer and surrender to the detectives. A charming contemporary has just confided to the world that she was the "original" of Beatrice in *Tono-Bungay*. It is the first intimation that has reached the author of this interesting fact. No one would have suspected it.

But this time may we have a truce to such artless tributes to the novelist's art? It was William Clissold, an entirely fictitious character, who thought out most of the problems of his life and made belated love to his fictitious Clementina in a fictitious *mas* in Provence, and in spite of the entirely imaginary wreckage of an automobile in the road to Thorenc the author survives. It is no good to look for that stone, with its simple inscription, in the Magagnosc cemetery. To the best of his knowledge and belief the author has never been buried anywhere. Even brother Dickon's allusion to William's good looks is not to be regarded as modest self-revelation. All novelists use actual experiences in their work. They must know things before they tell about them. But all novelists rearrange, sublimate, intensify. One turns over the sketch-book of one's memories and uses what one needs. One takes a lifted eyebrow here and a mimosa in flower there. The imagination discovers a certain congruity between some actual situation and some constructive necessity, and works in as much of the situation as it needs. But it alters and rearranges without scruple. The eyebrow is not a portrait; the parallelism of a situation is not a report. Surely there is enough to read in this book without reading between the lines.

And one other question may be glanced at here before this note concludes. There is much discussion of opinion in this book. Does that make it anything but a novel? Is it not quite as much "life" to meet and deal with a new idea as to meet and deal with a new lover? Must the characters in our English and American novels be for evermore as cleaned of thought as a rabbit is of its bowels, before they can be served up for consumption? This book, which contains religious, historical, economic, and sociological discussions, which expresses fits of temper and moods of doubt, is at any rate submitted as a novel, as a whole novel, and nothing but a novel, as the story of one man's adventure, body, soul, and intelligence, in life. If you are the sort of person who will not accept it as a novel, then please leave it alone. You are not getting sly peeps at something more real than the reality of art, and your attempts to squint through will only make you squint very unbecomingly.

# The World of William Clissold

(Παντα ῥει)

# H G WELLS

HOUSE OF STRATUS

First Published 1926



This edition published in 2002 by House of Stratus, an imprint of House of Stratus Ltd, Thirsk Industrial Park, York Road, Thirsk, North Yorkshire, YO7 3BX, UK.
Also at: House of Stratus Inc., 2 Neptune Road, Poughkeepsie, NY 12601, USA.

www.houseofstratus.com

Typeset, printed and bound by House of Stratus.

A catalogue record for this book is available from the British Library and The Library of Congress.

ISBN 0-7551-0430-7

TO

ODETTE KEUN

self-forgetful friend and helper

# Contents

# Book One

## The Frame of the Picture

## 1 – *The Beginning of a Book*

Yesterday I was fifty-nine, and in a year I shall be sixty – "getting on for seventy," as the unpleasant old phrase goes. I was born in November, 1865, and this is November, 1924. The average duration of life in England is fifty-one and a half, so I am already eight years and a half beyond the common lot. The percentage of people who live beyond sixty is forty-seven. Beyond seventy it is thirty. Only one in five thousand lives beyond one hundred, and of this small body of centenarians two-third are women. My expectation of life, says the table in the Almanac, is fourteen years and four months. That table in the Almanac is not a mathematical marvel, but it is close enough to the truth to serve my purpose here.

In the face of these figure I cannot hide from myself that the greater part of my life has been lived. So far I have had but few physical reminders of the ebb of the years. I do not feel that I am even beginning to be old. Perhaps I grow tired more readily than I did at thirty, and my tennis is neither so hard nor so quick-witted as it used to be, but my arteries, the doctors tell me, are still young arteries. I cannot read Bradshaw nowadays, I must put on spectacles for that, and I do not like to swim in cold water any more. Yet in good daylight I can still read ordinary print with unaided eyes, and, come to think of it, I have always gasped in cold water. Maybe I have not so much lost endurance as learnt wisdom. And generally my vigour is unimpaired. It is the dates and figures that will not be denied. They show quite plainly that at most only two decades remain for me, and when they are spent my strongest will be a white-faced, rather shrunken, assisted old man – "wonderful," they will say. I know because I say it now of Sir Rupert York and old Hayes. The greater chance is that I shall be no more than a jarful of ashes and a fading memory.

Possibly they may make something in time for me from these monkey glands they talk about; but I distrust these rejuvenescent extracts. I do not want merely to prolong my years as an unpleasant experiment. I may go on for some time yet by my own unaided strength, unless a serious illness catches me. Then, I have observed, if one comes back at all one comes back "aged."

I do not complain that I have to grow old. It is not a thing that I think about habitually. But the birthdays come round to remind me, and this year some journalist got hold of my date but added up the years wrong, and in the *Evening Standard* I found myself subjected to congratulations on attaining sixty. I was so startled that I did a little sum at once on the margin of the paper. For a moment I felt just as though I had missed a bank-note from a not too distended purse.

His mistake.

But today I find myself retrospective. I have been caught up for a couple of days in London before I go back to my sunshine in Provence, and I am all alone. Outside it is not so much day as a saturated piece of dingy time, a stretch of chewed and damp and dirty fourth dimension between two nights. It rains fitfully, now in fine clouds, now in hysterical downpours, now in phases of drizzling undecided intermission; and the shops are lit and there are lights in the windows. There is a sort of grey discoloration filtering down from above that I suppose one must admit to be daylight. Wet omnibuses, wet taxicabs and automobiles splash and blunder by, there are a few reluctant foot passengers under wet umbrellas. Everything shines greasily with the rain like the backs of rolling porpoises. What a climate! This intolerable place, they say, is the healthiest city in the world. Thank Heaven! I leave it tomorrow.

I do not venture outside this room today. At any rate I will lunch here. These excellent chambers of my brother's are kept by a French couple who combine English comfort with French cookery. No wonder old Dickon grows fat. He is in Brussels now – probably growing fatter. Inadvertently. He does not want to grow fat. He is dining with a curious little society for the promotion of scientific finance, of which he is one of the founders. That is all I know about his business in Brussels. Then he is going on into Germany, still in pursuit of monetary ideas. His energy and industry in the cause he has taken up are prodigious – and he is nearly three years older than I. He thrives on it. No wonder he needs a comfortable resting-place here. From these rooms one might imagine him sedentary. They make me feel sedentary. But even his sedentariness has directness and vigour. There is something about this room in particular, and this desk of his and this chair of his, remarkably conductive to not going out. Today especially.

Before me are good square sheets of paper and quill-pens and every provocation to write. The lamp is admirably shaded. So why should I not write, and forget altogether that visible chill, that inky catarrh of a climate which is snivelling against the window-panes?

### 2 – *The World in the Crystal*

For some time now I have had the idea of writing a book dominating my mind and never quite settling down to a positive beginning. I have wanted to begin so much, the thing was become so important to me that the very strength of my desire has restrained me. I have written one or two books before, but they have been technical works of no significance to the unspecialised reader. I have written various reports, too, and between thirty and forty scientific papers. Such things seem to write themselves. The book I have in mind now is something altogether more human and difficult than that.

It is not exactly an autobiography I want to write, and not exactly a book of confessions. My life has been largely spent in work; my only scandal was a public scandal and very fully reported. I do not see why I should repeat the newspapers again; much of my business I can only discuss in general terms because of my obligations to my firm and our associates, and there remains little for me to confess, even if I had the Rousseau streak in me. It is with larger affairs than my own that my projected book would deal. It is nothing, indeed, so systematic as a general philosophy of life I contemplate, but it is something rather more in that way than an autobiography would be. I should say that a description of my world best expresses what I have in view; my world and my will.

I want it to be a picture of everything as it is reflected in my brain. I want it to be a comprehensive picture. The book, as I see it, should begin with my – I suppose I shall have to say – "metaphysics"; it should display my *orbis terrarum*, and then it should come down to the spectacle of mankind as I apprehend it and my place in that history, and so to the immediate affairs of everyday life, to moods, passions, experiences, lessons, and at last to the faith and purpose that sustain me and fill my mind at the present time and make living on worth while. The main objective is that faith and purpose. All the rest will lead up to that, to how and why I accept life and go on living.

My metaphysics I can set about at once. I shall have chiefly to explain why I have no metaphysics. The reader need fear no elaboration of a system, not even a negative system. It is not so much a statement of scepticism that I have to make, as a confession of accepted ignorance. Yet that does not mean that I am – what is the word? – a Positivist.

I find most of the worlds that other people describe or take for granted much more hard and clear and definite than mine is. I am at once vaguer and more acutely critical. I don't believe so fully and unquestioningly in this "common-sense" world in which we meet and exchange ideas, this world of fact, as most people seem to do. I have a feeling that this common-sense world is not *final.* It is necessitated in many ways by the conditions under which we think and communicate, and I do not regard these conditions as being fundamental to existence. The common-sense world is a practical working world and so far true, but it is not necessarily ultimately true. There are times when I feel as though it was less the sphere that enclosed me and made my all, than a sort of magic crystal into which I peered and saw myself living. I have, as it were, a sense of externality and a feeling that perhaps it might be possible, though I cannot imagine how it could be possible, to turn away and look at something else quite different from this common-sense world – another world.

I never get to more than that in the way of detachment. I never get further from philosophical Positivism than that. Could anything be vaguer? It is the shadow of the ghost of a doubt. The individual in that crystal globe of time and space has a hundred thousand traits by which I know him for myself. How, then, can I be the onlooker also, of whom I know nothing at all except that he sees? This sense of externality is, perhaps, no more than a trick of my brain, like a moment of giddiness as one walks along the street. It certainly has no practical significance.

I am reminded as I write of this of a queer little thing that happened to me at times, most frequently in my adolescence and when I was a young man. I do not think that it has occurred at all during the last ten or fifteen years. It was this: The visible world, remaining just as bright and clear as ever it had been, would suddenly appear to be *minute.* People became midgets, the houses and the furniture, dolls'-houses and furniture, the trees, mere moss-fronds. I myself did not seem to shrink to scale; it was only the universe about me that shrank. This effect would last for a few seconds or for a few minutes, and then it would pass away. I have not found anyone else who has had this particular experience, but I am sure it has happened to many other people. I have never had the converse effect of enlargement.

I suppose a slight momentary change in my blood or breathing produced a change of phase in my nervous state, I perceived a difference in the *feel* of my vision, and my mind, a little perplexed, interpreted it in this fashion. If so there may be drugs that would have the same effect.

Or there may have been some little transitory fluctuation in my sensations of optical adjustment. Mental specialists connect doubts and confusions about one's identity in dreams and in cases of mental disorder with changes in bodily feeling. Yet one may argue that a conviction of reality which is so finely poised that it totters at a slight excess or defect of oxygen or suchlike factor in the blood cannot be a very soundly established one.

But it is not my intention to be mystical. It is the world in the crystal I want to write about, this crystal into which I seem to have been looking now and living for nine-and-fifty years. I will not question the reality or quality of the crystal further. It does not matter for my present purpose whether that is the final reality, or only a transitory moving picture produced by some stir of chemicals in a membrane of grey-matter inside my skull. I want to write of the motives of action in it, of its pains and pleasures, of its beauty and provocation, before my mental strength begins, as it must so soon do now, to ebb. I want to write of love and curiosity and habit and inertia and all the other motives that have kept me going. I shall write as a fairly fortunate and happy man, glad to have lived and very glad still to be alive, but wonderingly, more than a little regretful that this perplexing, interesting fabric of display and experiences, so incomplete still, so challenging a tangle of riddles, is drawing towards its inexorable end.

I do not want to go yet. I am sorry to have so little time before me. I wish before the ebb carries me right out of things altogether that I could know more – and know better. I came into the world with a clutter of protest; my mind is still haunted by protesting questions too vague for me to put into any form that would admit of an answer. If I had more time, I would like, just for a little while, in a winter's fireside talk, as it were, to have things made clearer before I go.

### 3 – *The Treacherous Forget-me-nots*

My life, I confess, seems to me to be short, distressingly short, preposterously short in comparison both with the vast range of my thoughts in space, and with the huge perspectives of the past and the future in which we think nowadays. I doubt if man had quite the same sense of abbreviation before this measuring by astronomical distances and geological ages began. And life is not only short, but things in it are out of proportion. The rules of perspective are reversed, and the remotest memories loom largest and are the most vivid. Things that happened five-and-twenty years ago are often distant and obscure enough, but the things that happened in my childhood are things of yesterday. I am no longer the young man I was. He and I have almost lost identity. Nevertheless, I am still intensely the child I used to be.

I suppose this is because most things are first seen and heard and felt in childhood, and our minds file these early impressions as key-pictures and refer the later ones to them. So they are continually refreshed. But later experiences are no longer used as new points of reference.

A hundred times, perhaps, in the course of my life and in a score of places, for example, I have seen autumnal horse-chestnut leaves reflected in brown water and the branches of a horse-chestnut tree coming down close to that still mirror, but it is definitely as a child that I think of seeing them, and all the other occasions are in comparison vague and unassigned. I was in the old punt on the great pond at Mowbray. The silvery sheet of water had that convex effect one always got there upon a day of absolute calm. It was like a very smooth broad buckler. I think that effect of curvature must have been due to the way the reeds and bushes shaded the edges, or perhaps to some trick in the angle of the reflection of the pines up the slope. Far away against a background of dark bushes, some of them still deep green and some a rusty red, floated a little squadron of motionless swans, the old bird marvellously tranquillised since his days of terrifying aggression in the early summer. Even the ducks and the friendly attendant dab-chick among the lily leaves were silent. Everything was so still that I remember being startled by the sudden "plop" of a falling husk into the crystalline water behind me.

I suppose it is the sodden horse-chestnut leaves scattered over the wet stone pavement in the yard behind this house that have released this group of memories. The armchair and Dickon's study fade to nothingness. I sit again in the punt with a row of glossy brown conkers all neatly bored beside me. I have bored them with a long nail rather tediously and have had to be careful of the palm of my hand. One or two I have broken. There are leaves in the bottom of the punt, and a thin and scattered remnant clinging insecurely here and there among the branches about me. I have been seeking a perfectly golden leaf without a patch of green or brown upon it, I have tried the taste of a horse-chestnut and have disapproved of it and spat out and watched the fragments of my mouthful sinking slowly and eddying down through the clear water, and thought how queer it was that some should spin and whirl about and some sink swift and straight, and I have wondered if the hooflike end of the leaf-stem accounts for the name of the tree. And now I am sitting motionless, suddenly aware of the tremendous quiet of the day.

It is as if the whole world paused. It is as if God was present, God whom they talk about so much in church…

Yes, I am almost as much back there as I am present in this room. Perhaps for the first time in my life I observed serenity on that day.

Half a century ago that was, right at the other end of life, and it is more vivid than yesterday. That must have been our first year at Mowbray in the beginnings of my strange father's last burst of success before his tragic downfall. We went to Mowbray from Bexhill, and everything was new and larger and finer about us.

I was nearly eight then, and at Mowbray I seem to have awakened quite suddenly to beauty and wonder. I do not recall any perception of beauty and loveliness at Bexhill. I think the summer must have been exceptionally fine and kindly. At that age I was entering upon a fresh phase of development, and the novelty and spaciousness of the new life stimulated me. As I sit here brooding at this writing-pad I live again a score of vivid, small, and yet intensely significant moments, and most of them are in the open air in the park and particularly round and about the great pond. Hardly any are indoors. I do not recall very much of the Mowbray interiors. Indoors at that time, I think, I was always reading, reading, reading.

In that punt it was I first became aware of the science of optics. I discovered something remarkable about the handle of a little fishing-net that I had put into the water. I was holding it quite still in the hope of presently whipping it up with some minnows, and I perceived that it was bent sharply at the surface of the water. I forgot the minnows and began to move the net to and fro and higher and deeper. It seemed bent, but it was not really bent. The bending shifted as I shifted the net. I puzzled over that distortion.

And in that old punt I puzzled over the riddle of reflection as well as of refraction. I found that if I crouched down with my nose just above the side of the punt I saw nothing of the bottom at all, only blue sky and tree branches. Then, as I rose, suddenly the still bottom with its roots and dead leaves and slimy weeds and the shoals of minute fish hovering above it came into view. I experimented. I extended and retracted myself. I tried to catch the exact moment between squatting and standing, when the mirror became transparent and the bottom appeared.

There was an afternoon at Mowbray, it must have been earlier in the year, in the summer, when I first discovered forget-me-nots. At the upper end of the pond near where the stream came in there were shallows and floating masses of green weed with pink blossoms and thick, widespread clumps of sedges, and half hidden amidst these sedges were clouds of flowers of a divine, incredible blue. Either I had never seen forget-me-nots growing before or I had never observed them. I went to and fro, peering from the bank, and then took off my shoes and stockings and waded into the water and mud until my knickerbockers, in spite of all the tucking up I gave them, were soaked. And I picked handfuls of these the loveliest of all English wild-flowers.

Then suddenly came horror, the unqualified horror of childhood. My legs were streaming with blood. The sharp blades of the sedge leave had cut them in a score of places. Fresh gouts of blood gathered thickly along the cuts, and then darted a bright red ribbon down my wet and muddy skin. "Oh! Oh!" I cried in profound dismay, struggling and splashing back to the bank and still holding my forget-me-nots with both hands.

Still do I remember most vividly my astonishment at the treachery of that golden, flushed, and sapphire-eyed day.

That it should turn on me!

THE WORLD OF WILLIAM CLISSOLD

## 4 – *Infantile*

Thinking of one's childhood is like opening a great neglected volume haphazard and reading in it. There must be many thousands of such pages that I might turn over, still bright, still fresh. The earliest pictures are the most fragmentary; they are vignetted in the unknown. One very early moment of self-discovery comes to mind when I was lying naked on my back gazing in a sort of incredulous wonder at my belly and knees. That must have been at Bexhill, although I have forgotten the background, and I could not have been more than three years old.

"*Me?*" I thought.

Use and wont have dulled that first astonishment at the conscious sight of my body, but I still retain something of the early incredulity. Mine is that baby body still, though my grandchildren would not believe it if I told them so; it is changed, but not out of recognition, it is younger than my face, yet in quite a little while now I shall see it for the last time and cease to see or feel it any more, and it will be altogether finished with, material for the undertaker and the crematorium. And that, I suppose, will be the end of all the pictures, and the volume will never be added to nor opened again. I know of no attic or store-room to which that great tome will go – even to moulder. It will, it seems, vanish.

I stare at this prospect in very much the same mood of wonder in which I stared at my foreshortened body fifty-odd years ago. My approaching disintegration is even more amazing than my realised appearance.

I think that discovery of my body must be one of the earliest pictures in my volume. But these vignettes of one's infancy are not firmly bound in nor properly arranged. Perhaps I was put to meditate upon that bed quite frequently. I remember my pink belly and the fat knees and toes that I recognised as myself, and how that then or later – it is not distinct – I discovered a most remarkable and most unaccountable button in the middle of my belly. At the point, through I did not know it, I had been cut off from the tree of life and made a separate individual.

Mixed up with that exploration of my navel is the hard long line of the rail of the bedstead and a memory of my mother standing at the foot of the bed and – strange and startling thing for my infant intelligence to realise – weeping very bitterly. I do not think I said or did anything about that, probably my mother never imagined I had observed it, but I remember it very plainly.

All these impression are bright and immense in my mind. The later things in my life, even when they are as vivid, are not as large. This I perceive is the common lot; nearly all autobiographers are disposed to develop the childish or adolescent experiences out of all proportion to the central realities of the life. But I shall not do that here; it is the maturer relationships with which I am concerned…

For a time I must discontinue making these notes altogether, for old Sir Rupert York has rung me up. He has discovered I am in London, and this dismal downpour has afflicted him so that he cannot endure to be alone. He must not stir abroad in the wet, so I shall break my resolution to keep in this room today and go out and lunch with him. I must make my apologies to Madame Deland.

## 5 – *Sir Rupert York*

"Wonderful" is certainly the word for Sir Rupert; he is close upon eighty, but his mind is as bright as it has ever been. He talks and moves slowly, and he confesses that he feels no longer disposed to work hard and is easily tired by any effort, but he misses no point in one's talk and his thought is candid and serene. On his desk were drawings and a photograph and a plaster-cast of a gorilla's foot; some American has been writing unwisely of the use of the ape's big toe in walking, and Sir Rupert has been demolishing him, patiently, unhurryingly, and completely. He is also feeling his way towards the use of a peculiar sort of early stone implement with a beaked end, and the room is littered with specimens.

He looks better than when I saw him last two years ago. Then he seemed to me to be greatly fallen away, and his skin had that rather shrivelled white delicacy that comes with age; now either I was prepared for it or it has really recovered tone and texture. He ate a good lunch; he is still far from the days of digestive paps, and in spite of the wet he came out on his doorstep without thinking of a coat to stand and smile his farewell.

Big and smiling he is and in some subtle way noble, and it is a comfort to me to have been with him, for in his case at any rate old age has not meant a lean and slippered egotism and jealousy of youth.

I told him about my project of writing a book, and he confessed he had had similar thoughts. They have come to nothing with him because rostro-carinate implements and suchlike riddles are more interesting to him than himself. But it was curious to see how different was his conception of autobiography. He is the least metaphysical of men; he has no doubts of the reality of our world of time and space; he will not trouble his mind with any speculations about his identity or consider any system outside the universe of science; he is even disregardful and a little impatient with the later analyses of modern physics. And the story he would tell would be a matter-of-fact record beginning with the sturdy boy full of material curiosities, fascinated by the discovery of strange mammalian bones in the Crag, and going on from that to collecting, to the systematic study of geology and morphology, and so to a fair full life of material gathered, generalisations sifted, facts insisted upon, and false conclusions exposed. I have always had a great affection for Sir Rupert since years ago we did some work together on the fracture of flints and bones; he had asked me to help him with an optical examination of flint under strain; and he still seems to me in several ways the greatest scientific man I have known, the greatest and the simplest. He is as simple as some fine animal that has grown to its full development under favourable conditions.

My own scientific work gives me the measure of his. He makes me feel no better than an excursionist in this world of science in which he is a prince. An excursionist or a prospector. I was not simple after his fashion. Wonder touched me as it did him in boyhood. It was not fossils that seized upon my imagination, but the riddle of double refraction and the perplexities of what we still thought of in those days as the "shapes" of atoms and molecules. Some of my work was quite respectable. Other men have gone along the road I opened; it was a sound piece of road. But I did not keep on whole-heartedly. In the end I deserted science altogether, as I shall have to explain. I am what passes for a rich man, an industrialist. I am one of the active directors of Romer, Steinhart, Crest and Co., and I have a share and a voice in most of their affiliated activities. I hold a considerable number of patents, and I am an exploiter of secret processes, which I recognise are offensive to science. The essence of science is open statement. During the war I was what they called an expert, and after the war I was foolish enough to dabble in politics. I thought a new and greater age was beginning and that the war had taught us a lesson. It did. But the lesson is slow in digesting, and I have experimented and tried this way and that in my effort to express and realise my conception of it. And I have let women deflect my life very considerably. I have been greedy for property and freedom and influence and for many sorts of experience I had better have avoided. But Sir Rupert with a large modesty and devotion has gone on serving the truth in that field to which he was called.

I do not think there has ever been any great conflict of motives in his life. Quite early and quite without reservations he determined to give himself to natural history. Other things have had to accommodate themselves to that. His circumstances made the gift easy; Professor Huxley was a frequent visitor to his home and Charles Darwin patted his head. And to be a naturalist then was a great adventure; science had challenged tradition and dogma, and the warfare that followed in the minds of men was epic warfare. We live in the liberties of thought that were won for us then. He has never married, and though I suspect him of no excesses of chastity, I perceive that the mixture of sexual need and the hunger for a dear companion that has so disturbed me has had no equivalent influence upon him. Nor has he ever displayed any religious impulse beyond an upright, unswerving devotion to his sense of truth. He has accepted the work that lay before him single-mindedly, living comfortably and happily and without any sense of sacrifice. He has done that work magnificently. Abundant it has been, and sound and wide, and strictly within the limitations of things as they plainly are. He questions so ably because he accepts so completely. Before I went to him today I had intended, forgetting a little his quality, to put my conception of the provisional reality of life before him and discuss it with him. Such an exchange would be as possible with a pensive lion in the Zoo.

Ever and again, as we talked together and ranged from this to that, he would return to gnaw the bones of his American professor. "You see," he would resume in a pause, "if anyone had been trying to make a case and deliberately faking the photograph, he could not have put the foot in a better light for his own ends than this fellow has done. If he made the photograph. But did he? He doesn't say whether he did or not. It may be the other way round. He may just have seen it somewhere and picked it up and run away with a misconception. That's not so bad. Then he's merely careless – and obstinate. He wanted to take up an original point of view and this made it seem plausible. But while this cast here of mine is from a living gorilla, *his* sketch is made from a photograph of doubtful origin of a foot which I am fairly certain has been taken out of spirits… Queer… All through he shows a sort of eagerness…

"Some of these Americans live too near the newspapers. They get the headline spirit. They want to make startling discoveries and startling reversals in a hurry…

"One has to understand one can't do that sort of thing…

"They must live under bad conditions over there. I don't understand what sort of surroundings a biologist can have – in a Western university, for example. They seem to be restless, excessively sensitive to cheap judgments. Over there – "

Sir Rupert paused and his manner became very earnest. "*They will let newspaper interviewers come into their discussions!*" he said. "They will let interviewers make statements for them, and they will attend to the stuff interviewers and paragraphists put on to other people. They seem to have no feeling for precisions in such things… This man seems to be afraid to admit details that tell against him… As though he might lose something…

"And yet, you see, they will make the rashest attacks…

"He brought it on himself."

He reflected for a moment and patted the plaster cast beside him on the table, and regarded it with a benevolent expression. He had brought it in from the study to the dining-room. He has the charming habit of carrying about with him everywhere the implements and bones that are interesting him. I have heard of him sitting at a large dinner party with a polished rhinoceros bone from which he would not be separated beside his plate, just as a child will insist on sitting at meals with some very dear new toy on the table.

He disentangled his mind from the cast and remembered his duty as a host.

"You like this Château Margaux? 1917. Good year, 1917."

## 6 – "*Die Welt als Wille und Vorstellung*"

I wish I knew more of the practical side of literature. I suppose that after a craftsman has written six or seven "works" he learns so well how to set about his business that he writes on strongly and confidently from the very first word, and has – I think Stevenson explains as much somewhere – the end of his book latent in his opening paragraph. But I have been beating about the bush for five sections and making notes for various matters that must come in later, and still I doubt if I have told anything at all about my world. Instead I have written about my childhood and made a sketch of my host at lunch. It is like the way one draws on the blotting-paper in a board-room. Unless – unpleasant thought! – it is the onset of the garrulous stage.

I shall keep the morning's writing and this note upon Sir Rupert at hand, but I shall try a fresh commencement here. Perhaps, after all, the proper way is to go directly to the core of the matter. Even though that may mean stiff going for a bit for both writer and reader. How in the most general terms do I apprehend life?

Metaphysically I have never been able to get very far beyond Schopenhauer's phrase: *Die Welt als Wille und Vorstellung.* Life to me as to him, when he wrote that title at least, is a spectacle, a show, with a drive in it.

Is there a plot to the show; is it a drama moving through a vast complexity to a definite end, or at any rate moving in a definite direction? To that question the various religions have given their various answers, and I will say at once that I have found none of their answers satisfactory. There is some invincible fact or group of facts outside of, or positively inconsistent with all their explanations.

Yet every one of them has some half-truth in it for me. Either the whole is too complex for me to perceive a plot or recognise the one the teachers would have me see, or there is no plot.

I admit a tremendous splendour, beauty, and delight in much of the scenery. The lighting effects are superb. For more than fifty years I have been turning the pages of the book of sunsets and never have I wearied. The texture and quality of the costumes, the subtlety, charm, and humour of the cast again, are often amazing. I rejoice perhaps excessively in the loveliness of the bodies in which we are clothed. But plot to hold together this vast display in one comprehensive system I cannot see. My mind seeks it and needs it; the spectacle remains incoherent in spite of all my seeking.

It is like one of those rummage-sale outbreaks of disconnected cleverness they give in the theatres nowadays and call revues. And some of the scenes and some of the actors are infernally dull, some of the cleverness is harsh and base, some of the turns bore to the limits of endurance, ugly and offensive things come on and spoil an act and will not go off for all my manifested disapproval. And like an Elizabethan gentleman I am upon the stage and not in the auditorium, and ever and again my stool is kicked from under me and I have to answer an unexpected cue, pull myself together, as people say, and improvise a part. Passive or active, I am always in the centre of this show of mine.

The shifting values of the scene at any particular moment, the distribution of importance and quality, come, I perceived, mainly from three groups of things. Firstly, there is what is fed to us – *dietary* shall I call it? – in which I include not only meat and drink and the want of them, but the reception or lack of all we can inhale or inject into our systems, fresh air or unexpected ideas. Secondly, come *infections and injuries* bodily and mental, and their feverish distressful stimulations. Thirdly, there is *irradiation*, by which I mean all that we call the weather, and heat and cold and sounds and light, and those subtler magic rhythms of colour and harmony that flow through eyes and ears and the substance of my body, to exalt or debase me. These three groups of things charge my life with its current quality and determine whether the mood of my part shall be urgency or valiant resistance, gay confidence, anger, repose, or despair. They determine, too, whether the tone shall be strong or weak, concentrated or diffused. There seems to be little or nothing in me that can resist these determinations. But manifest through all the phases they create there is an intermittent urgency of self-assertion and aggression upon which my poor simplifying and integrating human mind imposes a unity and continuity. This is the Me.

This urgency is, in the broader sense of the word, sexual: in that broad sense of the new psychology which makes sexual co-extensive with racial. Its drive is the drive of what Shaw calls the "life force" and Schopenhauer the "will to live." But it is concentrated about my egoism and divided off from the general life force of the world. It is protean; it involves an anxiety for present and future things outside myself, it seeks expression and recognition and response. Occasionally it becomes barely and plainly a clamour for woman. But – I speak for myself – it is reluctant to embody its desire in any particular woman for any length of time. Even when desire has run – as it has done once or twice in my life – deep and narrow and direct and passionate for a particular woman, my rationalising mind has still been disposed to invent generalisations that broadened and mitigated the intensity of that desire. There is a counterbalancing disposition of this force to admit the claim of a wider obligation, and to reconcile the narrow and intenser drive with that. This widening has increased with the years; the sexual has become more racial, and the will to live for myself has changed more and more into a will to live for life.

Such are the ingredients of my rôle in this tremendous, terrifying, delightful, exciting, unequal, indifferent, and irrelevant revue of existence. This is my personal analysis of life. This is the composition of my life as it presents itself to me. These are the threads of the stitches in the tapestry, the elements of my hours.

## 7 – *Immortality*

When the curtain of death comes down, is the *revue* over?

So far as William Clissold goes, I think it is. I think that death is a thing I shall never experience, for when it comes to me I shall be dead. I may see it coming, I may hope for it or fear it, but I shall never know it come. I shall never know it has come just as I never know that sleep has come. I do not believe in personal immortality. In my youth I struggled against the idea of individual extinction, but now I accept it quite tranquilly. I think there may be something immortal in me, and what that is I will do my best to explain in subsequent sections, but I do not think that immortal part contains any of the distinctive features that individualise me. The sound of my voice, the oddities of my mind, my likes and dislikes, and the great volume of my personal memories will, I think, end when my heart ceases to beat.

I have still enough greediness for personal experience to want, if not complete immortality, at least a little extension of my time. I am like a well-behaved child who is willing to go to bed but would prefer to sit up a while longer. But I can find no tittle of evidence that experience goes on after physical death. The phenomena of fainting, sleep, and unconsciousness all sustain my conviction that the immobility of the dead is also subjective. And I am quite unable to imagine any sort of living at all, any sort of conscious existence, without hands that feel, eyes that see, a sense of material substance, and a stir of bodily feeling. It is not strength but weakness of the imagination that enables people to think of themselves as bodiless "spirits." The idea that man is a threefold being of body, soul, and spirit, all separable and mysteriously endowed with his personality, seems to me a survival of remote barbaric speculations. I can no more think of myself living on as a spirit than as living on as a moving photograph.

The decay of the established religious beliefs which wrapped the life after death in a sacred reticence has let loose much popular necromancy. I was sufficiently involved with these curiosities at one time to be member of the Society for Psychical Research and to follow up some of the alleged evidence for personal survival after death. I found evidence of much deception and still more self-deception. And even if I had admitted the reality of all the phenomena tendered, which I would be very loth to do, they would have proved nothing except the survival of fragments of personal will and memory. Suppose a medium to produce some trivial secret between myself and some departed intimate, known to no one else; that no more proves that my friend is still mentally alive than a corrupting fragment of his face with a characteristic scar would prove his bodily survival. The mere fact of the medium being in possession of this confidence suggests helplessness and insensibility in the departed. Generally the supposed messages from the dead display great mental degeneration. The mediums produce no more than a shrivelled phantom of the sought-after dead. When Victor Hugo was summoned back from the shades, Anatole France told me, he had forgotten *Hernani* and *Ruy Blas* altogether, and acquired nothing to make up for this but the sort of moral platitudes one might get from an intoxicated concierge. If we are to believe the stuff at all, we must believe on the evidence that the next life will be no better than a tattered fragment of this. I had rather have the flame of my life extinguished at once than turned down and down to flicker at last in such a fashion.

The revelations of Sir Oliver Lodge's *Raymond* and of Sir Arthur Conan Doyle and the lucubrations of Mr Vale Owen confirm this view. The effect is not so much as if they had drawn the veil from a vision of deep and mighty things, as that the curate has bought a cheap magic lantern and got an enthusiastic and humourless spinster to daub his slides. I am prepared to believe the universe can be deeply tragic and evil or wonderful and beautiful, but not that it can be fundamentally silly. On the whole my presumption that there is nothing immortal in our individualities is strengthened rather than weakened by the evidence of this cloud of all too explicit witnesses to the contrary that has arisen in the past few years.

### 8 – *Crystalline, Atomic, Dimensional*

Though this is all that I can make of life, my mind is not entirely content to rest at this. I do not think that life is as entirely chancey and miscellaneous as my statement may seem to leave it. I do not believe that it is a succession of moods and impulses in an aimless confusion. There is order in the universe; there is law, essential and inexorable law. It is law outside of and independent of our wills, and perhaps irrelevant to our wills. But it is there.

It is not, I think, a habit of mind derived from early religious teaching that sustains this belief. It is much more closely related to the assumption of my scientific work. The world is in the nature of rational and explicable. At the same time it is not in any way subservient to human feelings and human ends.

I am reminded of a dear little grey kitten I had last year – I hope I have her still – at the Villa Jasmin. She was much intrigued by my cheval glass. She saw her reflection in it and she was greatly perplexed because she could not get at it. She struggled with the riddle. It was clear to me that she believed the damned thing could be understood. But it was more and more evident to me that her nice, quick, and in many ways very clever little brain had nothing at all in it to enable her to apprehend the nature of a reflection. She would pat the glass with her paw – after a time she patted the glass and did not attempt to put her paw through it – and then dodge round very quickly behind the mirror. Then still more quickly she would return to the front. She would stiffen her legs and bristle her hair and stalk off in a silly endearing way she had. It was just as though she raised her eyebrows and shrugged her shoulders. It was in the spirit of that grimace. She would give it up and affect boredom and go out of the room. And come back presently to give it up again. She gave it up on different days, a dozen times perhaps. By now she has probably given it up altogether.

But though she cannot understand it the thing can be understood. That is the tantalising aspect of my own insufficiency. If I were God enough I might so contrive it, not by adding anything absolutely fresh to her ganglia, but simply by strengthening and expanding one or another faculty, that she would theorise about light – to the Newtonian level. And with a little more knowledge and training to the level of Einstein and Weyl. And if there were a God above me, and it is just as possible as not there are intelligent being above me capable of watching my mental proceedings just as I watch hers – how should I know about them if there were? – I too might be expanded to – anyhow, a larger sphere of comprehension.

I have always had a persuasion that I have never got anything like its full possibilities out of my brain. Even for what it is, it may not be anything near its maximum of effectiveness. Ever and again I have been astonished to find myself in a phase of exceptional lucidity, I have seen my way through a game of chess or grasped a mathematical problem with a directness quite beyond my normal possibilities. Or I have had a rush of creative energy, and invented lovely things very rapidly and expressed them with unpremeditated skill. Something happened then to my brain, some exceptional aeration or other stimulation. It showed what it could do. But all the time it was no other than the rather foggy and uncertain brain of my everyday life. It is quite conceivable that our present atmosphere is not the best of all possible atmospheres for the working of the human brain, nor the normal current in our arteries its most stimulating food.

The inhabitations of Venus, if there are any inhabitants upon that steamy planet, see no sun in their sky. There is, the astronomers suppose, a complete cloud shell between its surface and outer space. Life beneath that canopy must be life in the hot twilight of a tropical forest; daybreak must be a mere rosy or orange brightening of the grey, and night a darkling into blackness. But perhaps there are storms there, and then on some rare occasion that flocculent, dense welkin may be rent and swept aside, and the stars may shine or the naked sun blaze down upon the tossing, waving jungle. A thousand things, faintly suspected, dimly apprehended hitherto, must be revealed for a little while, stark and plain.

But my everyday mind is a cloudy and misty mind. I grope, I do not see. So far as I can judge, most of my fellow-creatures are groping too, and many of them do not even suspect this possibility of clairvoyance. They think that what they do with their minds is all that can be done with their minds. I do not agree, but I have never worked out any very effective rules for bettering my mental operations. I have never been able to trace to my own satisfaction the causes that brought about those rare occasions of exceptional brilliance. I have never secured any command over them. But they have filled me with the haunting sense of something quite graspable if only I could close my fingers upon it, something just a very little way beyond my reach, quite visible had my eyes but a tithe more sensitiveness.

Yet even if some hitherto unsuspected God were to pour illumination into my mind so that, with all that intense realisation of beauty which is inseparable from discovery, a hundred obdurate riddles dissolved into obvious necessity, still I should have made, I feel, only one more step up an endless staircase. My kitten, could I put Newton's brain in control of its furry paws, would even then be patting pebbles on the margin of an illimitable ocean.

It has been necessary for me to keep in touch with current speculations about the constitution of matter, the nature of time and space. I have watched physical science, sternly self-disciplined, probing further and further, not only from ordinary human understanding, but from ordinary human feeling. The analysis of matter, in the last quarter of a century, has reached a point when it has ceased to be in any human sense wonderful. It is incomprehensible. Every statement is a paradox; every formula an outrage upon common sense. One is left baffled as by the hieroglyphics of some insane scribbler. In my curious childhood, when I browsed among that what were then already old-fashioned books in the Mowbray library, I read of atoms and molecules almost as kindly and human as Dutch cheeses. I write Dutch cheeses because I remember how later – I was just twelve and my mother had taken Dickon and me for a sudden furtive holiday in Holland to escape, as I realised years afterwards, from the sight of newspaper placards proclaiming the Clissold Smash, Clissold in the Dock, Clissold's Cross-Examination – when I saw the golden cheeses piled all over the market place, and the quaintly costumed porters carrying them in exact geometrically arranged batches to and fro between the gaily painted barges and the market, it seemed to me that in quite that fashion it must be that molecules moved about, and the atoms of matter combined and were distributed and re-combined. Everybody in those days thought of atoms as tangible things, and of space as a framework of three dimensions as rectangular as a window sash. The ether, the now vanished ether, wrapped about us like a garment, and time was like a star and dwelt apart. I remember when I was a science student, greatly torn between my search for knowledge and the urgent need of escaping from the wreckage of our family disaster, that in the college debating society we were already discussing the ideas of time being conceivable as a fourth dimension, and of a limit existing to material rectitude and exactness of repetition.

Since then all those easy old imaginings of quasi-tangible atoms and infinite incessant space have dissolved away insensibly. We have followed our deductions further and further into a stirring crystalline complex of multi-dimensional curvatures and throbbing reactions. Energy is and it is not, and then again it is, all Being flickers in and out of Not-being, there is an irrational bound set to motion, there is a limit to the range of temperature. Space is bent in some incomprehensible fashion so that straight lines re-enter into themselves, gravitation is a necessary consequence of duration, and atoms are the orbits and harmonies of infinitesimal electrical charges. Einstein's own description for popular enlightenment of his space-time system with its bent and possibly unstable co-ordinates, reads to me like the description of a clear vibrating four dimensional haggis. Weyl goes wider and further, and Bohr has imposed a rippling intermission upon the whole universe. In the depths or heights of physics, for one word seems as good as the other when all direction is lost, I find my mind sitting down at last exhausted of effort in much the mood of Albrecht Dürer's *Melencolia*. I have gone far along that way, and I can go no farther into that wilderness of vanishing forms and puffs of energy in a quadri-dimensional field of force.

The science of the elements is becoming to difficult for ordinary men to grasp – which must gratify every intelligent priest. But the mystical God of force and substance – if one may use the word "God" for so remote a conception – to whom the endless winding staircase of molecular science mounts for ever and never attains, is, I feel, no priest's God of sentiment and morality, no friend of man and pitiful judge of our peccadillos, but a God of austere complexity, a God of variable and evasive rhythms and unfathomable intricacy, the God of a philosophical mathematician.

I note as I write this that something has passed insensibly out of my mind since my youth, and that hitherto I have not observed its departure. And that is, *the awe of the inorganic*. During my student days I was drawn by an overwhelming fascination to the lovely facts of crystalline structure, and particularly of double refraction and the interference of light. I went into these mysteries exalted and intoxicated with wonder. Partly it was an intellectual exaltation; but partly it was sensuous, like the joy women find in the deep beauty of precious stones. Did I, in those days, in some faintly anthropomorphic way regard the glittering planes and beams and passages and patterning in those translucent depths into which I pried, as being accessible, as being physically accessible? Did I somehow conceive of myself as presently walking out of the ordinary paths of everyday into those magic palaces?

At any rate I cannot bring back any remnant of that wonder now. Neither in that connection nor in connection with that other profundity, space. There was a time, a rather earlier time in my life, when my little soul shone and was uplifted at the starry enigma of the sky. That has gone; gone absolutely. I could not have imagined that it would ever go. While I was still a little fellow at Mowbray I remember looking at the stars one winter night upon the terrace – it must have been a night winter because Orion was there – and I was in an ecstasy. I was rapt in a passion of wonder. I was lost to all other feeling. I had slipped out without a coat and did not care that afterwards my governess scolded me. For a time I did not hear her calling close at hand. But now I can go out and look at the stars as I look at the pattern on the wallpaper of a railway station waiting-room. About them I have become prosaically reasonable. If they were not there, there would be something else as casual, as indifferently sublime.

The more I have learnt about them the more coldly aloof from me have they become. What has happened to me? Is it the story of my little grey kitten over again? Have I grown tired of patting behind the glass?

### 9 – *Disintegrating Protestantism*

I return from the *coulisses* of physics and the deep dark outlook of astronomy, from the underworld and outerworld of material mysteries, to the spectacle upon the stage.

I have compared it in its casual inconsecutiveness to a London or New York revue. I cannot ignore the valiant attempts men have made to impose a coherent and comprehensive story upon it, to explain it as a drama with a beginning, a middle, and an end. Judaism and Islam give good but inadequate histories of how it all happened, and Christian teaching carries over some inexplicable gaps very ably and bravely; Buddhism, too, tells a tale with a curious affinity to the modern scientific spirit in its conception of impersonal retributions and its recognition of vast aeons. But Hindu thought is saturated with the cyclic delusion that things come back again. As my vision of the world has grown plainer and more assured, the last tinge of credibility has faded from these various dramatic diagrams of the universe. They have followed the fairies that I could still half hope to see and play with, when I lay down amidst the bracken of Mowbray Park.

I wish I could recall more of my early religious life. It developed in that late Victorian period when nothing had gone from the creeds but everything had weakened; people still believed in hell but did not like to have it talked about. Instruction was vague and allusive. I should call my upbringing "disintegrating Protestant." The idea of God was very much entangled with the disciplines of my nurse and governess, and the most vivid memory I have of the divinity teaching of my Bexhill days, was a highly illuminated card in an Oxford frame bearing the words –

"THOU GOD SEEST ME."

I believed that firmly, and it abased my private dignity to a reluctant propitiatory restraint of my private thoughts. I would try to pretend that I was not thinking something that I was actually thinking. I was told repeatedly that I ought to love God, but I cannot remember feeling the slightest gleam of affection for that silent, invisible, dominating, and dangerous spectator. Dangerous! – he could strike me dead, and was quite capable of doing so. On some mere technical point. How could one love a Being of that sort?

But certainly I never ventured to think that I did not love him. I was too afraid of him.

So was Dickon, although he was more than two years older than I. But we said very little about it to each other.

There was scant mention of the Crucifixion in our early teaching. I was told of it as a harsh matter of fact, but it was not dwelt upon. I saw pictures of it, and they filled me with horror that God should permit it, and there was a lesson from the New Testament read in church on Easter Sunday that dismayed and depressed a small soul already suffering from a surfeit of very new hot-cross buns. I was told to love this victim on the cross also, and there was nothing in my heart to respond. I felt that as a member of the deity he need not have put this dreadful thing upon me.

It was some transitory governess who insisted upon my loving the crucified one. I have forgotten her name, but she had a very long body in a green dress, a thick pink neck that rolled up over a slight swell of chin into a pink face, and a voice that impressed me as being rich. She always seemed to be leaning forward. When she found no spark of gratitude in us for the cross and thorns, she tried another aspect of her faith, and showed us a brightly coloured picture of Christ with a crowd of children about him and one upon his knee.

"Wouldn't *you* like to come to him?" she said, watching our faces for intimations of a response.

That estranged us in a different way.

I remember Dickon with his little freckled hands half thrust into his first knickerbocker pockets, looking very obdurate and saying nothing.

We wouldn't commit ourselves...

That is how I was taught about Jesus Christ. It is only in recent years that a personality has emerged through that curtain of mingled horror and mawkishness that was woven before him in my childhood...

My mother want to church and had us go to church. Under cross-examination she would perhaps have admitted finally, and with qualifications and evident distaste, that she was a Christian, but she would have agreed at once and cordially that she was a Churchwoman, and even a "good Churchwoman." I do not recall an occasion when she spoke to us herself of Christ or Salvation or any such topic, nor did any of our nurses or governesses except that one I have just mentioned. Our home had a religion, but it was an extremely restrained religion; it was felt to have passed beyond the bounds of delicacy; it was referred to rather than actually produced. At church one did not listen much, and only the more anaemic hymns were sung. Even those abbreviated Anglican services seemed tediously unnecessary. "Now to God the Father, God the Son, and God the Holy Ghost." I recalled my wandering thoughts. I might move about again. Pouf! what a relief! Nevertheless, the idea of God gripped me as a terrible idea.

For the life of me I cannot reconstruct the phases by which my mind recovered from the suggestion of that all-seeing, all-pervading, disapproving, and restraining deity. But when I was a science student I was in full revolt against that obsession and, more than a little scared at my own daring, I would invent "funny" blasphemous stories about "my friend Mr G." I would pretend to have special communications and revelations from this mythical person and to be exceptionally influential in my prayers. Sometimes I would call him "the other Mr G," because in those days British Liberalism was disastrously dominated by that astounding irrepressible person Mr Gladstone, and it was the custom of the reluctant impotent party his energy hauled after him to refer to him with a breathless reverential familiarity as "Mr G." There was a certain spice in confusing these two holy terrors, which lost none of its savour when presently, during my student days, the earthly Mr G embarked upon a ridiculously ignorant defence of the Book of Genesis as a trustworthy summary of palaeontology. He had so much the manner of a distinguished author replying to his reviewers…

Professor Huxley, his antagonist in the *Nineteenth Century* controversy, became a great hero to me, the valiant anatomist, the grave white-haired, yellow-faced dean of our college, who stood up alone and undismayed against both the Mr Gs and exorcised them together from innumerable minds that had formerly been oppressed by them.

I do not think enough attention has been given to the difference of our religious reactions at successive phases in our development. The great religions of the world come down to us from a time when the average age was shorter, when the world was relatively fuller of children and young people, when the emotional atmosphere was more in the key of adolescence than it is today. Life was short and thought was leisurely. Normally one believed what one was told. There were few things that were recognised as new and there was no appetite for novelty. The spirit of the times was against it. Ideas trickled then; in our times they jet. Notes of interrogation, those mosquitoes of the modern world, were scarcely known. Now they swarm on every path and infect us with a fever of doubt. Only a very few people grew out of the fears and beliefs they had acquired in childhood. Now very many of us do, and our unembarrassed actions and our freely expressed thoughts bring on the minds of many of the young towards our own stage far more rapidly than they would have come of their own accord.

It is difficult for me to judge how far the current generation is repeating the phases through which Dickon and I passed forty odd years ago, and whether there is the same necessity to minimise an early horror of God by familiar jesting. The edifying literature of our boyhood was pervaded by the idea of Providence, a fussy, uncertain, preposterous interface in human affairs, and we made my Mr G a symbol for all the petty malignities and kindnesses of the weather, and the chances of hill and road, and the turn of the cards, for all those caprices of accident indeed that were then called "Providential." And for every oddity of nature that jarred with our preconceptions of dignified benevolence. Our Mr G, by our insistence on his human absurdity, became indeed a caricature and a defiance of all anthropomorphic gods. "Upon any supposition," we would say of the hyena, of the wart-hog at the Zoo, or of the slug in the salad, "why did Mr G make *that?* If he hadn't been ashamed of his slug he wouldn't have hidden it in the lettuce leaf. And what a sell if Eve had obeyed him! She had free-will. What would he have done with all these nasty creatures? Dis-created them?..."

Dickon had a wonderful imagination of the Six Nights of Creation. These, he fabled, came after the Fall. So Eve was restored to her theological freedom. Mr G, he represented, after her vexatious indiscretions, in secret and much embittered, sabotaged a once perfect universe; for six nefarious nights he sabotaged it, put the taste of sin into his work, disharmonised sounds, invented stinks, created all the disease bacteria, supplied the wasps with stings, the flies with unsavoury instincts, and changed ten thousand once honest species into malignant parasites. Dickon would lie in bed shrieking with laughter, unable for a time to expound some new and still more awful dislocation that had just occurred to him.

"Didn't care what he did!" choked Dickon. "He *was* wild! Simply didn't care."

That old jest can still shock and please. Only this last June it was that I expounded the moods and character of our Mr G to my dear ridiculous Clem. We were walking up a winding, stony path, the old road from this place to that unaccountable village of Gourdon, which perches so high and splendidly above the Loup, and we sat down at a bend in the road which gives a particularly good view of the blue crests of the Esterel. In a flash she was up again with a short, sharp scream, and more than half disposed to scold me for the fact that she had put her hand upon a stunted little shrub smothered in a seething mass of nasty little crawling things, soft and distended purple larvae that were just exuding from the cobwebby nest in which I suppose they had been hatched.

"That was Mr G's bad hour," said I.

"What *do* you mean?" she asked.

The hour when the insects were made, an hour, I said, of feverish, fiddling, cruel industry, a morbid muddling of matter into life. "Well, wasn't it so?" I demanded, at the protest to her raised eyebrows.

I dilated, in accents of reproach, upon the innumerable varieties of insect species, upon their stings, bites, poisonings, infections, burrowings into living flesh, cannibalisms and hideous parasitisms, I enlarged upon the tortures they inflict and the filthy preoccupations of their activities, their immense destructiveness and exasperating uselessness. They and the spiders and lice and all the noxious creeping things betrayed a morbid streak in creation. "What was Mr G thinking of then? What was he about? Before the Fall, you know! Before the Fall!"

It was better than the view to see Clem's face – at the onset of an idea she ceases to be beautiful and becomes elfin – manifestly scared but much more delighted by the flavour of release in this new version of the Bridgewater treatises.

"After all," she said, coming up bravely to my level, "your Mr G made this view."

"And almost prevented your seeing it – by an ungentlemanly trick."...

We grow out of belief. All children are naturally and essentially believers. They begin with a sense of being completely protected; they trust unquestioningly. A cared-for child cannot conceive that there is a fundamental insecurity of life; that is an idea outside its circle of thought. It believes it is completely looked after and that all its proceedings are known; if it is good it will be made happy, and if it is naughty it will be punished. Only later does it begin to chafe and question under the restrictions of the law, and even then it doubts the justice of the control long before it doubts the existence of the control. Much of this childish mind persists with many people into middle age and even into old age. You will find quite old people under some mishap cry out upon the injustice of fate as though a promise had been broken. The other day I was told that Margaret Payton, that valiant sceptic and most clear-headed woman, had had a painful minor operation. Half submerged by the chloroform she betrayed her older, still persistent, preconceptions. "What have I *done*," she asked and asked again and murmured and muttered, "that God should make me suffer like this?... What have I *done?*... What right has God?... It is not just to me."

But we who really go right through into the completely adult stage come out at last beyond any sense of providence or responsibility. We realise the complete indifference of the universe to us and our behaviour. We know we are exposed and unprotected. "The Lord is my Shepherd," said the Psalmist, "therefore will I fear no evil." And again, "God is our refuge and strength, a very present help in time of trouble." But I cherish no illusions about my shepherd. For good or evil no God is dogging me. There is no shield at my back and no friend to guard me from the ambush. But no one reads my private thoughts before I can reads them myself as they well up in me. No one holds me accountable for my motives. No one complicates my conscience and thwarts my will by arbitrary imperatives. If I tell the truth it is because lying seems to me a servility or a treachery and I do not like it, and if I go out of my way to be kind it is just as if I went out of my way to visit a pleasant corner in a garden.

## 10 – *The Religious Mind*

In my earlier harsher phases of disbelief, while my conceptions of mental processes were still crude, I was very severe in my judgments upon the teachers and priests and professional servants of a revealed religion that was manifestly wrong in its revelations. I thought, for example, that it was only necessary to go to a clergyman and explain to him simply and clearly how this new Darwinism – how new it was in those days! – had swept away the historical Fall of Man, the very foundation of his scheme of salvation, to oblige him to cast aside his clerical collar and his specially cut garments, and, leaving them as a gift for any casual tramp, set out, in shirt and socks and braces so to speak, upon a search for some less superseded costume and some more justifiable occupation than the cure of souls. And when I saw the churches still open everywhere, and the preachers still preaching in the old terms and the congregations standing up to sing the old hymns and kneeling down to pray in the old confidence, I did not know whether most to blame the stupidity or the dishonesty of mankind.

And I still recall quite vividly my fellow-student, Davidson, at the College of Science, and how he would shrink and retract from my efforts to talk about the theological applications of the new biology. We shared a bench during the opening course of physics. He would lose his wind like a punctured tyre at the mere intimation of this topic; he would pant and his ears would grow red. He had a way of turning from me at the bench so that of all his features I saw just his red ear. It is only nowadays that I begin to understand the fear and disgust he felt for me. "I want to get on with my work," he would gasp at last, and there was hatred in his eye. "I don't want to talk to you. Not in the least... Please, don't speak to me please."

Although he had been quite willing to talk about all sorts of things before he discovered my heretical bent.

I do not know if Davidson is still in the world or whether he may read this, but at any rate I will offer him my belated apologies from my intrusions upon the sacred places of his mind. They were sacred and they had no defences. I was already so much at large then, and still so young, that I could not understand how rooted and vitally entangled he remained. Religion is only formally a thing of the intelligence; its substance is feeling and a way of life. Every religion pretends to rest upon facts and statements, but no religion really does so. The ordinary man has a private and personal world which is more or less completely ensphered in his religious beliefs, they give him a sense of being protected and of being accountable and of having a definite personal importance in the scheme of things. It is practically instinctive with him that this sphere of assurance and confidence must not be shattered. If it is, life will become as impossible for him as it is for the chick of a prematurely broken egg. And so he resists, and, indeed, becomes incapable of considering the most conclusive arguments against the formula on which his security depends.

He will not have them even as a recognised error in his world.

The other afternoon I was set thinking very vigorously by the face and behaviour of a priest, a man perhaps twenty years younger than myself, whom Clem and I found in the train at Vence. We two had been walking over the hills since the early morning, and we were very happy and a little tired and full of sweet air. We just caught the afternoon train with a run, and we got in breathless and a little clumsily and with a gasp of laughter; we threw a jest at each other about my Mr G – he'd almost caught us that time and had he meant to catch us or was it just his playfulness? – and disputed a little about the position of a cliff, the Baou des Blancs, marked on the map, and relapsed each into our own thoughts. And then I became aware of this fellow.

He was not looking at Clem. I have never seen anyone not look at anything with a more positive intensity. It was the exact converse of a hard stare. He was not looking more particularly at her flushed face and her pretty neck, his eyes were fixed on the panorama outside the window and his brow was knit and his lips moved – repeating some mental purge sovereign, I suppose, for such occasions.

It was as if his inner world was opened to me. I contemplated it as an explorer might do who has come over a crest to a tremendous declivity and contemplates a strange land. For the first time I think I realised fully the enormous distances between my peculiar world and the worlds in which the greater part of mankind are still living. I tried to put myself in his place and to imagine what sort of thoughts my ordinary thoughts would seem to him if suddenly they began to unfold themselves in his brain instead of mine, and what it would feel like to him to find himself living involuntarily for a day, let us say, as I live, neglecting all his offices, taking all my freedoms.

I used to think that bishops and clergymen and priests and teachers and all the Davidsons in the world doubted and went on from doubt to disbelief, and meanly concealed there disbelief in order to keep their incomes and positions. But indeed must of them are as capable of plunging into a sustained criticism of their beliefs as a passenger upon an ocean liner is capable of leaping the two hundred odd feet from the promenade deck to the Atlantic, in order to have a little swim in the sea. The liner has got him. And their worlds have got all these people, and no little cracks of inconsistent reality will be allowed to flood their mental holds with doubt. At once the pumps will get to work, the lips will be busy in exorcism.

What was my priest thinking, down there beneath the mists of his mind?

I doubt if his thoughts were definite. Here was a life different from his own, not merely in contrast with it, but in antagonism to it, and yet it was happy and betrayed no sense of Sin. It was evidently on the easiest terms with the hills and the sun. It jested – had he some English and did he understand our jest? And God permitted it! Suppose after one's years of meagre fare and tedious observances and shameful clothing and meek bearing and bitter and dismal restraint, suppose it should be that God could tolerate such freedoms? Suppose that God was different from what one had been taught? Suppose oneself, too, might have possessed some such glowing slip of slender womankind? To do with as one pleased! Help! Ave Maria! Help! Such thoughts were perhaps too clear for him, and yet I think a shadow after that fashion fell across his mind. And he muttered his time-honoured Latin specific: "*Ave Maria, gratia plena, Dominus tecum,*" or some such stuff, and did not look, oh! did not look.

My impression of this particular priest was that he was a fairly good priest; he had a grey distressed complexion, he was untidy and disturbed. But he was not disturbed enough to be dislocated. There must be priests who have gone much further than he from the perfect obedience of childish faith. There must be priests who neglect offices systematically, who drink or smoke unseasonably or excessively, or who have pilfered and continue to pilfer, who have mistresses and sustain intrigues. Here in the South of Frances there is much sly jesting about the priests' housekeepers. One sturdy fellow over the hills associates almost openly with a past or present mistress, goes to dine with her every day, and is the father of her son. I am filled with curiosity about the inner life of such priests.

I find it incredible that many of these sinful priests are unbelievers. There must be a strange jumble in their minds, and they must be accustomed to hiding themselves from the all-seeing God to their own satisfaction amidst the jumble. They must try not to think of him too closely. But they must feel that he is there still, the Hound of Heaven upon their track. Probably they find a consolation in exaggerating his mercy or in elaborating some fantastic childish belief in a propitiatory saint, a saint who is almost accessory to the offence. The good Saint Anthony will balance the cooked accounts. The Blessed Virgin loved greatly and is full of pity. God knows everything, it is true, but he ignores much.

Dickon told me a story the other day which shows how curious the jumble of a priest's world may become. Someone – Dickon or a friend of Dickon's, whichever it was – had taken a room for the night in an obscure and not too respectable hotel in a back street in Brussels. I think a railway connection had been missed or something of that sort, a cabman's advice taken too hastily, but I forget that part of the story. I rather fancy that Dickon, too, forgot that part of the story. In the dining-room was a priest, a big fat grave paternal man, dining rather guiltily with a woman. He had a rich unsubjugated voice, and he was doing his best to restrain her too public manifestations of personal devotion. Deponent's bedroom to which he retired some hours later, like most hotel bedrooms, had doors, locked of course, which communicated with the rooms on either side, and through one of these doors there presently transpired – an excellent word in this connection – the sounds of an acutely amorous encounter. Deponent moved about noisily and coughed, but the passions at large next door were too imperious for silence. They abated for a while, but a fresh and more violent storm followed the lull. The unseen lover, it became evident, was the priest who had been dining downstairs. There could not be such another voice in the world. In the morning he was visible in the corridor, departing, still grave, still paternal. But before he departed – and this is really all that matters in this distressing but necessary anecdote – he was plainly audible, very gently and sincerely, giving his fellow-sinner absolution for all that had occurred.

And she no doubt received it with an equal piety.

She, poor sinner, must have believed that that absolution was perfectly valid, and so believing she was absolved and troubled no other priest with the affair, but his case was not quite so simple. There were highly technical points about the matter, points above her understanding. She little knew what he had done for her. To cover a carnal he had committed a mortal sin, he had absolved an accomplice, and that the Church has very wisely forbidden. For a week or ten days perhaps he must have remained in danger of hell-fire, incapable of priestly functions, a man uncleansed. No doubt he was in Brussels away from his parish – if he had a parish. He confessed at once most probably, but absolution would have been reserved – for some days. Automatically an application must have been made to the bishop, naming no names, and automatically a faculty given to absolve. Then this curious transaction was completed and every shade of anxiety wiped from the soul of the wanderer. He, too, was safe once more. He could go his way in peace – until the next occasion.

He must have thought this out before and during his little encounter. He must have found it necessary to reassure his frail admirer. Perhaps he had not anticipated that necessity. How subtle and wonderful is the power of the human mind over contradictions! Both these people imagined they were living in the sight of God. Both of them believed that they believed that God was seeing them and seeing through them body and soul all the time! And both believed that what they did was Sin and point-blank defiance of His will.

Here again in this spiritual bookkeeping and quittance, in this simple deal between the carnal and the divine, is a glimpse of a mental world as remote from my present state as the life of some other planet from our earth's.

The human mind is at once complex and artless. Membership of a great organisation like the Catholic Church, which continues to fight for existence and power, must do much to develop the instincts and assumptions of partisanship. A priest, even a gravely erring priest, may still feel that he is on God's side and that God is on his side. Against a Protestant and still more against such a sceptic as myself, it must be easy for him to suppose himself a champion of God, and to feel in consequence a certain preferential claim upon Him. And even when the evasion of God's all-seeing eye has become habitual and loyalty had faded to nothing, that habitual evasion and that chilled devotion will still be far from positive denial.

I can imagine nothing more terrific than the outlook of a priest who really permits himself to disbelieve and allows his disbelief to be known. Before him are appalling difficulties and disciplines, difficult interrogations, struggles with his own still deeply rooted habits of submission, and at last expulsion into a vast, wild, windy, uncharted world of change and unknown dangers. Its usages are strange to him; it eats, dresses, washes even, in an unaccustomed fashion. He has for his stock in trade his poor ineffectual Latin learning. He left his family when he became a priest, and he has no friends now, no circle at all. For a very important part of the world, for the community naturally nearest to him that he knows best, he will be now a man with a black mark set against his name. To all the rest of the world he will be *queer.* I do not know what the market price of an unfrocked priest can be, but surely, unless he has what is called a "gift," he is among the cheapest of homeless men. Who will find work for him?

So I can understand that many a poor devil on the margin of the Church and with thoughts of rebellion in his soul, has stared out doubtfully at this greater world in which we live today, and felt the beauty of its breadth and freedom and heard the call of its ampler life, and then shivered and fled back headlong into the close and cramping but less perilous fastnesses of the faith, misapplying and crying, perhaps not altogether sincerely but with heartfelt passion, that ancient appeal: "Lord, I believe. Help thou mine unbelief!"

Were someone to discover some interesting well-paid employment for ex-priests, I do not know what would happen to the Roman Catholic Church. I believe it would collapse like a pricked sawdust doll. Its personnel would come pouring out.

With less vivid contrasts and a milder quality of tragedy, the inner history of a great multitude of people outside the Catholic Church must be very similar to that of the doubting priest; Anglican clergymen and ministers of Protestant sects and schoolmasters and schoolmistresses and the like, upon which the continuous active practice of religion is imposed. But outside the very precise and inquisitory disciplines of the watchful mother church, there is much greater latitude of accommodation, and the tragedy of apostasy is qualified by the comedy of prevarication.

It is very easy for me to be uncharitable in these matters. And perhaps I am. I have never had the least temptation to complicate my own thoughts about faith and philosophy, and so it is difficult for me to understand tortuousness in religion. What I believed and professed did not affect my material everyday life in the least. I had not even a friend who could be distressed by my opinions. It happened so. Dickon and I fell out of a shattered nest at my father's suicide, and if we found ourselves without any security we also found ourselves without any restraints. This is unusual freedom. Even the ordinary layman is obstructed in his free-thinking by a tangle of associations, by fear of hurting people he loves, by fear of offending people with whom he wishes to stand well, by an indisposition to break habits and reconstruct his days, and above all by the fact that as one goes out from formal religious associations one goes out from a complete institutional system into the wilderness, into a void. Negation has no schools, no ceremonies. Marriage and birth and death and the education of one's children must still, to a large extent, occur upon lines originally religious. There has been no revolution in religious opinion during the last hundred years, no new system ousting an old system, but only a creeping change, a crumbling down and a release. People drop one by one from perfect faith to imperfect faith and so to exploratory doubt, but there is never a day when they say *en masse*, "a new age has begun."

No new age has begun.

But while the Catholic Church, so elaborately organised, so stupendously systematic, has to a large extent kept its footing and stayed where it was, the Protestant world has passed through phase after phase of insufficient adjustment and is still as unstably adjusted as ever.

Throughout all my life there has been a great display of Protestant teachers who, if they were not precisely pouring new wine into old bottles, were at least trying to add just as much new wine to the old wine and pour out just as much of the old wine to make way for the new, as they thought the bottles would stand. The bottles were rectories, vicarages, manses, schoolhouses, college rooms, and cathedral closes; the bottles were habits and associations; the bottles were the phrases of creeds and articles that had become very familiar and sweet and dear; the bottles were all sorts of things, the daily stuff of life. In my lifetime I have seen Protestantism, wearing the same or but slightly more dandaical vestments, signing the same hymn tunes and sitting in the same pews, part from hell, fluctuate upon the nature and gravity of Sin, and play the most extravagant intellectual conjuring tricks with the Trinity, now professing to swallow it, now making it vanish, now reproducing it from the head or the elbow, expanding it to fill the stage or rolling it up into a small round pillule. Nothing could better illustrate the dominance of the daily circle of life over its theories and explanations. There is not a heresy in the whole cyclopaedia of Christian heresies that has not had the privilege of the Protestant pulpit during my lifetime. The pulpits creaked but remained. Their occupants remained.

From its beginning Protestantism was a departure. It goes on departing. In my young days I was greatly exercised by Matthew Arnold's modernisation of St Paul, and I am still entertained to find the anxious liberalising clergy trying to find recognition for their guarded misinterpretations of the explicit old creeds in Mr Shaw's "Blanco Posnet" and "Saint Joan," or extending an uncertain experimental hand towards faith-healers and even towards the spookeries of Sir Conan Doyle. Broad-minded Protestant clergymen are the best of company for a long thoughtful talk in the small hours. All things in earth or heaven become equally credible, and nearly everything is symbolical of something else. In that urbane atmosphere we discover after the flattest opposition that in the end "we all mean the same thing." We never define what that is. We go to bed on that. I find Dean Inge particularly sympathetic. He is a great modern Churchman, entirely honest but extremely devious. He is elaborately uninforming about the Virgin Birth, and courageously outspoken about birth control. His Gifford Lectures on Plotinus betray in every passage his preference for the light Moselle of Neo-Platonism to the emotion-loaded Port of Catholic mysticism. I suppose if he and I were handed over to some tremendous spiritual chemist and each ground to power and analysed to the last milligramme of his being, the report in each case would tail off with, "Belief in a living personal God – slight vestiges?" I met him a little while ago at a dinner-party and I found him all that I had hoped to find him – liberal Anglicanism incarnate, lean, erect, and – a little discoloured.

I do not know how Protestantism will end. But I think it will end. I think it will come to perfectly plain speaking, and it comes to perfectly plain speaking it will cease to be Christianity. There is now little left of the Orthodox church except as a method of partisanship in the Balkans. The League of Nations may some day supersede that, and then the only Christianity remaining upon earth will be the trained and safeguarded Roman Catholic Church. That is less penetrable, a world within a world, it shields scores of millions securely throughout their lives from the least glimpse of our modern vision.

## 11 – *The Paradox of Philip Gosse*

Philip Henry Gosse, the naturalist, made the most ingenious and delightful accommodation between his creed and his scientific beliefs. I read about him ten or twelve years ago in that little masterpiece, *Father and Son*, and my memory went back to a book upon shore life adorned with delicately coloured plates that I discovered in the library at Mowbray. When Sir Edmund Gosse, the venerable critic and poet, was a small boy he used, as he tells us in his memoir, to perch on a high stool and tint those drawings of sea-anemones and sea-mice and sea-slugs for his father. I am no collector, but for a time in my unsystematic way I sought the works of P H Gosse; they are rare and expensive now; and I need everything I could find of his. And so I learnt the completest defence of the literal interpretation of the first chapter of the Book of Genesis that has ever been made.

Gosse, the father, lived a simple, austere, and exalted religious life, and was evidently very happy in it – after his fashion. He followed the disciplines of the Plymouth Brethren. It was a life founded upon the English Bible, upon the most complete acceptance of the verbal inspiration of the English Bible. It was necessary, if this life was not to be shattered, that he should believe peacefully and fully in a special creation of the world in the year four thousand and four BC, in the establishment of the first man and woman in a garden of Eden situated in Mesopotamia, and in their almost immediate disobedience and misbehaviour. But Gosse, the father, was also a naturalist, and as a naturalist fossils and geological stratification forced themselves upon his attention; he was obliged to be aware of the contemporary controversy about evolution and to realise the existence of a mass of evidence that pointed to an enormous past for the world and life. A superficial mind might have considered he was in a hopeless dilemma, a Catholic might have been disposed to flee from natural history as a peculiar invention of the devil and seek refuge in the authority of the Church and Mr Belloc, but Philip Gosse neither despaired nor retreated. For some time perhaps he prayed and wrestled with the difficulty; in the end he overcame it, lucidly, simply, and completely – in a manner entirely Protestant.

For consider, he argued, what must be the conditions of creating such a universe as ours. It would have to be created as a going concern, for one can imagine it working from the outset in no other way. The honey must be ready for the moth at the moment of creation, the grass for the deer. The tree must be there for the woodpecker with its leaves and fruit and bark and grubs complete.

Consider now the trunk of the tree. It must be a trunk according to the nature that a tree must henceforth possess. There can be no cheap methods for the Creator; he gives the best. That tree-trunk therefore cannot be a flat stage-scenery trunk, nor a trunk of featureless pulp-like plaster or marzipan; it must have the normal structure of a tree-trunk – that is to say, it must have annual rings. What could the grubs of the woodpecker do in a plaster tree? And yet every annual ring would naturally indicate a year of growth, a year of previous existence. A sceptical fool at the very instant of its and his creation might declare therefore that that tree was as many years old as it had annual rings. He would be wrong.

Similarly every perennial in the garden of Eden, in the dew of the first Sabbath morning must have borne the leaf-scars of leaves that had never budded. At the root of every annual there must have been the decaying scales of a seed that had never been sown. And even Adam himself, at the moment of creation, must have been either an imperfect man – which is contrary to all religion – or he must have had a navel in his belly that had never linked him to a mother, because he had never had a mother. Moreover, since the animals directly they were created were living and modifiable and reproductive, the idea of their procreation and descent was in that instant made unavoidable; there was instantly projected into the entirely imaginary past their logically necessary ancestry. Fossils had to lie about in the rocks for the same reason that annual rings had to exist in the first created tree. The Neanderthal bones and the Cro-Magnon skulls, therefore, are no more proof of Adam's possession of an ancestry than his navel was of his indebtedness to a mother.

And so it must have been with the whole universe. Mountains of limestone arose built up out of the skeletal remains of creatures that had never really lived. The planets and stars spun out of nothingness upon orbits they might have followed for an eternity through phases of expansion and distortion, from nebula to night – if things had been different. Adam opened his eyes and saw the stars, all of them and in their order – though it takes years for the light of many of them to reach the earth. God who made the stars could make the ray. How else could it be done? The appearance of an immemorial past in the material world, then, no more disproves the simultaneous creation of everything at a specific date than the vistas one sees in two mirrors that are set face to face in a room prove that room to be an endless gallery.

This is logically perfect. One may even carry it a step further. For all that I can demonstrate to the contrary, I may have been created even as I write here, created with the illusion of past memories in my mind. Or the reader may have come into being in the very act of reading this sentence.

By this, to me, quite flawless argument Philip Gosse disposed of all the implications of Darwinism and could go on believing in the special creation of the world and man as the Bible recounts it, and in the doctrines that the Plymouth Brethren teach, and be able to have fresh spiritual difficulties whenever he wished and wrestle with the Lord in prayer in his evenings as he had been accustomed to do, and remain still for all this weight of conviction an honest naturalist collecting fossils and polyps among the rocks upon the beach without concealment or prevarication.

He must, I think, have made his discovery of this wonderful way out while he had been meditating, after the manner of the monks at Mount Athos. At any rate it was Adam's navel and not the annual rings of trees that had first directed him to his line of escape, and so he called his book the navel, *Omphalos*, and wise men still seek the surviving copies of it and read them and treasure them.

But Philip Gosse was a man of exceptional mental power, and few theologians have his clearness of head and his strength of faith. At the London Natural History Museum Sir Rupert told me they seem to show you Piltdown skull and Cro-Magnon remains and suchlike things, but indeed what you are seeing are most carefully and skilfully executed facsimiles. The originals themselves are locked away in safes downstairs, secure not only from fire and lightning, but from a far graver danger – the destructive arguments of the Creator's less intelligent partisans violent in defence of their threatened self-content.

## 12 – *Life Radiates*

I do not find myself under the same necessity to believe in a special creation of the universe as Philip Gosse, and so my mind takes the easier course of accepting this appearance of an immense antiquity – immense, that is, in relation to my experience – for my world as real. The vast age of the world is as real for my mind as my own individual existence. How far that is to be considered real and what "real" may mean are, as I have explained already, questions I have put outside my contemplation of the spectacle of being altogether.

And as the theological explanations of this spectacle have lost their grip upon me year by year and become unreal and incredible, I find myself passing under the sway of an entirely different set of ideas that seems to be taking hold of the modern imagination more and more firmly. They are called creative ideas nowadays, and they look for their justification not towards the past but towards the future.

Philosophically I am quite prepared to admit that there is no plot nor scheme nor drama nor pattern in the flow of events as they are apprehended by human minds, but my disposition is diametrically opposed to my philosophy. I have never encountered even a stain on a wall or a glowing cavity in a fire upon which my mind could not impose a design. It is still more natural for me, a moral being inherently, to impose some dramatic conception upon my universe as a whole – if only to get an orientation for my living, a standard of judgment by which to estimate the good or evil of my decisions.

Now the outline that modern science, with an ever increasing assurance, develops upon this common-sense spectacle of space is the story of progressive life. The black curtain of eternal nothingness rises to reveal the stellar universe, a whirl of matter like a puff of dust particles upon an immense scale, eddying through the endless emptiness of space. On one of its spinning, circling particles comes this life, at first not perceptibly more than a stir of complex chemical reactions amidst a warm wet slime. It is a new process in matter; presently it begins to display desire and discrimination, to seek nourishment, to seek the light, to move away from things unfavourable. At first it can exist only in warm and shallow waters, but its ability to spread and reproduce itself and to bring recalcitrant substance into the sphere of its desire increases steadily.

I pause and set a note of interrogation against that "steadily." I am not sure how far a case can be made out to show that life has continually grown in range, in knowledge, in continuity of will, in co-operative power. But there is much to support the assertion that life has been uninterruptedly progressive from its first beginning. The thrust towards greater range in space and time and an ever-richer and fuller mental being has been continual. Progression is not the same as proliferation; there have been secular massacres of animal and vegetable life, in comparatively brief geological phases thousands of species and genera have been swept away by rapid geographical change and there have been ages of great hardship for living things. But these severities seem always to have sustained exceptional strides in adaptation and to have prepared the way for a new phase of abundance upon a higher level. The swampy vegetation and floundering, basking reptile life of the Mesozoic Age was extinguished in perhaps a few hundred thousand years of adversity, but it was swept away by the same changes that presently evolved the grassy prairies, the rich forests, and swarming herbivora of the Miocene. Life had won the hills and dry places by the sufferings and disasters of that struggle, and now feathered birds and furry beasts could push their way towards the poles. The geological record, the archives of life's adventures, does certainly seem to so amateurish a reader as I a straightforward story of expansion and progress – and particularly of expanding intelligence. That is the thing these new views press most urgently upon me. Feeling appears, perception, restraint, and judgement, eyes that see ahead, and limbs that pause and hesitate. Mind grows – and grows at an ever-increasing pace.

The first elements of mind were assembled slowly and painfully through enormous ages. Among the invertebrata and among the lower vertebrated animals it is improbable that there are inner worlds beyond the scope of mere incidents; their most sustained mental operations may have a depth in time of only a few hours, or even of only a few moments, may be no more than a series of little puffs of consciousness connected by no unifying idea. The life of a frog or a fish is probably a life of transient awarenesses dying away at once after flight or feasting or fecundation into forgetting. The probability of a greater continuity than that appears only with the enlarging brains of the birds and mammals of the Tertiary Age. Manifestly these brains brought something quite new into the struggle, and thereafter the drama of life centred upon them. The brains in nearly every order and family of the mammals have enlarged relatively five times, ten times even, since the first appearance of this class in the world.

And it is not only by a mere increase in the size of the brain, we are reminded, that a great mental enlargement is indicated in the mammals. The peculiarity of the mammal, which the bird shows to a certain extent, is its continuing contact and fellowship with its young. Wisdom no longer perished with the individual. Quite early in their ascendancy the mammals began to educate. A wolf or a dog is elaborately educated morally and in the tactics of hunting; a young monkey has a powerful impulse to imitate and learn. With man came an ever-swifter process towards a mental continuum. In a few score thousand years he developed speech, picture-writing, writing, a distribution of documents, printing. In archives and literature he began a racial brain.

Each century, each decade in the last few hundred years, has made enormous additions to the speed and range of interchange between one man's brain and another's, and to the accumulation of more and more available store of knowledge. Telegraphy was still a wonder in my infancy. Now we can broadcast speech, will presently radiate drawings, and preserve a record of gesture and movement. The trace of the increase in man's powers of communication rises hyperbolically. Our minds are less and less isolated. They mingle and interact in a new common medium of published and recorded and universally accepted ideas and interpretations. A new common medium I write: for imposed upon our minds appears a mind. This is the mind in which exist science, history, and thought. It has the same sort of relation to our individual activities that a regiment or army has to its constituent men. It is a collective human person in whom we all participate and which invades all our personalities. It is no longer mortal as we are mortal. It is life awakening, breaking through the limitations of individuality and growing conscious of itself. We are all presented as contributory units to a Titanic being which becomes conscious and takes hold of this planet.

Is there any reason for supposing that this growing mental being has any limitations yet imaginable, set to the increase of its power, to its expansion, or to its invasion of our lives? I do not find any. It is said that it must be limited in time because it is limited to this planet, and that this planet is doomed to freeze and die with the cooling of the sun. but I do not see how anyone with a knowledge of the implications of modern physics or with any sense of the unknown knowable can believe that life is necessarily limited to this planet for ever. The premises are altogether insufficient. An observer of nature in the Cambrian age might as readily have declared that life was only possible under water, and that in a few hundred million years the last fish would gasp its last gasp as the last puddle on earth dried up. To me it is far easier to suppose that this present unfolding of consciousness and will is only a birth and a beginning, and that I am not merely myself but a participator in a Being that has been born but need not die.

This is the appearance on the face of things that best survives the test of my sceptical acids. It is how I see life. It holds my mind when all the older faiths have lost their last vestige of credibility. It is, I admit, a poetic and not a demonstrable idea. To accept it is not to return to religion. This Being is not to my mind a God, unless we are to invert the idea of God altogether. It is an objective and not a cause, and since it falls within the frame of time it can only have a proximate and practical reality. But it is great enough, I feel, to comprehend the utmost scope and outlook of my life and to rationalise its motives and relationships.

### 13 – *Promethean*

I have put this idea of the common mental being of our race, this Racial Man to which all our individual lives consciously or unconsciously are contributory and subordinate, as if it were an outcome of the new biological outlook upon the universe. In what I have just written I have told of it objectively as a history of our world. Seen thus objectively it appears indeed modern. But the same idea comes into human thought from another angle. We find it within us.

In the last million years or so our breed has changed from the most solitary habits to habits more social and co-operative than those of any other animal. The fierce, lonely, egoistic ape-soul has been modified and qualified, and had superimposed upon it an intricate fabric of mitigating and restraining dispositions. The superstitious fear which may not only overshadow childhood but last right into adult life, is only one of the earliest and crudest of these adaptations to social needs. The self-control of the primitive tabus is also among the merely initial amendments of human fierceness. There are not only inhibitions but addenda. The emotions of sexual abandon and maternal and even paternal love as the ape knew them have also been seized upon by nature and broadened and utilised for social ends. There is now in man a desire to serve. There is a pleasure in and a craving for co-operation and associated action. Curiosity has become disinterested, and the constructive impulse has been varied and widened.

The primary form of the human soul is still self-seeking, self-protecting egoism, as the primary scheme of the human body is still that of an ape's. But in contemporary man the gratification of purely egoistic needs is not sufficient for happiness, it does not satisfy completely. In the case of man in the case of the dog and other social animals, the individual soul has been invaded by the soul of the pack. A man has to be not only gratified but reassured. There is a conscience, there is a moral struggle, a conflict of motives. The cat, which is a solitary beast, is single-minded and goes its way alone, but the dog like his master is confused in his mind. And in our rationalising human minds it seems plain to me there is a continuing conflict between the intense and originally much more intense, crudely and definitely self-seeking factor, and a vaguer, wider, unselfish factor. The two are associated but not unified. They jar, and the rationalising mind struggles to account for the disharmony. I think that this less personal element of the self increases generally as we grow older and our experiences increase and widen, and that it is becoming more evident and important in the world's affairs. On the objective side there appears a race-mind, and this is paralleled on the subjective side by a great extension of individual interest to impersonal things. The race-mind, which is as immortal as the race, continually accumulates interest and attractiveness, and has more to offer the individual and more power over the individual. A large part of the waking hours of many people nowadays is occupied by activities that are of slight or no advantage to them whatever, although they may be of very great advantage to the race. A man may live a quarter or a third of his time in a study or a laboratory keenly engaged upon things that have nothing whatever to do with his intimate personal drama, activities that add only to the common inheritance. He may even neglect his personal drama for these things.

The last time I was in London I met a very stimulating man whom I had long wished to encounter, Dr Jung, the psycho-analyst. He had come from Zurich to London to give some lectures, and after one of these, the last of them, he had joined a party in a flat looking out upon the Thames at Westminster. I do not remember who my host and hostess were – Dickon had taken me there – but there was a pleasant and interested and not too numerous gathering to meet Jung, and we smoked and drank champagne and whisky and ate sandwiches and talked late. It was very good talk, no fireworks, no posturing in it, but close and clear. Jung's English is excellent, and an hour's lecture at the Queen's Hall had not fatigued him in the least.

I buttonholed the great man because I wanted to know how he regarded this conception of a sort of super-mind of the species, and he said that it was entirely sympathetic with his views. He made it clear I had not been following up that track alone; I had been running beside and responding to contemporary thought. One meets a phrase here and a suggestion there, and subconsciously they incorporate themselves with one's own ideas. I had thought myself original.

I quoted Paul that we were all members of one body, and remarked upon the ease with which one fell into theological phraseology in this matter. Someone mentioned a distant relative of mine, Wells, who had employed many religious expressions in a book called "God, the Invisible King"; a Manichean book, said somebody, neither Greek nor Hebrew, but Persian. The writer in question had gone very far indeed in his resuscitation of theological terms and in his recommendation of prayer and suchlike exercises. Too far, said someone. I agreed. I had already talked about that with Wells himself, and it was plain to me that this God the Invisible King of his was not so much God, in sense in which people understand that word, as Prometheus; it was a titanic and not a divine being. This unseen monarch was much more akin to Nietzsche's Overman than to a normal divinity. Frederic Harrison too, someone remarked, had said that God the Invisible King was merely the Humanity of Comte with a crown on. I had not heard of this before but it struck me as being a justifiable comment.

Yet I would not be too hard on my cousin for his use of the word God. For can it have other than a lax use? If you believe in good as an objective reality, in a sense you believe in God. I doubt if many Protestants nowadays believe in God in any other sense. The human mind had been struggling to apprehend this something behind and above and about individuality for thousands of years and insisting most pitifully upon exactitudes just where exactitude is most misleading. Theology has been experimental, and it had been angry and cruel because it did not realise what an experiment it was. It was worried by immediate practical needs. It has been dogmatic because it felt that its flimsiness could not stand the strains of inquiry. It felt it must take a standpoint if it was not to wander for ever. It has shown all the nervous irritability, rising at times to vicious violence, of a weak, well-intentioned man trying to carry out an important task with a defective equipment. But in all its aberrations it has clung to its essential, idea, the denial of individual isolation. The assertion of complete individual isolation is, I suppose, the essential idea of the dogmatic Atheist.

Jung laid great stress on the readiness of people to misconceive these ideas about a greater human being. They did not grasp how that being was supposed to be synthetic and comprehensive. They thought of it as something outside themselves, an individual of the same order as themselves, as someone put over them, and not as a being including and comprehending them as I include and comprehend my own nerve cells and blood corpuscles. Neither Nietzsche's Overman nor Shaw's Superman was really to be thought of as an individual person. Both were plainly the race development, the whole race in progress. But writers with the journalistic instinct to caricature got hold of these ideas and cheapened them irremediably, and the popular interpretation of these phrases, the Overman and the Superman, had come to be not a communion of saints but an entirely ridiculous individual figure, a swagger, a provocative mingling of Napoleon Bonaparte, Antinous, and the Admirable Crichton.

Jung came back to my quotation from St Paul about our all being members of one body. Evidently he attached much importance to that. He said that not only Christian theology, but nearly all mystical religion in the world, was saturated with the idea of a merger of the narrow self in some variously apprehended greater soul. So soon as religion began to develop theology and pass out of the phase of abject fear of the mythological Old Man, the tribal God, this conception appeared. The believer in the mysteries became more or less the greater being and the greater being became more or less the believer. In the phase of ecstatic communion the believer was lifted altogether out of his sinful and finite self and above all the frustrations of life.

You found this same idea of transcending individuality, in the Mass, in Mithraism and in many surviving hymns and phrases of ancient Persian and Egyptian cults. It was expressed almost in identical terms by Moslem and Jewish mystics. It was not a clear and cool intellectual realisation with the mystics; it was felt rather than thought, but clearly it was strictly parallel with the inclusion of the individual in a racial being that was so congenial to modern biology. In Christian mysticism it was obscured by the heavier emotional charge of that cult. In the case of women mystics particularly the suggestion of the phrase "the divine spouse" had been excessively powerful, and with such types as St Hildegarde or St Gertrude or the Blessed Angela de Foligno, Christian mysticism had sunken a long way towards a mere sublimation of sexual abandon. The Being became very personal and physical and responsive in their imaginings. The egoism was exalted rather than expanded to divinity. That, someone suggested, was what happened when women took to mysticism. A remark which started a detached wrangle in one corner of the room.

Jung listened for a while to that, and then he remarked that by his "Superior Person" Confucius must have intended the same generalised comprehensive man as this we had in mind, the racial and not the individual man. That again was new to me. "Superior Person," Jung remarked, could be translated just as well by Overman; but we Europeans had an unfortunate trick of misunderstanding and making Chinese thought ridiculous and unprofitable by using the least dignified words possible in our literal translations of its phrases. One can do that to European phrases with an equal destructiveness. Caradoc Evans, I remarked, degraded Welsh religiosity simply by translating the shining garments of righteousness as White Shirts. We had still the cloudiest notions of Chinese thought, said Jung, even of contemporary Chinese thought; the Chinese might be getting towards a working philosophy of the modern world, without our aid or sympathy, along a road of their own.

But so it was, whether one turned to the great teachings of China or the sacrificial mysteries of Peru, one found in forms that were sometimes gross and monstrous, and sometimes cold and enigmatic, intimations of an almost universal idea. Every great religion and every philosophy of life throughout the world seemed to have been feeling its way, often in spite of enormous initial difficulties of creed and training, towards this same process, the process of subordinating the egoism to a broader generalised being, the being of communion. Could one doubt that a common psychological necessity determined these agreements, that like parallel streaks on the surfacc of a great river they show the direction of a current that has been flowing with gathering force for five-and-twenty centuries?

The realisation of this inner psychological necessity which, under the suggestions of Jung and Freud and their groups of associates, we are now beginning to correlate with a new phase in the circumstances of human life, marks what one may perhaps compare to a coming-of-age. Just as we are disentangling our minds from the last lingering fears and submissiveness that marked the childhood of our race, so also are we growing out of the intense individualism of its romantic adolescence. As our mental range increases we realise that in the end frustration and extinction await everything that is purely individual in us. We are beginning, some of us, or even most of us, to develop a further, a more fully adult, mental stage. This adult mentality of the years ahead will be self-neglectful and scientific and creative in comparison with anything that had gone before. It will be consciously and habitually a contributory and co-operating part in the over-mind.

## 14 – *The Immortal Adventure*

These identifications of modern tendencies with old religious impulses are very curious, and I note them here on that account. But I do not find any necessity for religious phraseology to express my own apprehension of the drama of existence. If it is a matter of interest it is still a matter of secondary interest to me that anyone should have thought these thoughts before in other terms or from a different angle. I do not want, I am under no necessity, to be religious and mystical on this point. The science of physics has enough paradox in it for me, and about ordinary life I prefer to be matter-of-fact. I am much more inclined to use such new and unprecedented expressions as "The Adventure of Life," or what for all practical purposes is synonymous, the "Adventure of Mankind," or "of the Greater Man," for my general conceptions of everyday reality than any of the timeworn phrases of the older faiths. Those may be charged with emotion and reverence, yes, but also they are charged with misunderstanding.

"Adventure" is more in the quality of my character than any imperative to live in this or that particular fashion, and it conveys, what the theological terminology fails to convey, the suggestion that after all the limitless will of man for knowledge and power may not prove to be sanctioned by the nature of things. He may fail and freeze after all. He may smash to nothingness in some interstellar collision. Even with the admission of that uncertainty, the adventure is great enough and wonderful enough to hold my imagination completely.

This way of looking at existence differs from any religious interpretation in its entire voluntariness. We are not told dogmatically that we are so-and-so or that we must do so-and-so; but it is put to us, Let us be and do so-and-so. Let us gather knowledge and power, let us communicate and learn to co-operate, let us lay hands on life and fate. Let us at any rate make the attempt.

To give oneself knowingly to the Adventure of Mankind has this much to be said for it, that it is in the trend of current things. Whatever we may think of the universality of progress, there can be little dispute that the current phase of existence is by human standards progressive. We shall be in the movement whether we desire it or not. And since we are thus conscripted in the army of the Titans against the old Jove of chance and matter, since we are obliged willy-nilly to participate in the increase and creative application of knowledge to human ends, we may as well give our lives cheerfully and take a conscious share in the process. We shall be happier so. We shall be happier to extend our motives and desires beyond the tragic uncertainties of the purely egotistic life. We shall be broadened and steadied by that participation, we shall be released, we shall be very largely released from the worst intensities of personal desire and passion and from the bitter fear and still bitterer realisation of futility that haunt self-centred minds.

## 15 – *View from a Window in Provence*

It may be, the reader thinks that all these sections so far, were written on one wet day at Dickon's desk in his rooms at Bordon Street. The way in which I began this book may have given that impression. What a day's work it would have been! Indeed, I wrote no further there than the eighth section, and then I fell into a profound meditation in the armchair before the open fire – about electrons. And things like that. I had stirred up the long-slumbering curiosities of my adolescence by recalling them. I had a queer little idea, an imp, a paradox, an atom of explanation; I made some notes at last, but nothing to interest the present reader. Those notes will come to nothing; my day for such bright ideas is past. The rest of these pages I have written in my "bureau," as Jeanne will call it, at the Villa Jasmin.

I have revised all that I wrote in London here, and I find myself more and more interested in this enterprise. It is doing more for me than I expected. Autobiography, provided that it is not too severely disciplined, may be, I perceive, an almost inexhaustible occupation. Nothing is altogether irrelevant. Whatever interests one, or has ever interested one, is material. In due course no doubt I shall get to autobiographical particulars.

I have been back here in Provence now for fifteen days and everything is as it used to be last year, the same sunlit peace, the same delicate beauty and kindly freshness in the air, the same lean red-haired Clem, as absurdly insistent that she idolises me and will have no other man but me, invading me whenever she dares and protecting me against a score of imaginary onslaughts upon my peace and comfort: everything is the same indeed, except that my little kitten has grown into a very pretty grey cat with a quite extravagant sense of its own importance. It comes and sits in judgment upon each fresh sheet as I write it so soon as the paper is sufficiently warmed by the sun. At certain passages, upon no consistent principle that I can distinguish, it purrs.

This Villa Jasmin is an old Provençal *mas*, a small farmer's house set upon a hillside among olive terraces not far from Grasse. No automobile can come up to it and it is beautifully difficult to find, but there is a mossy stone track to us beneath the grey contorted trees by which we can supply our timber and coal and suchlike heavy needs. Let me describe it with some particularity. In it I hope to write most of this contemplated book; it is the foreground to all that follows.

The house is of three stories in front and has a tall bare face; behind, it nestles its rump, so to speak, into the hill; its sole decoration is a ripple of plaster beneath its ruddy brown tiles, a great scarlet geranium that sprawls up half its height, and a passion-flower; the narrow windows have wooden fastenings, and old wooden shutters on rusty hinges that a Cornish southwester would wrench off in a minute and scatter like dead leaves. Before the house in a broad terrace where I take my morning coffee and my midday meal. Blue-berried ivy climbs over the parapet; there is a trim close Japanese medlar in one corner, and in the midst, surrounded by a grass-rimmed oval of little respectful rose-trees, there is a very fine and flourishing palm. At the corner is a big olive-tree that now dots the gravel everywhere with its fallen black fruits. Beyond are other olive-trees and some fig-trees; a broad gravel path goes ceremoniously to a large oil-jar in which a genteel, glossy, flowerless plant is growing, and there it comes to a rounded and dignified conclusion. On the other side of the terrace there is a clump of thorny-bladed agaves, green-blue or green with yellow edges, a big stone-rimmed fountain where our washing is done and where Jeanne, in spite of the most passionate remonstrances from Clem, is in the habit of leaving her bowls and brushes and whacking-boards to desecrate our serenity, and there are two delicate grey mimosas, a great old Judas-tree, two pretty gracious trees whose names I do not know, and above and behind all a thick, tall hedge of bamboos.

There is always a sound of running water about this house. A stream comes down a little channel from above; close by the wall a mouth of stone, with lips like an angry ape's, spouts water into the big washing fountain; below the terrace a dispersed trickle of water falls from a domed niche adorned with an abundance of dripping hart's-tongue and maidenhair fern, into yet another basin of stone. There is a third fountain in a corner where irises grow, a little terra-cotta affair put there by my predecessor. It has an inscription in Greek letters, a phrase that Heraclitus made: *παντα ῥει*, all things flow. There is no enduring thing.

The hill descends steeply in front of the house, and paths sweep round from the front door on either side of the terrace and are hidden and unite before the fountain of the ferns below, and run straight down the hill in a broad, stony incline beneath now golden chestnut-trees and grey olives, to ruinous yet stately entrance pillars upon the rustic highway.

My study is on the top story and it is as far as possible from the kitchen, for Provençal servants prefer to converse when they are at some distance from each other, and always rattle plates and beat upon pots and pans for a time before they make use of them. It is a calm austere room. Its walls are painted grey and have nothing on them but six engravings, four by Mantegna and two by Dürer; there is a tall fine bureau, a large cupboard in which books are hidden – for the backs of modern books if they are displayed talk overmuch – a table on which papers are scattered, a table at which I write, and some rush-bottomed chairs. The floor is tiled, all the rooms in this house are tiled with time-darkened red tiles; the carpet is discreetly gay, and in one or two shapely old pots of white earthenware, very delicately crackled and discoloured, Clem puts bright flowers. And there is a stove, a good little hungry warming stove which burns wood and pine-cones.

My window looks almost due south over my palm and Japanese medlar and olives, and my view is wide and gently various upon hills and crests and further hills, a remote ridge from the Estérel and a sharp-edged inlet, a dagger-blade, of water. Beyond the last reluctant distances of the land appears the sea gravely blue and the horizon like the top edge of a blue silk barrier.

The hills are all terraced and planted; mistily grey olives prevail, but there are many sorts of trees and there are a few vineyards, rusty and yellow now, and other cultivations. The houses are solitary and plain, white or pink or pale yellow with little vertical windows like the toy houses of my childhood. There are many cypresses like black candles, like warning fingers, singly or in groups; I do not believe the land would be half as beautiful without its accentuation by these cypresses; and when the day is clear but overcast the trees upon the contours of the hills pattern against the soft grey-blue distances like a border of minute dark lace. Close to me on my extreme right is a single cypress against the butt-end of a lean high grey house; it is tall and like a plume, and for some reason it pleases me very greatly. A steep edge of precipitous walls above ravines and blank white factory-palaces clustering upon the hillside and partly veiled in haze is Grasse; it just comes into my view beyond the nearer olive slopes. A slender chimney minaret sticks up here and there, a steadying vertical white line; its rare, occasional smoke has, I know, the smell of incense. The cathedral tower is single and tall and square and outstanding. Right in the middle of my view behind a ridge and ten miles distant one feels rather than sees Cannes.

The whole of this land is a pleasant and prosperous region very indulgent to mankind. Its agriculture, like its scenery, has a delicate, fastidious quality. I never see a pig here nor any cattle; there are occasional sheep, genteel-looking sheep, there are disciplined grey geese and immaculate white poultry. Once or twice, in the more open and rocky spaces among thc hills, I have met small companies of goats with goatherds. They had a quality so harmonious with the scenery that they seemed rather like elegant quotations from Theocritus than economic facts. The farmer below me is employed in growing jasmine and violets, and a little way along the road there are fields of carefully tended rose-bushes.

In the early morning the stream-beds and valleys between the crests and ridges are filled with very sharp restricted banks of white mist, and then a conical hill some five or six miles away from here becomes an island of romance. All day long there is a quiet soft change in the features of this scene, hillsides hold the sunlight for a time and then fade away, spurs and summits grow from insignificance to prominence as the sun searches them out on its daily round. Towards sundown Mougins upon its ridge six miles away will at times shine out with such a brightness that I think of Bunyan's Celestial City. Everywhere at this time of year there are rubbish fires burning, and their bright down-feathers of white smoke expand and unroll and dissolve away continually and are continually renewed. Ever and again an absurd little single-track railway asserts itself by an acute long nose of white steam that burrows hurriedly across the bluish greens and greys and hangs for a time fades like an unimportant memory.

Almost always the sky above this land is a pure clear blue or delicately streaked with filmy cloud, and the sunlight is a benediction. Sundown brings a glow of warm contentment. Then presently the nearer houses lose strength, and faint and die and become white ghosts in the twilight. Amidst the darkling scattered lights appear.

I have never known a more intimate sky than this of Provence, by night as well as by day. Even the rain, the infrequent rain, is confidential, with something apologetic and reassuring in its whisper. Last night I saw the morning-star and the old moon close together above the crest of Peyloubet. My bedroom window looks our eastward, and there, in the deep blue of morning, framed in my window-frame like a luminous picture on my wall, was the old moon on her back with the young moon faint but visible in her arms. There is, I suppose, a slight astigmatism in my eyes, for I saw Venus not as the minute disc she is, but as an animated splash of laughing white light that made exhilarating gestures over this grouping. I understood suddenly why Czechs and Danes and Poles and Swedes and Englishmen and suchlike boreal and Baltic men were needed to realise the inhuman remoteness of interplanetary space. The stars and planets of the Mediterranean have no aloofness at all; Diana can still descend upon the hills of Provence, and for all our modern science the heavenly bodies move here as they did in pagan times, harmoniously in crystal spheres.

Possibly I dozed, for when I looked again moon and morning-star were gone altogether and the sky was flushed with the excitement of coming sunrise. I lay for a time and then got up and went to my window to see whether that little hill of mine towards Cannes had got its mists about it yet, and was sitting up and minded to play at islands of enchantment with me.

This is the present foreground of my world. Men have lived among these hills for scores of thousands of years, and one could think that here if anywhere in the world was peace and permanent adaptation. A short automobile journey to the east would take us to the caves of Grimaldi, where some of the earliest of human skulls were found, and Moustiers, which has traces of men even more ancient, is as close to the west. Cro-Magnon, in Dordogne, is five or six hours of motoring beyond. The soil everywhere is rich with human traces, from chipped flint fragments to Phoenician beads, Roman brickwork, and medieval crockery. The newest villas of Grasse stand on old foundations. This, one might say, is man's enduring home. The soil is generous; there is no persecution in the weather, no implacable animal enemy, and little disease. Here, it would seem, a man can still be born and live a life of immemorial usage, can believe and worship after the fashion of his ancestors, and die under the blessings of his church as a child falls asleep in the arms of a nurse.

But, indeed, this fair and spacious scene is a mere mask of calm beauty upon the face of change. As I sit writing I hear the sounds of chopping and sawing and ever and again a shout and a crash. Under the aged, wrinkled boughs a fire is crackling briskly. A farmer just beyond my cypress plume is busily destroying his olive orchard, and he is doing so in order to plant the ground with jasmine. He will have to stub those tough gnarled roots; it will be a heavy toil for him. All these peasants seem to be giving up their olives for jasmine, and they are growing that for the perfume factories in Grasse which serve the transitory, unstable world of luxury in Paris and London and New York. A change of fashion in scent, or some ingenuity of the chemist, may abolish the profits of this flower-growing, and then these hillsides will know trouble; for olive-trees that are gone are gone for ever. No one can wait nowadays for planted olive-trees to reach fruition.

The fate of this countryside, which looks so self-subsisting, is I perceive dependent upon the great consuming centres; those little hidden railways are like suckers from the urban fungi that have drained away all local autonomy. The rural life here has been insidiously and secretly and completely subjugated by Paris. Ostensibly this land is very like the countryside of hundred years ago, when its peasants could have gone on living if all the rest of the world had died, but in truth their lives now are hardly more secure upon these hills than they would be if they were dodging the traffic in the midst of the Champs Elysées. They are educated, they are tempted away, they are taken for the army and demoralised, they are pushed out of their homes to make way for artists and winter visitors like myself, they are pushed off their land to make way for villas and gardens and strange new cultivations.

Just out of hearing up the hill behind me is the main road through Grasse from Paris to Nice, along which drives the restless fever of a new breed of rich people, people cut off from the tradition of the past and incapable it would seem of any interest in the future. They have incalculable powers of manipulating the franc on which these peasants rely. Their great fat-tyred care go throbbing and hooting past, the chauffeur is glassily intent upon the road, the passengers – are passengers. Never were there people so entirely passengers. They are carried along like sacks. The clothes they wear, the very complexions of the women, seem to have been put upon their passive persons by the tradesmen of Paris and London before they were packed off in their cars. One cannot believe that their financial reactions are other than automatic. And yet they control. Or at least they are the instruments of a blind control. It is they who are sweeping away the olive orchards and turning the peasants into gardeners, speculative flower-growers for their parfumeries, and servants for their multiplying villas. Without premeditation, with no definite object, they change the face of the earth. Not merely here.

This window looks south and modern manufactures and mines and forges, the slums and the dismal industrial defacement of the world, are far away behind me and out of the compass of this picture. The plants I have helped to plan and reconstruct, the factories and sidings and warehouses of my group of companies and all our offices are forgotten here. There are hills and mountains gashed and tormented by us for minerals, far away to the right in Spain; and for all I know, though I should doubt it, there may be labour trouble and bad conditions in the scent factories of Grasse just round the corner of the hill. But such things are the mere fringes of the world of massed toil; there is no glare of foundry of furnace in this scene; between here and the equator there are no many-windowed factories lit up to break the visible night. The great masses of industrialism are at the back of this outlook, and as it were below my comfort, away deeply down through my sheltering hills and mountains, through the bulge of the world northward that robs them of our sun. They would be out of mind here altogether were it not that these people, hurrying in their automobiles along the road from Paris and Lyons and Grasse to Nice and Monte Carlo and Italy, and the still greater multitude in the lits-salons and trains-de-luxe that follow each other along the coastal railway, do in some subtle way recall that distant teeming darkness of toil. They come with a haste, with a headlong effect, crowding upon each other, as if they were in flight from things and suggestions and, it may be, apprehensions that they desire to forget.

Well, I at least do not want to forget. But I want for a while to be away from these things to think.

I sit now at my window after the sunset, and my cat is purring before the purring stove, within which the pine-cones have just begun to flame. My little study is bright and clear and secure in the light of my freshly lit lamp, but outside, behind a veil of blue silence that is deepening into darkness, is an incessant hurrying world. The rivulet that prattles beneath my window does not hurry half so fast.

If I could put out an arm of ten miles I could flatten down a little undulation of the land and see the lights of Cannes and Antibes and their hotels and villas-de-luxe, and if I could push away a few unimportant hills with my left elbow I could unmask the lights of Cagnes and Nice and, beyond those, Villefranche and Beaulieu and Monte Carlo and Mentone. From here they would look like patches of burning sand-grains along the dark littoral. In those places the evening is only a beginning. Through the nearer shadows among the hills the peasants are going home from their work, invisible in the twilight; they will eat and sit and talk for a while and presently blow out their lamps of American paraffin and go to bed. But all along the Riviera the immense ritual of dinner is in preparation, myriads of cooks and waiters are busy upon the endless repetitions of the standard meal, thousands of baths are in progress, hundreds of men are struggling at this moment with their heads in their dress-shirts, and women of every age are enhancing or creating their beauty for the illuminated and significant half of the day. They will eat rather too much of their magnificently commonplace food, they will drink rather too much, most of them, they will dance like automata to imitation negro music, they will flirt without discrimination, they will set out upon timid, dishonest, nocturnal adventures and arrange their poor little adulteries and fornications, they will gamble according to solemnly conceived systems against the facetiousness and disrespect of chance, and so come at last belatedly to inartistic lasciviousness or speechless grossness and sleep.

Nevertheless these people, individually and in masses, seem to make decisions, seem to have the direction of economic change. They have an air of being less mutely the creatures of fate than the peasants. It is hard to believe that it is so.

My mind takes a wider range beyond these Riviera resorts, these patches of luminous eczema upon the broad face of the earth. Out beyond is the Mediterranean, and across it, could my eye see through the smooth curve of the waters to them, go the lit ships from Genoa to the east of me and Marseilles to the west, and trailing my imagination with them go the slender threads of their wakes further and further round the globe, through the straits and through the narrow seas and into the tropics to the harbours and warehouses of India and the far East, and out by Gibraltar to South Africa and to South and North America into distant ports and up great estuaries. My mind hovers for a while over these ships, mere particles upon the homeless wilderness of the waters, and I think of grave engineers watching oiling and pressure, of officers in the chart-room, of stokers, excessively minute because they are so remote, sweating before their furnaces, and passengers – again those passengers! – congratulating themselves upon the calmness of the night and anticipating dinner. What a complex of habits and motives it is that drives those ships, with their ill-assorted cargoes, their vaguely directed passengers and their uncertain profits, about the world!

On my other table lie the English newspapers of three days ago, and the *Quotidien* of yesterday and today's *Eclaireur* and *Petit Niçois*. And there are various London weeklies and the weekly *Times* and *Manchester Guardian*. As I recall what I have read in them today the view from my window seems to extend further and further, my boundaries sweep forward across the Mediterranean eastward and westward to Oran and Morocco, to the Atlas, to Egypt and the Soudan, to Arabia Petraea and the Yemen and the Hadramaut, to Basra and Ormuz and India and China, and northward across the Pamir uplands, and on and on until at last they enclose the globe and meet themselves again in a shrinking coil and vanish. Over there in Africa, out beyond the hump of the Estérel and across the waters just over the roundness of the world, the Spanish are retreating before the recalcitrant tribesmen of the Riff under Abdel Krim. It is a hustled retreat, and the Spaniards are losing heavily and are likely to lose more. They can be having no rest tonight. Even now as I write some poor peasant lad from Andalusia or Castile may be writhing in agony with a sniper's bullet flattened among his freshly shattered vertebrae. Down he goes, and if there is no ambulance at hand they may have to leave him to the mercy of the pursuers. Or they may not trust that mercy. I can almost see those scattered figures of distress straggling across vast and lonely and rocky places and the crumpled bodies lying still, until the prowling beasts discover them. That, too, is in my present world as surely as these tranquil hills.

The Spanish retreat is leaving the French garrisons in Morocco very uncomfortably in the air, and all North Africa, I gather, is uneasy and dangerous – more uneasy and dangerous than the papers will admit. This afternoon there had been a great rattling of machine-guns from amidst the hills beyond Grasse. There is a garrison here of neat yellowish men, Malagasy I am told, and they are polishing up their tactics, for who knows what may happen? The other day as I came here from London I lifted the blind of my sleeping-compartment in the early morning and looked out on that queer contorted country about Toulon, which is so much more Spanish and African than French, and there in the crystalline light of dawn I saw companies of khaki-clad, brown-skinned men with mules and mountain guns engaged among the brown rocks in some manoeuvres.

A little further to the east in my outlook tonight there are British warships steaming through the darkness to Alexandria. Egypt also is astir. The Sirdar of the Soudan has been very deliberately murdered in Cairo by a band of students, and the new Tory government in London is showing the strong hand. Beyond the Red Sea, Mecca is in the hands of the Moslem puritans and the king the British set up has failed to recover the city. All along the festering lines of contact between Islam and the Western world there is crisis now. Out of hearing of me, out of sight of me, and yet wonderfully close to my imagination, there must be scores of thousands of human beings at an extremity of stress and excitement tonight because of reasonless conflicts, disorders of relationship, which are still almost as destructive and fruitless in human affairs as earthquakes and cyclones.

These newspapers just faintly visible in the shadow contain, I reflect, much other disturbing matter. There are particulars of religious riots in India, of the struggles of military leaders for power in China; considerable armies are in conflict there; the British Government had refused to ratify its predecessor's treaty with Soviet Russia, and there also trouble gathers. From America there was little to hand today except a tale of rising prices and a paragraph about a fight and bloodshed between the Klu-Klux-Klan and a State militia. But all these newspaper heading and items are merely the sudden swirls, the frothings – red frothings they are at times – and rapids upon the surface of the broad incessant rush of human affairs. The rest I apprehend but do not see. Between these various scattered and more or less significant items there are enormous intervals, great distances filled with unrecorded crises and unnoticed change. Everywhere older people have been dying and younger people have been asserting themselves for the first time; new practices and new ideas have gained a little ground and old ones lost it. The common mind of the world is not what it was last night nor what it will be tomorrow. It might seem that there was no permanent thing whatever in all this onward flow.

The more widely I extend my view from this window the more transitory the spectacle appears. Yet the books and criticisms of life that come to me do still, to a large extent, question change and repudiate progress. Men can still be found to write of the "enduring elements" in human nature and the "undying factors" of human life. Always by life they seem to mean the peasant's life, seed-time and harvest, desire and children, toil and rest. They see it associated with the soil, renewed by the soil, as necessary and inevitable as the succession of day and night. A denial of essential change is, I suppose, almost fundamental to the Catholic faith. And by denying essential change men solace themselves for the shortness of their self-concentrated careers. To those whose brief historical perspectives have been brought to a focus at the building of Rome and the Greece of Homer and Hesiod, this peasant life may well seem immemorial. But in truth there is no underlying permanent stratum to the changes of our world. It all changes, root as well as flower. Less rapidly, indeed, but as surely, the peasant changes with the rest of mankind. These terraces, these olives which now seem part of the scheme of Nature, have not been here for more than five-and-twenty centuries. And they go.

Before that time this land behind the coast was held by cattle-tending, barbaric tribes. And earlier they were more barbaric. Only a few thousand years ago this land was an untamed wilderness and its people savages. The man of the Grimaldi caves was of no European kin, and in his day it seems there was no sea out there beyond the hills, but a great valley in which men lived precariously and across which one might walk on foot to what were than the dense jungles of North Africa. And when one goes back a few score further centuries, back to the age of the relics that were found in the caves of Moustiers, then all about here there were bleak and desolate uplands where the cave-bear prowled, where the mammoth and the woolly rhinoceros crashed through the frosty thickets and the only thing to represent a man was grisly heavy-browed brute beyond our understanding.

Παντα ῥει, flux universal. It is only because I may sit at this window for so brief a time that I do not see this scene dissolve visibly and pass and give place to other unprecedented and equally transitory appearances. Of one thing only can I be sure, that all this goes, peasants and pleasure cities, ships and empires, weapons, armies, races, religions, and all the present fashions of man's life. Could my moment be enlarged to the scale of a thousand years, my world would seem less lasting than a sunset and the entire tragedy of this age the unimportant incident of an afternoon. I can discover in all my world nothing enduring, neither in the hills nor in the sea, nor in laws and customs nor in the nature of man, nothing steadfast except for this – a certain growth of science, a certain increase of understanding, a certain accumulation of power.

But there is that growth of science, there is that increase of understanding, there is that accumulation of power. I do not know why it should be so, but so it is. It gathered its force slowly before man was. It goes on now with accumulating speed and widening scope, and on it I build my working conception of the course of life. Man, unconscious at first, begins now, in an individual here and an individual there, to realise his possibilities and dream of the greatness of his destiny. A new phase of history is near its beginning.

But it has not begun. The world I have surveyed this evening is a world still unawakened. It flows towards its fate down the chance slopes and natural gullies of a will-less destiny. It obeys not a purpose but a gravitation. Its willful contribution is relatively ineffective. Such science as we have brings us suggestions rather than direction. It is not a dawn of power. But it is a small, clear, certain light, a morning star, tacitly hopeful, which it seems to me must surely and certainly prelude such a dawn. Implicit in the knowledge we now possess appears the promise of that comprehensive Greater Being, towards which thinking minds have been reaching for many generations.

I do not so much accept this conception of the coming of a general mind as find myself possessed by it as a natural outcome of all my mental growth. With the readiness of one completely prepared, I fall in with the intimations this new science of psycho-analysis gives us, that a new sector, a more completely adult stage, a stage of fuller self-knowledge and self-direction, is now enlarging the cycle of human life and bringing us into a comprehensive mental community. We become more impersonal, more co-operative, and more disinterestedly creative.

For long ages man has been the rebel child of nature; it is no new thing that he should attempt to anticipate and divert fate. Already this world is a man-shaped world; the water that runs beside the stone-flagged paths and the trickle of the soil down these slopes is guided and controlled by terraces and channels. Rain-water and earth go here as they are told. Scarcely a tree about this house but is here because it was planted or tolerated. Every beast that is too big to lurk or burrow is a subdued beast. But so far all this human control had been a control in detail; there has been no comprehensive understanding. Yet can that fail to come?

Since man in a few hundred centuries had travelled from that lonely savage in the upland caves to the engineer and chemist and psychologist of today, since today there is a constantly increasing stimulation and enlightenment of men's minds, since there are no real positive obstacles to human progress but only negative ones – ignorance, obstinacy, habit, doubt, and superstitious fear which vanishes before the light – it is not difficult for me to believe that in quite a few generations now, in quite a little time, our race, moving necessarily in the direction of its innate prompting, will enter upon a life that would be altogether wonderful to us could we but anticipate, it, that will be broad and gracious and lovely and beautifully eventful beyond anything we can dream of now or desire. That new way of living may be much nearer at hand than many of us dare to suppose, since its coming seems to depend almost entirely upon the conscious co-operation of men. No one has yet been able to gauge what increased power of co-operation of freshly conceived education may yield us. The long centuries that were needed to mould the life cycle of the early Palaeolithic brute-man, darkened and refractory, into our present freedoms, are no measure of the rate of change that is practicable to conscious effort.

As I look out upon this world, upon these hills so tranquil now under the glittering stars, I see as plainly as I see that those stars are rising and setting, our waste and disorder, our petty, distressful, and dispersed life, so intelligent and eager, so hasty and undisciplined and tragically silly, giving place to the advent of a conscious, coherent being of mankind, possessing and ruling the earth.

In the peace of this starlit hour one can see wide and far. I can put in their true proportions the fretting events in those newspapers, invisible now in the shadow beyond the circle of my lamp. That futile excitement about the gambling-tables beyond there is altogether swallowed up in night, and all the gambling and money manipulation in the world becomes scarcely more significant in this longer view than the rustling passage of a few autumnal leaves down the water-channel beside this house. They may choke a grating for a moment; they may waste a little water.

And the broad vision that I have from here is scarcely more troubled by those poor bodies in the desert twilight. The crackling of rifles and revolvers in the streets of Cairo does not reach up to this serenity. In some manner all men must die, and while their lives remain poor and little it is a small matter whether they die in bed or whether they die in battle. The great guns upon those ships have but a short range in time. That men should finish a trifle more painfully and a trifle less tediously than usual, by shot and bayonet, by gas and great explosions, is little worse than that they should die by fevers and famines and the cruelties of large beasts. Such things are aspects of our phase, and only in degree less transitory than the nightmares that may be troubling a score of pillows among the peasant homes near by.

There is no enduring pain, there is no eternal tragedy. Toil passes like the straining of a rootlet or the opening of a bud. Supreme above wars and disasters, surpassing and at last redeeming all the present torments of man, is the growth of a being of thought. Such circles of light as this beneath my lamp-shade are more formidable that all the armies and navies in the world, and stronger than the sum of human violence. They have an invincible tendency to run together like drops of oil. They grow brighter. It is because our light is growing that at last we apprehend the shadows. To realise the unacceptable evil in a thing is to begin its cure. Great as are the evils that we can see in life, the power of the will in us grows greater. I see the nearness of an order in the world like the order of a garden, of a work-room, of a laboratory, a clean life and a direct life and a powerful life for men; the jungle and all its sufferings gone at last for ever.

Nor will the coming to consciousness of this greater life of the race diminish or dwarf or fetter individual lives. They will be different, they will be enlarged. They will be passing beyond egotistical conflict and out of the age of jealousy, as we are passing beyond superstition and out of the age of fear. But they will be just as freely interested. They will be far more various and individualised. Their form of self-assertion will be different, it will have the form of distinctive service and distinctive creation, instead of being a blind insistence upon formal honour, upon possession, and upon stereotyped advantages. Today already in a thousand aspects of their lives people about us are anticipating this new phase, this completely adult phase of human life.

This is no act of faith I am making. I am not thinking against my own resistance. I am not declaring my passionate belief in something that the common aspect of things denies. I am writing down as plainly as I can what I believe to be plain matter-of-fact, as I see it directly my nose is sufficiently removed from my own affairs to permit a broad view of my world. This prospect of a saner, greater humanity controlling the world is as real in my sight as that faint light that came a moment since, and now I see has gone again, in a peasant's window there among the hills.

### 16 – *Pause*

I have made a long account of my framework of belief, much longer than I had supposed it would need to be when I began it in Dickon's London room. I turn over the corrected sheets and I still find matter for correction. I did not realise how much of the foundations of my life remained unformulated. At last I seem to have gathered everything together, everything essential, into the view from this window. Here I have got the present moment, the long past, the future, and the deeps of space. Here for a moment I may pause.

It is three o'clock in the morning, starry and immensely still. The moon is not yet visible; not even the pale stain of its light upon the edge of the sky. It will rise later, a hunted fugitive with the devouring dawn upon its heels. There is no sound in all this dark world but the soliloquy of the water under my open window. But at last I feel I have made my ground clear and disposed of my premises, and tomorrow I will go on writing about the more human things of life, about social organisation and toil and business and possessions, and about the hopes and desires of men and women, their loves and their ambitions, their generosities and disregards, and about the change that is going on in all human relationships. That change in human relationships is to be my expanding and increasing interest throughout. That was what I intended to discuss from the beginning, and it is only as I have set about my task that I have realised how much preliminary explanation had to be made – to myself as well as to the reader.

# Book Two

## The Story of the Clissolds:
## My Father and the Flow of Things

## 1 – *Fear Comes to Mowbray*

When I was twelve and my brother Dickon nearly fifteen, my father, Richard Clissold, having been found guilty of falsifying the books of London and Imperial Enterprises and sentenced to seven years' penal servitude, committed suicide and died in the passage behind the court just after he had left the dock. He had swallowed a small capsule containing poison which he had concealed in the lining of his waistcoat. While there had been a straw of hope left to him he had fought, but now hope was at an end. A few minutes later he would have been searched and they would have taken everything from him, and his way of escape would have been closed.

Neither Dickon nor I heard of this disaster at the time. Our mother had taken us abroad at the first intimations of the final storm. Probably our father told her to do so. We boys thought at first that we were going for a few days of holiday, but that holiday stretched out perplexingly from days to weeks and from weeks to months, and for all that time things were kept from us or mitigated for us. We went first to Holland and then into Belgium; we wandered from town to town and from pension to pension. For a time we were at St Omer, where there were mysterious comings and goings of my mother and various friends between France and England. We settled down at last at Montpellier – by that time we knew of our father's death – and there we began to realise fully that the spacious days of Mowbray were over and that we had entered upon a new life under a new name and more restricted circumstances.

I understood very little about my father's position in the world before our flight from Mowbray, and I doubt if Dickon knew much more than I did. I had known, however, that he was a very great business man. One of our many governesses – I forget her name – told me he was "very, very, *very* rich." Always with three "verys," and the last one stressed. That young woman, I realise now, had an admiration for him beyond her station; she liked to talk about him endlessly, she said he was "wonderful" and ought to have been knighted long ago, and she left abruptly and in tears.

I had still but the vaguest ideas of worldly position in those days. Mowbray effaced Bexhill. There our surroundings had been brightly and prosperously suburban in character; we had lived in a square-faced red house called "Sunny Beach" not five minutes from the sea-front, with a garden at the back where croquet – tennis had still to become universal – struggled against our infantile occupation of the lawn. There was, I remember, tamarisk about that lawn, ragged and ill-treated, and there was tidy tamarisk in front of the house, and everywhere about us there was tamarisk. Life at Bexhill was being a "kid" in a multitudinous jumble of "kiddies" amidst perambulators and nursemaids and pet dogs and iron seats and sand-heaps and boats and the stray balls of strange children coming out of nowhere into our play, and the legs of grown-up people. But Mowbray was a large and dignified frame for our lives. It conveyed a sense of social perspectives, and there I began to observe something of the relationships of things. I knew there were poor people in the world who had to be pitied but not encouraged, and that there were lower servants who resembled one another closely and upper servants of greater personal distinction like Mrs Praydo and Jenks the butler, and the current governess between heaven and earth, and mummy's friends who called in the afternoon and were shown the gardens, and daddy's friends, a gay and glittering train who came for weekends. Some of these were knights and baronets and even lords and ladies, and far away and over them all ruled the old, old Queen, Queen Victoria in Windsor Castle, who lived for ever and was halfway to God. There were a lot of foreigners also in existence; some of daddy's friends were foreigners, but foreigners did not amount to much unless there was a war. Then the Fleet would protect us.

I had not learnt very much in those days because my education had been so intermittent, but I was curious and fairly quick and I read voraciously. My education was intermittent because my father was imaginative and erratic and my mother fastidious and resistant. Towards the end of our great days he was talking of a public school for me, but he did nothing whatever to get me to one. "Which shall it be, Old Son?" he would ask. "Harrow and a halo or Eton in a topper and a bum-freezer?" I had a brief spell at a very select preparatory school near Guildford which I hated, and when I was eleven I began, by a special concession, to be a weekly boarder at Cossington's School. There I learnt to draw and the beginnings of science. I was taken away from that abruptly in mid-term. Dickon was then in the fifth form at Laxton after a good beginning at a preparatory school in Bexhill – his was a much sounder and more normal education than mine – and a few days later he too was jerked home and came back in a state of pleasurable excitement, with no idea of what impended.

"What's up?" said Dickon. "Is it to be Eton after all?"

I can still recall something of my mood when I learnt on the Monday morning that I was not to return to school. I went out on the terrace after Jenks had given me my breakfast and contemplated with infinite satisfaction the vast, empty, wonderful day that opened out before me, a surprise gift, a golden globe of sunlit time. It was a bright March day and the clouds were like great ships crowded with canvas that sailed before a strong yet kindly south-west wind. Everything was very quiet, there were no weekend visitors packing off and departing, because my father was away. I had no suspicion that life at Mowbray had come to its last phase of all for me. I decided I would begin by going to see if the primroses had appeared along the bridle-path through the wood.

I must have gone into the park and looked back at the house somewhen then, because it stands out so plainly in relation to this moment of my life. I see again the fair pale frontage under its pseudo-classical pediment; the dignified portico, the dining-room to the right, and to the left five windows of the long room both Jenks and my father always spoke of as the "saloon." East and west were stables and other offices, each with a cupola and a clock. The house was backed by woods, tall brown beeches, red-tipped before the first sharp jets of green athwart their lower branches. I can see it now. I can feel the freshness and release of that spring morning still. After the matter of the primroses had been investigated I proposed to strike back to the dip in the park and see whether the bracken had got its croziers above ground yet or whether I should find them by digging, and what our fallow deer were doing. Our new fallow deer. Only last autumn my father in his splendour had turned the cattle off the park and stocked it with nearly three score fallow deer.

Then probably after that I should cease to be a boy and become a Red Indian or an African explorer.

But the rest of that day and the two days of solitude that followed before Dickon's return have left no clear record in my mind.

Uncontrolled freedom at Mowbray seemed too good to be true to both of us. It was too good to be true, and we received the news that we were to go abroad to Holland "to see the lovely bulbs" with loud protests. "Oh *no*, mummy!" We had no desire to see the lovely bulbs and our mother's manner did not convey to us any great anticipation of pleasure in the spectacle. We wanted to go on mucking about at home. There was a dismay in our mother's dark eyes and a stress in her manner for which our boyish imaginations had no understanding. We argued that going to Holland was perfectly rotten and we made a stolid passive resistance to packing. One or two incidents before our departure struck Dickon as "rummy"; Jenks vanished suddenly, and a housemaid found in tears on the staircase said everyone was going to be turned off. She apparently, said Dickon, had been jolly well just turned on. Strange men appeared and moved the furniture about and treated a small boy accustomed to be taken notice of as if he was invisible. Mother appeared to be sniffing furtively that evening. Anyhow, when Dickon asked her if anything was "up" she turned her face away and dabbed her eyes with her handkerchief before she answered in a strangled voice, "*Nothing*. Nothing, dear. I have a little cold."

That first perception of something wrong in the air, something that was being kept from us, was greatly intensified by my mother's behaviour in the brougham on the way to Duxford Station. Dickon had, of course, collared the seat beside the driver but I was inside with mother. The excitement of travel was upon both of us youngsters by that time, we were disposed to forget our recent recalcitrance, but it was painfully evident she intended to continue depressing us. Dickon had made a sort of song about our departure that seemed to me the quintessence of wit, it was so perfectly innocent and justifiable in reality and yet so close to indictable offences. He had made it as we got up and we had been singing it all the morning.

"We're going to Rotterdam,
"Rotter Rotter Dam,
"We've both of us gotter
"Go to Rotter,
"Rotter, Rotter (*open out and let yourself go*)
"*Dam!*"

When I tried to cheer things up inside the brougham with this agreeable refrain my mothers quenched me with, "Don't, Billykins, I've got a headache."

We drove down the park road to the town ledge. I sat back subdued but resentful. At the curve where the woods sweep round my mother leant forward and became very still, looking back at the great house she was leaving for ever. It seemed to be smiling in the sunshine with the blandest indifference to her departure. I gave it one glance over her back, noted that her shoulders heaved and stared disgusted out of the other windows. What was the *good* of all this depression? What was the *sense* of it? It was *my* holiday that was being spoilt by her obstinacy, not hers. I remained stonily averted until we were close to the station.

Then she spoke to me and her voice showed that she had recovered herself. "Come, Billykins," she said. "Take your little bag."

I took my little bag.

Queer how just these scenes of five or ten minutes' duration stand out in one's memory. Queer, too, how broken and intermittent are all my memories of my mother, without prelude and without immediate sequel. It is as if that part of my mental record had been edited by some unknown power with a disposition to suppress her. I suspect a sustained inattention. It is only by an effort even now that I can restore her sufficiently to describe her. She was dark and slender, she was weak and gentle and ineffective; fear was in her nature and she would not, she could not, stand up to events. I think that both Dickon and I felt that fear in her as a thing excessive, and that it robbed us of much of the natural confidence and love that sons should have for their mother.

Her promotion to Mowbray must have frightened her very much. At Bexhill she had been able to manage fairly well, but Mowbray after Sunny Beach must have seemed like a white elephant after a governess cart. In the course of time she had come to like the place after her fashion and at the end she had become proud of it. Jenks and Mrs Praydo had made things difficult but not impossible for her during her period of responsibility; they had never failed to come to her to tell her what orders to give them unless they were very hard pressed. Some of the weekends must have been terrible – such a crowd of large, bright, brilliant, and various people, yet after all my father was there to manage them and she could wear her dresses very successfully – she had a lovely neck and shoulders – and even get into little sympathetic conversations with anyone who, like herself, seemed to be detached and shy. And in the quiet in between she could almost expand into a great lady and have local callers and see her own friends and take them to see the roses or the orchids or even, if they had suitable dispositions, completely "over the house."

I know very little of my mother's history. My father must have married her when she was very young; she could have been hardly three-and-thirty at the time of his death. I do not know where he met her nor what her people were; I may have first cousins quite unknown to me. I have no doubt he came into her world suddenly and splendidly and discovered her quiet, dark loveliness and decided to make her his with the same effective decision with which later he made Mowbray his. And to begin with for a brief year or so I am convinced she must have been a quite happy young woman. He was good-looking and charming and confident and kind. I imagine she began by believing him to be just exactly the nice and gallant, high-principled and capable husband that every Victorian young lady expected as her portion in life. Presently she must have come to realise that instead he was a strange and unaccountable animal, that a thousand things in the world could attract and excite him more than she could, that he could be unfaithful to her without a qualm, that without an antagonistic thought for her his proceedings could be utterly regardless of her security and of her standards of right and wrong and of everything she valued in life. I am sure he loved her ardently at first and then began to go away for a little while and then come back more ardent than ever, and so on for longer and longer absences and briefer and briefer spells of compensatory ardour, until it must have become apparent to her that he was developing the habit of forgetting her to very serious proportions. He was never, I am sure, positively unkind to her, he never in any material way neglected her, he showed her the greatest respect, but he forgot her more and more. It was his way to forget things. Negligence was the fault that finally destroyed him. At last it was all forgetfulness and there was no more ardour at all. In his forgetfulness of her he may have inflicted some terrible humiliations. He was a man of manifold activities. He went on with his career as he had been going on with it before he met her, his expansive, enterprising, erratic, dangerous, and occasionally forgotten career.

I think she must have known how dangerous it was, by instinct, by watching his moods, quite early in their life together. I believe she felt the quiver of the coming earthquake through all our comforts and splendours long before it came. In her heart she may have been praying desperately against an inevitable catastrophe.

I wonder how lonely that poor fear-oppressed lady was at Mowbray. She was a helpless nonentity on a ship that she felt might founder. She had no consolation that I can perceive unless it was the sense of temporary possession when my father was away. She did not resort to religion, at least perceptibly; I think she was too shy to take her troubles there. And we two boys must have been very uncongenial offspring indeed, intractable, difficult to pet and in voice and appearance very like our father, Dickon even more than I.

## 2 – *Carillon and Tragedy*

It was at Bruges that Dickon and I were told that there was to be no more daddy and no more Mowbray in our lives.

I have never been to Bruges since those days and I do not know how much that little old city has changed. I remember it as cobbled, with grass and moss between the cobbles, as built of very worn red brick and having a great number of courts in which big trees grew and into which one went through great archways. These I think were called Beguinages and I remember worrying my mother to show me a Beguin. "Mummy, is *that* a Beguin?" One might lark about among these places – discreetly. There were also numerous green-scummed decaying canals with grassy banks, sustaining a multitude of brightly painted and interesting barges. Also there was a very entertaining Grand' Place, above which rose a tall belfry that continually disseminated tunes like the tunes of a musical-box. It showered chimes and airs at the hours and the half-hours and quarter-hours. All Bruges lived as a vocal exercise to the accompaniment of this almost incessant carillon. One could ascend that belfry, but our mother would not let us do that. High places made her giddy and so they were forbidden us. Always there was a creaking and clatter in the cobbled square below, a coming and going of big two-wheeled waggons with the most interesting loads, a selling of things from booths, a shouting of hawkers and so forth. There was a great traffic of small carts and trucks drawn by dogs; we had never seen the like before. The dogs would bark at you but they would not go for you because they were fastened to the carts. They were always barking. We lodged in an inn upon the Grand' Place, an inn with some old Flemish name that I have forgotten, and it was in a little bedroom upstairs with an open window giving on the noise, on shouting, barking, chimes and clatter, that our mother told us that our father was dead.

We had known for two days that things were getting worse with mother, but we had said nothing to each other about it. She had kept us away from her as much as possible, sent us out to play, even given us francs to buy anything we wanted in the shops. When we drifted back to the square and the inn she had gone off for a long walk by herself – a strange thing for her to do. At bedtime there had been storm of affection, more especially for me because I stood it better. "My poor, poor darling little Billykins! My little Billy!"

Then she began to talk to herself, a thing she had never done before. "How can I tell them?" I heard her say as we sat at our lunch.

And also I remember, "I can't even wear black. I can't even do that."

She made us come up to her room after our lunch. We came the more reluctantly because she said she had something to tell us, something very important. We were both now in a state of extreme resentment at her odd and unaccountable behaviour. We knew nothing of her distresses and to her, poor woman, our minds were inaccessible. She had never known how to reach them, how to make herself in any way understood. From our earliest childhood she had never been able to imagine, much less to direct, what went on inside our little skulls.

"Sit down," she said. "No, don't look out of the window, please, *please*, don't. Sit down." Dickon she made take the only chair, and I was perched upon the bed. The room, I remember, struck me as untidy. The poor lady looked at her two difficult, obdurate offspring and stood clasping her hands.

"You poor dear children! Oh! dreadful things have happened. Dreadful things. How can I tell you?"

"You haven't had bad news, mother?" Dickon hazarded.

"Oom," said my mother, full charged with emotion.

"Boys!" she recommenced – she had never called us that before. "Boys, you are never to *speak* of your father again. Never. You are never to *think* of your father again. You will never see him any more – ever."

Neither of us, I remember, said a word. I glanced at Dickon for a cue and he was sitting stock still, not looking at her but, still hostile, taking in what she had said.

Her lips were compressed. She clenched her handkerchief into a ball and pressed it against her cheek and sat down abruptly upon her big travelling trunk. "Never see him again," she said. "Never go back to Mowbray. Never go back to England not for many years. Live abroad here. And your name isn't to be Clissold any more. None of us are to be Clissold any more. You will be called Walters – Willy Walters. Dickon Walters. Mrs Walters."

She paused. Then added an injunction: "Whatever questions they ask you, you are not to answer. Not to answer and not to listen. Whatever they ask or whatever they say."

Dickon, it was evident, intended to speak. She stared at him with dark apprehensive tear-stained eyes. Already he was so far his father's heir that she was afraid of him.

"But what's become of daddy?" he asked. "Why should we be called Walters? I think it's a *rotten* name."

"It was – it was my name – before I married," sobbed my mother.

"All the same," said Dickon. "And besides – where's he gone? I don't see it."

I was younger and blunter. I had had what I felt was a really bright idea, and I wanted to get it out before Dickon thought of it. "Is he *dead*, mummy?"

Dickon glanced at me as though he was minded to strike me. For a long time, as it seemed, my mother said nothing. Her brows were knit and her face was red. There was an immense silence in the room and outside a turmoil, a sudden dog-fight, men shouting, the clatter of cans overturned and trailed over the stones.

"OO! – oom!" my mother assented at last, nodding her head, her lips repressed tight. She choked, and then spoke very quickly in a sharp squeak: "*He's dead.*"

And then her face flushed transparent red and broke up like and infant's when it gives way to uncontrollable grief. She took refuge from all further inquiries, from all further control of the situation in a stupefying passion of weeping. I had never seen such weeping. I was astounded, I was horrified, I was ashamed. It seemed to me that even the noises in the square outside were stilled in amazement at her grief. "What *shall* I do?" she cried. "What can I *do?*"

"Leave me," she said at last. "Leave me. Oh! my heart's breaking."

How vividly those moments come back to me! I can see her still, see her thin red clutching hands before her face, and her poor silly little handkerchief so soddened with tears that it oozed and dripped. I can remember such a detail as that, but my own feelings I cannot remember at all. I do not think I had any feelings at all. Was I sorry for her? Was I sorry for my father? Was I even sorry for myself? I do not recall it. I was simply stunned with astonishment at the spectacle of a human being "breaking down." In all my life before I had never seen anyone "break down." And this was mother!

I do not remember the slightest impulse to console or comfort her.

I remember, too, almost as vividly how I walked with Dickon by the side of a canal that afternoon, though how we had got there from my mother's bedroom has quite faded out of my memory. I see Dickon with a white face staring blankly ahead of him, his eyes glassy with unshed tears, and I beside him waiting until it should please him to speak.

He spoke at last in tones of intense bitterness.

"Just as if nobody wanted to blub except her," he said, and wrathfully: "It's *our* father."

I accepted that and remained silently respectful as became a younger brother.

At length after a long interval his voice came again: "What's the sense of our not being called Clissold? Everybody knows our name's Clissold. Everybody."

That again called for no comment on my part. He brushed his eyes lightly.

Presently he thought aloud once more. "Why aren't we going to his funeral? It's our Right to go to his funeral. I am the Heir. I am his nearest. I ought to be there. Both of us ought to be there."

Again I had nothing to say. We went on silently side by side, silently comforting one another. We felt a hundred things we could not say. We both understood quite clearly that all we had been told was but an intimation of unspeakable things. The whole world had become dark; sinister abysses yawned beneath the Belgian cobbles; our feeble speculations and interrogations were as helpless as a weak wailing in an immensity of night. And we knew that so far as our mother went we should never be told, never be given any shape for his disappearance and death and this enigmatical collapse of our world. Some disaster, some frightful thing? In that our splendid, meteoric father was lost, dreadfully lost. Our hearts began to ache for him. His voice, things he had said and done were coming back to us. He had gone, gone for ever.

Towards our poor, fragile, incapable mother I can remember only that hardness of our hearts. It was almost as if we felt that it was she who had taken us away from him. And Mowbray and all we held dear.

### 3 – *A Stepfather*

From that time on Dickon and I became the close allies we are to this day. Before then we had not seen very much of each other;

we had gone to different schools and lived dissimilarly, but now we were thrown together in an almost constant association; we shared our troubles, and antagonisms, we were English brothers in a French school and Clissolds, suppressed but still obstinate Clissolds, crypto-Clissolds for a time, against the world.

We were poor in comparison with the Mowbray days, but not impossibly poor. My mother had property. Years ago my father, in a phase of clear prevision, had settled money upon her, and in particular some parcels of shares and some house property in Belgium and France. She talked freely and frequently during that phase of wandering, about returning this property to his creditors, but no creditors were ever about to take advantage of her mood. She presently adopted widow's mourning and put crape armlets upon us and established herself definitely in Montpellier as Mrs Walters, a young English widow, very inconsolable and quite devoted to her two sturdy boys. And we had to be the Walters boys thoroughly and suppress the Clissold in us even in our private thoughts. Imperceptibly we fell into a grouping in which she alone was the mourner amongst us, and we shaped our behaviour more and more easily to her assumption that it behoved us to comfort her and compensate her for all she had been through.

She made not great confidences to either of us. To me she talked rather more than to the silent and often preoccupied Dickon. I was younger and gentler in my manners and more flexible. "Ah, Billykins," she would say. "You're all I've got to live for now. You two dear boys."

And she would pat my shoulder and quite obviously let her thoughts ramble away to other things.

A more capable comforter appeared in the late August or early September in the person of her cousin, Mr Walpole Stent, a tall, shy, thoughtful, knickerbockered man with a very large forehead and an immense appetite for long, deep, confidential talks with her. He used to carry field-glasses in a leather case slung by a leather strap over his shoulders in order to examine distant landscapes with more particularity. Those field-glasses offended our sense of *comme-il-faut*. He put up at a little hotel in the Rue Boussairelles not far from our house, and he resumed a severed but never-forgotten friendship with our mother. With him we all went presently for a holiday to St Raphaël, which was then a comparatively unknown resort. He had persuaded her to this, she explained, and she had yielded because she thought it would do us good to go to the seaside before we recommenced school.

He was partner by inheritance in a firm of London solicitors, and I remember that even then I was impressed by the retentive and preservative quality of his mind. It was my first encounter with a well-trained legal intelligence. It was like some great furniture depository, safe from fire, corruption or admixture, nothing seemed to happen in it and nothing ever got lost in it, and he could, with every appearance of pleasure, reproduce the most commonplace facts at any time at the fullest length and in the completest detail. He did all he could to make friends with us in spite of his preoccupation with our mother. He liked us with the greatest determination. He told me a lot of natural history and scientific wonders that for the most part I knew already, and to Dickon he professed a sympathetic interest in cricket that his performance on the beach did not seem to justify. He was, most worthy man, the completest contrast to our father that one could imagine, and I perceive that the hostility to his memory that still smoulders in my heart is a quite instinctive reaction, unrighteous and unreasonable.

He reappeared at Christmas and found my mother almost out of mourning altogether, very animated and pretty in a dress of bright grey trimmed with black velvet. She began to make it after his departure but she did not wear it until he returned. We noted that, but said nothing. A paternal solicitude crept into his manner towards us, and he discussed our future careers with us at length. We did not, however, discuss them with him; we were already enormously self-protective towards him. We felt the coming usurpation. Within a year of my father's death my mother had married him.

She told us she did it entirely for our sakes. She said that we two needed the friendship and guidance of a good man. All boys needed that as they grew up, but we needed it to an exceptional degree. She was too weak for us and she knew it. For her it was implicit there could be no surcease from tragic memories.

There was a honeymoon in Switzerland while we two remained at Montpellier, and the French phase in our education was broken off abruptly and we were moved to Chislehurst. At Dulwich College, which was then a vigorously progressive school just taking up science teaching, we made up for a great deal of lost ground. We became boarders and went home only in the vacations. There was never any active dissension between us and our stepfather, but there was a sort of mutual estrangement. We differed. Even in our holidays it is remarkable how little of our waking time we spent at home. And in the course of the next three years our mother showed her further devotion to our needs by securing us first the friendship and guidance of a small but large-headed baby brother and then of a little sister, and then of a second sister.

Dickon was now nearly nineteen and I was sixteen, and as the Walpole Stent family fulfilled its destiny in this manner we two became more and more aware of our superfluousness therein. We proposed to enter at the Royal College of Science and set up for ourselves in London lodgings, and after a great deal of needless discussion, for our departure was manifestly a relief to everyone, this was conceded. But our stepfather loved weighing pros and cons fully and deliberately, and saw no reason why a foregone conclusion should be treated cavalierly. It was not difficult for our mother to give us an allowance of eighty pounds a year each out of the property my father had set aside for her; that was a quite possible allowance in those days, and so we two were able to establish ourselves in apartments in Brompton and face the world together.

When everything essential to that removal was settled, Dickon broached a matter of great concern to both of us.

It was late one evening that he found his opportunity. My mother and stepfather had been out to dine with a neighbour, and we had just come in from a music-hall. We found them refreshing themselves with biscuits and some lemonade. The bedroom candles were on the table. We exchanged colourless information about our proceedings. Then our stepfather asked some unnecessary question about the courses at Kensington I proposed to take.

"Oh, by the ways," said Dickon with a little catch in his voice and an elaborate casualess in his manner, "now that we are going away from here – and things have blown over a bit – I see no reason why we should keep up this pretence of being Walters. In fact – I'm entering at Kensington for both of us as – Clissold."

"But, my dear boy!" said our stepfather. "Do you know – do you know anything of the story?"

"Most of it," said Dickon. "Billy has looked it up in back numbers of *The Times*."

"*Well!*" said our stepfather.

"We don't like sailing under false colours," said Dickon. "We think we ought to stand to it."

"But how can we *tell* people?" cried my mother.

"You needn't. We can be Walters here. Whenever we come along to see you."

He lit his candle calmly and thoughtfully as though the matter was concluded. His hand was quite steady, but mine trembled a little as I followed him. I was sorry for my mother and I avoided looking in her direction. "There's much to be considered," my stepfather began.

"We've considered most of it," said Dickon and took up his candle. "You coming, Billy?"

My stepfather made no immediate answer.

Dickon went over to mother and kissed her good-night. "Good-night, father," he said. It was rare he said "father." I, too, saluted my mother, and just for a moment her hand sought mine and failed to press it. Her furtiveness made me as shy and ineffective as herself. We conveyed nothing and perhaps there was nothing to convey.

"But – !" said my stepfather as Dickon reached the door.

"If I go out in to the world as Clissold," said Dickon, turning to him, "I begin at the bottom – yes. But if I go out under a false name and then they find out I am Richard Clissold Secundus – where am I then?'

He did not wait for any further discussion, and my stepfather had no immediate reply. He had no readjust his point of view. And that he never did in a hurry.

But presently he began to assemble his considerations. Our bedroom was directly over that occupied by my mother and my stepfather, and I could hear his quiet, unhurrying voice unfolding the situation to himself and to her, amply, thoroughly, and needlessly, until I fell asleep.

My mother, I know, loved to have things explained to her. She did not listen, but she loved to have things explained to her. I am sure that she was in a muddled way distressed at our going, and that my stepfather's discourse comforted and consoled her. It was not that it met her fears and objections so much as that it anointed and soothed her mind. Dickon and I lay awake in our beds for a long time talking in fragmentary spurts, exchanging ideas about our own unforgettable father and about the world and about that battle with the world that lay before us, or following out our own thoughts to the accompaniment of that submerged, interminable commentary. I do not remember what we said to each other, but I have as vividly present in my mind as if I had heard it only a moment ago the muffled sound of that voice coming up through the floor.

### 4 – *The End of a Swindler*

I find it very difficult to recall what sort of figure our own father made in our minds at that particular phase of our lives.

Neccessarily his offence, his disaster, his career, and his punishment completely dominated our early outlook. He bestraddled our start in life like the Colossus of Rhodes; we sailed out under his shadow into the world. He overwhelmed us, immense and indistinct and enigmatical.

I knew he has died in some "dreadful" way after that scene at Bruges, but it is a curious thing, for which I cannot account, that I did not make any attempt to find out exactly how he had died for several years. I suppose when first I was told I was too young to know how to set about the inquiry, and before I had got the necessary *saviour faire* for such an investigation the habit of not inquiring was established. It was by chance one day at Chislehurst that I came upon a succinct notice of his tragedy in a stale Whitaker's Almanack. In those days nothing in print was unreadable to me. There in the Events of the Year my eye caught the name of Clissold, and I read, in small print at the bottom of a column amidst a crowd of other happenings: "Clissold, Promoter of London and Imperial Enterprises, having been sentenced to seven years' penal servitude by Mr Justice Ponters for fraud, committed suicide with potassium cyanide as he left the dock."

So that was it! That was my mother's great secret.

My first impulse was to go and tell Dickon all about it, my next to conceal my discovery from him altogether. For either he knew already and had been keeping this thing from me, or he did not know and we should have only this bare poisoned needle of statement to rankle in our minds and inflame us to painful, futile guessing about the details. Obviously a thing like that, big enough to be an Event of the Year, would be found in the newspapers of the time, and so after a day of consideration I asked one of the Dulwich masters – Graham Wallas it was, who afterwards became a great Fabian Society man and a professor of social science – how one set about looking up old newspapers. He was one of our keenest teachers, extraordinarily kind and sympathetic with anything responsive in his classes, and to him one went as a matter of course in any such difficulty as mine. I recall his little start at my request, his judicious self-control – I suppose he knew who I was really and guessed what I had in mind – and how he hesitated and considered and knitted one brow more than the other, with his kind brown eyes looking away from me over his glasses at infinity and his mouth screwed up in a way he had.

"Perhaps it's the best course," he said.

He could not tell me exactly on the spot how I could consult old newspaper files – I was too young for a British Museum ticket – but he would inquire and let me know the exact particulars. He would inquire.

"It's *The Times* you ought to read – certainly," he said. "You'll get the facts there complete and without – without sensation. Whatever facts it is you want to look up."

And at last at a charge, I remember, of sixpence, in a commodious room at *The Times* office, where a number of blighted, anxious-looking people were pulling big volumes about over the tables, I began to reconstruct item by item my father's dereliction and death.

As I did so a great cloud of long-neglected memories returned to me, memories of a big, kind daddy-giant, who came suddenly out of nowhere into one's childish world with a tremendous

"Hello, you kids!" and banished dullness. He banished boredom; that was his supreme quality. He is always a large, not very distinctly featured giant to me; my memory of his face is not clear. Chiefly I remember his red whiskers. My mother destroyed every photograph there was of him, and in those days the portraits of prominent people published in the papers were engravings – photographic reproduction for periodicals did not yet exist – and those I was able to dig up made a lamentable mess of him.

So he remains incurably atmospheric, red whiskers, a flushed complexion, a very reassuring smile, quick movements. A wonderful giver of "pig-a-bags" he had been at Bexhill, and at Mowbray there had been rare, memorable sprees, a time when a weekend party of grown-ups played rounders with wild enthusiasm on the great lawn, and Dickon, who was only fourteen, ran faster even than men of fifty and got rounder after rounder for his side, and several games of spoof cricket with the end pillars of the terrace balustrading as a wicket and a walking-stick for a bat and a rubber ball. He dressed up once as Father Christmas for us. He sang the "Two Obadiahs" and "Tommy Make Room for Your Uncle" to us – until my mother implored him not to make us vulgar. He would think of us when he was abroad and in all sorts of places where a daddy might reasonably forget his little boys; he brought us back delightful flat tin soldiers marching, cooking, camping, in oval wood boxes from Paris, and entertaining earthenware Nativities with kings, shepherds, and irrelevant crowds complete, from Italy. And he sent us coloured picture postcards from the ends of Europe, costumes or animals or railways or ships. He saw to it that we had toy railway trains on rails that really worked, from some special shop he knew of in Holborn. Such deeds fought for him eloquently. It was absolutely impossible for me to think of him as a villain.

I sat in *The Times* search-room with my cheeks flushed and my eyes growing hot and red, reading of growing suspicion and denunciation and insolvency and pursuit and trial, and never had I a doubt that he was an evilly entreated man.

He had almost got away from them. For days he was missing. He had danced off to Paris, taken a ticket and a lit-salon berth for Geneva, and vanished at Culoz. They had found him and arrested him nine days later in a little out-of-the-way inn in Biscay. When the detective broke it to him that he was known and under arrest he had remarked cheerfully: "Good old Scotland Yard! Have some déjeûner with us? It's awful stuff."

*Us!* He had travelled with a typist-secretary as his daughter. He thought, he said, that was a fresher disguise than wearing a false beard. His levity on this delicate matter told against him at the trial.

And his offence? That was rather a tangled business for a boy of fifteen. I will not attempt to summarise that complex story here. I could appreciate better the nine days' man-hunt that has preceded his arrest. Even in the decorous Victorian *Times* – a *Times* without headlines – I could detect the sporting zest his disappearance gave the affair, and when later on I looked up the case in other contemporary newspapers, I realised what a bright addition to the British breakfast-table of that spring, the chase of my father must have been. Tall Englishmen of easy manners had been arrested at Marienbad and in Stockholm; all over Europe his travelling compatriots must have been seeing him, sometimes several times a day.

I saw the chase from the point of view of the hunted. I suppose he knew how hopeless his flight was even from the first. But he was always for giving the thing a trial rather than for giving in. But there he was, dodging about at minor junctions and giving false names at inns and wondering what the devil he should do when his money ran out and, I guess, keeping up the delusion of his pseudo-daughter that she was having a romantic elopement. And treating her as it seems he did – strictly as his daughter. He would not damage her more than he could help. All the while he must have been going over the squalid sequence of rash falsifications and expedients that had ended in his crash. So recently as a year before he had been in no greater danger than that of a rather florid and extravagant bankruptcy. Even then he might have pulled through and recovered his prestige in the City. But he had been unable to face a merely legal failure when just a slight stretching, a further risk, a fraud that good luck would conceal again, might tide things over. He did not want merely to escape; his hopes grew with his dangers; even when the game was utterly lost he had still attempted victory. He had been careless in his manipulations, a little contemptuous, I am afraid, of the alertness of his associates, a little too confident of their courage and sympathetic dishonesty.

Towards the end he broke badly. His last exploits were hardly more planned or intelligent than the flurry of a harpooned whale. He plunged from misdemeanour to felony. His last falsifications were puerile, and on those he was convicted.

And so after a futile struggle over the extradition they took my father back to England. I imagine him concealing as much as he could of his chagrin beneath a bearing still hectically debonaire. Back he came to the City of London, where he had been so brilliant, so brilliant and meteoric a figure, and there he stood in the ill-lit stuffy court and was examined and re-examined and wearied and exhibited and disentangled and picked to pieces, picked to discreditable shreds.

I realise now that he had never taken business quite seriously. I perceive from one or two phrases of his under examination that he was immensely astonished that a little more or a little less sharp practice should make all this difference in his treatment by his fellow men.

Twice the judge, a fellow-member of his club, a successful youngish man who had once looked up to him, had to reprove him for "a certain familiarity" in his manner.

And then it become plain to him that it was really so, that he was in a trap and the spring had closed upon his neck. There was a line drawn between permissible and illegal sharpness, a miserable line, and they could not see how slight a thing, how playful and fresh a thing, it had been to overstep it. That dismally cheerful train journey with the detectives, the restraints of his present imprisonment, this dingy crowded court all eyes for him, were to be only the prelude to a long grey, chill, eventless, undernourished, unstimulated living burial. They meant it. Well, he, at least, had had one saving moment of foresight. Here the stuff was, close at hand. Here under his finger. Good!

So he held his chin up and answered firmly to the end. Was even humorous once or twice. There was laughter in court.

*The Times* search-room seemed to contract upon me until it become the waiting-room of a court and the helpful attendant might have been a warder. It was as if I stood in my father's place. I could understand it all.

Death is a very dreadful and tremendous thing to the adolescent mind, but I felt that I could understand. I wished that somehow when he stood up to hear the foregone verdict, alone without an overt friend in a court crowded to overflowing with his enemies and with merciless, curious spectators, he could have known that some day his son would be there beside him in imagination and feeling – not condoning but understanding. He would not have wanted his offence condoned. I am sure there was no nonsense of that sort about him. At last, almost as a relief, after his tedious drawn-out defence, the verdict and the sentence must have come; the old club acquaintance exalted and aloof, in his antic great wig and scarlet gown, a successful windbag, giving the reporters in particular his carefully prepared phrases, blaming, condemning, pronouncing a sentence heavy and exemplary. Well, some of us have to muddle and lose our game, but why add insult to defeat? Seven years' penal! And the rest of life, a few years of discredited, pauperised age. Thank you for nothing, my lord.

And then?

Did the stuff hurt? Did it seem as swift a poison as we suppose it to or did time drag? Were there some moments, some minutes even, while the capsule dissolved, minutes charged with fear whether it would act at all, and then perhaps a frightful pang, some numb horror or rending agony that none have ever lived to tell about?

Then the blow of the wall as he fell against it, if ever he knew he fell against the wall, and darkness.

## 5 – *Young Wolves in Brompton*

If I had had any faltering of sympathy for my father in his destruction, Dickon's sturdier simpler faith would have sustained me. When I came to tell Dickon about it, he showed, so far as I can remember now, that he knew most of the story. Perhaps he had been put through it by schoolfellows; at any rate, all his judgments were prepared. "They made him a scapegoat," said Dickon. "They let him down." And, phrase reminiscent of rafts and pirates and all the fierce imaginations of a boy: "He got the long straw.

"They never touched his co-directors," said Dickon. "They were too high up and too near royalty. Lord Duncomby was in it. Two others. What were their names?...

"But they took the stuff all right while it lasted... Trust *them*," said Dickon.

That was what I, too, wanted to believe. Our father had been careless, indifferent, and they had caught him. But he had only done what everybody did. "They don't catch *me*," said Dickon, gauging the realities of life.

Neither of us believed that he was essentially worse than the run of business men. We contemplated a brigand world.

In which after all he had made things that remained. All over London were great buildings he had promoted. He had altered the face of London – criminal though he was. He had been lavish with his architects, and his ideas about service flats and suchlike new methods of housing were far in advance of his times. Many of his failures have since become richly paying properties. And though he flourished in the worst period of English architecture he never put up anything absolutely detestable. I remember Dickon stopping me one day against the heavy but by no means ungainly masses of Cornwall Court.

"That's one of the Clissold offences, Billykins. They called him a scoundrel, but he gave them that. That's just one of his things. Catch a muff like Lord Duncomby doing anything as fresh as that!"

From the outset, because of our father's fate, we two saw the world lawless and adventurous. We were precocious in that. Children believe that in heaven and on earth alike there is order; they do so naturally and of necessity, and most young people and many people through life retain this early assumption that there is justice and benevolence behind and sustaining the law, that laws and customs are really wise and good. This is an illusion, or at least an exaggeration; of great provisional value no doubt in restraining youthful excess; but it was one that our peculiar circumstances forbade us to entertain. For if we agreed that the system in which we lived was a righteous one, what could our father be but a rogue? But if it was unrighteous and casual then he was merely ill-starred.

There was a strong suggestion of the predatory animal about both of us in those days after we had left Chislehurst and set up for ourselves in Brompton. We had a mean furnished bedroom with two narrow beds, a frayed carpet, a small wardrobe, and one washhand-stand, and a sitting-room lit by a central gas-light; the accommodation was greatly restricted by the mute corpse of a black piano the landlady refused to take away; and there was insufficient table-room and shelf-room for our books and work. Our elbows were therefore a good deal in each other's ribs. We neither of us betrayed by any word we spoke how sick with longing we were at times for the space, the freedom, and self-confidence we had had at Mowbray, but we both knew what was in the other's mind and our expressed intentions towards the future compensated for our silence about the past. We would talk long and intimately at times, late at night perhaps when there was a noise outside to keep us awake, or on the way to the College, or of a Sunday when we walked in Kensington Gardens or explored the endlessness of London to the north and west, and then through intervals of days or even weeks we would have no rational conversation at all. We would fend each other off with silly nick-names and playful and nonsensical insults and go our own mental ways alone. For days together we would elaborate some fanciful joke– our standing dish about Mr G for example – or invent and embroider upon a saga about some odd imaginary personality.

We had an underworld, ten times more foolish than this world of appearance, which underworld we called the Boops. The Boops followed the events of the day and the fashions of the time after their manner. The Boops had a Royal Jubilee; they had an Inventions Exhibition in which Mr Heath Robinson would have felt at home; they held reviews of army and fleet; they worshipped curiously a god after their own image, a Mr B. In the Boops we guyed much of our astonished chagrin at life and laughed it off. For we both had a cheated feeling about life as if something had been promised and snatched away from us.

Occasionally our excessive proximity got on our nerves. There were forces storming in us that made us want to be alone with ourselves for a time, made solitude an urgent need. Dickon would warn me of a brooding violence. "Billykins," he would say, "your little face fatigues me. Take it right away before I buzz books at it. Lose it somewhere. Pawn it for a day or so where it will be safe from damage. See?"

"Why the hell don't you go out yourself?" I would retort, savage but preparing to depart. "Look at the rain!"

"You're insoluble – worse luck," said Dickon. "The door, my lad, is there."

As he was nearly two stone heavier than I in those days I could not banish him when the corresponding mood came upon me. I would then go with my work into the Education Library in the South Kensington Museum and there until the place closed at ten I would read and write by the glare of great spitting violet-flushing arc-lights of a type that have long since vanished from the earth. Then home to a malignant silence and bed. Or it might be, with the clouds lifting, to a tacit amnesty and talk into the small hours.

It added to the natural restlessness in Dickon's blood that he had still to find his calling in the world. In the meantime he was working, but working neither so hard nor so well as I, first at mineralogy and then at mining. "There's always something doing with mines," he said, but he never seemed convinced that that was his proper line of attack. He would have moments of pure rage against the social system that environed us, that seemed so lax and yet was so difficult and dangerous to assail. I remember him once in Holland Park. "How the devil are we to *get* at them?" he cried suddenly as though he had been stung. "How the devil?"

"Get at who?" said I, in the London idiom.

"In these houses. *Look* at them! Every one stands for thousands a year. And I can't think of a dodge against them, not a dodge. Idiot and fool I am! – unfit to survive. Like silly fat sheep inside a wire fence they are, and I'm like some brainless wolf. Look at this outfit coming along! Perambulator, two nurses, and a

Newfoundland dog. Large expensive toy elephant and a ball. Fine fleecy blanket. All for one ratty, beady-eyed kid!… You ugly little mite! Where does daddy get it? Where does daddy *get* it?"

I was shocked. In those days I had not a tithe of Dickon's voracity. I did not want money then. I did not want money seriously until after I was married. I was under the spell of pure science then, submerged in it, and while Dickon's work was almost perfunctory I studied with all my strength. I was working in the Physical Research Laboratory under C V Boys, then a very young man, pink-skinned and flaxen-haired to the eyelashes, clever-handed, and delicate-minded, inspiringly ingenious, rapidly understanding. How many brilliant and delightful minds have gone and go to the making of science! Boys in those days was the worst lecturer I have ever heard, so bored, so devastatingly bored, so appalled by the hour of talk before him, but in the research laboratory he had amazing flashes, he threw out sparks that set one alight. I had been taken out of the ordinary class and allowed to do some special work under him upon mineral threads and particularly fibres of quartz, and it is difficult for me to exaggerate how much I owe to him. He developed and encouraged my innate enthusiasm for physical research. I began to dream of papers read before the Physical Society; of the Philosophical Transactions, of broadening explorations below the surface of matter. And my taste for such work reinforced my distaste for money-making.

After all what use had I for money? Given a laboratory and a lodging and a few pounds for a summer holiday, what else was there to desire? Nothing that I permitted to rise to the surface of open and confessed thought.

I tried to put my point of view to Dickon.

"You're dreaming, Billy," said Dickon. "You don't know what you're in for. You think you'll give your life to science. They won't let you. You've found your little corner at the college for a bit – but nobody wants research, pure research, and so there's nobody to pay for it. Try it if you want to, for a bit. Until you need money or the college turns you out to make room for someone else. The world's scramble and you'll have to come into it. Seeing what you are. Trust me."

### 6 – *Quartz Threads and Socialism*

Thoughts are parricides. Each phase abolishes and devours its parent phase. Thought is always trial and selection and discarding and forgetting. I can recall some of the things Dickon said in those old days, and some that I said, and they stand out like fragmentary ruins and seem to illuminate a little the past state of the areas immediately about them, but as for the detailed mass of that development it is gone, it is gone now as completely as the lie of the houses and frontages and ownership round about the Cathedral of St Paul in London before the Great Fire.

We argued tremendously about Socialism and Individualism, but what I meant by Socialism and what he meant by Individualism are now, I perceive, things almost beyond recovery. I think my Socialism and my passion for scientific work were all mixed up together and that it was my sense of the scientific process that dominated the mixture. I doubt if my views have changed fundamentally in the intervening years, but I perceive that what I called Socialism then is no longer to be called Socialism. Socialism for me was certainly something quite different from those vague aspirations towards a land of Cockayne professed by Mr Ramsay MacDonald and his party when they are out of office, and still less had it anything to do with the doctrines of Communism that have since swamped it. It was, indeed, little more than the application of the distinctively scientific spirit to human affairs in general. I wanted to be part, an honourable part, of this clean and orderly development of knowledge, strong, unhurrying, wonderful, that I found going on in the research laboratory, and from that point of departure it was easy to envisage the social struggle as an indecent and preposterous inconvenience and to want to extend the honourable openness, co-operation, and collectiveness of the world of science to human affairs in general. The social struggle impressed me even in those days as if I were required to fight for my chemical balance in the laboratory and knock out my competitor before I could use whatever was left of the weights and instruments. It was an intolerable distraction of attention, a destruction of possibilities. I did not stop to consider how it had arisen and whether, perhaps, it was not in some way necessary. Possibly even more necessary than the scientific process. I simply denounced it and demanded that it should be discontinued, that the private ownership of the means of research and economic exploitation should follow the private and secretive methods of the Alchemists to oblivion.

While I clung to the opportunities for pure research that, thanks very largely to Boys' good opinion of my work, I had had the luck to find, I was saying therefore, but only, so to speak, with the sides and back of my attention, "Get on to the Socialist State, the International Socialist Sate, social peace and world peace, and stop this tumultuous waste. Do in the search for food and comfort and security what we are doing in the search for knowledge." And as I was very much preoccupied then with the crucibles and cross-bows that were our chief weapons against the innate disposition of quartz to settle down into a compact geometrical form, and with the problem of how to fuse that refractory material to as fluid a state as possible and shoot it forth, as swiftly as possible, so as to draw it out into the finest possible threads before it cooled and set, I did not perhaps sufficiently consider the very much less congenial and very much more massive and refractory task I was proposing that other people, conceivably beside me and behind me, should undertake.

I just wore a red tie once or twice, called myself a Socialist – chiefly to my private self – and argued at nights with Dickon.

Now Dickon's more resentful turn of mind made him direct his attention to just those things, the blunderings, the casualness, the inconsecutiveness and injustice of the world at large, that I was most disposed to ignore. He was then much more irritated by life, much more *in* life, more combative than I was. At that period of adolescence every year of age means a great difference of temper and will. He had penetrated further into the jungle. And, moreover, he was naturally more energetic and realist than I, more aware of foreground things and less concerned about distant ones.

"You're trying to live in Utopia," he would say. "You're living in a dream and you'll awake with a bump."

Our difference exercised him; he felt the implicit criticism of himself. He would suddenly break into discourse – at the most unexpected times. His words are all forgotten now, but I will try to give the sort of things he would say; he would be sitting on his bed, perhaps half undressed, marking his points with minatory waggings of the collar and tie he held in his hand.

"You can't live in a world that isn't here, Billykins; that's what you don't grasp. That's what's the matter with you. This show is a scramble and it's going to be a scramble yet for centuries. You've got to look after yourself; you've got to look after the things that you care for, yourself. You may want to do the most disinterested things but you have to do them yourself – as your fad. Poor people aren't permitted to have fads. I'd be a Socialist just as you are if there *was* any Socialism. But it's only just been thought of; it hasn't begun to come. They call all this about municipal gas and water the coming tide of Socialism. Coming tide! It's a few Fabians piddling under a locked door. The world's world of private adventure yet for – far beyond our lives, Billykins. Take it or leave it, that's what it is. And as I want to live in this world and not in a world that isn't here, I'm Individualist. It isn't a matter of chance as you seem to think. It's a matter of necessity. I'm an Individualist and out for private enterprise – which means in plain English going through the pockets of some crowd one has coralled by dangling some commodity before them, or making some other looter disgorge. And then for freedom – and, if you like it, disinterested service – scientific research – or anything else – as the mood may take you."

No, that is too clear and quintessential, too hard and definite and contemporary, but it has something very close to his spirit, and it is as near as I can get now to the discussions of those days. The reality of our talks was much more loose and inconsistent. We were trying things over; we were feeling our way. We used claptrap phrases because there was nothing else to use, we came home with remarkable discoveries that evaporated, we went back upon ourselves, we jammed in flat contradictions and lost our tempers. But what I have written has the clarified essence of it all.

And here something strikes me. Until I began to write this account of the ideas of my student time I had always assumed that I was still a Socialist and Dickon still an Individualist. But now I begin to think it over and try to write it down I find my Socialism is very little more than an old railway label on a valise; it records an important journey, indeed, but hardly a scrap of present significance attaches to it. What I am writing here is, I realise, no longer Socialism.

Where is that liberal Socialism of the eighties and nineties now; that wide project to turn the expansive forces of the modern world towards organisation and construction? It has expanded to simple recognition and become incorporated in current thought, and it has evaporated altogether as a movement and a cult. It is not only that Socialism has become no more than a memory, a used label, in my own life; it has become no more than a memory in the world. That journey has been made. It has gone – gone like Chartism, like

Puritanism, like the naturalism of Rousseau or the civic virtue of Robespierre. And as I consider these things I wake up for the first time to the quality of the Socialism that remains. The movement did not realise the wider recognition of its broad ideas. It became sectarian with organisation, it gave way to impatient passion, it bore a narrow-souled, defective, and malignant child Communism, and that child has made away with it.

I am no more a Communist than I am a Catholic or a Conservative. It is not that I have left Socialism, but that Socialism has passed away from my world.

Socialist, Individualist; it is time we washed these old labels off our intellectual baggage. They are no longer of use to us, and they may easily send our wills and intentions astray.

## 7 – *Systems in History*

The Socialism I knew and professed in my scientific days was a project for a more spacious and generous ordering of the world. But gradually that propaganda for a larger, less competitive, scrambling and wasteful way of satisfying the staple needs of mankind gave place to a vehement campaign against existing institutions and usages, lumped together for convenience of invective as the Capitalist System. I seemed to hear more and more of the evils of the Capitalist System at every Socialist gathering I attended, and less and less of anything desirable that could be imposed upon its disorders. Gradually there loomed upon my consciousness the legend of a tremendous book, which was to set all other Socialist writings, teachings, and preachments aside, a mighty book, always spoken of in those days by its earnest young propagandists as *Das Kapital*, in which this Capitalist system was discovered and demonstrated upon as the source, the engine, the form of all the oppression and robbery and parasitism of man by man. A new sort of Socialist appeared, energetic, opinionated, and intolerably abusive, and the moral and intellectual decline of Socialism began. It ceased to be a creative movement, and it became an outlet of passionate expression for the inferiority complex of the disinherited. So it remains to this day.

It is so much easier to vilify than plan; it is so much easier to fix attention upon an injustice than a hope. All planning these new Socialists derided, and they succeeded not only in feeling themselves but in suggesting the feeling to others that "Utopian" was the word for something contemptible and unphilosophical. What need for planning? Had not the profound and stupendous Hegel, that master intellect, that supreme if slightly incoherent God of Human Thought, made it densely clear that the overthrow of the Thing-that-is was in itself the creative establishment of the Thing-that-it-is-not? And so all our young Socialists went about being a tremendously scornful and heroic, no longer working for a worldwide organisation of peace and staple supplies, but simply for the Thing-that-the-Capitalist-System-was-not, whatever that might turn out to be.

These things came to me intermittently. I had little time for Socialist discussion after I began to work with Boys, and I found these new views bored and repelled me rather than irritated me to the pitch of discussion. Now it is hard to recall even the substance, much less the method of various disputes. I remember making a bad impromptu speech at some meeting in Chelsea in which I defended Utopian Socialism and was derisively handled. But I do not think I was quick enough to realise in those days that the Proletariat and Bourgeoisie about which these new Socialists gabbled endlessly were absolutely indefinable classes, and still less to apprehend that this Capitalist System of theirs was a phantasmagorical delusion, a sort of Pepper's Ghost, thrown upon the face of reality.

Nowadays I do not succumb so easily to our human disposition to believe that where there is a name there is a thing, and I have learnt to look behind the logical surface of every argument and conviction. I find now in this retrospect that I can see round quite a number of corners that defeated me in those days. Mere everyday living is in itself a training against false classifications and the habit of accepting unanalysed terms. Which is one reason, I think, why we older people are more penetrating and less logical than our younger selves.

A recent chance encounter, when I was last in London, comes back into my mind, an illustration of all the qualities that make Communism a travesty of intelligent revolutionary theory. It was with a young man with a System to expound. If I had to argue a case against Communism now I should take all the possibilities of delusion that inhere in the one world "System" and rest my case on that.

This word "system" had done extraordinary mischiefs not merely with Socialism but in the whole field of political and social discussion. Its peculiar treachery is the insidiousness with which it imputes deliberate order to entirely unorganised things. A system is properly an organised relationship such as one finds in a system of pulleys or the metric system. But when the learned, confronted with some quite possibly planless, discrete assembly of facts, have sought to classify and arrange these in order to discuss them the more conveniently, these arrangements have also been called systems, whether the facts really responded or not, as in the case of the Linnaean system or the Copernican system. It was easy in the past, when men were entirely possessed by the idea of a supreme designer, to pass from these systems of description to the idea that the things classified were themselves systematically arranged. Men, for example, spoke of the miraculous order of the solar system as though it was something as definitely arranged as a clock, and so hid from themselves the extreme casualness of the relation of the sun to the more or less persistent satellites, the planets, planetoids, comets, meteorites, and so forth that go with it, like midges round a wandering beast, as it drifts through the scintillating disorder of space. And with matters of social arrangement this imputation of purpose and order where there is naturally no order at all, is still extraordinarily mischievous.

I remember how in my schooldays the endlessly complex social muddling of medieval Europe, the swaying smash-up of the Roman Imperium, was dressed up for us as the Feudal System. We were taught to believe that there had existed a neat, universally respected pyramidal arrangement of Society, in which everyone knew to the prettiest pitch of precision his level and his place and his dues and duties. The natural disposition of little scraps of floating wreckage to cluster about and adhere to larger lumps, the obvious phrases, flatteries and conventions of such vassalage, the customary humiliations of the abject and the ingenious devices of the medieval lawyers, were seized upon by the romantic imaginations of later historians and elaborated into a nicely balanced scheme. Hundreds of millions of perplexed, instinctive people lived and died while Feudalism floundered and changed through the centuries of its prevalence, and never had the remotest suspicion that some day earnest scholars would reveal how beautifully systematic were their lives. And today millions live and toil, suffer or prosper, and only by reading a very bad-tempered and unattractive special literature or by falling into some propagandist meeting do they get any explanation of what is meant by this Capitalist System under which they are supposed to be living.

Capitalism there is, no doubt; it is a complex of financial and economic events arising out of purblind attempts to organise the large-scale production rendered possible by modern knowledge and by the enlargement of the modern imagination. But it changes in its general facies yearly, monthly, hourly; it is never quite the same thing twice nor here and there, and people who scold and blame the Capitalist system and organise a revolution to overthrow it and behave as though the millennium will necessarily ensue when it is exorcised are wasting their strength upon a Protean shadow. They are "seeing things" and fighting phantoms. There is no more a Capitalist System now than there was a Feudal System in the eleventh century. These are systems of descriptions, far remoter from reality than the systems of Linnaeus or Ptolemy. There has never been any essential system in the general social and economic life of mankind. Some day men may make these things systematic, but the time is not yet. At present all these things are an immense driftage, with an endless multitude of counter-currents and minor eddies and a limitless variety of interactions. The most immediate task before Man in his great adventure, as I see it, is to make the system that is not yet here, to thrust and weld it upon this chaos of his economic methods and ideas, and subjugate it to his security and creative happiness.

I met a young man the other night at the studio of my nephew and godson, William Clissold, who helped me greatly to understand the working of this system obsession. "A regular intellectual stinker, he was," said William, who affects a remoteness from things of the mind. This young man, at once nervous, convulsive, and arrogant, fell in very illuminatingly with my present line of speculation. He was apparently incapable of thinking of human affairs except in systems. I could not make it plain to him that I believed there was no system at all in economic affairs; the idea was beyond his intelligence. His main obsession was what he called the Manorial System, a dressed-up revival on the economic side of the exploded Feudal System, and he seemed to regard it as the clue to all existing social and economic relationships, and was honestly shocked when I professed never to have heard of it.

He was a discordant person even to the eye; he was rubricated at the tips of all his features, he wore rimless spectacles, and his hair was black, wiry, and discursive. His manner had a kind of fierceness, his voice, which seemed to have corncrake blood, was permanently raised, and his occasional laugh was like the wheels of a heavily laden cart. How he generalised! There is nothing so invigorating as a good generalisation, but it ought to go through its facts and marshal them; it ought not to fly over their heads and expect them to follow. He floated over the confused procession of occurrences as irresponsibly confident as the spirit of creation once floated over chaos. He did it with such assurance that he did not even know he was floating.

"Oh, you *ought* to know about the Manorial System," he said. "It explains so much."

He expounded a little. He opened a picture of the Middle Ages as bright and clear as an illuminated missal. There was this Manorial System of his all over the country, with wonderful bailiffs and reeves and the court leet, particularly the court leet. The land in his clear, gay vision of those vanished times was cut up into nice little manors and rather larger little baronies, all dove-tailed together, all, it seemed, with vivid, quaint coats-of-arms upon them, and to balance and complete them a Guild System in the towns, sweet and subtle and humane. And happiness and homely justice and art – remarkably art. And the Church kind and grave in an attitude of benediction. And in the sky the stars and all the Sons of God purring together.

I hardly liked to press him to tell me how it was this dear Fairyland of his had collapsed into the evils of our own times. No doubt the Reformation was much to blame for it, but the discovery of America upset things; the Turks and Mongols were stupidly rough with the warriors of Christendom, and the Black Death took the meanest advantage of the merrie sanitation of the Manorial System.

Fairyland it was, a Scholar's Fairyland, secure and aloof from that dark wilderness which is history. For think of what those days were in reality, the life in fortresses and castles, the towns like criminal slums, the houses crowded together and locked and barred and fortified against each other, bodies unwashed and clad in coarse and dirty woolens as the finest wear, brutish communes here and reigns of terror there, gangs in possession, monasteries and nunneries illiterate and remote, sheer naked savagery in many districts, and mud-tracks through the unkempt roads between the towns, not a road except for some Roman highway in decay, not a bridge except by way of atonement from some powerful dying sinner, fierce dogs upon the countryside, hogs and stench in the streets of the cities, pestilence endemic. And endless breeding of children there was, to fester and die for the most part before ever they grew to youth's estate. Here and there would be a region where some accident of natural kindliness gave life a little space of April sunshine; here and there perhaps one might find a tolerant equilibrium of lazy lassitude, some lord or abbot in tidy or genial mood. A little space at most and a transitory phase it was in the ugly succession or cramped, distressful lives. And this fellow, blind as a bat to facts that scream aloud at us from every thick-walled, windowless, medieval ruin, from every museum with its instruments of torture and its girdles of chastity, from the stunted suits of armour in the old armouries, and from the flaws and indecisions in the fabric of the patched, unfinished cathedrals that were the chief achievement of that age, talked of his Manors and Guilds and seemed to think a kind of Paradise might be restored by setting back the clocks of history.

I questioned him, I argued very little with him. I went away to think him over in a mood of wonder.

Wonder! Yet perhaps not altogether wonderful. A student of physics or biology turns his back on the world at large and goes towards a more concentrated reality – in the chemical balance, the laboratory, the marine station. He must travel and explore. He must serve facts sublimated and released, facts that will blow him to pieces or corrode him to death at the least levity on his part. But a student of history or economics turns his back on his reality when he turns his back on the world at large; he goes into a cave of winds in which documents whirl about before imaginative gales. In that cave confident statements are stronger than facts. He may lie, misjudge, and blunder; nothing will hoist him sky-high or eat his flesh out or stain him purple for evermore. All the circumstances of a scholar's life conspire to turn the mind inward away from the dusty bickering of the common life. For him history is not, as it should be, an extension of reality; it is a refuge.

Perhaps there is something innate that in the first place disposes a man to become a University teacher or specialist. He is, I suspect, more often than not by nature and instinctively afraid of the insecure uproar of things. Visit him in college and you will see that he does not so much live there as lurk. He must find infinite assurance, infinite compensation for the threatening indignities of life, in the development of his lucid counter-world, so much simpler, so much clearer, so entirely logical. Once he has secured his cell he encounters little opposition; he may bid good-bye to his worst timidities, and set to work secreting his soul's protection. To deny a fact in that withdrawn and protected atmosphere becomes more and more like defeating it, and to impose a system on the confusion almost as good as conquering it. In his classrooms, his lectures, his written controversies, the theorising recluse can soon grow fierce and contemptuous enough; he can at last down and out with his facts that are so intractable in practice, to his own complete satisfaction.

And to live in agreement with a theory for any length or time is like what the Americans call a common-law marriage; you and it are wedded by habit and repute. A man wedded to a system is less and less able to apprehend contradictory realities. He becomes like the dogs and pigs people here in the South of France specialise to hunt truffles; he can at last discover his system at the merest hint of evidence, and all that does not countenance it ceases to interest him, ceases to exist for him; he thrusts past it heedlessly, scornfully.

### 8 – *Psycho-analysis of Karl Marx*

And now I can come to the maggot, so to speak, at the core of my decayed Socialism – Karl Marx.

To him we can trace, as much as we can trace it to any single person, this almost universal persuasion, which now Socialist and non-Socialist share, that economically we are living in a definable Capitalist System, which had a specific beginning and may have a definite end, and that current disorder of human affairs is not a phase but an organised disease that may be exorcised and driven off. Then after a phase of convalescence the millennium. For me he presents the source and beginning of one of the vastest and most dangerous misconceptions, one of the most shallow and disastrous simplifications, that the world has ever suffered from. His teaching was saturated with a peculiarly infectious class animosity. He it was who poisoned and embittered Socialism, so that today it is dispersed and lost and must be reassembled and rephrased and reconstructed again slowly and laboriously while the years and the world run by. He it was who was most responsible for the ugly ungraciousness of all current Socialist discussion.

I have always been curious about Marx, the Marx of the prophetic London days, and always a little baffled by the details that have been presented to me. He seems to have led a blameless, irritated, theorising life, very much as Lenin did before he returned to Russia in 1917, remote from mines, factories, railway-yards, and industrialism generally. It was not a very active nor a very laborious life he led; a certain coming and going from organisations and movements abroad in France and Germany must have been its most exciting element. He went to read and work with some regularity in the British Museum Reading-Room, a place that always suggests the interior of a gasometer to me, and he held Sunday gatherings in his Hampstead home and belonged to a club in Soho. He had little earning power, a thing not unusual with economic and financial experts, and he seems to have kept going partly by ill-paid journalism but mainly through the subsides of his disciple Engels, a Manchester calico merchant. There was a devoted wife and some daughters, but I know very little about them; one married unhappily, a tragedy that might happen to any daughter; of her one hears disproportionately. He suffered from his liver, and I suspect him of being generally under-exercised and perhaps rather excessively a smoker. That was the way with many of these heavily bearded Victorians from abroad. He grew an immense rabbinical beard in an age of magnificent beard-growing. It must have precluded exercise as much as a goitre. Over it his eyes look out of his portraits with a sort of uneasy pretension. Under it, I suppose, there appeared the skirts of a frock-coat and trousers and elastic-sided boots. He was touchy, they say, on questions of personal loyalty and priority, often more a symptom of the sedentary life than a defect of character, and the "finished" part of his big work on Capital is overlaboured and rewritten and made difficult by excessive rehandling and sitting over. Examined closely, many of his generalisation are found to be undercut, but these afterthoughts do not extend to Marxism generally.

He tended rather to follow the dialectic of Hegel than to think freely. There had been much mental struggle about Hegelianism in his student days, much emotional correspondence about it, a resistance, and a conversion. He competed with Proudhon in applying the new intellectual tricks to the new ideas of Socialism. He belonged in his schoolboy days to that insubordinate type which prefers revolution to promotion. He was, I believe, sincerely distressed by the injustices of human life, and also he was bitten in his later years by an ambition to parallel the immense effect of Charles Darwin. One or two of his disciples compare him with Darwin; Engels did so at his graveside; the association seems to have been familiar with his coteric before his death. And after three decades of comparative obscurity his name and his leading ideas do seem to have struggled at last – for a time – to an even greater prominence than the work of the modest and patient revolutionary of Down. But though his work professed to be a research, it was much more of an invention. He had not Darwin's gift for contact with reality.

He was already committed to Communism before he began the labours that were to establish it, and from the first questions of policy obscured the flow of his science. What did his work amount to? He imposed this delusion of a System with a beginning, a middle, and an end upon our perplexing economic tumult; he classified society into classes that leave nearly everybody unclassified; he proclaimed his social jehad, the class war, to a small but growing audience, and he passed with dignity into Highgate Cemetery, his death making but a momentary truce in the uncivil disputations of his disciples. His doctrines have been enormously discussed, but, so far as I know, the methods of psycho-analysis have not yet been applied to them. Very interesting results might be obtained if this were properly done.

He detected in the economic affairs of his time a prevalent change of scale in business and production which I shall have to discuss later. He extended this change of scale to all economic affairs, an extension which is by no means justifiable. He taught that there was a sort of gravitation of what he called Capital, so that it would concentrate into fewer and fewer hands and that the bulk of humanity would be progressively expropriated. He did not distinguish clearly between concrete possessions in use and money and the claim of the creditor, nor did he allow for the influence of inventions and new methods in straining economic combinations, in altering their range and breaking them up, nor realise the possibility of a limit being set to expropriation by the conditions of efficiency. That a change of scale may have definite limits and that the concentration of ownership may reach a phase of adjustment he never took into consideration. He perceived that big business methods extended very readily to the Press Parliamentary activities. He simplified the psychology of the immense variety of people, from master-engineers to stock-jobbers and company-promoters whom he lumped together as Capitalists, by supposing it to be purely acquisitive. He made his "Capitalists" all of one sort and his "Workers" all of one sort. Throughout he imposed a bilateral arrangement on a multifarious variety. He simplified the whole spectacle into a process of suction and concentration by the "Capitalist." This process would go on until competition gave place to a "Capitalist-Monopolist" state, with the rest of humanity either the tools, parasites, and infatuated victims of the Capitalists, or else intermittently employed "Workers" in a mood of growing realisation, resentment, and solidarity. He seems to have assumed that the rule of these ever more perilously concentrated Capitalists would necessarily be bad, and that the souls of the Workers would necessarily be chastened and purified by economic depletion. And so onward to the social revolution.

This forced assumption of the necessary wrongness and badness of masters, organisers, and owners, and its concurrent disposition to idealise the workers, was, I am disposed to think, a natural outcome of his limited, too sedentary, bookish life. It was almost as much a consequence of that life as his trouble with his liver. His work is pervaded by the instinctive resentment of the shy type against the large, free, influential individual life. One finds, too, in him that scholar's hate of irreducible complexity to which I have already called attention. In addition there was a driving impatience to conceive of the whole as a process leading to a crisis, to a dénouement satisfying to the half-conscious and subconscious cravings of the thinker. It was under the pressure of these resentments and impatiences – and with the assistance of the Hegelian doctrine which tells us that the Thing-that-is is always shattered at last to make way for higher synthesis by the Thing-that-it-isn't – that Marxism evolved its prophecy of the ultimate and not very remote victory of the idealised worker. The Proletarian would solidaritate (my word), and arrive *en masse*, he would crystallise out as Master, and all things would be changed at his coming. He would put down the mighty from their seats and exalt the humble and meek. He would fill the hungry with good things and the rich he would send empty away. The petty bourgeoisie he would smack hard and good. And everyone who mattered to the resentful gentleman who was making the story would be happy for ever afterwards.

It was a wish solidifying into a conviction that gave the world this wonderful and dramatic forecast of the dispossessed Proletarian becoming class-conscious, merging the residue of his dwarfed and starved individuality in solidarity with his kind, seizing arms, revolting massively, setting up that mystery, the Dictatorship of the Proletariat, "taking over" the "Capitalist-Monopolist state" and, after a phase of accommodation, dissolving it away into a confused democratic Communism, the Millennium. It is a dream story of things that are not happening and that are not likely to happen, but it is a very satisfying story for the soul of an intelligent and sensitive man indignant at the distresses of life and living unappreciated in a byway.

It is for the pyscho-analyst to lay bare the subtler processes in the evolution of this dream of a Proletarian saviour. Everybody nowadays knows that giant, in May-day cartoons and Communist pamphlets and wherever romantic Communism expresses itself by pictures, presenting indeed no known sort of worker, but betraying very clearly in its vast biceps, its colossal proportions, its small head and hammer of Thor in its mighty grip, the suppressed cravings of the restricted Intellectual for an immense virility. This Proletarian is to arise and his enemies – and particularly an educated world very negligent of its prophet – are to be scattered. There will then be a rough unpleasant time for the petty bourgeoisie. Things of the severest sort will happen to them. After the upper, they will get the nether millstone grinding into them...

The respectable leaders of British Victorian Trade Unionism upon whom Marx sought to foist this monster as their very spit and likeness, seem to have been considerably dismayed by it. They felt so much more like petty bourgeoisie.

One need only run over the outstanding names of the movement to realise how little the working man has had to do with the invention of this fantastic Titan or, indeed, with the development of Socialistic ideas at all. Trade Union and Labour leaders by the dozen and the score have called themselves Socialists and Communists in recent years, just as they called themselves Rationalists or Eugenists or Single-Taxers, but none of them have laid hands of power upon the central edifice of theory. That, on both its constructive and destructive side, had been the work either of prosperous men bored by social disorder and waste, or of irritated University students and scholars. Saint Simon was a benevolent aristocrat, Robert Owen a capable employer, William Thompson an Irish land-owner, William Morris and Ruskin belonged to the wealthy middle-class, Engels sold Manchester goods in Germany with reasonable success, and

Marx, our Marx of the relentless class-war, Marx, in the ecstatic language of his biographer Loria, "arose in a refined and aristocratic entourage," came from "an extremely ancient stock devoted to the accumulation of wealth" and was "united by marriage to the race of German feudatories, fierce paladins of the throne and the altar." Beer, in his history of British socialism, says Frau Marx was "related to the Argyles" – related to the Argyles! it is near divinity! – and speaks of Marx as a "proud mental aristocrat." The intense hatred and contempt expressed in Communist literature for the *petite bourgeoisie* is a further symptom of the element of down-at-heel aristocracy in a state of bruised self-conceit inspiring the movement. The stock Communist insult is to imply that an adversary isn't a born gentleman. I doubt if the theory of democratic Socialism owes nearly as much to real working men as the sciences do, as geology, archaeology, and physics, for example, do. It is a product not of the worker under oppression but of unprosperous expectant types irritated by exclusion and disregard.

In a tract by Lenin, *The State and Revolution*, written upon the eve of the Bolshevik seizure of power in 1917, I find the same smouldering resentment against all prosperous or educated people reflecting the economic argument, I find the same resort to the Armed Worker as the humiliator of negligent authority. Lenin discusses with evident distaste the probability that the Dictatorship of the Proletariat may need the services of educated people other than its own prophets. He writes of them with a sneer of the pen, so to speak, as "these intellectual gentry," and dwells with satisfaction upon the fact that they will be at any rate "controlled by armed workers."

Consider the values of that phrase.

A little while after this tract was written Lenin was dictator in the Kremlin and the "intellectual gentry" of Russia, the men of science and art and literature, were at his mercy. They might have starved altogether in those troublous times if Maxim Gorky, the novelist, who had a certain personal prestige with Lenin and a strong sense of the value of things intellectual, had not intervened. There was an attempt to organise their protection and maintenance, and when I was in Petersburg in 1920 I visited an old palace – the "House of Science" they had rechristened it – looking out upon the grey-flowing Neva, to which a number of "these intellectual gentry" had been shepherded. Control of the world of the mind by armed workers did not seem to be a very successful experiment. These men – and some of them had been very important figures in Russia's intellectual and creative life – were manifestly living in great misery and most of them were doing little or nothing. They were ill-fed, scantily and shabbily clothed, detestably watched, and with neither the books, papers, nor apparatus needed for their work. Poor Glazounov the composer was there, very wretched, the shadow of his former self, cold and ill; he could do nothing with his time because the Armed Workers would not hunt him out any music paper. He played some of his music to me on an old piano and talked of the days that had passed, and he wept. The chief Armed Worker directing the House of Science was a Mr Rodé, who before the revolution had kept an ultra-smart restaurant on one of the islands, a resort of gay parties during the white nights of the Northern summer. He had adapted himself to a Communist régime and he had a considerable control of the dietary and general comfort of the interned "intellectual gentry." Distinguished archaeologists, physiologists, chemists and historians, great mathematicians and brilliant teachers were in his power and fed from his hand. Maxim Gorky also was looking after the place with the breadth of intention and the practical incapacity of a genius and a Slav.

The social breakdown that had occurred in Russia is claimed by the Marxists as their prophet's social revolution. This they do in spite of the fact that he had pointed to England and the highly industrialised countries of the west as the lands of revolutionary promise. In truth the Russian collapse was like nothing Marx had ever dreamt of. The Russian peasant soldiers, having been robbed, starved, massacred, and misled by the Czar and his ministers – six or seven of these poor devils had to be killed in the battle for every one Austrian or German – reached the limit of their endurance when they found that the Kerensky revolution gave them no respite from the torture of the war. Two millions of them had been killed and mutilated. They had had enough and they would stand no more. They turned homeward to their villages. Once they had started nothing could hold them. The Russian armies melted away from before the Germans and Austrians and streamed home across the land. For a time Russia was in a state of social dissolution such as this Western world has not seen since the Thirty Years War; straggling bands of armed men did what they liked with the country through which they passed; robbery, rape, and murder went free and unavenged. In many provinces there was a Jacquerie, a château-burning. At times in bad places that Jacquerie rose to an extremity of horror. Yet there was a kind of crazy justice in it.

That was the true Russian Revolution, a social debâcle, a destruction of Czarism by its own weapon, the deliquescence of the army.

Admist the tumult of the disorganised towns there emerged the Russian Communist Party, the only association of men with any solidarity left in that frightful confusion. They were not workers, they were not proletarians – in Russia there was practically no Proletariat – they were a small body of Intellectuals with a following of youthful workers and students, greatly helped by sailors from the fleet. They grasped at power, they secured machine-guns, they organised forces of their own, including a band of Chinese, they shot, disarmed and restored a kind of order in the towns and as far as the railways reached in the country. "They had to shoot," President Masaryk told me on one occasion. "But they went on shooting."

They went on shooting. They were men of no experience; many were mere boys; they had fallen into irresponsible power and they had tasted blood. They had an orgy of blood-lust sharpened by fear. Then they set about the reorganisation of Russia upon Communist lines, declaring that the word of the prophet was fulfilled and the Capitalist System at an end.

They have held Russia ever since. They have held it because the Whites are worse then they are and because they fend off foreign interference and the return of the detested landlordism from the peasants. But there seems to be some uncertainty even in the party about the depth and quality of the resultant higher synthesis. There is a hitch in the Hegelian sequence, no system has appeared. There is no Communist system; it is a negation, a project-shaped vacuum.

Since I do not believe there is or ever has been a Capitalist System, I cannot get very excited about its alleged overthrow in Russia or anywhere. But I do find myself very deeply stirred when I think of the enormous wastage of good human hope and effort that has resulted from this falsely simple statement of our economic perplexities, this caricature of contemporary human life, as a simple antagonism of two systems that never have existed and never could exist.

I have been twice to Russia since the Revolution, and I was there several times before it. I should find it difficult to give a short general judgment upon the new ensemble there. With all the judgments I have encountered, from the violently adverse to the enthusiastically favourable, I find myself in disagreement. The peasant had got rid of his landlord, and if he is shot more frequently he is whipped much less; the hysterics of the Czar and his wife have given place to hysterical experiments; instead of

Rasputin's practical interpretations of Christianity one finds Zinovieff's practical interpretations of Marx; education is more general, but, if possible, less efficient; the railways are more awful than ever, and if there is more cruelty, filth, and disorder in the prisons there is less misery on the road to Siberia. If, as is highly probable, the Bolsheviki have killed more people than there are members of the Communist Party, we must set against that the far more monstrous war waste of the Czardom. If Zinovieff gets his way, the shadow of a giant war of the steppes against Western Europe may materialise, but many things may happen before Zinovieff gets his way.

I will not attempt to weigh the outcome of the Russian Revolution in the scales of my partial knowledge and possible prejudice – I had some irritating times in Moscow with the younger Bolsheviks and I dislike the type actively. The present "system" there, as I have been able to judge it, is just the same old Russian "system," with many of the parts missing, many of the wheels failing to cog, and many of its former patched-up compromises dislocated. In the old days my business could get along in a fashion at the price of a considerable amount of bribery; now they cannot get along at all; that is the most evident difference to me. Old traditions still make Russian officials hold one up, but the uncertainties of the new régime make them afraid to do a fair and reasonable blackmailing deal. One is just held up to no purpose. This is naturally irritating to a man who, like myself, had kept a certain pride in his work, and has always been a very temperate taker of profits.

The Communist formulae obstruct everything and have released nothing. I have been to Russia twice to get some little of the metallurgical wealth of the country out of the mess into which the Bolsheviks have dropped it; our aluminium works are still in a salvageable state at Dornoff, the only region of the world where there are deposits suitable for the new Manson process –

and if only they would do the work properly I would gladly put the Bolsheviks in complete possession rather then have all these carefully adjusted arrangements going to waste. But each time I have been treated with a stupid suspicion, kept waiting about for weeks, watched and followed, my rooms searched in my absence, and in the end I have been thwarted – for the mere sake of thwarting me. I was quite willing to tell them all I knew about the particular matters that concerned me, put all my cards upon the table; for I want cheap aluminium and light alloys in the world as badly as they want Communism. Why should they assume they are more disinterested than I? The impudence of it!

But their theory required me to be a subtle and treacherous representative of the Capitalist System, a thievish moneylender and entangler of simple, brave, good workers, and themselves, raw, young, and self-ignorant, the guardian angels of mankind. They had no shadow of doubt about these moral values. Their ambition was to lay me by the heels on a charge of "economic espionage." They had their dirty prison and they had me, and they felt an opportunity was being lost. The career of a good Communist depends upon conspicuous displays of zeal. Were they showing *zeal?* They would not listen to what I tried to tell them; that was obviously only a blind. One fool said my science was "capitalist science" as opposed to "proletarian science" – in metallurgical chemistry! I battered myself against that sort of thing in vain.

What can one do with men who are inexorably convinced, in spite of every material fact about them, that they have, germinating under their hands, a new and perfect social system, the Communist system, which they are defending from the subtle treacheries of a wicked Capitalist System; and whose entire intellectual outfit is unsleeping suspicion and a stock of ready-made nicknames by which they can misconceive everybody?

There is no way round these fixed ideas. You are put on this or that side of an opposition between entirely imaginary systems; and in whatever direction you thrust the end is futility. So there is our stuff in Russia untouched and badly wanted, and our works are going to decay – beautifully planned works they are, though I say it who shouldn't – doing no good to Russia or any human being.

And this is mainly if not entirely an intellectual trouble, a trouble of wrong statement, just as most of the great religious wars of the past were mainly wars of wrong statement. The world splits between Europe and the East and the limitation and misery of hundreds of millions of lives is the by-product of an incoherent argument about the interpretation of social interactions. An imperfectly aerated old gentleman sits in the British Museum, suffering from a surfeit of notes, becomes impatient to set a generalisation in control of his facts, and presently we have this harvest of tares. It is Arius and Athanasius and the camel driver of Mecca I think of in his case, rather than Darwin.

### 9 – *Reincarnation of Socialism*

Socialism which was creative is stunned, and Communism, which is the sabotage of civilisation by the disappointed, has usurped its name and inheritance. I have accused Marx as the prime mover in the destruction of Socialism. But the teaching of Marx would not have found impassioned and fanatical followers, if there had not been something deep and widespread in the human make-up to answer its appeal. This response came, I believe, from the natural hate of men deeply conscious of their own merits and conscious also of social disadvantages for those whom Fate seems to have treated better. It is a response easy to evoke in all too many people in world so chancy as ours. Malice is a necessary quality in an animal which has changed so swiftly from solitude to an exasperated gregariousness as man has done. The new Marxist Socialism, therefore, with its confident dogmas, its finality and hardness, its vindictive will, developed an intensity and energy that drowned and almost silenced the broader, more tentative, and scientific initiatives of the older, the legitimate Socialism. Communism, with its class-war obsession, ate up Socialism as Catholicism, with its facile consolations and definitive creeds, the Church militant here on earth, ate up Christianity. Communism may live as long as Islam; which is most like it of all other human things, as rigid and as intense. It may endure long after the Moscow caliphs have passed away, establishing a second system of fanatical resistances to the comprehensive organisation of the world upon modern lines.

But the constructive conceptions that inspired the earlier Socialism will not disappear with the fading-out of Socialism from general discussion. They arise too easily in the natural development of economic and social life. They may change their phraseology; they may cease to be expressed in the old terms and under the old name, but they will live. It may have been necessary that Socialism should die in some such fashion in order to be born again, revised, refreshed. There were extraordinary gaps and imperfections, I realise, in the liberal Socialism of my student days. The broad ideas of it, the ideas of a collective organisation of the basal needs of mankind, of a systematic economy of the energy that goes now to waste in competition for mere existence, the idea of a complete abolition of forestalling, of obstruction for gain and indeed of every sort of profiteering, these primary Socialist ideas are more living now than ever they were. They have infected the whole body of modern thought.

But among other obvious deficiencies, that nineteenth-century Socialism was almost wilfully blind to the necessity for a scientific monetary method, a proper reckoning of obligations and claims proof against manipulation, if any just and efficient system of production was to work. Owen, indeed, thought of that essential – Dickon has shown me recently a collection of Owen's experimental "labour notes" – but his smaller followers in their little wisdom dropped the question. If anyone mentioned money in a Fabian Society meeting in my Socialist time there wold be a kind of general hoot: "Oh Lord! Here's a Currency Crank!" Saying "Currency Crank" in a Fabian Society meeting was almost as deadly as saying "Boor-jaw!" in a modern Communist gathering. I have seen Sidney Webb, our London Lenin, flushed, flustered, and irritated, waving all that sort of thing aside. Bitter scorn, an earnest scorn. Let us get on to sensible things. Morris to judge by his *News from Nowhere* would have done without money; his other contemporaries, it seems, thought that any old money would do. But science is measurement, and money as we have it at present is about as good for the measurement of social obligation as an earthworm for the measurement of length.

Equally vague, evasive, and useless was the political attitude of that old Socialism. The Socialists were proposing to "nationalise" the means of production and distribution, but when one asked who or what was to be the operating "nation," they had nothing to suggest. Again came flushed impatience and a hasty waving of the disturbing question away. Socialism, they recited, was an economic not a political reform, which of course explained everything. It seems incredible, but they seem to have believed that economic justice and administrative efficiency were compatible with any sort of political rottenness, division, and absurdity. Never mind about that; the wise little officials would see anything through. You see while Marxian Socialism was invented by discontented professors, Fabian Socialism was largely the product of hopeful Civil Servants. The psycho-analysis of Fabianism is as destructive to its scientific pretension as the psycho-analysis of Marxism. The only difference is that it reveals a brighter type of soul.

These Socialists of my student days were entirely vague about international relationships. It was uncomfortable for those Civil Servants who did its thinking to imagine a world with quite a different sort of Civil Service altogether. So they did not imagine it. And though they could contemplate the expropriation of most people they had an habitual respect for the possible resentment of rulers and politicians and the governing class generally. None of these nineteenth-century Socialists I heard and read were clear whether they were nationalist or imperialist or international, or what they were. They shivered at the word Cosmopolitan and sneered at the phrase World-State. They did not even know whether they were Protectionists or Free-Traders; and to this day they do not know. You will find a Labour paper like the *Daily Herald* scolding vigorously at the private ownership of land and minerals in one column and insisting in the next upon the "right" of some little barbaric nationality to hold its territories and its natural resources, however vast they may happen to be, against the needs of all mankind. It would wrench the northern coalfield from the Duke of Northumbrland and leave all the minerals of the Riff to Abd-el-Krim.

The petty industry in research of these Fabians affected to be prodigious, but in general inquiry their inertias were astounding. They were all for municipalising and nationalising, and yet they would never consider with any patience or care the constitution, the methods of election, the areas of control of the municipalities and parliamentary governments to which with the utmost recklessness they proposed to entrust the land, the natural resources, the public services of the community. So long as it was an elected body and not an assembly of private persons they did not seem to care. The community was just to elect somebody, somehow, anyhow, and the clever little official would tell that somebody what to do. Gross energetic men, it seems, were to wait and plan and spend and fight vehemently for power – and then, whichever of them won it, would hand it over meekly and trustfully to the wise, good, quiet "experts" waiting in their bureaus.

Socialism took over a prevailing belief of the time when it took over the belief in the necessity for elected bodies. There was no need to take over that belief, and had the movement been a really full thinking movement it would not have done so. But in the nineteenth century AD it was believed as firmly that it was necessary to have some sort of election, any sort of election, however preposterously conducted, before the affairs of the community could be administered, as it was believed to be necessary to have some sort of blood sacrifice before seed-time in the nineteenth century BC. It was the current superstition. It fades. When creative ideas emerge again into a definite system of proposals, I believe we shall find them completely detached from this delusion that they can be realised only by, through, or with the consent of elected persons. There will be no further research for majorities. Realisation of a new stage of civilised society will be the work of an intelligent minority; it will be effected without the support of the crowd and possibly in spite of its dissent.

I am now, more than ever I was, a revolutionary. Every year of my life makes me more certainly revolutionary. I believe that before the muddled and very insecure process of the world's affairs now current can be changed into a stronger, broader, happier, progressive organisation, many habitual resistance will have to be overcome and many legally established institutions which will refuse to undergo the modifications and subordinations necessary to adapt them to a scientifically conceived world civilisation will have to be cleared away. The legal standing of such old, obstructive, entrenched rights will have to be changed by imposing – in a manner essentially illegal – a different legal standing upon them. No human legal system has ever voluntarily abolished itself in favour of another. Fundamental changes of political and social method must be effected by pressures exercised by the sort of people who have a will for the better order. There is no way round such a necessity that I can see. This may not mean actual violence, but there will be at least the intimation of superior strength. If that sort of thing is not revolution, then I do not know what revolution is.

I believe that ultimately man, collective man, has to suppress the sovereign independence of any part of the world as against the whole. He cannot get on very much beyond our present sort of civilisation until he has contrived a world currency, a world control of staple production, a world peace – and, in fact, a world state. He has to regard prescription and proprietary claims as entirely secondary and provisional arrangements in dealing with the land, with the natural resources and the material organisation of the earth. No quibbling can make dispossessions and redistributions of ownership and sovereignty, in the face of protest, legal acts; and no evolutionary process that does not involve death and birth, putting an end to old things and beginning again with new things, can ever bring about the new world implicit in science and in manifested human possibilities.

But when I think of revolution I have in mind something quite different from the idea of a Revolutionary that has dominated the human imagination since those violent days in Paris a hundred and thirty odd years ago. I have no use for that Revolutionary of the Communist placard type, that pithecoid Proletarian, dishevelled, semi-nude, making heroic motions with improvised weapons behind a casually assembled barricade of beams, paving-stones, overturned carts, pots, pans, railings. I look, indeed, for something antagonistic to that. I look to the growth of a minority of intelligent men and women for the real revolution before mankind. I look for a ripening élite of mature and educated minds, and I do not believe progress can be anything more than casual and insecure until that élite has become self-conscious and effective. I do not look to the mass of people for any help at all. I am thinking of an aristocratic and not a democratic revolution.

Except as scavenging or fertilising floods, I do not believe in democratic revolutions. I believe the multitude, when it is suitably roused, can upset anything, but I do not believe that it can create anything whatever.

I quite understand the dismay that comes upon every impatient world-mender when he seeks creative forces among the prosperous people of today. Most of them are prosperous by reason of some flaw or direct iniquity of the economic muddle, and they are vaguely aware of that; they do not want any examination of the complex of disarrangements that gives them the advantages of their property; as a class they are prepared to defend the stacked-up instabilities they call the "existing system" very stoutly. But there are exceptions to the conservatism of the prosperous. Many of these exceptions are personally or vicariously curious and spend their resources upon research; many, like myself, are bored to death by the poor mean pleasures, displays, and gratifications our prosperity can buy, and many have a really disinterested creative impulse. It is to the increase in number of these exceptional types and to the spread of an inquiring and adventurous spirit in this class that I look for the continuation, acceleration, and extension of social and economic progress towards a new and finer world order. If the class-war idea is sound and liberated people are necessarily less socially disposed than frustrated and limited people, then manifestly there is no hope for mankind.

No doubt our present social complex is still heavily loaded down by an accumulation of dull and heavy creditors, parasitic, greedy speculators, and unproductive spenders generally, but social life has always had to carry such a burden of selfish and obstructive prosperity since social life began. Relatively I do not think there is more of that burden now than there was two hundred years ago. I think there is less of it. And it has less pride and assurance. Read any eighteenth-century novel and mark the amelioration of social attitudes. There is no reason why we should go running off in a passion to fields, slums, workshops, mines, railway-yards, docks, the forecastles of ships, gaols, and institutions for the re-organisers of society, because the imaginations of the fortunate classes are still largely unstimulated by creative ideas that are hardly a century old. It is true that the lives of the majority of mankind today are insecure, anxious, limited, laborious, stunted, unfruitful, and generally unhappy, and that they will remain so until economic order is attained. But because masses of toilers and needy people are thoroughly uncomfortable it does not follow that they are capable of the subtle and intricate adjustments needed to make themselves and mankind free and happy. It does not follow even that they are capable of recognising those who are attempting to make them free. They are very properly disposed to discontent, and many of their livelier minds find the idea of a class-war attractive, but I doubt if their conception of that class-war is anything but vindictive. It is not a better order they want but – witness the Communist hatred of the petty bourgeoisie – malicious reprisals against the slightly more prosperous class immediately and therefore most irritatingly in contact with them. The most dreadful thing about their situation is their evident inability to imagine any better order. They do not want a change; they want an inversion without a change. They have grown up in a coarse and ugly way of living, and their first impulse, so soon as they realise the coarseness and disagreeableness that has been put upon them, is to extend it to everybody. "See how *you* like it!" They want that far more than they want a new way of living.

They know instinctively that a new way of living would be unpleasantly discordant with their established habits.

One may sympathise with that vindictive impulse, but I do not see that one is called upon to assist it. The sense of frustration in a hopeless toiler may be keen enough to make even sabotage a pleasure, but I have other tastes. For three-quarters of a century Socialism under the spell of Marxism has cherished the delusion that in the masses there is a huge reservoir of creative power. There is nothing in the masses as masses but an unreliable explosive force.

The greater revolution must be a deliberate and not a convulsive process. It has to fight against the egoist and fool in man, the ancestral, instinctive brute, as much in the suspicious and angry mob below as in the timid, mean, and violent propertied classes above. It has a far greater percentage of possible adherents among the educated and able than in the crowd. Just as we depend for the gigantic services of scientific progress upon at most a few score thousand rather unpopular individuals mostly of the middle and independent classes, so the task of bracing, ordering, and clearing this very cruel and wasteful jungle of human affairs may remain for some generations still in the hands of quite a few obstinately clear-headed men and women. They have to work hard and be patient; there is nothing else for them to do; they cannot indulge in the emotional gratification of premature organisation and simplified propaganda. They will be men and women of experience, who have learnt about human affairs by handling them; they will be prepared for formulae that will not simplify, and for incurable intricate problems. Ultimately this sort of people will acquire the necessary force and knowledge to change things systematically, and then they will set about doing so. Their convictions will radiate into the general mass. They will reshape the general conceptions of economic political and social life.

Their revolution will involve much greater and much more sustained operations than barricades in the streets and little squitterings of machine-gun fire. They will have a different sort of strategy than the disorganisation of political parties and subtler methods than sabotage schemed in cellars and the misdirection of honest discontent. I do not see why thwarted pedants and unlicked youngsters should be allowed to monopolise the excellent name of Revolutionary for ever, nor why restless shop-stewards and the sort of defectives who set fire to things should imagine themselves sole lords of human hope.

### 10 – *Irruption of Mimosa*

This morning my work has been interrupted.

I have been raided and assaulted by Clementina. She has come into the room with an armful of mimosa, iris, and white and purple stock, and stuck this pretty stuff all over the place. She has made a great disturbance because I was not going to have my lunch out of doors in the sun – they are laying it out there now all over again – and her beastly little animated muff of a dog has chased my grey cat up the Japanese medlar. It is the fifteenth of January, and she declares the Provençal spring arrived. But that is no reason why she should constitute herself Primavera and cumber my study with an excess of flowers.

"It's no good," she said. "I can't keep away from you today." And she hasn't. She has ruffled my hair. She has also ruffled my mind.

She seized upon some pages of this manuscript. "Oh! Marx!" she cried with a note of disgust. "Capitalism! Revolution!" she put the sheets down. "I thought you were writing your life. I thought I was going to read something about you. I thought it was going to be about yourself!"

"This book," I said, "is not for you."

"You told me about it one day."

"In a moment of weakness. It is hard not to talk at times to a woman who besets one as you do me. But what I said was – inexact."

"Obviously. If you are writing about *–isms,* I'm not sorry I interrupted you. I thought it was to be about yourself and what you had made of the world. I thought I should get an idea of what you were like when you were a young man."

"I have a section to finish. And the door is just behind you."

"I'm not going. I'm not disposed to go. It's spring. And near lunch-time."

"You are going," I said.

I do not know why I scuffle and romp so easily with Clementina. Certainly there is spring in the air today. But now she has a better idea of what I was like when I was a young man. She has been at last more or less thrown out of this room in a properly pacified, subdued, and crumpled condition, and I find myself turning over my writing and reassembling the ideas she dissipated by her wanton invasion.

It is true that the late three or four sections have been mainly devoted to Marx and Socialism, but that is no more than a digression from the account of my world than the theology of the First Book. Why should one entertain the idea that a man is no more than his face, his mannerisms, and his love affairs? A man, if he is to be rendered completely, must begin with the creation of the world so far as it specially concerns him and end with his expectations of eternity. If a man is to be given completely, there must first be the man and his universe, then the man and history, and only after that man and other men and womankind. My struggle to apprehend the social conflict about me in terms of Socialism was at least as much a part of me as the poor little marriage and the poor little half-divorce I shall presently have to reveal – and my subsequent proceedings. It played as large a part in shaping my life – a larger part.

It is plain to me that, having swept aside the Communist idea of a revolution and thrown some passing doubts upon the economic interpretation of history, I am bound to give a version of the human story that seems to me to be truer. I am bound to indicate and in a measure explain my conception of the world of toil and business in which I have struggled and won freedom and security for myself. Every autobiography that is written for more than a special circle of readers must be thus encyclopaedic. My eyes are astigmatic; my mind is no doubt ill-informed and incompetent; that is all the more reason why I should tell of things as I see them and of all the things I see, and not assume that I see them in some correct and standard fashion.

A writer may affect modesty and deal with these broad issues by reference. But is that modesty? He may defer to recognised authority. He may declare that so far as recognised authority goes he has no world of his own. He may say, "In matters of religion I follow the teaching of the Holy Catholic Church," or "Upon questions of economics I submit to the superior knowledge of the economists." But is not the good man assuming that he has so complete a knowledge of the teachings of his church or of the orthodox economists as to be sure to think upon all issues exactly as they do? He commits his church or his science to all his implications. Though he disavows authority, yet he presumes excessively to knowledge.

To achieve the perfect robe of perfect modesty should he not rather say, "I follow the teachings of my church so far as I know and understand them; I am conscious of limitation and even of error on my part, but I do my best," and then he should go on to set forth his own defective interpretation. "That as I see it," he should say, "is the teaching of the Church. That is my humble reading. By this I have guided myself. I may be in grievous error, but this is what my authority has meant to me." It is his interpretation that matters to us, and claims our interest in him. Or else, why autobiography at all? The existence of perfect solutions that he may or may not understand does not excuse him. These we can study without his help, but his reaction to them is another matter. We do not want him to give us these things in perfection; we do want to see them in fallible operation. And so we bring his modest gentility back, blushing prettily no doubt, to the full encyclopaedic range again.

In the next two or three sections I propose to write a short history of human society as a labour-money complex evolved out of the primitive patriarchal family. They will have to be highly concentrated sections. This book, at any rate, is not going to be a home of rest for tired readers. If presently Clementina repeats her aggressions, she will find sheets of discussion about how toil came into the world and what money did for the Roman Empire. "Old economics!" she will cry. For the life of me I cannot get either my father's disaster or the business achievements of Dickon or myself into any sort of focus without that background. And as for Clementina – !

Clementina has a mind like one of those water insects that never get below the surface of anything. Water-boatmen they are called, and they flicker about sustained by surface tension. She just flickers about. She professes an affection for me that is altogether monstrous, and she knows no more about my substantial self than the water-boatman knows of the deeps of the pond. She knows as little about the world.

Why is a person with so quick an intelligence and such wise instincts as Clementina mentally so superficial? Why does she habitually dismiss three-quarters of human concerns as uninteresting? For gossip, excursions, household matters, and making love, Clementina has an abundant, swift, penetrating, and indefatigable intelligence. She has subtlety; she has invention.

The poetry she writes shows at least a keen appreciation for poetry in general and also for a certain prettiness in things at large that she has not learnt from pre-existing poetry. But she will not even look at the framework in which such things are set and which is continually affecting and determining such things!

I am reminded of something I was told the other day by a man who is by way of being a prominent historical writer. He was "approached," as they say, by one of these big American film producers. People, the film man apologised, were displaying a certain curiosity about the general history of mankind. It was an unaccountable lapse, and no doubt a temporary one, but it could not be ignored. Would it be possible for my friend to prepare the scenario for a series of films of such a history? A glimpse was given, carelessly but attractively, of dollars falling in showers.

My friend considered various difficulties, but decided that something of the sort could be done. "The public wants to know about things," he agreed The film man expressed great optimism about the scheme – but in rather doubtful tones. His reason was in conflict with his instincts and mental habits. The latter were the better exercised and the more powerful. There was a pause in the discussion. It was evident that a difficulty had to be considered.

"I wonder now," said the film man, "if it wouldn't be possible to run some little *story* through this series, something about a boy and his girl and a bit of trouble between them or a revenge or something of that sort. *So as have a thread of human interest in it.*"

A thread of human interest – in the history of mankind! The conversation ended in discord.

For Clementina there is apparently no thread of human interest in economics – that is to say in the toil, payment, enslavement, or liberation of scores of millions of human beings. Of history she has much the same opinion as the film man. Geology, of course, meant nothing to her but "old rocks," palaeontology nothing but "old bones." It is inconceivable to her that anyone should be interested in theology. Sociology makes her impatient and politics rude. Yet though she has renounced all the vanities of the world in order to come and live near me in the less accessible lanes of Provence, she can still muse pleasantly, during one of our rare trips to Cannes or Nice, before a hat-shop window. That, she feels, is "life." As surely as biology isn't. And with her flitting glance she is just a sample of general readers everywhere. They do not care whence they came nor whither they go nor what they are doing. They just flicker about. They will be water-boatmen till the stream dries up...

But it occurs to me that Clementina has had to wait an unconscionable time for lunch. What patience she has shown! She is almost directly under this window and she has not called up once. Probably with a pensive calm that sometimes descends upon her after misbehaviour she has been eating up the beetroot and olives.

### 11 – *History of Toil Through the Ages*

Five thousand years ago our ancestors can have had no more economics than the animals; they lived from hand to mouth where the food was. If the food diminished they wandered away. If they could not find more food they weakened and perished like any other beasts. Their gear was just a skin and a stick and a stone or so, not more than could be trailed or carried. A stranger was an intruder and better killed. The old man killed or drove off his sons, and was the lord of all his womankind, lord indeed of his visible universe, until a younger and a stronger adversary came to dispossess and end him. If his equipment was simple his ownership at least was immense; he recognised no other rights in the world but his own, and he died fighting for them.

The first step towards human accumulation on a broader scale was taken when the Old Man came to recognise the right of another adult male to live within sight or smell of him. This first mitigation of the possessive instinct was the foundation of human society. The women trained their boys in the fear and avoidance of the Old Man, to regard all his belongings and particularly their mothers and stepmothers and sisters as tabu, and in return they persuaded the Old Man to tolerate the existence of his sons, and at last, in the course of ages, even to allow them the right to possess the strange girls they caught and dragged home with them to the family fireside. That is the only credible story of the beginnings of human society I have ever found in anthropology. It explains the primordial incest tabu, and the worldwide traces of marriage by capture, and a score of worldwide primitive customs that are otherwise fantastic. And it marches with most of the complex suppressions that lie at the roots of our modern mentality. It follows that the first private property to infringe the universal dominion of the Old Man was property in a woman.

One can still hardly speak of economics even after the ape family had passed into the primitive human tribe. The tribe personified in the Old Man still owned so far as it ranged; it hunted in a pack and feasted from one carcass; most of the implements it used were made by those who were going to use them; there may have been a little bartering of ornaments and curious oddities between individuals and mutual present-giving, but there was still nothing in the nature of work, of employment, as we understand these terms. Mothers worked for their children and got them food and watched over them, as animal mothers do. Probably children and inferior women were the first human beings made to work beyond this instinctive devotion; they were sent out to find and bring home sticks for the fire or berries or small edible creatures. The first reluctant worker may have been a fire mender. The first workers were in much the position of the modern labouring man's wife; they did all that had to be done, and they got no pay beyond their keep and their owner's attentions. Maternity had given woman a greater submissiveness to routine drudgery than man, and probably the greater part of the simple duties of the cave and the squatting place fell to her.

The early Palaeolithic human tribe could have been only a stage more advanced economically than a pack of wild dog. They had their fire and implements to the good. They had become more carnivorous and had perhaps grown bigger and stronger than their more solitary ancestors. The expansion of toil as the tribe grew and possessions and elaborations increased, fell no doubt upon the shoulders least able to evade it. There is no natural instinct for toil in man. He likes to make things but with as little trouble as possible. Already in Palaeolithic times a considerable and increasing amount of human intelligence and energy was being devoted to shifting toil upon the shoulders of somebody else. As human societies grew larger and better equipped and the necessary labour increased, oppression became more intelligent and systematic. The Old Man in the ape-man stage just killed and maltreated; the chief of the primitive human tribe directed and employed his folk, the women almost naturally and the men as much as he dared, and punished the idle among them. Sometimes perhaps there was not one single chief but three or four big fellows who had learnt to respect each other.

That was the quality of the "primitive communism" so many worthy anthropologists have seen fit to idealise.

As hunting tribes and herd-following tribes developed into cattle-herding and cattle-driving, and as agriculture, first of snatch crops and then of settled regions, appeared, an ever rising tide of labour poured into human experience. The hungry picnicking freedom of primordial man gave place, age by age, to the more and more regular work and regular meals of the agricultural man, under the guiding compulsion of the chiefs and elders of the community. The children as they grew up found they had to work; the young men had to work. That it had once been unnatural to have to work was an idea beyond the brief range of human thought in those days. As soon could a draught-horse think of freedom. An anxious industriousness was gradually imposed upon the men of the agricultural regions, a moral impulse towards activity. To be an idler became a new shame almost as great as the older one of being a coward; one pretended not to be lazy just as one pretended not be afraid; and man began to store like the squirrel and worry about the future.

It was only with the development of agriculture that man became a truly economic animal; the first of the vertebrata, I suppose, to be truly economic. Hitherto the chief economic creatures had been the ants and termites and bees. To become economic is first to become the watchful servitor of vegetable growth; that is the essence of it. Nomadic predatory peoples never succumbed to the delusion that industry is in itself a virtue. It seems to me fairly certain that there was a barbaric stage in human development when most of the tribe worked on such occasions as demanded work, under the direction of the chiefs and medicine men, and that they did it as a matter of course, without wages or personal reward. The labour was communal – that is to say, only the very strongest could shirk it; the product was communal – that is to say, the weaker got what they were permitted to get out of it. Probably there was little private personal property beyond wives, ornaments, weapons, huts and suchlike things. The cattle and lands belonged to the head men. Or some cattle on the common land were perhaps ear-marked for individual owners and the rest belonged to the tribal heads.

I think it is a fairly obvious and very important thing that, to begin with, trading had little or nothing to do with the economic life of the tribe. In out present life, trading, with its later instrument, money, is so intimately mixed up with staple production that people are apt to forget the two were once separate processes and dealt with different orders of necessity and desire. A barbaric agricultural people could, if necessary, live a fairly full and complex economic life without any trade or any pay whatever, and with scarcely any private property. Trading was an extra thing, a function, and not the most important one, of such seasonal gatherings as may have occurred.

An early enrichment of the primitive economic scheme must have been the slave, either the stolen child or the spared captive. Just as the stolen woman came into the early Palaeolithic human group as the first private wife, so as the Neolithic order developed, the slave came in as a more amenable worker than the tribesman. Before the Neolithic stage there was little use for slaves. A stranger child could be taken along with the tribe like a captured wolf-cub, and petted or ill-treated, outraged or adopted as luck would have it. It was agreeable to have a human being to do exactly what you liked with, a motive which, as the Society for the Prevention of Cruelty to Children knows only too well, still leads queer people to take over the care of orphan children. And all sorts of small irksome services could be put upon a youngster too timid to run away into the wilderness.

That was probably the limit of slavery while man was still a wanderer. An adult male slave was of little use to nomads; his escape was comparatively easy. If he proved to be a helpful person it was better to make him a member of the tribe. But as agricultural work increased, men and women captives, used hitherto chiefly for sacrifice and torture and suchlike amusing but transitory ends, began to have an economic value. The heads of the tribes got a more tractable service from them. Their spirits could be broken entirely because they were not wanted for fighting purposes like the young men of the tribe. They could be used up more completely. The Egyptian turquoise mines in Sinai, as early as the days of the First Dynasty, were worked by slave labour.

There must always have been great local variations of the early barbaric state. We make a great mistake, we fall into the System myth, when we suppose the early barbaric community to have had a stereotyped pattern. It had certain common tendencies; it developed under certain common necessities; all the world over, men's minds are much alike. And though communications were difficult, men were as imitative and perhaps more imitative than they are now. The tradition of the Old Man of the primitive days gave here a God and there a God-King and there a King-Priest. Wherever agriculture went there went with it the traditions of a blood sacrifice, a human sacrifice. I have never been able to imagine satisfactorily why this should have been so; but very plainly it was so. In the old world that blood sacrifice became very generally mitigated; in America, under a mysterious tendency towards harshness manifested by that continent, it developed to tremendous proportions until it obsessed a civilisation. The Maya, the Aztec religions were insanely bloody. With agriculture, too, came an enormously clumsy primitive astronomy to determine the coming of inundations and the propitious phases of the year for sowing. Pyramids and obelisks acted as gnomons, temples were oriented to stars. It is wonderful to think how widely and vividly those opening phases of civilisation have been studied and made plain, within my lifetime.

Side by side with the largely agricultural hard-working communities of the warm alluvial countries there developed endless less agricultural and mainly nomadic groups, grazing sheep, driving cattle, and in Central and Eastern Asia keeping herds of horse. They traded, they conquered or were driven out again from the agricultural lands after a phase of conquest; they developed institutions after their needs, and these came in to modify and confuse and complicate the customs, institutions, habits of mind and points of view that grew up from the ploughed lands. Among the cattle-tending nomads and in mountain glens one may even imagine a sort of justification for that "ancient gentilic (tribal or clan) organisation" which Engels, the fellow-prophet of Marx, declared by some inner light to be the primitive stage of human society. Only instead of his amiable Elders, enjoying "the spontaneous informal regard of Society," there must have been a reality much more after the vivid pattern of a Highland chief. All these things, we must remember, were worked out by thousands of communities through hundreds of generations, over plains, uplands, gorges, valleys, forests, steppes, and deserts, and the more simple and exact we make our classifications and explanations the easier they will be to carry in our minds, and the farther they are likely to be from the truth. Human society did not develop through an orderly progression of stages, but by an infinite diversity of temporary equilibriums and blundering innovations.

All the anthropology I have read seems to me almost without exception to assume that the man of six or seven thousand years ago was more lucid and systematic that the man of today. But plainly he must have been very much less so. It is not that he was intellectually inferior – there has probably been little if any growth of the human brain since Palaeolithic times – but that he had nothing made ready for him. His language was still a relatively poor instrument, there were no accumulations of recorded and established general ideas. Logical reasoning and systematic thought did not begin until about twenty-five centuries ago; Plato struggled mystically with the species and the individual, the One and the Many; and the syllogism is no older than Aristotle. Our classical scholars never seem to be quite sure whether in the dialogues of Plato they are dealing with a Cyclopean clumsiness of argument or philosophical profundities. Before that time men thought, as children and under-educated people still think, by imagination. They tried to express things beyond the immediate daily life by symbols and mythical stories which were promptly misapprehended and retold in a different sense. And there was infantile wonder and emotion still flowing undisciplined through their minds. They could find some numbers beautiful and others flat or obnoxious. They were as childish as that. They were capable of immense inconsistencies. Habit and imitation held people's lives together throughout wide districts and regions in a general likeness. They attempted, they got, they prevailed, or they submitted, they told or robbed the toil of others, they feared and hated, killed and triumphed. This was life, they said, for what else could there be? They bred and passed on the mysterious appeal of life, they loved their children violently and their grown-up offspring less, and they died and forgot and were forgotten.

Seven thousand years ago you had, at a generally more simple level, all the elements of the social problems of today; oppressors and oppressed, luckless wights born to toil and suffering, lucky ones to veneration and delight, genial, kindly recipients of good-fortune, patient drudges, people cruelly misunderstood, souls in wild protest, cunning, wary winners in the game, perplexed losers, and it was all unsystematic, no one had planned it. It had grown unawares as a jungle grows, it had drifted along the stream of time, expanding, multiplying, complicating into an ever broader and vaster spectacle, out of man's solitary past.

It seems to me to be enormously important to stress this casual, complicated, and incoherent quality of man's past. I reiterate it deliberately. I return to it again. It is a conviction fundamental to the edifice of my ideas; it is as much a part of me as my eyes. I do not believe we can deal properly with our current problems until we are saturated with this realisation. I have watched political thought with a very close interest all my life, and I perceive the urgent need to purge from our minds the disposition to think that at certain phases of human affairs something wicked was done, that a few men, priests or kings or rich men, plotted against the rest to deceive and enslave them. Or that at a definite time something wise was done and a new direction given to affairs. I can find nothing of that sort in my vision of history. What are called turning-points in history are significant and not directive. Life is more muddled and more innocent than we are inclined to think it. Men accept their lives as they find them, and all human beings are greedy, something disingenuous, and inapt to sympathise with the unlike. Some are pressed into the position of devourers and some find themselves stifled and preyed upon. But change priest and victim and with scarcely a hitch the sacrifice would go on.

Man's soul and mind in those days were already a palimpsest. It is only nowadays that psycho-analysis is beginning to work down through the superimposed layers and to reveal the restrained and baffled solitary-minded Old Man of the pre-Palaeolithic days, peeping up through all the obliterations of training, custom, law, and religion that have been imposed upon him. But there he is at the bottom of things, the reason why men will combine far more readily for warfare than peace and for persecution than worship, why they are so easily "anti" and only by repercussion "pro," why they must grab beyond their utmost needs, why restraining laws are necessary, and why we all seek instinctively to ensure our own private security against the promiscuous motives of the general herd, that uncertain currish mob-soul of our kind.

## 12 – *Money*

No other part of history so interests me as the opening chapter before the documents begin. There is no excessive presentation of persons and personal names; egoism has left nothing but defaced monuments and disconnected boasts, and we seem to come nearer to the realities of human life than we do in many a later age when kings and princes and their policies monopolise the foreground.

Certain great enlargements of human life came about in the period between ten thousand and two thousand years two. They came about very gradually and it is only nowadays that we begin to reconstruct the story of their appearance. One of these enlargements was writing and another was money. Even in the Palaeolithic age, thirty thousand years ago, men were very near to writing. They not only made beautiful pictures like those in the Altamira caves, but they simplified drawings down to conventional signs and wrote them rapidly and kept tallies. I remember being shown some tracings of Palaeolithic rock paintings in the Madrid Museum five years ago. There was a hunting scene, a dance, some men gathering honey, and what were perhaps hunting tallies done in red paint. I do not know if these latter have ever been published. They might be primitive Chinese; the sign for man, for example, a swipe of the brush and two legs, is very similar. Matters remained at that stage for a long period. Hunting and herding people need tallies and route pictures but have little other use for writing. As trading developed the need for record increased. The evolution of trust and commercial patience must have been a slow affair. Such things crept into life and became domesticated and familiar by degrees, age by age. As picture writing passed into syllabic writing and became more and more capable of rendering the subtleties of speech, much more extensive possibilities of communication and of the extension of power opened out. Laws and claims and pledges could go farther and endure longer. Men could be documented and "fixed."

With this enlargement out universal disposition to shift toil to other people and get them working for us discovered a rich mine of new possibilities. The man with the upper hand was no longer obliged to beat his slave or peasant to his task and stand over him.

He could check his output. Much fine intelligence went to the elaboration and enforcement of "bits of writing" by which men were entangled.

Money, too, came creeping into the elaborating scheme of human economy. It was not so much invented as discovered to be present. We are told, or at least we used to be told, that the first money was cattle. That seems quite plausible. Cattle must have been exchanged for women in marriage and for other desirable possessions very early in the human story. The herdsmen, one can understand, were among the first traders; the nomads no doubt began merchandising. I suspect that nomads were among the first metal and mineral miners, but I do not know how far archaeologists would countenance me in that. In many parts of the world tinker and blacksmith and "cheap-jack" are still gipsies. They brought metals and precious stones along from the mountains and passes and gorges to the alluvial plains where minerals were rare. Possibly the first approach to a coin was a metal tally with a cow stamped on it. But metals were rare in themselves and highly desirable. I have read somewhere that the Hittites and Spartans had money of iron. It is only twenty-five or twenty-six centuries ago, it seems, that coined money came into use in human affairs, and for some centuries it belonged only to the superficial world of trading operations; it had little to do with the broader, more fundamental economics of the community. Most of the food was grown, most of the houses and temples were made, even possibly most of the ships were launched, without a resort to money.

It has struck me, as a man coming late to such studies, that our histories of mankind do not attach sufficient importance to the gradual but profound alteration of phase, the reorientation that occurred in human affairs as documentation and money, from their first sporadic superficiality, crept into and changed the massive substance of economic life. These two things must have varied and elaborated the fundamental game of shifting the toil enormously. They cast the cloak of personal invisibility about owners. And they fixed obligations with a new relentlessness. As the broad lines of the money convention were more and more widely understood and recognised, as its purchasing power extended from a few to more and more commodities, the novelty of abstract wealth arose. Men found themselves possessed, not merely of cattle, olive orchards, ships, slaves, and so forth, but of an amulet which would call all or any of these things into their service. They could be mortgagers instead of worried owners, and they need keep no slaves, because now every penniless man was at their bidding if they so desired it. Money had generalised slavery. They had no need to insist upon the status of a slave. They found very soon that it was superfluous even to have the coined money in a strong-box; they need only have the documented promise to pay money or an acknowledgment of receipt from a sufficiently solvent creditor. Parchment money was already in use among the Carthaginians.

Money has always had about it something indefinite. It varies and has varied widely in its nature. It was not invented by any particular person. There never was, today there is not, a complete system of money. That has still to come. Money crept into human concerns insidiously, century by century. It is a variable, many-faced thing. It is a token here, and there a piece of metal of intrinsic value. It will breed like a rabbit where Usury is permitted. The Catholic Church once sought to sterilise it, but now she holds her peace and makes no trouble over a pious legacy of debentures. It breeds, but it is subject to degeneration. It can be debased and manipulated in all sorts of obscure and furtive ways. Men can operate upon its moods and fluctuations and snatch profits, but even the most cunning operators must sometimes guess. In modern life it has become so intimate and so fundamental that most people have a kind of horror of thinking too closely about its uncertainties. We will not even ask ourselves why it should be sterile in our pockets and prolific when we hand it to state or bank. We feel that to speak to a man about his dividends is an immodest act. With most of us money is protected from ruthless investigation by an emotional fear analogous to that which veils sex in the minds of the young. We realise a helplessness.

In the period when Dickon and I faced the world money was fairly stable. We accepted it as a trustworthy measure of values. Most of the world was on the gold standard, fluctuations in exchange were fractional, and there was a slow general fall in prices going on, a fall that scarcely anyone discussed. But the worldwide stability of money throughout most of that half-century before the war was an exceptional phase in its history.

Almost the whole story of mankind from the days of the Roman Empire onward could be told as a history of the fluctuations and variations in the behaviour of money and of its sublimated form – credit. The older civilisations of the Orient did, no doubt, use the precious metals abundantly; all Asia Minor and Greece coined money before Cyrus; the latter days of the Jews were dark with debts and usuries; there was lending and banking in Babylon and Carthage; but the cash nexus first sent its ramifications deeply into the general life of the community in the triumphant years of the Roman Republic. Did men, common men, pay taxes normally in money, anywhere at any time before the Roman days? I doubt it. And with the rephrasing of transactions in terms of money in that age ownership attained a novel fluidity, interest could expand to gigantic proportions, men could borrow with an unprecedented, dangerous readiness, and be ruined and sold up with amazing rapidity. The punishment of the bankrupt was merciless. The history of Rome seems to me to be full of the entanglement and dispossession of small men, of great inflations and explosions of debt, of popular attempts to repudiate debts and of aristocratic suppressions of repudiation, of moneyed men becoming for the first time more powerful than lords and rulers. It is the history of a series of events of a different type or order from those of any previous history.

There are historians – it does not dispose of them to say they are mostly Germans and so, by nature and necessity, wrong – who declare that the Roman collapse before the barbarians was essentially an economic collapse due to crude finance. The slave estates which had succeeded the debt-consumed free cultivator had given way to the serf cultivator, who was born and lived and died the debtor of his lord. And the serf had no spirit to resist the invader. For him a barbarian lord was little different from a Roman lord – himself perhaps only a very imperfectly assimilated barbarian in the imperial service. The outer barbarian had indeed the merit of cutting off the visitations of the imperial tax collector. Disorder and political disintegration were welcome then for the common man, since they meant a disappearance of the taxes and debts and deeds that crushed and held him down. Illegal exactions and outrages might be substituted, but these were, by their nature, transitory things.

This interpretation of the fall of the imperial system seems very plausible to me. It is fairly plain that the money and credit nexus which first pervaded the Roman Empire, and which was ruptured and left in tattered fragments by its fall, was mended very slowly and crept back throughout our Western community again in the later Middle Ages. Today it is the method of nearly all our economic intercourse. Except the toil of mothers for their children and the toil of the wives of poor men, I can think of no large class of services that are not appraised and paid for in money. Hardly any were so appraised and paid for in the early civilisations three thousand years ago. In the old civilisations one was paid for one's toil by a specific easement or reward; nowadays one is paid by this abstract token, this coin or note, which is understood to carry with it a power of command over a certain quantum of whatever pleasures or possessions we desire. So long as that understanding holds it will work. In the ancient world services were simply and personally reciprocal. They are no longer so. Even the traditions of that reciprocity are lost and I do not believe they can ever be restored. And this has come about not by any revolutionary substitution of one organised system for another, but by an extraordinary growth of contrivances, conventions, tacit, unreasoned acceptances, establishments of usage. Money is not an institution that has replaced simpler and less convenient institutions, it is a tradition that has grown and exfoliated and crowded older usages out of existence.

It is not a safe device. It can fail to keep faith. It had failed and recovered in Russia and Germany. Nowhere is it proof against fresh failures. If men lose confidence in it sufficiently, our civilisation, which is now entirely based upon it and which has no reserved alternative to it to fall back upon, will clog and cease to work. It is at least as indispensable now as housing and clothing. Modern civilisation is like an aeroplane in mid-air, an aeroplane with one sole, imperfect engine which is popping and showing many signs of distress. It may win to an aerodrome and repairs and replacements. Or it may make a very unpleasant forced landing presently with little hope of immediate recovery.

## 13 – *Change of Scale*

In the last three centuries there has been a great expansion of the scale of economic process. This change of scale is one of the outstanding facts in the general scheme of history. It has inaugurated a new phase in human experience. It has an effect as though upon the customary succession of day and night there were to dawn an unfamiliar illumination from some strange new star, a light altering all visible values, dispelling accepted shadows, revealing things hitherto unknown. There seems to be no simple cause of this change. There may have been an almost entirely accidental confluence of favourable conditions.

Through stimulations that I will not attempt to classify or estimate, European business in the sixteenth and seventeenth centuries was in the state of vigorous renascence. Shipping was pushing with an unwonted boldness round the continents and into unknown seas, there was a great influx of silver from America, towns were growing rapidly. There were also great intellectual liberations, the rediscovered Greek literature was releasing the long-restrained imaginations of men, printing was making reading easier and cheaper; but how far this mental enlivenment really affected economic developments it is impossible to calculate. The eighteenth century carried on the expanding stir; there was much experimenting and innovating in financial method; there was a rush of inventions; coal was utilised for metallurgy, and that led to a bigger scale use of iron and steel; the machinery made possible by this opened up new possibilities of organised manufacture, and the facilities of intercourse began an astounding increase in scope and pace that still goes on.

Most of these things seem to me to have arisen detachedly. The more one looks into their history, the less connected they appear to be, and the less ready one is to accept simple explanations. One is apt to think of the steam-engine, for instance, with its intricate, tremendous influence upon transport and upon the development of mass production, as arising out of the scientific thrust. But did it? Were the inventors and exploiters of steam – Watt watching the dancing kettle lid, for example – really scientific men? Were they influenced very much by the science of their time? Did they owe very much to Bacon or the Royal Society? And for the matter of that, to take a later case, was the aeroplane a scientific invention? Was it not rather the creation of odd experimenting out-of-the-way people, a little distrustful of the mathematicians' assumptions about the air?

The proper triumphs of science no one can deny. Indisputably the whole development of electrical appliances arises out of systematic scientific research, and so do most medical progress and most metallurgical and chemical improvements. But it is worth noting that the experimenting, innovating spirit of the last three centuries was also active outside the strictly scientific movement, and that historically the scientific man has rather pursued and overtaken and studied and organised, first in this and then in that province of creative knowledge, than directed the opening inquiries. In the last three hundred years inventions and new ideas have come faster and thicker like flowers in springtime; the scientific man has gathered rather than sown. In the world of psychology he is only now really getting a grip upon the stuff, and in the world of social and economic relationship and in relation to law I am doubtful whether, even at the present time, science has fairly begun. Yet there have been tremendous changes and enlargements in these latter fields, changes and enlargements almost as considerable as those in natural science.

But though I see the expansive forces which distinguish the life of man in the last two or three centuries as multiple in their origins and defiant of any comprehensive explanation, it does seem to me, nevertheless, that one can throw at least two generalisations over the whole. The first of these is the sustained widespread appearance of this change of scale in human possibilities. Suddenly the world has grown relatively much smaller. Man had acquired new power over matter. He can handle masses and produce commodities by wholesale methods absolutely undreamt of before the present time. And, secondly, he has now so mastered the utilisation of fuel, wind, and water for the production of power that a large part of the burthen of sheer toil imposed hitherto since civilisation began upon the unwilling shoulders of our kind may now be lifted. Human intercourse need no longer be mainly a toil-shifting tangle. I take it the main features of the present phase of this property-money give-and-take which is human society are due to the confused and mainly selfish efforts of people to adapt themselves to the releases of these new conditions without any clear understanding of their nature.

This change of scale and all the disturbance and opportunity it brought with it was going on even in the eighteenth century, but it was only becoming the completely dominant fact in the world's economics when my father was growing up. He was already alive in the early days of railway speculation. I remember he told me when I was a small boy that he was married in the year the *Great Eastern* was launched, which was, I find, 1859. He was showing me a picture of the monster hung up in a bedroom at Mowbray. She was a prematurely big ship of eighteen thousand tons. I doubt if her engines were up to their task, and I believe she was a financial failure. She was beyond the limit set by circumstances at that time to the change of scale in shipping.

My grandfather was a not very leading partner of a not very prominent firm of stockbrokers. So my father grew up, indigenous to that dark hive, the City, in the days when London was really the head and centre of the business enterprise of the world. The new phase of civilisation had first become manifest in England; she was leading with iron and steel, cotton, wool, railways, steamships, finance. In those days the English were regarded, not only by themselves, as a people beyond all other peoples, more energetic, more practical, cold and high and wise. And Providence had favoured His new Chosen by putting their coal and iron very close together and planting them in an island at the geographical centre of the trading world. It was their mission to develop the rest of this planet, patronisingly, profitably. France, their most serious rival, was, they declared, "fickle," Spain sunken in Catholic decay, Italy a protégée, Russia barbaric, Germany poverty-struck and impracticable, lost in dreams of music and philosophy; America from north to south a continent of unstable republics, fields for enterprise, of no financial importance at all. The chief manufacture of the United States in those days was supposed to be wooden nutmegs. English schoolmasters teaching Transatlantic geography never failed to mention them with a kindly you-may-laugh-now smile.

In those days all the nations of the world were resorting to the dark and narrow ways of the City for credit to make railways and harbours and to reorganise their industries along the new lines. If any refrained, energetic young Englishmen went to inquire into the matter and if necessary compel them to come in. The solicitation of China and Japan was forcible. French enterprise had a narrower range in the Mediterranean and the Orient, and was always rather too closely entangled with its Foreign Office. In the Far East the Englishman sometimes met a stray American, for a mysterious instinct drove the Americans very early across the Pacific, but in those days they did not seem to amount to very much there, and presently their Civil War engaged them. That was supposed to be the end of all their democratic hopes. North America would "split up" as South America had done, lacking the golden bond of a crown. Amusing it is to recall that in the political cartoons of those days John Bull figured as a wise old giant and Jonathan as his untidy, ill-behaved nephew. Neither American nor German enterprise had ruffled the hustling, muddling self-confidence of London in the days of my father's youth.

The industrial and mining developments of the later eighteenth and early nineteenth centuries were largely proprietary. Landowners prospected for minerals under their own lands; cotton-spinners bought machinery and reduced their cousins and neighbours to economic servitude, and presently resorted to the foundling hospitals and workhouses to increase their supply of tractable cheap workers. There were companies, but they were mainly just multiple proprietors. With the coming of railways and steamships and power machinery, however, the change of scale passed further and further beyond the dimensions of ordinary individual fortunes. Before a man could set about trying to handle this or that still incompletely developed economic activity in the big way he found he had to associate himself with someone who would bring in the large amount of credit needed for the attempt. He had to go the City.

By the middle of the nineteenth century two contrasted types of exploiter were trying to draw wealth, ease, and power out of the new forces of enlargement; one the reorganiser of employment upon new lines, and the other the operator with credit. The method of the latter was to saddle the new production or the new service with as heavy payments as it could stand – or at any rate to operate and get away with a profit before the limits of payment were apparent. The former was a cheap producer and seller who sought new customers; the latter was a collector of savings which he led towards investment in the new enterprises, and deflected more or less on the way thither. The organiser encroached upon and destroyed the freedom of the small man; the financier enmeshed the organiser. That stately process continues. To nowhere in particular. The smaller people, superseded by the new machine and power-using enterprise, had to take care of themselves as well as they could. Most of them the new developments took by surprise and they were impoverished or pauperised before they realised clearly what was happening. After the immemorial practice of mankind, the new labour needed was obtained as cheaply as possible and left to get as much above a bare subsistence from the social economics effected as it could.

Among the early victims of the new drives towards larger scale business were the small cultivators whose way of living was knocked to pieces by the Enclosures Acts, and the weavers and spinners and other workers who were crushed or devoured by the factories. The railway put an intricate and picturesque high-road life out of action, ruined coach-owners, horse-owners and horse-breeders, wayside inns. On the whole the new methods were increasing production very greatly, but they were requiring a smaller proportion of skilled and capable workers among the people they employed, and so the larger share of the increased output went to support a great expansion of population, a proliferation of low-grade human beings. Everywhere arose great new towns, vast sprawls of mean streets and slums, in which the bulk of this additional unspecialised and unselected population sheltered.

It is one of the dearest assumptions of the Marxist theorists that there has been a concentration of wealth in the hands of a vigorously acquisitive and steadily concentrating minority throughout the last two centuries. It is amazing how many of us, with eyes in our heads, with museums, ancestral mansions, and collections of old furniture to refer to, with pictures and books at hand, novels, plays, collections of letters, poems with dedications, have come to accept that concentration as a fact. But relatively to the common lot the life of the rich and noble in the seventeenth century was manifestly finer and ampler than it is today. They had far more space and beauty, more respect, more servile human service. Music of the finest quality, delightful art, every sort of decoration – such printing and bookbinding, for example, as we cannot rival today – mental freedom, existed for them alone. It is preposterous to say that the rich have become richer and the poor poorer in this last phase of history. The increase in production has gone along quite another channel. It has neither been monopolised by the property-owner nor distributed throughout the general mass. It has merely expanded the general mass. It has been absorbed by blind breeding. Since my father was born, in that little space of time, the population of England had doubled.

So has the population of Germany. By internal increase and in spite of considerable emigration. Since 1850 the population of the world must have increased by many hundreds of millions. No one is much better off nor worse off as yet for the change of scale; there are only more people.

## 14 – *The City and My Father*

Short-sighted rearrangements of production under a conspiracy of helpful circumstances, and then blind borrowing and purblind lending, reckless breeding; evasion of toil and responsibilities above; congested, reluctant, protesting labour below; and nowhere any clear vision of the whole – that was the substance of the nineteenth-century spectacle, and it followed logically and necessarily in the vein of all preceding social life. Knowledge had so grown by the middle of the nineteenth century that there might have been enough for all and unprecedented freedom for all. But this possibility concerned nobody in particular. The practical fact which concerned everyone was that there was not nearly enough for most people because of the primitiveness and incoherence of proprietary and monetary methods.

Quite the strongest and most remarkable of the impressions of financial men my own dealings with finance have left me is their superficiality and inattention. Men follow science and art, pursue agriculture, organise manufactures, or go upon the seas to trade, *closely*, because these things are profoundly and sustainingly interesting. But no one is in business in the City for the sake of business in the City. Men go there to come out of it again, successful. There is no instinct for arithmetic, no lust for computation, in the make-up of a normal human being; I doubt even if those abnormalities they call calculating boys get any pleasure from their gift until it is applied; the only living interests in the City are acquisition and the excitements of risk and conflict that might be pursued as easily at Monte Carlo. The activities of the City and its younger, perhaps stronger, offspring in Wall Street – for who knows now which is leading which? – affect the intimate lives of all mankind, but this is not present in the consciousness of the City. It is the peculiar quality of money and credit to abstract reality from transactions and remove it to an immense distance. Finance is forgetful of the world in its processes, and the world thinks as little as possible about the finance that thrusts it along and pushes it about. Hardly anyone in the City is going an inch further than he is obliged to do beneath the surfaces on which he moves his pieces. The City has grown up from forgotten beginnings; City men accept it as it is and follow its rules and traditions. They no more want an inquiry into what lies beneath it than cricketers want people to geologise beneath their pitch.

In the course of my life I have met a certain sprinkling of bankers, and I do not think there is any sort of human being more marvellous and incredible. They take money for granted as a terrier takes rats; when they see it they go for it; but they are absolutely immune to any philosophical curiosity about it. From no other profession do men fly so rapidly to the distraction of other occupations; bankers become collectors, naturalists, historians, critical writers; the profession is a hotbed of amateurs. The world of banking and finance draws princely incomes from processes it does not understand clearly and that, with a strong self-protective instinct, it will, if it can, prevent anyone from understanding clearly. I can imagine no more preposterous caricature of reality than the representation of the City and Wall Street and the bourses and exchanges of the planet generally as a sort of synthetic, wicked, watchful, many-headed spider, scientifically sucking the life-blood from the world. The spider sucks blood because it wants to do it, but banking does it merely because it does it.

No doubt the activities of the City tangle the whole world, but they do so aimlessly. The men who rush about its narrow ways do not what they are up to. They would be very angry to be told as much, but so it is. They impress themselves and each other and their clerks and their typists and the anxious, greedy, investing public as strong men and bold men and decisive men and little Napoleons; some of them are controlling altogether colossal sums; but in their heads are brains that still remain – it is offensive, but it must be said – inadequately developed. They are youngsters who have never taken time to grow up, youngsters overblown. They have never struggled on to the fully adult stage. They are ignorant of fundamentals, they do not see themselves plainly, they are individualistic in their aims, the sense of being a possible part in one complete social organisation has not come to them, and all these characteristics are the characteristics of immaturity. Their great enterprises, their debts, their loans, their technicalities and methods are solemn vast puerilities; it does not make them any the less puerilities that all mankind suffers because of them.

That congested City is still the chief credit whirlpool of the world confusion, and thither the money goes and there it must be sought again. About its ways went our father in his time, in a becoming black top-hat and an impressive frock-coat after the fashion of the period, red-whiskered and comely and engaging in his manners, bold and enterprising to his own undoing. And thither came Dickon and I later on, sniffing after the credit and the money which are the keys of personal liberty and without which there is neither food nor freedom nor power in the world.

I will not disinter my father's story here. Indeed, many essential phases of it are now so covered up and hidden and untraceable that I do not think I could, even if I wanted to do so. He seems to have worked with his father's firm for a time and to have been at first an alert but quite wary speculator. There were many people in the City who liked him and who kept their faith in his ability and recuperative power right up to the wild preliminaries of the final disaster. He did very little with railways; railways had been built, had been over-capitalised, had failed to pay, and had been made to pay – by excursion trains and an educational campaign – before his time. The railways were settling down after a wild youth. But the new possibilities of large-scale retail trade the railways had created were still in process of active exploitation. It was an open question then whether the greater changes would follow the lines indicated by the increased ease with which customers could be brought to centres, or those defined by the increased facilities of distribution. Bright, pushful men were looking for presentable aspects of both these possibilities with which to woo the City and, in co-operation with the City, the investor at large. My father was early in this field, and he seems to have done very well along both lines.

He looked for easily transported goods and hit upon tea; he brought together some tea wholesalers, some lead-packet people, and a small retailer in Clapham named Partington, whose shop it was possible to claim was "Established in 1810," and out of these ingredients he created "Partington's Pure Packet Teas; Partington's Own Delicious Blend." At first there was to have been a postal order business, but, instead, the packets were found to be particularly marketable on the counters of small retailers. People with sweetstuff shops and confectioners and so on, who had never weighed out tea, could sell packet tea. Simultaneously he revealed to Nickleby's, the drapers of Camden Town, that they were the North London Central Bazaar, "the shopping and social centre of North London Life," and got them into a phase of hectic enlargement. He worked with sustained energy and very closely in those early years; there was reality and substance in both these concerns, and it was rather through the pressure of natural business development than any nefarious intention that by the time he had altogether disposed of these organisations he had sold them for about ten times their actual value as going concerns. Partington's, with a group of other firms of very unequal value, presently became the London United Tea Company, and then launched boldly into World Tea Plantations; Nickleby's also expanded into London and Empire Stores, with shops at Brighton and Manchester and a place in Durban, and another, a shocking failure, in Bombay. The belief of the investing public, and particularly of the small investor in associated shop constellations, was growing steadily all these years, and my father took his own where he found it.

In those days my father was by the best City standards a sound man. He was watching what he was doing quite carefully. His reputation for soundness was greatly enhanced by the Red Gulch and Throttle Lode affair. Either he got a tip in some way, or he made a happy fluke with a large parcel of copper-mine shares and was out and away with his profits before anyone had noticed what had happened. It seemed a desperate fling to many City sages. But after that raid he never went near that market again; they never had a chance to get back on him. This resolution as it became more evident turned people's momentary doubts into an accession of confidence.

Nevertheless, it was the beginning of his undoing; his natural belief in his instinct and his luck was stimulated; he became greedy and hasty, he spread himself out over ground he had never explored with any care, he took liberties with his associates and lied where before he had simply exaggerated. He went out for the promotion of seaside resorts, for big housing schemes and especially for service flats in huge architectural piles, for gas-lightning – more particularly in South European countries – and, arising out of that, for soft coal. I do not even know the succession in time, much less the inter-relations, of Cornwall

Court Limited, the London Buildings Company, Seabreeze Estates, the Gas and Metallurgical Coal Group and Mediterranean Gas and South Coast Development; I know only that the mounting pile culminated in London and Imperial Enterprises and crashed. But I know enough of my father through my own nature to know that what was the matter with him was boredom, the frightful boredom of City life, the boredom of enterprises getting more and more remote from any living and breathing reality, the boredom of arithmetic in little offices, of bluffs and misleading statements in board-rooms, of deposit-books and cheque-books that one had to remember didn't mean what they appeared to mean, and of remembering what So-and-So didn't know and what Such-and-Such did. Stuff like that in the brain must be like dry chaff in the mouth on a hot day. The City is a trap for human energy: it promises life more abundantly and wastes it ruthlessly. It is like the bottle of nuts with the monkey; he can get his hand in and he can get his hand full, but to get his hand out is another matter. And until he can get his hand out the nuts are uncracked nuts.

My father must have felt that beneath the florid appearance of success his life was passing away. I realise only too vividly his desperate determination to clutch some concrete happiness, some vivid splendour, high place or power, out of that mocking hurry of dingy and doubtful trnsactions, before age or death overtook him. Our removal to Mowbray was the first early symptom of his possible impatience for realisations and expenditure. Afterwards, nearer the end, there was some gaudy pleasuring; I have heard since of brilliant but costly ladies assisting him to taste "life," and there was a great time in a hired villa at Monte Carlo, of which except for a few postcards no intimations ever reached Mowbray; and a theatrical venture with a now forgotten actress, Lillie Morton, whose private may have been greater than her public charm. I hope it was, for my father's sake. Before he had reached my present age the whole feverish story was over.

And so he passed, and so, with less acutely tragic incident, a great multitude of brave and eager lads have passed through the City, growing old as they passed but not really growing up, a swirl and a superficial consequence upon a deep flood of changes beyond their understanding.

# Book Three

## The Story of the Clissolds: Essence of Dickon

## 1 – *Dickon Finds His Purpose in Life*

My brother Dickon was physically very like my father, but he had a sturdier quality of mind. His imagination was as bold, but his self-restraint was steadier. Both of us indeed were honest to a greater degree; our consciences were livelier and more watchful, the sense of an obligation incurred gripped us more firmly and did not so readily slip its hold. Some ancestor of marked integrity must have been latent in my father. We were both mainly Clissold, but physically Dickon was nearer to my father than I. He was a better-looking youngster. He had my father's reddish hair and something of his physical swagger, while I mingled threads of my mother's darkness with streaks of paternal gold.

Dickon, I have told, professed individualism, but he has always been a very sociable individualist; I was an unsocial Socialist from the outset, with a greater disposition to go alone or with one companion. Clara once said that Dickon was canine and I was feline, and I think that expresses something very elemental between us. Dickon's pink skin freckles at a mere glimpse of the sun, and he was carried my father's sanguine amplitude of limb and body to a considerable massiveness. He is now, in fact, a very fine figure of a man indeed, a stout tweed-wearing man, "Nordic," they would say in America.

In the preceding Book I brought the account of Dickon and myself up to the later "eighties," when we were studying science very unevenly at the Kensington schools, and considering our attack upon the world. Then I went off on the trail of Marx and the economic history of the world. I left Dickon at loose ends.

He did not long remain at loose ends. It was at night in a show called the Inventions Exhibition, while we were sitting watching a crowd of promenaders and listening to a band, beneath festoons of fairy-lights – little oil lamps they were – and in front of a grass plot on which yet other fairy-lights, blue, red, and orange, made a flickering guttering enchantment, that Dickon's ends ceased to be loose and he unfolded to me his plan of campaign. It was to be his life's plan of campaign, but I believe that it had crystallised out in his mind only that afternoon.

That Inventions Exhibition was one of a series of annual shows; there was one called the Healtheries and another the Fisheries, and others, in what was then a great area of waste land in south Kensington. Now most of that land is filled up by the Imperial Institute and by Museum galleries and buildings belonging to London University, but in those day these exhibitions were able to spread from the Exhibition Road to the Albert Hall, the upper galleries of which building were somehow included in the spectacle. These grounds were put in order and laid out with beds of geraniums and calceolarias; they were illuminated in the evenings, and the Exhibition was favoured by a succession of fine summer nights.

It would be interesting now to disinter the plans and guide-books, if any copies survive, to that Inventions Exhibition. It was before the coming of the safety bicycle or the automobile; the gas-lamp still held its own quite hopefully against the dangerous uncertainties of the electric light, and gramophones, cinemas, wireless had hardly germinated in the womb of time. The germs existed, but nothing had come to exhibition pitch. I remember some very attractive omnibuses, driven by compressed air, wallowing to and fro in a confined space. They were the only anticipation of automobiles in the show, and I remember, too, how Dickon that afternoon doubted whether electric traction could ever be anything more than a scientific toy. It might be done, he said, but it could never be done to pay.

Yet what we had seen had stimulated our imaginations considerably, and while we listened to the band in the evening after a frugal supper, we were both much more prepared to expect great changes during our lifetimes than we had been when we pushed through the turnstiles in the early afternoon. Our talk had ebbed for a time and we were smoking unaccustomed cigarettes which Dickon had made with a machine for the occasion.

"It is no good inventing things if you do not get people to make use of them," said Dickon, coming up to the surface, so to speak, after a profound meditation.

"No," said I, not in the least aware of his drift.

"There's no money in anything until people have been told of it."

"The money?"

"No," contemptuously, "the anything."

I perceived that he was taking up his standing problem of "how to get it" again. "I suppose new things have to be sold," I said.

"Exactly. And you have to make people *want* them."

A pause.

"Advertisement," said Dickon. "Advertisement is only beginning. Billy! – I see it. That's where my money is. Advertising."

The distant band was playing a waltz tune just then, for I remember the rhythm of it. (Tra-la-la la pum pum, pum pum. Tra-la-la la pum pum, pum pum. Tra-la-la-la pum pum, pum pum, Tra-la-la-La pum, pum, pum, pum, it went. Am I filling in detail from my imagination or was it the Blue Danube waltz?) And the promenaders passed, keeping step to it; mysterious, romantic promenaders, for the fairy-lights were not enough to show their faces plainly.

With something of the manner of an explorer, the voice at my side began to talk of the dark and dismal advertisement of that time and to point out its defects and its possibilities. I understood now why he had been so silent and preoccupied throughout the afternoon. He had been reading all the advertisements in sight and thinking about them. He had been struck by their limitation of range; their crudity and formality; their inapplicability to the sale of new devices. A realisation of unworked opportunities close at hand had struck him dumb at first, and was now moving him to speech. He began to talk of advertisement, and to the best of my recollection he talked of advertisement for the next year or so.

That evening I had a lecture on the things advertisers did and the things they failed to do. It was delivered with the dogmatism proper to an elder brother, and with a note of reprehension as though I had in some way participated in the negligencies of the commercial world. I said little, and what I said was brushed aside or crushed. I did what I could to find excuses for backward and unskilful advertisers and was soundly scolded for their sins.

I recall the feeling rather than the substance of his outpourings. I remember that after a time we got up from our seats and walked about the grounds, and Dickon was still weighing pros and cons; we went into the more or less deserted exhibition galleries, and he held me remorselessly before silent exhibits and denounced the futility of their appeals. He was still at it as we made our way at the close of the exhibition, with other *jusqu'au-bout*-ists, along a tiled subway that echoed to our feet and led to the Metropolitan station.

"Look at that thing!" he would cry. "Look at that *silly* thing! What's the good of sticking that here?"

I recall distinctly my agonised protest. "Damn it! *I* didn't put it there!"

It restrained him not at all.

In the small hours he was sitting up in bed. "Advertisement, Billy," he said. "Advertisement! And the School of Mines may go and blast and burn and fuse and run itself to Jericho. The voice has reached me, Billy! Come over and help us! The Hoardings call to me, the Magazines are moaning, and I come. I come."

"Oh, *shut* up, Dickon! Good-night!" I said, pulling the bed-clothes over my ears.

He dropped his work at the School of Mines almost immediately; he made no pretence of finishing off his term, and for some weeks he divided his waking time almost equally between an intensive study of advertising methods and brooding in Kensington Gardens upon his course of action. His first definite step was to go, after a very careful and elaborate preliminary exploration of the special field in question, to an advertising watchmaker in Cornhill, to get an interview with him, and tell him why his watches were not selling nearly so well as they might do in the West-end, in various suburbs, among the City clerks, in the East-end, and what he thought might be done to stimulate their sale. He had brought notes and sketches of almost all the advertisements the firm was using, and very politely and clearly he pointed out how stereotyped was their appeal and how mechanical their distribution. He convinced his hearer of advertisements going to waste and reaching nobody here, and of areas neglected there, and in the end he was allowed to make a scheme for a more scientific campaign. Hitherto the work had been done in an almost routine fashion from the office. His scheme was accepted. It succeeded, and his path in life was open before him.

## 2 – *Milton's Silver Guinea*

I do not know whether it was luck or some mysterious flair that made Dickon pitch upon Milton for his first attempt, but I doubt if he could possibly have chosen better. Milton liked him from the outset; and with Milton, Dickon at the ripe age of one-and-twenty fixed up his first contract and began pushing Milton's

Silver Guinea by the score, by the hundred, by the thousand, into the waistcoat pockets of the middle-class. Faster than Milton could assemble his watches Dickon assembled his customers. That was only a little while before the mass production of watches was fully under way. Milton's watches, I fancy, came in whole or in part from Switzerland. And when presently the Waltham watches came, ticking very loudly from across the Atlantic, Dickon made a brave and successful fight for Milton for some years, with "Milton's Silent Silver Guinea; each personally tested, numbered, and individually guaranteed."

In the end Milton left the field of popular sales and became a professor of quality. Milton's Limited now sell "watches that are beautiful and intimate," but Dickon still steers the bulk of the output along the path of assertive veracity to the grateful customer. Only last summer I discovered him in his smoking-room at Dorking meditating profoundly over Milton's current advertisement in *Punch*, a most gentlemanly affair.

"Do you remember Milton's in the old days, Billy?" he said, handing it to me.

"Rather."

"Changed since then. The money I've brought these people! Used to be cheap stuff."

I considered the page of *Punch*. I know of no other periodical whose advertisements so exactly catch the tone of the morning-room of a good West-end club.

"There are times," he reflected, "when I almost think of buying a Milton… Beautiful and intimate… They seem to be first-rate watches."

### 3 – *Forty Years of Advertisement*

Milton's was only Dickon's point of departure. A great light had come to him, and for a time he saw life wholly as a field of action in which he was to create appetities in people for commodities they had never in the least desired hitherto, or to direct their attention to the great superiority of common necessities when they are labelled distinctly with a proprietor's name.

Immense wealth lay in convincing people that an article could hardly be considered to exist unless it was vouched for by a respectable firm. In the day of our youth an enormous number of things were sold anonymously that are now sold under the brands of makers and packers. Our father had been one of the pioneers in this christening of goods with his Partington's Packet Teas. When I was a child every grocer had his own sorts of tea, his tea-chests with different qualities, and he weighed the tea out and packed it up for each customer. I can remember seeing that done. Almost everything he sold them – bacon, butter, lard, pickles, jams, biscuits – he sold from stocks of his own buying on his own individual reputation. He had pickled onions and cabbage in a great tub, as they still have them here in France. He used to display sugar-loaves in his window and chop them up in his shop; I would gaze fascinated at the sugar-chopping in the Duxford grocer's. And the oilman sold his own lamp oil, and no one asked where he got it. Mustard used to be bought for Mowbray at the chemist's.

But even in our childhood there was already a number of vigorous firms reaching their hands over the retail tradesman's shoulder, so to speak, and offering their goods in their own name to the customer. As an infant I used to love a particularly fascinating Oriental who infested the back pages of magazines, pouring stuff into the mouth of a forked fish in the interests of Nabob Pickles. He seems to have vanished utterly. Colman's Mustard insisted already upon being the only English mustard. It just stuck up its name in bright letters – everywhere. I do not know if it ever became the only mustard, or if there are other mustards now. There was also a "Keen's Mustard." Is "Keen's" still with us? "English" mustard that is – there are all sorts of other mixings here in France. But I saw yesterday in the window of an *épicier* in Grasse neat little tins of Colman's, with the same vivid yellow ground and the lettering I remember spelling out from a train window in my childhood. If it is not the only English mustard everywhere, it is certainly that here.

Then there was soap. The great firm of Pears in those day had already thrust an individuality upon soap. *Pears' Soap* marks an epoch; I hope history will not neglect it. It was advertised with an unprecedented swagger; there were magazine and newspaper articles about how the firm did it; Pears bought Academy pictures by RAs to reproduce in a sort of facsimile, gilt frame and all, and were among the first of all advertisers to be funny and laugh at themselves. Harry Furniss did a picture in *Punch* of a dirty tramp writing a soap testimonial: "Two years ago I tried Pears' Soap; since when I have used no other." They secured it and made a great thing of it.

These and a hundred other siren voices had called to me from wall and hoarding and printed page from my childhood up, but it was only now that Dickon was talking about them that I gave them more than a casual attention. I had never yet stirred up a restaurant by demanding Nabob Pickles and rejecting all inferior imitations, nor refused mustard until I was reassured by a sight of the Colman tin; but now I began, if not to clamour, at least to watch and discriminate under Dickon's critical guidance. He was grappling with a multitude of curious problems, and he insisted upon discussing them with me to the exclusion of every other subject.

"You see, Billy, you help me. The things you say – not much in themselves but they give me ideas."

Queer amusing problems some of them were. Cocoa had come into English life, and a number of firms were struggling to monopolise the market, among them Van Houten, probably a

Dutch firm, and Epps and Cadbury. I do not know if Rowntree's came then or later; I fancy they were never very deeply in the cocoa fight, but only came in later with chocolate, but I may be wrong about that. Dickon was making a careful comparison of their different methods. "*Epps' Cocoa, Grateful and Comforting*," Dickon would repeat. "Wonderful words. Wonderful! Genius in them… Billy, do you think *any* of these cocoas are the least bit different from the others?"

So earnest were our researches that we tried them to see. We sipped our cocoa and regarded each other with grave, inquiring faces.

These were purely English firms, I suspect. The battle of the cocoas, if it was fought in America at all, was probably fought under other names. I doubt if any commodity straddled the Atlantic in those days.

Another of our investigations was an attempt to discover why there was no advertising campaign for a salt or a pepper to put beside the omnipresent clamour about mustard. We never got to the bottom of the pepper problem. We decided that an opportunity was being lost there. "Harvester's Black Pepper Stimulates and Enlivens without Harmful Mechanical Irritation" we believed would have driven nameless pepper from the cruet. White pepper could have been denounced as an effeminate powder. There could have been bright attractive pictures of a stomach curly and vigorous rejoicing in its strength under the cheering influence of "Harvester," and of another, lax as a dead slug, debased by common white. Salt, common salt, we guessed, was deliquescent stuff to pack and handle; that was why no one touched it – except for Tidman's – was it Tidman's? – bath salt. Salt, for a proprietary sale, would have to be salt with a difference, we concluded, and we came very near to forestalling the dry table salts warranted not to cake into lumps, that presently appeared. "Cerebos," I think, was the leader.

I remember him sitting on the hard, wooden seat of a compartment in the dingy, dirty, sulphurous Underground Railway of those primitive times, with three or four magazines on the seat beside him, discoursing of the advertisements of a medicine called, if I remember rightly, "Owbridge's Lung Tonic." Always those advertisements were encircled by a monstrous O. "Now, why that O?" he demanded. "It individualises. It is also probably on the bottle. If there is any other lung tonic going, it serves to make the other fellow seem an undistinguished nobody. But does it make people want to take the stuff much? Does it do anything to catch the eye of consumptive people? Think of anyone with lung trouble and a cough. Suppose he had this advertisement on one side, and on the other side one that said quite quietly, 'Clissold's Lung Tonic soothes and gives peace. And in that peace you heal,' which would you want to try? Think of those words, Billy, not too big and noisy but put where they seem to catch the eye almost by accident! Just whisper it. *'And in that peace you heal.'* "

In that period there was a great clamour of pills and proprietary medicines generally; I think they were far more vigorously pushed then than they are now. Hardly anything in domestic medicine that was not being dragged out of its anonymous phase in the prevalent research for big business in small things. It is natural that many people should experience a certain internal dullness on occasion, and require artificial animation. In the pre-Victorian days this was almost always supplied by homely remedies; castor oil which chastened and sweetened the soul, rhubarb pills and antibilious pills, Epsom salts, and, for the defenceless young, flowers of sulphur. One took these things and corrected oneself as a cat eats grass. But no philanthropist ever filled columns with the praises of these more immediate gifts from God. So they were thrust aside by Beecham's Pills, Worth a Guinea a Box (marvellous words, oh!

marvellous words!), Eno's Fruit Salt, and a crowd of other highly named and vividly packed proprietary mixtures.

The age of the secret remedy, says Dickon, is drawing to an end. Advertisements of medicine decline. Not that people are giving up their resort to a tabloid or a cupful of something out of a bottle directly they feel out of condition, but they are more and more disposed to take known and specified drugs and preparations. This does not mean a return to the little chemist's scales and measures – in Britain the little chemist has been almost syndicated out of existence – but a development of the great-scale marketing of tabloids and capsules, made up to this or that prescription, by firms of manufacturing druggists. Dickon has been pressing manufacturing chemists to bolder and bolder advertisement for some time. He wants them to market attractive little medicine cases for dressing-bags. The ordinary citizen will then have his physic at hand, like a case of golf-clubs, to meet all occasions. He will play upon himself as a conductor plays upon his orchestra, summoning the drums, soothing the brass. Far more entertaining this will be than the tin-whistle solo of the old panacea. There will certainly be great changes of fashion in the contents of these cases, and the objective of the advertiser of the old-fashioned proprietary medicine will be more and more to get and keep a footing in the case; to ensure his position as a contributory instrumentalist, so to speak, in the internal symphony of the citizen. He will become like the advertiser of automobile accessories instead of a principal dealer.

But this is by the way. I was telling of the advertisements of London and the London press of forty years ago as I remember them. Even when they were not concerned with medicines they dealt largely with the comfort of the human interior. In addition to those things I have named, there was in my adolescence much propaganda of Cod Liver Oil; Elliman's Embrocation, always well advertised, flourished then as now; and the abolition of home-made beef-tea and mutton broth was beginning. Liebig's Extract of Meat was widely pushed, but I cannot now remember whether Bovril was already afloat; Oxo I am almost certain came later. We were to watch some pretty fighting presently over those meat extracts. The small tobacconist was still a single-shop adventurer, unaware of his approaching doom; he sold loose tobacco and cigars and matches and pipes and walking-sticks; the propaganda of cigarettes had scarcely dawned in those days. Cigarette smoking was a picturesque exotic habit that middle-aged people associated with Italy and Spain and the laxer morals of the south; one rolled a cigarette with a luxurious nonchalance and felt oneself a villain; the American machine-made cigarette was just creeping up by way of the shop-boy and art student. No one had heard yet of Russian cigarettes.

Besides these things I have named, and a few others at the same level which I have no doubt overlooked, there was really no very big and sustained advertisement going on at all. Big central drapery and provision stores had not yet learnt to advertise continually in the daily papers; many of them were still developing from moderate sized local shops in the footsteps of Nickleby's. Bicycles had not yet arrived, nor margarine, cereal foods, fountain pens, typewriters, kodaks, automobiles and all their accessories, and scores of other such things.

To compare one of the great American magazines, or even a modernised London weekly, with its equivalent of forty years ago, is an amazing revelation not only of the increased equipment of life nowadays, but of the continuous extension of strongly organised big businesses into what were then the trades and occupations of a great multitude of independent individuals. When I was young, England was far in front of America in the process, but American advertising has long since overtaken and outstripped anything we do on this side. France still follows us – now rather rapidly. Many of these big organisations seemed and still seem to be aiming at monopoly, but their sustained advertisement is the proof of their sustained sense of insecurity. Some have failed to achieve their object. Nobody has yet succeeded, for example, in replacing the small baker, though there have been various well-supported attempts; and cheese remains, like art, above all standardisation.

I suppose that, as far as provisions go, it helped greatly in the concentration of the distribution trade into big stores in England that so much of the food of the country was imported. The shipping of it necessarily accumulated it into bulk, and made bulky handling easy. And the fact that America and other new countries were exporting so much of their food production developed a collection at centres there, and so made concentration easy for them also.

It was after some rather unfruitful work for an advertising shoemaker that Dickon began to interest himself in the bicycle. Big-scale selling of boots and shoes, he said, would come a little later, when machine manufacturing was better developed, but the bicycle would not wait. The bicycle was here and now. So he jumped on to the bicycle and travelled some way on it. The more he inquired into this then fashionable toy, the more convinced he became of its future as a normal means of transport. First it would develop as a holiday amusement, and then it would cheapen down to the daily worker's needs. He attended early shows and races and himself rode with fury. He was an early believer in the diamond frame which has long since ousted all others. He was in bicycle advertising from the first, and he started one of the earliest bicycling weeklies, the *Flying Wheel,* which he afterwards sold and which still survives in an incorporated state. He made great efforts to organise the advertisement of wayside inns in cyclists' magazines. For a time he was very keen indeed upon what he called consumers' magazines. The ordinary citizen, however, refuses to accept the specialisation implied in a specialised magazine. In the case of bicycles, motor-bicycles, and automobiles in the world of pet-fanciers and photography, such publications have worked fairly well, but they have never yet superseded advertising to the general consumer.

Quite early in his novitiate as an advertiser, I remember Dickon pointing out to me the interesting conflict between the advertisements in what he called Trade Papers and advertising to consumers. By Trade Papers he did not mean the Trade Papers of such great industries as iron and steel, but the Trade Papers of the smaller distributor. These latter appeal to the retailer, shop-keeper or hotel-keeper or whatever he may be, and the goods advertised are often just those plausible imitations against which the big advertiser is warning his public. Often these less well-known goods are the output of minor packers and manufacturers selling on too small a scale for a public advertisement campaign, but supplying a quite sound and honest article. These typical Trade Paper advertisers want to sell their stuff to the man behind the counter and not to the public; they are on his side against his big enemies, and they expect him to pit his personal recommendations against the pervading public advertisement. The retailers' Trade Paper was in fact, according to Dickon, not advertisement, properly speaking, at all, but anti-advertisement.

But for Dickon, I suppose, I should never have seen an inch below the superficial appearances of countryside commerce. But because of the education he was given me, I recognise still in every wayside advertisement, in every article in every shop, in the steep streets of Grasse here, and upon the highway through Magagnosc to Nice, in the patches of cultivation about me, and the inscriptions upon my wine bottle and mustard jar, the flying fragments, the living details of the great battle between small and big, between the standardising organisation and the huckstering individual, which is still a dominating aspect of human life today.

## The World of William Clissold

### 4 – *Media*

One of Dickon's main discussions in those early days concerned what he called "media." A medium for him was anything you stuck your advertisement upon – a wall, a hoarding, a railway station, a landscape, a public conveyance, a book, a newspaper or other periodical. Or it might be an Exhibition or a Market Show. And then there was the house display, the shop-window, the imposing premises, the van. He invented for these primitive explorations of what has since become, in America at least, the great science of advertising, two beautiful terms, thc *advertisand*, which was what you wanted to sell, and the *advertisee*, who was the person you wanted to sell it to. A good advertisement had to reach as many advertisees as possible as inexpensively as possible; it had not only to reach them but it had to create a buying desire for the advertisand; it had not simply to do that, but it had to make the route to the purchase clear and plain. These were his criteria in his judgments on the advertisements we saw about us, and by this standard he judged his "media."

He would weigh them against each other with extreme gravity. Walls or hoardings lasted longer than any daily or weekly periodical, and he went to great pains to estimate the life of a poster; he would even waylay and talk to bill-stickers. Enamelled metal was already in use; sheets of that, he reflected, talked for years. But they were difficult to place, and if there was any need for a change of appeal they were hard to recall. Also, they tired people by repetition.

"Imagine passing the same plaque every week-day for a year! There's season-ticket holders have to. Horrible, Billy!"

He was far in advance of the times in perceiving that an advertisement should not bore; the advertisers of those days sought strenuously to bore. He held also that landscape should be respected; he believed that it was very easy to arouse an antagonism to a commodity by rude and blatant methods. He considered the advertisements he saw in stations and vehicles abominably ill-done. They shouted where there was no need to shout. In those days railway advertisements were almost conscientiously ugly, and they vied with each other in the size of their letters. "No need for such an uproar, Billy – no need for it. You've got your people there – they're standing about and their minds are unoccupied. They're quiet and at your disposal. Ready to take an interest. Why bawl at them?"

He was the first to offer the public anything of length and interest to read upon a railway platform.

Yet he could be compact with the best of them when the medium required it. It was he who thought of advertisements on the risers of the staircases going up and down to railway stations, spaces hitherto neglected and mute. How well I remember the excitement of that novel idea, the weighing of considerations, the problem of who to take it to, the feverish hope of great developments. "It must be witty," said Dickon. "Short and witty. I won't have them just yapped at." To whom should he take it? For a time he hovered between a flea powder and a chewing gum.

It was in periodical publications that the greater future of advertising lay, he believed, and particularly in monthlies and weeklies. They were left about in the house and were turned over again and again by different people. "But advertisement must be fresh and different each time. This sort of thing – "

Yes, it was. I remember, that same conversation in the Underground Railway I am recalling, and he pointed to a standard announcement in the back pages of some monthly magazine.

"This sort of thing is as exasperating as hiccoughs. It comes up again and again and you can't control it."

He doubted whether the daily newspapers were very much good for proprietary articles. They were good for theatres and amusements of all sorts, but not for an advertisand that had to go on selling. He watched people reading papers in trams and buses. They showed a vulture's eye for the news they wanted and a wonderful capacity for sweeping disregardfully across the most treamendous displays of advertisement. He declared it was possible to print a newspaper advertisement so big that it was totally invisible. People would not read type that was visible three yards away. Their eyes went through the gaps.

"But any sort of stuff that has a quality of news – 'Salmon is exceptionally cheap today,' for example, with a reason for it, or 'Mackerel in the Channel and Oranges in the Bay,' would get them. *What* Bay? There you are! People would read that sort of thing like any other news."

He weighed that idea carefully. Fishmongering and fruit selling were still far from any syndication or he would have started a scheme for a "Fishmongers' Chalk Board" and a "Fruit Shop Bulletin" in some of the old dailies, a sort of eleventh hour announcement of goods to hand.

And as the grouping of shops into big centralised stores, which my father had done so much to promote, went on, Dickon became more and more keen on what he called bringing the shop window into the morning paper. In those days it was beneath the dignity of the London *Times*, for example, to admit what are called displayed advertisements or break its grave gray expanses with pictures. The other papers in those conservative days did not care to be very different from *The Times*, and for a long time, indeed until the great Americanisation of the press by Harmsworth and Pearson, Dickon's idea remained an aspiration. Long before it was done in England, the stores' advertisements flared all over the American papers; there was an interval of a quarter of a century or more before the big London stores were brought into a similar intimate relationship to the popular press.

How recent all this seems to a man of my age! I remember when shop windows were made of little oblong panes, and lit in the evenings by a few jets of unassisted gas or an oil-lamp or so, and when the aim of the window-dresser seemed to be rather to impress the amount and nature of his stock upon the observer than to interest and attract him. Then came plate-glass and a depth and vastness of window-front hitherto undreamt of, and gas-mantles and electric light. People found a new interest in looking at the long array of shop windows, and the enterprising heads behind them realised by degrees – and there again my father with his "Shopping and Social Centre of North London Life," was a pioneer – that it might be wise to allow people to make a resort of the interior of their establishments without being compelled, as they used to be compelled, to make purchases forthwith or get out. But for a long time the big stores were content with the local crowds they assembled, and I believe it was Mr Gordon Selfridge, coming from America with the brightest and newest ideas, who at last realised my brother's anticipation and carried his shop window into the London daily paper.

My brother has a great admiration for Mr Selfridge, and I have been privileged to meet him, an unobtrusive man with something of the shy quiet of a poet. My brother compares him to Mozart on account of his interest and variety. "He makes some of the older advertisers sound like the village idiot at a fair beating on a pan," said Dickon. "A great artist! Oh! a very great and subtle artist! Some day people will make collection of those Selfridge advertisements."

So it was Dickon developed. The lax and incidental student of pure became the enthusiastic specialist in marketing, an active force in that change of scale in distributing methods which is one of the most striking aspects of my immediate world. He began as I have told, with watches and boots and the early bicycle. He extended his interests into the special journalism of the bicycle, and then into a great variety of magazine enterprises. He found helpers and confederates, associates with capital and partners. He has always had the gift of being liked, and, oddly enough, his name helped him. It gave people a shock to begin with, so that they always remembered it distinctly, and then as they got to know him they went about remarking upon the paradox of his sterling honesty. He always kept faith not only with what he said but with what he thought the other fellow understood by it. In a little time he was the essential partner of Clissold and Breakspear, and he had his active fingers in several of the most promising of the new popular magazine firms that were then appearing.

In six or seven years he was already very well off, able to marry and establish himself in a fine house in the Cromwell Road. Quite early he relinquished in my favour his share in the hundred and sixty pounds a year my mother allowed us, so that I could go and live in more comfortable apartments near to the Royal College and carry on as a research student there. He went eastward to a flat in Bloomsbury until his marriage brought him west again.

But of that marriage and of mine I must tell later.

### 5 – *Phil. Trans. as a Medium*

There drifts into my mind the substance of a silly little conversation that must have occurred somewhen in those old days before our divergent marriages had diminished our mutual familiarity. It was before my marriage anyhow, because I see Dickon in my only armchair as he talks, and there is a litter of notebooks and drawing material on the table.

He had been asking questions about the drift of my stuff and confessing himself baffled by it. "You're the brains of the family, Billy," he said a little ruefully. "Undoubtedly you are the brains of the family."

"Different brains," I said. "There is one glory of the sun and another of the moon and another of the stars."

"And another of the hoardings and magazine-covers," said Dickon – still a dozen years from sky-signs and twenty years from smoke-writing on the blue.

He fingered the pages of my first paper in the Philosophical Transactions, a tetter of formulae, and then ran his eye over the rest of the contents.

"Blastopore of the snail," he objected. "Fancy poking about at the blastopore of the snail! It's – indelicate. And cryo-hydrates! This chap Oliver Lodge seems to be all over them. Wonder what they are! Well, this is your affair, Billy. It's up to you to display the name of Clissold properly in these Philosophical Transactions. If that is the end of life. Not my pitch. Not in the least my pitch. I wouldn't try to sell even a stethoscope through these Philosophical Transactions. No."

He ran his hand over the edges of the pages with a shuddering sound and reflected profoundly. A liveliness became apparent presently beneath his depression.

"But all the same, Billy, one of these days, mark my words, I'm going to cheer up this respectable and awe-inspiring periodical. Just to please myself. I know exactly what I'm going to do. I'm going round to the Secretary of the Royal Society, and I'm going to put such an innocent-looking contract past him that he won't see for a moment what I'm up to, and then I'm going to give these dull old Philosophical Transactions of yours a real, spirited Christmas number, a genuine advertisement display. I'm going to have everything – coloured inset leaflets, extra sheets in the cover, cosmetics, lip-salves, hair-dyes, wigs, corsets – *men's* corsets! – scents, sensational pictures of lingerie, toilet fittings in ivory and silver and gold, the Parisian note loud and clear, soaps recommended by Lillie Langtry and Sarah Bernhardt, and complexion stuff by Mary Anderson, ravishing portraits of these ladies in colour, super-colour, bath scenes by Alma Tadema, Lucullus bathrooms, smart restaurants, hotels, plages, Monte

Carlo, Ascot week, Cowes, grey toppers, hatters to the Prince of Wales, manicure establishments, turf commission agents, dealers in real diamonds."

I said his advertisers wouldn't like that.

"The poor old dears! Temptation of St Anthony wouldn't be in the same field with it!" said Dickon with the confidence of a man who knows what advertisers will stand. He did not worry about them. He was thinking of grave, earnest men in spectacles, aghast.

"Tonics," he said, as an afterthought. "Cures for debility. Ginger. Do you sing in your bath?"

Dickon never had a proper respect for the Royal Society. "They lead devoted lives," I said.

"Bah!" said Dickon. "I know 'em. I know their secret cravings. They'll eat those advertisements. Doctor Faustus asks for his youth again! Mephistopheles restores it – small bottles, one guinea. You bet."

"Confound it!" I remonstrated. "Dignified work! Vital work! Why *will* you always insult men of science?"

And then at the sight of my artless indignation he threw a great fit of chuckles. "Oh, Billy!" he cried. "Oh, Billy! I got you," and kicked his legs about…

Always a great lout, my brother Dickon.

### 6 – *Dickon Reflects*

Watching Dickon and watching the world through Dickon's eyes has been at times almost more instructive than watching it through my own. He embarked upon advertising at first, as I suppose most of the early advertisers did, in a cheerfully piratical spirit. It was to be his way of "getting it" – and that was all that mattered.

But as time went on and his interests spread and his wealth and power increased, he was obliged almost in spite of himself to recognise the part that he and his like were playing in the rephrasing of human life. They were assisting at a synthesis that was replacing the scattered autonomous various individualism of the past by a more and more intricate interdependent life. He began to think of advertising less and less as an adventure, and more and more as an integral social function, with obligations and standards of its own.

Temperamentally he had never liked falsehood; he had disliked even reserve if it misled; he always kept as clear as he could from the pill and patent medicine field, in which lying and bluff figure so largely, but he had never felt quite happy in his assertion that in the long run it was better to understate than overstate in an advertisement. It is largely true, but it has never been wholly true, that for the individual in business honesty is the best policy. For a trade as a whole it is certainly true, but not for the incidental adventurer. He can achieve his "get away," as the American criminals phrase it, leaving his trade discredited.

Dickon has been a prime mover in the organisation of advertisers into a professional organisation since the war. He has helped to found lectureships and establish examinations in advertisement. I believe he would like to see a special university degree, Bachelors and Doctors of Advertisement. Some day we may come to that. Even before the war he was thinking of schemes of making deliberate falsehood, either in an advertisement or in the news columns of a newspaper, a felony. "If it was felony for our father to issue a false balance-sheet which only caused people monetary loss, it is far more felony to tell some poor old woman in a cottage that the filth you want to sell cures the pain in her back, and so waste her last chance of proper treatment for kidney or cancer."

"Proper treatment!" said I. "Where?"

Dickon stuck to his own line of thought. "Here we have people making fortunes by keeping people ill, misinforming them about their symptoms, inducing them to trust in misdescribed goods. Billy, it's a crime against the Empire. It fills the streets with uncomfortable people. Poor mothers, induced to give the children they cared for innutritious muck, so that they grow up disappointing weeds. All these weedy people in the streets, in the buses, everywhere – just because you let advertisers say their muck is flesh-forming and frame-building and bone-making when every competent authority knows that it isn't. The poor mother isn't a competent authority. How can she be? She finds it out too late. Can't help herself. And in the long run it's bad for advertising. *It's bad for advertising.* The advertising world has to sacrifice its black sheep. *Has* to! Advertisement, Billy, is too big a thing for lying – too big a thing. Much too big a thing. It's the web of modern life; it's the call of the flock. For most people, flat statement in advertisements is warranty, absolute warranty. And it ought to be. They take it as they take the news in the adjacent columns. The voice of print, Billy, is the voice of God. To them it is. And it's up to us to see that they get it divine and true."

I raised my eyebrows.

"Divine and true," said Dickon, raising his voice above me massively.

I said I supposed our legal theory was that if there was misdescription there could be an action for damages.

"But how can the poor mutts bring actions against a firm with scores of thousands to play with? How can they do it? No, I want the fellows handled by the Public Prosecutor at the instance of a properly constituted Advertisement Society, and sent to jail."

I was amused. It was down at Dorking, and in 1912 or 1913, that he discoursed in this fashion. We had been playing tennis and we were on the terrace above the court. Dickon was sitting in a deck-chair looking flushed and freckled and over-healthy and very, very earnest, drinking an inadvisable whisky and soda.

I raised the old issue between his individualism and my Socialism. What was all this talk about? Where were his lifelong principles? He was preaching rank Socialism. Wasn't *caveat emptor* the sound principle for an individualist world?

"Individualist be blowed!" said Dickon. "*Caveat emptor* was all very well between two Latin peasants at a bargain in that little old parochial Roman world – as it *was*, Billy, as it was – but the odds have altered now. I'm thinking of those weedy children and the old woman with a pain in her side."

## 7 – *The Advertiser as Prophet and Teacher*

The Great War did much to develop Dickon's conception of his rôle in the world. He expanded mightily upon a diet of propaganda. There was a phase in the Reconstruction Period when it seemed to him that only an adequate advertisement campaign was needed to achieve the Millennium. I have given these vignettes of him in the eighties, in the later nineties, and in the pre-war days as he grew in strength and confidence. Let me anticipate for a section and complete his apotheosis of advertisement. I must recall what I can of a discourse of his towards the end of 1918. Then you will see how the imagination of Dickon the advertiser grew from that of the watch peddler he was forty years ago to its present dimensions.

If the Great War made nothing, it did at least appear for a time to have disorganised everything. The idea that society had been shattered and would need rebuilding was very prevalent in 1915. Everything was going to be rebuilt, fairer, sounder, juster, happier; that went without saying. That was the justification for a war that was otherwise inexplicable; it was a Phoenix flare. By 1916 this had become a standard promise for all the optimists who were engaged in whipping up the flagging enthusiasm of the nation. It crystallised into the word Reconstruction. All our

English world talked Reconstruction, from the pro-war intellectuals, who dropped off from the war propaganda into silence or opposition after the collapse of the Stockholm Conference, to the deep *John Bull* bellowings of Horatio Bottomley, most popular of patriots and stimulators. "A world fit for heroes," said Lloyd George – phrase unforgettable. How tremendously that word Reconstruction was bandied about! It waved as gallantly, it vanished at least as abruptly, as a contested banner in a riot. Many of us can still feel uncomfortable if some thoughtless person chances to revive it.

There was much pitiful moral tragedy in that fiasco, but to begin with Reconstruction embodied some bold and righteous hopes. And it completed the evolution of Dickon. Under its spell he became temporarily a Utopian, more Utopian even than I in my Brompton days, and planned a world which never had been, but which, it seemed to him then, might very easily be. He had realised the tremendous possibilities of handling people in great masses revealed by this war advertising, in which he had played a conspicuous part; possibilities of teaching hygienic practices for example, suggesting new habits or routines, restating and changing general ideas, altering outlooks altogether. For a time these realisations possessed him completely.

His Utopianism was amateurish; he had all the crudity of a sudden convert. He wanted to see the energy that had been gathered into the great Ministry of Munitions turned directly to the material rearrangement of the country, the railways re-made, the countryside re-planned, slums swept away, old beauties restored, and much of our present towns and cities rebuilt. Then manifestly the war would not have been in vain. He saw himself directing the demobilising millions back to abundant work, and homes renewed and happy, through a vast advertisement organisation. "A land fit for heroes," he quoted continually – in his profession they call that sort of thing a "slogan" – and it seemed plain to him after the vision of large-scale human co-operation the war had given him, that the whole food supply of the world was capable of control, that population could be poured from district to district like water, instructed in the requirements of its new surroundings and held to it effort. He had some magnificent moments in that Utopian phase of his.

"The war's been a bloody mess, Billy, but at least it's taught us to handle things in the big way," he said: "the advertising way. We learnt it by selling mustard and motor-cars, but these were only the things we learnt upon."

And again: "Advertising; what is it? Education. Modern education, nothing more or less. The airs schoolmasters and college dons give themselves are extraordinary. They think they're the only people who teach. *We* teach ten times as much. Why! even the little chaps who write the attractions in the big weeklies and monthlies, Kipling, Jack London, Bennett, Galsworthy, Wodehouse, all that lot – teach more than the schoolmasters do.

"Schoolmasters! What do you mean by education? When you get down to hard tacks. *Just old-fashioned, primitive advertisement done by world of mouth in a room!* Why! a class-room schoolmaster teaching by shouts ought to be as out-of-date nowadays as a town-crier!

"The only use I've got for schools now is to fit people to read advertisements. After that, *we* take on. Yes, we – the advertisers. You may laugh, Billy; it's true. All new ideas come as a shock at first. Don't just laugh at it like that. Don't sit like an oaf and grin. Tell me what's wrong with it.

"And even *in* the schools we could put ten times better lessons over the heads of the masers now – with a properly organised cinema. Ten times better. But we leave the cinema to a lot of music-hall muckers and close-up chorus girls, as though it wasn't worth using."

He laid great stress upon the cinema, but I do not recall him saying anything about broadcasting in those Reconstruction days. But, of course! One forgets how fast the world moves. In 1919 there was no broadcasting. With broadcasting I can see Dickon reducing his poor schoolmasters to the last extremity of usherdom – mere conductors on his omnibus to knowledge. Before broadcasting he had at least to leave them an occasional use of their voices. Now they would just hum on the loud-speaker and stand about and mark registers. Gagged, perhaps, to prevent any personal intervention.

His denunciation of schoolmasters increased and intensified, of schoolmasters and the clergy, as his imagination of what might be done with the crowd developed. He would talk to me in his hectoring, elder-brother way, but always with a twinkle in his eye and a touch of burlesque in his tone and an evident readiness to jump overboard from his argument at any time with a sudden splash of laugher if it became too difficult to maintain; and his argument was always exaltation of the modern advertising method and always contempt for the refinements of the intellectual world.

"These fellows in caps and gowns think you can make things decent by being genteel in a corner and shuddering and sneering whenever you hear a noise. I ask you! You've got to *explain* your Millennium to people, Billy; you've got to make 'em want it, and you've got to tell 'em how to get it. Then they'll get it. Just as they get Lucas lamps and safety-razor blades or any other old thing. The advertisand is different, but the method is the same. Why, Billy! Look at things plainly. With all reverence – "

He adapted his ruddy face roughly and quickly to express all reverence. It was just an habitual concession unnecessary in my case.

"What were the twelve Apostles? Drummers, just drummers. Travelling in salvation. Introducing a new line. Why did Paul raise his voice at Athens? Because he hadn't a Megaphone. And the miracles they did? Sample bottles. To this day it's advertisement. What is a wayside crucifix? – an advertisement of the faith. What is Christianity? – an advertisement campaign. Tell 'em. Tell 'em. Tell 'em all you can. It's the method of social existence."

He turned to biology, to the poetry of life.

"The very flowers by the wayside, Billy, are advertisements for bees!"

My grin armed the fighting spirit in him.

"Vulgar you think it is?"

"Frightfully."

"If there's anything vulgar about modern advertisement, Billy, it's because it's been so concerned about pills and soap and pickles. Just a passing phase. A man or a class or a religion or – anything that will not advertise isn't fit to exist in the world. It means it doesn't really believe in itself. To want to exist and not to dare to exist is something beneath vulgarity… That's why I have such a contempt for your rotten, shy, sit-in-the-corner-and-ask-the-dear-Prince-of-Wales-to-dinner-once-a-year Royal Society.

"If the soap-boilers did no more for soap than your old Royal Society does for science," said Dickon, "nobody would wash."

## 8 – *Dickon's Marriage*

But this post-war talk, is, as I intimated, out of place. I will return to the Period of Reconstruction later. If nothing else was reconstructed then, we were, and out post-war interchanges form a distinct and separate chapter in our history. Before I go on to tell how the war shook up and released and stimulated our ideas about things in general, I must tell of his marriage and of a considerable divergence of our ways of living. When I was three-and-twenty things happened to make me break away from the life of pure research I had seemed destined to follow. I became an employee and later a director of Romer, Steinhart, Crest and Co., I left London to live at Downs-Peabody, and I became more and more involved in the huge industrial developments that have occupied the greater half of my life. They had little or no advertising side. They brought me into a world of associates quite apart from Dickon's; they carried me abroad for long spells and made me by comparison cosmopolitan.

He remained extremely English. He lived for some years after his marriage in the Cromwell Road, and then he bought Lambs Court near Dorking and became a substantial figure in the substantial suburbanism of Surrey. I, too, married a little while after he did, but marriage, which stabilised him, disorganised all my intentions about life. My marriage was a failure. I will tell of it in due course, but for some years a certain chagrin may have helped to make my visits to Dickon's home less frequent than they might otherwise have been. His marriage was heartily successful, ostentatiously successful; and for a while I suspected him, I think now unjustly, of feeling that I was to blame for the muddle I was in.

Ostentatiously successful I write, but whether it is to be regarded as a perfect marriage I do not know. I doubt if there is any such thing as a perfect marriage. It may happen – as an accident. To this day I find a certain lurking perplexity about my sister-in-law in my mind; I have never been able to exorcise it. There was something extraordinarily fine about her – and something cold and aloof. Nor do I yet see as a clear and consistent thing Dickon's relations to her. He was so incapable of aloofness. He was floridly and magnificently loyal to her and she was profoundly loyal to him, but I do not know, I cannot imagine what there was down there at the very bottom of things between them. Was it love, the tenderness and infinite consideration she had for him? It was love at first, no doubt. And mixed with his infinite respect for her, his pride and his rare overwhelming tenderness, there was something resentful. Did he always suppress that resentment in her presence? I do not know. I will tell as much as I know, what I saw, what I inferred, and leave it to the reader. Plainly there are things here outside the range of my feelings and experiences.

She was a very small person; she had fine exquisite features; she was not a short woman, not dwarfish in any way, but simply made upon a delicate scale; she looked much more fragile than she was, and when I first encountered her she was a little strained and artificial in her manner because she was so valiantly resolved not to be shy. I met her only a month or so before the marriage, and when the marriage was already fixed. Dickon had discovered her in Bloomsbury, and I had a sense that she had been sprung upon me after a period of uneasiness and concealment on Dickon's part. There was a sort of tea-party in Dickon's sitting-room, and she was there under the protection of a cousin, whom I forget altogether, and I had the spectacle of Dickon, my stern, dogmatic brother, almost dishevelled with nervousness, proffering tea, handing cakes, asking me – *me!* – if I took sugar, and watching my face for the faintest intimations of a judgment.

She was little, not very well dressed, guarded. That much I saw at the time. We talked about pictures, about which none of us knew very much, and about music. At Lambs Court there is still a photograph of her in those early days. One had to sit quite still for some seconds in those days in order to be photographed, and so if one did not get blurred one looked like waxworks. She had contrived to sit quite still. How unaccustomed now are our eyes to those later Victorian costumes! She had a collar to her dress that reached to her little ears and great puffed sleeves and a whalebone figure.

I forget most of the incidents of that meeting now, but I remember Dickon afterwards parting from me at Hyde Park

Corner. "You don't see what there is in her at first, old man," he said, for the third or fourth time. Though I had never said a word to betray that I did not think her the most obviously and instantly desirable of all possible sisters-in-law. I had hardly said anything. I did not know what to say.

On our way on Hyde Park Corner he had told me things about her. She was the daughter of a doctor in Bloomsbury, a very competent general practitioner. She was a connection of his early partner, Brakespear. She had passed some examinations – I forget what they were but they were difficult ones. She drew beautifully. She was clever at music and spoke French and German wonderfully well. She was an only child, which, I think, accounts for a sort of reserved inwardness in her manner; she was untrained in the exposures, criticisms, recriminations, and habitual intimacies of family life.

She read, I was to discover later, and she studied, but she was not accustomed to talk. There were moments when I was to watch her listening to Dickon's discourse and compare her in my mind with a passenger waiting for a ferry with the river in flood. Waiting as one waits on a fine agreeable day when waiting is no hardship. Waiting, moreover, with no intention of travelling on the stream. And – to begin with, she was, in a peculiar still way, in love with Dickon and devoted to him. He, too, was in love with her, but just the least bit disappointed, I felt, that she did not make a better show in front of me. Once or twice during those early encounters he tried to draw her out and exhibit her paces, but she had little, scarcely perceptible, ways of stopping that. It was amusing to see Dickon interested in an article that declined to be pushed. He would have been a terrible impresario for a showy woman.

I began to think her a little less undistinguished after a fourth or fifth meeting, and at the wedding I had a feeling that for some obscure reason she had hitherto been concealing from me and the world in general an ability to be, if she chose, conspicuously pretty.

But I still didn't see why it had been necessary for my bright and exuberant Dickon to marry her. I did not see why he of all people should be mated to incarnate restraint.

It was a thoroughly respectable wedding, and the household they set up in the Cromwell Road was in the highest degree respectable. A time was to come when I was to think a lot of Minnie's taste, but in the furnishing of that first house nothing of her sensitive fastidiousness appeared. Perhaps it was not yet fully awake. I suppose Dickon must have just carried her through the furniture shop with him and given her no time to meditate. The house was, my brief disturbing wife declared, when she paid her introductory visit, "utterly and hopelessly *banal*."

I was married, as I will tell later, about a year and a half after Dickon, and my marriage took him by surprise as much as his had taken me. I kept Clara an even closer secret from Dickon than he had kept Minnie from me. Perhaps I felt what his opinion would be of the Allbut ménage. I sprang her upon Dickon and Minnie within a few weeks of our marriage. I took her to call upon Minnie. I went in a faintly irritated mood because Clara had seen fit to supplement her wardrobe from an aunt's supplies, and had suddenly become much more a woman of the world and much less of a hard-up art girl than was seemly in the future wife of a struggling research student.

A natural antagonism flared up at the first encounter of Minnie and Clara. Clara was an effusive human being, and particularly so with strangers. She fell upon Minnie with cries and embraces. "What an exquisite *little* dear you are!" she said.

I was beginning to forget that Minnie was so very small; I saw her disentangling herself with an unobtrusive distaste from those swift familiarities. Clara praised her clothes loudly – they were in the current fashion of the time – insisted upon regarding them as the triumph of a special effort, and then, with an obscure perception of rebuff, turned her enthusiasm to the house and the furniture. "Jolly *good* things you have!" she exclaimed. "Where did you get them all?"

"Dickon and I went to Maple's," said Minnie, regarding her strictly later Victorian surroundings for a moment as though she had just seen them for the first time.

Clara looked round for some piece that might be exceptional. There was nothing exceptional. So she pounced on a book.

"*You* read George Meredith too!" she said.

"Here's Dickon!" said Minnie, relieved as the door opened...

I became more acutely aware of the sketchy quality in Clara's smartness as Dickon came in. It was my turn now to watch for unspoken verdicts. Clara's way with men was sometimes a little over-confident...

It was not a good call. Dickon, I could see, did not warm to Clara. Minnie seemed deliberately to be refrigerating the conversation, and we left with Clara in a splendid rage.

"So *that's* my prospective sister-in-law!" I remember her saying on the doorstep.

She paused. "*Watchful!*" she whispered. "She watches."

And then she embarked upon an exhaustive summary of Minnie's deficiencies. The burthen was that there was nothing in Minnie, but for all that it was clear that there was much to be said about her. Firstly, she was personally insignificant. Secondly, she was cold-blooded. Next, her style of dressing was provincial, timid, genteel. She was under-dressed. On such an occasion as this it was rude and offhand to under-dress. One was expected to dress a little. To meet a chosen sister-in-law was an important occasion and ought to be treated as such. One ought to make an effort.

The ashes of our controversy over the borrowed finery glowed again for a moment.

Minnie's furniture and her household management, insisted Clara, had the same limitations as her costume and the same uncivil negligence. The tea, for some reason, had greatly offended Clara. There had been a lack of variety in the tea; for the first visit of an imminent sister-in-law there ought to have been display; everybody nowadays gave little sandwiches, cucumber sandwiches, paste sandwiches. Amusing things. Light things one just took in one's hand. It looked skimpy not to do so. And dull. Buttered buns were ridiculous; hefty things like that ought to be relegated to the nursery. (At tea Clara had "adored" buttered buns, had received them with acclamation.)

And that furniture! That *heavy* furniture! Maple's! Carte blanche to them to furnish, no doubt. No individuality. No character. Where *could* my brother have met her? No doubt we should have to go to dinner there so soon as we were married. It would be our first dinner party together. Could we last two hours? What should we talk about? Even in that forty minutes' call the talk had caught and hung time after time.

"Well, anyhow," reflected Clara, "I shan't want much of a frock for *that!*"

I said very little to Clara's tirade, because it shocked and irritated me to hear my own secret judgments on Dickon's wife caricatured, made monstrous and preposterous, and expressed in terms of intense personal hostility. "She isn't so bad," I said. "And she makes Dickon happy."

"*Does* she make him happy?

"Your brother," said Clara, following up her own question, "would never own to a failure if he felt he could pull it through to look like a success. He's – stiff stuff. As stiff as you are. Obviously she's as flat as ditch-water. Uninteresting. Prosaic. She paralyses him. If she hadn't been there – he would have been different… Sooner or later he'll be going round the corner. You mark my words, Billy. But he'll never own up."

I detested her for saying it, but there was something of a likeness to Dickon in that.

"And she won't either," jerked Clara, suddenly completing her impression.

"Won't what?"

"Own up."

## 9 – *Lambs Court*

There with the help of Clara's vivid expressiveness, which sometimes succeeded in being on the whole unaccountably right with every detail wrong, you have a sketch of Minnie. She was neither flat nor prosaic; she was never uninteresting; but it is true that she never seemed to take hold of Dickon, and that she did not seem to take hold of life. He had taken hold of her, and she liked that; it warmed her as much as anything could warm her, but there was nothing about her holding on to him if presently he let go. She was, I had long realised, a creature of fine secondary shades and complicated shynesses and reserves, and I have never known anyone with a less voracious will to live.

I doubted from the first whether he appreciated her fine shades. His natural disposition was towards poster colourings more suitable for display. But gradually I came to see that it was not the delicacy not the fine shades that he cared about. He had a profound unshakable belief in her honesty, loyalty and common sense, and she justified his belief. Whatever else she may or may not have been to him, she was, so to speak, his treasury, his brake, his wary councillor. And though she was never a brilliant talker in society, I noted that when he quoted her sayings and cited her opinions, there came out a shrewd individuality quite different from his own.

They did not have children for a while. Then in the course of four or five years came a couple of sons and a daughter, and they went to the space and dignity of Lambs Court and took a great flat in Queen Anne's Mansions as their *pied-à-terre* in London. It was only after her death and the marriage of young Richard that Dickon left Queen Anne's Mansions for the chambers in Bordon Street in which this book begins. There were gaps sometimes of two or three years when I would be abroad, or in the north, or in the Midlands, and when I saw little of Dickon and Minnie, and so my memories pass almost abruptly from that rather commonplace, rather nervously self-conscious and apologetic home in the Cromwell Road to a very prettily furnished and well-ordered country house, with a small but very well-dressed and maternal Minnie, keeping a competent eye on her nursemaids and instructing an entirely respectful gardener in the development of the very beautiful terrace gardens she created. The two figures do not merge so completely as they would have done if our acquaintance had been continuous. In that case I have no doubt the earlier, immature, more fragile and shyer Minnie would have been replaced day by day and bit by bit and effaced altogether from my memory.

In the second phase Minnie had far more confidence, far more grip upon the world, than in the first. There was a subtle difference in her relations with Dickon, but it would be hard to define what that difference was. Perhaps she had passed through phases of dismay and reassurance. I thought his attitude towards her was a little more effusive and formal that it had been, and more habitual. I thought that she seemed no longer to be observing him with the happy interest of their earlier time. It was as though she had got used to him and had accepted something that had not been present in the beginning, or resigned herself to the absence of something she had once thought there.

She had become a great gardener, which was rather wonderful after a girlhood in Bloomsbury, and she was also beginning to know quite a lot about furniture and pictures. Later on she was to become something of a buyer of pictures and etchings. She would help struggling artists, until she felt the touch of proprietorship to which the helped are prone. The children were happy and delightful then, in a perfect nursery and with an excellent, kindly nurse; but I do not remember ever seeing Minnie romp with them, and I doubt if in all her life she ever lost her temper with them. Yet she loved them. Flowers and furnishing, I think, she cared for more than living things; she could do so much more for them without provoking them to come back upon her clamorously. They did not climb upon her, they did not shout or hammer at her, as human beings might at any time do.

After a time I went no more to Lambs Court. I stayed away for nearly seven years. While Dickon's marriage had turned out successfully, mine had ended in the uncomfortable tangle I describe later. I was tied to Clara legally for the rest of my life, and unable to marry again. I was welcome at Lambs Court as a sort of bachelor brother, very welcome, even after I had been cited as a co-respondent in the Evans divorce case, but I felt a certain exemplariness in Dickon's attitude towards me and an implicit criticism in the immense discreet silences of Minnie. There were times when Dickon's gestures, pauses, acts seemed to say almost as plainly as though he spoke the words: "My dear fellow, why are you in this uneasy mess? It is so perfectly simple. All you have to do is to marry Minnie, make much of her, stick to her, stand up for her, stick to business – and keep strange women in their proper place. Out of the picture. And there you are, you know!"

Quite possibly my suspicions were unjust. At any rate he was habitually proud of her and as good and faithful a husband as most of the rich and rising business men of Surrey.

Then came my attempt to live with Mrs Evans. That was in the turn of the century and people in England were still unprepared to tolerate a ménage, however stable, of two unmarried people. So long as I was a man of the world, carrying on a series of incidental intrigues almost openly, I was socially acceptable anywhere; but an attempt at illicit domesticity, with a still undivorced Clara, however disreputable, in existence, was too much for the standards of the time. If I could have divorced Clara and married Sirrie Evans, all would have been well. I wouldn't accept that verdict. I fought. I betrayed excessive resentment. I would not ask Minnie for any help in thc matter, I made no attempt to bring her and Sirrie together, I said nothing to Dickon, but I felt acutely their failure to apprehend our situation. Minnie ignored it. She did not know this Mrs Evans, apparently she would not know this Mrs Evans. She asked me to come to Lambs Court alone, and I never answered her invitation. I did not see her again or communicate directly with her until a year or more after Sirrie's death.

To this day that lack of initiative perplexes me. By the time of the Evans affair she and I had become very friendly. She did not know Sirrie, she may not have been prepared to take any very serious risks about her, but still she might have assumed that I should not have become attached to a woman without good qualities, and it would have been quite possible for her to have found out and met Sirrie in some roundabout way before committing herself. But she just did nothing. She was one of a number of people who just did nothing to help us. Something cold and distant there was in that. Or something profoundly timid? Or some aversion from relationships into which there entered a possible thread of passion?

Dickon knew Sirrie slightly. One might have imagined that he could have broken down that icy barrier by a word or so. But he did not, and perhaps he could not. The barrier may not have been solely for the benefit of Sirrie; I do not know. Sirrie may have symbolised many things for Minnie and Dickon that had little to do with me. I continued to meet Dickon in London. We had both become members of the Ermine Club, and we would lunch or dine and gossip together without any allusion to the complete separation of our households. Nothing was ever explained. We belonged to the same group of after-lunch talkers. We gibed at each other's opinions and went to one or two theatres together. But about the rest of his life during that estrangement I made no enquiry beyond such information as he volunteered. I continued to be aware of Minnie only in relation to him.

He varied towards her no doubt. Sometimes when I met him in London Minnie was as remote from him but as necessary to the world and as much taken for granted as the Atlantic or the Equator. At other times he was full of quotations from her and references to her. Then, oddly enough, I was not so sure of his serene and complete assurance about her. It has been the common habit of our two lives never to pry into the intimate proceedings of the other, but I have had a feeling that in these phases of allusion, these passages peppered with "My wife says this" and "Minnie does that," he perceived himself under a necessity to maintain her. Yet it would be difficult to define what it was he maintained her against.

Whatever imperfections and difficulties there were in his married life, whatever hidden relaxations there were of its outward integrity, none of them ever came to the surface as a visible infringement of Minnie's dignities. There were, I happen to know, what the French call *passades,* but the heroines were obscure young ladies, amply compensated and silenced. He was, I repeat, as good and faithful a husband as most honourable, prosperous men.

One spring day in 1910 I found myself put down at a Romer lunch party next to Minnie. I was sure they would put me next to her as soon as I saw her in the drawing-room. She had altered very little; she was, perhaps, stronger and firmer and better dressed. She looked like very good porcelain amidst the metallic splendours of Lady Romer's assembly.

I put as good a face as I could upon the encounter. I asked after Lambs Court and the children.

"William the Second," she said, "is absurdly like you. He has a gift. He is going to draw – wonderfully. The two brothers together are like Dickon and you – even to the way they insult each other."

She said something about my coming down to see them.

Then in a pause she made a great effort. "Billy," she said very softly, "I was so sorry to hear of your loss."

I was too astonished to say anything.

"I wanted to write. I was stupid... I often don't do – things I want to do."

She was feeling her way towards an apology, and she was flushed and sincere. It was a sort of confession – for one who could not confess. She became more incomprehensible to me than ever. I was quite unable to get her into relationship with that old and now healing sore. I dismissed the attempt.

"I would like to see something of William the Second," I said, after a clumsy interval, "I've neglected my godson."

"Next weekend?" she said as awkwardly...

It was the most intimate moment we ever had together.

Thereafter our outward friendship – and I can imagine no friendship of Minnie's that except for the rarest moments was other than external – was resumed.

### 10 – *Honours List*

Between that meeting and my later memories of Minnie, streams all the storm, tragedy, and illumination of the war. The war that has changed so much and yet at times seems to have changed nothing.

I never expected the war to happen until it was actually happening. Romer, Steinhart, Crest and Co. were naturally in touch with much pre-war armament business, and armament seemed to us – to me, at any rate, it seemed – a foolish way of using up good metal that fools had got to pay for as highly as possible. I still think the war need not have happened, and that the amount of good that has come out of it is incomparably smaller than the waste and evil. It is easy to be wise after the event and say how inevitable the catastrophe was, but I do not think it was inevitable even so late as July, 1914. More intelligent men in the Foreign Offices could, I think, have averted it even then. But few of us were intelligent and imaginative enough to realise the enormity of the disaster until it was upon us. We expected a quick war, possible humiliations, great changes of the map and far less strain, destruction, and uprooting. Most of our Governments and rulers were as little able to foresee and fear as so many mentally defective children with a box of matches in a powder magazine. At last a match was dropped. Then for a time the skies were darkened, the world was full of thunder, the torrents of disaster poured. There was a clatter of falling things, a flare of burning. Millions of young men suffered detestable things and died and passed. And at last when it had come to seem that no end would ever be possible, the storm was over and the skies cleared magically.

The tornado struck Lambs Court, seemed likely to extinguish the life of Lambs Court altogether, and left it a last – with scarcely a flower-bed ruffled. Dick and William, my nephews, both went into the war and survived it, William unscathed, Dick with a bullet wound and a six months' spell of prison in Germany after Gough's disaster in 1918. Indeed, Lambs Court came through it amazingly. Weekend parties were already resumed in 1919. And Dickon was made a baronet! Dickon was made a baronet and Minnie became Lady Clissold – to my infinite amazement and perplexity.

The war, I say, took me by surprise, but so soon as it was under way my rôle was marked out for me. I was too old for the earlier enlistments, and I doubt if in any case I should have volunteered. I gravitated naturally to technical work, and was presently involved in the new-formed Ministry of Munitions. I did four years of bitter contentious work, and I should suppose that Roderick and I between us saved the British taxpayer many, probably negligible, millions of pounds. My estimates of current honesty and current intelligence were considerably lowered by those experiences; I conceived a passionate contempt and distaste for the higher ranks of the British Army that I still have trouble in controlling, and I came to consider and treat the military, naval, and aerial expert, salaried adviser of the War Office today and highly salaried official of an armament group tomorrow, as the moral inferior of a Constantinople tourists' dragoman.

At the end I dodged the shower of honours with considerable difficulty. There were a number of people who were deeply concerned that I should get something and be generally soothed, pacified, implicated, and shut up. I transferred a particularly persistent suggestion of a KBE to a useful subordinate who might have been passed over, the sort of man to appreciate it, and I tried to use whatever claim to attention I might have in hunting down one or two exceptionally scandalous cases. In that I failed completely. The Press would not touch my entirely convincing facts. Nobody would touch them. One of my worst offenders married his loot to American money and became a bright ornament for any London dinner party; another took the fancy of Royalty; another embarrassed me by appearing on the board of an allied steel firm with which we had the friendliest relations. After a while I realised that I was being unreasonable and self-righteous.

I began to laugh at my own virtue. If there was to be a real inquisition into stolen goods, where should we end?

Dickon was more surprised by the war even than I was. He had never believed that these European armies were really in earnest, and he had been inclined to approve of German imperialism as of something pleasantly flamboyant and picturesque in a age inclined to be prosaic. It advertised amazingly. When the guns began to go off he was outraged beyond measure at the breach of faith. It was as though a large bill-stickers' hoarding had begun to kill and eat people. There seemed nothing for it at first but violence with an axe.

He was furiously indignant against the Germans. So indeed was I in the early months. So was all England. At this resurrection of war. The awakening of England in the autumn of 1914 may have been uncritical and foolish, but it was thoroughly honest, and so far at any rate as the million odd volunteers were concerned, heroic. By the end of the year Dickon had somehow contrived to get into khaki. He was fully fifty, and I do not know how he managed it, but he did. He had once in the early bicycle days spent some months in that now forgotten supplement to the military might of Britain, the Volunteers. He was keen then on cyclist riflemen. He may have exaggerated his former standing in that force. At any rate, he was taken on. I cherish a snapshot of his substantial figure with a lieutenant's star upon his collar, looking very earnest and unsuitable. Afterwards, for some reason of etiquette in connection with supplies, they jumped him up to be a temporary colonel, and at that he could stand beside the stoutest of them, stouter than any and taller than most. He was trained at Checkershill and then on Cumberbatch Moor, but that was as near as he travelled on the road to the trenches. He went to France, indeed, but by a different route. They found they wanted him on the commissariat.

A man who could advertise things for retail sale was naturally supposed by the military authorities to know how to buy and distribute anything. He did some thoroughly sound work for them, and afterwards he became a great factor in civil food-control organisation. He worked hard under Rhondda, an able, ailing, concentrated man who might be alive today, perhaps, if it had not been for the strain of that work, and after Rhondda died Dickon went on with Clynes, a Labour leader, who had joined the Government. Through Dickon I met Clynes on two or three occasions. He was a little intelligent-looking cockatoo of a man, who, like Brer Rabbit, kept on saying nuffing all the time, in the face of every conversational allurement. Perhaps, like one or two others of his colleagues, he needs a platform, a large hall and adequate interruption, before he can really express what is in him.

"Does he know anything?" I asked Dickon afterwards.

"He knows what he doesn't know," said Dickon. "He's perfectly satisfactory to work with."

A foretaste of the Labour Government of 1924.

Dick, my elder nephew, volunteered before his father at the beginning; William was taken later, protesting, but without bitterness, that it wasn't his fight; Lambs Court was presently filled with convalescents and a trained staff, and my niece Winnie was sent up to London, out of sentimental range, to work with great energy at the manufacture of bandages, a little resentful because her mother would not allow her to drive a car for the Ministry of Munitions. Minnie presided capably at Lambs Court, and presently, after strains and endless petty hardships, scanty food, darkened homes, tiresome air-raids, gleams of leave for the boys, almost overwhelming anxiety over Dick's disappearance – he was "missing" for three weeks – and a sort of universal neurasthenia, the war came abruptly to its hysterical end. Down either side of Pall Mall hundreds of captured guns were displayed, the streets of London were alight again and swarming with a vast, wearily enthusiastic multitude which laughed and shouted because it did not want to howl and cry, and the war was over. And Dickon was talking with passionate conviction of Britain born again out of these troubles and of a "reconstructed" world.

That was the background so to speak to the affair of his baronetcy.

I realised that he did not intend to refuse it, with an indignation that now strikes me as excessive. At the time it seemed extravagantly important to me that my brother should not accept this thing. I suppose I was overworked and worried, in a state of inflamed honesty, more indignant and less cynically patient than I have ever been before or since. I was in conflict with my business associates. Perhaps I should have been better employed in watching them. Brampsheet particularly – he had just got his peerage – was against all post-war scandals and enquiries, and my anger extended to the social world which was sheltering the men I wanted to expose. This had been the war that was to end all that sort of thing. These exasperations made me see Dickon's title as a sort of treason to the insurgent radicalism that had always been implicit between us.

"Dickon!" I protested. "That old livery! In an age of Reconstruction!"

"Historical, time-honoured."

"Everything we want to say good-bye to."

"All the same – "

"You mean to take it, Dickon?"

"Yes. Yes, I think I may take it."

"You'll have to kiss the king's hand?" I invented.

Dickon pretended not to hear.

"You'll have to kiss his hand," I jeered.

"No more than kissing a book."

He went off at a tangent to answer unspoken objections of mine. "You live in a sort of dreamland, Billy," he said. "Science and the future and all that. Even now. In spite of your business and money. But I live in the present time. I'm here and now. I'm contemporary. A child of the age. This sort of thing is the fashion of our time. It's just a symbol of success and service. Very well. It may not be the best of media, but it's one way of saying 'I'm here!' That's how I look at it."

It was as if we were back in our Brompton diggings. That, I remembered suddenly, had been his standing argument against my Socialism.

"It's bolstering up the old order. You take the honour, yes – but you give your adhesion."

He said I lacked *savoir-faire*. That if one went on those lines one would become a "lone wolf." One didn't bolster up the old order. On the contrary, it acknowledged itself subdued. It stood on one side to make way for one. Saluted. And besides – with a quick change of line – he wanted Minnie to be Lady Clissold.

"Have you asked her?"

"And the old man's name," said Dickon, with a second flash of deafness. "I've always had a feeling about the honour of the old man. Here it is at last – his name rather than mine. Sir Richard Clissold, Bart. After the way they let him down. After that last scene at the Old Bailey."

"Sir Richard Clissold Boop," said I.

"Eh?"

"Boop. The Boops and their Jubilee. Good God, man, you haven't forgotten the Boops, have you? All this, Dickon, strikes me as the most infernal Boopery. You'll have to wear a little Boopy sword. And silk legs! And the Boops will stand round in their little Boopy robes, dressing-gowns and tea-cosies and table-cloths and curtains and antimacassar wigs and newspaper hats, all very solemn and solemn, to welcome you. Don't you remember?"

He did. But he didn't want to do so. He embarked upon an insincere defence of royalty. "They" were so hard-working, so devoted. "Hardest-working couple in the Empire."

"To no purpose," said I, "except to stick on."

"So much to do," said Dickon. "Reconstruction everywhere. Why divide people by quarrelling with that?"

I told him that people of his sort defended the crown because they were too lazy to set about getting it out of their way. They only pretended to like it. It obstructed the traffic. It falsified realities.

"Bit too many royal visits and processions just now, I admit," said Dickon. "Still – they *are* the decentest!"

He shrugged his shoulders, and tried to look indulgent and reasonable and as much like *The Times* and *Punch* and a white top-hat in Ascot week as possible.

It was not only the traffic in the streets, I said. It was the traffic in men's minds. It put the common people wrong about the purposes of the State.

"They love it," said Dickon.

"That's just it," said I. "It's a lumbering perversion of human respect. A modern community can't afford to waste its respect like that!"

That consideration has been my unwavering objection to monarchy and has made me that rare being, an English republican. I am puzzled by the readiness of liberal-minded English people to acquiesce in and conform to the monarchy. The king is necessarily the head and centre of the old army system, of the diplomatic tradition, of hieratic privileges, of a sort of false England that veils the realities of English life. While he remains, the old army system remains, Society remains, the militant tradition remains. They are all bound up together, inseparably.

The people cannot apprehend themselves in relation to the world while, at every turn and crisis of the collective life, the national king, the national uniforms, the national flags and bands, thrust blare and bunting across the realities. For millions these shows are naturally accepted as the realities. They personify and intensify and ensure the national distinction, the separation of the marching, fighting, grabbing Empire from the general business of mankind. How else can a monarchy work considering how monarchs are made and trained and flattered?

For a time Dickon and I wrangled over the issue between monarchy and republicanism. The United States, said Dickon, could be republican and intensely nationalist; France – this was in 1919 – was republican and militarist. Americans, I said, were not nationalist, but were obsessed by an unavoidable sense of difference. As for France –

"King!" said Dickon, with a nimble change of front, "but after all what's the king got to do with my baronetcy? I shall scarcely see him long enough to make a face at him. He'll ask, 'Who's that fine man?' And forget when they tell him. It's LG's affair. You're taking the whole of this business too seriously, Billy. You are indeed. You're putting it on too broad a basis. You're so fierce a republican I doubt if you'd read a book if you found it was printed on crown octavo."

He followed that up. "It isn't as though LG's title were so damned serious as all that. There's something like derision in most of his creations. They're just a flare up at the end. The last dance of the old costume ball. Before it is all swept away."

"In that case Lady Clissold becomes a comic title."

"If it was only for the pleasure it would give the servants at Lambs Court I'd take the title," said Dickon.

"You won't take it," I said.

"I'll do it – if only to annoy you."

I laughed.

"It's just like buying a fur coat for Minnie. It's a decoration. It's a way of putting her over the heads of a lot of showy, chattering bitches that aren't worth a tenth of her."

"There's no need to make Minnie a Lady by the King's grace," I said. "And as for putting her over those other – ladies, you're just putting her among them. And that reminds me: have you asked her about it?"

He had not. And I realised in a flash he was not quite sure what she would say about it. That was why he was trying over the proposal on me first of all, to get a review of the possible objections.

"She won't let you," I said. "She won't let you."

But she did let him. Dickon took his baronetcy.

## 11 – *Minnie's Farewell*

Minnie died very suddenly in the early part of 1920. She died under an operation that no one had thought very dangerous. But though she told it to no one, she had a feeling of danger, and she did a thing that was to reveal to me as nothing else could have done, the real quality of her relations to Dickon and the world, their aloofness and their filmy tenderness.

Her presentiment of death was very strong. But I do not think she was very deeply troubled at the thought of dying. I suppose that people who live with delicacy rather than intensity can die without any great mental agony. She was troubled about Dickon much more than on her own account; she thought her possible death might be a shock for him, and she feared that shock. So she wrote him a letter – a letter that was only to reach his hands if she died. Otherwise it would just have vanished like many another thing she must have thought of and done in that reserved life of hers. I saw that letter. He was impelled to show it to someone, and he showed it to me.

I was at Dorking with him after the funeral, and he suddenly came into the library with it in his hand. It was already a little worn with much re-reading. He looked at me with eyes that were distressed and perplexed.

"Billy," he said, "I want you to read this. I want you very much to read this. From her. After she died."

I was inclined to demur.

He pushed it into my hand. "Read it," he said, and again impatiently as he went out of the room, "*Read it.*"

A pencilled note, it was, but in firm, clear hand. Written without haste. Punctuated, so that one seemed to hear Minnie's characteristic little pauses for deliberation. No outpourings. No abandonment to her impulses, no confidence in her impulses. A skilful letter written carefully for a definite purpose.

It was Minnie come back to life. It was Minnie quintessentially. Except for one or two phrases at the end that stuck in my memory, I cannot remember much of its exact wording. I read it only once. But it was, I think, the tenderest of all imaginable caresses that she reached across the grave to give him. Like Minnie, like all of Minnie, it was faintly aloof from complete participation in life. Because it was faintly aloof it was also faintly insincere. Insincere, I mean, in the sense that she did not seem to believe completely even in her own life and death. But not in any egoistic sense insincere. She was not posing. She did not seem to be thinking about herself at all. She said not a word of any unwillingness to be torn untimely from life. So far as she was concerned, I feel she was capable of saying: "Have I to go, then? Very well, I am ready," even with the faint shadow of a smile upon her lips.

But Dickon in distress, Dickon left alone, big Dickon with his capacity for vivid remorse hiding a heartache, and with no possibility of a word to cure it, was another matter. That had got through to her as a real and dreadful possibility, and she had done her best with it.

"If I have to leave this queer, wonderful existence," she said, "I want you to know how happy you have made me in it."

That was the text of it, that was all she wrote about, the value he had given life for her. Nothing else.

I thought of many things between them. I saw for the first time as I read her letter with what comprehension she had understood his quality. I saw how well she knew him, and how she feared his easy and abundant remorse. She said nothing of any contentious things, harped upon no forgiving for the derelictions she must have known he had committed, but she said how happy and full she had found every hour with him, she reminded him of many kindnesses and generosities he had shown her, and of the great joint adventure of their worldly success. She recalled a score of little intimate delightful things, mostly from their early years, that she had treasured in her memory.

"The fun we have had, Dickon! The dear boys and Winnie! They were such fine and happy things to have launched into the world. And they get their brightness and courage, my dear, from you."

All things must end, she said, and if this was the end of this strange, lovely, difficult world for her – well, she was sorry to leave him, sorry indeed, but thankful for all she had had, and thankful to him.

"Dear Dickon, my own, be sorry – I know you will be sorry for the parting; but do not grieve, dear Dickon. Do not mind too much about things that never really mattered, do not mind about them. Think of the life that has been so good with you and not of the death at the end. Think of the work that lies before you and the big tasks you have to do. You are only beginning. I know there is endless work before you yet. I wish I could have watched you and stood beside you a little longer. Dickon, my *dear*, thank you and thank you and thank you... And again, dear Dickon, thank you and God bless you, and, if it must be, good-bye."

In that manner, in such words, it ended.

Dickon stood before me again and I gave him back the letter.

"You've read it?"

I nodded.

"Well... Tell me something... Was she really happy, Billy? Did I really make her happy? As she says I did?"

"Certain, Dickon."

"Then why should she doubt?"

"Doubt what?"

"About what I should feel. If she didn't think that perhaps I had seen that she – she wasn't quite as hard and happy as she braved it out she was. There were times – "

"You're tormenting yourself."

"But isn't she just saying those things – She may be just saying those things – Thinking of me... She did things like that. She couldn't bear – hurting. Anybody being hurt. She'd a kind of terror of anybody being hurt – or remorseful...

"You don't know, Billy, at times when I've been a bit disposed perhaps to be heavy-handed with the boys – how she's stood in...

"And the thought she had – for old servants. For people in trouble... I could tell you things... Noticing when an old housemaid wanted glasses. Feeling when people were overworked or burthened. Things like that. Always for going gently..."

He stared at me. "A man lives with a woman all his life, Billy. Eats with her, sleeps beside her. Happiness. Tears. Endless... And he doesn't know much about her. At the end, he doesn't know much about her."

"She loved you all right, Dickon. More than you deserved, old man. And you made her happy. I've watched her. She was a happy woman, proud of you, proud of the opportunities you gave her, proud of this house and life here – and content."

"But you know, Billy, and I know – I've been like most men..."

"So far above such things, Dickon," I said; "they never touched her."

"But many a time I must have been – a bit of a lump to her... A man's so much rougher and clumsier."

"She didn't feel it like that."

"Eh!" he said, and then for the first and last time in my life I saw my brother weep.

Never in our childhood and boyhood had I seen his tears, not even when our father died. But now he did not conceal his distress. "Tears won't bring her back," he said. "Not tears. Not wishing. Not repenting... Nothing will bring her back to me... Not for a word. Not for a moment – to tell her... *What could I tell her?*"

He went to the window and stood there with his back to me to hide his face.

"If I could be sure," he said. "If I could believe it! That I made her happy?"

He became quite still, an immense broad back against the park and the sky.

"Kindness," he whispered to the unresponsive heavens. "Kindness, tenderness, the years of it, from the beginning to the end... That quiet kindness."

He turned and addressed me – how can I put it? – as though I wasn't there.

"Nobody knew her but me," said Dickon. "Nobody knew anything about her really but me. Nothing at all. Nobody thought enough of her. Nobody had any idea. I've been her husband for thirty-one years, Billy – I've never found her lying to me or herself. And courage – I've never known her flinch. A little thing she was and she could look pain in the face. Take it as something one had to take. And when Dick was missing – that April! Three weeks we had of it and never a flicker because she had to stand by me. I just saw one day how white her face was. Or else I might have thought she didn't feel… But she felt…

"What a time that was!… Loyal! Strong! And I've let her be in the background. I've let it seem as though she wasn't anything so very much… didn't matter…

"Billy, I was silly to take that old title, but don't you see how desperately a man may feel that his wife ought to be honoured? Somehow. When she won't take any honour! So that he sticks tinsel on her – in desperation. She let me do it. She understood… My lady! Princess she was! Princess – with something cool and sweet. Like moonlight… Silver… All my days ought to have been gratitude…

"Oh, what *good* is it talking?"

He looked out of the window again and I could have imagined he was expecting a reply from the twilight.

"Silence," he said, at last.

## 12 – *Period of Reconstruction*

Was she a cynic? I think the answer is Yes. On that basic I can explain her but on no other. Hers was a cynicism fine as carved ivory, but it was cynicism. It had neither aggression nor insult in it, but for her I do really think that Virtue, as the Ancient Cynics meant it, and Freedom, were the only good things. She was as completely disillusioned about the pomps and vanities, the received values and accepted gratifications of the life we live as I, but in addition she was disillusioned, as I have never been, about the power of the life within us. She was weak in effort and she knew it. So she would not thrust out to blunder. She accepted. She accepted good and avoided evil. She thought fighting evil was itself an evil. It made one hot and angry. So one went by on the other side. She could not understand the sort of drive that achieves, even if it achieves blunderingly. She could not understand the "dust and heat" of endeavour.

Because of that way of thinking she came a little to underrate Dickon, I suspect, after his first glamour had faded. His infidelities, his urgencies, his sudden changes of direction, his excessive admirations of questionable leaders – of Lloyd George, of Milner, of Northcliffe, for example – his storms of combative energy that had to find an outlet and so often found a wrong one, were incomprehensible to her. Yet as that last letter showed, she kept an infinite kindliness for him to the end.

Dickon, as people say, "adored" her, and yet he never seemed to me perfectly self-forgetful and at his ease with her. Even if she did not underrate him, his tender conscience made him feel she ought to do so. He was capable of a good deal of expressive coarseness in his conversation, but in her presence he was always rather carefully decent. He never talked before her of his sincere enthusiasm for his calling. The rising tides of Advertisement broke and recoiled from the gates of Lambs Court. The best conversations I had with him during her life were away from her, and it is since her death that he seems to me to have developed most interestingly and boldly. Dickon was incapable of amateurism, and not only his life, but his whole view of life, had to centre upon his occupation. Even more than in my own case, his activities had to be related to the beginnings of things and the utmost star. But he felt her gentle irony at the gravity of his prolusions, her scepticism of the values in her drama, her recognition of his egoism. She was terribly, because so unconsciously and inevitably, a delicate lady, and not an actress upon the stage of life.

This contrast between them intensified as the years went on. At first he carried her with him much more than he did in their later years. He talked most of his thoughts to her. When he talked to her he could persuade her. Then, I think, he became shy of something passive in her assents. She approved, but she never came to meet him. He felt that in her presence his ideas became huge and clumsy, sweaty and crude – as new things must be crude, and that he forced them on her. So he ceased to force them on her. There is a vein of self-distrust deep in Dickon's nature.

His ascendency over me was established so early and so firmly in our student days that it only dawns upon me now that at times Dickon must have been sensitive to my opinions. Innovation, experimenting, "giving the things a try," were the quality of his life. He felt the risk in some of his views and acts. And she so manifestly favoured ripened and finished things, fine old furniture, works of art rather than works of science, polished conduct and acts as perfectly adjusted from their very inception as the muscles of a Persian kitten.

Dickon was greatly stirred by the war and by his own experience of the war. As I have told, he was attaching very broad ideas to advertisement even before the war. Propaganda was an immensely stimulating discovery for him. And the idea of Reconstruction after the war seized upon him, interwove with those expanding ideas about advertising, and for a time possessed him altogether.

The Period of Reconstruction is still only five or six years behind us, and already it is difficult to revive its emotions and expectations. Even more difficult is it to recall the mental states of the war.

We began with heroism and sacrifice. I shall insist to the end of my days that the last months of 1914 were a tragically splendid phase in European experience, months of high, heroic, terrified living for a great multitude of people. I do not think that so far as we English were concerned the war degenerated greatly until the latter part of 1916. Then with conscription the mirage of greatness vanished. Like a mirage its disappearance was imperceptible. One became aware that it had gone. The war was discovered to be a daily tale of stupid and beastly destruction, moral even more than physical.

And then it was that the clamour for Reconstruction became strong. All this bloodshed and waste was the agony in which a new and fairer world was to be born; the war was to end war and social injustice. This slaughter was the seed-time sacrifice from which we should reap the brotherhood of man.

In the years immediately after the war, with the frightful squalor and suffering, the fear, pain and stress, the atrocious wastage and tragic heroisms of the struggle fresh in our minds, it was a moral impossibility not to think that there must have been something more than mere destruction, mere warning, in this immense disaster; that somehow a price had been paid and a gain achieved. I suppose I am an exceptionally sceptical man, but I confess that was my conviction for some time. Only very slowly did I begin to accept the possibility that the abyss had swallowed up that enormous wealth of life, effort, and material accumulation, that it was gone for good, gone never to return, without recompense or consolation.

*Now* we can begin to face that monstrous verity. The war did no more for mankind than the Black Death or a forest fire. It solved nothing, inaugurated nothing. At best it swept away illusions. The Period of Reconstruction was the hectic death of one of the greatest of these; that good arises automatically out of suffering.

But while my resort to the consolation of the Reconstruction Period was at least temperate, Dickon's acquiescence in that idea of a comprehensive and forward movement in human conditions was passionate and complete. "A world fit for heroes," he reiterated. "Magnificent phrase, Billy! And it's alive. It will do things."

He did think it would do things. But what he thought it would do I still do not find very clear.

Across the seas came Woodrow Wilson, with that large, gaunt face of his, solemnly inscrutable, bringing his schoolboy essay in politics, his Fourteen Points. We knew nothing then of his vanity and narrowness nor of his limited authority. Nor did he. He seemed to promise the organisation of a world peace. Within the framework of security this ensured, there was to be a sort of voluntary collectivism. It was not to be Socialism we were assured – because a great number of influential people had declared they were not Socialists, and it would be embarrassing for them to contradict themselves – but it was to have the effect of Socialism. There were to be worldwide labour laws, health laws, protection of women and children, protection of races at a disadvantage, throughout all the planet. Just how it was to be done Dickon seemed to regard as an unimportant detail. He was too full of the spirit for any such particularisation. He would do his job of propaganda and preparation and the other fellows would do their jobs. In that magic word Reconstruction there was no really definite constructive idea at all, no taking apart and putting together again, but instead there was undeniably an enormous amount of what Americans call "uplift." Something was to be done, very large, very generous, very beneficial and splendid; and that was all it amounted to.

I write something was to be done, but now I come to consider it, I believe that what we really thought was that something was going to do itself. And we were to be its ministers and henchmen.

The Lytton Stracheys of 1990 or so many find in this Period of Reconstruction material for much amusing writing. My own failure to be thoroughly amused by it is due, I admit, to a want of humour. I am still too close to it and its immense, if irrational, disappointments. It was a movement of the extremest incoherence and inconsistency. Men full of undisciplined individualism were rushing about talking about collective effort and the subordination of every enterprise to social ends. Men of the rankest patriotism were rushing about talking of the League of Nations. Scheme for re-housing the people of London in great and admirable buildings in London jostled amicably with schemes for scattering the population of London over the countryside. Everywhere beautiful houses were promised for the populace, and nowhere did they appear. Also there was to be a great exportation of the unemployed to the Colonies. On scientific lines. And a colonisation of England that would render emigration unnecessary. There were to be wonderful new high-roads. London was to have a railway clearing-house and save incalculable acres of wasted building land. Civil air transport, moreover, was to make both roads and railways superfluous. Productivity at the touch of the new spirit of collective organisation was to leap up like a man who has sat on a wasp. Everything was to fetch a good stimulating price, but then wages would be enormous. Charing Cross bridge was to be rebuilt very gloriously as a war monument, and everybody was to go to school up to the age of sixteen. The output of blue prints must have been enormous in those wonderful days. The projects were upon every scale and with every amplitude of scope.

Entangled with a number of self-mobilised business men and jarring upon them every moment was a miscellany of young University "authorities," economists, sociologists, professors of political science, very convinced and guiding and empty; and there were temporary and permanent Civil Servants in the movement, all mysteriously devious with the devious discretion of men who have to think of their chiefs and their departments; and journalists and novelists turned statesmen, making generous vacant phrases for us in the utmost abundance; and inventors of this, that, and the other implement for altering human life completely; and so down to pure faddists and founts of richly printed matter with which one's letter-box was choked, beings who filled the souls of men of affairs with terror and contempt, and drove them back in panic from their new viewpoints to their old business ways.

And the moral hotch-potch was just the same as the intellectual. Mixed up with the entirely honest types like Dickon were the complicated and half-honest; and about these again a considerable crowd of adventurers who were not honest at all, who canted reconstruction and presently canted de-control, and whose one clearly apprehended reality in the pother was an opportunity to snatch. Some of them snatched amazing handfuls. Though perhaps it is not for me to complain of that, seeing the derelict Government undertakings that have fallen back into the hands of Romer, Steinhart, Crest and Co. and their associated enterprises.

## 13 – *The Abortive Spring*

Then there came a chill. There is a book of Tarde's called *Fragment d'histoire future*, which Mr Brereton has translated into English as *Underground Man.* It describes the unexpected extinction of the sun. A sudden extinction, like a gas-light being turned off. It is springtime in France, the almond blossom has come, the birds are nesting, people are going afield, when the catastrophe occurs. The sun rises already shorn of its radiance, cools to a red orb at midday, is dulled to a sullen coppery glow, and a snowstorm that grows thicker and thicker fills the air, driven before a cold and devastating wind. The young elder leaves, the almond petals whirl past and are forgotten. Everything is presently in flight for shelter and searching frantically under cover for fuel. The icicles gather along the eaves and fall clattering like broken glass before the freezing gale. The plants bud no more, the birds sing no more, a great darkness comes upon the world. Naturally those who have fuel cling to the fuel. The quicker-witted start for the coal-mines and begin to burrow down towards the central heat.

In much the same fashion did the hope of Reconstruction vanish from the sky. Peace conditions had returned and the phase of ready borrowing was at an end. The golden sun of credit veiled its countenance. A heavy ground swell in the European currencies gave place to a storm. The States had over-borrowed and mankind was collectively in debt.

Even during the war the belligerent States had rarely dared to take men's possessions outright. Lives and bodies they had taken freely and recklessly, handing over millions of men like cattle to their poor bluffing and blundering military chiefs to waste and torture as their fear and folly determined, but the property of men these Governments would not conscript. Because, you see, *human society is a labour-imposing, labour-shifting, property-money complex, and life, the more or less of it, only an unpremeditated by-product.* It ought not to be so, perhaps, but it is so. The human complex has grown in that fashion according to its nature, and it is not to be hastily and easily changed into some different play of relationships.

When they might have taken the warring Governments had bought, often at exorbitant prices, and they had borrowed to pay. The bills of these usuries were now being presented. Dickon and I and a number of others of us, business men first and money men afterwards, went to and fro in the year of the Versailles Conference, making a great noise about Reconstruction, putting heart, temporary heart, into a multitude of depressed people; and we no more realised what our real circumstances were than so many bumblebees in a roomful of spiders' webs. But as the grey filaments wrapped round us and wrapped round us, the note of our buzzing and booming changed. Only those who have hard and vivid memories know how much it changed. But it would be interesting to take a newspaper of the year 1918, let us say, and another of 1924, and count how often the words "Reconstruction" and "Debts" are to be found in each.

The era of Reconstruction faded out, with practically nothing to show for its enthusiasms; it gave place to the era of Debt-collecting and what is apparently a strained and painful attempt to restore the comparatively stable state of affairs that had prevailed in the three or four decades before 1914. Finance and the manipulation of money became the burden of life. The voice of the "constructive" business man died away; nobody wanted to hear it any more; he himself did not wish to hear it any more; and all the world watched the quiet whispering goings to and fro of the bankers and finance ministers.

But though debt and debt-collecting now dominated our thoughts, I do not think that the rapid evaporation of human hope was entirely due to the entanglements of finance. It was certainly not due to any plotting and scheming and foresight on the part of the financiers. No little, diabolically intelligent knot of men had waited at the centre of the threads and said, "Patience! Presently all these poor fools will be in our nets. Then we'll stop this nonsense of hope."

Finance is not a malignant conspiracy; it is only a malignant stupidity, a stupidity we all share actively or passively. It is a persistent, timid adherence to conventions and methods that cannot possibly work out beneficially for the mass of mankind. I have lived near and in business and finance for a large part of my life, and I here declare with the fullest deliberation that I do not believe there are any men of supreme intellectual quality, good men or bad men, now active in the world of finance. There are no doubt many very energetic and quick-witted men, but their acquisitive process is essentially automatic, arising out of the current methods of monetary issue and credit. Every human being alive is something of a toil-shifter, and happier in getting than in yielding; most human beings have, in addition, a sneaking craving for power and precedence over their fellows, and the weakness of the system are found out by the pressure of these common tendencies, quite mechanically, just as the weaknesses of an embankment are found out by the weight of every particle of water it restrains.

Dickon, as he saw his dream of heroic Reconstruction stained and crumpled and spoilt and defeated, was disposed to be very fierce about the Money Power. He would talk of the Money Power throttling the Productive Power, and assert that at last all great combinations of industrial plant fell into the uncreative grip of the banks. He deplored his share in popularising loans when he ought, he now declared, to have been explaining and steadying the country under the "conscription of wealth." But I was never with him in that direct antagonism between money and productive organisation. Finance, I agreed, had sewn up the world in a shroud of debts, but it did that almost as innocently as a blow-fly lays eggs in a carcass. Without a carcass a blow-fly is a merely secondary nuisance easily driven away. When you end litter you abolish flies. Had there been sufficient constructive will and knowledge in the world it would have made short work of that web of debts, that enslavement of the world to the counting-house.

It became very plain to me as things went on that Dickon and I were impractically vague in our intentions. Yet we two were among the more clear-headed and capable of the active hopes of the Reconstruction movement. He had considerable prestige as a propagandist. I was a successful industrial organiser. Until we came to this test we had neither of us realised that in practical affairs we were mere fortunate amateurs following the inertias of our early successes, and no longer in the habit of solving novel problems. We were two samples of a body of perhaps a few hundred, or at most a few thousand, would-be Reconstructors. All of us, individually and collectively, were entirely inadequate to the task we imagined we were attempting. Opportunity gleamed upon us suddenly and found us unprepared – and passed.

How shallow was our conception of Reconstruction! – was every conception of Reconstruction I ever encountered! To most of the hopeful people of that time Reconstruction meant simply – all they wanted – at once. Labour, for example, demanded an immediate shortening of hours and a rise in wages, and was blind to any necessity for intermediate phases or auxiliary constructive effort. In England, trade after trade struck vigorously, and got its advances, its eight hours' day, and crowded off at once to see the cinemas and football matches, leaving the working-out of the Millennium to anyone else who chose to bother. Nobody chose to bother.

I do not blame labour; it acted according to its nature, just as the creditors and investors acted according to their nature; but the Reconstruction collapse was, I think, brought to a crisis quite as much by the failure of labour to understand as by any exactions and obstructions of finance. Neither the unhelpfulness of labour nor of finance was the primary factor. The primary factor was that the organising and administrative people like Dickon and myself, men of concrete affairs as we professed to be, men who ought to have known if anyone did, how to set about reconstructing things, were caught without a scheme of action – without the ghost of a scheme of action. We had no sense nor measure of what was happening to us and the world. We ought to have known that labour would be obdurate, and finance insist upon its pound of flesh at any cost to the body politic. Labour always has been and always will be unwilling, and creditors will cling to their claims and have to be dispossessed as firmly if as gently as possible, to the very end of human existence.

We learnt our measure in those days. We were as planless as the Bolsheviks in Russia. We were planless for exactly the same reason – because there never had been any plan. There is no plan. There is no Capitalist plan; there is no Communist plan. There is no plan at all. We have traditions and usages on which we innovate timidly, and they have the claptrap of Marx and Lenin. Both capitalists in the West and the Bolsheviks in Russia extemporise and experiment – with an air of knowing all about what they are doing. We big business men had seemed to be running the economic system in Britain, but, put to the trial, we showed we had no power over it at all. Things had happened and we had happened in consequence.

I do not see that we Western Reconstructors have much excuse for looking down upon the Bolsheviks on the score of failure. They failed to reconstruct from the ground upward amidst the ruins of Russia, and they had a very bad famine and a series of foreign raids to complicate the job for them. We in a shattered and impoverished England failed just as much as they did. But since everything was smashed in Russia before they took on the attempt at reconstruction, their failure showed starkly. In the West nothing was smashed, although everything was strained, and the social and economic inertias carried us through. Our gestures and essays in reconstruction were swept aside by the virtual resumption of the old order, and there was no open revalation of futility. In March, 1925, under Mr Baldwin – we seem almost back in March, 1914. The difference between the failure of the constructive spirit in Russia and in the West was the difference between a man on a desert island where there is nothing to eat and a man on a walking tour in France who finds he has forgotten to put food in his knapsack. Both may have intended to be self-sufficient, but the former starves, the latter takes refuge in an inn and says no more about it. He eats his dinner and reads of the other fellow's death with a feeling of superiority. But the money with which he pays may be borrowed money, and financially his balance-sheet may be even worse than that of the dead man. Debt is not so bad a thing as death, but it lies in the same direction. It is a parallel road to frustration.

There was no plan and there is no plan. When the restless, enquiring minds among us have worked out the broad lines of a plan – and that is being done now, and in a generation or so it will be sufficiently worked out – when we have painted and established upon the screen of the future the realities of human possibility in terms that will convince and compel, then the real Age of Reconstruction will have begun, and this queer phase of hope and insufficiency that came to mankind in the beginning of the age of confusion that followed the great war, will be recognised as the first uneasy stirrings of the sleeping world-state before its conclusive awakening.

### 14 – *Northcliffe as Hero*

Looking back at it now, as it settles itself into the general perspective view of our lives. I see that this effort, this disappointment of the Reconstruction Period and the reaction that followed, was a cardinal phase both for Dickon and myself; a being born again or – a better image perhaps – coming-of-age. It is easier for me to see the change that happened to Dickon than to trace it in my own case. So far as one's own self is concerned, when one gains new perspectives and gets one's conception of thing expanded and cleared, the new vision is apt to swallow up the old, and so one forgets one's earlier limitations. But I remember Dickon before the war as fragmentary and dogmatic and instinctive, in comparison with his more recent self. He took the world for granted then, he took it as established and in all its broader aspects beyond his control. The stress, excitement, hope, and frustrations of the last ten years have pulled him together.

Before the war I was a revolutionary, a theoretical revolutionary, decidedly unreal and amateurish in my views, and he was not. My insistence upon change and the need to change, such as it was before the war, he was always putting aside until tomorrow. It was interesting but impracticable; it was Utopian; he lived for the world as it was. But after the reconstruction effort, and particularly after the death of Minnie, he changed – almost fundamentally. The world had hitherto been open to criticism indeed, but good enough for him. He could still take a baronetcy in 1919. He is no longer like that.

The war was the beginning of this new birth, but like so many violent accidents, its real quality and consequences were masked by the immediate shock. Even now they are only beginning to come through.

It is curious how irrelevant the actual details of the war seem to be now, and how enormous the effects we begin to realise. I could tell a hundred stories of the war, of our special productions, of hunts for raw material, of ingenious substitutions, of our tragic explosion at Lembury, of our replacement of men by women workers, and how good the first lot were and how bad all the others, of the spies we suspected and the spies we had, of our poison-gas work, and of how we sank a hundred tons of that filth in the North Sea after the war was all over, because there was nothing else to do with it – stories interesting enough in themselves but of no wide significance in my world now, even to me.

Nor do the accounts of the air-raids we stood, the persistent attempts of the German raiders to localise our works and particularly the plant at Downs-Peabody, seem to matter very much now. One moonlit night of crashes and vast silences, in a wide empty street near Victoria, I came upon a man clinging to a railing and mooing like a cow, and his intestines protruded from his waistcoat; he had just been torn open by anti-aircraft shrapnel; I made up a bed for him with some cushions I borrowed and went off into the wilderness of Pimlico to find an ambulance, and when I got back he had disappeared and nobody knew what had become of him – or the cushions; I had to pay for the cushions; and I was dining not a hundred yards from Buckingham Palace with Stetson during an air-raid when a naval shell, which happily proved a dud, I suppose from some boat in the Thames, danced in from somewhere at the back, made a vast smash of falling brickwork and broken window-frames, and came to rest among the hats and umbrellas in the hall without injuring a soul; but these things are now like something seen in a show or dreamt or read about. They join on to nothing. They are like travel snap-shots or like the promiscuous collections of picture postcards my nephew Dick used to make when he was a very little boy. They call for no more than a passing allusion here. What is of infinitely more moment is the revelation that they brought home to us of the undirected instability of the world's affairs, the realisation that we were not mere passengers but as much responsible navigators upon the ship of human destiny as anyone.

In the winter of 1920 Dickon and I had a long discussion. We had indeed several, we were much together at that time, but it will suit my purpose best to concentrate the substance of it all into one conversation. It crystallised out a number of ideas that I had had in solution for some time. That week or so of discussion marks the establishment of the new phase, the definitive phase, of our attitude of life. I find as I recall it, already well in evidence, the embryonic but recognisable from of that revolutionary project which it is the main object of this book to state, and to which I shall come after our own story has been sufficiently told.

It was influenza that had thrown us so much together, and fever maybe quickened our ideas. It was in the early days of the Bordon Street Chambers. Deland, to whom we were a great find, could not do enough for us. The influenza of that year was rather more feverish and bronchial than the current one and a little more prone to unfavourable developments. Deland would permit us to take no risks. We sat indoors of an evening, and before us was a big copper kettle steaming on a bright coal fire. We had screens about us, screens that Deland had insisted upon, and we drank hot whisky and Dickon opened his thoughts to me abundantly and frankly.

He certainly said or implied most of the things I am now going to make him say.

I remember him sitting in the low armchair, in a blue dressing-gown under a shaded light, that made his head by contrast look like a great orange, ruffled by eyebrows and split by a smiling mouth below, and with the unusual trick of producing two level blue eyes from below the eyebrows at salient points of the conversation, and I remember, too, that he grunted more than usually when he moved. At his elbow Deland had put a low table and the tray and all our convivial material. And his discourse, which arose out of his complete admission of the failure of the Reconstruction Movement, went in this fashion:

"Addison" – Dr Addison was the Minister of Health then – "won't get his half-million new houses; he won't get sixty thousand, and Fisher" – the Right Honourable H A L Fisher was to have been the great light of a better education – "won't get the school-leaving age raised to sixteen. That's all as dead as mutton now, Billy. Addison may make some sort of fight for it, but it won't be any good, and Fisher will let it go because he's that sort of a chap. Then it's ages since we heard a word about that State-controlled milk-trade which was going to save ten thousand babies a year, and your people and people like you are going to take over those national factories that Chiozza Money said inaugurated a new economic system, take them over at scrapping prices, and run them on strictly profiteering lines. Oh! I've been watching you, Billy. Well, perhaps not strictly profiteering. Business lines. I've been watching you and I've been watching

Brampsheet follow his nose. What a nose he has! And it's true there's no one else to run them. No one. But the mines are different. That's not true about the mines. Nothing is going to be done about the mines either. That's a clear miss. The mine-owners are mucking along in the dear old fashion in spite of the Sankey Report – and elementary common sense. Public health is as you were, or a bit worse, and nobody will get anything much done except the money-bugs. And so we go on. Reconstruction was quack medicine, and Lloyd George is a liar, and here we are bilked and done."

"And men of our age," I probably remarked, "ought never to have believed that anything else was possible."

Dickon reflected over his tray.

"And yet, for all that, there is a lot in this idea of Reconstruction," he said. "I've acquired that idea of Reconstruction for good. It's like being vaccinated."

Some sound of guarded assent from me.

"Bigger job than we thought it was," said Dickon, shaving delicately at the lemon peel with the razor Deland had brought for the purpose.

"We aren't going to make over this old muddle of a world yet for a bit," he said, and cut a translucent slice and rejected a pip fastidiously. "I shall leave you to put the sugar, Billy… No… But it's been a lesson."

He completed his duties as host.

He made a compelling gesture toward me with the open razor to hold my attention until he began. Then he composed himself to talk.

"I perceive, Billy, that this little old world of ours has been ready and asking for a revolution, a complete and through revolution, for three years. Three years. Since about the middle of 1918. The market was ready, the demand there – and no supply. What has been missing has been somebody to know what was wanted and able to produce it. The world had its mouth open. It was scared tame. Lord! Billy, how funny all this is really. The expectation! The result! That solemn goose of a Wilson laying his addled egg in Paris. Day by day, each day a little more of it out. Mankind awe-stricken. Go on, Great President! Go on! And the Bolsheviks – Not even an egg – "

He sought for an image.

"Making a mess," I suggested hastily.

"Making a mess – a little weak mess – in the middle of the remain of Russia."

He shook his head at the fire. "Tremendous pause. Mankind puzzled. 'That is all, gentleman. No, there is nothing more; nothing more at all!' And then presently the old things, the dreary things, the slow and pompous things, the shams, the vested interests and the ancient rights, the kings that mean nothing and the uniforms that mean nothing, come crawling out of their shelters and hiding-places, scarcely able to believe they are still alive. As they are, Billy. As they are!"

"Yet there *was* that pause," said Dickon. "There was a time when the door stood open."

He surveyed history at large. "I suppose there never has been much imaginative greatness in the handling of human affairs. The greatest of men is still an ape – what was it? – imperfectly depiled.' Good phrase that! All damned nonsense about the dignity of history. Dignity hasn't begun yet. We've had great figures stuck up for us. Caesar and Marcus Aurelius. Really no better than Winston or Wilson. It's always been this sort of thing really – or worse?"

Dickon returned to his main discovery. "These have been extraordinary years. If there had been a clear project ready and men to put it over, it could have been put over. It was the psychological moment for a great change... I for one thought there was going to be a really great change. A new age. Here and now, Billy... We seemed to see the promised land. And now, where is it?"

"But isn't there something still to be done?"

"I don't know," said Dickon, and added – though he poised the name in his hand – "there's Northcliffe."

"Northcliffe!" said I, and sat amazed.

Then I reflected that Dickon saw all the universe through a haze of publicity. Hadn't he called the temples of the world God's advertisements?

He began to talk about that great newspaper adventurer in tones of affectionate perplexity. In some obscure extensive way outside my sympathies, Northcliffe had taken a very steady grip upon Dickon's imagination. He had become more than himself for Dickon; he had become a symbol for forces Dickon partly apprehended and partly hoped for in the world about us. He spoke of the "New Men," the "New Adventurers," and at a scrutiny of these phrases he always fell back on Northcliffe. Northcliffe was still the master of *The Times* then and of a powerful group of newspapers, but for a year or so he had been making a poor figure in the world's eyes on account of his concentration upon a bitter personal feud between himself and Lloyd George. This after clambering courageously through a phase of great unpopularity to a commanding influence in national affairs. His war services had been enormous and on the whole sound. There was a story that Lloyd George had led him to hope he might go to the Versailles Conference and had then disappointed him. At any rate, Northcliffe had behaved like one who had been stung by an intolerable treachery. For a time his conspicuous vindictive resentment had robbed him of largeness of effect. It had disappointed and estranged many who like Dickon had hoped for great things from him. But Dickon stuck to him. "He is a big man," said Dickon stoutly, "he is a big man."

Northcliffe, said Dickon, had never known what a big man he was going to be until his greatness was upon him. Opportunity had taken him by surprise. As it takes most successes nowadays by surprise. He had found himself powerful before he had time to turn round and realise what he wanted to do.

"That's more or less the history of all our sort," said Dickon. "We strive with all our little mights – just to get freedom, just to get out of the ruck – and what we thought was a wall of stone and iron turns out to be cardboard and *phut* it goes, and we find ourselves right through, with power in our hands and nothing in the whole universe between us and the ironical eye of God."

"Mr G," I said.

"God I mean in this case," said Dickon.

He sketched out the adventure of the Harmsworths. The father was an Irish barrister who had come to London and been called to the English Bar, and who had died before success could be won there. He seems to have been an able man who died too soon, with a restless, ambitious, stimulating home and a wise, strong, patient wife. His chief delight, I have been told, was to speechify in a mock Parliament in some Camden Town tavern. From that he hoped perhaps to clamber to the other mockery at Westminster. Alfred, the son, went to a little private school in St John's Wood, and began a journalistic career with a jelly-graphed school magazine. The schoolmaster knew how to seize an aptitude and develop it, and he promoted Harmsworth's purple smudging to the dignity of print and periodicity.

"I've seen some numbers," said Dickon. "It was pretty common stuff; cricket scores and school news and so forth. Northcliffe never wrote a distinguished line in his life… Well – writing distinguished lines isn't – everything. Though, of course, it helps."

While still in his teens, young Harmsworth launched out with a weekly paper called *Answers*. Then came some awful things for errand boys and the cheapest public, *Comic Cuts*, that crying outrage. "Great money makers, I'm told," said Dickon.

The *Daily Mail* followed and was a brilliant success. The world become aware of a personality different from the ordinary newspaper personality, an influence and an energy. Then came opportunity, and this Harmsworth of *Comic Cuts* secured a controlling interest in *The Times* and became a power, presently a very considerable power. The peerages of himself and his brother were formal recognitions of his substantial success. Northcliffe and Rothermere became the golden flowers on the stem of Harmsworth Brothers. He pushed forward to something like a commanding position in the country among the uncertainties, hesitations, and novel occasions of the war.

"It makes our little rush up look quiet a gentle ascent," said Dickon.

Dickon had become associated with Northcliffe during his propaganda activities. There was a real liking between them. "He's got imagination, real imagination, the quality that makes a great man, Billy; almost the only man he is with a touch of greatness in our public affairs. The only one."

"You don't think there's something great about such a type as Arthur Balfour?" said I.

"That damned Madonna lily!" said Dickon. "He grows where he's planted," and came back without further comment to Northcliffe.

"He knows that we are a new sort of men, and that this is an age of new things. He knows there is the possibility of great reconstructions in the air. He's not clear about it, but he feels it. He's alive to it. He's not afraid to change the world. That's what makes him signify, Billy."

Dickon gave me a little vignette of Northcliffe and himself sitting in a room in Crewe House, a fine town house of the old régime that had been requisitioned for propaganda headquarters against the Austrians and Germans, an easy spacious town house with a garden of its own up behind Shepherd's Market in the heart of the West-end, full of eighteenth-century dignity and eighteenth-century furniture. "They talk of revolutions," Northcliffe had remarked in that soft whispering voice of his. "Our being here *is* a revolution."

"That," said Dickon, "is Northcliffe near his top note. A bit exalted. None the worse for that. But seeing things. Seeing changes. Seeing forces."

He leant forward, poked the fire, and spread his amplitude before the blaze. "In a sense," said Dickon, "it was true. In a sense – it was nonsense."

"Potential revolution," said Dickon. "There I agree."

He frowned; he shook his elder-brother finger at me and frowned. "There is something wrong about Northcliffe, Billy. Something grotesque and tragic. Like a string that jerks him back."

The man, he said, had moods, alternations of moods that went beyond the limits of sanity. At times he had to go away and hide from everything. He would fly off to his wonderful old mother at Totteridge. His brother, his secretaries and subordinates took charge. Dickon knew of these dark interludes already three years before Northcliffe died insane. But all through Northcliffe's life was a succession of moods and phases – vast inequalities. His boldness, his vision, seemed to come in phases and vanish again. Sometimes he had the assurance of immense power – "and it's there for his using," said Dickon – and at others he was just vain and empty, in the air, "posturing or frightened, fat and frightened, and no sort of good at all."

Dickon shrugged his shoulders. "And there you have – in his hands – with no one really able to control him, a gigantic Publicity, the supreme power still in modern life. Yes, Billy, there is no power now, none in all the world, like the power to speak plainly and uninterruptedly to the crowd. My God! The power he and the other big newspaper people could exercise even now, if they chose to take it up and use it. Even now – still – today – the empire and the world are absolutely in the hands of the big press owners and the new men they ought to work with. This is their time of opportunity. The situation stiffens; if stiffens every day, but it hasn't congealed yet. There may be years yet before it has completely congealed."

A note of lamentation crept into his voice. "Not twenty men," he said. "And nine-tenths of the British newspaper sales in their hands. And all concentrated in London, not scattered like the American papers in a score of places. They might march this country wherever they chose and the rest of the world would follow. If they had the dignity of their power. Who could stop them? How could you stop them?"

But they drifted. They achieved nothing except great, clumsy, overwhelming fortunes. Opportunity was a touchy visitor if you didn't go down at once to receive her. Northcliffe felt that, but the others didn't. That was where he was different.

I suggested that Dickon overestimated the strength of these newspaper proprietors. They would lose circulation at once if they tried to put big things over. Dickon was convinced they would not. "The public likes initiative," he dogmatised. "Wants it. And besides, altogether, they control the paper supply and distribution. And there's still no one yet with the courage and decision to stand up against them if they chose to begin!"

And even if the public didn't like them it would have to stand them, now. Who would they lose circulation *to*? The public must have some sort of paper. No other sort of paper was possible at the present time. These press barons had the power surely enough. But they had no common idea. They had no idea of themselves. And the power slipped away from them. It was like the moment when Wat Tyler, the Kentish rebel, was killed. The crowd stood irresolute. There was the Press, as the prince had been, mounted and in full view, capable of saying what it chose to say and take control. And there it was with nothing to say – exposed in that expectant silence.

"These men," he remarked, "came up by being new. If they stop being new, they fall back into a position of subordination to the old gang, and cease to matter. They amalgamate with the old crowd and are lost... They don't know their opportunities. They are afraid of their opportunities. Too big for them... Except possibly Northcliffe. I'm not so sure of Northcliffe."

Dickon made a gesture of despair and dismissal, with a glass that was fortunately nearly empty.

"They could say what they like," he said, "even now. The whole world still listens for an idea."

He went on to a general review, an irritated, exaggerated, influenza-touched review, of what he called the new forces in English affairs: "The men like us." Those new forces had never realised their quality and their outlook. That was our trouble. No mental synthesis, no clear understanding, was there.

I give Dickon's views as well as I can. They are not precisely my views, but they are the brothers of my views. He saw things from the angle of a great advertiser, he overvalued the conspicuous, and his choice of new men was very different from mine. But I do not remember that I argued with him that night. I let him cite his own cases.

Lloyd George, Dickon insisted, was one of the "new forces." In 1920, certainly, he was still a very big figure. "In politics he's just what I am in advertisement, and Northcliffe is in journalism, and you in metallurgy – a new sort of man with new scale methods." None of us could have existed in 1880, neither Lloyd George nor Northcliffe, nor ourselves, nor any of the prominent men of the day under sixty. Asquith and Balfour and Grey were by comparison just dignified statesmen in the Victorian tradition. They had learnt to be British statesmen at the

Universities under the best tutors. They were incapable of freshness or adaptation. "Locums," said Dickon. They had been pushed aside for a time, and all their type and tradition could still be thrust aside. Thrust aside for good. An active figure like Lloyd George made them look like historical monuments.

But in Lloyd George also there was something that made for futility. "He's just a magnificent weed. In flower. Where one might have a great tree. He lives from hand to mouth. He's as clever as six foxes. Sane – too sane. Meanly sane. What's the matter with him? Just the opposite of Northcliffe. No end of cool, clear brains, but they don't seem to be in the right place or the right way up, or something. No length of vision. No imaginative warmth. There Northcliffe has the pull of him. And Lloyd George can't wait. You must have long views before you can wait. Temperamentally he can't wait. And he's broken with Northcliffe. He ought to have let Northcliffe take a hand in the Government and sent him to Paris. It might have changed the course of history if Northcliffe had gone to Paris.

"But, of course, the Paris show was too big a temptation for George, just as it was too big a temptation for Wilson.

"And here we are!" said Dickon.

He passed the other great powers of the British newspaper world in review and dismissed them all. Imaginative insufficiency. They could do so much if they chose. And they did not choose.

"Riddell – a clever man. A cynic. Laughs at his peerage. What is he after in life? Beaverbrook? He has as much brains and imagination as anyone. But – he's impish." Where Northcliffe was disposed to be grandiose. "Northcliffe," said Dickon again, "that's the *big* man." Beaverbrook was devoted to Bonar Law – they came from the same Canadian village, Dickon believed – and he meant to make his friend Prime Minister. "Possibly he will. And beyond that, so far as I can see, he regards the world as a playground, and isn't quiet sure of his fun. Eager, feverishly eager, to be all alive, and no idea what life is. Will he ever grow up? If he grew up… He's young still."

Dickon turned away from that.

Lord Burnham of the *Daily Telegraph* was a good sort, with a greater sense of public obligation than the others. But no inner light, no drive, and no desire. His idea of a newspaper, a pillar instead of a power.

"Lords of Journalism," said Dickon. "Newspaper nobles."

Scott of the *Manchester Guardian* was a star apart. "But you can't do very much as a star apart," said Dickon. "Twinkling is good enough for him. He doesn't *want* to do." The *Manchester Guardian* and the *Corriere della Sera* of Milan were after their fashion the two finest newspaper in the world, but anything might happen to them at any time because of their isolation. So Dickon prophesied in 1920. For the *Corriere* now it is prophecy no longer.

Dickon sees as drama what I see as process. He sees it as a drama of publicity. What is not seen and known by the public is not reality for him. That night he reviewed our political world entirely as a display of these newspaper adventurers and "new men" of his – Lord Birkenhead, with his careless freedom of word and act, and Lord Reading, who was Rufus Isaacs, almost as "new" in type, he held, as Lloyd George or Northcliffe – and he declared that only a realisation of their common interest in a boldly reconstructed political and social order could prolong and stabilise their adventure. The old things were biding their time, reaction impended, and these new men were attacking and undermining each other, doing nothing revolutionary, and letting the weeks and months slip by. They did not seem to think they had anything to fear from the old conservatives. "Wait," said Dickon. "I've seen and heard a thing or two."

He made me realise the latent power of what he called the "old gang" in things British and American, less audible, less brilliant, slow and tenacious, the old gang of long-established property, of banking and rent, the implacable gold standard and the unwearying creditor, the old gang who want nothing more to happen for ever. He made an acute guess that found its confirmation in the General Election of 1924, when almost all the residue of his "new men," battling one against the other, were swept away or driven into secondary positions. The chill of the coming day when Mr Asquith would become an earl and a Knight of the Garter, Lord Birkenhead a minister-journalist, and Lloyd George a comparative nobody was upon him. Though he foresaw the coming phase of reaction, he was not yet reconciled to its inevitability. He still clung doubtfully to his hero, Northcliffe, a loyalty that was so soon to be shattered by a pitiful death.

### 15 – *Advertisement for a New Sort of Man*

The fever and the whisky and the whisky and the quinine that were working together in Dickon's blood that night seemed only to give his mind a wider sweep. He generalised with unusual freedom. He expanded his discourse upon British affairs, until it became an exposition of a worldwide struggle to remake. He saw that struggle everywhere as a triangular conflict. First there were these "new men" of his, the Sons of Light, still uncertain in their quality; and next there were the "haves," the holders, the creditors, the financiers, the antagonists weaving the nets about these extraordinary Sons of Light he had chosen; and thirdly there were the "have-nots," labour that would not labour, that did not want anything that anybody else wanted, but did not know what it wanted, the retrogressive obstruction, the massive veto, the eating, breeding crowd.

We two had grown up in an age of rapid progress, and we were too much disposed to take progressive change as the natural order of the world. We were only beginning to realise that the rush of progress had brought also a stimulation of the defensive, a strengthening of the resistances that protected established things. The forces that had been disturbing and enlarging the scale of human affairs of four or five generations might have exhausted themselves in the catastrophe of the Great War. "Crashed," said Dickon. It was an unpalatable line of thought for him, but he followed it manfully for some time. The owner was resuming his loosened grip everywhere; the creditor was recovering from his earlier dismay and confusion, and there was no residue of creative force to resist his return.

Perhaps we were in for a phase first of stagnation and then of retrogression. It was, yes, it was possible. It might last as long as the forward rush and undo much of its achievement. The conservative forces wanted, indeed, only to fix and retain; they were as unwilling to go back as to go forward, but you cannot fix and retain without stagnation, you cannot have stagnation without decay, and you cannot have decay without disorder. For a while Dickon was morbid. Life asserts itself in the unused organ as putrefaction or cancer. Decay meant conflict even more certainly than did such an excess of energy as had led to the Great War. But the conflicts of a phase of decay had not even breadth of motive. The creditor, the property-owner, might avert the confiscations of a creative revolution, but at the price of reviving the brigand. "That begins already in Italy," said Dickon. China, India, had passed through "ages of confusion." Why should not our Western world do the like? Why should there be any recovery at all in human affairs?

But this was too depressing for Dickon's temperament. I have never known him keep a purely pessimistic poise for long, and presently he was saying that the real age of Reconstruction – which he had tacitly restored to the scheme of things – might still be centuries away. To talk of the world not really going forward was for him just talking; it signified nothing at all – a polite gesture to the insanities of possibility. Wasn't he himself going forward?...

He sat staring into the glowing coals.

The influenza germ reasserted itself.

"Unless you have men to tell people how things stand and what they have to do – " he said, and broke off.

"Where are the other men to be looked for?" he said. "Where shall we find the new forces? Perhaps this is naturally a conservative and creditor country. But – for example – America?"

He returned to his main hope. "Northcliffe is talking of going round the world," he said. "I wonder if he will. He seems to have this same feeling we have that a big reconstruction is due. Somewhere that isn't perhaps London or England. He wants to look for it. He talks of greater Britain, of the Empire. I wonder if that's it. I wonder what he will find if he does go round the world. I wonder what he expects to find. Banquets he will get everywhere. Flattery. An immense publicity. No rest. No thought. But his instinct is sound. That man, Billy, is like a big lonely wasp at a grocer's window-pane. He knows there is something important to him behind it, but he doesn't seem able to get through. He tries to find a way. Perhaps he will never get through."

He never did get through. Two years later that poor giant with the feet of clay, that great vulgar man of energy whom Dickon had idealised to the level of genius, went round the world even as he had proposed. His progress is to be found recorded with a straining amplitude in the files of his *Times*, and as he journeyed his exorbitant brain glowed and became more and more confused. The problem was too vast for him, he was too utterly uneducated, he staggered with a fundamental instability. His desire to do great things in the world gave place to alternations of childish grandeur and frantic suspicion. The little folks about him whispered and soothed him and tried to put as seemly a face as possible upon the dismal business, and then presently, close home again in Germany, suddenly he became hopelessly mad and violent and was overcome and restrained and passed altogether out of the comity of men.

I doubt the reach and power of imagination that Dickon ascribed to him. But I agree that there was greatness in him and that his story is a tragic one and his destruction a loss to the world. And I agree, too, that he did embody forces that are still operating largely about us.

From his exposition of Northcliffe, Dickon began in a large febrile way to seek through all our world for what he called "creative far-reaching men." The world needed them; the world was ripe for them; these "new men" of today were only the precursors of the men who had to come. To him it seemed essential that they should appeal to a great multitude of hearers, be audible to the ends of the earth. Until a thing had been put through to the multitude and had taken hold of the multitude, it had not, from his point of view, been done. From the very nature of the case it was manifest that the primary thing in the career of these redeeming advertisers would be that we should know about them. And we did not know about them.

For a time he discussed the American publicity people and such great newspaper men as Hearst and the Pulitzers. From that he spread out upon a general comparison of English and American. "I've met Hearst," he said, "as often as I've met Rothermere; I've spent days with both the Pulitzers, and do I begin to know anything about them? No. I've not the faintest idea of what they are up to, or what they *think* they are up to. Billy, why are Americans, all Americans, Americans without exception, such mysteries to us? European race. More often than not *our* race. Our language. Conditions after all very like ours. A bigger country, of course. A different pace. Difference of phase.

But while you seem to get Englishmen and Frenchmen all round and through and through, half an American is in a loud glare and the other half is darkness. It's like seeing things by the beam of a searchlight after you have been seeing them in a light that is soft and grey and generally diffused.

"That's it, perhaps, Billy. A profound difference in their publicity, using publicity in its widest sense. From the way that a child gets looked at and talked about, onward. They're lit up differently, inside and out. And what is life but a consequence of illumination? When you go to America and see headlines and interviews with a girl about her engagement, or with a professor about his resignation, you at first say, 'Good God. There's no privacy here at all!' And then you discover that outside that crude, cheap, hasty, flat misleading lighting-up of salient objects and events, there's abysses of darkness, immense pits where much goes on and nothing is exposed – and people, rich people especially, unobserved in them and doing the most extraordinary things.

"In Europe a man may have a private life, yes, but in America he has a secret life, lit by sudden shouting judgments and flashes of journalistic lighting. In which you get an impression – vivid enough but wrong. Things about him that would be plain here are invisible there, even to himself. And other things come out with a kind of scream, all out of proportion by our standards. It's because of that, Billy, that to our European senses Americans never seem quite real. The quality of the exposure, the method of illumination to which they have had to adapt themselves, account for nearly everything between us. That sort of watchful reserve they have, mixed up with a desire to make general, over-simplified explanations of themselves. The queerness of these greyish-faced, slow-speaking Americans in grey, who watch your face as they talk to you! If the searchlight jumps round upon them they are ready all the time. They talk about themselves as we never do. They try and hide their nakedness behind autobiographical statements. They instance themselves as types. They snatch suddenly at your verdict upon them. They have none of our sense of sustained scrutinies and slowly maturing judgments; none at all."

Was there any such gathering and influential body of men and women in America set upon Reconstruction as we two were set upon Reconstruction?

"Allowing for all the differences in pace and phase," he said, "the fact remains that we and they are going along the same road in the same direction." The need for a great reconstruction was common now to all the world; there were only these differences in phase. Business had grown there faster and bigger than it had grown here, and their banking was rapidly overshadowing ours. They were bound to lead the world's affairs for a time. But how far were they able to keep the lead or do anything with it?

He sized up the prospects of a world under American leadership. Where the Americans producing an American mind that would be large-thinking and powerful enough for the whole world? In certain things they were broader-minded than Europeans. The United States had always been more curious and intelligent about China and Eastern Asia, for example, and more restrained in its imperialism. It had been far ahead of the European intelligence in its grasp of the importance of a properly regulated currency and credit system to economic life. It had got currency into politics long before Europe suspected there was such a thing as a currency riddle. But, nevertheless, it was – shallow. All its energy – and its energy was tremendous – seemed to be on the surface. Woodrow Wilson was typical of the American quality that perplexed us. The idea of some great settlement of world affairs, some world peace organisation, was magnificent. Quite beyond the scope of the European outlook or the compass of European statesmanship. One saw the United

States leading the world into a new age. Then for the realisation of that vision, the Fourteen Points, as trite and superficial as a magazine article.

And after that – America the Creditor.

"And while we sit here asking, 'Can the Americans develop a world mind and lead the world?' there may be just such another pair of brothers as we are, Billy, in Indianapolis or Chicago saying, 'Why don't the Europeans show a sign of a world mind?' I believe our sort of ideas are fermenting in the world everywhere. We're not such original chaps as to be very far from the general trail. What brings us here will bring others here. And Americans most of all...

"It's just that we don't know about them. They aren't talking yet...

"This new reconstructed world, Billy, is like a big dragonfly jerking itself bit by bit out of its larval skin. Jerking and then resting. It's wet and quiet just now, a little disposed to quiver, making no noise, but it's nearly here; it's almost out; it's coming on."

"And presently, all at once, it will spread out its wings and buzz," I said.

"And then we shall know about it."

He looked at me with that queer experimental expression of his, like a small boy who has given his little brother a dose and does not quite know how it will agree with him or he with it. I looked back at him and laughed. "You'd like to be sure."

"There is a lot in what your friends the Communists call the economic interpretation of history," said Dickon. "If material needs make political and social forms, then big business and international finance will presently develop a soul of its own, become really conscious of itself and make itself known to the world. The same experiences will beget the same ideas. There must be fellows not only in America but Germany and France who are getting, as we are getting, towards their idea of positively making a new world system – not letting it happen merely, but making it happen."

Dickon reflected. "China? Japan? India? It can't be all aimless mooning. Here two or three are talking, there someone is writing. Convergent thoughts perhaps. Surely convergent. Every day there must be someone pushing the new ideas just a little further, clearing up, rounding off, maturing, making possible and practicable. That is the real Reconstruction. But for the world in general they are still inaudible, smothering, unable to speak out yet within the swelling, uncomfortable old institutions. Then someone says something, definite effort is started, the trouble begins."

He paused, a little troubled by his growing and distending metaphor. He was always begetting these metaphors and finding them too much for him.

"Then is the time for the man-midwife," I suggested, "the propagandist, the advertiser, to set about his task, and bring the new order into the world."

As we talked we replenished our glasses with a reasonable moderation from the decanter and the kettle on the hob, and I think we talked on at last partly because the influenza made us feel as physically lazy as we were mentally flushed, and disinclined us for the little effort needed to get ourselves from the fireside to our waiting hot-water bottles. And it was interesting to have my brother spreading out his general ideas to me again after so many years. It was interesting to see how close he had come to certain speculations of my own.

At last the little clock upon the mantelshelf pinged one o'clock in the morning, and Deland, whom we had supposed asleep, coughed rather markedly in the passage. He would not go to bed before his precious charges were safely tucked away.

Dickon stood up, a great bulk, and stretched out his freckled fists.

"That whisky and the talk has done me good, Billy. Well, the Reconstruction of the world is going to be a long job – but it's going to be done. Even if *we* die – futile. The present muddle isn't going on for ever… Reconstructing the world. It's interesting. And besides, Lord! *What else is there to do with life?*"

He drooped and stood with his hands in his pockets staring at the fire.

"Minnie. And the children married and scattered. It's passed like a dream."

### 16 – *Vishnu, Siva, and Brahma*

So, in effect, Dickon talked and thought four years ago – nearly five years now.

I think it was Dickon who first hit upon the image of Vishnu, Siva, and Brahma, the Indian triad of fundamental gods, to express the main forces in the world about us. We found that a very happy symbolism for our ideas. Neither of us can stand a dualism in politics or social life, a mere antagonism of the ins and the outs, the haves and the have-nots. Both of us have an instinctive hatred of eternal rhythms. Dickon, even more than I, insisted upon the triangularity of human affairs. The war of Vishnu, the stubborn conservative, against Siva, the democratic destroyer who ploughs up and inundates, would mean only a dreary alternation of dullness and catastrophe, if it were not for Brahma the inventor, the creative spirit, for whom politics has so rarely found expression. He is the innovating thing; he is always young and being born into the world, always struggling to become effective. That Hindu trinity is far nearer to political and social realities than the Persian dualism of light and darkness, the dualism of the good and the bad, that the party system suggests.

Like modernist theology, like all such applications of ancient and time-worn phrasings to new necessities, it fails a little under scrutiny. Dickon's treatment of Lord Northcliffe and Mr Lloyd George as Sons of the Morning, lit by the spirit of Brahma, is decidedly unsatisfactory. Something has gone wrong there. I make identifications in quite another direction, but of those I will tell later. My identifications, too, are provisional and for want of any better. But I think they are nearer than Dickon's. Mr Baldwin is better as Vishnu's Prime Minister, and there is much to be said for the view that the Duke of Northumberland is a modern incarnation of Vishnu. But the genteel Ramsay MacDonald and the inexpressive Clynes, man-of-the-world Thomas, and Catholic Communist Wheatley are not very good as – shall I say Sivatheria? Siva keeps his temple, if he keep a temple anywhere, in Moscow. Does Siva tolerate temples? One thing I know, that in the heart of every youngster forced at the very dawn of adolescence to accept a destiny of obedience, inferiority, and uncongenial toil there is a potential altar to Siva with the red fire waiting to be lit.

Perhaps it would be better to stress the eternal intermingling of the triad. The spirit of Vishnu – that is to say, the stiff, fierce cowardice of established advantage, the spirit of Siva, the wild resentment of exclusion and imposed inferiority, the spirit of Brahma, the urge of curiosity and creative experiment; all these in varying degrees work everywhere and in all of us. Wherever there is ownership and government Vishnu installs himself; wherever there are dispossessed masses Siva reigns. Brahma, who makes all new things, dominates neither ruler nor crowd, but moves throughout the universe, progress eternal…

If Vishnu rules among the creditors and conservatives and Siva is the god of debtors and the parties of the left, does it follow that Brahma is to be identified with liberalism?

This is a matter for discussion not so much for me as for the bright young gentlemen, often now quite middle-aged, who spend their vacations reviving the Liberal Party in conferences and summer schools. I admit that liberalism has always attracted me, and even in my socialist days as a student I called myself also a liberal, I still call myself a liberal and my views liberalism, but the repulsion of the Liberal Party has been as strong as the attraction of its name. When I dabbled in politics in that rather excited and uncritical reconstruction period after the war, I joined the Labour Party – I do not now recall exactly why. Possibly because of the little bunch of intellectuals who gave it a delusively constructive air. Under democratic conditions all parties are the same stuff and all politicians are alike; the game they play is the same for all of them, and every team must be made up of much the same sort of men. But nevertheless – though Mr Vivian Phillipps, Chief Whip I understand of the surviving fragments, would not own me – I am a liberal. And so is Brahma the Creator. Though I do not think he would own Mr Vivian Phillipps.

Of all kinds of men who have ever been active in affairs, I suppose the English Whig of the eighteenth century is most after my heart. Yet I doubt if the real Lord Brahma is very like an eighteenth-century English Whig...

Since Dickon took to monetary reform as his special and comprehensive task, he has, I remark, restricted Vishnu more and more to the creditor spirit and the power of gold. And if he were pressed for some evidence of the existence of Brahma, he would find it in the projects for a regulated currency as they have been sketched by Mr Maynard Keynes. But where he will find the spirit of Brahma expressed in the public affairs of America I do not know. I hesitate between Mr Henry Ford and —. But why should I be thus specific about men so far away from my continual observation? Let me keep my personal allusions for the lands I know. Here in France they are quite sure that the one God of America is Vishnu, the Transatlantic Brahma is as inaudible to them as he is obscure to us, and Siva, they gather, is either detained at Ellis Island or safely in gaol.

A golden incarnation of Vishnu rules America, as they see it from these broken European countries, rules America absolutely, sitting upon a Treasury full of gold. Indeed, the American Vishnu sits, in this vision, like a golden weight upon all the world, smiling gold stoppings at the figure of Hope. But I am an Anglo-Saxon myself and I know that I do not know America. More may be hidden in a market-place then can be hidden in a desert. America seems to be leading the world now, and seems likely to go on leading the world for some time, in the reconstruction of economic life upon this new scale, the scale of the great modern business combinations. It cannot do this, I hold, without producing, in addition to a vast encumbrance of merely wealthy common persons, a great number of energetic and capable directive men and women of a definable type, people who will ultimately be bored and irritated by existing political institutions and current ways of living, and who will set themselves, more and more intelligently and co-operatively, to the entire reconstruction of human affairs.

At present such types are still ineffective in America, because among other difficulties, they have to struggle towards understanding through thickets of mind-destroying slang and swamps of verbose cant. You do not hew your way across a great continent in three generations and carry your vocabulary intact. America has partly lost the ancient gift of rational speech. American thought is more hampered than we realise by the necessity of expressing itself in a language that is habitually depraved. It is kept at a low level by the universal resort to the common school, with its badly trained teachers and poor equipment, and by those peculiarities of illumination upon which Dickon expatiated, which sacrifice clearness so ruthlessly to vividness, and precision of dealing to harshly dramatic effect.

## 17 – *Sense of Humour*

One other aspect I want to give of Dickon before his picture is completed, a glimpse of something very deep in him. What I have to tell may seem extraordinarily nothing to the reader, but to me it is the very heart of Dickon. It was one day, at most two years ago, after my very first discovery of Provence and before he went off to Brussels, that this incident occurred. I was sleeping that night at Bordon Street, and when he came in I was reading by the fire.

It was late. He was a little flushed and crumpled, in dinner dress and with his decorations. I did not know at the time where he had been; I learned that afterwards.

There had been a great dinner of Advertisers – I rather think it was one of the organisations he had created – and he had spoken and let himself go. A little warmed by champagne and professional fraternity, he had spread out his dream of the Advertiser as prophet and teacher to a pleased but incredulous gathering. Someone had laughed, and he had sounded a prophetic note in reply. "We are the masters of the newspapers and they know it," he had said. "We and we alone have the ear of the world. We can dictate what shall be know and what shall not be known, what shall exist and what shall not. We can educate the people or degrade the people, exalt right things and humble base things. We can be the guide, philosopher, and friend of the common man – working together (renewed laughter). Why should we not rise to the full height of our possibilities?"

Then he had paused and come to something like an anticlimax.

"Are we never to reach beyond motor-cars and medicines, cigarettes and pickles?"

He glowered impressively for a second or so and then sat down.

The Organised Advertisers cheered and hammered the tables, but also they looked curiously at one another and glanced at Dickon, flushed and already doubtful of the wisdom of what he had said. They had heard some of this before from him, but not so much nor so plainly.

"There was moderation in all things," commented a subsequent speaker. "Our energetic and masterful friend to whose organising fervour our profession owed so much," was, he thought, a little prone to exaggerate. It was not perhaps altogether a fault in an advertiser (laughter) within limits (renewed laughter). But though it might be good business to exaggerate, it was not wise to threaten (hear, hear). We had our share, a great share, he would indeed go so far as to say a vital share, in stimulating and in sustaining the currents of trade, the prosperity of our mighty empire, but it was a share – in subordination. It had its place and its limits. There was such a thing as taking one's bit too seriously...

Possibly through sheer clumsiness he had circled about and repeated this thought three or four times. But he was encouraged by "Hear and hear" and some gentle rapping on the table. What had been intended as a friendly reproof became an attack upon Dickon, and at the end what they call a trouncing.

Dickon was a respected and popular figure in the advertisement world, but his was the reluctant popularity accorded to success. His associates liked him but they felt at times, I think, that he did a little to compel them to like him. This talk of their high responsibilities after dinner had not so much flattered them as made them feel uncomfortable, and the gathering fell back very readily into a sympathetic deprecation of "exaggeration" and "lack of humour." They applauded warmly; they nodded their approval. Later speakers showed an increasing disposition to echo and even exceed the trouncer, and a funny man saw his opportunity, and the applause and laughter grew.

The arrow still chafed in Dickon's hide. He stood before the fire and brooded immensely before his explosion.

"This damned sense of humour!" he cried suddenly and violently.

"Eh?" said I, looking up from my book.

"You might do a decent thing that would make you look a bit high-falutin'. And so you do a shabby, lazy, second-rate thing instead, and grin and say, 'Thank God I've got a sense of humour.' That's what it amounts to."

"Is this me, Dickon, you're talking to?"

"Oh no, Billy! I never talk to you. I was thinking. Man I heard speak tonight. Took me up – for blowing a bit too strongly about advertisement...

"Perhaps I said too much... Perhaps I did."

He went on as if he addressed some third person.

"But *Modesty*! Knowing your place in the world! Rot it all is! Rot I tell you. Cringing, shamming, shirking muck they bully into boys in public schools. And from an Advertising Man of all people! An Advertiser! Think of it! Modesty! Not going all out for the things that have to be done! Let a child drown under your eyes! Thank God *you* don't profess to be a swimmer. *You* don't take upon yourself to rescue all the drowning kids in Christendom. If some presumptuous silly ass who can hardly swim at all chooses to go into the water and gets himself into a mess, *you* aren't going to do anything but smile. Flick a pebble at his head as he comes up for the third time. You're a quiet smiler, you are!"

I learnt back in my chair to appreciate my brother better. There was nothing else to do. I was still at a loss to know what it was all about. He was just the slightest bit drunk, but mostly this was, I perceived, a rational passion.

"Sense of humour!" said Dickon. "There isn't much of that poison in Advertisement, anyhow..."

He seemed to recall my presence.

"You may laugh, Billy! But that blamby-pamby idiot tonight has got my goat. I've been a hot man tonight in a world of quiet smiles. Fuming. He let me up to seeing what all this gentlemanly grinning and smirking and enjoying the fun of it quietly and unassumingly really means. Why should a man be guyed for taking himself seriously? What else *is* there to take seriously? Those chaps who won't take themselves seriously ought to have been headed off by birth control and never begun. All this half-doing things! All this living with the guts out!... A joke's a joke in its place, but most of this not taking yourself too seriously is a dirty sin against heaven."

And suddenly Dickon soared above me. He became a pulpit and my admirable armchair a pew. His voice mingled expostulation and passionate assertion in the most extraordinary way.

"Because one sets out to do big things, Billy, because there are big things to be done, because one works until one gets ragged and sore, it doesn't follow one is presumptuous. We two are successes, Billy; life has pampered us, petted us, put its best carpets under our feet. Have we a right to be anything but serious men? *Damned* serious men! It's no want of modesty to attempt everything one can; to play as big a game as one can; it's a sense of obligation. What we *are*... That's another question.

"Don't we know each other through and through, Billy? Do we pretend? Do we put on airs? Don't I know what asses we are, I who can't leave a scrap on my plate and you who brighten at the swish of a girl's skirt? But you *do*, Billy! Everyone sees it. Don't we know how we blunder, how we lose our little tempers, the endless *silly* things we do? Yes, and all the same, with all our weaknesses upon us, we've got to be in deadly earnest and do our biggest job.

"If we don't, who will? Look here, Billy… Is there a race of Gods among mankind, that you and I can slack? Which will do things if we don't? If we stand aside, smirking in our elegant modesty, who is there to take hold of things? A sense of humour, I tell you, Billy, is no fit possession for a decent man. Let the failures have their damned sense of humour! Cuddle it and nurse it. They need it. Let them snigger and sneak and steak and steal, and make funny faces behind the backs of the men in earnest. That's *their* road, the low road. But for us – things have been put before us, Billy, and we have to take hold of them. We may not be aristocrats; our luck may be all chance; but for good or evil, God has put us among the masters in the affairs of men. And a master I mean to be. Oh, I'd rather – "

He paused to assemble it.

"I'd rather be a skunk and set myself to outstink this drain into which I have fallen, stink and stink hard, instead of making for fresh air, than be one of these damned sense-of-humour business men."

Queer how Dickon could be stung at times!

He was quiet for a moment. "I know I'm a fat ass," he said in an altered voice. "Oh, I know I'm a fat ass and deserve to be grinned at. Don't I *know* it!"

He went on talking to himself in broken sentences. "Taken the second plateful… Go to the club. How can one help eating too much at the Ermine? Sleepy afternoon… Half one's efficiency gone… Things like that. Temper over a tight collar… The times I've shocked Minnie! Such a poor *comic* thing!…"

The muttering died away into an incoherent rumbling that was presently ended in a nod and a "Yes."

Then he stood quite still. And suddenly whispered something that gripped me strangely. He whispered it quite forgetful of me, as one whispers a phrase that one has thought out and chosen long ago and repeated many times. I perceived at once that it had been his ultimate consideration on many such occasions of trouble.

"*Weak as we are*," said Dickon, "*those others are weaker.*"

I stared at him. I had known Dickon all my life, and suddenly it dawned upon me that in some things I hardly knew him at all.

He woke up again.

"Pity I got in a temper!" he said. "Oh! – a damned pity!

"I could have murdered that fool…

"I showed it an they grinned at me… I'm glad I had you to blow off to, old man…

"I shouldn't have slept all night. Sometimes cursing him and sometimes cursing myself. No one knows that nights we spend, some of us, Billy…

"You see, Billy, what I said wasn't exactly what I meant to say. I overdid it. What I said was right, but somehow I overdid it. I gave him a loophole. I don't say things exactly. It's too beastly hard to say things exactly.

"But they got what I was after all right… Damned sight too much for them…

"They like being funny little nibbling beasts. They *like* it…"

I forget what else he said. I was not listening any longer. I was turning over his astonishing aphorism in my mind. "*Weak as we are, those others are weaker.*"

That, I think, is the quintessence of Dickon.

## 18 – *Stratum of Futility*

It is curious show the social uses of Lambs Court have dissolved away since the death of Minnie. Richard Clissold Junior has married now, and Winnie has gone to live with her husband in Italy, and young William, my godson, is something of a rebel and a painter (but I begin to think after my last visit to his studio, a very good painter), and until my great-nephews and great-nieces repopulate it Lambs Court above stairs is an empty place, left more and more to the routines of old and trusted and conservative servants.

Dickon's life, for all our early divergence, reverts to the pattern of mine – the life of a man who has come through the ordinary drama of the world with the sense of a part played out, who is yet full of vitality and anxious to get things done, who still has strong and deep desires, but who is no longer swayed by that intensity of personal reference that narrowed his life before. In that period of renewed intimacy that followed Minnie's death we discussed almost as if we were students again what we were doing with the years that still remained to us. Both of us were at loose ends. Both of us were becoming acutely aware of our dwindling handful of life, and both of us were asking ourselves, as it soaked away between our fingers: "What am I doing with it? What is the best that I can do with it?"

We were pulling ourselves together for the last lap of coherent living. We were entirely vague then about our objectives. I had been so for some years; but with Dickon the phase was more acute. And more decisive. Since then Dickon, with characteristic concentration, has settled down to a task of his own, a task that will need all that is left of him to accomplish, and I, for more complicated reasons, am no longer under the same cloud of feeling that then made me unhappy. But for a while it was as if something long forgotten – anxiety of youth, anxiety about the purposes of life – had come back to us out of those far-off adolescent days.

I find myself wondering how many of our contemporaries have experienced such a fresh start, such a phase of doubt and resumption in their middle years. I question if many intelligent people escape that sort of trouble in adolescence. It is so universal that I would call it distinctively "anxiety of youth." Then for most of us comes immediate necessity, the pressure of events; we are caught up and hustled along and excited and distracted and amused, and many of us, perhaps most human beings, never reach those open and interrogative silences again before death ends the storm of experience. Unless there is a space of leisure, a release from the thickets of need, I do not see how that trouble can return. And some happy souls hear no more of these interrogations, because, like Sir Rupert York, they have answered them once for all. It is well I have already given a picture of him in this book, because there at least you have one man who has said, simply and completely: "This work is good enough for me." He will go on unhurryingly, with his bones and his other specimens and the subtle and satisfying problems that concern him, until at last one morning he will not get up, but lie, peaceful and done.

He is one of a number of men of a science whom I know to be men serene in their souls and happy in the essence of their lives. But scientific work is a world apart, a magic island cut off from futility. Music, too, may be another magic island, cut off not only from futility but from reality. There is a protective isolation about most of the arts. But Science has most of this precious detachment. And is yet profoundly real. Scientific workers work to the end, though at last they may go gently like a boat coming home as the wind falls in the evening. I was once upon that island of enduring work. Had I kept upon it I should not have been writing this book now and making these half-envious, half-admiring reflections.

Even when there is a space of leisure I doubt if that phase of middle-aged unrest happens very generally. It is natural for me now to find the quality of middle-aged people's lives particularly interesting. I am impressed by the present proliferation of the middle-aged. They form a larger proportion of mankind than was ever the case in the world before. And I am more aware of them.

Quite as important in human affairs as that change of scale upon which I have been dwelling in recent sections is the prolongation of life now in progress. I do not think I am being led away by my own circumstances to exaggerate its importance. The average age of the English, for example, has risen steadily for the last century. For that, at any rate, we have fairly trustworthy figures. In Elizabethan times one was mature at thirty and old at forty; Shakespeare was already a worn-out, unproductive old man in retirement at fifty. Everything was earlier and younger then; Romeo had the years of a raw undergraduate, and Juliet was a child. One loved and loved again and married and had children, and by the time they were of age the game was done. The ordinary man of fifty was fat or grey or bald and his teeth had gone beyond repair. There was no repair.

Young people died freely at all ages; more children died than lived to maturity. There was a fever, therefore, to get to the crises of life before the chance was snatched away.

> "What is love? 'tis not hereafter;
> Present mirth hath present laughter;
> What's to come is still unsure:
> In delay there lies no plenty:
> Then come kiss me, sweet and twenty,
> Youth's a stuff will not endure."

That was the note of it. To be old and hale was remarkable. It was to be distinguished and isolated. The aged of fifty and upward formed a dwindling chorus to the song of youth. They sat and looked on at the dance – a little outstaying their welcome. The literatures of the world still preserve the spirit of that more transitory time, and its tradition dominates us today.

In all classes now, but particularly in the prosperous classes, people do not die as once they did. More and more hold on. And they are cared for and mended; it is not merely life that is prolonged, but vigour. Vigour and the desire for living. An accession is developing to the human life cycle; a stage after the family life, which itself grows less and less prolific and uses up the available energy less and less completely. And this elder stratum has no traditions as yet to shape its activities. Literature has not prepared us for it, and we come through to it with a sort of surprise. As soon as they have done with loving and getting, the novels, the plays dismiss us with a phrase. We are supposed to be enfeebled, sated, and done. We discover we are not so easily dismissed. We have not finished. We are not enfeebled. We demand a better rôle than to act as chorus to the next generation and offer it out-of-date advice. Here I declare on the edge of sixty is living still to be done, in a new mood and for a new end.

I believe that as civilisation develops this elder stratum is going to play a determining rôle in human development. In the first part of this book I told of a talk I had with Dr Jung of Zurich. Among other things that I brought away from that evening was the fruitful idea that the prevalent states of mind of quite grown-up people in past ages are preserved as phases in the development of the immature today, and that a new, more fully adult phase is spreading from the fifties and forties downward in human experience. This proportionate increase in the elder stratum will contribute greatly to the intensification and extension of this new adult phase. It will ultimately make life more disinterested and more deliberate and less romantic. It will make novels and plays that set out to present life aspects of history instead of stories of mating. But that will only be when this stratum has developed a consciousness of its distinctive quality and rôle. Then it will impose its standards upon the younger generation and assist it sooner and sooner to maturity. At present things are still the other way about, and the elder stratum is dominated by the overemphasised standards of the younger generation. At present it has still to realise itself. It is like a new actor thrust upon the scene before a part has been found for him. For a time it is a conspicuous encumbrance even to itself.

What an extraordinary spectacle of waste do the lives of the great majority of us middle-aged and older prosperous people present today!

An immense proportion of the property and spending power of the world is now in the hands of old folks, who would in every previous time have died and left things to their heirs. The heirs remain allowanced and functionless, going about the world in a state of arrested reality. They are amateurs of everything, provisionally active, waiting for a call that lingers.

About here in Provence, and especially along this coast from Saint Raphaël to far beyond Genoa, there is gathered an abundant assemblage of this old, prosperous multitude for my astonished observation. Under eighteenth-century conditions not one per cent of these people would be alive. Now their still peculiar sham youthfulness sets all the fashions of living. The amount of altogether futile vitality upon these hills and coasts is incredible, until one has gone to and fro through it and mixed with it and watched it.

There is, first of all, a very considerable resident population here of oldish wealthy people. They build, they own or lease beautiful villas with great gardens and lovely prospects. There must be hundreds of thousands of such people along these coasts; from England and America alone they must number scores of thousands; and they must represent an aggregate income of hundreds of millions of pounds. They employ the lives of hundreds of thousands of servants, they spread their gardens over great areas of land, they send up the cost of living for everyone, and they crowd the pulmonary refugees out of the sunshine. They are often men and women who play a vigorous game of tennis, stand the fatigues of whole days of motoring, they come and go among themselves, lunching, dining, assembling, dispersing, and I cannot find a soul among them that is doing anything of large importance in the world or stretching its energies to the full, in any direction whatever. They declare they have played their parts in the world and finished. There are women who have borne and brought up one or two or even three children, and women who have produced none. I could assemble a score of men within an hour's motoring of this *mas*, younger men than I, who say they have "retired." Under that phrase they contentedly rule themselves dead for all effectual ends. They are just playing about, the little innocents, until Nurse Angel-of-Death comes to put them to bed.

Close to me here is a fairly representative sample of these Riviera residents; she is the widow of old Sir Ralph Steinhart, and she was a niece of the original Romer; she inherits an interest in the activities of Romer, Steinhart, Crest and Co. and their subsidiaries from both sides. Every time I have done a hands-turn for any of our concerns I have made her richer. Here she is, within half an hour's drive of me, silver-haired – the natural grey made an even white by skilful bleaching – high-coloured and bright-eyed. She is a little bent and restlessly active. Her gardens are very spacious and fine. We pass them usually when we go to Nice. She has, I observe, obstructed a number of the peasants' paths to make her domain more secluded; she threatens them on boards with *pièges à loup*, and they must go round by a longer way outside her fences to do their business. Inside one rarely sees anything moving among the olive terraces and the frequent stone jars; it is still and deserted except that sometimes in the cool of the evening a manservant is visible taking a pet dog for its sanitary stroll. Nearer the house there are great hedges of agave and cactus, groves of palm and glimpses of glorious colour which, save for herself and a few guests, delight only God and her gardeners. She had bought and evacuated half a dozen peasant houses, she told me one day, to assure the amenities of her view – which, on the whole, is not so good as mine.

I am obliged almost in spite of myself to know something of her house and her life. When she is here – for two-thirds of the year she is not here and the house stands empty except for a caretaker or so and a casual priest or so, a luxurious blank on the face of the earth – when she is here, she makes continual efforts to cultivate my acquaintance. It is not that she likes me or that I even pretend to like her, but because she is inordinately curious about my relations to Clementina, and because generally I perplex her and because, more than anything else, she has nothing better to do. She persists in raiding me with parties of high-coloured, bright-eyed, observant Romer and Steinhart nieces and in-laws. Or with a literary party of those beastly little cigarette dealers who write novels for the English country families, and their crumpled and dishevelled womenfolk. Or with a scratch lot from the dramatic world. Or even with the one of her selected collections from the aristocratic Catholic circles of Paris. But these last are rarer. That is the side of her life she turns away from me. Her car does its best and sticks inside my pillars, and up they all come on foot, either quietly agog and staring about them, or else with an impelled reluctant look, according to their race and breeding.

As soon as the car is observed below, Jeanne flies upstairs to put on what is known with us as a Lady Steinhart apron, and while I entertain the party upon the terrace with a taciturn amiability, tea is served in cups of coarse Provençal ware. The party is made to spread a peculiarly fluid and difficult cherry jam on toasted crusts with large holes in them, through which the red stuff drips on anything below it, and I converse about the Provençal climate – which has recently developed Anglomania – and intimate my readiness to hear the purport of the visit. If

Clementina is present she is silently polite, and regards the visitors in a way that serves at least to embarrass their scrutiny of the books, newspapers, and other oddments scattered about the terrace. Her dog goes a little way off and yaps protestingly and usefully, in a tone that shows that the whole affair is to be considered unusual. After a time something seems to break, and her ladyship and party gravitate down the hill again. I never ask her to repeat the visit, and she always does.

She cannot understand why I should live here for so much of my time in a house that I rent for three thousand depreciated francs a year, wearing dirty old flannels and employing a solitary servant. She knows that I pay ten thousand pounds a year or so in super-tax and income-tax, and this way of living seems to her like a wicked waste of God's bounty. She cannot understand why I sit for so many hours in this upper room to which her way is always barred. And, above all, she cannot understand why Clementina sometimes isn't here and sometimes is; why she has so many meals here, and why she sits dangling her long legs over the wall of my terrace and smoking my cigarettes with an air of complete domestication, while I am upstairs writing. As I never explain Clementina to anyone, as I shall probably not explain her completely even in this book, it is natural that to Lady Steinhart she remains unexplained.

Consequently Lady Steinhart never quite knows whether she really knows Clementina and whether she may, or possibly even ought to, invite Clementina to lunch, and what would happen if she did. And all that is excellent exercise for Lady Steinhart's mind.

Visits like this seem to take up a large part of her time. She and a multitude of other people are always rushing about this country seeing each other; and I will confess I cannot imagine a less interesting series of sights. Like all Romers and Steinharts, she is addicted to discovering and dropping young musicians, and for these special parties have to be assembled. And also she gets through a considerable amount of time altering her house and garden. She is always digging something up or laying something down, or planting out something or opening out a vista, and if she can manage it she takes you to the spot affected and asks your advice. And while you are giving your advice she is thinking of the next thing she will bother you about. She pursues and buys old furniture, pictures, pottery, and jewellery remorselessly and voraciously. It's a clever little fifteenth-century pot that gets away from her once she is on its trail. And when she has bought a thing she glories in it for a little while, and shows it to her friends and makes them guess what she gave for it, and puts it in her already very congested house, where it presently sinks down out of sight among the other stuff; and when she has forgotten all about it, as she must do. I hope her tremendous and implacable major-domo steals it and sells it to someone to sell to her all over again. Then there is also much to be done about her clothes and her dresses and her hair. So her days are always emptily busy and the net result of them is exactly nothing at all.

But you must not think that Lady Steinhart's life is wholly consumed by these activities. She is a very moral woman; there is no talk of a lover for her although she is still short of sixty, and she does not dance more than two or three times a week. But the gap thus left is filled in by a rather distinguished serious side. This serious side she does not let me see as much of as I should like to do. It is the one thing she does not press upon me, and it is the one thing about her that interests me. She is a little bashful with me about it; I do not know why. It reaches high and far. You might imagine that a born Romer, who is a Steinhart by marriage, would be a Jewess, but this is not the case with her. She is hostile to Jews. She is a Catholic. She is substantially one of the old noblesse. She is a Catholic and a reactionary, and it is alleged that she made even Sir Ralph a Catholic after he became speechless before his death. She is involved in French politics at an angle proper to an aristocratic and pious woman. Priests, bishops, monsignori are to be found at her house, moving about quietly, speaking in undertones, forming little black clumps in the bright flower-gardens, obscurely active, mysteriously wary. She has done much for the Church, and she may do more.

And the Church which has always had a weakness for pious women of property makes her a great concession. She has a private chapel of her own to play with; it is her dearest interest. She buys it petticoats and lace and ornaments and jewels and metal pots and pans to put on and take off. It is in the house somewhere, and often when one goes in, one is reminded of her serious side by a whiff of incense from some recent function. She can go there alone and meditate, and I suppose she can regale herself with special services, but what she thinks of God when she meditates is as hidden from my imagination as what God can think of her. There is usually a subdued-looking priest or so at her table. Not excessively pampered. The Romer blood is in her veins, and you feel, and you can feel they feel, that they have been paid for.

That private chapel is the crown of her life. It is a great privilege, and she must have sought it for many years. It is the consummation of her bric-à-brac. No doubt the Church weighed the matter and decided that it was worth while to respect her spiritual possibilities to that extent. Perhaps the Church does not know the Romers quite so well as I know them. Anyhow, she has it. The chapel is her distinction. Take that away and substitute a lover, or bridge, or the higher amateurishness in art or criticism, or a specialised collecting mania, or a cherished illness, or just blank interludes, and you have the life of quite a large number of these great ladies of the Riviera. And the men, the "retired" men, the resident sort, cultivate their gardens also, play tennis, make love in a vague, furtive way, indulge in wistful reminiscence of the days when they were alive, and are on the whole much less animated than the women. Some are vicious in an elderly, elaborate, Roman way, and their establishments are barred and secret, and their rather too smart menservants go about visibly clad in light and becoming blackmail. French journalists are modest upon such questions, and the Riviera has no Suetonius. There are not many married couples in constant association among our residents. The prevalent thing is a single personality engaged, with the widest, most dignified, and expensive of details, in futility.

But the residential side of the Côte d'Azur is not, after all, its most typical aspect. Where the big hotels cluster, the multitude grows dense. Sooner or later everyone in the Western world who has more than three thousands pounds a year must come to the Riviera. An invisible necessity seems to bring us here just as the souls in the Swedenborgian books go undriven to their ultimate destinies. I am here, and, after all, I am rather pretending not to belong to it than honestly detached. For so many of us there is nowhere else to go – quite remarkably there is not. To the north are murderous climates and to the south murderous discomforts. A few come once or twice and then not again, but most who have come continue to come. A middle-aged hunger for the sun is an active, physical cause. The transients come and go tremendously. Many of them still function in some reduced or inattentive way elsewhere; some of the younger set between forty-five and sixty are frankly recuperating; but most have altogether discontinued any contribution to the world's affairs. In the hotels we sit and watch them, guessing ages. The average is astonishingly high. Golden lads of sixty step it briskly with gay girls of forty-five. The grey heads bob to the black music. The other day we found an incessant couple in a Cannes hotel, who golfed all the forenoon and danced together until one in the morning, and both were over seventy. The only young people here seem to be subsidiaries. I make no objection to all this activity on the part of old people. I would rejoice to see them dancing and generally active at ninety and a hundred, but my perplexity is their universal disregard of anything else in the world but amusement taken in a quasi-juvenile form.

For a large proportion of this multitude the belated juvenility finds more questionable expression than golfing and dancing, Darby and Joan. Since they have yet to discover that there is any graver business in life than getting, they must gamble, though they are rich and easy; and since they know of no livelier desires they still want most desperately to go with the adolescent modes of love. With a little care and effort much may still be effected in that matter. One can still be jealous and vindictive, still charm here and break off there, be cold and cruel and fitful and make the yearning lover realise the wretchedness of an insecure allowance. When one is no longer over-anxious to steal away with one's dear mistress, one can still be seen about with her. Which accounts for the prevalence here of a large number of really very beautiful and brilliant and highly decorated young women between the ages of fifteen and forty, and a large variety of utterly detestable young gentlemen. A mistress must look the part and have a lavish and pampered air. And for some of those who have had a hard struggle to win to this Paradise of ease and power, there seems to be a peculiar charm in gilt-edged passions; Russian exiles, often with quite genuine titles, nobility from almost everywhere, countesses, duchesses, princesses divorcing or divorced, royal bastards (in profusion and with every degree of authenticity), ex-royalties, and even precariously current royalties are here, and only too ready to oblige. The Americans, they say, are particularly generous and abject paymasters to such people. That is probably a libel on the Americans; there are merely more of them with money.

And, thirdly, there is the sport, the mechanical gratification of shooting pigeons, the assembling to look on at racing, polo, flying, fencing, tennis. The worship of tennis becomes more amazing every year. The papers that come here, even the *Manchester Guardian* and the *Nation* discuss it earnestly, deeply. Photographs of its heroic figures fill the illustrated weeklies. The women have a sort of wadded look about the feet and ankles; the men's faces, in the absence of a ball to hit, are alertly empty. We study the characters, the mannerisms, of these gifted beings. Minniver, it seems, is amusingly short-tempered; he insults his partner and swears. You can hear it all over the court; you can hear about it all over the world. Judkins has a peculiar penetrating sniff. It is, I understand, to be broadcasted.

In relation to all these things cluster the shop-folk and all sorts of dealers, the professionals, the teachers of dancing, the manicurists and complexion specialists, the hoteliers, restaurateurs, and so forth, with their own sympathetically imitative tennis and sport and private vices out of business hours.

It is still full season down there on the beaches, for I got my *lit-salon* reservation for next week from Cannes at only eight days' notice – I have to run to London for some business and leave this writing for a few weeks. But presently this widespread crowd of aimless property will begin to pour home like a sluice along the roads and in the expresses *de luxe*, and so to Paris and more especially to England in May and June, to the Paris dressmakers and body-makers and face-makers and on to the jostling splendours of the London Court, and the culmination of all things at Henley and Ascot – especially Ascot. Grave men will wear grey top-hats with the serious elation befitting such an act, and every sort of dress except the old and shabby will be displayed. The King and Queen, those perfect symbols of the will and purpose of the British Empire, will be gravely presiding over the parade amidst the clicking cameras. Wherever there is a foreground there also will be the Countess of Oxford and Asquith, and no doubt some oaf of a Labour member will be well in evidence in a white bowler hat and a loyal grin – just to make it clear that there is nothing different about Labour. And if you study the photographs and pictures of this immense inane gathering you will see they represent mature and oldish people in an enormous majority, deliberately and gravely assembled, dressed with extraordinary attention, and doing nothing, nothing whatever except being precisely and carefully there.

In the wane of the season here, to replace our first-class assembly, there will come a char-à-banc crowd of the merely prosperous, also middle-aged and getting on with it, filling the Monte Carlo Casino at reduced entrance fees, gambling at five francs a go, and learning how to be rich from the margin. They will envy, they will emulate, they will peep over the villa walls and up the Casino staircases to the private rooms. Some may even go up those staircases. Adventurously. The wives will return to Sheffield or Main Street of Pernambuco marvellously changed about the hair and the skirts and the souls. These are the reserves of the great spending class. They are learning. They spread the stratum wide and deep into the general life. Tons of illustrated papers go out weekly to them to keep them in touch; books and plays of a special sort are made to satisfy their cravings. They have no God, and Michael Arlen is their prophet.

I have written of the "elder stratum," but when I think over my occasional glimpses of life at Monaco and Monte Carlo and Nice I am doubtful whether "elder fester" would not be the better expression. When one traces it away from here to Paris, London, Vienna, New York, California, to Biskra and Egypt, to High Savoy, to Biarritz, Palm Beach, and endless other places, to race meetings and summer resorts, to Scotland and New England, and so to its town houses and country houses and its places of origin, one realises something of its scale and significance in our Atlantic world. It is all that pays super-tax; it is the surplus of the world's resources. Yet extensive and impressive as it is, it is nevertheless, so far as its present characteristics go, almost as new as the great growth of advertisement in Dickon's lifetime. Its precursors in the town and Court life of the eighteenth and seventeenth centuries were relatively younger, more actively self-assertive and more assured, and incomparably less abundant and diffused. They were a little intimate community, and this is an auriferous flood. I do not believe that its present development is anything more than one distinctive feature of a transitory phase in the great unfolding of human society that is now in progress. This way of living is no more permanent than the way of living one finds recorded – in caricature indeed, but in illuminating and convincing caricature – by Petronius in his *Satyricon*. It is an overspill of gathering human energy like the spots on an adolescent face. No state of human affairs that releases so vast a splash of futile expenditure can be anywhere near equilibrium. It must be, it manifestly is, undergoing rapid changes. Intelligent people, even the intelligent people in the rich elder stratum itself, will rebel against this mode of life, as Dickon and I have rebelled. And all those who are outside of it have only to learn of it to desire to end it, because it is so plainly a vast waste of spending power by essentially powerless people.

Circumstances may have made Dickon and me rather tougher and more refractory stuff than most of our class, less afraid to lie awake at night and look what used to be called the Eternities in the face. But none of these people can be of a very different clay from Dickon and myself, and what has happened to us must happen with slight differences in quality and quantity to most of them. There is a great dread of lying awake at night manifest everywhere. The activity to escape mental solitude is remarkable. Most of the rushing about in motor-cars is plainly due to that.

The rich, ageing Americans in particular seem constantly in flight across the Atlantic from something that is always, nevertheless, waiting for them on the other side, whichever side it happens to be. There would not be all this vehement going to and fro if they were not afraid of something that sought them in the quiet places. And what else can that something be but just these questions that have confronted us. "There is only a little handful of water left now. What do you mean to do with it? What under the stars is the meaning of your life?"

"Oh, hell!" they say at the first intimation of that whisper, "where are we going tomorrow?"

Below and behind and all about the petty glittering activities of the elder fester a sane and real next adult phase must surely be preparing even now, the realisation that life can be lived indeed to the very end, and that learning and making need never cease until the last hour has come. Surely there dawns the immense undying interest of social development, of the establishment of a creative order, of the steady growth of human knowledge and power upon the blank outlook of the present. Can these poor, raddled, raffish, self-indulgent, aimless, wealthy types of today go on existing as that grows clearer? There is no need of any great convulsion to chase them from existence; they will fade out of the spectacle. Some will learn, some will be expropriated; many types among them will be made impossible by less speculative methods of production. In that direction things must be moving now.

If I could return to this countryside in only a hundred years' time, I am sure I should find the villas, hostels, roads, promenades of all these places, and all the life that fills them, changed profoundly. The buildings will be for the most part rebuilt and less miscellaneous in their quality. Villa Cocotte in its louder variations may have gone; the gaudy casinos and dancing restaurants will have been cleared away; the gardens will be more beautiful and less strenuously exclusive. The present fences of wire, the *pièges à loup*, and fierce little intimations against trespassing will have been abolished noiselessly by a general amelioration of manners. The peasants' homes will have got bathrooms, and their cultivations will be less laborious and more skilful.

These bathrooms may be already close at hand. Jeanne tells me that one reason given for the cutting down of olive-trees here is that the olive harvest comes in winter and that picking olives swells and stains and chaps the hands. Enough labour cannot be got for the picking. People will not lend their hands to such work. A new phase of civilisation is near when the human hand has won to this much respect.

Swift, silent cars will run about this fairer land on smoother roads, less numerously perhaps, and with a greater appearance of purpose. The advertisement boards, like a clamour of touts that ruin so much of the roadside scenery, will be banished altogether. This Provence is too kind and lovable not to remain the resort of great multitudes of people, but they will no longer be living days of busy inconsecutiveness and pursuing the shadows of unseasonable pleasures.

Perhaps my hopes run away with me, but it seems to me that even in so short a time as a hundred years there may be a far larger proportion of true adults amidst the retarded adolescents of our elder stratum, and that their tone of thought and their quality of conduct will have soaked far into the whole social body. Youth is eager and passionate, but youth is not naturally frivolous, and at present an artificial and meretricious frivolity is forced upon the young by the greedy urgency of their aimless seniors. Youth also may be something graver and stronger a hundred years from now.

However evident its approach, it is certain that the coming adult phase is not yet in the ascendant. And since it has still to come as a general thing, and since its essential quality is a merger of one's romantic, adventurous, individual life into the deathless life of the being of the species, manifestly it is not to be attained in its fullness by a few isolated pioneers. The men of science of this time are as a class more nearly able to be adult-minded than any of the rest of us – so far, that is, as their science goes. They are more in touch with an enduring reality; they have their side of the world comparatively organised, and they are joined up into a kind of collectivism. The rest of us are rather people who have heard of this way of living and are seeking it than who are actually living in the new stage.

Meanwhile all the available forms and conveniences necessarily remain those of our stratum. We must wear the clothes the fashions prescribe unless we want to have our lives eaten up by minor troubles and explanations. We must live in the usual way, for how else can we live? If we want to travel we must travel by trains-de-luxe or go slow and dirty, catch colds, and be crowded, stifled, and disgusted; we must go to the hotels that quiver to the strains of jazz, for there are no others at present to go to; and eat either in restaurants amidst processions of mannequins or with dancers jogging our elbows, or perplex our poor stomachs with questionable fare. And if we want air and exercise, is anything so convenient as tennis? Which demands all sorts of conformities.

So we two Clissolds go about the world looking like any other fairly rich spenders – crypto-adults at the best. If I live upon the hills here, and very simply for a part of the year, it is only because I have hit upon a remarkable young woman who has seen fit to make it possible for me. And Heaven knows how long that will last! It is only here that I can live like this – it is a little abnormal adventure of my own – and for the rest of my existence there waits a setting of hotel managers and porters and maidservants and valets and all that is *comme-il-faut*.

Yet we appear to be much emptier worldlings than we are. We are both, after our fashion, refusing to accept the fundamental stigma of the elder stratum – which is the cessation of all serious work. We have no blank enjoyments and we work as long hours as ever we did. Longer perhaps. Dickon grapples now day and night with the mysteries of what he calls the Money Power. To release our dear Lady of Business from the paralysing grip of the Creditor is the final quest of his life. He is thrusting in a sullen, persistent way through a dark jungle of finance round about her in search of something vulnerable. He believes there is a concrete dragon somewhere in that darkness to be slain, and if so he will slay it. Wherever there is a promise of light upon these obscurities Dickon goes. Last November he was in Detroit in earnest conference with Henry Ford, who possessed, he thought, a peculiar point of view and special experiences about the evil thing. He crossed the Atlantic in winter for that. And he is developing an angry, industrious patience with currency and credit theorists. When he catches me in England he makes me talk about them. He wrangles with me and will not be denied. He talks now about money just as he used to talk once about advertisement – continually, with his heart as deeply in it.

I am quite unable to estimate what his activities amount to, whether he is just hammering at a door which isn't a door but a rock, or whether he is getting through to some working generalisations. In the past Dickon had a way of getting out results, but this is an immense business.

Apparently he cannot wring anything fundamental out of the bankers. I have heard him in his wrath denouncing them as "beastly little Abacuses; rotten little roulette wheels, bagging the odd zero chance." He clings to it that they are automata and have not the least idea of their rôle in the general economic life of the world. He compares them with the Freemasons, who "had some sort of a secret once and have forgotten it." He talks of "going into banking" to find out. A pretty manager he'd make for a local branch! The district would wake up.

I cannot write down his opinion of various Chancellors of the Exchequer. The Treasury he sometimes reviles and sometimes only bemoans. "Some of these chaps seem to think," he says. "Seem to be able to think. But being officials by nature – they won't let on. They control it. Or they might hit on something important and upset their nice little lives." He wants to have the Treasure "dug up and replanted." It is "pot bound" – which is, I believe, some sort of horticultural metaphor. (I am no party to these criticisms.) Certainly he has hit upon nothing definite yet, or we should have had him at once setting about to "put it over." Just as once he "put over" Milton's Silent Silver Guinea.

May he do so before I die! I dream at times of my dear old Dickon, so amazingly stout and still so amazingly active, engaged upon his last and greatest campaign, leading a band of big manufacturers and engineers, Titans of industry, mammoth distributors and cosmic shippers, piling Pelion on Ossa, newspapers on hoardings, and cinematographs on wireless, shaking all the markets and shocking all the mints in the world, in a stupendous effort to scale and storm the Olympus of Wall Street and the City and dethrone the golden usurer who reigns there.

As for me, I work along a different line. I doubt if this simple treatment of the Money Power as the One True Devil gets to the bottom of things. We need a true sound money, yes; but that is only to be got with quite a number of other developments that belong together. I have failed to find any place in politics, which is just as well for me; I have satisfied myself that I was in a state of dangerous fog about economics and education, and at last I have come to this quiet and seclusion in the sunshine – I said last year, to think things out, and now as I get them thought out, I say, to write my mind clear and try my creed over by making this book.

# Book Four

## The Story of the Clissolds: Tangle of Desires

## 1 – *Stress of Youth*

But now I must come to my own personal history, which perhaps I have kept back unduly. Must tell of my own marriage and my lapse from scientific work to industrial chemistry, and how I also like Dickon became a rich man, as perplexingly aware as he of creative power almost in reach and yet evading us. To tell the story fairly I must go right back again to our student days.

It is part of the romantic travesty of reality that youth is a happy trivial time. Childhood can be made happy and is made happy nowadays for an increasing number of children, but I doubt if very many human adolescences can be truthfully called happy. For the enormous majority of human beings since ever humanity began to develop social life, adolescence had been anxious and perplexed. The creature is still at bottom the child of the Old Man of the rough Stone Age, half-man, half-ape, and wholly egoist; its adaptation is imperfect, and as adolescence comes on there is a struggle between the necessities that keep it tame and social and the deep-seated urgencies of its past. As the instinctive obedience and trustfulness of childhood fades, the natural man, the natural boy or girl, is discovered to be reserving a personality, becoming self-assertive, difficult, recalcitrant, and interrogative. "*Why* should I?" is the note of youth, and usually it is consciously a resentful note, a plea in opposition.

The parents and schoolmasters of our simpler past made no concealment about the matter. They understood the reality of original sin, and they did not spoil the child by sparing the rod. Youth was a sobbing, snivelling, howling time, jackets were dusted thoroughly and great girls trounced and spanked, and withal the Old Adam was never very thoroughly beaten out. To this day, smacks, blows, shakings, bangings, confinement, privations, and threats are the normal fare of ninety-nine out of a hundred young people. So soon as they come out of the gentle shelter of parental affection – and even that is sometimes very free with hand and slipper – the storm begins.

People so intelligent as to read a book like this are also probably intelligent enough not to have many children, and to provide those they have with a skilful, kindly, healthy upbringing, and it may seem to them that this is a too distressful view of human existence. But let them think not of their own clean nurseries, but of all the world from China to South Africa and Peru and of all classes of people. We are too apt to think about life in terms of cultivated homes in hygienic Atlantic countries. Taking the whole world over, almost half the children born into it are dead before they reach twenty-one, and most of the survivors have suffered great hardships. It is a quite unnecessary state of affairs now, but so it is. The process of getting dead before you are twenty-one cannot, I maintain, be a very jolly and amusing one – all the optimists and kindly smiling humourists of the world notwithstanding.

By the time they are eleven or twelve most of the young people alive in the world – less than two-thirds of the children born, that is, for more than a third are already dead – are put out to toil. By toil I mean uncongenial exertions that are imposed upon their free activity, exertions we would all shirk if we could. A few advanced countries hold off the curse of Adam until thirteen or fourteen, and some are making a serious effort to retain young people at educational work, and to make that attractive and even joyous, until they are sixteen. The rest of mankind is neither consulted nor persuaded in this matter of toil; hardly any have a choice between this toil or that; they are put to it and there is an end to the matter. And they hate it, and if their lives are not altogether unhappy it is not because they do not suffer humiliations, frustration, physical deprivation, and futile desires and hopes in abundance, but because they are submissive and forget.

They can forget and they can hope and they can forget their hopes and still hope again. And at length as energy ebbs comes resignation.

The common human life is a tissue of expectations that are never realised and anticipations that are never fulfilled, of toil for unsatisfying ends and pursuing anxieties, of outrageous, tormenting desires, of fever and fatigue, anger and repentance, malaise, and death.

I state these facts as brutally as possible because I think they are excessively disregarded in the art, literature, and general thought of prosperous, cultivated people. Perhaps in the past it was necessary to disregard them because there was little power to alter them. But now there is power to alter them, and literature may venture to make a step from poetry towards sincerity. We can face the fact that a very large proportion of human beings are still fobbed off with the mere offals and broken meats of life, because now we are beginning to realise that there is a possible salvation for them. It is no longer necessary to pretend that youth and everyday life overflow with excitement, fun, and happiness.

In the past I cannot imagine how the ancestral ape could have been carved into our present poise of tormented association and dawning collective power without the sufferings of billions of lives. That struggle was a necessary thing – so far as I can apprehend any necessity in things. It was in effect an immense surgery. It was not indeed an immense cruelty, for the sufferings of a million people are no greater that the sufferings of a single soul; such things do not aggregate because there exists no central brain to aggregate them; nevertheless, the operation was immense. The chloroform of a thousand illusions and distractions was unavoidable, but now those fumes pass off – and may pass. The price of power has been mainly paid. Where once the ape lurked in the thicket there are fields and houses and the lowly multitudinous rich material for a secure, powerful, and generous society.

It is possible now so to launch human lives and so to care for them that they may be balanced and serene, full and creative, eventful and happy, from beginning to end. And, moreover, these human lives we set going can be so directed that death will no longer appear as defeat; they will rather broaden out and flow on into the general steam of perception and effort than end, in any tragic and conclusive sense, at all. We are living in a cardinal change of phase in the history of conscious and wilful being. For the first occasion, it may be, in the whole process of space and time, a star of conscious and immortal resolution has been born out of the dreaming inconsecutive sufferings of animal life into the night of matter.

But we are still begotten carelessly, and we are still foolishly prepared for life.

When I go back among my memories I find the partially effaced evidences of profound conflicts. These are largely effaced, because that is the self-protective habit of the mind. But infancy and childhood are normally distressful for human beings. They are not necessarily such happy phases as they seem to be in the case of a kitten or a puppy. Much of my subsequent life, though it has been full of activities and satisfactions and the liveliest interest, has often been far from happy. There were long phases of sustained strain and dissatisfaction. And yet I have been one of the fortunate few. I have had physical vigour, I have had worldly success, I am comparatively rich, and have won through to freedom and monetary power, and it is this that gives me the measure of the common lot. What has distressed me must have distressed and distresses most people more than it has done me. My difference is only in my luck and in my escape to consolations and security. If life has not been wholly happy for me, if it has been troubled and vexed, then much more so must it be for most of the people about me.

When I probe among these faded and suppressed recollections of the unpleasant side of my past, I find among the early scars the traces of a queer instinctive struggle against instruction and direction. As a little child I had already a lively and curious mind. I wanted to learn, but I wanted to learn in my own way and for my own ends. But this I was not allowed to do. So that from an early stage I seem to have been protecting my personality against invasion almost as strenuously as I was attempting to add to its powers. Instinctively I disbelieved in the good faith of my teachers.

I believe most children have a similar instinctive disbelief. At the bottom of my heart I realised that the teachers did not particularly want to teach me; that they found the job irksome, got through it as easily as possible, and cared scarcely at all whether they distorted me by their reluctant and insufficient direction and the pressure of their compulsions. They hated me as the keystone of a hated but unavoidable job, and subconsciously they sought to injure me. They, too, had personalities in defensive revolt.

My lesson-times with my governesses and tutors were full of petty malignant conflicts of will. It was so with most of my schoolmasters. Their work, I knew, was jaded and insincere. Gilkes at Dulwich I came to believe in, Wallas, and one or two others, but even under these exemplary teachers I was jealous of direction.

The same self-protective conflict went on against the customs and procedure of out-of-school life. Why did they shove all these good manners on me? My recalcitrant soul objected obscurely but perceptibly. Why should they be so insistent that it was for *my* good that I had to keep these observances? And new clothes? Things that altered one's feeling of oneself and made the mirror unfamiliar. Were these changes really for me or for the sake of some hostile subjugating outer power? There was always a fuss, persuasions, resistance, slappings, and scolding, and when I had new clothes, until I was ten or twelve, and even after that I was darkly suspicious about them for some years.

At first I was horribly frightened about religion. Then, long before I had come to clear-headed scepticism, I became incredulous and began to detest the people who were trying to put this dismaying obsession upon me. I cannot remember a time in my boyhood when I really believed that a clergyman went about his business in good faith. It was his business, and a jolly rotten business I thought it was.

And as I grew up I began to apprehend the confused dangerousness of life and to perceive that I was being driven into the scrimmage anyhow, that though my mother and stepfather made large, copious gestures of concern, yet at the bottom of their hearts they did not care very much what kicks and shames, what subjugations, servitudes, and frustrations awaited me in the struggle.

Aided by Dickon, encouraged by one or two teacher, helped by my astounding luck, I found myself doing intensely congenial work before I was nineteen, but I went through enough conflict, anger, and anxiety to realise what must be the obscure inner tragedy of a lad who, without any special gift or advantage, is sent to drudge in a shop or office or mine, just when his intelligence is awaking to the interests of life at large. That is the common lot. That is what happens to ninety-nine out of a hundred youngsters in a modern civilised community. They are pushed into work they do not want to do, and it cramps and cripples them. It is the meanest cant to pretend that we people who succeed are in some way different from the general run, that "they" don't feel it as we did, that "they" are really interested by subjections and routines and duties that would bore us of the finer strain to death. Going to work is a misery and a tragedy for the great multitude of boys and girls who have to face it. Suddenly they see their lives plainly defined as limited and inferior. It is a humiliation so great that they cannot even express the hidden bitterness of their souls.

But it is there. It betrays itself in derision. I do not believe that it would be possible for contemporary economic life to go on if it were not for the consolations of derision. I suppose nearly all servants and employed people find it necessary to ridicule their employers and directors. They find it necessary to divest these superiors of their superiority, give them undignified nicknames, detect their subtler frustrations, and then with a gasp of relief, ha, ha! life become tolerable again.

The root of all laughter lies in that whim of Fate which in the course of a brief million years or so made of the fiercest and loneliest species of animals the most socially involved of all living things. The adaptations are complex and clumsy and lie heavily upon us. We live under the tension of an imposed respect for our fellow-creatures. When that tension snaps, when the compelling orator sits down on his hat, or when the neatly dressed dandy struts defying our depreciation, all unconscious of the flypaper he picked up from his last chair, we shout with joy at the release. And none of us likes to be laughed at, because we feel that thereby our protection from our fellow-creatures is stripped from us. Our claim upon their respect is torn and flung back at us. There is sublimated rebellion and menace in all laughter.

Dickon and I in the days of our youth were both great laughers. We showed our teeth at the toils of existence about us, at the religious fears we struggle to escape, at the dull pomp and circumstance of monarchy and law, at the vast solid arrogance of well-off people. I have told of our standing jests of Mr G and the Boops. I have told how for days we hardly spoke to each other except to talk facetious nonsense. Almost all our reading beyond the bright circle of our special interests was in funny books, and all we really cared for in public entertainments was the comic part. We read Mark Twain and Max Adler; Jerome K Jerome rose upon us and seemed to us a star of the first magnitude; Dickon and I were both married men and very busy when W W Jacobs began to write, but my discovery of him was a matter to tell Dickon with haste and enthusiasm. More laughter we sought, and yet more. We had, and I believe the whole human race in bondage has, an unappeasable craving for laughter. Nearly all our world could be made digestible with mockery, and it was intolerable to us in any other mode. But there was one thing we two could not laugh about, could not talk about, and which, indeed, we never tried to talk about, and that was the immense urgency of sex.

So far I have been able to tell of the forms and quality of my world without very much more than a passing allusion to sexual things. But now I must begin to deal with that vivid and disconcerting reality. From my late days at school onward I was tormented by sexual desire. It was not desire for any particular person; it was plain unassigned lust, and the tension grew with every year of my life. And interwoven with it, a thing springing up with it in me, and not, I am certain, derived to any considerable extent from teaching or other outer influence, was a feeling of intense shame and an impulse to conceal this burning appetite.

I do not know how far I was abnormal, or how far it is the common lot to be thus obsessed throughout adolescence. I can only tell my own story. I think perhaps Dickon and I were both rather more reserved and restrained that the average; our circumstances reinforced our natural character and developed our distrust of our fellow-creatures very early. I did not betray this red secret, I know, to any living being, nor did I attach my desires to any living being. I do not remember that I ever looked to any human being for their gratification except in the most transitory fashion. I kissed the servant at my lodgings once in a sudden tumultuous fashion, and was instantly disgusted with myself and ashamed. She was, poor girl, so manifestly a substitute for something else, with her untidy hair and soiled apron. My desires were developed in relation to nude pictures and statuary, they were stimulated by monstrous dreams, they were directed by glowing imaginations that arose unbidden. And since I was convinced that they were essentially enervating desires, I kept myself, except for the most incidental lapses, under a rigorous restraint.

That sexual desire arises of itself in young people in their early teens, that it is something quite distinct from personal love, and that it may never become closely associated with personal love, are facts that run altogether counter to the romantic travesty of life upon which most current moral judgments are based. Edwin, in a state of spotless purity, encounters the lovely and if possible even blanker Angelina. Innocent toyings lead to the naïve discovery of passion. Which burns, without heat or smoke, with an instinctive moderation, and Edwin and Angelina are happy ever after. So it is supposed to happen, and generation has followed generation with the strangest, richest, most terrifying, distressing, and debasing tumult in their blood and in their moods and dreams, and a bright pretence of never having heard of the business in their general deportment.

I doubt if there was anything in my behaviour during those strained years before my marriage to betray, except to a skilled observer, the tormenting distraction within. My work suffered from phases of inattention, and I had moods of sullen and sometimes frantic anger. At times the drive in my nerves would summon up alluring visions of sweet, lovely, and abandoned women, and I would count the scanty money I had available and leave my work and prowl about the dim London roads and streets looking for a prostitute, and when I approached one her poor painted charms and cheap advances would seem so repulsive that I would quicken my pace and hurry past her in a commotion between desire and disgust. I would wander for hours in that fashion, and return fatigued and footsore and still incapable of restful sleep.

I do not know if this sort of thing happened to Dickon. I can only guess. We never betrayed our sexual life to one another. We were too close together and unable to escape from each other to risk even the beginning of confidences. To this day Dickon and I have never talked about sex.

I want to insist upon the fact that this wolfish impulse, with its disposition to carry me out with it and prowl in the twilight with me, did not lead me to fall in love with anyone and was on the whole a barrier to my falling in love with anyone. It was something much deeper, more animal, more elemental in my being, pre-human, something a tom-cat could understand. There were women students at the college, some very clever and attractive; there were friendly girl students in the Art College near by; they seemed aloof from passion and preoccupied with minor interests; I did not associate them with my hot desires. They had an inordinate liking for walking about the Museum and making tea and conversing in groups after the tea was made.

Such entertainment offered small solace to my feverish cravings. I can guess now that they were not so serene as they seemed. And no doubt I seemed to them also cool and detached, and very self-controlled young man reputed to be good at molecular physics.

Since those days fiction and conversation in England have grown much more outspoken, but I doubt if that increasing frankness has done so much as people pretend to assuage this part of the stress of youth. That was an age of repression and concealment, yes; and to bring a thing into the light is the first step to dealing with it sanely; but mere frankness and exposure alone will no more cure these troubles than they will heal a broken leg. So far as I can judge, humanity suffers from periodic waves of putting too much clothing on and then of taking too much off. From round about the end of the century up to the present time we have been flinging aside everything, from top-hats and collars and neck-wraps and boots and shoes, down at last to the fig-leaves. And the breadth and freedom of our conversation, and particularly the conversation of some of our clever young ladies, leaves nothing unspoken and everything to be desired. But the questing beast does not fly from the sight of itself; lust does not evaporate under the influence of chatter. Lust remains lust and is going to be a monstrously troublesome thing to human beings, whether we hide everything and never speak of it, never name it, never think of it, or whether we decorate our nurseries and elementary schools with nothing but undraped marble and wax models, and treat all conversation that is not directly sexual as improper. I have studied these affairs, not always theoretically, through nearly forty of my fifty-nine years of life, and I am inclined to think that between the utmost frankness and the severest concealment there is very little practical difference. It is a matter of usage.

Some there are, going a little further than the frank exposure school – moral homoeopathists – who would allay by gratification.

There is something to be said for that doctrine; it abolishes most of the morbid repressions and shifts the stresses from the deeper to the more superficial strata of the mind, but it does not end the trouble. I am for moderation, for moderate gratification, but it is not always easy to arrange or define moderation. It is in the nature of sexual desire to be inordinate. That is the crux of this perennial perplexity of our species. That is the justification of decency and restraint.

This is a thing that I now see I realised instinctively in my youth, and which is present and very important in all adolescents. Sexual enterprise grows with success. It clamours of more. Give it an inch and it take an ell. Permit the song of Pan to be sung and presently it will be demanded with variations. Nothing complicates so easily and rapidly. Nothing is so steadfastly aggressive. Noting is so ready to enhance itself with insane fantasies. Nothing under check of defeat is so apt to invade and pervert other fields of interest and take substitutes and imitations rather than accept complete denial. I can quite understand the disposition of most churches and religions to fight sexual desire from the beginning, to kill it at the door rather than fight it when it is already half in possession of the house.

A point that I think is very important if one is to see this business clearly is that I never really identified my lust with myself in these early phases. So far as I can ascertain how matters stand with other young people, that is the normal case. I can best express my state of mind by saying that I felt it to be a damned thing that had come in me. It did not seem to be myself as my passionate desire to carry on research in crystallography and molecular physics was myself, or as my care for my future or my affection for my brother and my few friends was myself. St Austin has drawn the most interesting theological deductions from this autonomous detachment of carnal desire from the essential personality, and it is plain how easily it must have led to a belief in diabolical possession.

If anything was needed to clinch our belief in the naturalists' explanations of man's origins, it would be this extravagance of our sexual side. No designing mind, no mind, at any rate, with a glimmering of human reason, would have produced a sort of life so dominated and swamped by sexual desire as we are, nor have permitted that desire to escape so easily from fruition to quite fruitless gratification. But a mechanical process whose variations of method were subjected to no other criterion but survival would plainly have produced just such as state of affairs as exists. Only such a process could have made an unconditional clinging to life, hunger, and an insensate direction of every accumulation of energy into the reproductive channels, even when that channel led almost certainly to nothingness, the crude elements of existence. The billion futile pollen-grains of the cedar-trees are no more astonishing than the futile cravings, love-makings, couplings, and sexual tumult of human beings. "What matter the waste," says old Nature, "if there is a chance of one pollen-grain reaching an ovum? What else do you think you are for? Why should I economise? What is economy? I neither need you nor hate you. Take your chance. More of you. More of you to live or more of you to die. What does it matter to me?"

So it is that for the begetting and bearing of three or four children, a matter of a few minutes in the life of a man and of a few months in the life of a woman, the sexual shape is imposed upon almost all their activities. No other shape has any appeal to Nature. We are driven by imaginations, feverish wishes, rivalries, hostilities, hates, resentments, all arising out of sex; we dress for sex, we disport ourselves for sex, it drenches our art, our music, our dreams. For that much practical outcome our whole lives are obsessed. And if it were not for that obsession, for its hopes and excitements and collateral developments, I do not know where the great majority of lives would find the driving force to continue.

## 2 – *The Crewes at Home*

So I remember my adolescence and my young manhood as a period of hidden struggle and sustained anxiety, mitigated by ridicule and laughter. Careless youth indeed! Within was this ever-recurrent, alluring, and terrifying attack of sex upon my freedom and activities; without was the dangerous world, the hostility of the tradition of the Old Man to youth, the social obstacles and imperatives, the powers of direction and the powers of denial and restraint that manifestly meant to trip up and capture and subjugate the vast majority of my generation to lives of subservience, self-effacement, frustration, and toil.

I had no objective clearly before me, which I believed to be the realisation of my essential self; I wanted to saturate myself with immediate experimental knowledge of molecular science and to give all my energies to its prosecution, and I knew that I had to win and hold, against a mass of adverse influences, the necessary position and opportunity. Research in those days was even more scantily endowed and permitted than it is today. But I had got my foot in the door, so to speak, and I think I could have won through to an assured place if I had kept myself steadfast and concentrated. But I could not do so. Sex caught me unawares one day and wrenched away the mastery of my life from science. I fell into a passion of desire and I married. It was as if the walls of my laboratory collapsed, and my instruments and notebooks were overturned and scattered by a rush and invasion of stormy, commonplace, ill-conceived purposes. I married for the sake of a kiss, and I made a great entanglement for myself in life.

I do not know whether even now I have emerged from the developments and consequences of that great entanglement. It diverted me altogether from the narrow scientific trail I had intended to pursue. It turned me into the paths I have followed. I fought my way through it to this very different sort of freedom that I now enjoy. It is, perhaps, a broader freedom. But is it an encumbered freedom; it is not aloof and serene like the freedom of science. All the problems and cares of life seemed enmeshed with it.

I dislike having to tell this story of my marriage. I perceive I have delayed it as long as possible; that I have, for example, told almost everything I have to tell about my brother first, very largely because of this reluctance. There is no sound reason now why I should not face the facts of this the most remote phase of my past – for it seems really much remoter than my childhood – but I have suppressed it so long that the habit of suppression has been established in me. I find it difficult to recover the facts in their order, and about many of my moods I must needs be as speculative now as though I told of the acts of someone quite outside myself.

After Dickon went to Bloomsbury I was very lonely for a time in Brompton, and then the gaps of time his departure left me began to be filled by other people. The social life of the South Kensington student in those days was hardly organised at all; there was no Students' Union as yet and no tennis clubs nor suchlike facilities for meeting. There was not even a students' refreshment-room. There was a small debating society very much in the hands of a little gang of biological and geological students, from whom I got my first ideas of socialism. I scraped acquaintance with a youngster of my own age named Crewe, who was also doing advanced work in physics, and with him I began to walk and gossip in the park and gardens, and I became fairly intimate with one or two of the debating society men. Crewe had a brother in the art school, and introduced me through him to that more picturesque side of South Kensington life.

The London art student in those days was still only very imitatively Bohemian; he was very new to the art of being an art student; but there were Morris dresses and florid ties and velvet jackets and casual meals in studios and a research for conversational brilliance. Presently I found myself rather shyly a visitor at the Crewes' house.

The Crewes occupied a large, ramshackle, grey, semi-detached house in a road that branched out of the Fulham Road; though I went there scores of times, I cannot now remember either the name of the road or the number of the house. They had gatherings there every Sunday afternoon and evening; open house and a cold supper with sandwiches and salad and stewed fruit. The paternal Crewe was a very old, mooning gentleman with a long, thin beard, who seemed always to be standing about with his hands in his pockets, wishing he was somewhere else. He had kept a private school and retired. The presiding spirit was Mrs Crewe. She was much younger than he, very pink and very ample, with a shapely wrist, a harp, strange, elegant gestures, and a remote allusive style of conversation acquired from the novels of Mr George Meredith. She was a woman of letters; she wrote charming little love stories and children's stories in the magazines, and poems and criticism. She did not get much money for these things, she made you understand; so far she was among the elect. She loved youth and youthful hopes; she had a devouring sympathy and a great craving for confidences. She was constantly trying to "draw one out," as the phrase went, but as there was very little in the depths of my mind except quartz fibres, certain little riddles about the relations of various triclinic crystals to their monoclinic cousins, and an impatient but very formless rage with nature and the social order, it was very difficult for me to respond as freely as I wished to her kindness.

She wrung from me that I had scientific ambitions, and that for her meant that I wanted to be "like" Professor Huxley or

Lord Kelvin. That I could possibly want to know things without dramatising myself as a copy of some eminent savant never entered her head. And she was restlessly eager to find out that I had someone, a girl necessarily, who "inspired" my ambitions, although I should have thought that feminine inspiration was biological rather than molecular. I evaded her probings – sometimes, I fear, a little ungraciously – and it is only now in the retrospect that I realise how sedulously she must have restrained her appetite for confidences in the matter of my father and mother. And it was also an alleviation of her inquiries that the influence of Meredith robbed them of any brutal directness.

She irritated me, she embarrassed me, and I liked her – I don't know why – very much. She liked me too. I would find her very bright little brown eyes seeking me across the room, and her funny round face, under the tremendous cap she wore, bobbing and nodding to me, with an effect of encouragement and reassurance – I cannot imagine what about.

She would even beam deep understandings at me while she was plucking her harp strings and exhibiting her Victorian wrist. Always every Sunday she played the harp for a while and all the talk was hushed. And one of us would always be caught to sit on the little stool close beside the harpist. But usually this fell to some unwary newcomer who had not discovered the imminence of harping. He had to look rapt.

"Young Sir Philosopher still brooding over his crucibles," she would cry across the room to me.

"Beware the witch's warning!" And she would shake her finger. "There are cauldrons as well as crucibles, Sir Alchemist."

I would pretend to understand what she meant.

"Not only the stars can twinkle," she would throw at me and turn for some other victim.

I had never before encountered such perplexing brilliance.

All sorts of people came to these Sundays of hers. One or two were quite well-known literary and dramatic people, people whose names you saw on programmes or at the bottom of signed articles, but mostly the company consisted of beginners, some of them manifestly late starters, but as portly and important and whiskered as the well-known. There were early Fabians and eccentric thinkers. A modestly resolute man in a drab kilt with wildernesses of hairy knee was frequent; he was Erse or Gaelic or one of those things, and he explained to me on one occasion that properly he ought to be wearing a broadsword. He felt "incomplete," he said, without it. One evening Mrs Crewe's conversation was exceptionally delirious; "red hair from green meals," she said, "warbling his Dublin wood-notes wild. That delicious accent!" and I became aware of Mr Bernard Shaw in his celebrated Jaeger costume talking in a corner. At that time he was a lean young music critic with an odd novel or so to this credit, giving few intimations as yet of the dramatic career that is now culminating so magnificently – if even now it is culminating – in "Saint Joan."

But the larger element was undistinguished youth. There were three Crewe girls, each with a large circle of intimates, and both the sons also brought in their friends. And often youth prevailed to such an extent that the pretence of a conversazione was abandoned and we played juvenile games. We would play dumb-crambo or charades, and in these charades a certain inventiveness I have, and a certain capacity to act preposterously and gravely, gave me a kind of leadership. Dumb-crambo is an inferior entertainment to fully developed charades, and after a time the latter banished the former from the Crewe household and grew into a kind of consecutiveness. We contrived to make many of them into quaint little three, four, and five act plays. Those were the absurd days of the British theatre; Barrie and Shaw had yet to dawn upon us; even the mockery of Wilde's *Importance of*

*Being Earnest* had not relieved the pressure of the well-made play, and two leaden masters, Henry Arthur Jones and Pinero, to whom no Dunciad had ever done justice, produced large, slow, pretentious three-act affairs that were rather costume shows than dramas, with scenery like the advertisements of fashionable resorts, the reallest furniture and the unreallest passions and morals it is possible to conceive. This sort of thing lent itself to joyous burlesque. I remember we spent one very happy evening in the big ramshackle drawing-room with the folding doors upstairs, reading and rehearsing a play called *Michael and His Lost Angel*, by one or other of those twin glories of that departed age. I was Michael, very dark and high and gloomy, as far as possible in the manner of Mr George Alexander, and there was misconduct "off stage" in a lighthouse or down the barrel of a big gun or in some such bed of roses.

The Crewe gatherings went on until the schools broke up in the summer, and in May and June they flowed out into the garden, a town-stained garden of gravel and plane trees, which owned whatever magic it possessed to twilight and darkness, assisted by perhaps a dozen Japanese lanterns.

And it was in that garden one moonlight night that Clara was suddenly transfigured a beauty and mystery, and that we whispered very close to one another and hesitated and kissed. For the first time in my life I knew what it was to hold a sweet and living body in my arms and drink the passion of a kiss.

In that moment all the diffused disturbance of my life became concentrated upon one desire, to posses Clara. I held her to me, but abruptly her responsive passion ceased, and she wriggled out of my embrace.

The door had opened and someone was coming out of the house into the garden. "It's late," she said. "They will miss us. Let us go in."

We two went back into the gas-light and the belated dispersal of the party with scarcely a word more, but I knew that we were affianced. Clara, now that I could see her face, seemed to be lost in some remote, faintly triumphant dream. She did not look at me. I do not think she looked directly at me again that evening. Our hostess was in the passage and saw us come in.

"Is it a flush of warmth at last," she whispered darkly, "on Sir Galahad's white shield?"

I said I had had a very pleasant evening and asked whether I might come again when the Crewes returned in September.

"I feared the dawn would never come," said Mrs Crewe. "*Now!* Ah! – you will be human."

No doubt I made some sound like a reply, but I forget that now. I remember I wanted to walk to Clara's home with her, but she was entangled with a party of cousins, so instead I went off by myself for a long prowl in the flooding moonlight along the Serpentine and across Hyde Park.

### 3 – *Inadvertent Marriage*

I cannot recall my first meeting with Clara. She had emerged by degrees from the little bunch of young people who frequented the Crewes' house. I would find her looking at me or fluttering to my side. She intimated a distinctive friendliness by a multitude of trivial preferences and attentions. She was a dark-haired, slender, restless, talkative girl, with aquiline features and hazel eyes. At first I had not thought her very pretty. Until this great desire to possess her seized upon me I had learnt nothing of her parentage or her worldly circumstances.

Now here it is that I find my story most difficult to tell. Except for one or two vivid memories, I really do not know how I felt during the phases of this love affair. I suppose I must call it a love affair, and I suppose my state was what is called being "in love," but I cannot for the life of me recall any such moods of tenderness and self-forgetfulness as a romantic tradition requires of a lover. I will admit that the record has been thrust aside and out of the light and out of the way for many years; it has its pages blurred and discoloured; much may be absolutely forgotten. But it seems to me now that I wanted Clara with a simple, hard desire to own her and keep her. And I am in doubt whether she felt more towards me than a reciprocal extravagance of desire.

Perhaps while one can still remember tenderly one still loves, and love only ceases with the effacement of tender memories. The effacement of memories about love relationships and acts of love may be exceptionally easy in the mind; there may be some biological reason for that. Scenery, a great variety of casual incidents, chains of reasoning, passages from books, live far more vividly for me than what I am convinced must have been high moments of intense sensuous and emotional experience. I am sure there is something lost altogether between Clara and myself, and that this hard story I tell is a mere framework of facts, a skeleton robbed of all living substance and significance.

Apparently at this time there were in my mind two sets of motives so entirely inconsistent and incompatible that I sit and ask myself whether I am not seeing all this phase of my past through some distorting medium. There was my passion for research which called for all my best energies and my most lucid and energetic hours, and there was this new passion for Clara, which also was bound to develop into a whole-time job, and yet for more than a year at least I do not seem to have realised any contradiction in these matters. I seem to have gone right on with both, and to have been sincerely perplexed and astonished when at last their divergence took so practical a form that it was no longer possible for me to ignore it.

In some way surely I must have sought to reconcile them. I doubt if I could have adopted Mrs Crewe's idea that the desire for the constant companionship, kissing, fondling, and embracing of a young woman constituted an "inspiration," that it disposed and empowered me to speculate deeply and subtly upon the constitution of atoms and the nature of electrical charges. But I may have had a persuasion that these love exercises gave pride and energy and peace of mind.

I do not remember that I ever talked very much to Clara of the work I was doing. I recall her on one occasion when we were at Deal, praising the beauty of a lighthouse, and saying that with its steady light, its smooth and certain rotation, its beautiful adjusted mirrors, it was "like science." I was extraordinarily pleased at her saying that. I was so pleased that it is plain she did not often say things like that. But generally our nearest approach to my scientific concerns was the canvassing of the characters of Professor Guthrie and Dr Boys and others of the Royal College workers in those days, and speculations about the fortune of Lord Kelvin, and the possibility of making artificial precious stones, and so forth. The thought that I might make diamonds dazzled her. On the side of my socialism we were better able to meet. She, too, called herself a socialist, but she approached it rather as a campaign of benevolence towards the "slums" – supplemented by a general preference for wool garments, red ties, art fabrics, and archaic oak furniture.

If I can remember no moods of actual lovingness between us, I can at least say that we were greatly interested in and desirous of each other. We must have gone for walks together, walks and talks, from first to last, for many hundreds of miles. She had read much more widely than I had in the literature of the time, and she instructed me in the study of Meredith and Hardy and Walter Besant and Swinburne and the Pre-Raphaelites. She introduced me to the writings of William Morris and the early Bernard Shaw, the Shaw of the *Star* days. She was keen on pictures, keen on music, keen about the theatre. She was keen about the movements and characters of public people; keen about fashions and social events. So keen she was upon so many things that at times her whirling conversation seemed to whistle like a blade through the air about me. She made me feel thick and slow and under-informed. This lively diversity of her attention was mainly due to the fact that she had no objective in particular – unless it was her adventure as a sexual animal in the world. She was acutely aware how literature, art, the drama, and every social subject turned upon sex as a door turns on its hinges, and towards all other things except that hinge she was an active amateur.

She acted; she was almost on the edge of things theatrical, but she had no intention of becoming an actress; she sketched cleverly, but she had no intention of following art. When there were elections she became an excited political helper, but she pursued no sustained political aim, and though she was poor and keenly interested in success, she made no movement towards business activities. She had, indeed, no intention of doing anything seriously and steadily but living as a sexual consumer, and talking about it, and she approached life with an immense receptivity. She was a feminist after the manner of those ancient days, the days of George Egerton and *The Woman Who Did*.

Soon after that first kiss of ours she took me home to see her "people." They lived in a rather crowded little house in a square near Earls Court Station. There was an obscurely silent father – their name, by-the-by, was Allbut – who came in at odd times, and did not seem to like me; he was an architect, I learnt at once, and later on I realised he was also a speculative builder. He was one of those people who have quite a lot of money that is always "locked up" in something or other and meanwhile the household "carries on."

Mrs Allbut was very like Clara, except that in her a certain Mediterranean flash of dark alertness became distinctively Jewish. She seemed to be running her household with an acute watchfulness towards material things and an evasion of any control of her four fuzzy-haired daughters. Clara was the second of this band of sisters. They displayed on this opening occasion a cheerful harmony that was, I found later, exceptional with them. They all talked with incredible rapidity and a tremendous *savior faire*, so that all I had to do was to bear myself meekly under their swift, critical inspection. We played a game suitable for harpies, called demon-patience, a game of pouncing and snatching in a snowstorm of cards, and I got a new measure of the limitations of the philosophical mind. I was so inferior at first that my masculine self-conceit took refuge in a puerile burlesque of myself.

How different was the outlook of those girls and myself, and how unaware all of us were of those very profound differences! To them I was Clara's captive, one of her captives, for they knew, even if I did not, that she had other possibilities, and my rôle was to be retained captive so long as suited Clara to retain me, and then either to be discarded or to be converted skilfully and surely into a secure and permanent basis for Clara's miscellaneous keenness, whenever and if ever it became desirable to effect that conversion. They also were doing their best to secure a selection of practicable captives. They appraised me; they petted me and drew me out; I suspect they speculated secretly whether it was possible and worth while to filch me from Clara's bundle to their own collection.

My reading of my part was entirely different. I was, I conceived it, the masterful male, recipient of Clara's furtive but extremely effective endearments, conqueror of her heart and instincts, aspiring to be her kindly owner and ruler with the privilege of soothing and entertaining myself with her easy delightfulness whenever I chose. Her physical docility, her lively attention, was the cause of an enormous pride in me. She ruffled my hair and called me "Flosopher-lost" when my demon-patience was particularly disastrous; she seemed unable to keep her quick hands off me, and all four of them evidently found my ineptitude a very promising and endearing trait.

I remember that first afternoon very vividly; the rather dark room, the circular table from which the cloth had been removed, the bare arms, the soft glowing faces close to mine, Clara's hair sometimes brushing my cheek as she reached across me with a card. Doris, the third sister, was the quickest of all. "Stop-Out! No you *don't*!" she would cry, return some belated card to its player, and cut short the pelting struggle.

Later on I stole an evening or so from my work to study this demon-patience. I was not used to cards, but I perceived that it was absurd for a fairly good mathematician to be unready with the groupings and variations of four sets of thirteen cards. I drilled myself a little, thought out a few principles of action, and afterwards made up in science what I lacked in speed. Until at last I could truncate a hand with "Stop-Out!" as often as Doris and win a hundred up against her.

I was rewarded for these infidelities to my work by Clara's brightly expressed approval. Doris was amazed and dismayed at certain tactical inventions of mine; she would scream and lose her head as I slapped down an accumulated series of cards, humming distractingly as I did so, and Clara would slacken her play and come near to applause. It was evident her sisters had pronounced me stupid after my first début, and that it pleased her to see me vindicate myself.

For more than a year Clara filled all my waking thoughts that were not given to my work, and she dominated my dreams and reveries. All my vague and dispersed sex fantasies gave place to the thought of her. She was a very exciting girl by nature, bold in her thoughts and for that very remote and decorous time very bold in her talk and acts. We found a thousand opportunities in that ill-lit old Kensington for kisses and embraces, and she taught me everything that there was to be known in the fine art of caressing. For that she had a natural genius. It is wonderful what lurking places and kindly shelters there are to be found in streets and parks and house-porches and passages and gardens that seem quite open and exposed to unimpassioned eyes. Since no other girl now existed for me I could not imagine that any other man existed for her. And she volunteered the information time after time that none did.

After a time I defied the possible disapproval of my landlady, and Clara ventured with books and parcels and messages to my lodgings for bouts of philandering. I can see again the little circle of light upon my scattered notes under my shaded lamp as we stand body to body in the shadow.

"*Shall we turn the key in the door?*" she whispers.

And in the summer she went with her mother and sisters to St Margaret's Bay, and I went to Deal so that I could walk over and discover them by accident and share their bathing tent and join them in the sea. Clara and her sisters were good swimmers, and we would float side by side or bask on the beach in the sun together, and in the night I would lie in bed and bite my wrists and arms black and blue with the violence of my desire for that wet body in its closely clinging dress. She had a project which was never realised of a great swim by moonlight. It stirred my imagination greatly, and in my reveries we struck out from shore – and, at last, faint with effort and delight, turned with our arms wide open towards each other. And sank.

But there were various other youths and men about, and they made it very difficult for Clara and me to get at each other alone. A certain Billy Parker was particularly obnoxious. His elder brother was affianced to Marjorie, the elder sister, and he had a stupid proprietary way with Clara, hovering about her, joining in her conversations. She assured me he bored her to death, and that when they were alone together she said the most humiliating things to him and praised me continually. Clara, not to lose a moment of me, would walk part of the way with me back to Deal, and Billy would always insist on coming with us, so that she should not return to St Margaret's Bay alone. She would take my arm up to the parting and do most of the talking to me, and then as she and he went off back she would take his arm, no doubt to hold him the more firmly while she drove the barbed humiliations home. And there was a Mr Crashaw staying at St Margaret's Bay, quite a middle-aged man, a friend of her father's, she said, but evidently focussed upon her. He had twice asked her to marry him, she told me.

"I'd send him packing altogether," said Clara, "if it wasn't for his kindness to mother. You see, he's got no end of money."

Until that seaside holiday I had not been jealous of Clara nor even very urgent to be finally engaged to her. Now an irrational jealousy infected me, and also an extreme impatience to possess her wholly. But she would not be engaged to me until there was an immediate prospect of marriage. "You can't doubt I love you," she said, "but life *is* life. Marjorie marries Fred Parker this September, and then mother will be at me to get out of Doris' way. Night and day she'll be at me."

"But you don't mean – !" I was breathless.

"It's tragic, Billy. It's horrible. How can I love an old man like that? How can I endure him? After your kisses. And babies! Little old babies they'd be! Oh! Don't let me think of it, Billy! Don't make me cry! Let us be happy while we can."

My soul went cold and white within me. I thought no more of stresses in crystals for a time. I was filled with an angry resolution to marry Clara. If research was to suffer it had to suffer; if it stood in the way it had to be pushed aside. But I still hoped, in spite of the manifest fact that I was now parting my life into two unequal portions and giving the greater part to Clara, to hold my own in science. The staff in the department of physics was being rearranged, and I knew that I had merely to ask in order to get a demonstratorship at three hundred and fifty pounds a year. It would of course mean a serious invasion of the of the time I could give to research, but there the job was, with a room of its own separated by only a wood partition from the research laboratory. Three hundred and fifty pounds was not so small an income in those days as it would be now. In addition, there was the hundred and sixty pounds a year coming from my mother. I went to know how far that was the limit of my interest in my father's savings. She was troubled in her mind by my questions, and retired upstairs with a headache, but my stepfather took me into the garden, and in the course of an hour or so of carefully worded explanation made it clear that he found any increase impossible. Still that made five hundred a year, and in those days one could get charming little houses in Kensington and Fulham for fifty or sixty pounds a year.

"We need not begin with a baby right away," said Clara.

"I don't want to do that," said I.

"I'm dying to bear you a child, Billy," she said. "But for a time – we must wait. Your child. Your life. All your warm life in me! But I'll be patient…"

I was prepared to be enormously patient. I could think of a child only as something that would come between me and Clara.

"It ought to be enough," she said. "With management that ought to be more than enough. You should see what mother has to get along with at times."

### 4 – *Lair in Disorder*

It was only after we had married that I began to realise fully the extraordinary dislocations of motive that had occurred in me. Sex, which had been like a foreign thing inserted in my being, had become fully incorporated and was now the dominant thing in my life. It had expanded from a physical need and developed into a great power of self-assurance, a restless, recurrent triumph in possession. My researches went on for a time without notable deterioration. I had been so interested, so fertile before Clara obsessed me, that my work had got an immense way upon it. I ceased indeed to invent new things, to have flashes of intuition, make dazzling and ecstatic leaps upon remote lurking connections, leap out of bed at night to scribble sheet after sheet of notes. But I had enough in hand to go on with fruitfully. To that period belongs almost all the work upon the strains at the contact of dissimilar crystalline masses in rocks that was published between '92 and 1901, and secured my fellowship of the Royal Society, and I worked out also in this time those methods of examining by reflected light the ruptured faces of crystallised alloys that later stood me in such good stead with Romer, Steinhart, Crest and Co. It would have been imperceptible to anyone else; for some time it was imperceptible to me that the mental exaltation of the work had vanished.

I had grown up, I had become fully adult, I had consummated my life; I had bought my young woman and held her exultant in my arms. We made an excellent festival of each other. And presently we emerged from our mutual preoccupation a little habituated to these excitements with most of the problems of life still before us.

As I have told, we called upon Minnie and Dickon.

I suppose it was – if one may use a preposterous metaphor – the intention of old Mother Nature that we should now produce a number of children, and that while Clara bore them and cherished them I should go hunting for more and more food and comfort. That also was the tradition of human society. Some of the children would live and some would die, and by the time the task was done, our jokes exhausted and our tears dried, we should be ready to depart. In those days it was not the custom to correlate the large developments of human affairs with the things of the individual life, and so it was only vaguely and personally that we apprehended that children were no longer wanted in such abundance as heretofore and that a new sanitation, new methods of education, were lifting the burthen of complete reproductive specialisation from womankind – and putting very little in its place. For a time upon quite personal grounds we were resolved to have no children. We had insufficient money; we had insufficient room; and Clara, with her all-round intelligent amateurishness, was left very much at loose ends. I, too, with my ill-paid, pure research was far away from the traditions of the normal breadwinner. I needed time. I was always in want of more hours, hours for thought, hours for calculation and experiment. Clara on the other hand had nothing to do with her time. She was quick and clever with her little home, and through with its monotonies in an hour or so. Between our séances of love-making, therefore, I was hurried and driven, and she was slack and bored.

Though neither of us was nearly as avid of life as young people seem to be nowadays, we were still sufficiently impatient to develop the discordances of our position into very great distresses. The once wonderful house in Edenbridge Square with a green door and a brass knocker, brightly furnished with money that Dickon had lent me, which had seemed at first the most delightful of love-nests, become a lair from which we both absented ourselves more and more. I would steal an increasing proportion of our waking hours for the laboratory, and she would be driven abroad, almost penniless, in her cheap but clever clothes, to find some amusement, some excitement, for her vacant hours. For a time she came to the laboratory to help and work with me, but her nimble hands were more often than not in the wrong places and her quick inaccurate wits were extraordinarily fertile in faintly irritating misconceptions. And after a while she found laboratory assistance, without complete intellectual participation, boring, and took offence at my frequent disinclination to knock off and make love to her in my private room. It seemed to Clara the primary use to which a private room ought to be put.

She thought she would act; she thought she would develop her gift for painting and drawing. Philip Weston, who afterwards as Dickon's prize artist was to do so much to make the London poster artistic, was very ready to give her lessons. She made considerable progress and attained to everything except originality and intensity. She rejoined the Fabian Society, which she had left before her marriage, and various other societies that promised drawing-room meetings. But most of these things were things of the evening, when time and the exigencies of life were not so heavy on her hands. Art in a convenient studio is on the other hand naturally an affair of the afternoon.

Across the interval of a third of a century I can look back at the strains between these two young people, one of whom has become myself, and I can see that neither she nor I can justly be blamed for our disaster. Like all human beings we were borne upon the great flood of change, and it chanced that we were caught in an eddy. She did not know the forces in her and without her that had taken hold of her and were spinning her so giddily, and I had as little self-knowledge. I wanted to drive on with my work and drive on with my work. In such times as I could spare she could minister to my love and pride in her. For the rest of her days I had no care except that she did nothing to infringe my lordship over her. And being anxious not to distress me unduly, when presently under the urgency of her need for entertainment she began to infringe upon my lordship, she saved my pride and temper by some very excellent lying.

What a vivid silly creature she was, and how inevitable was her drift to that exciting exploitation for her physical personality which was her instinctive gift! It needs all that third of a century for me to record with detachment that while I was sitting over my petrographical microscope, getting nearer and nearer to the interference colour scale that enabled me to determine the proportion of the bases in the micas and felspars, she and Philip Weston, having discovered they were perfect physical types, were obliging each other as models for a series of drawings from the nude. In the atmosphere of aesthetic gravity thus created, what the world in general calls misbehaviour become an almost negligent extension of their interesting studies. And I admit she was a pretty thing, well worth drawing and deserving to be drawn, and for the moment less mischievous when posed than active.

I did not know of such little adventures in liberality at the time, but I felt them in the air. I become curious about her movements. I was horrified to find myself suspicious and jealous. I did not think of Weston at first, but I was startled to find that Billy Parker had turned up again with a touching disposition to take her out to rather expensive lunches. Billy was her sister's brother-in-law, a privileged relationship; and she talked of him so frequently and needlessly that a wiser husband would have perceived that he was not at any rate the central figure of the situation. But after a time I began to see all sorts of things about Billy down the petrographical microscope.

Now it was against all my conceptions of our relationship that I should question her, much less make any objection, about her use of her leisure. We had had many very liberal and far-reaching talks about the relationship of men and women before we had married, and it had been agreed between us that we should not be "tied" by that antiquated ceremonial. We were both to keep a "perfect freedom."

I suppose young people of high and advanced pretensions have talked in that way for generations. It pervaded the brief life of Shelley, and in his letters and recorded conversation the phrases of a noble sexual generosity have already a used and customary quality. I suspect the revolt against marriage, and against the fierceness of marriage, has been growing with changing social conditions, with increased social ease and security, with the decline in the necessity for the lair-home, for a long time. It can be remarked in the social life of Imperial Rome; it peeped out in a score of usages during the days of chivalry; the last two centuries are full of it; half our novels are about it. I doubt if an animal can become so rapidly economically social as man has done in the last million years without becoming also sexually social; a solitary beast is a pairing beast, but man is almost the only gregarious beast that attempts to pair. But at the time I did not philosophise so broadly as that. I did not realise that half the trouble in the little houses round such squares as Edenbridge Square and all the similar and kindred squares and roads and suburbs of London and Paris and New York – and I suppose Pekin and Bombay – is a struggle between the dispositions of the lair and the dispositions of the herd. I happened to be on the liberal side, by chance as much as by anything; I preached the tolerations of the herd with the exclusive passion of the lair rich in my blood. I controlled my instinctive impulse to dominate and monopolise. But the tension of these suppressions found an outlet in other directions. The things I would not allow myself to say about Clara's morals I said about her meals. I become abruptly aware of a galling disregard for my comfort in our little home. I became acutely sensitive to Clara's domestic casualness, to the indiscipline of her one servant, to her absence from home if by any chance I came back at an unusual hour. I began to nag, I became irritable and objectionable. We quarrelled, we sulked, we made it up without explanations under the compulsion of our vigorous young appetites. Presently we found ourselves in money difficulties. She had supplemented her pocket-money by diverting various sums due on our tradesmen's bills. On our first year of housekeeping together we were nearly a hundred and seventy pounds in debt and with nothing in hand.

And just at this inopportune time she became extraordinarily preoccupied with the idea of a child. She declared she wanted a child passionately, that it was dishonourable for us to go childless, that it was our duty to balance our peculiar gifts against the rapid multiplication of the unfit. And she was going to waste. She was demoralised through her thwarted instinct of maternity. She was no good without a child. Anything might happen to her unless she had a child to steady her. She expressed herself with extreme impatience. I objected. While we were entangled and short of money a child wouldn't have a fair chance with us. Couldn't we wait a year or so?

"While I muddle about," she said. "Billy! I'm going to have that child."

"Not yet," I said.

She spoke slowly and with her utmost emphasis. "Billy, you don't understand. I'm going to have a child."

"But, good God!" said I. "How is that possible?"

She made no answer. Suddenly I took her by the shoulders and looked into her face.

"How is that possible?" I said.

She explained garrulously and unsoundly. One was never sure. In a dozen ways it might be possible.

But my doubt of her had been a very transitory one. My solicitudes as a reluctant breadwinner came across my mind to shield her from my scrutiny. And as yet I did not distrust her to the extent of that doubt.

"Well, we'll have to face it," I said, singularly free from the joys and exaltations of fatherhood. "Will you be ill, do you think? So far you've carried it well. You'll carry it off all right. You're a very perfect female animal, you know, made for the business.

And we must squeeze some sort of nursery into the house... I wonder what it will cost us... We'll manage... But it will be a tight job for us. You're a devil, Clara, at getting your own way– in spite of science and art."

She seemed, I thought, to flinch.

"Nothing to be afraid of," said I. "You're one of Nature's daughters."

There was something already at the back of my mind which had been there, indeed, since I realised the deficit on our first annual budget. But I did not tell Clara of it, because I hated to think of the alacrity she would have displayed in grasping all the possibilities it opened to us. I knew that I could carry off all this trouble quite easily by a simple transfer of my activities from the laboratories of the Royal College of Science to the laboratories of the great metallurgical and chemical firm of Romer, Steinhart, Crest and Co. They had heard of me, they wanted me badly, although they did not nearly know all I might be able to do for them. But at any rate they wanted me to the extent of eight hundred pounds a year, rising by increments of fifty pounds to twelve hundred, and that seemed to offer an immediate surcease of all my present anxieties. The heavy work of the elementary course of the college was over for the year; it had finished in February, and there would be little difficult about my resignation.

A year before I should have told Clara of this possibility and discussed it with her, but now I kept it to myself. Even in that moment of acceptance of the new situation I wasn't quite sure of myself. I though it over for three or four days still before I went to Romer, Steinhart's. I seem to remember that I was on the whole amused, bitterly amused by what had happened to me. I realised quite clearly that I was bidding a long farewell to the living realities of research. In all probability it would be a lifelong farewell to the service of pure knowledge. For the rest of my life, as I saw it then, I should be nosing out artful ways for underselling magnesium or making aluminium cheap. Fine fun! I was to be a scientific truffle-hunting dog for predacious business. Which was predacious by instinct and did nothing worth doing with the money. I remember recalling one day how old Mrs Crewe had said to me, "Ah, now – you will be human!" and laughing aloud in the street. This was being human.

I did not pay very much attention to Clara during these days, but afterwards I perceived that she, too, had been greatly preoccupied. She was manifestly dismayed at the prospect of bearing a child in our diminutive house, and though I could have relieved her of that apprehension in half a dozen words, I did not find it in my heart to do so. At times she would express an effusive penitence for the trouble she had been the means of bringing upon me; at times she would be extraordinarily thoughtful and aloof. One of the chance things I had said to her stuck in her mind. "I'm one of Nature's daughters," she said. "And she's got me."

I wonder if I felt tenderly for her. I do not recall any tenderness at all.

I had an interview with old Romer, and then with him and three other of the directors, and after that we clinched our arrangements. I informed the Royal College people of their approaching loss, and still I forebore to tell Clara of her improved prospects. Perhaps I wanted it to be a pleasant scene, and I feared that her joy and relief would provoke my resentment and make me say something bitter.

Then one day at breakfast I saw she was looking unhappy. I had never seen real unhappiness in her face before. Hers was a very animated face, and I knew a thousand of its expressions – angry, bored, and forgetful – but this was something different. She thought I was reading my paper; she had forgotten I was there, and she was sitting quite still and staring in front of her – as though hope suddenly gone out of her being. "Cheer up,

Clara!" said I, and she became aware of me with a violent start. She looked at me with a question in her eyes.

"I'm all right, Billy," she said.

I glanced at the clock. "It's nothing to be afraid of," I said, getting up and gathering together some papers for my despatch-case. I took her in my arms and kissed her. She kissed me back, but how forced was her kiss and how dead she had become to my touch!

I had to hurry away or I would have told her of the Romer-Steinhart arrangement there and then. But her expression of wretchedness went with me. It troubled me all day. She showed deep feeling so rarely that the idea of her being miserable came with a special painfulness. I felt I had been too hard with her over a misadventure that was as much mine as hers. And generally lately I had been hard upon her. She was in for much the worst side of the trouble before us. I wasn't playing the game by her; I was being a vexatious and unhelpful partner. I was making her suffer for my disappointments, disappointments she could not possibly understand.

I was so concerned to relieve her worries that I came home early. But she was out; she did not come in until past six. When she came in she was no longer wretched looking; she was flushed and grave-faced, but extraordinarily alive. I had been sitting in the little drawing-room and living-room that was also my study, poring rather inattentively over a file of notes upon some work I was closing down, and waiting for her to come in. I stood up as she entered.

"Back early?" she said.

"Before five."

"Your fire's out."

"I didn't watch it."

"Ellen got you some tea?"

"She was out. I got it myself."

She stared at the things on the table, with her mind far away. "Billy," she said, "I want to talk to you."

"At your service," I said.

"It's – serious stuff."

I stared at her, unable to guess what was coming. She did not look at me. Her eyes looked at me at the blank fireplace behind me.

"It's got to be said," she remarked. "Sooner or later it has to be said."

Her voice quickened. "It's better to have it out – than to go away with nothing explained. It's better to have things said. Better to be plain. It's something I've had in mind for weeks. Now it has come to a head. I don't know if you remember all we used to talk about before we married, about either of us giving the other their freedom if they wanted it. I don't know how much you meant about that sort of thing, or whether you mean to stand by it now. But all these months while we have been so unhappy together I have been thinking of what we used to say. I've been thinking of how we used to declare that no law, no marriage, ought to hold a man and a woman together if they did not love. And all the while you have been growing colder and harder to me and making life more difficult for me. I have been asking myself, Billy, more and more if you and I are really lovers any longer, if you and I can even pretend any longer to be in love."

"Quite recently," I remarked, "the pretence has – worked."

"Oh! Proximity! Habit! How can one save oneself? But is it love, Billy? Is it truly love? For that matter, has it ever been love?"

I realised that I was facing something absolutely strange to me. This was new, a different Clara who stood before me. I remember vividly the picture she made in our darkling room and the effect of discovery her words produced. And I noted for the first time that she was already physically changed. Her pretty shoulders seemed a little broader and lower, her neck softer and whiter. Her eyes; there was something changed in her eyes. I observed, but I do not remember what I thought nor what I said in reply to her words. I observed that she was declaring that we had never loved, and I apprehended, with a kind of astonishment at not having had it clear before, that that was true. Why had it not been clear before?

This opening comes back to me very plainly, but much of the talk that followed must have slipped out of my memory altogether. I cannot remember in what phrases she made me aware that she meant to leave me nor by what transitions my mind adapted itself to the new situation. Then in harsh relief against that fog of forgetfulness I see her with her hands gripping each other and a sort of swallowing movement in her throat before she blurted out: "I'm not going away alone. You don't understand, Billy. You don't understand what I am trying to tell you. I'm going away with Philip Weston. I have been at his studio all this afternoon."

In a flash I saw everything plainly. I recall a gleam of sympathy for the wincing courage with which she faced me. A dozen different mental processes seemed to be going on in my mind, quite independently of one another. I remember quite distinctly that I thought I ought to kill her, and that it would be extremely agreeable and exciting to take her pretty neck, which I had kissed with delight a thousand times, and squeeze it, squeeze it in my hands. I was dangerous, and she knew I was dangerous. And yet at the same time, in the same brain was a leap of relief that I was quit of her. And then a pang of exasperation because my agreement with Romer, Steinhart was signed and fixed and my successor at the Royal College already appointed. For a time I didn't think much about Weston. Clara in the foreground blotted him out.

I stood still on the hearthrug, and the moment for murder passed.

"So that, in all probability, is where the baby comes from?" I said.

She moistened her lips with her tongue and nodded, with her eyes still warily on mine.

"And Weston – is in a state to believe that?"

"He loves me, Billy."

She felt she was over the worst.

"He doesn't know you yet. All this – puts one out to a certain extent. I didn't see it coming. Where for example, do you propose to sleep tonight, Clara? Here? We might fall victims to – what did you call it? Proximity. Habit. And then I might strangle you. And that would surprise and annoy Weston."

She did not seem to have thought that out yet. She decided to take a few things and go back to Weston. He would be waiting in the studio. He would be sure to be waiting.

"I ought to be strangled," she said, with that idea still lingering in her mind. I perceived that she would have liked a little strangling – and then perhaps tears. But I was immeasurably remote from tears.

It came to me as I stood on the hearthrug before her that I was gathering and expanding and spreading out a sort of peacock's tail of derisive hate. I had no feeling for her then but derisive hate. It was as if I had never done anything but hate her. I was teeming with insulting phrases like a thundercloud ready to burst, and saying nothing. At the same time I realised that this was not how a civilised man of advanced views ought to react to our amazing situation. It was before me, but I did not grasp it yet.

"I don't know what to say to you," I confessed. "Get your things together. Tell Ellen some old lie. Tell her your mother is ill and you want to be with her. And go. Get out. I shall go out – now. And just walk about and try and figure out what has happened. I shan't come back for an hour or so. I promise you that. You'll have plenty of time to pack and get off… It's sudden. And yet I suppose I ought to have seen it coming…"

I considered. "What else is there to say?" She appeared at the door of the sitting-room as I was going out of the house. An idea had dawned upon her. She spoke with a note of perplexity.

"Billy," she said, "this may be our good-bye!"

I stared at this new aspect. She wanted an emotional parting! She wanted a scene in which I was to play the part of poor old Billy. She felt a certain remorse and pity was due to me. She conceived the situation as cheaply as that. She had no sense of the murderous fury that filled me.

"Well," I answered, after a pause, in a brutal voice; "what the hell else do you suppose it to be?"

"*Billy!*" she whispered, aghast, and gripped her hands together. "Oh, Billy!"

I did not slam the door wilfully, but it seemed to slam itself.

## 5 – *Queen's Proctor*

It is a difficult undertaking to reach across the interval of thirty-odd years and reconstruct the state of mind of that dismayed and angry human animal who walked about Hyde Park while his wife, dismayed likewise, and as troubled, perhaps, at herself and him and the universe as he was, packed for her departure from the poor little home that had contained their passions and dissensions for a year and a half. There was no tenderness, no pity in my mood; it was almost entirely a state of rage. And I do not think that even then it was directed against Clara. What I raged against had the shape of Clara, wore her delightful body, but it was really the passion and desire in myself for the glories, thrills, and gratifications she could give me that maddened me. She had become a consuming necessity in my life, and I had lost her.

I do not remember that in all the storm there entered anything at all that one could speak of as love. In most – in ninety-nine per cent of love affairs, there is, I am convinced, hardly any love at all. There was hate. Hate, a wildly scornful hate for Clara's nimble lying, would come over my mind like the quivering red glare one sees for a time among thunderclouds, and pass again. It was not a very pointed and personal hate. I hated the situation and her share in it, but even then I knew that she was as much the victim of uncontrollable drives in her own nature as I was.

But what in this belated retrospect impresses me most about the state of mind of this young Mr William Clissold in Hyde Park one April afternoon in 1891 was the primary important in it of wounded vanity and self-love. I realise again as I sit and think these things over and write about them here the profound mental effect a woman has upon the man to whom she gives herself. She becomes the sustainer of his self-esteem, she imposes her values upon his vanity; she secures an enormous power of humiliation over him. In every love affair there is a campaign of flattery and reassurance. It seemed of the first importance to me that evening that I should not be the rejected one, that I should, so to speak, shout it at her: "I don't want you. I never want to touch you again."

What an incredible thing that young man of twenty-three is to myself of fifty-nine! I am astonished as I look back into this little pit of memories at his narrowness and violence. Maybe I am self-righteously astonished and nearer to him still than I like to think myself. But how entirely self-centred he was! I suppose every young thing has to be self-centred if it is to get anywhere in a scrambling world. Youth and individuality are self-assertion; they have no other possible significance. Yet I cannot but feel that my self-protection was excessive.

I had a great desire to lie to Clara and tell her that I, too, had been unfaithful. It filled me with shame and anger that I had been steadfastly faithful to her and content with her. It would have been so much easier to have been able to write to her magnanimously: "Go your own way. I, too, love someone else."

It appeared, indeed, as I walked about Hyde Park, fantastically important to me that I should balance Clara's infidelity with equally liberal behaviour of my own. Just to define Clara's place once for all and banish this "poor old Billy" business from the world.

I doubt if my behaviour was very abnormal by our present standards. Human society had passed beyond the phase of passionate possession between the sexes, when it was natural and proper for the husband to kill the wife for her treason and the lover for his robbery. That "Old Man" husband is buried deep now beneath whole mountains of suppression. But not so deeply as to be beyond danger of eruption. The mountains of suppression quake and move. I had trained my mind in the fashion of our time and held Clara to be a free person on an equality with myself. It remained to me, therefore, to solace my shattered vanity as well as I could, and above all to release myself as soon as possible from the ascendancy that Clara had gained over my senses. Because I knew quite clearly, even then, that if I did not do that, if I let myself dwell upon her relations with Weston, I ran the risk of an exasperation of mind that might fling me back again, in spite of all my civilisation, towards archaic violence.

And so for a time I though very little either of my science, my teaching, or of the new position I was to take up in the autumn. I set out upon a search for sexual adventure, and, with the advantage of such knowledge as my marriage had given me, it was not long before I had distracted myself from the obsession of my divorce proceedings with several intrigues. So long as one did not love and was not too scrupulous about the truth, making love was by no means a difficult art. I could be plausible and talkative, and had the instinct that restrains a caress until it is desired. I could soon count "successes" and had a healing reassurance that I could be desirable. For illicit love in London it is not so much charm and splendour that are needed as convenient premises and a certain leisure. There was hardly a particle of love, it seems to me now, in any of these businesses, and in the intervals of my various adventures I found myself wildly and terribly unhappy. Yet it may be, so queerly selective are our memories in all that touches sex, there was much tenderness, gratitude, friendliness that I have forgotten. Yes – there was friendliness; of that I may tell later.

It was profoundly necessary to me that I should flaunt my freedom before the eyes of Clara, and since I had refused to play the part of "poor old Billy" in the drama it became almost as necessary to her to demonstrate her satisfaction with Weston. One among my three or four "affairs" had emerged to a sort of predominance. It was with a girl named Jones, who was a model, a sunny-haired, smiling, amoral creature whom everybody called Trilby. I had met her in some studio party. Du Marier's *Trilby* had been the success of a publishing season, and the name itself was being splashed about the whole English-speaking world. She was blond and handsome and more effective than Clara; she knew her and had some obscure hostility to her, and so we contrived to be seen about together and even to encounter Weston and Clara on one or two occasions and go through the gestures of a liberal amiability.

And Clara and I were sedulous to assure everyone in our two little worlds that what we were doing was high and calms and exactly what ought to be done, that we had parted because we did not love each other as people ought to do if they were to live together, but that we maintained the highest esteem and the utmost affection towards each other. Our marriage had been a mistake. An agreeable mistake that had not lasted. She was drawn to Weston by an old and natural passion. We said little or nothing about the decisive intrusion of the coming child or of any doubt that had ever troubled us about its paternity. After all, very few people were likely to check us back with a calendar. And in my heart I hated Clara with a virulent hatred.

For the life of me I cannot now recall the exact motives and intentions of these posturings and pretendings. I know we were all set most resolutely upon being emancipated, unconventional, free, and natural. I think we all had a muddled sense of changing conditions, of the obsolescence of the standards of the past, due to the altered population question and of the necessity of readjustment; we young intellectuals were among the first detached particles to fall into what is now a great whirlpool of almost instinctive readjustments.

Unhappily in all the proud and magnificent disengagements and renunciations of our readjusting process we took no account of an important legal functionary, who was called in those Victorian days the Queen's Proctor. It was this gentleman's business to investigate the particulars of such divorces as the resources of his office brought within his scope, in the six months between the granting of the decree *nisi* and its being made absolute and final. To this day English law has no tolerance for divorce by consent. Its conception of marriage is the orthodox Christian one; its attitude towards divorce is punitive. There must be a party who is aggrieved and a party who is blameless, a party rolling and wallowing in "Sin" and a party of unspotted purity. The latter longs to continue the marriage, but the former has made it intolerable. The petitioner must to the climax live in a state of chaste grievance and hold out hands of reconciliation. It is the business of the Queen's Proctor to see that he or she does so. If the petitioner is rich, the petitioner goes abroad and, with a few expensive but simple precautions, is relieved of this obligation; the King's Proctor cannot, in the interests of national economy, pursue such a petitioner. But if the petitioner is poor, cheap, unpleasant persons of the minion type conduct their rude inquiries into his or her purity. They did into mine.

I petitioned. I got my decree *nisi,* and while Clara was in the amphibious state of a wife living in sin and under legal notice to quit, a daughter who is legally mine was born. Then the Queen's Proctor intervened, and I failed to get my decree made absolute. I was already at the laboratory at Downs-Peabody – I had been there two months – when I learnt by telegram that our iniquities were discovered and that since we had made it manifest that we *both* wanted a divorce, Clara was still, and was going to remain for the rest of our lives so far as I could see, my wife.

### 6 – *Clara at Large*

None of us had reckoned with the Queen's Proctor. We had all been told of his legal possibilities, but we had answered airily that "they don't do that sort of thing now," and we really believed it. That was the *fin-de-siècle* assumption, that unfair or unpleasant laws did not work in the case of agreeable people, and it needed the startling trial and condemnation of Oscar Wilde that year to remind the world that even in the end of the most wonderful century old laws might still crush the wittiest, most impudent, and debonair of offenders. Elderly judges sat in the divorce courts delivering judgments that were none the less operative because all the clever people thought them half a century behind the times.

For my own part I was infuriated beyond measure by this smashing vindication of established institutions against our modernism. My hatred of Clara was overshadowed by a comprehensive rebellion against the world. It remained inconceivable to me that I was to have the burthen of her support and be barred against any decent remarriage, perhaps for all the rest of my days. I thought quite seriously for an hour or so one day of killing the Queen's Proctor to "ventilate" my grievance. I wonder what sort of dried-up old lawyer would have been swept out of existence if I had consummated that impulse. But that such a though should have crossed my mind is a measure of my estimate of the situation. And I made a resolution, and kept it for three years, that whatever Weston decided to do about Clara, and however the law might stand in the matter, I would contribute nothing to the support of either her or her child.

She wrote a letter saying she wanted a good talk in private with me – "just to ourselves" – about "our daughter's prospects," but the latter phrase so irritated me that I did not answer. She wrote again twice. I was now getting deeply interested in the peculiar needs and conditions of Romer, Steinhart, but it happened that I had to come to London for a conference upon a more economical rearrangement of the refuse tilts at Downs-Peabody and that I had to visit the house in Edenbridge Square which I had at last let, in order to see a man and arrange for the forwarding of some of my books and the sale of the rest of the furniture. Accordingly I made an appointment with her there, and there it was we met for the last time.

(Except that once about fifteen years ago I saw her pursuing an omnibus in Trafalgar Square, I never set eyes upon her again. She died of influenza at Nice five years ago.)

She had arranged herself for my reconquest, very plainly but very prettily, and no one would have suspected her of a baby four months old. But I had determined to be insusceptible. I had hardened my heart and fortified myself. She asked me what I meant to do and what I thought she ought to do. Nothing, I said. She could go on just as if she had been divorced. She could call herself Mrs Weston. The press notices of the dismissal of our decree absolute had been very inconspicuous; even the notices of our brief trial had been rare and compact; we were too obscure for attention, and if she stuck to it stoutly that she and Weston were married, no one was likely to make any trouble in the matter.

She said that was reasonable, very reasonable, but there was something troubling her mind. She faltered for a moment and decided to be blunt.

"Philip," she said, "isn't sure about the child."

She eyed me. She seemed to be weighing my receptivity for some elaborate and circumstantial confidences. "Nor am I," she added meanwhile.

I shrugged my shoulders. "I don't feel an interested party," I said.

"*Billy!*" she cried. "You're pretty tough... Legally anyhow – it's yours."

That stung me. I swore compactly.

"Well, we have to face facts," she said.

"Philip's your man."

"I shan't feel safe with Philip. I don't feel safe with myself. I was a fool, Billy."

"You were careless about yourself, Clara. And about me. Haphazard is the word. I've never thought of you as a fool."

"There's still the old tang in the things you say, Billy."

I had no defence against that. There was no one she had ever found so satisfactory to talk to as I was, she said. I put things so clearly and freshly. We had had some great times together. She glowed at her memories and sighed. "I suppose I've learnt too late," she said, "that everything one does has consequences. I've made a beastly mess of things." Life was like turning on taps that wouldn't turn off again. When one was a child one squalled and somebody came and slapped one and shut the tap off and put everything back. Then suddenly one was grown-up and nobody came. But the slaps came. "I've had some bad times, taking that in," said Clara.

I was touched, I relaxed a little in my manner. I said that what she needed in life was not a husband like myself, but a large sedulous male attendant of about fifty. Perhaps it was too late now to prescribe that. Old Crashaw for example. Where was he?

"He's married," she said, "and idiotic about her."

"So that's no good."

"No," she said, "I was a fool. I should have played the game by you."

I said that some day perhaps we should defer the age of moral responsibility until people were thirty or thirty-five. "As if I didn't know how I have spoilt things for you!" she exclaimed suddenly, the most successful thing she said in the whole conversation. It had never occurred to me before that she could recognise the damage I had suffered.

"I bit it off," I said, "and I had to chew it. You're not to blame for that."

"Poor old Billy! You've had a beastly time."

She was positively embracing my admission that the affair had hurt me. The mule's ears went back again.

"Suppose now after all I come back to you," she threw out, so that it was doubtful whether it was an idle remark or a serious suggestion.

I forget the exact form of my reply. I considered the possibility for a moment. I told her that then, very carefully and deliberately, without causing her unnecessary pain, I should set about killing her. But if I forget my exact words I remember hers.

"That's the most attractive thing you've ever said to me!" she cried.

"All the same, you'd better stick to Philip," I said. "You can explain things to him so that he will believe. Unless you've muddled already with his confidence."

She was not quite convinced now of her power to humbug Philip, I could see. And once she had been so certain.

"I don't know what you're up to, Clara," I said, "but your one chance in life now is Philip. If you try any second string business with him he'll smell it, even if he doesn't know about it. Have you been shaking him already – by something? You pile your little all on him. I swear to you I'll go to gaol for ever rather than do anything to help you."

"I've never asked for that, Billy."

"What good would it be?"

But she still hovered undecided before the course she had to take.

"It gives Philip a frightful power over me. Whatever he does I shan't be able to divorce him."

"No doubt you'll contrive some consolation for your wounded pride," I said.

"You can sting. You could always sting…"

It was clear our talk was coming to nothing for her. Whatever vague intentions she had had, whether of a reconciliation, or an entangling afternoon's adventure, had failed. I wonder to this day what she had wanted in that interview.

At the end we shook hands and then with my hand in hers her eyes scrutinised mine. Mine told her nothing. She hesitated. She took her chance with me and flung her arms about me, and gave me the last of those wonderful kisses of hers that I was ever to receive. Her first kiss had seemed to me to come straight out of heaven; this last, straight out of stock. I accepted the favour without excitement. I held here in my arms – considerately, even appreciatively. "Ah!" she sighed, detaching herself and scrutinising my face again.

"You'd better play a straight game with Philip," I said, as though nothing had happened. "You won't – but you'd better."

"Why didn't you *make* me play a straight game with you?"

I don't think I answered that.

"You could have done it so easily."

I shook my head.

"You had everything in your hands."

After she had gone I sat for a long time at the little table in the drawing-room at which I had worked so often, thinking.

I was extremely sorry for her. Suddenly having thus beaten her off from me, I was sorry for her, as I had never been sorry for her before. This futile attempt to raid back to my affections alleviated my hate for her by its very futility. I saw her flimsiness at last plainly, the poverty of her equipment, the adverse chances against her. Our separation had robbed her of her personal hold over me; I saw her now as a stranger, as detachedly. For the first time in my life I realised that pity for women which comes to all decent men sooner or later – in spite of our endless humiliations and subjugations and the way we spoil lives through them. For it is not they who spoil men's lives, but the accidents of a bad time and a misdirection in ourselves that misuse them to our own hurt and belittlement.

But was I to blame? What else could I have done from first to last except the things I had been impelled to do? And now what was there to do? It was impossible for me to take her back even were she prepared for that. A little more kindness perhaps? But even that might prevent her from doing the one wise thing before her, which was to make herself Philip's only woman and he her only man.

I had a half-generous, half-insulting impulse, and I found a sheet of paper in my bureau and wrote her a note telling her to take all the furniture left in the house for herself. She had bought it with a certain avid interest; she was always a bright-eyed buyer, and suddenly I saw clearly that its poor little pieces and arrangements were personal to her and I had no right to deprive her of them. Fortunately the furniture man had made so poor an offer for the stuff that I had held it over to consider, or I could not have done even this petty act of decency. The real owner of the furniture I reflect now with a smile was Dickon. I had still to repay his brotherly loan. But I did not see it in that light then. Possibly because I knew certainly that I would repay.

I did everything I could to keep Clara out of my mind for some years and to heal the scar of her excision. But presently came a time when she was in dismay. She wrote to me pitifully and shamelessly. The ménage with Weston had broken down; I do not know how, the truth in these things is always obscure and complex and indescribable even to the principals in the quarrel. Her family had turned against her, and not one of her three sisters was well married. She was evidently as concerned for our daughter as for herself, and I have every reason to suppose she was by nature and intention a good mother. She was always cleverer and kinder with dogs and cats than I was; she had quick responses to all living things that came near her, and I have no doubt she was exceptionally attentive and kind to her own child. I decided to help her. But I helped her in such a way that even now I am not a little ashamed to write it down. The truth has to be told because it is an illuminating truth. It shows the make-up of the human male. I arranged she should be paid three hundred a year, and I saddled it with an ungracious condition that the money should be paid to her "while she remained chaste." She had to swallow the insult. My solicitor saw nothing objectionable in this ugly proviso, and would even have amplified it by a clause against "annoyance." But the law still keeps its moral ideas in cold storage in the vaults of the seventeenth century.

Two years later I made it an unconditional three-hundred a year. What right had I to dictate her conduct of her life in this fashion? And when things were already going well with me and the sense of security and property was established in me, I heard that our daughter was being ill-taught in a National School in Hoxton, to the great distress of her mother, and suddenly I made a settlement of thousand a year on Clara. My solicitor advised me to make it on the daughter with Clara as trustee, but I had as much confidence in Clara's maternal instincts as I had in her inevitable unchastity. It worked quite well, and she brought up her daughter as a very pleasant young lady, and married her off finally just after the war when the marriage market was good, to a prosperous doctor in Cardiff, who had met her first on war service. Then Clara travelled for a time. With first one woman friend and then another, visited Egypt and the Garden of Allah, and acquired a taste for roulette at Monte Carlo. Of her sisters I never heard anything more. I have been told she dressed young during this final phase, and was sometimes charming and sometimes rather haggard. She always had one or two very old men or very young men in attendance. Her death was due to the impatience that made her get up for a dance before she was well of her influenza. The fresh chill, and the casualness of the hotel where she was staying alone, killed her. She was about four hundred pounds in debt and overdrawn when she died, which sum seemed to me to be almost exactly like her – neither very scandalous nor quite solvent.

I made the acquaintance of our daughter as a schoolgirl at a vehemently healthy, manly girl's school at Brighton. I had learnt from Clara that she was a little worried in her mind, assisted by her schoolfellows, at the aloofness of her father, and so I went in state on several visiting days and showed myself with her and was introduced to her friends and found occasions to take her about in London. She was quite easy to be nice to. She did not resemble me in the least, but also she did not resemble Weston; I have sometimes fancied a resemblance to Billy Parker, but that may be a morbid fancy. She played and plays tennis very well, and is ridiculously grave and important in the art, practice, and politics of this epidemic.

I liked her, and I still like her, and I perceive that I loom large in her scheme of things, but I have never warmed to her; I do not feel and, to be plain about it, I do not believe, that she is bone of my bone and flesh of my flesh. I feel none of the instinctive harmony and intimacy that I do with my nephew William or even with his brother Richard. But I love William. I was temperately generous at her marriage, and I know that she has expectations that my will must not altogether disappoint. Sometimes I pay her a flying visit when my business takes me to Cardiff, and sometimes there will be a dinner and a theatre party in London. On occasion she sits on my knee, ruffles my hair, and calls me "Daddy." But always a little tentatively. I am gracefully responsive, and all the while I feel as unreal as if I were acting a Charles Wyndham part in a play by Sir Henry Arthur Jones, and she were the celebrated and charming Miss So-and-So. The doctor is good, solid stuff, though rather too prejudiced against psycho-analysis, and the two children are healthy, jolly little experimentalists with life, as amusing to play with as puppies. If they are not exactly bone of my bone and flesh of my flesh, I have no doubt they would be quite willing to be so. It is not their fault if they are not.

## 7 – *Empty House*

I sat for a long time in our empty house after Clara had departed, with my note about the furniture on the table before me. I sat there long after it was quite dark. Then I found a candle and lit it and went about the house musing over the things that had happened in the various rooms, incredulous of its evaporated happiness. What a poor, stuffy little house it had become, and how proud we had once been of it! I came down to the drawing-room again and sat there.

It must have been half-past ten or even later before I closed the door behind me, because when I went by the Underground Railway to the Strand to get some food I found the people streaming out of the theatres. It was the narrow old Strand that is now being swept away; it was lit then by a queer mixture of gas-lamps, mantle-lamps, and fizzling arc-lights on trial that made variegated glares and pallors on the bobbing heads of the crowd. The people jostled me because I was still half lost in thought, and when I sat down in Gatti's I remember the waiter annoyed me because he would not take "Oh, anything that's going" as a definite order, but insisted upon making suggestions.

That session with myself in that dusk-invaded room, in my first and last home, became for me a cardinal point in my life, the end of a chapter, the beginning of a new phase. It stands out in my conception of my life as our departure from Mowbray stands out, or the night when Dickon and I announced our secession from the Walpole-Stent household stands out. It marks the real beginning of the man I am now, the passing of a much more instinctive, passionate, and direct being. I have described my youthful self as a very detached scientific intellect in conflict with what seemed an alien and destructive sexuality. The two had fought a battle that was really an admixture. For a time sex had stormed along its own path with me, had seemed to carry all before it. It had made me aggressive and combative; it had turned me to acquisition and had made me aware of the need of power. My intelligence had not been so much defeated as hammered into new recognitions. The two had come now to a phase of balance and understanding, I still thought that research, the clambering to new visions of reality beyond any limits of knowledge yet attained, was the best thing in life, but I knew that I could not go on with that toilsome ascent until the craving hungers that torment and distract unless they are satisfied were assuaged, until my personal pride was secure, until I could command beauty in my hours if I desired it.

I had realised at last the profound importance of the sexual motive in life. I could not live fully without that self-respect, that zest in my personal life that only woman could give me. I had to discover now how I could come to terms with womankind. I had to do this under the handicap of my entanglement. I had so to frame my life and to achieve such relationships that I should be safe from such another disaster as this empty house embodied. I had to gain a certain security and amplitude in the world, so that if presently I was able to build up some more than temporary liaison, it should be secured from the tension of wants and debts and safe against the attractions and distractions of a more prosperous Philip Weston. I has not realised before the *quid pro quo* in love. It was plain to me now and plainly reasonable. I saw why Clara with the thought of motherhood had been scared from the narrow bleakness of our little home, and I saw, too, the manifest connection of her attempted reconciliation with my new prosperity.

Can a creature made for motherhood be indifferent to a lair? I will not say coarsely that I learnt that women are to be bought, but I saw quite clearly that they have to be paid for. Well, I must be able to pay for them. I could not think now what it was I had expected from Clara. I had made vast assumptions. But though a man does research, so that new light and wonder such as no one has every known before pour into the world, so that new things begin and all things are altered and turned about, yet if that involves personal poverty, a certain preoccupation of mind, an inability to cherish and supply, no woman has any use for him.

I was not man enough, I saw, or perhaps I should say I was too much of a man, to accept the rôle of a scientific devotee, vowed for the best part of his life to celibacy and poverty. That would cripple me with a suppressed sense of inferiority and all the mental distortion that entails. I needed material success, embodied in its living symbol. I must have that living symbol. I had learnt now in terms of Clara and bitter experience what I had disregarded when Dickon told it to me in words that then had no meaning for me. "Research!" he had said. "Please yourself for a bit, Billykins. So long as you're let. But there's not even freedom of thought in the world for a man who isn't his own master. The show is a scramble, and it's going to be a scramble yet for centuries."

So I, too, would become predatory and set out to overtake Dickon in his scramble to possession and freedom and purchasing power. And, freedom and power assured, I must square my account with this craving that obsessed me. Then, as Dickon had said, for disinterested service, scientific research, or anything else, as the mood might take me.

Already I had learnt a great deal from the beginnings of my work with Romer, Steinhart. I had been able to measure myself against most of my directors and get some inkling of the scale and vast possibilities of their organisation. For those days it was a very great company, though it was a mere infant compared with the giant ramifications of annexed, subsidiary, dependent, and associated concerns into which we have since grown. We had practically no relations with America or Sweden at all then, and towards our German and other continental homologues our attitude was still one of naïve rivalry. The authorised capital of the mother company is now thirty-two million pounds; in those days in was seven hundred and fifty thousand. The works at Downs-Peabody were still the largest part of our plant. But even then in the early nineties the firm's rate of growth was sufficient to foreshadow its present scale. Our ordinary shares of a pound were creeping up and round about thirty shillings. And it was clear to me that with my quite special knowledge and my peculiar aptitudes it would be extremely easy for me to secure a fair and handsome participation in the big things coming.

My directors had not yet made up their minds how I was to be handled. But I had already formed very clear ideas of how the firm was going to be handled. I had been brought in by Julian Romer, the younger son of old Romer and the brother of the great Roderick, the head of the firm. Julian was, perhaps, the best equipped technically of all the second generation of Romers. Roderick was a far better administrator, but of no account from the technical standpoint. Old Romer had been the business organiser of the concern; Steinhart had been the scientific spirit; but both the Romer sons – Steinhart had daughters only; Ralph Steinhart is a nephew – were sent abroad to learn something sound about modern chemistry and metallurgy before the intellectual lassitude of the English public school could submerge them. Julian had a real aptitude for scientific work and also considerable business ability. He had marked the drift of my early papers and leapt, long before I had a suspicion of that side of the matter, at the industrial applications foreshadowed. He had explained me to his co-directors and sought me out. He was a high-coloured, black-haired, warm-blooded, bright-eyed little man, very quick in his movements, very confidential in his manner, coming up very close to you, insinuatingly. We were to work in the same laboratory for a time. He was, if possible, to pick my brains; I was to be the auriferous quartz, and he was to be the extractor. His sedulous amiability, his pressing persuasiveness, were, however, just a little too warm and eager for the metallic Clissold temperament. We exchanged. He learnt something of what I knew – enough to realise the full value of what I could do for the industry – and I learnt very rapidly of his business and productive organisation.

I perceived I could be, that I was made to be, the goose that could lay golden eggs for Romer, Steinhart, Crest and Co. I did not intend, however, to lay them in full sight of my employers. After a week I found Julian's interests in my private thoughts so lively that I took all my notebooks out of the laboratory back to my lodgings and bought a safe to keep them in. I just carried one notebook in my pocket. When Julian embarked upon discussions with me I stressed the philosophical side. Julian showed a real feeling for pure science, and I saw to it that he got it chemically pure. I carried our talk at times, I believe, to a very close approximation to some of Einstein's subsequent work, but I doubt if Julian fully appreciated the high and novel matter I was giving him. One day he made a sort of quarrel because I didn't let him know what I was doing upon the crystallisation of alloys, and hinted quite plainly that I was paid to confide all my notions to him – at least all that occurred to me in business hours.

"Results," I corrected. "But I have to follow the laws of my being. I couldn't think if I thought I was watched while I was thinking. It would make me self-conscious and nervous. But when I have results I shall give them to you properly, ready for use. They're coming, rest assured."

"But I could help you so much more," said Julian, "if I could follow what you were up to."

"Couldn't bear you at my heels," I said. "It would paralyse me."

"I've got ideas."

"Don't I know it? But you will to bear with my limitations."

He shrugged his shoulders and pouted and looked hurt and unhappy. "I had looked forward so to working with you, my dear fellow."

Quite at the outset I did some good work that proved my value to the firm. It was nothing out of the way; it was the natural consequence of bringing a fresh young mind to bear on an established routine. The system of the refuse tilts had grown up bit by bit, had been adapted several times to changes of method, had become a thing of use and wont to all the directors, and an increasing element of waste had crept in with each adaptation. Things had moved fast; there had been a lot of patching. No one had thought of standing the whole thing on its head, so to speak. I saw almost at once that that could be done at a very considerable profit, simply because I was not habituated to the old sequence. If I had been in the firm for ten years, I should have been just as blind to it as the others were. They saw my points and nodded to each other.

Julian behaved at the meeting as if he had begotten me, trained me, and taught me what to say. Also he prompted me. But this first golden egg established me with the firm and gave me time to work out my more primary and extensive problems in applied metallurgy and to devise a method of conceding them upon terms where by the profit should be mutual.

My mind was already full of that possibility when I sat and thought in my empty house.

I remember very distinctly thinking over Julian, Clara quite forgotten for a while, and smiling to myself in the darkness. I was already very fond of him then, and my affection has grown with the years. He is one of the few men I can bear to play golf with. He knows so much, he puts his heart into every game, and he achieve even worse results than I do. With outcries, with something near tears. "What have I done?" he cries, to God and me, to the caddie and the earth and the sky and any casual birds or beasts that chance to be within earshot. "My God! But *look* at it!" He had left London directly after the meeting on the previous afternoon for Downs-Peabody, and he had been most solicitous that I should do all I had to in London before I returned. I had thanked him warmly. I had expected something of the sort and prepared for it.

When I had unpacked at Downs-Peabody I had found, among other things in my boxes, two or three fragments of meteorites I had brought away from the Royal College. Just before leaving to come to London, I had fused these up together in a dark and intriguing lump. One side I cut and polished beautifully. I had marked this lump "B. in reserve. Final phase," packed it away in a little box, and left it, as if inadvertently, in the drawer of my laboratory table for Julian's benefit. I felt sure it would amuse him while I was away. He was probably busy with it now, missing his dinner to examine and perhaps analyse a scrap of it, and it was pleasant to calculate what he would make of it.

It *was* "in reserve" and "in its final phase." What else was there to be done with it?

No doubt my meditations wandered for a time to the characteristics of his people. I do not believe very much in all this modern fuss about races; everyone alive is, I am convinced, of mixed race, but still some of us are more white, some of us more negro, some of us more Chinese than others. Compared with me Julian was Mediterranean, South-Eastern, Jewish; compared with him I was Northern and Western and blond. And our minds worked with the most entertaining differences. In his presence I felt slow and stupid – but solid. His mind could dance round mine as it marched. It came into a question like a brisk young dog, which comes into a room, seems to see, hear, and smell everything, knows what you feel about, wags its tail all the time, makes a remark or so almost absent-mindedly, and goes out again quite assured there is neither biscuit nor bone there. He thought so quickly that he never stopped to think. I had as little chance against him at chess as a gorilla. And yet I could get to things and do things that seemed impossible to him and that he knew were impossible to him. I could produce a path where he was convinced there was no path, and I could see, and make him see, things he had never see. While he raced through the labyrinth of a question, learning its every turn, I seemed able to look over and reach over.

But the more one tries to state these differences, the more one realises how subtly they defy formulation. These brunette peoples, these dark-whites, made civilisation for us. I doubt if either we blonds or the yellows or the blacks could have done as much for ourselves. Then we came in upon an established system, we Northern and Atlantic peoples, migrants, invaders, sceptics, protestants, obstructive questioners, slow, recalcitrant learners, less brilliant but more original, rupturing conventions, releasing debtors, opening new ways, resuming the forward movement upon obscure new lines...

Perhaps Julian and I represent a blend that may become very effective in human affairs. We two and Roderick have done quite a number of things together that none of us could have brought off in exclusive association with men of our own type.

But I see I am astray beyond my thoughts in my empty house in Edenbridge Square. From Julian my musing probably passed to my other associates at Downs-Peabody, and so came back to more intimate questions. For the first time in my life since I had begun to observe and think I had come into contact with rich people and with able people engaged in getting richer, and I was beginning to apprehend a number of points about human motives and my own possibilities that had hitherto escaped me. I had not properly understood before what there is in this process of getting and keeping rich; my estimate of motives had been too simple. I had regarded only the forms and habits of life. I was now getting a grasp upon the driving forces of life.

I can best put it by saying that in my younger view of the social order into which I had been born I had seen it mainly as a business of toil-shifting and a struggle for freedom. People were poor, limited and oppressed because they had had too much of the necessary toil of the community thrust upon their shoulders, and my early socialism was a simple and reasonable scheme for the redistribution and economy of toil. Everybody might be relieved from any excess of toil and given leisure and a sufficiency of freedom. Then – seen from the angle of back streets and the common life of worry and insufficiency – it seemed reasonable to expect that everyone would be happy. But now I had begun to share the lives of these Romers and Steinharts and Crests and their womankind, and to realise the power of pride among their driving motives. I had come back into large houses and parks and gardens and into an atmosphere of many servants and abundance and display; a multitude of dormant memories of Mowbray were revived in me, and I was reminded that so soon as a human being is housed, fed, and made to feel secure, it proceeds at once to seek occasion to swagger over other human beings. It seeks reassurance.

That everyone should have a fair prosperity, no one toil, no one be enslaved, would not simply leave this overbearing and conquering craving unsatisfied; it would release it to unexampled activity. The Romers and Steinharts spent and swaggered like English county families out of the best novels, with touches of Oriental splendour they did their insufficient best to restrain. Roderick's dressing-gowns are indescribable, and I have always suspected Julian of secret cloth-of-gold pants. The Crests, an old English family born to coal and ore, were in comparison coldly and haughtily victorious over the common ruck of mankind. Crest was about as intelligent in our business as a horse, but his very incapacity increased his effect of being thoroughbred. He was silent in the board-room and very cunning; for generations the Crest family had grown richer and richer by being in the way and having to be bought out, and I think that both he and Lady Muriel, his wife, despised the Romers and Steinharts for actively creating wealth instead of passively insisting upon it. Julian in lapses from his habitual ingratiation had had occasion to remind me once or twice that I was a salaried employee, but the Crests made me feel it from the moment we were in sight of each other. They were going to walk on me. They were going to be aloof, condescending, unaware. Such ascendencies were what life was for.

I had been over to lunch with the Crests at Folingden, and Lady Muriel had made it abundantly evident that I was unsuitable for sustained conversation. I had to be addressed with polite consideration, I had to answer when I was addressed, and then I had to lapse into respect. Heaving honoured me as one might pat a dog, she proceeded to talk across me with Mrs Roderick Romer about the condition of the poor in their respective parishes. The cottagers in the Crest Village were not providing sufficient girls for domestic service; the Romer village had plenty of girls, but our works at Downs-Peabody were too near and were beguiling them away.

"I want Roderick to close the works to Brampsheet girls," Mrs Roderick had said.

"A girl who is not broken to service by fifteen," Lady Muriel had generalised, "will never make a good servant."

"I tell him he's destroying the breed. He's destroying all their standards."

Difficult stuff for the excluded middle to cut in upon.

A sad and handsome "Nordic" face with an expression of enigmatical aloofness had hovered behind Mrs Roderick's Oriental opulence. It was the Crest's family butler, waiting with the peas. He might have been Crest's first cousin. He was exactly the same creature – minus the acres that had the coal and iron below…

I sat in my empty house and I found my irritation against the Crests and my sense of the exuberant triumph of the Romers and Steinharts over the Oreshire domestics and poor, interweaving with my bitter realisation of the share that economic inferiority had played in my disaster with Clara. I philosophised widely. I was beginning to understand how the issues and ramifications of sex spread into the whole complex of social life. I had thought two years ago that sex was simply a sensuous craving, an appetite needing assuagement and trailing with it a sense of beauty. I knew now that that was not the tenth part of it; that was merely the red centre of a far ampler desire – a desire for possession, assurance, and predominance. I understand now how that spread out into the general competition of life. The desire of a woman to own and dominate a man, or the desire of a man to own and dominate a woman or women, is only the intense focus of a vastly greater nimbus of purpose, to dominate men and women at large. It spreads out into a craving for servants, for dependents, for wills that wait on our wills. It branches out into a desire for possessions of all sorts; it finds a grotesque specialisation in the accumulation of pets, This hunger for the sense of mastery over life accounts for the otherwise idiotic pleasure people take in the shooting of pheasants and suchlike poor, attractive creatures. The ultimate expression of dominance is to kill. The specifically sexual drive is merely the apex of a drive which at its broadest is a desire to own and dominate all life.

And I was, in fact, as sexual, as aggressive upon life as these Romers and Steinharts and Crests, as Dickon and all the rest of the world. Only I had failed to perceive it until Clara had developed me.

So I saw it in my empty house. I saw life stripped bare and plain as a struggled from which there was no remission. One might have the freakish desire for scientific knowledge; it was no excuse. One had to fight for its gratification just as one would have to fight for any other fantasy that caught one's will. One had to fight or gratify the lust and the craving within one before one could serve it, just as one had to fight the conflicting purposes of one's fellow-men and the antagonism of nature. The service of mankind through science gave one no natural claim for help or consideration in the scramble of life. One had to struggle with one's enemy and beguiler, woman, just as much as one had to struggle against one's enemy and rival and would-be subjugator, man. That was the quality of life. Fight, establish yourself, or go under – go under even though your every wish was benevolent. And happily for me I had a weapon in my special gifts and in this metallurgical knowledge I had chanced to acquire.

I would fight. What else was there to do? The prospect of a frank struggle to get the better of the world bored me but did not dismay me. I was fairly sure of myself. I would somehow get to power and freedom round the reservations of Romer, Steinhart, and the Crests, as I would somehow get round the entanglement Clara had made for me to the gratification of my desires. And that was how the prospect of life spread itself out before me. To that I had come at that time. Such quasi-scientific, quasi-religious mysticism as I have now is all of later growth. In those days I had no intimation of that wilful reconstruction of human affairs which now dominates my activities. That came during and after the war. That was a result of the war. Simply I contemplated and nerved myself for struggle. If I contemplated anything at the end of that struggle it was a resumption of pure research, aloof from and disregardful of the common affairs of me. I was a hard young man, far more narrowly egotistical than I am now.

The memory of those hours is all dark loneliness and stern resolve. Clara was already at an infinite distance, clean out of my universe. I had parted from her and given her the furniture, and she was, I thought, handsomely disposed of.

The candle flared down to extinction at my elbow, and made the shadows dance about me. Outside a bleak gas-lamp lit the railing and black bushes of the unfrequented square.

## 8 – *Window Wide Open*

It was not until nineteen seven or eight that I could feel I was accomplishing what I had set out to do and that the Romers had accepted me for good and all as a necessary part of their combination. By that time I could count myself a rich man as riches go now. It would be a long and tedious story to tell, full of petty manoeuvres and cunning shifts and counter-shifts, before my group came to realise that they had to pay fairly for the science and initiative I could give them. Crest did his best to block my intrusion upon the board-room and even drove me to negotiations with a German-American group. He would not understand what I signified. His preponderant inheritances were against me. To this day he treats me with a sort of provisional equality, as though he had somehow mislaid his social ascendancy over me, but that at any moment his butler might find it in the hall or conservatory and restore it to him. But Lady Muriel, with the social flexibility of her sex, now consults me about the incipient love affairs of her grandchildren.

Within four years I was a director of one of our subsidiaries, our queer little profitable Clissold Mineral Paint Company, but I did not become a director of the mother company until after ten years of steady work. It was interesting, this business; it was exasperating and it was boring; it was difficult at times to resist the temptation to smash the game and get out of it all, and the years between twenty-five and forty-five slipped away almost unperceived. Meanwhile I continued a respectable scientific career with a steadily ebbing freshness and vitality of thought. I got my FRS in 1902 chiefly on the strength of my papers upon intercrystalline stresses, but two young Germans, Stahl and Bütow, were already running away with my ideas and getting at things I had been too preoccupied to see. And so my purely scientific career petered out.

In 1907 I made an attempt to revive my scientific passions. I organised a private laboratory. It was beautifully equipped, but from the first it had an incurable flavour of the amateur. Julian had just such another. His was as neat as a dressing-bag, as lavish and handy as the things on the toilet-table of a professional beauty. It had everything that heart could desire in laboratory – except the heart to use it. Julian even had an assistant, a London BSc., a sort of intellectual valet who brushed and folded his researches and put them out for him when he wanted to resume them. I didn't go to that length. I did some reading, brought myself up to date. But the glory had departed.

I do not think I have spent three hundred hours in my private laboratory altogether since it was finished eighteen years ago. And half that time was given to special war stuff of no scientific value. I feel that such seclusion is now an affectation for me. I am no longer a leader anywhere upon the scientific front, and I lack the special energy to push up again. For the last year Siddons, not the astronomical Siddons but the Cambridge brother, E A P Siddons, has been using the place and justifying its existence. Siddons, I think, will presently come in with us and take his place beside Trippmann at the head of the firm's central research station. When I came into the firm we had exactly twenty-one men working in our laboratories, from myself to the bottle-washer and counting in Julian. Now we have four hundred and seven qualified men doing scientific work for us. It is all I can do to keep in touch with the new stuff they are opening up. Most of them are, of course, of the "trained" type and their research is routine inquiry, but ten or a dozen are fairly original men, and one or two of these are personalities of quality who promise well for our future.

Between 1908, when Sirrie Evans died, and the beginning of the war I passed through several phases of deep discontent and unhappiness; I shall say more about these experiences later. I was dissatisfied with life and restless. Whatever I did, I wanted to be somewhere else. I found business excuses for travel; I went into Russia, into further India and stayed for the better half of a year in Siberia. But nowhere was there any escape from this uneasiness of mind, this persuasion that in some essential respect my life was not right.

Then came the profound excitements of the war, and for a time it was possible to believe that real and fundamental things were happening. I have already written about that period in my account of Dickon. As I have told, disillusionment was harsh and speedy. Another phase of profound distress and unsettlement followed. It was complicated by a queer irrelevant passion that distracted me excessively. The need of a clear unifying purpose in my existence became imperative if I was not to go to pieces altogether. It rose to complete ascendancy over the confusion of my desires. It brought me at last to this tranquil sunny room in Provence and this pause for a final assembling of my purposes, before it is time for me to go altogether.

I have been working here at this book – with three brief intermissions in England – since last November. It is now June. Once more I note with gratitude the intimated and tranquillising beauty of this land. In April there was a great blaze of blossom; the big Judas-trees flowered magnificently, and a lot of little and medium sized Judas-trees I had hitherto not observed, its family, flowered in unison. There was also a great foam of lilac. All sorts of iris clamoured successfully for attention, and the roses, always more or less in flower here, suddenly took their task of beauty seriously and did wonderful things. That was our spring after a wet and windy March that flooded our kitchen. Now the days are baths of warm sunshine, and my common daily wear is pyjamas. The nights are nights of magic. They are scented nights. This week they are saturated in moonlight, and they abound in fireflies, fireflies that prick the darkness intermittently as they drift athwart the pallid roses and lilies and the black, still bushes and branches. In the depths of the ivy lurk green glow-worms. I find the nightingales too abundant and very tiresome with their vain repetitions, but Clementina does not agree; her mind has been poisoned by literature, and she does not really hear the tedious noises they make, she hears Keats. On the other hand, the carpet of sound made every evening by the frogs in the valley below is indescribably beautiful in itself. We disputed agreeably, and now she has gone and left me to my study table and my thoughts.

Here, tranquil before the still moonlight, serene as shining silver, defended from moth and mosquito by an invisible gauze, I can brood over my papers into the small hours. I have been sitting here not troubling to write since eleven. It is now nearly one. Here I can get all that Romer, Steinhart turmoil into something like its proper perspective against the world at large. I can look back upon it now across an interval of five-and-thirty years and make a companion picture to those still hours I spent in Edenbridge Square when my adventures with Romer, Steinhart lay all before me. Space, time, and the pressure of life are all altered in their values now. I can see our huge combine broadly, and my work for it as a quite typical item in that change of scale and material that is the essential fact of current history. I can see how extraordinarily representative we are of the general quality of contemporary life, both in its large wilfulness and its retarded consciousness of itself.

## 9 – *The Market Tree*

How new and significant a thing we are! Of the various substances that we extract from crude matter and pour into the workshops of the modern world there is scarcely one that was even thought of a hundred years ago. Even the various steels we co-operate with White and Halbow in producing are new. Steel was a fudged, rule-of-thumb product in 1825; nobody knew what it was exactly; it was variable and uncertain, and to have produced a hundred-pound lump of it would have been thought a miracle. Now we can make steel play its tricks like a performing seal; we can make you steels as brittle as glass and steels almost as flexible as rubber, we can make crystalline steels as obdurate as carbon and malleable steels that at a temperature below red heat you can draw into wire and beat into leaves hardly less thin and ductile than gold. All you have to do is to pay the price. Some of these steels are still expensive toys, but tomorrow they will be staple needs. But that is only an overflow of our metallurgical activity. Steel is not our main interest. In ten years' time every other automobile body will be made of our light alloys, and in twenty there will be scarcely an aeroplane in the air that is not made of some stuff of ours. Again, for main roads, for all roads and streets where the wear is hard, Romer, Steinhart in twenty years' time will supply the only possible road metal, all over the world. There is hardly a modern contrivance from an incandescent lamp to a gramophone needle and from a toughened lamp chimney to the type that will print this book, that does not owe something to us – and pay it.

All this has grown from nothing in less than three-quarters of a century. In 1858, the original Steinhart, who was a Swedish chemist of Jewish extraction visiting England, met the original Romer, who was then travelling in mohair trimming for his uncle. They met in a train between Sheffield and London, and Steinhart talked about the slackness of the English and the peculiar opportunities that were, he thought, going to waste upon the coal and iron properties of the lordly Crests. Romer, who was a youth of nineteen at the time, and who detested mohair and his uncle, jumped at the possibilities of independent action these remarks opened out, and made himself so ingratiating to Steinhart and afterwards so importunate to Crest, our present Crest's father, that at last he brought together the first experimental company, the founder company of all our branching tree. This was the Crest Slag Works, and it was afterwards reconstructed as the Crest Bye-Products. Romer, who had a really vigorous intelligence, went off to Germany and studied metallurgical chemistry for two years to fit himself better to control this business he had made possible.

In 1879 he succeeded in shifting the central works from the Crest properties to Downs-Peabody so as to be in easy reach of the Brampsheet and Hinton-Peabody deposits, and the Crest Bye-Products Company was swallowed up in the bolder enterprise of Romer, Steinhart, Crest and Co. with a capital of fifty thousand pounds. The rearrangement of the names showed, among other things, that the Crests were no longer on the back of the concern but dragging along at its side. Where alas! they continue to drag.

But I do not see why I should write here the details of an industrial development which are easily accessible to the curious in a variety of forms. The external facts have always been stated very plainly and fully at our annual meetings; we are widely documented. What interests me now is the social and mental significance of this rapid and amazing growth. It spreads through the once formless worldwide commerce in metals and raw material for mechanical production, it sends out processes, it joins on to cognate bodies and bodies that become cognate in a way that is extraordinarily suggestive of the appearance of a vertebral column and its linking up to rudiments of rib and limb in the body of an embryo. And side by side with it and capable of either consuming or amalgamating with it are similar and rival organisations. Parallel with it are other great organising systems dealing in oil, great food trusts, cotton, shipping combinations. It is a new economic structure where formerly there was fragmentation, open market, and crowd commerce. It is only being recognised for what it is. We ourselves, Romers, Steinharts, Crests, and all the other twenty-odd outsiders who have come into the direction of our main or openly associated concerns, are only beginning to see what it is we are doing. Hardly any of us realise the full extent of our tentacles; we expand as if by instinct, and at times our right hand has scarcely a suspicion of what the left is closing upon. It is still more interesting to compare what we are, we creatures inflated by expansive forces beyond our expectation, with what we might be and what perhaps we ought to be.

I do not believe that our primordial Steinhart dreamt for a moment of the nature of the egg he was laying in the nest of the conservative Crests. There was a bolder imaginative touch about our ancestral Romer; he may have had previsions of the things that are coming. Not one of our present gang has ever seen what we are doing as a whole. Or if anyone has, the vision has vanished again instantly like the Holy Grail. Here am I in Provençe, the new Thebaid, living the life of a hermit – with Clem installed within a mile as the official temptation – in order to get a view of it. Possibly Roderick comes nearer than anyone to a comprehensive conception of our rôle in the world's affairs. He is something of a statesman. He made a mistake in taking a peerage. He is rather lost up there as Lord Brampsheet. He has barred himself out of the House of Commons by this splendour, and only discovered too late that he can make quite good political speeches. It was some feeling between the wives about the Crest barony that added Brampsheet to the glorious roll of Lloyd George's peers. Crest wanted his caparison, Lady Romer saw an opportunity of drawing level with Lady Muriel, and manifestly it was impossible to honour the impassive Crest and leave the energetic and possibly malignant Sir Roderick untouched. And Sir Roderick at the time did not realise what he was doing for himself. Perhaps it is just as well, for him as for us. He likes to argue, and this vice of debate might have grown upon him until he gave to party what is meant for the business of the world.

He has imagination; he has ideas; he is aggressive; he is not content to fall into the moulds of preceding things. He will talk at times in quite revolutionary fashion. He respects Crest more than I do, but he hates him just as much. He respects Crest more than I do, because there is still a lingering instinct in the Romer blood, due to a thousand years of pogroms, that these hippoid types should be propitiated. He dare not believe as I do that modern science and mechanism have made cavalry and the landed gentry obsolete. Apart from this weakness my Lord Brampsheet is as progressive as myself and much more energetic. To him we owe the steady extension of our interests beyond industrial production to international finance. Through his tentacular instincts and intervention of banking it is that we are in co-operation instead of cut-throat competition with our German and French and Swedish parallels, and allied and linked to mining and coal interests in all parts of the world, to cotton growing, and gold and diamond mining, which were once as remote from us as concerns in another planet.

Roderick is physically a bigger man than my Julian, and his methods of address are less insinuating and more familiar. Occasionally he seems to be trying, as the Americans put it, to "jolly" you. By an odd coincidence he resembles the Bolshevik leader Zinovieff so closely that when first I met the latter in Pertersburg in 1920 I laughed aloud. They might be identical twins. Yet neither is pleased to hear of this resemblance.

The parallelism is more than physical. Their imaginations are similar, constructive and a little grandiose; they have an enormous amount of mental energy, and mental energy, I should think, of very much the same type and grade. In 1920, after the phase of extreme Communism, Bolshevism in Moscow was as intellectually bankrupt as any "capitalist" government. In spite of such purely comic efforts as Lenin's "electrification of Russia" and Trotsky's valiant splutterings, it plainly did not know what to do next. But Zinovieff had already hit upon the spacious idea of an appeal to Asia, and the evocation of a sort of godless Islam out of Russia and the Turk and Central Asia. So far as any politico-social idea has ever realised itself, Zinovieff's dream might realise itself. And so in this vastly richer Western muddle of ours, which has so much more time and stuff to waste before it gets down to bare realities, I find in Roderick an idea where other people seem to have no ideas; not, indeed, a clear idea, but an adumbration with something very like an outline, the idea of a sort of shelving or subordination of political forms and a reorganisation of economic and social life under the control of a union of big financial and industrial groups. The same idea looms up even more distinctly in some American circles. It foreshadows a statecraft of realities. Beside Roderick, our old Asquith seems to me as unreal and empty as one of those figures of Chinese porcelain that nod their heads and move their hands in country houses. I do not mean that Roderick has ever sat down and worked out his idea to even its broad implications. He has never detached himself enough from current activities for that. But he has it. Power has happened to him. In this present world he is one of number of men who wake up in middle age to find power flowing past within their grasp. He has at least awakened. He blinked, he snorted and made startling sounds, he shut his eyes again, but he had awakened.

He knows as well as I do that the politics, the parties, the governments, and empires of the world today are all a swiftly passing show, masking, but growing at last dimly transparent, to reveal the real processes that are going on in human life.

But these things belong to a later part of this book. I am discussing now the motives and ideas that have made us what we are. Roderick interests me most of all our group, and I watch him as closely as anyone. What do these gleams, these phases of broad politico-social vision amount to altogether with him? Very little – yet. To me they amount to much more, but with me also they are conceptions that stir rather than conceptions that control. With him they have a quality almost of improper thoughts. When we talk of these things and I betray a belief that there is a vital reality in our talk he becomes manifestly a little shy, a little scared. "But to come back to business, my boy," he says. "To come back to business – "

He has not made himself. He has been made. His motives in building up this great system about Romer, Steinhart, Crest and Co. have been all of a piece with my motives. He wanted to live, to assert himself vigorously upon things and upon life, and he came in at a lucky angle. I believe, with the same differences that make him physically a contrast to myself, his mental and moral life is very parallel to mine.

And for the rest of our people I find no driving forces at all commensurate with the great plant which nominally belongs to us, but to which we indeed belong. Men like Spink and Gedge came in by making themselves useful, young Brand by making himself agreeable. Trippmann is able and alive, but almost wholly a chemist. Siddons may develop; there is more in him than in the others, and he is still very young. The rest are wheels or links. Several do good research work and make excellent arrangements to exploit their results, but they do not seem to apprehend the business as a whole and in relation to the world as a whole. They run after fine houses and fine wives; they appreciate knighthoods and baronetcies; or they sniff after the imaginative excitements of the artistic and dramatic world, and the sands of their lives run out.

None of us are very great sportsmen; it is too heavy a call on our time. Lord Crest is still under the impression that he is a great English country gentleman a little distended by commerce, and so in need of a sort of moral tight-lacing. He is enormously respected in the Carlton Club, and both his sons have been through the Guards. Everard represents Offerton in the conservative interest and will some day succeed his father as the drag on our wheels. Sons and father are all associated with various attempts to create strike-breaking and quasi-Fascist organisations in England against the active Labour people. Gods!

how that sort of prancing and threatening exasperates some of our men, some of our very best men! Crest has recently had his portrait painted in the Ruritanian style as Lord Lieutenant of Oreshire, scarlet and splendid. The background even is romantic. No chimneys are visible. There is a beautiful carriage with horses in London for Lady Crest, as well as several cars. Lady Muriel is a friend of the Family, of the most exalted Family.

"My boy," said Roderick, when I was letting myself go one day upon Crest's costliness and general ineffectiveness, "have you ever thought of his value as our shopwalker?"

"Mask," said I.

"Mask!" said Roderick with a sudden outbreak of racial self-derision. "You've said it, my boy! He can go and do our business where I can't show my nose..."

I sit here and think over these things, I think of Roderick and Julian and the rest of our group, and the wives and houses and dinners and weekends, I review the galaxy of our chief shareholders and dependents and profit-spending associates, not forgetting my little neighbour Lady Steinhart, whom I have already described; I recall what I can of the phases and moods, the cravings and pettiness of my own story, and then my mind wanders off to our works, to our wonderful plant with science and subtle ingenuity in every trough and tap and furnace and mould, to our staffs of skilled workers, to our collateral associations with mines of every type in every climate, to the great regions we search for ores, fluxes, solvents, to the cultivators whose output we buy by the countryside. When I think of this worldwide system, seeking, extracting, recovering, and sorting the crude substance of the earth, fusing, sublimating, condensing, fining, allaying, placing its finished substance at last in the hands of ten thousand sorts of manufacturer and returning its sifted by-products to fertilise a hundred lands, when I think of the myriads of workers whose lives we direct, the hundreds of myriads with which our work is associated, and the far greater multitudes whose employment we make possible, when I contemplate the totality of all this achievement threaded through the jostling human crowd, and then put the swift, incessant efficiency of this human process of ours, side by side even with the best of the motives that move us who are its nominal directors, it seems to me it is not so much we who have got all these things out of the earth as the things themselves that have called to us and compelled us to extract them.

They have compelled us as the soil of any place selects and determines the trees that shall grow there and stunts them or gives an extravagant vigour to their growth. Romer, Steinhart, which began as a single sapling, has become a great tree, that like a banyan, the Indian market-tree, expands into a grove and joins to other groves and shelters great mutitudes and may at last coalesce into one single canopy of confederated business to cover the economic life of the world.

## 10 – *Old Style and New*

Our main plants, our essential companies, are things of a new economic type. I doubt if many people realise how new they are. Our business are not only new in scale and correlation; they are new in their internal constitution. There is not the same necessary antagonism of employer and employed in them, because they are not merely nor mainly toil-shifting organisations. We employ hardly any brute labour at all in our own concerns. Almost all our labour is either skilled or semi-skilled. Over three thousand of our people draw more than a thousand pounds a year each from us, and that number increases in a larger proportion than the increase in our general employment. There is nobody at all with us on a flat subsistence wage; not a soul. And since our plants have been costly to construct and are destined to be superseded by better plants within very definite limits of time, since many of them would deteriorate rapidly with disuse, it has always been the policy of the firm, from our early Crest Bye-Products days onward, to keep its workers content and interested in our common welfare, and so never to have a break in production. We have never been held up by a strike in all our history, and we have never closed down a plant upon its staff because of trade fluctuations. We have kept our workers together and our plants going steadily – if only for the sake of the machine. Business shrewdness and a certain goodwill were both active in determining that policy; the original Steinhart was, we know, a student of Robert Owen, and regarded his employees with an amiable generosity of intention. His idea, and it is still a tradition of the firm, was that there is a sort of moral partnership of the business inherent in those who have been employed by it for some time. But I won't pretend that our virtue has had to struggle against out interests; old Steinhart's good intentions happen to have yielded the very best policy possible for us.

Whenever we have bodies of our own workers in sufficient numbers we subsidise the science teaching in the elementary and continuation schools in that locality as generously as possible, and at Downs-Peabody we run a big technical institute at which scholarships can be held, side by side with our research laboratories. We have nine professors with salaries far above the normal University scale. Spink and Gedge are both sons of men who worked in the Crest Bye-Products for weekly wages. We have a savings' bank organisation and an investment system; we have workers who, some of them, hold up to two thousand pounds' worth of our ordinary shares. We pay no day wages at all, and we are steadily changing our weekly wage-earners to a monthly and quarterly salariat. In alliance with our staffs we participate in subordinate housing companies, recreation grounds, cricket clubs, swimming-baths, two art museums, and a number of social clubs. We subsidise two weekly newspapers to explain what is going on in our business and what becomes of our products.

All this is just sound modern business. We cannot afford to use our premises as social battlefields. We do not discuss the right of this or that person to a greater or lesser share of the surplus profit of our activities, but we mean to keep our processes going on as largely, handsomely, healthily as possible, and this is the way it has to done. And one must remember we are not demoralised by any vehement competition – which is the true cause of most sweating and commercial ugliness. The sweating system is only an economic expression of fear and greed, the economic bad manners of rush conditions. But we happier moderns are working often with patented processes, often with a monopoly of raw material, with a staff of workers that it has taken half a century to assemble, and always with a scientific and technical superiority that makes us unapproachable. Energetic new people do not seek to wrest things out of our hands; it would be hopeless; they come in and offer to work with us.

We do not spread our broad methods about the world without internal friction. The Crests have held lands in Oreshire since the thirteenth century; great grabbers and savers they have always been, a hard-fisted, firm-mannered race; they guessed right at the dissolution of the monasteries and grew mightily at their expense. Galsworthy's Forsytes are mild stuff compared with our Crests. Crest seems to have kept the beastly economic medievalism of his ancestry intact. He is as hard and mean as a French peasant and a British duke rolled into one. In the unproductive disorder of the Middle Ages the only ways of getting rich were to oppress, compel, sweat, or rob outright. Usury was forbidden, and besides, usury required arithmetical gifts accorded only to the Jews. Trade was a rare occupation, and as a trader you monopolised naturally, even if you had to fight and murder to do so. There was no increase in values going on; what you gained someone else lost. What you got you held with a scowling, swaggering dignity tempered only by the showiest possible largess on holiday occasions. When some unasked improvement in our workers' condition is in contemplation, Crest will still come to our board meeting with the clatter of rusty armour in his voice and demand where all this sort of pauperisation is to end. Where is the money to come from? he asks.

Nothing will ever convince him that our dividends do not come out of the pockets of other people, nor that our profits are not abstracted from the wages of workers who have been held down while the abstraction is effected. He is equally persuaded that the object of foreign trade is to pauperise foreigners. He is not really an employer as we conceive it; he is a medieval robber baron who offers terms. He is always trying to force our people into rifle clubs and the Territorials because it would give them a sense of discipline, and once he wanted a man dismissed because he did not touch his hat to him outside the works. The man was, unfortunately, a humorist. "Hey, my man!" said Crest. "I don't think you know me!"

"Don't think I do," said the man. "Who might *you* be?"

"I'm Lord Crest."

"I'm Billy Watkins. What aba't it?"...

It took nearly half an hour of our time at the next board meeting to convince Crest that gestures of social abjection were not among the duties for which Billy Watkins drew his pay.

"We can't interfere with their manners, my boy," said Roderick, pawing Crest's shoulder with a familiarity that made Crest pale with anger, and infusing an unusually Eastern oiliness and the shadow of a lisp into his voice, "and that's all about it. Why! if we began on that sort of thing where should we end? I'm always speaking to Julian now as it is about tapping in the tops of his eggs. *Will* tap 'em in. It isn't done in the best families. It gives us away. All of us Romers. And Clissold went out of this very room before me only yesterday. He's equal to going out in front of *you*. No sense of precedence. You've got to put up with this sort of thing these Bolshevik days, Crest, and thank God if they do their work."

"If you *want* to see discipline go to the devil – !" Flashed my Lord Crest, and dropped the subject…

But as our tentacular connections have spread our interests from our original mineral and metallurgical operations, we have come into relations with labour and with organisations for production developed upon less fortunate lines than our own. There we find ourselves tangled in responsibilities of every grade of difficulty. That's the less pleasant side of our picture. In the early days, for example, we bought the whole Crest Collieries output upon a sliding-scale arrangement and left the treatment of the miners to the parental Crest, their Union and God, and afterwards we filled our increasing need for coal in the open market. Now we have the infernal Crest mines practically on our hands; we hold all their shares, we are bound in a Federation to this, that and the other line of action, and indirectly by various purchases, working agreements, and amalgamations we have become miners and sellers of coal as well as consumers, but we have no finger in the direction, nor in the labour organisation.

Mining is as ancient a business as the first Pharaohs; it has always been a form of mass labour, and, like all labour which draws its traditions from the ages before machinery, it is a very unpleasant, inhuman, and wasteful form. That side of our great machine remains excessively unsatisfactory to me. It runs along, jarring and occasionally jamming, wasteful in substance and wasteful of life. The typical British mine-owner still belongs very generally to the horse-headed class; the equestrian tradition still dominates mine-owning. Economically he is an antiquated nuisance. Since he gave nothing for his coal and ore he does not care how much of it is wasted so long as the royalties come in. Royalties to these landowners are a tax on every coal-consuming industry. Cheap coal is necessary to the industrial life of Britain as good roads. Coal winning is a common interest that we industrialists are fools enough to treat as a private trade.

I am not on the Crest Collieries directorate, and it is difficult for me to do more than gibe and grumble at this equestrian inheritance. Our mining and mineral interests are dotted all over the world, and conditions in the mines that concern us, here and abroad, are determined by conditions in the others beyond our reach, and one set cannot be changed without the other. Before we can begin a fight with Vishnu we must be reasonably sure that Siva will not rise against us both. Much the same sort of thing applies to our transport interests also. We are big enough to be affected, but not big enough yet to exercise an effective control. I would like to see our tentacles grow and grow, bigger and stouter, until a single combine could take the whole mineral resources of the world into one problem. But that seems a long dream still, and before it can be realised and creative Brahma can get to work, Siva, in other words the passionate destructiveness of labour awakening to its now needless limitations and privations, may make Brahma's task impossible. I would even favour nationalisation if I believed, which I don't, that there was even a sporting chance of the politicians sustaining a competent management.

I am afraid of the obstinate injustice of all these ancient forms of employment, mining, shipping, transport work – which still carry on the traditions of the gang slavery of the ancient world. There seems never a day when one can turn them round into a new path and animate them with a new spirit. Yet on their present lines they are accumulating wrath and disaster for the whole system. The wastage of life is frightful. There is no more reason now why coal should be picked out from the seam bit by bit by hunched-up men working in darkness and dirt and foul air than there is that steamship furnaces should be hand-fed by sweating stokers or the harvests of the world reaped by hand.

Some day I may begin to see more clearly than I do at present a way of extending our hard and scientific methods into these old industries that the needs of finance and the markets have obliged us to annex to our comparatively clean, original system of enterprises. I would like to tackle a whole coal district as one system, survey it and sound it, reassemble the housing and surface cultivation, burrow into it with passages and air tubes and pour out coal tar, carbonised road-metal, pipe-steam and electric power for the towns and houses and factories, and so let the whole countryside run happily until nothing more was left below to burn. That might not be for a century or so, and by that time our industrial people would be moving on quite cheerfully to some new district and some fresh phase in the exploitation of natural resources, and we should have the old Black Country coming back daily and beautifully to agriculture and horticulture again. And as for our miners I would have them on salaries instead of day wages, work them at most five days a week and ten months a year, pay them for two months' annual holidays, pension them comfortably when they had done thirty thousand hours' work, even if they hurried up and did it soon, and get tons of coal out of them where now we worry out hundredweights. This is no dream, but an entirely practicable possibility. Only Crest and his kind, and the general foolishness that tolerates and supports them, stand in the way.

### 11 – *Sirrie Evans*

This book, however, is not to tell of my social and economic imaginations and desires, but about the conflict of motives that has gone on in me, beneath the surface of my very considerable business activities. I write about my motives not because I suppose they are at all remarkable, but just because they are not at all remarkable among my class. I try to lay bare in myself the soul of a successful business man. A considerable number of active men nowadays are in much the same case as myself. I am a fair sample of a new attitude of mind which is appearing here and there in the world and becoming more and more common.

I worked. I succeeded. I appeased myself with women. That is my history in brief. I followed out the programme I had planned in my empty house. But I was not satisfied. Always I was restless. And since mine is an intelligence which dresses itself up very little, this unrest of the spirit found its chief outlet for many years in fresh sexual activities. I suppose all the energy of life is sublimated from the sexual energy; the waters have a compelling tendency to return to the ocean from which they arose.

I have been what the eighteenth century called a rake. It is natural for me to find redeeming characteristics in a rake, to plead that he is at least obliged to be personally clean and fit and seemly, and that he must needs be of some imaginative activity and responsiveness. And also that no mere force of physical desire makes a rake. Grossness is no incentive to change and exploration; there is no need in modern life for a simply lascivious man to betray that quality to the world. The house of ill-fame is the natural resort of the man of good repute. But to me such conveniences, such imitations, have always been shameful and abominable. Bodily desire has been the lesser part of this business to me. Whatever else I have desired, invariably the leading thing I have desired has been personal response. And the next thing to that has been something hard to name, a kind of brightness, an elation, a material entanglement with beauty.

And still there was something more. I think now that I have been victim of one of those exaggerations of promise that our restless, purblind old mother Nature never hesitates to put upon us. Always through my fuller years there was a feeling, a confidence I never had the power or will to analyse, that somewhere among womankind there was help and completion for me. How shall I express it? The other half of my androgynous self I had lost and had to find again. You remember the fable Aristophanes told in the Symposium.

I have never found that completion. For me, at any rate, it has been no more than a sustaining illusion. But I do not repent of my love experiences. I am glad old Nature put that *ignis fatuus* into my wits and nerves to lead me the dance I have had. All these affairs have been touched by imagination and have revivified my imagination. I have nothing to reproach myself about in them. I have never prostituted a human being in any of them, I have never cheated, made dishonest promises, nor wilfully inflicted humiliation. If I have lied at times I have lied in small matters to mitigate or reassure; I have escaped from essential and fundamental lies. I am a rake unrepentant and unashamed.

I state these things here not by way of apology, but because they interest me as matters of fact. It is too often assumed that a rake is necessarily a seducer, a sort of area-sneak of the affections. He breaks down the sweet temple of virtue in spite of its pitiful pleadings and resistance; ransacks it, leaves it hideously and incurably defiled, departs with triumphant mockery. But that is pure romanticism. There are just as many women, in this modern world at least, as ready for love and as impenitent about it and as little desolated by it as men.

If I were seeking an exoneration for my life I suppose I could make great play with the fact that I was so tied to Clara that I could not marry again and live in a seemly, ordinary fashion. I am sorry for that fact because I would have like to have sons and daughters; I envy Dickon his youngsters, those sympathetic, organically linked extensions of oneself; but if I am to be frank with the reader as with myself, I am not sure that if I had been married and tied to almost any one of the women I have known intimately, my life would have been essentially different from what it has been. I understand how deeply husband and wife may trust one another, but there must be excitement in love and a sort of magic and adventure. It must be difficult to sustain the excitement, magic, and adventure year after year, with anyone whose every gesture and intonation one knows by heart. A separation and then a homecoming to dear familiar things? That is a different story.

But then, as I have written already in my account of my own futile marriage, I think that the same forces that the breaking down the separations between small businesses, fusing production into concerns upon a world scale, and driving the peasant from his immemorial holding, are breaking down the walls of the home. The faithful, fruitful wife was a possessed and secluded woman. But now the home is a service flat, a lodging, a suite in some hotel, and the man who once tilled the soil his ancestors tilled before him wanders from job to job about a world that is almost as homeless for him as the high seas. Man, who settled down to plough and increase and multiply twelve or fifteen thousand years ago, is now getting adrift again in great streams and clouds; it is a sort of harvest of mankind from the fields into the great camps of the new towns, and the woman who was his helpmeet is becoming once more his camp-follower. Or is ceasing even to follow his camp and, against all nature and precedent, setting up one of her own. Or is simply at large in the streaming crowd and amazed.

My life has been spent where the disintegrative forces are most at work. As a young man I was living rather exceptionally the sort of existence a great and increasing number of young people are living today. I indulged in great freedoms that are no longer freedoms but widespread practices. From the days of my separation from Clara until I was nearly thirty-two my opiate for that recurrent hunger in my heart was a series of intrigues that often overlapped and sometimes went on simultaneously two or even three together. The facts of these relationships are so flat and commonplace that it is hard to convey the glamour, the sense of depth and delight and reassurance they could afford.

Most of that satisfaction was the most patent illusion. I have to confess that, considered as a man, I am the least marvellous that can be imagined; the chief word in my description upon my passport is "normal," repeated several times; remarks, "none"; eyes grey, hair brown. A new hat makes me unrecognisable to most of my acquaintances. I suppose I am fairly alert and interested in people, and that is my most attractive quality. Yet my entire lack of personal splendour has not prevented my being the happy lover of a number of charming and interesting women. I can only suppose that they wanted to make love as much as or even more than I. I admired them, I was grateful, I delighted in them, and as a man I was good enough to pass muster. Of course, we called each other "wonderful" and "delicious," and so forth. We were so, I suppose, in that light – as any meadow may be wonderful at dawn. What I gave them was almost exactly what they gave me – an exquisite sense of personal reception, a vividness of being, a surcease of this pursuing hunger of the heart that overtakes us in leisure and security.

Women have gained great freedom even during my lifetime. A few generations ago a woman's work, as the proverb said, was never done. Now for many it is over before it has begun. It is not that they are better paid, but that they are wanted less. Much knowledge that was once hidden has come to them. Motherhood is no longer an oppression, nor even the fear of motherhood. For a great number this means a release of sexual imaginations. They have blank time, unexpended energy, and an inherent predisposition for the excitements and beauties of love.

I do not think these modern women want men very badly; they want love. Usually they are married women or women already possessing lovers. But their man is masterful and oppressive, or he is negligent or wandering in his attentions, or preoccupied and dull. Mr Smith or Brown reminds our lady too plainly, too flatly, that she is just Mrs Smith or Brown. He ceases to make her a goddess for his adorations. In a life of thin, unexacting routine love also becomes a routine. She has no sense of glorious giving, no sense of self-escape. But when she steals away to a lover all that is changed. You can hardly call her an unfaithful wife, for when she steals away she is no longer a wife. She ceases to be Mrs Smith or Brown. That is the gist of the whole thing. As her lover ceases to be Mr Jones. They both keep holiday from these commonplace verities. They go out of the world. She becomes as much a goddess as Diana visiting Endymion. As Mrs Brown she would no doubt be betraying Mr Brown, but as Diana in a secret cave remote from the things of everyday she betrays nobody. Restored to her self-respect, to her belief in her possible loveliness, she can return to her too casual and negligent husband with a pleasant sense of dignity preserved and equality restored.

It is a fundamental convention in the romantic version of life that when a married woman takes a lover she prefers him to her husband. In three-quarters of the illicit love affairs in such a great centre as New York, London, or Paris, this is not true. It is probably less true even than the converse proposition about men. And the mere suggestion to most of these modern women rakes that they might go off and live in blissful union with the lovers they have been adoring would, I believe, be quite sufficient to end the affair for them. I cherish no illusions about my relations to the goddesses for whom I have been a worshipped and worshipping god, dear friends though they have been to me. For only one of them have I been the anti-husband. For most, I have no doubt that if the husband's life or prosperity or pride had been seriously threatened I should have been sacrificed with about as much regret as, let us say, a once worn dinner-dress that he had found too frank and discreditable, or a pet dog he did not like.

And yet in the secret cave we would be very earnest about our business and things would be very lovely between us. In all these affairs there are not only questions of more or less, but each one has its distinctive elements that do not enter into the others. Athwart my memories of these little opium doses of love there flits the tall, slender figure of Sirrie Evans, with her fever-touched cheeks, her strong profile, and her burning, deep-set eyes. She came into my life like any other adventure, but perhaps a little more vividly and happily. There was nothing to tell me that she was destined to live with me for nearly seven years and die at last exhausted in my arms.

I met her first at a dinner party in London – I think at the Rudhans'; it was a large white dining-room with grey marble pillars – and she did not sit next me but across the table. We glanced at each other and liked each other. We were both being held rather tenaciously by dinner partners of the low-voiced, semi-confidential type, the sort that cut up dinner parties into horrid little cellules of viscid duologue. I seem to remember that my own lady was plying me with questions in an old Confession Album in a search for common ground, and I rather suspect that Sirrie was being subjected to arch and clinging compliments. Our eyes met in a common distress which changed to a mutual appeal. We recognized kindred. "Let's get out of this somehow," we telepathed.

The couple at the end of the table were talking rather loudly; the man was a challenger, the sort of man who makes controversial statements and looks about him. "The Russian moujik," he said, "will be the Saviour of Europe, simple, industrious, profoundly

Christian, worshipping his Tzar as God's Vicegerent." They all said that before the war.

I let a question on my left fade out neglected. "I don't agree with you," I said. "Have you been there?"

"They have divine beards," said Sirrie, grasping the situation with decision and directly to me.

"They are extremely kind to animals," said the lady at the end.

"I judge by the evidence of the Russian literature," said the man I had contradicted. "Dostoievsky in particular."

It was a large reply, but I took it up manfully.

The others fell helplessly into their proper places and we kept the conversation at our end of the table general until the ladies departed. By that time we had discussed Russian literature and Russian characteristics, peasants, and primitive people generally, whether peasant art and peasant costumes were not everywhere very much the same in Europe and Eastern Asian, and whether the essentials of peasant life had altered very greatly since the Middle Ages, and so it was natural for me when presently we went upstairs to go across Sirrie and pick up the threads again.

It was not so much a case of love-making between us as of mutual attraction. We arranged to meet next day to see what there was of peasant art in the Museum at South Kensington, as though that was the most natural thing in the world to do. Later I learnt her name – I had missed it before – and discovered that a sturdy, dark, thickset man with an expression of defensive self-satisfaction was her husband. I saw him watching us, and when he was aware that I observed him he turned away. She ignored him. Always she ignored him. And I ignored him too, as completely as I had ignored the Queen's Proctor in my separation from Clara.

It is impossible to convey by writing and telling the distinctive effect and charm of Sirrie as I knew her at that time. She was a brave thing – essentially brave. It was not the thing she said or the thing she did that seemed to matter so much as her style and carriage. She had a gallantry all her own, an alertness, very fine dark blue eyes, very fine brows; her cheeks were a little hollow and her voice very beautiful. But altogether she was beautiful. She had a lovely adventurous humour that seemed always seeking for the fun and quaintness and colour of life. She had a strong impulse to travel, to wander into fresh surroundings, to discover freshly different things. She was a born explorer.

The greater substance of our early escapades was altogether innocent. She loved to prowl in out-of-the-way parts of London, to peer into queer shops, to see contrasted sorts of life. She wanted a congenial man to go with her. We spent days exploring Whitechapel, Shoreditch, Clapham, the Crystal Palace. She would laugh with delight at the old and neglected exhibits at the latter place. Her sense of the absurdity of forgotten pretensions was very acute. "What were they up to here?" she would ask. "What did they think they were up to?" We never missed the stuffed animals; we traced the decay of the ethnological groups. The Picture Galley was a great joy to us. And the "antediluvian animals." Seeing things with her was like looking through a telescope in the sunlight at familiar garden flowers. We stole a night or so from our outward for our inward lives and went for walks and boated together upon little flower-smothered Surrey and Sussex rivers and canals. They were not so much passionate times as glad times that were spent together in those days. Never before had I known so keen a flavour of pure holiday.

It was only very gradually that I came to understand that the underlying force in her life was an intense hatred for her husband, and that beneath her keen superficial interests and quick responses she hid the wounds of some profound exasperation. She had been one of four brilliantly pretty sisters, and he had married her before she was eighteen. I do not know what particular things had happened between her husband and herself; she never talked to me about them and I never questioned her; but they had so scarred her that even her happiest moments at that time were touched with the quality of something done in his despite. I am by no means sure that she was altogether in the right. Possibly her hatred of him was unjust and freakish. She was quite capable of inexplicable animosities. She had neither justice nor morality in her apart from her aesthetic standards. She never said an action was wrong. She would condemn it as "not pretty." A gallant act was good enough for her.

Even in those days Evans was rich and growing richer in that slow, unproductive, creeping way that adds nothing to the wealth of the world. To him a wife also was no doubt an acquisition. From his point of view he had bought her, but the four lovely sisters thought they were a gift to the world. He had to beg for her thrice; when he married her I imagine he was already exasperated by the resistance to his wooing and by her gay flirtations with other men. She on the other hand may have been exasperated by the fact that she had yielded. He was the sort of man who is filled with dull, deep anger at the idea that he is not the most attractive and irresistible male in all time and space. The Old Man of the primordial tribe must have been much the same. He seems to have tried to break and subjugate Sirrie so soon as she was legally his. She tried some "nonsense" with him, and he stood no nonsense from her.

But I do not know what happened. I do not know what happened and I do not care to know. Perhaps very little happened. Perhaps she merely discovered that Evans was Evans and that she was inseparably linked to him. She had sold something for too low a price, something of fundamental value, something without which life was spoilt for her. And she had sold to an ungracious purchaser. At any rate, within a few months of his marriage he had this slip of a schoolgirl fighting him bitterly and successfully for her freedom – for her quite excessive conception of freedom.

The weakness she seized upon at first was his inordinate tender vanity, his fear of appearances. She made him realise that at any moment she might appeal against him to friends, to servants, to passers-by. Her appeal might be startling and unjustifiable; he was not safe from her unless he let her go her own way. I know that quite early she ran away from him for two days and dealt with him from an unknown address by telephone. "Leave me alone," she said in effect, "and I will still appear to be you wife. Otherwise, though it tears my world to pieces, I go."

But even though in a sort of way he left her alone, she would not respect his public honour. She despised and hated him too much for that. She broke the treaty, not he. I do not defend her. I set these things down. She came to me out of this ugly past, and it was not my concern to judge her.

Evans, blinded by his essential vanity to the fact that the most animated of women can still find many men entirely unattractive, sought to awaken her jealousy. She should be kept short of attention, kept short of money, left about and humiliated. She retorted by a scarcely ambiguous friendship for a young Guardsman, Lord Hadendower, about whom I know nothing. I never met him; he was killed at Soissons. Evans made his infidelities conspicuous and stopped her allowance altogether. She concluded rather rashly that the former action made a divorce impossible, so she, too, made her infidelities public and met her financial inconveniences by running up bills. All their world talked. He did not like advertising to restrain her credit and her allowance was turned on again. For a time she had the upper hand, and Evans was her suitor.

This bickering, dismal business developed. He shirked the rude publicity of a divorce for five or six years. She tired of Hadendower very soon and flung him away from her. But that meant no kindness to Evans. She was not a woman of strong passions, but an absence of passion is often associated with an absence of shameful emotion, and she was lively in her imagination and wild in her talk and letters, and quite reckless of appearances. Somewhere she had met a dangerous and folly-begetting word, the word Orgy. She was much sought after socially, a brilliant talker, a mimic, unfeelingly funny, capable of a calm indecorum of speech that left people gasping but delighted, and Evans was acutely aware of the powerful support she would have in any open breach in which he was not entirely in the right. So he waited until he was entirely in the right. For a time he made no breach. He had developed a consuming desire to recover her. He tried to buy her back, threaten her back; at last even to win her back. But nothing he could do now could touch her detestation. Her life became more and more a scoring of pleasures, social successes, stolen outrageous adventures that had a subsequent publicity, defiant freedoms, against him, the heavy thing go which she had got herself chained. His love, such as it was, became at last a deep vindictive hate. That was the bristling situation into which my wanderings had led me.

I just imagined I had had the good fortune of an exceptionally refreshing passade.

I had known Sirrie scarcely four months when Evans exploded his long-prepared mines under her feet and commenced proceedings for divorce. It was his amiable intention to make it as scandalous and dirty a divorce as possible and ruin her completêly. Since at last he must come to complete publicity, he seems to have decided, then the uglier it was the better. He wanted to drive her into hiding and exile so that her visible existence should no longer trouble him. She should know what poverty was. She should appreciate the rare and precious advantages she lost by despising him. Every possible or probable man was cited as a correspondent so as to present her as entirely abominable, disgust her lovers with her and deprive her of any help in the world. It was a great case for the newspapers.

None of her lovers stood by her at the outset. Not one. I was as bad as the rest at first, jealous and ashamed. I had not known a third of the things thus dragged into the light. My first feeling was anger, because she had troubled so little about my being implicated. She must have known of the gathering storm.

So far as I was concerned we had been cleverly watched and documented. The other side got at me very neatly with a nasty little clerk who broke things to me. They were so quick at the crisis that Sirrie had no chance to tell me beforehand of what was coming. I managed to be out of London when the case came up. I read the first day's proceedings in the morning paper.

"Damn!" said I, over my breakfast things at Downs-Peabody.

"Damn!" became, so to speak, the password of the day.

I took my little car and started vaguely north before Julian could get at me.

The plain English of that is that I ran away. I ran away for the better part of a day at an average speed of about thirty-five miles an hour and left my reckless, shameless, brilliant fellow-sinner to face her consequences alone.

In the morning I was blindly angry with her, merely angry. I saw myself – I remember the phrase among my self-reproaches – as "one of a row of accursed fools." My views about the charming levity of promiscuity were badly shattered. It was only as the morning wore on that she became anything more in my mind than an object of anger. Slowly she came through the wrathful mist, no longer as a feminine mischance, Eve and be damned to her, but as herself.

I began to see her face and hear her voice. And – for all the circumstances – her form was still slender and her face still fine.

How was the business taking her? After all, it wasn't going to be such very great fun for her. She must be having a nasty time up there in London while I was motoring northward, a very nasty time. She would have to go into the box. That was the idea that stuck itself like a thorn to my mind and gradually changed its tone. I tried to think of her still as a shameless woman, exposed and exposing all her friends. But I could not do so. I ceased to think of what she had deserved by making me ridiculous and asked myself what she must be feeling and how she would be carrying it off.

I began to be obsessed by the figure of her as she would stand there, with the court staring at her and the clever ones sketching her, slender and flushed and holding her head up – I knew she would hold her head up. Whatever happened to Sirrie, she would certainly keep her head up. That, you see, was how it was set on her neck. And there would be no whimpering or being overcome. Once I had surprised her at a theatre with her eyes bright with tears and that memory supplied the highlight of my picture. Tears were possible to her but not weeping. "If I did these things I did them," she would say. "But I didn't do them like that." And that would be true. The more illogical the distinctions she made, the sounder they always were.

They'd ask her filthily intimate things. The old judge and lawyers would gloat over her. The court would be crowded. At the back all the young lawyers would be packed, alert not to lose the chance of a juicy line. Evans would see his lawyers did the job properly and that the juicy lines were forthcoming. She had written some exaggerated letters. She had a trick of using improper words – almost as a child uses them to startle. She had done that in her letters to me, and I had no doubt she had done it to everybody. They wouldn't give such letters a chance, I knew; they would read bits out without the qualifying context. The pure-souled gentlemen in the wigs and gowns would boggle modestly at her worst expressions as they read them. The court would blush to its straining ears. "I'm afraid I must paraphrase this, me lud." She had been wild and fantastic. These comparatively passionless woman can say and do the most outrageous things at times – through a kind of insensitiveness. "Why not?" is their formula.

"How old is she?" I asked, and did little sums. She had been married at seventeen. She was now four or five-and-twenty.

I can only recall dimly now what sort of see-saw went on in my mind. I have to guess at most of that as though it was something in the mind of a stranger. I must have felt a great disgust at the whole business, I must have been indignant with her and have condemned her or why should I have continued to travel north hour after hour?

But I must have dismissed all that indignation later. I cannot recover it. It is like trying to reconstruct the torn letters from the wastepaper basket of the day before yesterday. Perhaps it was a sort of inertia kept my foot upon the accelerator.

"If I go back to her," said I… "It's a complete return."

My decision hung fire all day and then it exploded. Suddenly I knew what I was going to do. As if I had known all along. It was the last possible train to London I took that night. It was behind time, and I got to London in the small hours. She was all alone, I found, except for one sister, at Berridge's Hotel. I telephoned and was answered by the sister – she was in bed and asleep, tired out. The next morning I went to her.

"I've come to stand by you," I said.

"You'll learn a lot of new things about me," she answered, looking me squarely in the eyes. "Not very graceful things."

"I've read the morning papers."

"You could hardly help it. It isn't a pretty case, is it?"

"Unpleasant for both of us," I said. "I admit the surprises. Nevertheless, I'm going to stand by you."

"You know – the things – They'll bring them up in the ugliest way – but substantially – they will be true."

"I don't except to see you vindicated like a Drury Lane heroine. I've thought that out."

"What does this mean? What do you mean to do?"

"Stick by you."

She stood without betraying any emotion, rather like a woman who weighs a business proposition. Then she turned to me with the same air of entirely controlled reasonableness.

"But you didn't know of these other affairs. You came in late and innocent. I gave you no warning. I ought to have had the sense – There is no earthly reason why *you* should come into this mess. It's *my* mess. My little affair with Jim. Silly to think so much of Jim – to hurt oneself annoying a thing like that! I drove Jim frantic and he's got me. I've... There's been some rotten men in this. I've been an utter fool at times. No one will blame you for standing out."

"No one will blame the other fellows either. I see that. But you want someone. In this business. After all, I'm the last on the list. Forgive me if I'm unsentimental; I won't even pretend to be in love just now – but I'd as soon see a little child drown under my eyes, a little child I knew, as let you go through this alone."

"But after?"

"I've thought of that."

"What do you mean?"

"I mean – I like you. More than I dreamt I did."

"What's that?"

"I stand by you – now and afterwards. I'm not a green youngster. I've told you – how things are with me. You won't be taking advantage of my innocence. I know a little about women. It's easy to love you. But somehow also in spite of all this – I respect you. I'm not shocked. I don't care what their evidence is. It can't alter the knowledge I have of you. You have – a crazy side. I don't know all you may have done, but I have some idea of what you are. For me you began when we met. Have I seen nothing of you? All the exidence in the world won't convince me that your soul – if I may say so – isn't as straight as your body."

She did not speak at once. She shrugged her shoulders at my last sentence. She seemed to be taking in the new situation.

"You'll come to the court?"

"Every day. Your brother. Your friend."

"Like someone holding my hand! Oh!… Billy! when you know the sort of thing – !"

She stopped short. The tears flashed for a moment in her eyes.

"Friendship," said I.

"Friendship," she echoed, and her eyes questioned me, and then slowly she smiled at what she saw in my face. "You old brick," she said, and for a moment her mouth was awry before she recovered her smile. She held out her hand. "All right."

We clasped on it, a hand-clasp that was better than any embraces.

"I've been playing rather a lone hand," she began… "I've deserved what I've got…"

She bit her lip and looked helpless.

"Put a hat on," said I with my spirits rising unaccountably. "Run! The court won't wait."

And in that way in the lounge of Berridge's Hotel I married myself for all practical purposes to the scandalous Mrs Sirrie Evans and faced for the first and last time the legal consequences of my adultery. For two days I sat in court, to the great interest of the smart women who crowded it, and was conspicuously assiduous to the needs and comfort of the respondent. And when it was all over I carried her off and put her in a flat and for all possible purposes treated her as my wife.

It was an irrelevant accident, an extraordinary digression in my life. I went to her and I went to the court primarily because of a sense of obligation. I was bound to stand by the consequences of my own misconduct. But insensibly and very quickly my attitude changed to one of what was I now admit unreasonable championship. It was unreasonable, it was instinctive, I felt that

Sirrie was essentially as honest as, and finer spirited that I, that her sex put her at a frightful disadvantage and threatened to penalise her horribly for acts no more immoral than many I had committed with impunity. I took up the cause of laxity in general, in my appearance at her side. I defended the whole series of my paramours in her. We were fellows in the common business of erratic and forbidden adventure and desire. But from championship and fellowship I passed very rapidly to a keen affection and pity for a creature misused by herself and by the world that had produced her.

And the affair opened a new phase in my own life. I had been hitherto an exceptionally lone animal. Now I found myself carried completely out of myself by care for another human being. I did my ineffectual best to reinstate Sirrie socially, to mitigate the penalties of those sins of hers that I could understand so well. I enabled her to take a pretty little house, secured her good servants, and would not dine nor associate outside my business with any people who did not treat her as my wife. We travelled and visited together. We were faithful to each other, and every moment that my very active business occasions permitted we spent together.

Weighing this phase over now, I am most struck by the fact that our living together was not the result of any passionate crisis, not the outcome of any grand passion. There was no tremendous declaration, no irresistible elopement. I do not remember any strong desire to possess her or be with her before we lived together. There was no such urgency. Our union was forced upon us by Evans' malevolence. I am not sure that I should have gone to her if I not been cited in the case. Before the divorce we had liked each other greatly, been pleasant to each other, made love lightly. My dominant mood at the trial I can best describe as a sort of indignant tenderness. That so fine a thing should be treated so scurvily! So fine thing!

It was only after we had kept house together for some time that we developed very deep personal feelings for each other. We grew into one another by imperceptible degrees.

I have never been able to make up my mind whether my early life was one of exceptionally starved affections or not. I know of no quantitative standard by which one can measure oneself against others in these matters. I have never been able to determine whether young people are as capable of love as their elders, whether disinterested love is not necessarily a concomitant only of the fully adult state. My own youth was certainly a very loveless time. I had an imaginative love for my father, and a brotherly affection for Dickon was always present, but beyond that there was very little. There were no passionate boyish friendships, or if there were they have faded out of my mind. Even before our mother estranged us by her second marriage I did not care very greatly for her. Either I never loved Clara or that love is effaced. I was on good terms with many men and woman, but none seemed necessary to me, and for none was I prepared to sacrifice myself in any way.

My impulse to defend and vindicate Sirrie surprised myself. It also surprised Sirrie. She had liked me greatly from the first, but after her divorce she became acutely interested in me and curious about me. There was a phase in our life when she seemed always asking me questions about myself – questions that were excessively difficult to answer. I had not been in the habit of answering questions about myself. I was something new and unexpected in life for her, and, as it appeared to her, something unexpectedly good. She had had bad luck with her men. She threw over her idea of being a wicked woman, a sort of defiant insistence upon it as her *métier,* without another thought. I heard no more of it.

She set herself to understand my motives and the way I worked. Her social outlook had never included a laboratory, a railway, or a smoking chimney, and she thought that the lower classes were all either cottagers or servants. Trade unions were as much outside her world as totem groups. She thought that when you wanted anything you went to the best West-End shop that sold it, and I doubt if she realised completely that the first step to getting it was to wring or wrench its substance out of the soil or out of the rocks. How far she ever came to understand my ideas I do not know. She accepted my urgent preoccupations with business as a strange but forgivable thing in my composition. Since it mattered to me, it mattered to her, but it might just as well have been the Turf or a preoccupation with big game.

But if she did not understand my ideas, she came to understand many things in my character that are still hidden from me. She controlled me for my own happiness, invisibly, imperceptibly. She gave me a disinterested friendship, which is so much greater a thing to give than sexual love. While she lived my discontent with life was greatly allayed. I never worked so well as I did during those years.

When I had made a home for her I had had a streak of warm self-approval in my mind. I had thought I was doing something rather handsome and generous. Instead, for the first time I was getting the most precious things in life, love, faith, understanding, fellowship, and the reality of home. I was getting all that was good in marriage except children. But plainly she was tuberculous; we knew from the outset that her lungs were "wrong," and we did not dare to have children.

It was a friendship, it was a fellowship; it was these things first and foremost. We made love; we had spells of intense happiness of that kind, but our reality was our friendship, based on our unfaltering belief in each other's soundness and goodwill and our common repudiation of the current moral verdict upon us. I do not think we would have been very jealous of each other if there had been any real occasion for it, but there was not. I was too busy in those days to follow up any competing interest, and she was too tired of men to experiment with them further. Jealously is an active reaction to a sense of insecurity, and we were both very secure with each other.

Our first home was a little pinched-in house on Richmond Hill with an iron balcony in front and a wedge-shaped walled garden behind. There Sirrie could be ingenious and decorative and house-proud. But later we had to move to Bournemouth because of her health; I was growing in wealth, I could give her a fine new house there, gracefully designed, and she made a pretty garden amidst rocks and pine-trees on a slope that looked towards the sea. I would run down by the afternoon express like the most orderly and moral of business men, and she would meet me in her car. How well I remember her erect figure and her fine thin bright face, brightening still more at the sight of me. And every time I settled down in the car beside her to be driven home, to my home, I would have the same thought pass through my head – the wise that she was really my wife and that this pleasant security against passion and unrest could last for ever.

But I had the best of these two homes. While I was there we had each other, and she was very skilful in making me happy. What did she do when I was away? The "nice" people kept away from her both at Richmond and Bournemouth – which did not prevent them from being endlessly curious about her doings; and the incorrect people who did call were for the most part rude or dull or humiliating with their freedoms and confidences and assumptions. She took my name of Clissold; she was my wife in the sight of the butcher-boy, but everyone who mattered knew about us and remembered about her. She was wonderful stuff for the imaginative anecdotalist *sotto voce*.

She read enormously. The house was always full of new novels. She was acutely critical of the problems in conduct they raised. We had great discussions. She made me a reader of contemporary novelists – a thing unusual among business men. She also played with her garden endlessly. But she was an impatient gardener. She suffered a few acquaintances. She must have spent endless hours staving off the talk and tedium of their limitations with the new game of bridge, that presently developed into auction bridge. She became a great bridge player – when I was out of the way, and if these callers and associates bored her at the time, she got a certain compensation in preserving their choicer fatuities for my entertainment. She could be extraordinarily funny, but at times more than a touch of bitterness was mixed with her derision. She developed an acute perceptiveness for furtive tentatives to gallantry on the part of timid, vain, mean, and unsubstantial men and for the elements of pose and falsehood in the romantic confidences of the women.

Those years we spent together seem to me now in the retrospect to have passed very quickly. They were broken up by long journeys I had to make through the Urals, into Siberia and into the Canadian Rockies. It was impossible to take her on these expeditions. But wherever I could I took her, for her passion for travel was insatiable. She went to the Argentine with me and to Sweden. It was only very slowly and too late that I realised how rapidly she was dying. The last three winters of her life were spent, one in North Italy and two in Switzerland, and it was in a sanatorium in Switzerland that she died.

I do not remember when her cough began, but it is an essential part of my memory of her. She grew thinner, her cheeks more hollow and more flushed, and her eyes intenser. As she grew weaker she grew more daring. A craving, a great love for speed grew upon her. Motoring was developing, and I got a big Italian car that could jump up to eighty miles an hour on a straight. She would crouch together by my side, wrapped in her furs, her eyes gleaming over the grey stole that covered her mouth, silent, ecstatic. "Faster!" she would whisper.

Once or twice she drove – and these were memorable experiences for me. I held myself still beside her, controlling an impulse to snatch the wheel from her poor wasted hands.

As I realised her weakness and her sufferings, insensibly companionship gave way to protection. For the last four years her movements were more and more restricted, rain and sundown drove her indoors; she had to live in rooms at a measured temperature; she could no longer face exertion. Her restlessness increased perpetually; she did not like any place she was in because she did not feel well there; she wanted to go on, where the sun was still kindlier and the air easier to breathe. She had phases of acute unhappiness, but her hopefulness always rescued her. She felt the shadow of social isolation that lay upon us as though it was a chill, and that, too, drove her on. She fretted, she had a vague, shamefaced ambition for some social demonstration, some vindication, some recognition imposed upon people. I cannot imagine her troubling about anything of the sort if it had been freely available. But she felt and imagined exclusion. The further one is abroad, the less evident is that exclusion. At an infinite distance from London all English people meet. She wanted to be met. It was childish, no doubt, to feel desire for a worthless thing simply because it was denied, but are we not all children when it comes to such social uneasiness?

When she died we were planning a journey to the South Sea Islands and afterwards a tour right round the world. I could contrive it without breaking up my own activities too much, for everywhere now there are minerals and possibilities for Romer Steinhart. She would sit with a soft green and blue and crimson Spanish shawl about her, the most fragile and ethereal of creatures, with a dozen travel books upon her couch and one or two on a table close at hand. "I must see Easter Island," she would say. "It cannot be far out of our way to see Easter Island."

I would bring the Atlas and sit down on the couch beside her. "Let us see where it is. Yes… Yes, I think we can bring in Easter Island."

Her hand would stroke my head.

"Billy Cook, the dear World Tourist Organiser. You can really spare me all this time?"

"I want to see these places," said I.

"I'm rather a lump to take about. But down there I shall recover. Last week – unless that machine is wrong – I gained two ounces. And we will swim in the warm, warm sea."

"And I will guard your toes from the sharks with a cutlass between my teeth."

"Brave Billy! Of course you will! Kiss me, Billy dear."

She hoped and longed for the south seas to the very day of her death. She hoped to the end. On the morning of the day when she died, she explained how favourable a thing haemoptysis was.

"I believe that was the last of that stuff," she whispered. "One coughs away…all the diseased tissue…all the tainted blood…and then, of course, one heals…heals."

"Be quiet, my dear," I said. "Talking isn't good for you. You will have to heal quickly if we are to start next month."

She was very tired that afternoon. She had had a spell of coughing so violent that it had alarmed me; she had nearly choked with blood. The flow ceased at last; the doctor gave her a sedative and she went to sleep in my arms. "Stay with her," the doctor. "You had better stay with her. If she wakes she may cough again. She is very weak now."

But she did not cough again. A tired, flimsy, pitiful frame she had become, something that one just took care of and treated very gently; her motionless eyelashes touched my cheek, and she passed away so softly that until, with a start, I noted her coldness, I did not suspect that she was dead.

## 12 – *Mirage and Moonshine*

She died in 1905, and I was just forty. Her death left a very great gap in my life. While our relations lasted my life had an effect of being filled and my hunger of the heart was assuaged. I was needed, I was necessary. If I was not fully satisfied I was at least fully occupied. Since then I have never quite lost the sense of loneliness as a thing painful in itself. I had acquired a habit of looking to someone else for kindness. I wanted someone to smile a welcome to me and be glad when I came home. It was a new need.

During my years with her I had parted from an earlier, harsher self and become the more tolerant and less intense self I am today. My earlier self seems to me to have been tacit, whereas now I am explicit; it was, in comparison with what I am, compact of self-reliance tempered by lust. Only through desire did I ever trouble myself in those younger days to propitiate my fellow-creatures. For it seemed I could get everything else without propitiation. But that had now been changed. In part that change may have been a natural change as one ripens, but far more I think it was the effect of my relationship to Sirrie. With her friendship, her charm, and at last her weakness, her involuntary appeal for kindness and service, she gave me in a few brief years all that is given to most men by marriage and parentage. I had acquired the habit of referring myself to the needs and standards of a life that was not my own. From her at least I did not take. From her I had learnt the fear for something one desires to protect and cannot always protect. Her death, moreover, coincided very nearly with the close of a phase in my relations with Romer Steinhart. The fun of winning my way to the inner fastnesses was at an end. My position was acknowledged and my share established; I was Roderick's most trusted colleague; I was becoming free to do something, if I would, with our great businesses.

I remember myself during that decade of copious low-grade living that passed at last into the Great War, as empty with the deprivation of my lost solicitude for Sirrie, consciously lonely, and with my old dissatisfaction with the disconnected multitudinousness of my impressions greatly deepened and broadened. The world as it ceased to be a battlefield became a riddle. The struggle for existence being won, came the less natural question of what to do with existence, to which question – except for reproduction – nature offers no instinctive reply. So we fiddle about with reproduction and do not even reproduce. I will not say that such moods of discontent possessed me, but they were always in waiting for me when I was not vividly active. They did not hinder me from continuing to play a leading part in the aggressive extension of Romer, Steinhart, Crest and Co. through the world.

Copious, low-grade living seems to me to express the quality of that time very exactly. The automobile was becoming prevalent, and prosperous people were using it more and more in headlong attempts to escape from their tedious and uneventful selves. The vacuous face of our collective life grimaced with the pretence of a solemn grief at the death of plump old Edward the Seventh, and then went through expressions of grave expectation at the accession of his worthy, conscientious, entirely unmeaning and uninteresting son. Save for some irreverent verses by Max Beerbohm that solemn front was scarcely broken. The parading attention to the immense passings and comings of our intrinsically insignificant royal personalities, blocking the traffic filling the papers, delaying business and legislation, caught the mood of disillusionment, and accentuated for me the extraordinary triviality of human association. These pervading unavoidable royal personages stole dignity from knowledge, mocked progress, an dishonoured all life for me. When they went in public procession to thank the God of Earth and Heaven for an averted illness or a fresh addition to their respectable family, or to open something or come back from somewhere abroad whither they had expensively, ridiculously, emptily gone, I found the closed streets, the oafish spectators, incredibly exasperating.

This stuff was the formal crown of my existence. This was the Empire, the legal purport of my world. For this, I reflected, our great organisation was supposed to work, for this we won our beautiful metals from the obdurate earth, and fought nature and human indiscipline. To this end we increased the wealth and power of mankind. The German cousins, the Russian cousins, in their still more gaudy uniforms, came and went; envious rich American women crowded to London, bowed down and worshipped.

It seemed to me that this sort of thing might go on indefinitely. Life was not even tragic in those days; it was neither tragic nor comic; it was elaborately silly and vaguely dangerous. Flags, armies, national anthems, stuck upon my world like straws and paper gewgaws on the head of an idiot. But I did not conceive this idiot could blunder into actual war.

The result of maintaining political forms that are beneath human dignity and religious pretensions that are beneath human belief is to impose a derisive cynicism upon great multitudes of people who would otherwise live full and vigorous lives. I link the feverish playing of games, the onset of rowdy dancing, the development of night-clubs in every city in the world, the hunt for immediate pleasures that was already in full tide before the war, with this dominance of outworn loyalties and faiths that block out any living vision and sustaining hope from the general mind. Amidst the rhythms of jazz and the heavy blare of national anthems, what other voices could be heard? Industrial recriminations there were – strikes. The mere shadows then of our present considerable discontents. They brought no hope to me.

My unhappiness in those pre-war years, you may say, was essentially grief for Sirrie. And the personal loneliness to which she had left me. But that is not exact. The loss of my preoccupation with Sirrie exposed me much more than I should otherwise have been exposed to the clamorous futility of the times. But it was the time that distressed me, the times and a certain growth of my mind, my powers and my sense of responsibility. I wanted not simply a better life for myself, but a better life altogether. Thousands of people were as consciously bored and distressed as I was, by the resonant emptiness of those years. Millions were bored and feverish without any clear apprehension of their trouble.

It is one of the most respected conventions of the contemporary literary man that people's lives and actions are never determined by political and social conditions, but only by personal reactions. That preposterous limitation may be the reason why so few fully adult people read modern novels. Life is more coloured by the morning paper than the literary man will admit. I know, for example, that the enormous preoccupation of the community with the fuss of the king's coronation and with the posturings of the German Emperor, irritated and depressed me far more than the actions of any individual with whom I came in contact during that foolish period. I was a unit in a half-witted social body quite a much as an individual, and I suffered acutely from the mental degradation of the half-wit who included me.

For a little while I was interested in the new invention of flying. I worked upon a group of light alloys with special reference to the elimination of wood from the framework, and I was a good deal at Eastchurch in 1911–1912. Those were primitive times in the air. I used to have joy rides in aeroplanes of 35 h.p. and less, and Shortt was considered a bold pioneer when he put 80 h.p. engines into his machines. But after a few flights I lost any sense of wonder when we ceased to bump along the earth and roared up over the cows in the meadows and worked our laborious spiral way up and up until we were over the Medway and looking down on the Thames and Essex coast. There we hovered, churning the sweet air, rather conscious that we were holding ourselves up and that it was undignified to come down too soon. It would have been a fascinating method of travel if there had been anywhere to go, but the only really long journey aviators made in those days was a sudden, unexpected nose-dive out of the world. They were only discussing air-pockets in those days; no one was ever strapped in, and every landing was an adventure. But the essential things were done.

"This we can make," said I to myself, high and swaying unstably above the Thames estuary. "This we can improve. This is only the beginning..."

And then: "What will be the good of it?"

It was this pointless achievement of flying that first forced upon me the realisation how largely inventions were being wasted on mankind. That foolish gift-giving uncle, Science, was crowding up the children with too many mechanical toys. The children I half discerned could only misuse them and hurt each other. Or fail to use them at all. I recall that thought, and with it I associate a downward vision, washed with bluish haze, of little fields, a pale yellow thread of road along which a slow-moving black dot was a motor-car, and a group of farm buildings seen in plan, all roof and hayrick.

"What will be the good of it all?" said my private devil in my ear. "Why bring the duffers sailing up here? Leave them to grow turnips and swap diseases till the crack of doom."

I suppose I did quite a lot of promiscuous love-making in those vacuous days. It is nothing to boast of and nothing to conceal. For a long time I found no one I could love very much, and I began to prefer women who plainly did not care for me very greatly to women who brought a personal passion, or the pretence of one, into the game. I was ready enough to admit they were charming and delightful creatures, but not that they were personally indispensable, and that I was tormented by yearnings, uncertainties and monstrous fidelities on their account. I began to feel a tolerance for meretricious love which I had once thought revolting. But I rarely came to absolutely meretricious love. If I had been a poor man and manifestly ungenerous I should have failed in some of these love affairs in which I did not fail, so much of paying was there in it, but that is not quite the same thing as meretriciousness.

Such was the quality of my life in the middle forties. Cut down in this fashion to its heart, it was friendless, loveless and aimless. But that is not to say that there was not steady, extensive, interesting toil, much fellowship and kindly commerce with pleasant men and women, aesthetic gratifications, fun, excitements, a great deal of incidental happiness in it. But always there was dissatisfaction waiting for me in the shadows and the quiet moments. It was not good enough. Life was passing by. I was not being used to the full. By all the common standards I was a winner at the game of life – and I was doing nothing with my winnings. Romer Steinhart was a big thing to be in, but I was not taking Romer Steinhart anywhere; it was talking me nowhere in particular. If I had been a less successful man I might never have discovered my unhappiness. But then I should have had no story to tell. I should have lived, suffered, spun my hurried time about the whirlpool and vanished according to precedent.

Came the huge, thronging, deafening excitements of the war, the stresses and fatigues of the war, the headlong hopes of that period of Reconstruction that I shared with Dickon, and our rapid and immense disillusionment. That disillusionment, I see, was necessary and had to arise from vast and tragic events. If it did not seem ungracious to the valiant dead and to those who still suffer in body and memory from that tremendous catastrophe, I could find it in my heart to say the war was a good thing for the world. Not in what it destroyed nor in what it achieved, but in what it released. I have told of our reactions to the war in my account of Dickon. I have told of our realisation of our own haste and superficiality and how at length we subdued our minds to the real nature of world reconstruction, which that period of frothy projects had only caricatured. Of my ill-conceived attempts to enter politics I will tell nothing here; they were tiresome, humiliating, expensive and absurd. We had, we realised, to brace ourselves to serve in a cause for which we might never see even the beginnings of a triumph, but an imperative and unavoidable cause, a cause identifiable with the main process of life.

That needed a great effort in me, all my mind, a re-examination, a reorientation of my ideas. Without that effort I should fall back into the dissatisfied cynicism of the pre-war period. But my efforts to pull myself together, for what I have already termed the last lap of living, were complicated and impeded by an emotional entanglement into which I had drifted without any appreciation of its possible power. I was deeply in love, in love in a fashion that was new to me, and I was in love with a woman who had no knowledge of nor interest in these vital troubles.

Once more, just as in that early passion which led to marriage, I found my double nature tormenting me. I had vowed in my empty house in Edenbride Square that no woman should ever again turn my life about. I would take my freedoms and have the better of women. And for all my incidental adventures and digressions I had, in the main, kept my course. Suddenly now I found myself in the toils again. I had a mistress without whom, it seemed, I could not live. And, equally, I could not live with her and continue myself.

This story I have to tell about myself and Helen is, I perceive, an experience different in kind from any other love affair in which I was ever involved. It is too recent for me to write about yet with complete detachment. In a sense Helen has been exorcised here in Province; I can hardly trace how; but the scars are fresh and plain. The essence of every great passion is by its nature a thing untellable. We do not tell our love experiences; at best we tell things about them. Only the reader who was in love with Helen could see her as I saw her. For other people she was a strong, clever, ambitious actress with a charming smile, an adorable voice, a reputation for a hot temper, and an ungracious way with obtrusive admirers. Many people found her beautiful, but no one called her pretty. She was a mistress to be proud of, but only a brave man would attempt to steal her.

For me she was wonderful and mystical; she was beautiful and lovely for me as no human being has ever been; she had in my perception of her a distinctive personal splendour that was as entirely and inseparably her own as the line of her neck or the timbre of her voice. There was a sideways glance over her shoulder full of challenge; there were certain intonations, there was a peculiar softness of her profile when it was three-quarters turned away, that gave me an unanalysable delight. My passion was made up of such things. If that explains nothing, then there is nothing that can be explained.

We met before the end of the war, and then she was a comparatively unknown young woman, very fearless, and quite prepared to be interested and excited by a man of my standing and reputation. She fell in love with me and I with her, and I ceased to trouble myself about any other woman. We loved romantically, ostentatiously. Hitherto she had despised her suitors. We became lovers, friends, allies and companions. For a time I was very happy again. I immersed myself in the reconstruction movement, and I spent all the time I could spare and refreshed myself greatly with her. She, too, was busy with her profession; she was doing fine work and becoming well-known, and almost from the first we had to fit our times rather carefully to get together as we did. But to begin with we did not mind that trouble.

How easily can we fling one common name over different things and believe they are the same! I suppose everyone would say that with Clara, with Sirrie, with Helen, just as with the chance love affairs that have happened to me, I was a lover and the business was love. So far as the chance love affairs go, they had many things in common – the furtive elation, the gratified sense and vanity; but all these three relationships, these relationships that signified, were unique in root and branch and substance. With Clara I was animated by the sexual egotism of the young man, with Sirrie by a profoundly tender protectiveness, with Helen by the glamour of a beautiful personality. Only when we began to be estranged did I realise the hold her quality had taken upon me and the depth of my feeling, my utterly irrational feeling, for her.

What a lovely thing Helen was – and is! She not only evoked and satisfied my sense of beauty in herself, but she had the faculty of creating a kind of victorious beauty in the scene about her. She had a vision that transformed things, annexed them, and made them tributary to her magic ensemble. It was our custom to snatch a day or so and go off together from my business and her career, and I do not remember a single place we ever went to that did not reveal, through her, the most happy and wonderful qualities. It was if the countryside turned out to salute her.

We frequented the Thames Valley, and I shall never go there again for fear of finding the soft morning mists over the brown mirror of the water, the deep shadows of the trees, the tall attendance of the still poplars, and the brightness of the little inns all disenchanted. There is a small, squat hotel under the shadow of Corfe Castle. Is its sunlit garden of flowers among the grey stones the loveliest in the world? I remember that it was. I will never risk a disillusionment. I will never drive my car again through old Wareham's streets and along that white causeway beyond the prehistoric earthworks and so to the Swanage Road. That was the way to Corfe and to a walk over the grassy hills above, commanding vast distances of marsh and woodland and inlet, that touched the heavens of loveliness. Thrice we went there. There is a great park near Tunbridge Wells and an inn with some quaint armorial decorations of gates and chains; is it the Marquis of Abergavenny? I think it is the Marquis of Abergavenny. That also is an enchanted pavilion. A tall, broad-browed, smiling woman will haunt that place for me to the end of time.

I remember, too, an inn that cannot really exist, but I remember it as out beyond Staines and Egham – the inn at Virginia Water. One goes southward along a broad tarred road, bearing red omnibuses and charabancs and tradesmen's vans and tooting motor-cars and motor-bicycles and bicycles, a dusty din of traffic hurrying to no end of places. That stream flows on into the twilight and presently, with an outbreak of headlamps, far into the night. It is as modern and prosaic an improved and enlarged motoring road as can be. One comes upon this inn I write of at a dip in the road; comely enough it is and busy all the day with excursionists and trippers, but apt to become empty and quiet after sundown. At night the passing headlights flare upon its face, and its face is very still.

One descends to be welcomed by an easy, accustomed waiter. It seems no different from score of such good wayside inns. You do not see at first what it and the tall trees about it are hiding. But there is a great winding artificial lake there, a queer freak of

George the Fourth's. It stretches away with wooded islands and a further shore of woods for six or seven miles into the Windsor Great Park. This is the Virginia Water. It is not without some daylight vulgarities. There is a cascade of the utmost artificiality close by the inn, and further away some quasi-classical ruins, made of polished pillars and marble capitals that were stolen from Greece in the great days of Lord Elgin and intercepted royally on the way to the British Museum. These are unimportant accidents. By day the trippers swarm about them and gape and go away, and more trippers come. In the evening all that is changed. The black knots of trippers vanish before the gloaming. Sounds of the road become quite remote and negligible. The stolen ruins are wrapped up in a deep blue veil and disappear. Perhaps they are carried away. Perhaps they go back to haunt their proper place in Greece. Imperceptibly beauty prevails and is presently discovered enthroned. The still water reflecting the slumbering trees and a hemisphere of afterglow becomes a magic mere in a world of infinite peace.

"Death will be like this," said Helen, standing white and shadowy beside me. "With the high-road we have left – near and yet – suddenly – quite away from us. Perhaps we shall come to a place like this some day, my dear, and we shall scarcely realise we are dead."

"The high-road matters no longer," I said, and believed it as I said it.

I had a new and interesting car in the garage behind us, and some faint memory of its presence may have passed by me and faded into the shading tranquillity about us.

Our hands touched.

"We have done with the high-road tonight," I said. "I wish we had done with it for ever."

How vividly I remember that quiet moment side by side, and how passionately I longed later to recall its quality! And yet it was as unreal as a picture painted on glass. It was a picture we had found to buy and hang up and presently forgot. It was the loveliest shamming.

We stood in silence.

"What a scene this would make!" said Helen in a voice that was almost a sigh...

How vividly, too, do I still remember her shadowed face as she watched the reflections from the wavelets dance upon the brickwork of a bridge across the Thames.

She had discovered that there was a definite pattern at play in them.

"Like thoughts – with a sort of order, a sort of logic," she said, and it seemed the wisest thing I had ever heard said.

How was it that at times she could say such things? She did say them.

I thrust an oar into the reasoning liquid and turned its argument to quivering ecstasy. The reflection danced upon her face. And I, too, was all a-quiver with love for her...

But such memories as these will mean little to the reader. It is only for me that they are charged with beauty. They have the intense, irrational significance of some of my childish memories. There were moments, many such moments, with Helen that seemed to be worth all the rest of life put together. Inexplicably and incommunicably.

And we quarrelled and parted. We quarrelled and parted because neither of us, when we were put to the test, would consent to regard these moments as worth any interference with our work and the things we wanted to do. We did not really apprehend them as real. We could feel together, but we could make no sacrifices for our feelings. Ours was an intensely sympathetic and an intensely selfish fellowship. We were exacting with each other and grudging.

I confess I had little respect for her work, and she regarded mine as coldly. What was this making that I found worth while? What was this business of producing strange and untried materials from which ten thousand beautiful devices and creations could be wrung? She could not and would not understand. She thought one did such things to make money. And then when one had made money one sought the proud and magnificent Queen who satisfied pride and dispensed happiness. Her imagination lived in a world of brave men and beautiful women, and would have no other.

I could as little understand her ambitions. The exploitation of a personality in public was a thing incomprehensible to me. She, on the other hand, was the conscious priestess of her own divine qualities, her grace and dignity, her wonderful voice, her power to evoke the lurking emotions of her audience. She could not see what better rôle there was for me than to be her champion and supporter in this lovely self-absorption.

I put our antagonism plainly here, but it was not apparent in our earlier relations. It came into them by little degrees, and surprised and amazed us as we discovered it. At first we were greatly in love with each other in the sense that we felt an extreme need for each other. It was from my side that the first revelation of dissevering motives came. But when I had been with her a little time, and when I was fully assured of her, then aglow with happiness and fit and energetic, I would hear the call of my business operations and of my political interests as a call to self-completion. All the other women I had ever had to deal with since I became an actively prosperous man had accepted these inattentions and disappearances as things in the course of nature. I had been used to go away to my real life. But my going away, becoming customary, must have impressed Helen as the supreme outrage. Because, you see, it was not that I went away to see to tiresome, necessary things; that might have been forgiven. But I went away to things because they were more important to me. She was incidental and they were essential! It was incredible. Could anything be more important in life than the service of personality and the mood of love?

I knew I was costing her tears, but I could not suspect how much I hurt and stung her. She was not jealous; she was too magnificently sure of herself to be jealous; but she was superbly angry. I threw her back, amazed and wounded, upon her own proper work. She had loved me, she made me her lover, and I was only half a lover. She had sailed into life very bravely and confidently, and a perfect lover had seemed one of her elementary rights. I had failed to be the perfect lover.

I am telling all this with the utmost simplification, but to tell it in any other way, to relate comings and goings, moods hidden and betrayed, insensible changes of attitude, would mean an inordinately long and complicated story. It would need the intricate faithfulness of a Henry James. I doubt if I could retrace my steps through that maze. At first I was stronger than Helen, and I was overbearing with her and thoughtless and cruel. But she was younger than I was and with greater powers of variation and recuperation, and a time soon came when she was stronger than I.

The life of any actress is a life of uncertainties. Now everything falls away, the sense of frustration and failure is overpowering, and the poor lady is beyond measure miserable. This is the lover's moment, to console and sustain, to make life worth living. Then, quite irrationally, things conspire to make the actress queen of the world. She blazes into success, her personality is illuminated and admired from every point of view, she is talked about, sought after, she blossoms gloriously. The lover must run in the shadow then, carrying the cloak, ready for the moment when she will have to go out of the warmth and light again into the chill.

I perceive that always it was impossible for me to have been a worthy lover of Helen. In Paris – or, at any rate, upon the Parisian stage – there is the sort of lover I ought to have been. And there are such men – indubitably. But there was something in me, whether it was innate or the result of my upbringing I cannot tell, which declared that though I found Helen almost intolerably lovely and necessary to me, I would be damned if I waited about for her in the shadows with a cloak. And there was something equally powerful in her which insisted that, although she was intensely fond of me and fond of my company, she would not bother her head for a moment about me while she was actively warming her hands at the great blaze of applause and adulation she had lit. Meanwhile there were quite a lot of arms ready to hold the cloak in the shadows, and many intimations of consolation for me during these periods of neglect.

I had seen very little of the world of theatrical folk before my relations with Helen took me into it. I found it saturated with an excessive self-consciousness, with a craving for strong unsound effects; its lack of intellectual conscience continually amazed me. It was pervaded by sly and hovering young men and by habitually self-explanatory women who made up their personalities as they made up their faces. It never seemed sure whether it was smart or Bohemian. It affected a sort of universal friendship and great liberties of endearment. It sat about at unusual hours and gossiped and talked about itself, endlessly, emptily. And collectively it was up to nothing at all.

At first I could not believe it was up to nothing at all. For me the theatre hitherto had been something to which one went occasionally and contemptuously, preferably to see something laughable. I was prepared to concede there was a serious drama, outside my range of attention, but I did not really believe in its existence, I merely avoided dispute and inquiry. I liked and admired Shakespeare, though I did not find anything fundamental in him; I regarded – and I still regard – most popular fuss about him exactly as I regard the popular fuss about the smile of the Prince of Wales. I mean, there is about the same amount of original judgement in both these cases. The rest of the Elizabethans I thought to be highly artificial or rather drunken or delirious stuff. I like a good many English and French comedies from Congreve and Gay down to Barrie and Noel Coward. I lumped Ibsen – except for *Peer Gynt* – with Pinero and Jones and all the other "serious" dramatic shams of the Victorian time. I knew that such people as Granville Barker read lectures about a National Theatre and produced intricate and industrious plays to substantiate their talk; but that mattered as little to me as the Turf. Shaw alone I read with interest, a perverse but entertaining Manichean, an elusive wit, who took refuge from solid, sober expression on the platform or behind the glare of the footlights, and then repented and came back in a preface to say plainly all he had not said plainly – a preface that itself became forthwith as tricky as the platform speech. But always in the clearest, easiest English prose that was itself a delight to me.

Now with the advent of Helen I did my best to modify these views and believe that behind the "Drama" was some reality that could be correlated with my general vision of life, just as I assumed that within her was something fine and immortal that also could be correlated with that general vision. I tried to impose a grave attentiveness to things theatrical upon my unformulated subconscious conviction that a show is a show and the stage of the very slightest importance in serious human activities. I went about as far as possible with the air of a man who regards the Theatre as a great human institution.

I became more and more like a playwright soliciting the great actress with an inappropriate and unattractive play. My play, which I had been working out all my life, was the drama of our whole universe, the soul of man growing conscious and wilful out of nothingness under the silent stars. I wanted Helen, with her grave beauty, her air of tender wisdom, to be a heroine in that eternal play. But Helen had no suspicion of the existence of that drama, could apprehend no hint of it. Her idea of a play was one with a sustained series of emotional states and a crowing situation that would do justice to her fine voice, her lifted face, and the inimitable gestures of her arms and hands.

Absurd that two people so incompatible should have clung together, with conflicts and quarrels and partings and reunions, for nearly six years! My own obsession I can understand, but I have no inkling of hers. Perhaps she realised her peculiar hold upon me and knew that such a power might never be given her again over any other man.

My love for her and my jealousy of her deepened together. I was jealous of her, not on account of any rival, but on account of the world of display that was taking her away from me. From indifference I passed to an irritated detestation of most of the people who gathered about her, the serviceable young men, assiduous dear Bobby This or dear Freddy That, who were always free to fetch and carry for dear Helen because they were doing nothing that mattered, the over-familiar journalists who intimated by a sort of cringing patronage how necessary they were to her publicity, the little agent fellows entangling her in vexatious agreements, the galaxy of women intimates who consumed dear Helen's time with lunches and confidences, the large, idle, rich men exuding vague suggestions of taking a theatre for her, the men of letters about town who lifted her reputation to the higher levels of culture, the hostesses with an air of helpfulness in their stupendous exactions, the intrusive Americans coming frankly and blankly to admire, loudly, interminably, unprofitably – a lengthening, inexhaustible queue of them. I had to wade, ankle-deep, knee-deep, and at last waist-deep in this swamp of people to have any time with her at all. I performed incredible gymnastics of civility.

Year by year and month by month I saw her subdued to the likeness of this crowd, becoming more insolently assured of its incense and attendance, less and less free for any privacy and depth of living. If at first I had gone away from her overmuch, she, as her successes grew, became more and more deeply embedded against me. And yet we retained an obstinate attraction for each other. I had long days of anger and frustration, and then an hour or so together would silence every discord. By act and letter we could slight each other unendurably, but we could not continue to quarrel face to face. Her smile enchanted me, and she had a habit of affection for me.

Yet we had some sharp encounters.

"Damn that telephone!" said I, in her flat.

"Oh! – *you* want a slave in a harem..."

"You ought to make your private secretary your mistress," she said, coming back from her conversation. "Then she'd be always at your disposal."

"You will end by marrying your impresario."

"Well, I may have to. If I can't manage him without it."

Anger.

"He'd know his place. He wouldn't make me cry. Why do I stand you? Why on earth do I stand you? Why do I let you bully me? Nobody has ever made me cry but you."

It was a ridiculous and pitiful situation. Our several careers, our several conceptions of what was good in life, a deep obstinacy in both of us, tore us apart inexorably, and yet we had a primitive and essential affection for each other. For the reader this can be nothing but comedy, but that does not alter the fact that these things wrenched me abominably and hurt her very greatly. We were not only hurt but perplexed by ourselves. That quarrel in her flat recalls another preposterous occasion. We had gone to an inn near Petworth for two or three days, and she brought down a new play by Lawrence Lath with her, an utterly empty play, twenty thousand words of smartness, called *The Golden Woman*. She was learning her part; she was full of little ridiculous problems; how to treat this foolish line and what action was best to bring out the flavour of that. Consultation was imposed upon me. An exegesis of Lawrence Lath!

"I can't stand this rubbish," I protested. "It is cheap, knowing, vulgar – Rue de Rivoli. Why have you got yourself mixed up with it?"

"How can I learn my part when you talk like that?"

"Why are you in the position of having to learn such a part?"

"It's a part. My dear, what does it matter? I shall come right through it."

"And what do you come to when you come right through?"

"Is this to begin all over again?"

"And meanwhile have I no existence? Is there nothing in me, no obligation to call me away from this – this vacant pleasantness?"

Helen became an indignant queen and the manuscript part of *The Golden Woman* a sceptre. "Go back to your money-grubbing!" she cried.

"I'll go!"

"Go!"

A sudden appeal to high heaven for justice against me. "And I have to be ready with this for rehearsal tomorrow afternoon! How can I *think?* How can I do any decent work?"

We broke off with each other and repented and came back together again with tears and tenderness. We renewed our conflicts. There loomed up a tour in South Africa for her, a tour which might extend to the United States and become indeed a conquest of the Anglo-Saxon globe. She would cease to be an ordinary human being; she would become as universally visible as some celestial body. I protested selfishly and savagely at this vast separation.

"Your wife is dead now," she said suddenly. "You could marry me."

"What difference would that make?"

"We could go about quite openly. We could travel together."

"You mean you would give up the stage?"

She appealed: "What would be left of me if I did?"

"You mean I am to marry myself to the theatrical profession and follow you about?"

"You put everything in such ugly fashion. I am asking you to marry me..."

She became obsessed by idea that I must marry her, and then "everything would be different."

It was only too plain to me that nothing would be different. We parted again with some heat and bitterness and had a second inconclusive reconciliation. I had never before begged for mercy from a woman, but I confess I did from her. What did I beg of her? That she would be in some profound and fundamental way different, that she should not be herself in fact, in order that I should be myself. What did I really want of her?

There were times when I behaved like a thwarted child. She had become a habit of mind with me. I beat myself against her. I stopped thinking about things in general. I neglected business. She had got my imagination so entangled with her that for a while it would not serve me for any end of my own. I came near to a complete surrender and to giving her a marriage that would have done nothing at all for either of us. And then, filled with wrath, not so much with her as with myself, I set myself, sullenly and steadily, to break those humiliating and intolerable bonds.

I told her that now at last we had come to the end of our relationship.

We parted in a phase of grim anger – and she started out upon the subjugation of South Africa.

How completely had this hard, ambitious young woman changed from the dark, tall girl I had loved! And how swiftly so soon as she departed did she become again the dark, tall girl I had found so splendidly lovable! How I longed to hear her voice once more and see her again with my eyes! Directly she had gone I was asking myself why I had let her go. I forgot that for three years she had been going away from me far more than I had been going away from her, and it seemed to me simply that I had let her go. The love alone was remembered; the quarrels all forgotten. Why had I let her go?

And at the same time, cold and clear in me, disregardful of my general tumult and dominant over all, was my decision that we had to part.

## 13 – *Revolt against Love*

I was left in England with my nerves, my personal pride, and my imagination jangling unendurably. Gusts and eddies of unreasonable anger whirled about in a vast loneliness of spirit. I did my utmost to pull myself together, and for a time I could not do so.

This phase of distress is still very present in my memory. It seems the worst phase I have ever been through, and perhaps it was the worst phase. The perennial conflict in my nature between sensuous eroticism and creative passion had come to its ultimate crisis. I had made my last attempt to reconcile them, and it had failed. I had decided for creation and broken my servitude to this romantic love, but at a price. My will went about now with a white face and no power to do anything further.

The universe said to me in effect: "You are founded on sex. All you call life is founded on sex. You have been given the woman who is the loveliest woman in the world so far as you are concerned, and you have refused to give your life in return. Very well, you suffer. You have some gimcrack idea of getting the best of me, me who made you yesterday, me who need not trouble to destroy you because of your own self you die tomorrow. Success is yours and the beauty of that women might still be yours. And yet you cannot be content until this gimcrack idea of service rules it all. You have a sense of obligation! What sense of obligation? To whom? You insult my gifts. Victory and possessions, women and spending-power are all the gifts there are for men, and all these have come to you. Not good enough for you! Then somewhere beyond sex and hunger you must find the thing you need. I cannot give it you. Go your way, but I doubt you will end your life on a pillar like St Simon Stylites, cut off from earth and not much nearer heaven!"

For a while it seemed to me that I had at last brought my life, outwardly so successful, to a revealed defeat. My will was crippled by the strength of this desire for Helen that I had still in me; it had exhausted itself in the effort to break free from her, and was left incapable of any vigorous initiative, neurasthenic and suffering.

I thought of making a tour of the world to get away from the thought of her, but I knew that flight would accomplish nothing real. It would mean at best the stupefaction of fatigue. The other end of the world had no secrets and no releases for me that were not also in London and Paris. Excitements were mere temporary refuges; I might as well take to drink or drugs. Flight was not to be thought of, therefore; I had to sit down in front of this desolation and dig myself in and fight and beat it. I had to set my scattered thoughts in order and arrange my work for the last years of my life.

I had become so used to the delight of Helen's company, her voice, her careless close affectionateness, that all the world seemed haunted by her. For five years I had never been outside the beaten track of business except to go with her. I had been moved neither to happiness nor anger except through her. I had referred my pride to her; she had been my sufficient satisfaction. In England I was quite unable to escape from my memories. I went abroad. I wanted something which might excite and revivify my imagination. I thought I would go to the meeting of the Assembly of the League of Nations in Geneva and interest myself in such hopes of world peace as that gathering could afford. I flew thither on a private plane from London through a great storm of wind and rain that fell from us like a cloak as we crossed the Jura; and that at least was entertaining.

It was the year when that queer, vain, simulacrum of a statesman, Ramsay MacDonald, was posturing with poor Herriot as his rather abashed protagonist. MacDonald played to an imaginary audience, a Victorian audience that had been dead five-and-twenty years. Herriot and he, he intimated, were two great, noble, and righteous men in an otherwise wicked and foolish world. He made dramatic scenes with Herriot, holding out his arms to him from the rostrum and almost embracing him. Mighty things were to be done against "the powers of darkness." Beyond that he was vague. His second in command, Lord Parmoor, amazed the gathering by a display of simple evangelical piety unusual in European statesmen. I sat with cramped knees in the stuffy gallery of the Assembly and listened to the slow unfolding of the slow unfolding of these discussions that discussed nothing, in which there were no exchanges, in which every prepared and inconsecutive speech was duplicated by an interpreter's rendering. I listened. I laughed bitterly at some of the phrases my representatives used. I could not even be indignant. These political men seemed now all flibber-gibbers and phantoms, who could do nothing but recall the forms and gestures of a life that has passed out of reality. What substance, what nearness was there in all this stuff compared with the substance and nearness of a remembered face?

I went about Geneva in a state ripe for disillusionment, and I was abundantly disillusioned. The gathering was enormously polyglot and various, and there was a tremendous lot of lunching, dining, meeting and talking, plotting and intrigue going on beside and beyond the formalities of the Assembly. It was too crowded for me altogether. There were deputations of all kinds of odd people seeking all sorts of queer ends. I remember a charming Red Indian from Canada with a wonderful belt of wampum; it was a treaty all done in beads; by it the British Government gave sovereign dominion for ever and ever to the remnants of the Five Nations over a long strip of country running right through Canadian territories, territories in which prohibition and all sorts of bizarre modern practices now prevail. The Canadians were infringing the freedoms of that ribbon of liberty by sending in excisemen and the like. So the Five Nations, with a grave copper face, wampum treaty very carefully wrapped in tissue paper, were appealing from the British Empire to mankind.

Another figure that stands out in these recent memories of Geneva is Dr Nansen, tall, white-headed, with the big black slouch hat of an artist. I do not know him, but I saw him about everywhere. He was tremendously set, I was told, upon the inclusion of the Germans in the League of Nations. They refused to come in prettily, and he was spending considerable sums in cables of exhortation to Berlin. There was also a little group of German socialists, sadly, endlessly explanatory of the obduracy of their Government. There was a score or so of shock-headed, bright-eyed boys and girls from some Maori school in New Zealand; they all wore hat ribbons of red, white and blue, and what they were doing in Geneva I cannot imagine. They exercised Swiss curiosity considerably but not sufficiently. I was told by my hotel porter that they were Siamese, and by a policemen that they came from Madagascar, while a cabman said Mexicans without hesitation. After a day or so I never set eyes on any of these Maoris without at once seeking a new point of view from the nearest Swiss, and I never failed to get one. It was the most cheerful item in my Geneva pilgrimage.

There were unofficial as well as official Chinese about. There were Druses with grievances against the French, and Turks and Kurds with grave charges against the British. There was a strong contingent of representatives from the various societies, unions and so forth formed to sustain the League by propaganda. They were there, I suppose, to administer first-aid if it showed any signs of distress. And there was a vast concourse of Americans. One was always coming upon them having large luncheons and dinners and meetings or going for excursions on the lake, in the interests of this League their country had put upon us Europeans and then declined to support. I met scores of them. Brilliant rich girls in enormous automobiles; small, grey, rich men with great retinues of stenographers and secretaries. They were prepared to champion the League of Nations against all comers. They took enthusiasm in enormous volume into the Assembly galleries, ready to endorse whatever happened. A little gentleman named Filene – they told me he was the Selfridge of Boston – had been offering some huge number of dollars for a solution of the problem of peace, and a considerable proportion of the less attractive American men appeared to be candidates for this reward and would at the slightest provocation draw duplicated manuscripts from their hip pockets upon totally inoffensive strangers.

It was sunny and close and dusty in Geneva all the time; there was no air that did not seem to have been breathed several times by every nationality on earth; to respire properly one took a motor-boat out upon the lake or an automobile far up into the mountains. My central memory in the scene is that long bridge which spans the Rhone from the principal hotels to the Assembly. Everybody seemed to be always going or coming over it. There anyone could be waylaid. Heaven knows how many times I myself did not tramp to and fro across it trying to get away from myself to something that would hold my interest.

In any other state of mind I should have found much to watch and think about in that astonishing gathering, but my mind was heart-sick. The Labour Bureau of Albert Thomas was something escaping from the initial foolishness of that polyglot sham Parliament of Mankind, and men like Salter and Maderiaga, whom I met, might have told me, had I been tuned to listen, of many less conspicuous and more important activities that were arising in this meeting-place, out of the mere fact that it was a meeting-place. Some day soon I must go back to Geneva and look at it again from the angle of these things. In a hotel lounge one afternoon I saw Lamont, of J P Morgan and Co., and Lubbock, of the Bank of England, sitting together with an air of having met by chance and fallen talking about nothing in particular. Yet these two, while Ramsay MacDonald and Parmoor waved arms and bombinated in the Assembly, were doing things of fundamental importance to human life. And I saw my friend Loucheur, who is now taking his turn – a transitory turn, I fear – at saving the franc in Paris, very busy eating in the Restaurant du Parc, and wondered for a moment what schemes he might have brought with him and why he had brought them.

But I could not induce my distracted mind to penetrate below the most superficial aspects of Geneva at that time. Wherever I was I fretted to be somewhere else, and there was no peace in me. Everything irritated me. This is all, said I, that humanity can muster to make a world order. This is, perhaps, as near as it may ever come to establishing a world state. Compared with the size of the world and the immensity of the problems the League pretends to face, this is a small city and a small multitude of debaters and workers, and yet nine-tenths even of those who are here are trivial, frivolous, dishonest or absurd!

And then in this phase of discontent Helen suddenly came back bodily and took possession of Geneva.

Of course she was away in South Africa, but it chanced there was a woman about in the town sufficiently like her to play the part of her double. I was lunching with Edwin Mansard at a restaurant on the lake when I became aware of this woman sitting with a man at a table a little way off; she was talking to him, and as she talked her very pretty hand, exactly like Helen's hand, was playing with her roll and the things upon the table exactly as Helen was wont to do. My imagination was so out of control that I could hardly keep my talk with Mansard going for watching her.

My intelligence, my eyes, told me that it was impossible that this could be Helen; nevertheless, the resemblance released a storm of pent-up longing.

"I'm not boring you with all this?" said Mansard, pulling up in the account he was giving me of the International Labour Bureau. I suppose I had answered him vaguely.

"Not in the least," said I. "Not in the least. Go on, my dear fellow." But I spoke with my eyes still on this double of Helen's.

Then with a wrench I turned myself to Mansard's offended face. "You were saying?" said I.

Presently the couple got up to go. She held herself like Helen. She walked like Helen.

With a renewed effort I returned to Mansard.

Afterwards I saw her, high up above me on the balcony of some hotel looking on to the lake. She was wearing a blue dress of a shade that became Helen extremely. Helen had just such another dress, and would lean on a balcony rail and look at a sunset in just that fashion. I stood gaping. I was filled with the fantastic idea of seeking out this woman and getting into talk with her. But this was madness. I pulled myself together, packed up, and fled to Paris.

As I pitched about in the *wagon-lit* through a sleepless night I argued with myself. In some way I must get back my control over my mind and drive my thoughts away from this obsession. I was persuaded that the best thing to exorcise one woman from one's mind is to invoke another, but so far I had not been able to get up sufficient interest in another woman to make love that was in the least degree convincing either to myself or to her.

I found myself envying the good Catholics for whom there were cloisters and retreats, cool, quiet places in which one could escape from galling suggestions and inflammatory reminders, and settle one's business with one's soul, deliberately and definitively. A time may come when we who have parted from the old religions long ago shall also have our retreats.

As the train tossed about, tearing along too fast on the bad French permanent way, with a clumping rhythm of the wheels and strange roarings and echoings as we passed over bridges or through tunnels and cuttings, I found myself wishing there could come a conclusive smash, a wild clatter, blows and crushing impacts, fire perhaps, and one last ecstasy of pain that would take me out of all my perplexities. I have a strong conscience against suicide, but latterly I had been flying a good deal and with a preference for a defective engine in an overworked service in bad weather, and I now realised how this smothered desire for a release was at work in me. It was impatience. It was cowardice and indolence. I knew in my heart of hearts that I was not beaten, that at last I should come out of these distresses of desire and be my own master again and serene; nevertheless, they did so weigh upon me that the chance of death had become a temptation.

I talked aloud to myself in the swaying, jangling, creaking compartment. "Now what are you going to do with yourself?" I said. "What are you going to do?"

*Whump, bump,* went the train over some points, one was tossed up and jolted sideways, a receding diminuendo of bumps.

There was a beastly contrivance in the compartment so that you could not turn out the light completely. When I turned off the full light a nasty little mauve lamp came on and threw a ghastly pallid illumination on racks and curtains and the greasy shining panelling, and there was no way of extinguishing this.

"What are you going to do? Since there are no monasteries for you, you must go into retreat by yourself. Be a hermit. There were hermits before monasteries...

"What you have to do is to get it plain – write it down... Get it plain. Write it down. Get it plain. Write it down."

I argued the thing out with that accursed railway playing cup-and-ball with me and shaking the teeth in my jaws, roaring and chanting my thoughts into rhythms.

What was wrong with Geneva? What was the good of turning my back on that attempt unless I had something better in mind? It missed its object, but what was the object it had missed? It didn't deal with realities. Very well, think how men were to deal with realities. That wasn't clear. Then get it clear. No one had got it clear. Then someone had to begin.

If only the train would run smoothly for a moment I felt I should have everything right.

The vile uproar of this train was only an intensification of life. One never had time to assemble one's ideas. Never. One was always being hurried on, always being forced to think in rhythms and refrains because of the beating oscillations of the vehicle. Through it all quivered that idea of a retreat, a hermitage. It must not be a place with a lot of other people. It must be a little house alone. My mind insisted, for some obscure reason, on a little white house, very low and long. It was to stand in sunshine and air. Plenty of air – not like Geneva. And isolated. Far away from people with arguments and irrelevant grievances, wampum treaties and telegrams to Germany; and, above all, far away from anyone who looked like Helen. There I could live very simply for a time. I might look after myself and walk to an inn for a meal.

And there I could have a table – I saw the table, too, very stout and plain – and at it I could jot down all the heads of my difficulties, and balance this against that and *think*. There would be no hurry; day would stretch beyond day. Then I could decide what I meant to do with this universe, which hitherto, it seemed to me, had done what it liked with me.

And there must be no more women in it – no more women.

The engine, as if I had amused it, set up a whooping, derisive scream, blundered clumsily over points, and rushed through a station, and a flicker, flicker, flicker of lights in fives and fives glared and swept and vanished one after another, athwart the walls of the compartment.

I felt that I should never sleep again and that for all the rest of my life my head would ache. My throat was dry, I was excessively thirsty, and my mouth had the evil taste of sulphurous coal fumes.

Nevertheless, it had suddenly come into my mind that I was fighting my last battle with my universe and that I was going to win. Perhaps the metallic uproar of the train had suggested the metallic uproar of a battlefield and stirred some slumbering imagined wilfulness the wartime had left in me. I became militant. I swayed and vibrated through that noisy night, but now, within an infinitude of vain repetitions, I was making definite plans.

Where was I? There were to be no more women at all – no more women. That was it. I was losing all purpose in my life because I had never faced and fought my essential weakness. I must do without women. Henceforth I must do without women.

Henceforth I must do without women. Henceforth I must do without women. That is what I ought to have decided in Edenbridge Square a third of a century ago.

I talked aloud against the loud mockery of the train. "This is the end of women. Overdue that! Long overdue! I have wasted time and strength and influence upon them. I deserted science. I deserted science."

My mind held to that. Clara became mysteriously identified with Helen, and Helen with Clara. They were my enemies, my wasters, Alpha and Omega, the chiefs of a great array of adverse women.

"But what are women for?"

I thought for an interval and then raved.

"Never mind. Leave them alone, my boy. Get on with your job, damn you. Get on. Do it, as you *can* do it, alone. Tackle these half-condensed ideas and get them clear. Think it out. Work it out. What else is there to do? What else is there to do?"

The train accompaniment changed into a genial, obstinate, confidential "Get on with your work, *alone*. Get on with your work, *alone*." And then burst into a clatter that was like the laughter of a giant gear-box in hysterics.

"The little white house, anyhow," said I. "And if the worst comes to the worst and the old craving must be drowned again – the brothel in the valley."

For a while I held myself still and stared that mauve light in the eye. Hell will be lit by such little, insufficient, unquenchable lamps. I do not know if hell is hot or cold, or what sort of place hell may be, but this I surely know, that if there is any hell at all it will be badly lit. And it will taste like a train.

I must have slept. I found myself standing up in the swaying compartment, raising the blinds. Trees and fields were visible, hurrying past me. The dawn had come, the sky was flushed and clear. There were exquisite bands of cloud, band beyond band, like luminous rose-coloured knife-blades.

Nothing lasts for ever, I reflected. Presently I would breathe fresh air in Paris, I would hold my head under cold water for a bit, and then for a bath and that cottage, and we would see.

## 14 – *Reculer pour Mieux Sauter*

I put up in some rooms I had had before at the top of the Hotel Meurice and looking on the gardens, and I recall it as a quite extraordinary thing that this fancy of a little white house high up in the hills, where the ordinary passions of life are allayed or forgotten, so comforted me that for a day or so I was almost at peace. And then I began to be troubled by the problem of where I was to find this house and how I was to obtain possession of it. And in the lounge I turned over a back number of the *Bystander* and came upon a portrait of Helen that I had not seen before, and that also ruffled me. It was not Helen as I loved her, but it was Helen looking very magnificent and successful and triumphant, Helen more of a banner and a challenge than ever.

It is queer what limitations there are to everyone's ability. People call me a fairly competent man; I have planned great works and carried through great business operations, but I found myself now quite incapable of discovering any such house as this I dreamt of. I have not that delicacy of touch. I could not imagine how to set about looking for it; I did not know even whether I should look for it in Italy or Greece or Austria or France, and I felt I could neither secure it nor furnish it and organise its service if I found it. I saw all this as an impossibly complex and labourious task. Largely this was due to my neurasthenia, which deprived me for a time of any power of effort, but it was also due in part to the fact that I had never done any of these things; always before I had got someone to do them for me. I thought vaguely of sending over and borrowing old Deland from Dickon.

I stayed two or three days at the Meurice doing absolutely nothing, and then came a warm, serene and illuminated day, a quintessentially October day that would have lifted the heaviest heart a little, and in the afternoon, as the sun was setting, I turned out for a walk, and I crossed the Place de la Concorde and set my face towards the Arc de Triomphe.

Far away the outline of the great bluish arch stood up without a feature visible against a sky of intense pale gold. The upper lines of the remote, tall houses on either side of it were faint yet clear, the nearer trees very bright and hard and black against their softness. A few lights were appearing in the distant shops and windows; some of the hurrying traffic in the roadway had already lit its lamps. Nearer to me was the space and dignity of the gardens that set back the exhibition palaces from the broad main avenue. What a gracious and splendid vista is that of the Champs Elysées, the finest, I think, in the world! Even the late afternoon loungers seemed tall and dignified as they strolled past.

For a time I was filled with the golden beauty of the scene, and then the faint sadness that lies so close to all purely aesthetic pleasure took possession of me. I reflected again that I was solitary and now not very far from being old, and that I had made myself solitary all to no purpose, with such a waste of will-power that I seemed unable to do anything now to justify my revolt against Helen. I had worked all my days to make myself one of the leading slaves of a great industrial machine that was as will-less as myself. And that was all I had been able to make of life.

It is a habit with me, and I suppose it is with most men, to note the women I pass. It is an almost unconscious habit of observation. Only now and then one notes what one's mind is taking in about them. Then one not only notes but notices. My life has had little occasion for casual encounters, but in some parts of Paris and London at certain hours one is aware that one is walking through gossamer filaments of adventurous invitation, faint elusive provocations, delicate strokes of not too critical approval. These gossamer threads become more perceptible the blanker one's thoughts. "Turn your back on your problems," they insinuate. "And if the problems return tomorrow you may find something else to amuse you."

So in the Champs Elysées I became interested in a graceful woman with a slender neck and a wisp of hair that was darkly ruddy against the light, who was going in the same direction as myself. She was promenading so nearly at my pace that only presently by quickening my steps did I overtake her. She walked easily. But there was that indefinable quality in her gait, a faint aimlessness, I think it must be, and something a little careless in her smart-spirited costume, that told me she was one of those who wait upon the accident of an encounter. She had not put on her clothes for herself or for anyone in particular. When she was still far off I saw her twice turn towards men with the unmistakable forced invitation of her kind and turn away. Then she ceased to heed the passers-by.

Her brows and cheek and chin I discovered as I came nearer to her were prettily drawn. A vague curiosity, the absurd and instinctive curiosity of the wandering male, brought me up alongside of her to see her profile.

So it was I first discovered Clem's abstracted countenance, elfin and pensive, infantile and sage. The uniform amber light revealed her professionally undisguised make-up and robbed it of personal significance. Those dabs of paint and powder were nothing essentially hers; it was as if her face had been ill-treated by some alien thing. Beneath these addenda she was perceptibly pale. She was looking at the great arch and the shining sky, forgetful for a moment of the hungry business that had brought her out, oblivious of the awakening interest of the quite possible Monsieur who was walking beside her.

I do not see why one should intrude upon a woman because, roughly speaking, it is her calling to be intruded upon. She paid no heed to me. I walked past her and went on before her. But her quality remained in my mind.

Old Nature – I sometimes suspect the old harridan of a visible body and a mocking mind – must have been cheered by this new interest of her rebel son's. He had with immense exertion cast himself off from Woman, and here he was back at the old lure.

Clementina had seemed rapt in the beauty about us. That marched with my mood. And there had been something sad and tired in her abstracted face. That, too, appealed to me. And she was very graceful. Here was an extraordinarily interesting young woman, I said to myself.

"But hadn't I perhaps just imagined things?" said the Vieux Marcheur in me.

So often I have imagined things. I did not want to stare round at her. I dropped back to see if I should still find her off her guard.

She was, and then she woke up to my presence. Instantly her expression changed and her face became a mask, defensive but seductive. She was the woman of her class at the moment of invasion. And her personality and privacy hustled away out of sight. "Ware Man!" What sort of loose, detached, occasional male was it this time? Was he of the impossible kind instantly to be got rid of? Or was he to be considered, attracted, dealt with? Two very intelligent hazel eyes met mine, businesslike and scrutinising, under long slanting brows.

I passed muster, I perceived, by such standards as she could maintain. She decided to smile interrogatively, but her eyes remained guarded.

I made up my immediate mind forthwith. For an hour or so I would forget my ache.

"I am all alone in Paris this evening," I said. "Would you care to dine with me?"

"This is very sudden," she answered in English, with a faint accent that for a moment I could not place.

"But will you?" I said, also in English.

"It is early for dinner yet."

"We could walk on to the Arc de Triomphe and then come back."

"Why not?" she said, no pretence of pleasure.

"There is a comfortable restaurant at the Rond Point, the Franco-Italian. We could dine there."

She aroused herself to appear interested.

"That would be charming," she said.

"I want only companionship," I said, and she looked at me to read the significance of that. "Let me be pleasant to you for an evening."

"As you will," said, she, and braced herself, I fancied, for the task of being pleased. Had she been free, I felt, that evening would have been her own.

"You like walking?" she asked.

"And you? You walk too easily and gracefully not to like it."

She smiled with a little less effort. "I could walk for miles… Often I prowl about Paris – for no purpose."

"It is the most amusing city to prowl about in the world."

"There is a cheerfulness. Until the winter comes."

"Even in the winter."

"Even in the winter. If one is warm."

"There is a hard, clear animation on the coldest days."

"When it does not rain. But sometimes in the winter there are days – When the gutters swill and the river is swollen and watery and Paris is wet and disgusting. Now, at any time, such days may come. And, anyhow, I feel the cold."

I had jumped into the encounter on a momentary impulse, and I had no intention of inflicting myself upon her to any extent that she might find disagreeable. I was buying her company for an evening; that was my conception of the affair. I had to treat her like any other pretty lady I might happen to know except that I must not press my attentions upon her as I might have done upon anyone who was quite free of me. I had no compunction about being seen about with her; that sort of thing had never troubled me. I began to talk of Paris to her and praise the place, its gay urbanity, its spacious grace, its light and freedoms, its brilliant kindness to the stranger. I supposed she was a Parisienne, and that this would flatter her.

But she made it appear that she was not a lover of Paris. "It is crowded. It is full of noises. They talk of the roar of London; it cannot be worse than this. London may roar; Paris – barks. Everything thinks only of itself, and yet everything clamours for attention. And nobody attends. They push against you. Everything pushes against you. I am always just missing being killed by taxi-autos and automobiles."

She spoke like one who was tired and at an ebb.

"But you were thinking Paris beautiful tonight."

"When?"

"Just now when I overtook you."

"No. The sunset made me long for the south. I was dreaming of the warm sunshine down in Provence. Where I spent a holiday – it seems ages ago."

I made her talk; I was surprised by my own interest in her. It was good anyhow to stop thinking about myself – and Helen, even for a little while. In some way I didn't clearly understand at the time this red-haired, pale young woman was also a disappointed and perplexed person.

I have learn more since. Nowadays I am almost a specialist upon the subject of Clementina. She was the daughter of a Scotch engineer who had worked upon tramways in Athens and Asia Minor, her mother was Greek, and she had had a chequered and polyglot upbringing. She had grown up strongly patriotic both towards Britain and Greece, and she had had the unusual advantage of two sound religious trainings, Greek and Presbyterian. Her social experiences were jagged and distorted by the gradual lapse of the Scotch father from honourable employment into continuous but still dignified drunkenness. In the absence of an income the family, I have gathered, subsisted by the economies effected by the mother. In the distressful years at the end of the war Clementina, who was then one-and-twenty and fatherless, fell in love with an amorous, romantic, carefully beautiful but quite orthodox French subaltern in Athens, followed him to Paris, transferred all her patriotic emotion to France, and all her waning but still considerable gift of faith to the Roman Catholic Church. There was a ménage in Paris which went on rather happily until it was time for the orthodox French subaltern to marry the featureless but entirely eligible wife selected for him by his aristocratic family. The parting was upon the correctest pattern. He wept very freely and frequently over Clementina, he contemplated suicide from a safe distance and found it inconsistent with Catholic principles, he declared he would never love any woman but her, he promised always to seek her advice and help in moments of difficulty, and he gave her a ring of no great intrinsic value that had belonged to his mother and a quite surprisingly small present of money. He declared that he would not insist upon her subsequent chastity, and that he had abandoned any right to do so, but the bare thought of his being supplanted evoked passions of such splendour and violence in him, such tearing of hair, such clenching and waving of virile fists, that he broke two ornaments in her flat, pawnable ornaments that under the circumstances she could ill spare, and departed to his own aristocratic milieu in a mood of the utmost nobility before she had time to estimate the dimensions of his parting present. The Greek mother had already died and left her daughter a small, untraceable, and possibly imaginary house in Smyrna. So equipped Clementina had to face the world on her own account.

In quite a few years she had become a woman of considerable experience, experience rather than wisdom. Scotch heredity and Greek heredity do not mix; they make a sort of human Macedonia, a mélange of hostile and incompatible districts in the soul. Clementina is in streaks beautifully logical and clear-headed, and in streaks incoherently but all too expressively passionate; she is acutely artistic and rigidly Philistine. Flung across this piebald basis are the three great religious cultures of Christendom, not so much following as traversing the racial boundaries. There are chunks of intense Catholic, Greek Orthodox, and Calvinistic feeling in Clementina, pervaded latterly by a broad disillusionment and scepticism.

Her social ideas are also of very confused origin, drawn on the one side from the home life of a high-minded and influential Scotch engineer, whose austere respectability increased rather than diminished in his drunken phases, and from the excellent if extremely snobbish English school in Athens to which he sent his daughter, and on the other from the abundant voluble family of the Greek mother, aunts, cousins, uncles, hangers-on, which infested the sinking home, critically and voraciously, up to the very moment when it went right under water and ceased to be a home at all. She has the defensive disposition due to the mixed and uncertain social status of her childhood; she is alert to detect and resent imaginary slights and insults and to magnify negligencies into cruelties.

Imposed upon her heterogeneous traditions are the impressions and suggestions of two or three European literatures, for Clementina is a swift responsive reader. And then just at a susceptible age had come the dignified and dishonest conventions of Catholic France, which has sanctioned and codified even the fornication of its tenderly fostered but otherwise gallant young men. One must know only the right people; one must behave with an icy loftiness in the nastiest situations; one must keep one's wife and one's mistress apart; the meaner the act the finer the gesture, and so on. So constituted there was and alas! there still is a very considerable amount of jangling in Clementina. Through it all, I declare, runs a thread of gold, which I discovered at the outset and select as the real Clementina. She is delightful in that phase and for its sake I am prepared to accept or forgive all her other phases.

I will not venture to guess what rôle in life Clementina was originally best fitted to fill. She was certainly not fitted to become, at the age of three-and-twenty, a brilliant adventuress with no social position in Paris. There may have been something meretricious in the Greek heredity, but whenever she was involved in a love affair that was not an earnest business of body and soul, the Scotch engineer arose staggering but resolute and damned it root and branch. She had learnt to dance beautifully from the charming young aristocrat; his name, by-the-by, was René, but she always called him Dou-Dou; and she did her best to make something more than a sexual liaison out of her affairs with a series of the kind of men detached young women meet in dancing places. I am carefully incurious about all this part of her life; it has nothing to do with me; she was, I believe, given an establishment and put among her furniture once or twice, and each time her Presbyterian father or her Catholic puritanism or her fundamental veracity made a shipwreck of the business. Her native pluck was very great, but there must have been times when she looked at this amazing universe with considerable dismay. Where was this sort of thing going to end? And how long would it take before it ended?

There had been some great row just before I happened upon her. Neither Clementina nor I have any disposition to gossip about it, but I am inclined to believe that it was with a rich and agreeable gentleman from the Argentine who had carried his confidence in his personal charm and his general right to do what he liked with his own so far that it had become suddenly necessary to smack his face, throw the more suitable of his presents at him, say a selection of unforgettable things, and depart from the flat he had taken. It was a mess, and there no going back on it.

Clementina had reverted to a single room in an obscure street and to perplexity about herself and God's intentions. She experienced a great longing for Provence. She had gone thither in the Dou-Dou days. It had not been really smart enough for Dou-Dou, but he had laughed and shown his beautiful teeth; it had been inexpensive, at any rate, and they were able to descend once or twice upon the Riviera coast, where he could display her quality to his similarly provided friends. There had been mistress-parades no doubt in Cannes and Monte Carlo, and everybody had shown off tremendously. All that she had largely forgotten. But the warm and gentle quality of friendliness in this land among the hills had sunken deeply into her spirit.

The better I know Clementina, the better I understand how hopelessly she was caught in a net from the very moment she was conceived. She feels and understands beauty exquisitely; she has the finest sense of intellectual and moral values, and a fire of disorder burns within her that will not let her rest. And also she has a passion for writing poetry in languages whose finer shades of sound she misses or misconceives.

Now in a mood of extreme disillusionment with Paris and all that Paris concentrated for her she was idealising this Provençal countryside and longing to be back there. She was under the charm of a dream of living in some extraordinarily cheap pension, walking, brooding, possessing herself. Then she could think over her life and its riddles; then she could make decisions.

In Paris one was hustled from day to day. Things happened to one; one did nothing to determine them. She talked of this dream of getting away as we sat at dinner together with an admirable frankness and freshness of feeling. It fell in very aptly with my own desire to get away.

She might have gone to Provence a month or so ago; she had had money then, a few thousand francs, but she was not the sort of person who could make simple, quick decisions. She had lingered and her money had run out.

She talked easily and unaffectedly in her Scotch-English, a little Frenchified, helped out with French words and phrases. There was nothing common in her voice or gesture or the quality of her thought. Her thought was fine-spun silk, and in that at least there was very little mixture. She was open and wholesome in her mind, very outspoken, but never indecent. She was instinctive enough to know that I had a directness of mind to match her own. She talked of the inevitableness of prostitution in some form for women like herself. She had had no training of any sort, she explained; she was not capable even of hard physical work. She fell into no place. She had no race, no nation, no people, no class. She was the sort of bird that other birds peck at. Her manners were samples, and her social code a patchwork. She had tried dactylography, but she could not spell; she was bored, and ceased to attend to a task at once difficult for her and inane. She was not steady and continuous enough for a workroom. She had been rejected as a governess and as a companion. She was too distinguished for the one and too disrespectful for the other. Marriage of any sufferable sort was hopeless for her. The stage was beyond her. She couldn't act. What else was there to do but trade on her sex? She might be "rescued," but for what? Rescue in France meant a sham penitence, a surrender to the subtle Catholicism that had smiled on her relations with her first lover; it meant a subjugation to narrow and authoritative nuns, scrubbing, meticulous needlework, and being driven and sweated in those close, inevitable economies that underlie all Latin benevolent institutions. She would come out of that worse than she went in – and with her pretty wardrobe scattered and her hands rough and spoilt.

"Nothing for it but the streets of Paris."

"Thank your stars they are not the streets of London," said I. "But aren't there girls in shops?"

"Vendeuse? I'd rather sell myself straightly and simply than give myself in as a tip to my employers…

"There are too many women in the world," said Clementina.

"Too many pretty women," said I.

"I see no advertisements for the plain ones."

I reflected. "Tell me more about this Provence of yours. I am interested. Are there little houses, little isolated white houses that look in the face of the sun and are simple and quiet?"

"White?" said Clementina. "No. they paint their houses pink or yellow. But there are many pleasant little houses among the grey olives, rather *austère*, but always with a *terrasse* in front of them with flowers and trees – where the peasants dine and sit. A Provencal *mas* can be very delightful in its plain way."

"I want a little house," I said. "Let me tell you something about myself. You are bored with Paris, but I am bored with the whole world. I wan to get away from it and think. I want a respite for thinking. Every now and then – for I am still a very busy man. I have thought of a little white house in the sun, very quiet and simple. A little white house where I can think things out and recover my will. But I do not know where to go to find it; France, Spain, Italy, Greece? I do not know where to turn for it."

"You might find it in Provence," she considered. "I remember a little place where we had lunch one day, named Châteauneuf, the most adorable of villages. Perhaps one could be quiet and happy there."

I had had an idea germinating in my mind for some minutes. It shot up suddenly now, complete.

I broached it. "I think," I said, "I could give you a rest from the streets of Paris. I think I could find you a job that would take you back to your Provence for a time."

She scrutinised my face and waited.

"Suppose," said I, "I made you my house-hunter and sent you to find a little white house down there in Provence."

"Pink is more probable," she said.

"A pretty house, anyhow, tucked away out of sight. With a quiet white room and a table to write upon. To which I could come and go. And if you found me also a discreet servant who could cook and look after me, and if generally you established me there. Could you do job like that? Can you be practical enough for that?"

"I'd try," she said. "Why not?"

"I have to go back to England in a day or so for some business. I shall have to be there a fortnight or three weeks. But I could give you my address, and you could pack off to Provence at once and begin looking, and when you had looked for a bit write and tell me all about it. Eh?"

"Why are *you* tired of things?" she asked. "You don't have to prowl about accosting people."

"One gets tired. I can't tell you my history now. And it would be unnecessary. And too complicated. But I want that job done for me, and you could do it."

She had dined, and she was warmed by my friendliness. The face that had seemed jaded was now ten years younger and very animated and pretty. "I think I would like to do a job for you," she said.

"Well, do it."

"You would be a pleasant employer."

"For once you need not sell yourself. This is straight employment."

Our eyes fenced. I could not see the Scotsman anywhere. "Tell me more about the sort of house you want," she said.

I sketched a house for her briefly, as I desired it.

"I am to find it and arrange it for you?"

"So that I can come and go."

"How could we do it?"

"I shall give you ten thousand francs for the job right away – I will give them to you at my hotel tomorrow – and afterwards you will tell me what your out-of-pocket expenses are, and I shall pay those."

"Your mean to give me all that money right away?"

"Why not?"

"But shan't I vanish into Paris with it and never appear again? Shan't I go off and spend it with my *maquereau*? What sort of woman do you take me for?"

"I don't think you will," I said. "For example, you don't keep a *maquereau*. You've no use for that sort of pet. If you do vanish there is nothing to prevent you, of course. I shall have guessed wrong, that is all. I shall have lost my stake. I shan't set the police after you, I promise you. You'll be perfectly free to steal the whole lot of it. I shall have to try some other way of finding a house."

"I will take that job," said Clementina. "You are not the sort of man one wants to vanish away from."

She came to a delicate question with the aid of a liqueur. "I am to live in that house?" she tried and blushed under her paint. She could blush, for all her *savoir-faire*.

"No," I said. "That is exactly what you are not to do. I shall live in that house alone. I want you to take this job as a business job. Forgive me if I am plain with you. I am tired of love affairs, grave or gay. I am near to being old. I am not making love to you.

I… I have recently had my heart completely and finally broken. I don't see why I shouldn't tell you as much. You had better understand now. When it's mended I mean to keep the vestiges locked up out of harm's way. You said yourself you were tired of that sort of thing. You are going to be my house-hunting, servant-finding secretary. It's a purely business arrangement."

"I wonder," said Clementina.

"This is plain business," I said, "and you will be free."

"Still – I wonder."

"No," I said very firmly, and we smiled at one another. "Does it seem too good to be true?"

"I'll get you the house you want if I have to build it myself," said Clementina in an agreeable burst of approval.

She rested her chin upon her hands and looked at me. It was still all east and south in her eyes, and they were very charming eyes. There might have been no Scotland in the world.

"It can't stay like that," she said.

"I mean it to."

She fiddled with a grape upon her plate. "As you will," she said modestly. "I will try to be a good secretary."

We were now feeling very friendly towards each other. Friendly and rather amused at our strictly defined relationship. It seemed to me that she was disposed to linger, but at last I carried her off in a taxi-auto and dropped her at her obscure address. We did not loiter at her door. I made my parting salutations with a respectful decisiveness and returned to the taxi. Tomorrow she was to come and lunch with me at the Meurice and receive her ten thousand francs. She came, very resolute and businesslike. There was just a little more of that tentative lingering, but not very much of it, and then, after a warm handshake, off she went with her money.

But the affair still seemed, I suppose, unsettled and incredible to Clementina. And in a sense wrong. Her father had been Scotch and conscientious, her mother Mediterranean and very feminine. For once the two strains worked together. She had not been gone two hours and I was writing some letters in my sitting-room when there came a *petit bleu* from her.

"You have left me humiliated," it said. "Please come to see me for a little hour before I go south. There is something important I really must say to you."

It proved to be of no importance to this history. She went south, and I returned to England.

The amazing part of the story is that within a week she had found this delightful Villa Jasmin for me and she had discovered my excellent Jeanne, which are all and more than I could have desired. At times I am tempted to believe that after all there must be a Providence, but one more lax and sympathetic than the nineteenth century supposed. She wrote me several long, charming letters, in a sort of Scotch-French-English, describing her success and asking for instructions, and I astonished her by sending more money to get the garden and furniture in order before I came. So soon as I could get my hands clear I followed her and installed myself amidst her simple and clever arrangements.

But now began a serious trouble that still clouds our tranquillity here. Deep in Clementina's nature is an exorbitant desire to love, a possessive, protective, active and caressing love. She had done her best to lavish it upon the Catholic young officer and experimentally upon a diminishing series of unworthy successors. It was like a beautiful gift garment for which she could find no suitable wearer and not even a peg to hang it upon. This robe of passionate abandon had not been apparent in Paris; it had been packed up and put away, but now it became extravagantly evident in Provence. She declared with plainness and fullness and inflexible resolution that I was the Heaven-sent recipient of that delightful, soft and clinging cloak. She demanded the right to protect and cherish me for the rest of her days.

My own mind was fixed in the idea that I had done with love and love stories. I was kind but hard with Clementina. I insisted, and still insist, upon my inviolate study and my inviolate hours. I do not object to her being the official salaried guardian of my garden and my household, but I make her go on living in the little pension on the main road up the hill, in which, with that small, muff-shaped dog of hers dating from the Dou-Dou days she had taken up her quarters. After all, it is not ten minutes away, and when it is dark I go with her up through the olives. We lunch and dine together, we go for long walks and keep holiday together, but my life as a whole remains my own. To these terms Clementina agreed with a feminine insincerity that never ceases to encroach.

So we go on. She has stayed on here, and in spite of some dangerous struggles I have been able to sustain my tyranny. We are intimate friends, and for the most part I keep her at arm's length from my personal freedom.

It is not always harmony here. Clementina can display some astonishing moods. The Scotch engineer must have had the devil of a temper, and the Greek mother transmitted a pagan streak straight from primordial times. I feel, too, that there must have been unrecorded odd elements on the side of the Scotch engineer's mother. She was I guess, an extremely argumentative person. Rhetorically argumentative. Swift and fierce in her opinions. But all the Clementinas are swift and fierce in their opinions, whichever constituent opinionates. Sometimes everything is judged from the standpoint of a château in a backward part of France (Dou-Dou), sometimes from a Parisian parterre (various other authorities), sometimes from the Piraeus (mother and the relations), and sometimes from the Longer Catechism. This complexity is perplexing, but by no means repulsive to a scientific intelligence. And in the end Clementina herself adjudicates. Through all these moods and confusions flows – sometimes in the sunlight and sometimes underground – a stream of affectionateness and whim and generosity that is all the Clementina that matters. It makes the final decisions.

There are occasions when I wish she would not ask quite so many questions about this book I am writing or that she would ponder some of the answers more profoundly. And generally that she would construct more of her conversation in some other form than the interrogative. But that is a minor trouble.

I know too vividly how Clementina in a stubborn or a storming mood can disturb and upset this philosophical tranquility, but I doubt if I begin to estimate how much I prey upon her, what a stroke of luck this freak of devotion is for me, and how entirely she makes things possible here. Here I can come and go, working out the last phase of my life. Here at last I seem to find complete unity and peace of mind. I lead a full man's life here, and yet I exist also in London and at Downs-Peabody quite as fully and competently.

My life has, in fact, been doubled. If my mind stales in Provence, I go to the stir of England again, but I am glad to come back. Always a little more pleased to find Clementina still besieging me. I can appreciate my contentment with this place more easily than I can explain it. There is a novel and peculiar liberty in this seclusion. I am able to think in it without haste or disturbance. One came into the world to think. I am astonished to consider how little I have thought consecutively before I came here. Now I can live for days together without restlessness or urgencies, without invasions or distractions, apart from the world and yet still in the sunshine of life.

This house, this room, give exactly the aloofness and the detachment I was seeking – a detachment so animated and qualified by Clementina that it neither bores nor distresses me. I am never lonely spirited here.

With some hope of results now I can review my world as a whole, balance alien considerations, work out the form of the great revolution that is happening in human affairs and in the human mind. Here I can define at last the Open Conspiracy that arises in the human will to meet and wrestle with the moulding forces of the universe, the Open Conspiracy to which in the end I believe I shall succeed in correlating all my conscious being.

# Book Five

## The Next Phase

## 1 – *Metamorphosis of Mankind*

Now with my story told I can come to the gist of my matter, to the new ways of living that are, I believe, opening out before mankind. I will at first set out only the broad lines of my ideas. After I have written this book I hope to return to the questions I am now raising and work over much that here I give in skeleton.

I will write as clearly as possible, but I must ask the reader to be patient if at times I am a little heavy and reiterative in this part. I am not a professional man of letters; my interests have been in things and practical ideas rather than in fine and graceful writing, and my utmost ambition is to be plain and strong. If I could set out what I have to say with charm and brilliance I would be only too glad to do so. I would make it as attractive as I could. But I am writing for the sake of the matter and not for the sake of the writing.

I have already given a sketch of the development of life and of the forces and accidents that have made human society out of what was once a sub-human species, rare in its numbers and scattered and almost solitary in its habits. In a few thousands of centuries this profound essential change has been brought about. From being a prowler man has become a hunter, a hunter in packs, and in the last hundred centuries or so he has taken to agriculture, become the first of the mammals to be economic as well as social, and developed societies on such as life had never known before, not even among the termites and ants and bees. This process still goes on with if anything an increasing rapidity. No living species except such as have passed under catastrophic circumstances towards extinction has ever been under so violent a drive of change as man.

The violence of the drive is even more conspicuous when it is measured against the length and scope of man's individual life. In my own lifetime his usual food, his range of activity, his rate of reproduction and the spirit in which he reproduces, his average length of life, his prevalent diseases, his habitations and his coverings have changed. No animal species has ever yet survived such rapid and comprehensive changes.

I have sketched a brief history of the beginnings of habitual labour, of the network of money and debt which holds us now all dependent upon one another, and of the rapid expansion of scale which had been the dominant theme in our affairs for the last two centuries. I have shown the lives of my father and my brother and myself as whirled along the lines they have taken by the forces of this enlargement. My father with the swift poison gripping his heart and holding it suddenly still, Dickon bashfully accepting a baronetcy, and I, with Sirrie Evans sleeping and then dead in my arms, Minnie and my mother, Helen and Clementina, Roderick and Julian, are all no more than minute specks upon the figure, atomies in the body, of this synthetic evolution of human society that is in progress.

I would compare what is happening to the human species with what happens to an insect that undergoes a complete metamorphosis. Man was a species living in detached and separated communities; he is now being gathered together into one community. He is becoming one great co-operative interplay of life which is replacing a monotony of individual variations. He is changing in every social relationship and developing a new world of ideas and mental reactions, habits of mind and methods of feeling and action, in response to the appeal of the new conditions. Nature, I take it, is impartial and inexorable. He is no specially favoured child. If he adapt he passes on to a new phase in the story of life; if he fail to solve the riddles he faces now he may differentiate, he many degenerate, he may die out altogether. One thing Nature will not endure of him – that he stay as he is.

I do not regard the organisation of all mankind into one terrestrial anthill, into Cosmopolis, the greater Athens, the Rome and Paris and London of space and time, as a Utopian dream, as something that fantastically might be. I regard it as the necessary, the only possible, continuation of human history. To fail to take that road will mean a fraying-out and a finish to that history, a relapse through barbarism to savagery, to the hard chances of animal life for a creature too scarce and long-lived to be readily adaptable, and so at last surely to extinction.

None of this is theorising; it is a statement of truths, austere and manifest. These alternatives are as much a matter of fact as the starvation of a large majority of mankind if ploughing and sowing were abandoned.

Another aspect, another idea of the human synthesis I have also developed throughout these papers, and I return to it now and take it up again. It is this: that since the earlier stages of the individual development through its embryonic and childish and youthful years are more or less mutilated vestiges and imperfect recapitulations of earlier adult states, fish, reptile, early mammal, monkey and savage, so all the moods and motives of adult life in our nearer history must now, if the race is to achieve its necessary accommodations and survive, be in process of relegation to the status of puerility and adolescence; and a new phase of wider, less personal feeling and outlook, must be expanding to fill the main years, the lengthening span of years in the individual life of the coming generations. Man like any other living creature must change with new conditions, and this, if he is to go on, must be the direction of his change. The new stage of human experience demands what I have already been calling a new adult phase, and conceivably also a new post-adult phase, in the normal life based on broader and sounder common ideas, expressed in new terms and new artistic forms, and accompanied by profound nervous and other physiological changes. From man's soul to man's chemistry this necessity to change and expand extends.

It involves altogether new political habits, a rearrangement and readjustment of moral and religious ideas and feelings, a new conception and method of education. The religious teachings of the past, the honours, loyalties, heroisms that adorn history, its science, its philosophy, its artistic expressions take on from this standpoint a juvenile and incomplete air. They will seem, they begin to seem, childish, falsely sentimental, greenly youthful. The great kings and conquerors of the past are already apprehended, and will be more and more apprehended as naïve and short-witted; we realise how egotistical and vain they were, egotistical and vain as leading and clever children who "show off" are egotistical and vain; we see them in their glory, tawdry, limited and artlessly, almost innocently, wasteful and cruel. We see war no longer as a tragic necessity in human life, but as a horrible arrest of development. Conquest appears now as cruel blundering, and patriotism like the barking of village dogs.

Many people in this present dawn of an age of conscious change are coming to accept this transfiguration of the dignities of history; but such a realisation of the past as preparatory is only a prelude to the realisation of the present as provisional, in form and in texture. This next mental step has still to be taken even by the majority of educated and intelligent people today. They have still to apply *Παντα ῥει* to their own affairs, to their activities today and their plans for tomorrow. That is less easy for them to achieve because it implies a revision of their habits of living. Many stick at the mental, and almost all of them stick at the practical, recognition that the traditions, morals, political and economic usages of this time, dissolve, cease to be imperative or make new demands upon them, year by year, as they live out their lives. They feel the times toss and jostle and strain them, but they are not yet prepared to thrust back against and control and steer the changes of the times.

This is a transitional state of affairs. Almost all this revelation of the current metamorphosis of human society and relationships has been made quite recently, since indeed my father was a young man. What I have been writing here in the last few pages of the metamorphosis in progress is now known in matter-of-fact guise, by any well-read, well-educated person. The statement is made very clear-cut here and put aggressively, but there is nothing absolutely new in it. Yet it would have seemed fantastic beyond description, shockingly fantastic, to anyone born a hundred years ago. No one was fully awake then to what was already going on. It is no great wonder that a vision so newly attained had yet to produce the changes it is ultimately bound to produce in our ways of living and in the spirit of our lives.

It is, as I pointed out in my introduction, in the nature of childhood to believe this is a permanently arranged world. In the past hardly anyone got beyond childhood in this respect. People thought that change was incidental, upon the surface of permanent arrangements. It is only now that a few of us begin to realise with any fullness that it is change which is fundamental and permanence which is only apparent and incidental. It is a natural thing to think in the former way; it is a result of experience and thought to awaken to the latter. And so it is that people are everywhere going on with old, and now often mischievous, loyalties and patriotisms, with old economic habits and old social assumptions that are no longer valid, that they are failing to make the new generation that grows up under their care realise the insecurities among which they are living, and that the metamorphosis of human society proceeds against such increasing resistances that it may even fail to achieve itself, and end in the failure and death of the species.

The present opposition to the reconstruction of human affairs comes quite as much from the uninstructed young as from the unconverted old. Conservatism is not merely due to the inadaptability of a generation that will presently die out. The young are revolutionary, inasmuch as they rebel naturally against constituted authority, but they are also reactionary in so far as they recapitulate the mental phases of the past. And we are doing little or nothing to correct that innate disposition. Our educational methods do not merely fail to inform the young of the immense demands life is making upon them – they conceal those demands. Humanity is confronted by the necessities and opportunities of a great metamorphosis, and our wills and imaginations are lagging and we are failing to square ourselves and prepare our successors for the great tasks of our inheritance.

This "Open Conspiracy" I am now setting myself to explain, is a project to make the apprehension of this metamorphosis fundamental and directive in human affairs. It is an attempt to harmonise people's lives with this metamorphosis and to undermine and remove the resistances that may divert its forces towards destruction.

## 2 – *Open Conspiracy*

I do not see this attainment of a new maturity for our race, which will thrust back what have hitherto been the adult characteristics of mankind into a mere phase of development, as a necessary and inevitable one. The attempt may fail. It may fail and mankind may fail and become extinct; there is no guarantee whatever against that, no modern rainbow of assurance in our ampler skies. The metamorphosis of mankind calls imperatively upon the will and effort of all who grasp its significance. By their response it succeeds or fails.

And now I come to the question of the gathering together of this Open Conspiracy to change the laws, customs, rules and institutions of the world. From what classes and types are the revolutionaries to be drawn? How are they to be brought into co-operation? What are to be their methods? How much are they to have in common?

To begin with the answering of that. Manifestly it is absurd to think of creative revolution unless it has power in its hands, and manifestly the chief seats of creative power in the world are on the one hand modern industry associated with science and on the other world finance. The people who have control in these affairs can change the conditions of human life constructively and to the extent of their control. No other people can so change them.

All other sorts of power in the world are either contributory or restrictive or positively obstructive or positively destructive. The power of established and passive property, for example, is simply the power to hold up for a price. The power of the masses is the strike, it embodies itself in the machine-breaking, expert-hunting mob. I have written already of Vishnu and Siva. The point I want to make clear here is that it is only through a conscious, frank and worldwide co-operation of the man of science, the scientific worker, the man accustomed to the direction of productive industry, the man able to control the arterial supply of credit, the man who can control newspapers and politicians, that the great system of changes they have almost inadvertently got going can be brought to any hopeful order of development.

Such men, whether they mean to be or not, are the actual revolutionaries in our world. Among them it is and in no other direction that we must look for the first effectual appearance of the new adult mind in co-operative association. If they cannot lead mankind forward to an assured possession of its new ampler life then I do not see how that necessary forward stride can ever be made. Humanity may stagger for some time if they prove insufficient, for a few score years, a few centuries perhaps, upon the verge of a world unity, thinking great thoughts, expressing noble sentiments, making some lovely things, to relapse definitely into a decadence, a slipping back, a slackening hold, a sliding and a falling.

I admit how poor are the present materials for this creative conspiracy. In what had gone before I have examined the scope and motives of the possessing, directing sort of people in the world and in particular I have done what I can to lay bare the quality of my brother and myself. I believe we two are fair average specimens of the outlook and impulse of our kind. I have tried to show how tentative we are and how we are entangled at every turn with – shall I call it Crest? The Crest tradition. The necessary start from a partnership with Crest. I have done my best to confess my own tangle of desires, to indicate at least my warring impulses and obsessions and indisciplines. Yet, as Dickon said, "Weak as we are, those others are weaker." It is out of us and our sort, and from among the scientific workers we can associate with us, that the consummation of the great revolution must come. There appears no other kind of men better able to carry it through. There are none. If we did not start through Vishnu as partners of Crest, then we should have to start as officials for Siva, fags for the doctrinaires, after a Communist revolution.

Give me the armorial Crests! Rather the dukes than the doctrinaires. I have no doubt – after my glimpses of Bolshevik industrialism – that ours is the more hopeful method of beginning.

I know some good men who are of the other way of thinking, but they are scientific rather than directive men. For my own part I shall keep to the right now and not try the left. Neither road goes straight to the goal we have to attain, the goal of a scientifically organised economic world unity, but though the right road be rocky and tortuous, it is I believe far more likely to get there in the end than the left. I may be influenced by my own economic position: every Communist is trained to that explanation; and if I am wrong, well, then good luck to the left! I shall travel by the blue train to the end of my story. I shall look to America rather than Moscow for the first instalments of the real revolution.

It must be quite evident that we and our generation of enterprising and power-attaining men are only are only a beginning, that we are a mass of unrealised possibilities. As Dickon said of Northcliffe, power took us by surprise. We are not the finished samples of the new sort of men; we are only the raw material. We were not told, we were not educated, we were not aware of our kind; we had to disentangle ourselves from a world jungle of misleading representations. It is not necessary that those who follow us should be at such a disadvantage.

I believe that Dickon and I are not abnormal types. I believe that we industrials and the financiers are beginning to educate ourselves and broaden our outlook as our enterprises grow and interweave. I believe that if we can sufficiently develop the consciousness of contemporary business and associate with it the critical co-operation and the co-operative criticism of scientific and every other sort of able man, we can weave a world system of monetary and economic activities, while the politicians, the diplomatists, and soldiers are still too busy with their ancient and habitual antics to realise what we are doing. We may grow strong enough not only to restrain, but suppress their interference. We can build up the monetary and economic world republic in full daylight under the noses of those who represent the old system. For the most part I believe that to understand us will be to be with us, and that we shall sacrifice no advantage and incur no risk of failure in talking out and carrying out our projects and methods quite plainly.

That is what I mean by an Open Conspiracy. It is not a project to overthrow existing governments by insurrectionary attacks, but to supersede them by disregard. It does not want to destroy them or alter their forms but to make them negligible by replacing their functions. It will respect them as far as it must. What is useful of them it will use; what is useless it will efface by its stronger reality; it will join issue only with what is plainly antagonistic and actively troublesome. It seeks to consolidate and keep alive and develop the living powers in the world today by an illumination, a propaganda, a literature, a culture, an education and the consciously evoked expectation of a new society.

It is only natural that a common interest and understanding should develop among all of us who are dealers in world realities as our enterprises extend and intertwine more and more. The nationalist groups and cliques that divide us today, the feuds and rivalries, are mere legacies from the passing order from which we release ourselves. Their persistence is part of our crudity and inexperience. Our true quality is cosmopolitan. We become the true International, because our activities extend throughout the world. Our international ideas are complex, material and real. When we cease to think ourselves British, American, German of French, we do not become vaguely cosmopolitan; we become world-steel, world-shipping, world-cotton, world-food.

The International of the Workers, in spite of its more explicit organisation, is even now an altogether less substantial affair than the business-International. It has been easier to organise for that very reason. It is so of necessity because of the limited outlook of the common worker, put to toil too soon, ill-informed and easily misled. He has feelings in the place of ideas. His International is a mere community of resentful sentiment directed against the general order of the world and against us as employers. And we I think incur that hostility not so much on our merits as on account of our association, as successors and partners, with the Crest tradition and its disregard of common human needs, and because of the aggressive extravagances of expenditure in which we permit our creditors and our Lady Steinharts – and ourselves in our laxer moments – to indulge. If European business men are men tainted with "Crestism," the Americans seem to me to carry a heavier load of useless women and heirs. These are matters needing correction. But a clearer day may come when the improving manners and intelligence of the employer and the better information of less stupidly directed workers may bring these now hostile Internationals to an understanding.

Many things that now seem incurably conflicting, communism and international finance for example, may so develop in the next half-century as to come to drive side by side, upon a parallel advance. At present big distributing businesses are firmly antagonistic to co-operative consumers' associations; yet one or two of the big distributors have already made important deals with these large-scale economic organisations from the collectivist side. Both work at present upon very crude assumptions about social psychology and social justice. Both tend to internationalise under the same material stresses.

I find it had to doubt the inevitability of a very great improvement in the quality and intellectual solidarity of those who will be conducting the big business of the world in the next century, an extension and an increased lucidity of vision, a broadened and deepened morale. Possibly my temperament inclines me to think that what should be must be. But it is patently absurd to me to assume that the sort of men who control so much of our banking today, limited, traditional, careless or doctrinaire, are the ultimate types of banker. It seems as irrational to suppose that such half-educated, unprepared adventurers as Dickon and myself and our partners and contemporaries are anything but makeshift industrial leaders, and that better men will not follow us. Dickon and I are, after all, at best early patterns, 1865 and

1867 models. And the spirit of the money market and of business enterprise today is far finer that it was in my father's days. These things in the logical course of their development must improve.

Equally absurd is it to suppose that the modern newspaper is more than a transitory medium of communication and discussion, and that we shall not presently produce men who will handle the press and the new powers of public suggestion and education still latent in the cinematograph and broadcasting, with a creative intelligence far beyond any present experience. Economic life in a few score years ahead may be carried on in a light and with an education and inspiration almost incomparably better than ours.

And the labour leader that we know today, so vacuously emotional and unsound, is equally a transitory type. The younger men are different, clear, harder, less disposed to clasp hands with us and more able to lock minds with us and come to practical understandings.

None of these new types of men that begin to appear can have had anything but sentimental and acquiescent regards for the things of the past. It is incredible to me that many of them have not been thinking as Dickon and I have been thinking, and that their thoughts will not presently find expression in discussion and literature, and that they will not produce a distinctive culture, affect education profoundly and develop an international social life of their own. Sir George Midas is half a century our of date as a study of the *nouveau riche*. After all he was only emphasising the glories of the old order when he got himself cigars and diamond rings a trifle too large and filled his marble halls with footmen in plush. The Victorian Crests were foolish perhaps to sneer him on to better things. Most of the big business men I know today are men of unassuming presence and temperate expenditure. They dislike display and evade Society. They practise much private civility. They seem to be illiterate and Philistine at present largely because contemporary literature is so extensively concerned with fantasies and imitations and allusions that have no significance for them, and art with the vogues of the studios. The insufficiency is rather in the art and the literature they disregard than in themselves. The art and literature of the eighteenth century were done to please an aristocracy, and those of the nineteenth century to please a bourgeoisie. They have still to develop a relationship to the modern man of energy.

As these new powers realise more and more completely their distinctive quality, and produce fresh aspects and complementary functions of this new adult phase they are constituting, they will automatically evoke types of literary and artistic work in harmony with their general activities, and depart more and more definitely from the second-hand social customs to which they now rather ungraciously adapt themselves.

Because of its continual progressiveness this great revolution which is now becoming apparent must necessarily continue to be open and explicit, continue to appeal to fresh types and extend its spirit and understandings into the lives of a larger and larger proportion of mankind. In no other way can it escape frustration. In that sustained openness it differs from any preceding process of success and replacement. History is full of the rise and fall of classes, priesthoods, dynasties, aristocracies. Each class as it comes up to predominance in the story sets itself to establish itself for ever; makes laws, constitutions, to fix its characteristics and defy all subsequent change. It rules, it tyrannises, it loses vigour and flexibility; with a diminishing resourcefulness and a fatal obstinacy it fights the slow and merciless will that has ground it out and will grind it away.

That is the common history of all past ascendancies. Such attempts at fixation were possible because the rate of change in their conditions was not fast enough to make such hopes of permanence manifestly futile. But the modern maker of values never reaches a breathing point for such delusions to establish themselves. The adaptation of modern enterprise is unceasing. Each victory is no more than a foothold for the next phase. Success is not a throne but an entrance. We of Romer Steinhart do not *dare* to disregard new suggestions or exclude new able men from a share in our directorates. All our monopolies are conditional monopolies; our patents pass out of our hands if we do not avail ourselves of them. We live only if we keep alive.

This which I call a conspiracy to reconstruct human life is therefore necessarily open and outspoken because all who are concerned in it realise that their utmost knowledge is provisional and their utmost achievement experimental. There is no part of the world, no race, no station, that presently may not be able to contribute something essential. This Open Conspiracy is indeed the application of the scientific method to the whole of life. Since scientific research ceased to be a secret occupation, since its great expansion began three centuries ago with the beginning of frank publication and unrestricted discussion, miners, cobblers, lapidaries, grocers' assistants, rustic priests (not least these last), side by side with noblemen like Cavendish and great professors like Huxley, have contributed inestimable things. The social and political revolution before us must cast its net as widely. Necessarily it begins in practice in and about the direction of great financial and industrial developments because these things are the vital centres of social existence. There we are likely to find the greatest concentration of energetic types. But the greater these grow the less can they remain proprietorial. The less can they sustain any privacy about their general operations. The less can they exclude the outside man who is able and determined to participate in their control, who is able and willing to criticise and offer suggestions.

Exclude! We invite! In spite of Crest we keep up a perpetual hunt for capable and vigorous men whom we can bring into our operations. So do such systems as the American Steel Trust and J P Morgan and Rockefellers and Brunner Mond and Schneider-Creusot and Krupps and Tatas and the German electrical and chemical combines and the Ruhr steel group and the wonderful Zeiss firm and Kodaks and Fords and so on and so forth up and down and all through the tangle of modern productive and business activities. It is a far simpler, more honest and more certain career now for a poor and gifted young man to set out to make himself a director in the Romer Steinhart system than to become an office-holding politician. The work is cleaner, the pay better, the position more assured.

This disposition towards the open board-room had increased conspicuously during the last few decades, and it will go on increasing. We industrials have got our affairs on to a scale when we want to hear them discussed and avail ourselves of every suggestion. The financiers are following us towards the light. We all realise the need of being understood. We realise the danger to ourselves and to our concerns and to the whole world, in secret operations. We are more afraid of our own shadows than of anything else whatever. We want to be lit on every side. We do not want to cast shadows because the shadows we cast are so large that the most destructive mischiefs, thefts of energy, diversions of purpose, can hide and mature in them.

I think now I have made plain what I mean by Open Conspiracy. It is the simplification by concentration into large organisations of the material life of the whole human community in an atmosphere of unlimited candour. It is explanation and invitation to every intelligent human being to understand and assist. It is the abandonment of all reservation in the economic working of the world. It is the establishment of the economic world-state by the deliberate invitation, explicit discussion, and co-operation of the men most interested in economic organisation, men chosen by their work, called to it by a natural disposition and aptitude for it, fully aware of its importance and working with the support of an increasing general understanding.

## 3 – *World Directorate*

How does this Open Conspiracy stand to the governments, the legal systems and the politics of today? These governments embody the evaporating ideas of the past. They occupy the ground we need. They are now largely entanglements and obstacles. They are like deadweight debenture-holders or old plant in the face of revolutionary inventions. They have a certain value in maintaining order and suppressing local violence, but they carry very poisonous traditions with them, they function inadequately, dangerously and at a heavy price; they divide, they waste energy upon false rivalries; they may quite possibly check the development of new methods altogether.

The larger part of human troubles at the present time, the undiminished peril and pressure of war, the recurring waves of financial and economic disorder, are due almost entirely to the relative inalterability of political and legal methods in the face of a general process of material change. Types of ships, railways, roads, machinery of every sort, methods of manufacture, methods of credit, are superseded, scrapped, replaced; scale of business, areas of operation enlarge; systems of production and distribution absorb, extend, amalgamate; they do so against friction, sometimes against friction that becomes nearly overwhelming. The kings, the parliaments and congresses, the law courts and flags and boundaries, on the other hand, stick on with the imbecile inadaptibility of inanimate figures.

Their relative inflexibility is enormous. They are not regarded in general as methods at all; they are regarded as sacred conditions to which the living activities of human society must adapt themselves. They are sustained; they sustain themselves by an immense propaganda of conservatism. The chief problem before the progressive revolutionary, after he has secured his primary need, freedom of speech and discussion, is to bend, break, evade, minimise, get round or over or through the political institutions of the present time. The political history of the world since the war has been largely a story of conference after conference. Washington, Geneva, Locarno, for example, in which in a sort of blindfold way the better sense of mankind has striven to release itself from these stupid and dangerous entanglements and feel its way towards a wider welfare.

Our purpose in this Open Conspiracy, in which we do not so much engage ourselves as discover ourselves engaged, is to build up the organisation of a world state, a single terrestrial system of economic production and social co-operation. We do this not upon an open site but upon a world already mapped out in an extremely impracticable and inconvenient fashion into sovereign states, empires, kingdoms, republics, each of which is fenced in by the most elaborate defences against overt absorption. Each sovereignty is an implicit repudiation of our purpose. What is going to be our strategy in the face of this opposition?

There is a disposition apparent in many quarters to mitigate the present political fragmentation of mankind by methods drawn from the old politics. Eminent statesmen of sovereign states, unaccustomed to anything between themselves and high heaven, are to meet and arrange for very considerable mitigations of sovereignty. They are to bind themselves and their national governments to respect the arbitration of largely alien tribunals, to agree to various measures of disarmament and mutual assistance, each according to his own measure of efficiency and good faith. This is no doubt the only strictly legal way; none the less is it a way of highly improbable issue. In the end it might, under the most hopeful conditions, give the world a sort of super-Washington, a Supreme Court of international law and a confederated world government with a limited ability to call upon national armies and navies to enforce its decisions. But though this is the only proper legal way, I doubt if it is the effective or desirable way, and I doubt still more whether the sort of Federal World Congress it might ultimately produce, with its delegated and attenuated powers and its constitution repeating the most approved features of its constituent governments, would be able to perform any of the chief functions of an adequate world control.

It follows therefore that the way we have to pursue must be – how shall I phrase it? – sub or super legal. That is to say, revolutionary.

People are too apt to assume that a world directorate, a world republic, would have to be just the sort of government we find today in a typical sovereign state, magnified to a world size – a sort of Parliament of Mankind with a World President, a World Emperor, in some suitably placed palace. They imagine someone hoisting the "world flag" amidst an uproar of military bands and a blaze of "world" uniforms. I think that is an entirely misleading assumption. All the governments that exist in the world today are combative governments fundamentally; a world directorate would be on the other hand fundamentally a government for the preservation of peace. The old type of government from which our present ones derive, regarded war as the primary fact in life and took the small scale multitudinous economic affairs of its people almost for granted. The world government we desire will be primarily social and economic. It will have hands instead of teeth and claws. It will not be a descendant or a direct development; it will have evolved along a different line.

No existing government seems capable of doing without a flag. Yet a flag has no real significance for peaceful uses. The head of the current state is traditionally a fighting figure. Before the war the numerous royal families of Europe almost lived in uniform. They were ready, aye ready. Their survivors show no disposition to relinquish the swaggering rôle. Wherever the remaining monarchs go the soldiers still turn out and salute, and every loyal Englishman ceases to be a rational creature and stiffens to the likeness of a ramrod at the first blare of the national anthem. No king would ever dream of turning out and inspecting the electricians or the economic entomologists or the medical officers of health. He is a soldier by blood on the distaff side quite as much as on the other. Not an old lady among these royalties that is not at least a colonel two or three times over. Even the aunts and grandmothers of monarchy are carried to the grave on gun-carriages and buried with military honours. At the slightest provocation to the national consciousness at an Empire Exhibition for example, or at a patriotic tattoo, the Prince of Wales and the Duke of York leap into scarlet and bearskins and become almost magnificent figures.

No doubt the multitude feels its dread of foreign foes and their knavish tricks greatly assuaged by these displays; it likes to think of those dear old ladies as Brunhildas and Bellonas and of pleasant young gentlemen as War Gods, but the whole spirit of this royalty business is flatly incompatible with world unity. And let me remind the American reader that this essentially combative attribution is as true of the White House as it is of Windsor. The presidential office only reaches its full development when the States are at war. Then in sentiment if not in practice Mr Coolidge is expected to buckle on the sword of George Washington, summon his levies and lead out the embattled farmers of New York, Chicago, Fall River, Detroit,

San Francisco, Los Angeles, Atlantic City and Denver, to victory or death.

But a world government will not be a combative government; there will be nothing to combat. The world republic will be fighting nothing but time and space and death. It will have no foreign minister. It will have no army or navy. Its general suavity will be tempered by an effective intolerance or armaments and of the making of lethal weapons anywhere. Necessarily. It will have no need to express itself even by the most generalised of flags, the most amalgamated of uniforms, the most attenuated of breastplates, swords and spurs. It will neither expand nor conquer nor subdue nor include the governments of today; it will efface them.

If on the one hand the coming world directorate will obliterate many of what we now regard as the most essential aspects of contemporary governments, it will on the other penetrate far more deeply than they do into the current life of mankind. It will be actively organising the world production and world distribution of most staple products; it will have incorporated the steel trust, all the mineralogical industries, all the chemical industries, power production and distribution, agricultural production and distribution, milling, catering, the transport organisations of the world and the chief retailing business into one interlocking system. It will exploit all the wind and water power of the world. It will in fact be the gigantic world-plant of which Romer, Steinhart, Crest and Co., their allies, subsidiaries and associates, are the germ. It will be not a world kingdom nor a world empire nor a world state but a world business organisation.

Its constitution will have grown with its development; it will no doubt have an extremely intricate constitution but one nevertheless in practical harmony with its functions. It will be checking its efficiency and varying and improving its processes easily and naturally through the research departments it will have evolved. It will be making a record of its proceedings and exposing itself freely to criticism. And it will be directing the education and biological life of the world community because of the same necessities that have already made Romer Steinhart's, almost in spite of themselves, founders of technical schools, library and theatre proprietors, builders of industrial suburbs, vital statisticians, and keepers of their workers' health.

It is because of this essential difference between the old order and the new that I disbelieve in any political methods of effecting the change. The difference is so wide that to a certain extent the two orders can have a collateral existence. For nearly a century the new has been able to develop very considerably in despite of the old. But the two systems are necessarily entangled, and sooner or later thy must interfere and come into conflict.

Political activities on the part of those who are renovating civilisation may then be necessary, but even so they will remain secondary activities. It may become imperative that men of the new type should throw their resources into the scale with or against Vishnu or Siva in the supreme interest of free discussion and personal liberty. Some bravo government may have to be lifted from the shoulders of a people. Or the gags of some doctrinaire domination may have to be relieved. But though the old-type ruler and politician may often be an antagonist and sometimes an ally, he can never be an instrument. The further he is kept away from economic and biological administration the better for the world. He is the wrong man to look to. Creative-minded people have been wasting themselves for a century by looking to him.

It is not only that by his nature he would be obliged to operate these new worldwide processes within the localised limits of national and imperial boundaries, but also that by the very conditions that raise him to power he is always either rigidly traditional or tempted at every turn to sacrifice sound working to a reassuring effectiveness. And whether his transitory power is the outcome of inheritance or of an election or of a pronunciamento, he will still be profoundly inexperienced in the intricate balances and reactions of economic life.

It was by turning towards politics and deserting the vigorous initiatives of that inspired industrialist, Robert Owen, that Socialism went astray, and it is to the political delusion that we owe now, in nearly every country under the sun, the spectacle of a large futile Labour-Socialist party which clamours while it is in opposition for the nationalisation and socialisation of everything, and gives way to a helpless terror of administration so soon as it finds itself in office. The public meeting where every breath of response is magnified to an immense impressiveness, the party committee rooms, the fretful attic, are the worst of all possible preparatory schools for business management. The only people, practically, who know how to manage transport, the exploitation of natural products and industrial activities generally are the people who are engaged in doing so now.

This is an unpalatable truth for other kinds of men, but it has to be stomached. What we have to do is to develop the common consciousness of such directive people and liberate them from the traditions of the past. We want them to extend themselves to the moral and biological consequences of their activities. We want them to realise themselves completely. It is equally futile to think of putting them under Lenin's dreadful "armed workers" or leaving them subject to the interference of the traditional rulers of the western world. They themselves have to rule.

If we set aside political methods as hopeless for the purpose of replacing the present fragmentary and combative governments of mankind by an intelligent world rule, then we must cast about for other ways of forwarding that revolution. It needs no very profound analysis of the situation to show what these must be.

The first group of activities is mental. We have to exhibit and persuade. The new phase in world affairs has reached a point of development at which self-assertion is not only possible but imperative. The world republic must begin to explain itself, to challenge the still dominant traditions that impede its full growth, to make a propaganda for the conscious adhesion of men and women. It has to call for its own literature and use the press it already so largely sustains, explicitly for its own creature ends. Big financial and big business men have often, I know, a considerable fear of publicity, but it is a fear out of which they must grow. They dread Siva too much and tolerate Vishnu too easily. It is high time to end this furtiveness. We have to remember that the sole strength of the political and social institutions amidst which we live and make our way today so tediously and wastefully and dangerously, lies in the fact that they are traditional and established. If we could start humanity afresh, wipe out its memories, and confront it only with the material, apparatus and problems of the present and the future, no one would dream of setting up the nationalisms and particularisms and privileges that entangle us today. Their sole justification lies in past engagements. They are not painted in fast colours and the memory of them needs to be continually renewed. For them at any rate there is no recuperative force in the silent touch of living realities.

When the old order tootles its trumpets and waves its flags, obtrudes its tawdry loyalties, exaggerates the splendours of its past and fights to sustain the ancient hallucinations, the new must counter with its tale of great bridges and canals and embankments, of mighty ships and beautiful machines, of the subtle victories of the laboratory and the deepening wonders of science. It must tell of lives lit up and life invigorated, of new releases and new freedoms and happiness ensured. The new world we establish is visibly greater and nobler than the old; it liberates the last of the slaves, rejects servility, calls on every man for help and service. It gives finer stuff for poetry and – better news for the press. I would lay stress upon that point that even now it gives the better news. The old stuff bores. It is no mere detail but a fact full of hopefulness that, for all its affectation of romantic interest, the old stuff bores. Patriots are bores; nationalists are bores; kings and princes are *ex-officio* terrible bores. Boredom is a great motive power. I myself am a revolutionary mainly because the formal and established things, the normal entertainments of a successful man, have bored me to the limits of endurance. I am convinced they are beginning to bore multitudes of people.

You can see the still almost inadvertent conflict of the new and old in the vague, copious, inattentive newspapers of today. Here, ignorantly set out indeed but still arresting, is the intimation of some new discovery, some mechanical achievement, the martyrdom of a man of science, a vivid statistical realisation. Side by side is some dull picture of a row of politicians, the latest cabinet of Briand for example, or a still duller display of royalties in wedding dress or highland costume, doing nothing in particular. Most significant of all are the photographs of some huge dock or novel engineering structure, a towering display of mechanical achievement, and President This or Prince That solemnly "opening" it, doing his poor level best to look as though he was in some remote way responsible for it and not indeed a fetish as casual and irrational as a black cat put upon a first-night stage.

But though mental preparation for the revolution is fundamental it is after all only preparatory. While that preparatory process still gathers force, there are already, and more and more there will be, a series of issues breaking out between the new ideas and the old. These must be the second series of activities of the Open Conspiracy. An enormous quantity of power is already in the hands of the new sort of men, and every day their proportion of power in the world increases. It is only now that the men of finance and industry are coming together freely and talking plainly, that we begin to realise how much of the old order is already existing merely on our sufferance. It is within the power of the bankers of the world now to forbid the growth or even the maintenance of armaments. They can forbid the building of battleships and insist upon education. They can turn expenditure from unproductive channels. If they do not do so it is because they are disunited and unaware or unsure of their power.

And this is even more true of the big industrial organisations. If the Romer Steinhart group of firms and their allies throughout the world decided now to restrict the supply of certain products and munitions to any particular power, or any particular body of persons, that power, that body would be given an overwhelming military advantage. No soldier in existence can stand against the general will of the chemists and metallurgists of the earth. He is, from his under-exercised brain to his over-decorated buttons, antiquated and altogether ineffective without our help. If he get the usurer and credit manipulator upon his side, he is still incapable of producing the weapons he now requires without our assent. Sooner or later people like Dickon will throttle the soldiers' publicity and tie the hands of the credit manipulator.

As the story of the Tanks and a score of kindred experiences make plain, the generals cannot devise nor even use novel apparatus properly without unprofessional instruction. Indeed they cannot understand them. Tanks, said Kitchener, the British War Lord, were "mechanical toys." Professional soldiers love to "use" men instead of mechanical toys. The men feel. The history of the war is one long record of the bloodstained obstinate unteachableness of the professional soldier. To the end of the struggle, with excellent telpherage systems available, the British military authorities kept thousands of live men in toil and torment and danger, bearing burthens along the communication trenches. The men panted and were exhausted, many fell and were drowned in mud, but the alternative would have been for the military gentlemen to think out the use of telpherage systems. That was an impossible alternative. Slowly, slowly, at a great price of lives, they did indeed learn a little about gas, about modern transport, about the use of aeroplanes. But to the last they choked their lines with cavalry and great stores of fodder, and to this day they clink about in spurs. There was no military conclusion to the war – it was a moral collapse.

The general's elder brother the Admiral is no better stuff. A generation ago we took away his sails and wooden walls and put engines in him and wrapped him up in steel plates, in spite of him utmost resistance, and now today he still clings to his battleships – and will, until we send him and his gold lace sky-high in one. No one has ever yet written our private thoughts about the exploits of the British Navy in the Great War. There were some cries from the Admiral Fisher, but he died. At Jutland the guns, range-finders, submarines, torpedoes and aeroplanes of this huge spending department were all behind the times. But to this day the Admiral lords it amidst this machinery that has out-grown him. It spite of the protests of Weir, Parsons, Thornycroft and our own people, the naval engineer remains a civilian officer under these splendid militants in blue and gold lace. It is the current state of the affairs in one vivid instance. And – is it wonderful? – there is a dearth of able naval engineers.

In 1914 the financiers and industrial leaders were taken by surprise and the gentlemen in uniform got loose. It is our fault, our want of vision, if ever again they get loose on that scale. It becomes increasingly unnecessary every year that they should get loose at all on any scale or that we should bear the burden and incur the dangers of their continued existence. The struggle of the financiers and business men of the world to tie up the professional soldiers of the European states again after the war, and to impede and mitigate nationalist extravagances, though it has been instinctive rather than deliberate, has been an extraordinarily interesting one. Scattered and unorganised though we still are, things have on the whole gone our way. As I write they are singing the Treaty of Locarno in London. This is bad news for the dealers in national flags. And the Compagnie Internationale des Wagons-Lits, stimulated by this triumph of cosmopolitan business interests over the dreams of national revenge and readjustment, is, I learn from today's *Petit Niçois*, building a new type of blue sleeping-carriage that will soon be traversing all the main lines of the continent from Calais and Cadiz to Moscow and Constantinople.

## 4 – *The Capital of the World*

As the new order struggles to assure itself against a repetition of the disaster of 1914 and is forced towards self-realisation in the effort, its peculiar characteristics become plainer. The world republic is going to be as different from any former state as, let us say, an automobile from a peasant's cart. Its horse-power will be in its body. There need be no visible animal, no emperor nor president at all; and no parliament of mankind.

It is an anthropomorphic delusion that a state must have a head. A world republic needs a head no more than a brain needs a central master neuron. A brain thinks as a whole. And as for Assemblies and Councils, why should people meet to talk nowadays – especially to talk different languages – when they can exchange ideas far more effectively without doing so? Writing and print have been tested now for centuries; they are quite trustworthy contrivances. They admit of pithy and precise statement and exact translation. Why overwork the human throat? Polyglot debates are a delusion, a horror of empty noises and gesticulation.

The boredom of these sham discussions! In which no one ever answers anyone, in which sudden interventions are impossible! Twice, at Washington and Geneva, I have sat out multi-lingual debates, and God save me from any more of them! As the interpreter, a Dutchman with an extraordinary quickness and aptitude for the task, rose to perform his incredible feat of promptitude, to say at once all over again, within measure, what had just been said, an audible groan passed like a breeze through the gathering. His voice rose and fell imitatively, his arms swayed out in alien gestures, as he tried to reproduce the actual speaker. Sometimes there were three versions, when the speaker used neither French nor English. With a further displacement of gesture and stress and precision. A few rare prigs in the galleries followed the paraphrases and noted differences and defects with an intelligent interest. The rest of the audience marvelled at the interpreter's gifts and creaked and whispered and suffered. After the interlude of translation, proceedings mumbled forward for a while and then halted again.

These things mock reality. The decisions of importance to mankind grow silently and deliberately in the minds of those best placed to make them, and are no longer to be arrived at – or upset – by dramatic scenes and feasts of eloquence in senates and assemblies.

In the world republic we shall need rather parlours for informal conferences than parliament houses for stirring debates, and great libraries of current statistics, competent digests of complicated facts and a concentration of administrative headquarters convenient for intimate talks and settlements. These facilities need not be all in one place. There need be no World Capital. The swifter and safer air travel and the easier transmission of speech and diagrams become, the less is a capital city necessary. Men can do their business now without swarming like bees. Even now you could steal and hide Washington away for weeks and, if the newspapers made no fuss, the average citizen of the United States would be unaware of his loss. A modern government of the world should never be in session and always in action. Men of importance would come and go, as the Caesars did, where and when occasion required. The main structure, the constitution, the directorates if you will, of the great republic, may be in active existence long before it is clearly perceived and described as such.

## 5 – *Geneva*

I have already told something of my flying visit to Geneva the summer before last, but I have told of it so far as an aspect of an emotional state and laid stress only on the overcast mind I brought to bear on it. I wanted to give my own experiences of motive, my conflict of desires, a conflict to which I will presently return. But I perceived and heard more at Geneva than I was aware of at the time.

The proceedings of the Assembly, as I have confessed, disappointed and bored me. I was prepared to be bored and disappointed. I had never been in love with this idea of a world league with a written constitution and two chambers and fittings complete that came over to us from America. It did not come to us from the practical intelligence of America, nor had it, at first, any great support among big business men; It was engendered by professors, very pedantic professors. Their minds were strictly legal, and they were too self-sufficient to consider any criticism that came from a non-legal standpoint. Wilson was a law professor quintessentially, an American law professor with historical perspectives that hardly went back beyond the War of

Independence. He had no mental nor moral humility, and he lacked any proper pride in the greatness of his opportunity. The queer parliament of nations he created, based upon obsolescent ideas about sovereignty, was unattractive from the outset. Everybody in council and assembly alike was there as a national partisan. Nobody represented mankind. Sooner or later Geneva was bound to become an arena for disputes between nations, with a sounding-board to carry the passionate notes of these disputes to the ends of the earth. The civil war that nearly tore up the American republic was brought about by a dispute about the representation of states in congress and the efforts of one faction to secure an advantage over the other. The League of Nations seems constructed to engender a parallel quarrel. Its Council and Assembly are still a greater danger to the peace of Europe even than Italy.

Yet there are certain possibilities of cosmopolitanism at Geneva that I did not a first foresee, and things are germinating there that may grow and flourish as instruments of the world republic long after Council and Assembly have been wrecked, abolished or reconstructed out of recognition and any power of mischief.

I have mentioned my conversation with Mansard one sunny morning while we lunched at a lake-side restaurant, and how my attention wandered from what he was saying. Mansard was one of a little group of men who set themselves to explain Geneva to such curious visitors as he supposed me to be. A lot that Mansard had to tell me I hardly heard at the time, and yet I must have heard it, because afterwards I found it in my brain. His estimate from the Assembly and the Council was not much higher than mine, but what he was driving at all the time was the possibility afforded by the League of developing an international secretariat for a great series of world functions. He was insistent upon the possible importance of Albert Thomas' Labour Bureau, its independent importance. He said that the various officials came from their countries to Geneva in a national or at best an international spirit, that the first effect of the place upon them was often to stimulate comparisons between nation and nation and exacerbate their patriotism, but that presently their interest in their work almost imperceptibly "cosmopolitanised" them. There was a real cosmopolitan *esprit de corps* arising in Geneva.

That was Mansard's besetting theme – the growth which he professed to detect of a cosmopolitan mentality, an "international mind," he called it, among the permanent officials in Geneva. When you gave him your ear and encouraged him, this germinating seed would grow with extraordinary rapidity into a plant, that spread and branched until it overshadowed the world. He quoted Sir Mark Sykes, who had been advocating a League of Nations militia when he died in Paris in 1919, for the sake of just the same end, a cosmopolitan *esprit de corps*. Mansard would quote the church in the middle-ages, its religious fraternities and orders, and particularly the Knights Templars as instances of a successful cosmopolitan loyalty in the past. His imagination would go on to a dream of the British Navy, detached from its parent stem, developing an autonomy of its own, and becoming the sea police for all mankind.

"And how can you run air routes except as a world service with a cosmopolitan *esprit de corps?*" asked Mansard.

So Mansard. I quote him because he strengthens me here, but I will not even comment on his ideas.

### 6 – *David Lubin*

If ever the history of this great revolution in human affairs that may now be in progress should come to be written, there must be at least a vignette of that prophetic American Jew, David Lubin. He was a precursor, a figure rather like Roger Bacon in his unappreciated anticipations. He left a very sharp impression upon my mind. We dined together twice and exchanged several letters. My last letter from him is dated October, 1918.

I met Lubin by chance in the boat train from Dover to London, some three or four years before the war. He was dying to talk to someone and I was the only other occupant of his compartment. He was indignant at some incident of the Customs examination. I think they had scrutinised some French books he was bringing with him. They had, he thought, betrayed a suspicion that he – he of all people! David! King David Lubin! – would import improper books.

I was quite prepared to sympathise with him. I hate Custom houses as I hate kings, as salient reminders of the foolish barriers that cut up the comity of mankind. Encouraged by my sympathy he opened himself out to me. That was altogether his spirit, he agreed. But he explained that so far as he was concerned he had done tremendous things to bring these separations to an end. He had a flamboyant, overwhelming manner and an exaggerated style of exposition; he was obviously extremely vain, and at the time I gave what he had to say a very measured amount of belief.

He was already on oldish man then; he had the burning eye and the gestures and intonations of a major prophet; I can imagine a certain resemblance to the great Mr Gladstone, the other "Mr G" of my childhood. What he had to say was mixed up with the most remarkable theories about Israel and the world; he was a Jew, intensely race-conscious, Bible-fed, Hebrew-speaking, born in Poland and brought up amidst the excited sentimental and democratic enterprise of developing western America. He had, he told me, started work with some cheap jewellers in Massachusetts at the age of twelve, first as a polisher of scarf-pins – he had got into trouble by polishing too hard and getting all the gilt off when he began – and then as a maker of blue goggles which the firm contracted to supply Sherman's army. He had gone west at sixteen, he had travelled in oil-lamps, prospected for gold, packed lumber and launched the first "one price" store in Sacramento City. "One Price" meant in this case fixed prices; it was not a one-price store like Woolworth's in London. That "one-price" store had been the foundation of a substantial fortune. "David Lubin," he said with a sort of shout, "*one price*," and pawed towards me with his hand. He had slept under the counter of his store in a bunk of his own making. He had known thirst and hunger. In ten years he had the largest Department Store and Mail Order House on the Pacific Coast. But also he had been lost for two day in the desert during his time as a prospector, and the sense of God, that Desert God of Israel, had overwhelmed him. So he did not "eat pork," like so many successful Jews, when wealth came upon him.

"Not for *me*, your monocle, your girl with the yellow hair!" He took his old mother, who had taught him to sing Hebrew songs and read Maimonides, on a pilgrimage to Palestine. He was giving all his life now, subject to such attention as the Mail Order House still required, to the God of Israel and the service of mankind. After the success of his store, had come experimental farming to restore the simplicity of his soul, and then great economic discoveries and his Mission. Throughout our conversation it never dawned upon him that I too might have had something of a fight with the world, or any idea of a function towards mankind at large. He talked to me as I must be a perfectly stable Englishman, as I had been exactly what I was for centuries at least, as though no one ever rose or fell in Europe or felt the call to service there, so that the Transatlantic marvel of a man working his way up from small things to considerable wealth was bound in itself to fill me with amazement and admiration. It did nothing of the sort. But it interested me acutely just then to hear his interpretation of his Mission.

My first impression was that he had used it to treat himself to an eccentric tour of the heads of all the governments of Europe. He said he had just been talking to the Grand Vizier in Constantinpole; that he was corresponding with the Queen of Roumania; that he had called on the King of Italy on his way back; that he had been in communication with Stolypin, who was at that time the Tzar's Imperial Chancellor, and visiting the home of the Russain Minister of Finance in Finland. He added that he had made treaties on his own behalf with more than forty separate governments – I forget the exact number – which at the time I supposed to be either some fantastic metaphor or a downright lie.

Yet it was not a lie. It was literally true. This crazy-mannered, posturing, one-price merchant had a real Mission, and was doing a work of the utmost significance. He was, upon one side of him at least, a very great man. He had enlarged his experiences as a successful mail-order merchant and an unsuccessful Californian fruit shipper, until they embraced the economic life of mankind. His inner vanity was not blinding him in the least to the broad realities of human economics. Within him there was a life of almost childish fantasy; he seemed to find a Messianic significance in the fact that he had been christened David the King and not Pinchus after his grandfather, because his face had been burnt by a candle flame when he was four days old and an old Rabbi had foretold a great destiny for him to comfort his mother; he identified himself with a mystical immortal Israel that was linking all the nations. Isaiah was his dialect. By Israel's scars the nations should be healed. But directly he turned his face outward he was the western prospector, farmer and trader, and his eye was clear and keen.

The International Institute of Agriculture which his persistence, emphasis and audacity had already called into being by 1905, and which was now seated firmly in a building of its own in the grounds of the Villa Borghese, embodied a vision of one worldwide human community leading a righteous, productive and happy economic life. It quite justified all he claimed for it and for himself. He had gone to Rome, thrust himself amazingly into the royal shooting-box at San Rossire and prohesied to the young King of Italy, extraordinarily after the fashion of some prophet in goatskin from the desert standing before a king of Israel or Judah; and the king had built this institute for him and had given him facilities that had opened doors to him in Washington and every country in Europe. He appeared as if from nowhere, prophesying and not so much organising as provoking organisation. He played off America against Europe and Europe against America in the astutest fashion, while he brought this Institute into being. He had projected the thing, American fashion, as a sort of economic parliament with an upper and lower house – what a curse to the human imagination the British and American Constitutions have been! – and I rather guess that his last years were overshadowed by the fact that there was hardly any recognition that it was he who had invented the "Original League of Nation"; but the reality he had begotten, as he expounded it to me, was something much more modern, practicable and far-reaching than any League of Nations. It was not organised talk but assembled knowledge he had evoked.

The International Institute of Agriculture, to begin with, was a census of world production. It was sustained by subsidies from fifty-two governments, each subscribing to an identical treaty, and it was administered by a permanent committee of representatives of the sustaining nations. It kept a record of the state of the crops and the general agricultural outlook throughout the world, based on telegraphic reports from the boards of agriculture of its constituent countries. Week by week and month by month production was recorded, so that the destinations of all the prospective supplies could be adjusted to the probable demands.

In addition the Institute had developed departments dealing with the world prevention of plant diseases and with meteorology and agricultural legislation. That much existed.

But Lubin was quite clear and resolute that matters could not stop at that. As this fabric of economic intelligence was built up, there would arise the plain necessity of a world revision of transport conditions. On that second step he was working when I knew him and up to the time of his death. The current interstate and international transport of commodities was, he recognised, altogether too haphazard and speculative for world welfare. Given a centralised control, an all-seeing eye, a regulated system of warnings, it could be made as clear and as definite – as a mail-order business. And moreover, he argued, agriculture was not the whole substance of economic interests; the methods of the Institute once they were established could be applied with suitable adaptations to the other main staples of human consumption, to coal, to oil, to steel and other metals. So this mail-order prophet from Sacramento reached out until he touched hands with Romer, Steinhart, Crest and Co. Instead of the dark, crowded, unco-ordinated adventurousness of contemporary business, we could, he maintained, following along the lines of his Institute, substitute an illuminated, orderly, worldwide merchandising. I told him Romer, Steinhart, Crest and Co. would be quite willing to subsidise his Institute whenever the Kings and Viziers failed him.

The storm of the Great War submerged Lubin's internationalism. There was a dismally sentimental little dinner in August, 1914, when the French, German, Austrian and Belgian members of the staff drank together to the world-peace of the future, talked of their immediate duty and dispersed in a state of solemn perplexity to their several belligerent countries. It was the beginning of the end of that chapter in the history of internationalism. Presently Italy was swept into the war, and what was left of the Institute – staffed now by women and by the mutilated and the unfit – devoted itself to the problems of the allied food supply.

Since the war I have heard little of it. It has passed into obscurity in the shadow about the eclipsed king. Lubin died in the influenza epidemic at the end of 1918 before he could think out the war at a sufficient distance to get clear of the combatant note; he had been altogether pro-ally, and when he died, the hand of the Lord God of Israel was still heavy against Germany in all he said and did. For some time, I think, Lubin had been ailing and losing his grip upon things. The war posed a multitude of troublesome riddles to him, and it was not always easy for his undisciplined mind to find where Isaiah had hidden the answer. Almost his last effort was to commend his Institute to those who were concerned with the prospective League of Nations. His last letter to me was about that.

He was buried at Rome early in January, 1919, and his funeral passed disregarded through streets that were beflagged and decorated to welcome the visit of President Wilson.

Wilson ignored him and his Institute and his suggestions.

## 7 – *Assembling the Conspiracy*

I will return now to something I have already used once as a point of departure. It is that I am projecting, not foretelling. All this estimate of creative forces here is speculative; the revolution I write about is not assured. For all I know it may be inevitable, it may be in the very nature of things; I have no evidence for or against that view. But I am convinced that it will remain only a possible thing, an unsubstantial appearance, until it is embodied in a wilful understanding among the people who can carry it out.

I write of the increasing power of the financiers and the big industrials to control human affairs, to prohibit wars, consolidate international production and distribution, restrain and direct governments, dictate policies; they are the great Barons for a World Witenagemot, but at present their power is either partial or unconscious in its use, or merely a potential power. It does not follow they will every use that power systematically or use it for great ends. The metamorphosis has gone so far I think that one can distinguish the broad lines of the new social Leviathan, the world republic; but it sleeps, it does not move, it has not yet awakened to its possible existence. The assembling of this "Open Conspiracy" remains a thing for the future.

The fact that I am writing my own mind clear about these things down here in this tranquillity among the olive trees is evidence enough that what I am propounding concerns a merely incipient reality. The substance of the preceding book is mainly the history of how I and Dickon came to these still developing ideas. But my case is that we are not abnormal men but samples of ordinary successful modern men, and that what we are thinking a lot of other similar and similarly circumstanced people must be thinking also, with individual differences but on the same general lines. I have come away here to Provence and made myself a sort of hermit for the better half of the year, in order to get on with this complex readjustment of my vision. It has been and still is for me a task more important and urgent than any concrete business operations.

To some extent I may be exceptional in this direct transfer of my attention to the general problem. No one else among active business men so far as I know has come away like this for an exhaustive consideration of the general position of business. Such moods and disappointments as have rendered it not only an easy but an almost necessary thing for me to concentrate on these questions, may not have chanced as yet to anyone else. Accident may have made me a sort of pioneer in expressing these views.

But Dickon, though he has not come away and is much too busy, I think, ever to come away, has developed quite similar views. He however has made no such attempt to crystallise them out. They come and go in his mind. His must be the more usual state of affairs. Such a pause for self-expression, such a realisation of the need for statement and a clearing up of the outlook has not yet come to the world of great business as a whole. It think it is nearly due. The new order is still mute; I chant my saga of the future without accompaniment; the politicians and political personages, journalists, religious teachers and schoolmasters who supply together the ordinary forms of political thought in use, repeat nothing but the accepted formulae of the passing state of affairs. But the phase of self-realisation and self-expression may be close at hand. It may come very fast when once it begins to come.

There are, I grant, few signs of its coming. As yet we think by ourselves alone as I am doing, or we talk only by twos and threes as I shall do when I return to England. We have still to talk by groups and then in books and organs of our own. Clearly while this mental fragmentation continues the world of contemporary expansions will be deprived of the larger part of its sustaining power, and the old order will still be in a position to hold on and recover its losses to us. A time comes when every social process must become conscious of itself. No great creative development can go on in modern social life beyond a certain point without a literature of explanation and criticism. We talk, I say, by no more than twos and threes. Almost all the talkers are me. Few if any of the womenkind of men of affairs seem to share these ideas that the practical handling of power is evoking. Nor do we make any éclaircissement with our business partners; we educate no successors. We hand on our impressions and vague intentions only by the most fragmentary hints and suggestions to our sons.

Our homes, our families, our social life, are still quite submerged in traditional ideas. We world submerged.

This is a state of affairs that is necessarily transitory. The men who have been the means of developing the large scale methods thus far, the men of science, the inventors, the men of imaginative business enterprise, the men of financial understanding, cannot leave human affairs in this present crisis of discordance between worldwide achievement and nationalist outlook to which they have brought them.

But they cannot go on to the subtle and enormous tasks of intellectual and moral adjustment that are required of them without a consolidation of their own still largely scattered activities, and the support of a widening confidence and participation in what they are doing. They have to bring not only the world of science but the world of literary activities and their own womenkind and families into understanding relationship with themselves. They have to produce a social life of their own that will sustain and ensure the continuance of their world and be harmonious with that work. They have to evoke a literature and an education that will record and continue and spread their awakening creative spirit. They have to bring that spirit out of their laboratories and works and offices and country houses into all the concerns of mankind.

I do not know if they can do that, but I do know that if they do not do it, a long period of violent stresses and probably of degenerative disorder lies before mankind. The old order of things such as it was can never recover its former confident stability; it had been sprung like a worn-out tennis racket; it has lost its moral ascendancy over men's minds even if it has kept its grip on their affairs. But the new scale world can achieve itself only under onerous conditions. Economic revolution trails with it every other sort of revolution. It involves a new way of living, new habits, new relations between the sexes, an artistic and literary renaissance, a new handling of the methods of publicity, an educational revolution. And it is only people of our type and freedoms who can have the knowledge and experience to plan and the courage, ability, and worldwide advantages to achieve, so great a reorientation of human attention and effort.

## 8 – *A New Social Routine*

A new social life must necessarily develop step by step with the progress of the world republic. It will be aristocratic in the sense that it will have a decisive stratum of prominent and leading individuals who will wield a relatively large part of the power and property of the community, but it will be democratic in the sense that it will be open to everyone with ability and energy to join that stratum and participate in its work to the extent of his or her ability and energy. It will have routines of its own, and they will be widely different from the routines of the present time.

The social routines of the present are determined largely by the assembling of government and the existence of a court. Society gathers at some sort of capital and entertains and is entertained. There are routs, parties, pageants and theatrical displays. Then it disperses to carry on the traditional motions of the conquering nomads from whom most old-world governments derive, to hunt, shoot, frequent the open air. There is no need to hunt or shoot now; the hunting is a public nuisance and the shooting a massacre of tamed birds, but still the thing goes on. At convenient times society races, bets upon and trades its now rather obsolete horses. Its costume, its language, is gravely equestrian.

This seasonal coming to town and return to the country that was once necessary to powerful people in the past, has undergone great elaborations and modifications as these powerful people have become more and more a creditor community no longer in direct contact with realities. All the procedure has become more formal and more trivial. Games have become displays and functions rather than general exercises. I have told already of the disillusionment of Dickon and myself as we clambered up from the struggle for freedom and power and realised the nature of the feast, the feast of honours and satisfactions, at present spread for success.

The new social life will be the life of people in close and keenly interested contact with the realities of economic, directive and administrative affairs. They will have no time for systematic attendance at courts, parliaments, race meetings and the like; they will find much better fun in the work they are doing. And there will be no capital, no court, no parliament and no race meetings. I doubt if these adults will have any use for mass assemblies.

The present disposition of people to assemble in monstrous crowds, the great Epsom festival of Derby Day for example, is a very curious and probably a now passing phase in the human development. The crowds seem urged to gather by an immemorial habit, but they do not seem to be very happy or busy when they have gathered. They stare about. In India immense congestions of a religious sort occur. In the past there were great fairs and pilgrimages; Mecca is still a pious Epsom. There appear to have been such assemblings at Avebury and at Stonehenge, with races and sacrifices. Solutré, to judge from the vast accumulations of picked horse bones, was an annual camp and fair for the horse hunters of the Palaeolithic period many thousands of years earlier. This custom of seasonal assemblies goes back therefore to the early beginnings of social life. It was dictated first perhaps by the habits of the grazing animals to scatter when the food is scarce and the calves of fawns are young, and to reconstitute the herd at the breeding time. Man the hunter followed the herd, and learnt to assemble as the herd did.

All need for these swarmings has evaporated now with increased freedom of individual movement. They are survivals. All the world is a meeting-place for the new type of man. An uncrowded meeting-place. All the world is our court and our temple, our capital and our fair.

This disappearance of a "social round" from the lives of the more modern types of people does not mean a decline in sociability – but an intensification. Just as a king or a president becomes ridiculous now as a symbol of the will and purpose of mankind, so jostling innumerable people, roaring in unison with them, cheering some regal mannequin, promenading in our best clothes and eating by the hundred, fail to satisfy our deepening sense of intercourse and co-operation.

We want to get at other individuals closely and effectively. We want to develop resemblances and understand differences. For that purpose social life needs to be a series of small duologues and group meetings. Its encounters cannot be very definitely arranged. Staying together in a well-managed country house for a few days' holiday, joint membership of a club, meeting frequently to lunch or dine, taking exercise or sitting in the sun together, working in proximity or co-operations, going on an expedition for a week or ten days, sharing a walking tour, a day or so in yacht or the like, these are surely the best forms of contact. What more does one want? All the other social things are mere occasions for mass excitement. And when we come to contacts of personality, the actual encounter is often the least part of the relationship. I am reminded of Heine's visit to Goethe and how the chief blossom of that long anticipated encounter was a remark upon the excellence of the fruit trees by the wayside. Out reallest intimacies are often with people we have never seen.

Writing often affords a closer encounter of minds than a personal meeting. After all I am living here in this *mas* up a byway in Provence, not because I want to get away from people but because I want to get more effectively at them. I have so much to say, and the saying of it needs such careful preparation, that it is absurd to think of saying it by word of mouth. I want to say it when the people to whom it appeals are ready to hear me. I want to lie ready for the mood of attention, and as a book on a table or even as a book on a shelf I am sure at least that I shall not be met in a phase of defensive disregard. At a set and dated meeting, especially if it lasts only an hour or so, anything may happen.

I once met J M Keynes at a lunch party. I rather think I had asked to meet him. I had and have a great admiration for him. It is the only time I have ever encountered this idol of my brother Dickon. I could have imagined all sorts of topics we might have discussed together, but as a matter of fact all we did on that occasion was to fall foul of each other rather sharply about a book called *The Mongol in Our Midst* and the way in which a gorilla sits down. Neither of us really cared very much about the way a gorilla sits down, but we both chanced to be wickedly argumentative that day. We scored off each other, and that is all that passed between us.

Yet Keynes has affected both Dickon's ideas and mine profoundly, and I shall be disappointed if this stuff I am writing here among the olives does not reach him at last in Cambridge – with my friendly greeting.

A life of active work that continues to the end, a life in which everyone goes apart at times to think and write things out in order to communicate them better, a social life of meetings by twos and threes and fours, a social life that has no use for crowds and for crushes and for mere passing salutations, a social life where men speak to one another by books or by pamphlets more effectively than by speech, in which there are no debates, no public decisions by means of oratory and voting, will necessarily produce its own forms of house and garden, its own apparatus of intercourse. One needs a place or places to work in, and that accommodation must vary enormously with the nature of one's work. It may call for indices, libraries, laboratories, secretaries; assistants, colleagues, summaries may need to be readily accessible. And away from the working place, but not too far away, one wants to dine and rest in some unexacting beautiful apartment, a flat in a retired quarter, rooms in a riverside inn or the like, some corner of freshness, light and quiet. And then one wants a break in one's work, the sort of break people now call a "week-end," and for that is indicated the pleasant country house, with good company and tennis, or racquets or lawn tennis or swimming or good walking. Or this *mas* here. And further one needs the occasional refreshment of going abroad to a different climate and of encountering a different fashion in all the incidentals of life.

I say "week-end," but I will confess I wish the ancient people who invented the week had invented it longer and larger and with more than one day of rest at the end of it. Six days' work and then one day off may have been all very well for the peasants of ancient Babylonia or among the vines and fig-trees of Palestine, but I find it one of the tightest misfits of the modern world. The English "week-end" lasts from Saturday afternoon until Monday at lunchtime, and leaves four days and two half-days for getting things done. One is always knocking off too soon. I could do most of the things I have to do in England far better in spells of from six to eight days of steady work to be followed by three of four days of play, gossip, laughter, and rest. But people treat this neolithic week as though it was an astronomical necessity, like day and night. For one person who will be shocked by my republicanism, a score will cry impossible at a ten or twelve day week, with a three or four day Sabbath to it.

Here in Provence Clem and I can practise it, and it succeeds wonderfully. I can call up a little automobile I now keep in

Grasse for our Sabbath, and we can go anywhere within a hundred and fifty miles, to the sea, North Italy, Avignon, Nîmes, Grenoble, or just down to Nice or Marseilles for an urban day or so. I believe a longer week would suit almost everyone in a modern community better than the Babylonian legacy.

The freedom to get away that a longer week would give the ordinary worker would revolutionise the everyday life of labour. His present Sabbath is merely a pause in his toil; it is neither a rest nor a change. Before anything can happen it is over. The ordinary wages-worker comes back on Monday morning less disposed for work than when he left it on Saturday. He wasn't worked out when he left, and he isn't refreshed when he returns.

Some day perhaps the world will keep such an enlarged week. This change in the timing of life to a longer, slower rhythm, this relinquishment of mass gatherings and periodic and formal social functions, this intensification of personal encounters, this expansion of interest to worldwide activities, this resort not only to reading but to writing and publication as a normal part of one's social existence, must be necessary aspects of the development of a new adult stage in human experience. The new sort of people can no more submit to the social routines, the time apportionments, the etiquette of the eighteenth and nineteenth centuries, than they can keep an automobile in order with tools of wood and flint.

## 9 – *Heirs at a Discount*

This new way of living demands not only different rhythms and routines, it demands also a changed spirit of conduct for women, differing from any that prevails at the present time. How far women will come with us and how far they will let us go is a question I must tackle in a separate book of its own. But here I will venture to say that family life will be less the habitual mode than we now pretend it is.

It is a venerated assumption among lawyers and suchlike preservers of antique psychology, that men work and organise great industries in order to "found families." I cannot imagine how anyone with the most rudimentary powers or observation can repeat so foolish a statement. I doubt if any big business man or any big financial man for the last hundred years has done what he did for the sake of his family. Far more was it for the sake of the business. In former times of insecurity one may have looked to one's sons and connections by marriage to hold together the estate one had created, but even then I believe the care was mainly for the estate. And nowadays, though sons or nephews may often prove congenial junior partners, a really vigorous business man is much more likely to care for a capable stranger than for a disintegrative son. The later Caesars did. They were constantly adopting colleague-successors. The most disastrous of the Caesars were the ones who were born to the purple. And look at the families "founded" by the earlier American millionaires!

No energetic directive people are deeply in love with inheritance; it loads the world with incompetent shareholders and wasteful spenders; it chokes the ways with their slow and aimless lives; it is a fatty degeneration of property. If Romer, Steinart, Crest and Co. could avoid carrying Lady Steinhart and the Crests on our backs we should all rejoice. Our only reason for resisting the heaviest possible death duties is that the alternative to our present load of heirs would probably be the active interference of some rascal appointed by political intrigue to look after the growing share of the old-style State in our concerns. Rather Crest, rather a score of Crests, than one of Lloyd George's convenient friends. Rather Lady Steinhart's possessive bad manners, her fences and her *pièges à loup* for a mile or so and another generation or so, than a network of tiresome unintelligent restrictions over the better part of the world.

In course of time these great business systems as they become the ostensible as well as the real government of the world may evolve some method of voluntary dispossession. We may for example return our individual shares of the capital into the business and become annuitants after sixty-five. Or we may devise ingenious Trusts that will save our work alike from the paralysis of the politician, from the weight of a layer of rich widows and from the ravages of the heir. We may make the personal share smaller while retaining the power to wield large masses of property so long as one is on the active directorate.

Few of us realise how rapidly family life, home life in a little group of parents and young, fades out of modern existence. Royalty makes an immense parade of its family life because that is its *métier*; but a great majority of the more influential people in the world, though they keep quarters here and there, no longer centre upon a home. Lambs Court is a sort of home for the Clissolds, but now only servants inhabit that place continually; Dickon who for a modern man of enterprise was exceptionally domestic, hardly ever goes there now; for nearly half his life he has been as homeless as I have for nearly all of mine. Family seats are traditional things, and they may be pleasant things to sojourn in for a few happy years, but they are no longer any more necessary to human life than capital cities. Half the great country houses in England are for sale today. Just as all the world may some day be the seat of government, so the common safety and welfare may at last dissolve the walls and seclusion of the family altogether.

I do not think that this reduction of cohabitation and this diminution of inheritance in property involves a disregard of blood relationships. A man may come to a care all the more for his kin, because he is less encumbered with them. A son who no longer regards his father as a tyrant or a lock-up investment may come to realise his value as a friend and as a kindred experiment in living. The less perhaps the habit of proximity the more the magic of consanguinity. Where there is a natural peculiar sympathy it will out, in association and co-operation, and where there is not there is no profit to parent or child or the world in a forced succession. If the son becomes a competent director, well and good, but we do not want him as an inert shareholder. Let the son justify his sonship. Let the widows and feminine dependents be limited to comfort and security, house and gear. A man who has been privileged to direct great business has no right to encumber its controls or impoverish its reserves with his domestic bye-products.

## 10 – *Civilisation by Newspaper*

This increasing, free-moving cosmopolitan society of vigorous individuals, with its habits and methods spreading out into larger and larger strata and sections of the human community, will produce its own literature. It will live very much by and through its literature. Literature will be a form of social intercourse.

There will be much thinking and reading and writing in the next phase, but it will not be delegated work. It will be a literature of activity. It well not be a professional literature. A modern man of affairs, like an Athenian gentleman or a Chinese gentleman, will work out his own philosophy and make his own comments and records. A few may specialise in expression, but I do not see that we need continue the vicious practice of the Roman plutocrats and keep a class of philosophers and men of letters to ease us of our responsibility for these things – and lose them at last in the necessary pettinesses and pedantries of men without experience.

We shall need newspapers that will give us facts simply and plainly. We shall certainly have no use for the vast sheets of advertisements set off with inaccurate news. Quasi-amusing trash and political frothings that now invade our homes every twenty-four hours. The daily papers of educated people half a century ahead may be a tenth of the size and ten times the price of these wildly flapping caricatures of contemporary happenings.

I am not even sure that, so far as our own interests go, we want them daily. It is the betting man and the stock exchange speculator who follow the fluctuations of the day and hour, and if our sort of people gets a real grip on the world there will be very little betting and speculation. For most people the daily paper is a daily disappointment – to which they are drawn by habit and against which habit forbids them to rebel. I lie in bed here of a morning with a mind at peace, inaccessible to any correspondence, and think of the hundreds of millions of rustling sheets away in England that are being opened with a sort of jaded eagerness for something really wonderful. Recently our postman here has become erratic; he brings the Paris papers, the London papers, sometimes at eleven, sometimes at four, sometimes not at all. Americans over the hill get them; to him one Anglo-Saxon sees as good as another. It matters hardly at all. There are four packets unopened now on the bench at my side. I may rip them open and glance through them today or tomorrow.

The weeklies interest me much more. The new order may find a weekly newspaper sufficient. In seven days things have had time to shape themselves a little. Ten days would be still better. The best of all newspapers, to my mind, is *Nature*. That tells you of things that matter, and tells you adequately. The weekly *Manchester Guardian* or the *Weekly Times* too are good, but they would be better if they left out more of the literary stuff and gave a fuller abstract of the news and more articles of relevant information. I do not know enough of the American press to say whether there is any periodical at all over there, daily or weekly, which gives as competent a digest of the general news as *Nature* does of scientific happenings.

I may seem perhaps a little too ample in this criticism of the press. I may seem to some readers to be enlarging on a superficial matter. But indeed it is not a superficial matter. The press colours the general tenor of life now and makes the background of all we do. If it is noisy, uninforming, inexact, we live just as though we had to live in a house with all the windows open upon an incessant railway station or an unending fair. The hurdy-gurdy of a roundabout is an unimportant instrument of music in itself, but not if it drives the workers in a great laboratory frantic and makes their work impossible.

And it is not only as the background of our own lives that the press is essential to our social life. It is the medium of relationship between the active directive people and the mass of the population which, consciously or not, is in co-operation with them. It is the only medium through which the bulk of the community may ultimately be brought into conscious co-operation. But at present it fails to possess that function. At present the great distributing businesses which provide the financial basis on which our newspapers rest and which dictate their tone are not sufficiently self-conscious to see beyond mere circulation. The newspapers tell of the lines and bargains offered by the distributors to their customers, and what else the newspapers may be doing with those customers does not seem to concern the advertiser. So long as the advertisements are carried far and wide, so long as there is no hostile discussion of the advertised commodities and so long as no plainly subversive doctrines are preached in the papers, the big distributors do not care what else is or is not given to the public. They are still too new and too untaught to maintain any conscious relations of policy and action with the transport organisations of the world as a whole, with the merchandising of staples in bulk and the general industrial network, and they behave as though they had neither come out of a past that was different nor as if they headed, as they surely do, for equally great changes and developments in the near future.

The newspapers on that account are still quasi-independent of the distributing trades. Because of the inadvertence and inconsecutiveness of these latter. But that is a conditional and transitory freedom of the press. It is diminishing rapidly. Newspapers have nothing like the power they had in their hands during their period of opportunity at the end of the war. I have recorded my brother's lamentation of their blindness already. In the long run newspapers may become merely instruments in the hands of the retailers.

There is still a delusion which many business men share, that it is the public that determines the pattern and sets the key of the press for which it contributes its pennies. This is no more true of the newspaper than it is of the theatre or the cinema. The rôle of the public in these affairs is to endure. You can feed the public anything you like in all these things, within the limits of its endurance. It is helpless against you. Its only possible veto is to die, riot *en masse*, be ostentatiously sick or abstain from what you give it. Short of these extremes it must accept. It may grumble but it must accept. Given competition it will prefer whatever bores and repels it least, but its freedom of choice is limited by the very great and growing limitation of competition. Exceptionally great masses of capital are needed to start a paper nowadays or to make any sort of big public show. The public may wish for all sorts of things in its paper, but unless it carries its wish to the effective point of refusing to take the paper altogether unless it is satisfied it will not, of its own initiative, get them. Nearly everyone has the newspaper habit; and the newspaper proprietors can defy your individual objection so long as they maintain a general understanding among themselves.

The only possible effective control of all these processes of publicity, so that this shall be given and that withheld, is to be found in the hands of the active proprietors and directors of the great newspapers themselves, and in the advertisers who sustain them. If these people choose to give the public well-written daily or weekly papers, responsible and large-minded, the public will get them, but it will get them in no other way.

The public does not make the newspaper nor the cinema, but on the other hand the press and the cinemas do more and more make the public. They provide the social background for an increasing proportion of people, they determine the characteristics of the modern social atmosphere as nothing else now does. The pulpit and the home circle sink to relative insignificance. And if we men of large material influence propose, as I am proposing here, to accept our manifest responsibilities and reconstruct the world as we can do, upon broader, finer and happier lines, then it is in the world of the press and the show and the new methods of publicity that our first overt struggle must occur. If the conspiracy of circumstances that has put power into our hands is to be changed into an open creative conspiracy, it is to these things that we must first address our awakening intelligence.

And it is with Vishnu rather than Siva that Brahma must struggle here, Vishnu who wants the people blinded and divided and misled so that he may rule unchangingly for ever. But Vishnu's way is always either to suppress newspapers or make them so dull as to be unreadable, and Siva tears his own papers to pieces and will not tolerate success even in a labour journalist. But Brahma is persistent and inventive, and if one way is blocked to him he will find another. In the long run the press comes back into his hands because he interests.

Open, candid, exact, full and generous, these are the qualities the newspaper of the new life must possess, for these are the necessary qualities of the new life. It must suppress nothing, lend itself to no shams and outworn superstitions, throw all its weight in the scale against particularism, sectarianism and traditionalism. Day by day or week by week, by text and picture, it must bring to every mind capable of receiving it the new achievements of human effort and organising power, the victories of conscious change. Even in its reports of litigation and police courts it will display the struggle of the old Adam against the needs of a growing society. There is never a case before the magistrates that does not afford either a criticism of law or custom, a lesson in psychology, or the revelation of some educational defect. Life will be shown as incessantly interesting, and the anniversary, the ceremonial and the crowded occasion, so necessary to mankind amidst the dullness and deprivation of medieval life, will sink down to unimportance.

By an organisation of publicity and suggestion and entertainment, upon wise and liberal lines, the new social life can be sustained and reflected in the minds of an increasing proportion of the people of the world, and the growth of the new order in the body of the old assured. The press, the cinema theatre, broadcasting centres, book publishing and distributing organisations, are the citadels that dominate Cosmopolis. Until they are in the hands of the creative revolution human progress is insecure. They may be held by brigands, they may be gripped by the forces of reaction and the life of the world may be starved or stifled. The firm establishment of a great press throughout the world, reasonably free from the interference of national and local politicians, and, in the last resort, capable of assailing them effectively, is the first course in the foundation of the conscious world republic.

## 11 – *Force and Violence*

Human society rests upon physical force. Law is in the first place the systematic forcible suppression of instinctive and incoherent violence, so that property and life are generally safe. Law in the past may have been at times little better than the will of the ruler or the pressure of tribal opinion, but it has always had in it a certain element of system, the implication at least of a definite pledge to protect and observe conditions. But hitherto it has been applied only locally, it has been reserved for the subjects of a state; it still varies enormously from land to land.

It would make an extraordinarily interesting book if someone were to give us history of the extension of legal protection to the stranger and the alien, the growth of the idea that a man could have rights not only as a citizen, not only as the protégé of foreign state sufficiently powerful to avenge his wrongs, but simply as a man. There would be some entertainingly tortuous chapters upon extra-territoriality and diplomatic privilege. It must be quite recently that the conception of a worldwide protection for anyone whatever, an even justice for the stranger and the native, has become practically effective. It has been associated with the general widening of mental horizons in the eighteenth and nineteenth centuries. It has been accompanied by certain social developments of the most interesting and promising sort.

Quite the most significant of these is the modern policemen. If we could bring back to contemporary London or Paris or New York a capable Roman administrator, he would, so soon as he had got over the enormity of the traffic, the astonishing width of the roadways, the plate-glass shop-windows, the artificial lighting and suchlike obtrusive material differences, concentrate upon those rare impassive persons who smoothed and pacified and assured and facilitated the thronging concourse. For the modern policemen is something new in the world. He appears in history even later than the modern press. He is something very essential and very significant in the new phase of human association in which we are living. He embodies new ideas. He has great possibilities of development.

I suppose the learned could give us a long history of constables, watchmen and the like throughout the ages. I suppose there was some sort of watch and controls in ancient Rome and Babylon. They were not so much sustainers of order as a prowling reminder of order in dark and dangerous places. Rarely have such arrangements created enough confidence to dispense with the bearing of arms by private citizens. How recent and how complete is the individual disarmament of mankind! I have been round and about most of earth, and in some very lonely and desert and wild places; I have flown thousands of miles, been under-seas in submarines, had my fair share of personal dangers, but – except as a formality during the war – I have never carried a weapon upon me. How astonishing that would have been to my Tudor and Plantagenet ancestors! How different a mental atmosphere it implies! Before the Tudor Clissold went out at nights, he made sure that his very ornamental dagger came easily out of its decorative sheath. He put a wary hand upon the hilt at every corner.

So unobtrusively that there is little about it in the histories, these new police organisations came into being and spread, with macadamised roads and gas-lamps and newspapers, into a changing world. All these innovations seem commonplace, almost vulgar, nowadays. But they transfigured the tenor of social life. Very rapidly it appeared that with the aid of print and telegram the common man also could apprehend the world as a whole. Imperceptibly it was realised that life and property could be made so secure that it was reasonable to demand release from anxiety upon either score. It was demonstrated that freedom of movement and freedom of activity wherever in the world one's interests might take one, might be conceived of as common rights.

The ideal of the civil police developed in the eighteenth and early nineteenth century. Though I imagine it arose first in France, it developed in England more rapidly and completely than anywhere else. It was, as the English mind apprehended it, a new organisation of force for novel ends. The policeman was to be the servant of all, he was to be kept entirely out of politics, his use of force was to be strictly limited, he was to be unarmed or very lightly armed with a truncheon or suchlike blunted implement, and he was to protect and not infringe private liberties. He had to be alert but not inquisitorial, warn rather than command. If he did not hit hard, he was to hit surely; instead of a spasmodic and vindictive omnipotence he was to embody a gentle, inevitable omnipresent urgency.

In England and America and every European country there has been a struggle of these profoundly modern ideals with older and baser applications. Every British Home Secretary has felt the temptation to give the policeman a political twist, and almost always that temptation has been resisted. Both the United States and England have felt a certain pressure to set him such difficult and unsuitable tasks as the regulation of sexual morals, insistence upon bedtime, restrictions upon drinking and eating; and every attempt of this sort has been found to overstrain him morally and make him inconvenient. But he has never been so far demoralised anywhere yet as not to be a betterment in every community in which he appears.

Police force and military force, in their typical and contrasted forms, might almost be taken to symbolise the new human order and the old, the one candid, universal, protective and releasing, the other selective, combative, secret and compulsive. In the French and English newspapers during the last week or so there has been a curious display of both types of force. A group of criminals with romantic political pretensions had been forging French paper money in Hungary, and they have been caught by the frank concerted action of the French and Hungarian police. A robbery in England has been brought to book in Paris by an equally frank co-operation of the police of France and England.

By being kept out of nationalist politics, the European police have been free to form a sort of international of their own to the universal benefit. There one sees the filaments of the new order leaping across the separations of the old. But at the same time a very nasty little affair has come to light in Toulon; mysterious Englishmen, it seems, have been in the stews of that city, inciting poor little prostitutes to worm secrets – what secrets can they be? – out of French sailors and arsenal workers. Secrets got in this way are not worth the stink they are wrapped in. But there you have the old order at work and there is your contemporary nationalism in its logical development. My intellect is cosmopolitan but my pride and instincts are patriotic, and I am not pleased by the suggestion in the French papers that my Admiralty has been caught under the beds of the Toulon brothels.

A civil police is the proper method of force in the modern state, as a regenerate press is its proper method of mental intercommunication, and so the civilisation, the internationalisation of the police mentality is plainly the second line of work to which the creative revolutionary should address himself. The development of a great world press with common ideas and a common aim, and the development of an intercommunicating network of police forces throughout the world, animated by a common conception of security for life, property, movement and thought, constitute the two main practical activities to which those who wish to secure the metamorphosis of social life should devote their attention, their energy, their ambitions and their resources. An International Court between nations is all very well in its way, but far more penetrating and significant would be the organisation at Geneva or elsewhere of a central police bureau to co-ordinate the protection of life, property and freedom throughout the world without distinction of persons under a universally accepted code.

## 12 – *Race Fantasies*

There is a vast amount of racial prejudice in the world, and perhaps I am disposed to undervalue its importance as a force antagonistic to the development of a world republic. I am fairly alive to small differences and with quickly roused racial feelings, but though they affect my personal relationships in all sorts of ways, I do not find they are any encumbrance to social and business co-operation and interchange. It is quite plain to me that there are, for example, subtle differences between the reactions of Clissolds as a class and of Romers as a class to the same circumstances, and it is amusing to observe them and play with them and natural, a natural extension of one's self-love, to arrange a scale of values in which these differences are so estimated as to count in favour of the Clissolds. But my affairs have brought me into contact with most sorts of European transplanted to America, with Indian iron-masters and Chinese and Japanese business men in some variety, and while everywhere there were differences, differences in quality that were almost always exaggerated by differences in culture and training, nowhere did I find anything that could be considered an insurmountable barrier against their common citizenship in a world republic. The negro is the hardest case. But the negro has hardly ever had a dog's chance of getting civilised in considerable numbers, and yet his race has produced brilliant musicians, writers and men of scientific distinction. In the eighteenth century he was the backbone of the British navy. I refuse to consider even the black patches of the world as a gangrene in the body of mankind or shut any kind of men out of a possible citizenship.

It is foolish to deny the variety of human types. There are strains with an earlier maturity, a shorter span of years, quicker, more vivid sensibilities, less inhibitory, less enduring. There are heavier and slower strains. There may be a great range of susceptibility to particular shocks and diseases and stresses. I doubt if there is any strain at all that can be picked out and isolated and described as being an all round inferior stain. At the utmost I will concede that some strains may give a larger proportion of feeble and inassimilable individuals. I do not see why all of these varieties should not mingle and play different parts according to their quality.

The great society of the future will call for a large range of special aptitudes. Uniformity to type is impossible in it. There is already a natural segregation of the extremer types. They are subtly adapted to particular rôles or to special climatic conditions. You might pour Cingalese by the shipload into Norway or Highlanders into the Congo forests; in a few centuries you would look for their type in vain. However much humanity is stirred together, however much it interbreeds, I see no end to its variety so long as its opportunities vary. Some types may disappear but new ones will appear to replace them. The pattern of the kaleidoscope may change but there will always be a pattern. A time may come when we shall talk no longer of a man's race but of his temperamental type. But the number of temperamental types will have increased rather than diminished. As the world republic develops there will be a general lengthening of life and a longer phase of fully adult living, but every race may reveal its own distinctive possibilities of ripeness.

This book is to give one man's vision of this world; it is not a controversial book, and I do not propose to write any formal reply to the many preposterous volumes of incitement to race jealousy and conflict that have been published in the last few years, books about the Yellow Peril, the Rising Tide of Colour, the Passing of the Great Race, and so forth. Even the titles are banners and aggressions. Most of them impress me as the counterparts in ethnology to the profound historical researches of Mrs Nesta Webster. There are scarcely the shadows of facts to correspond. I was sufficiently concerned about this suggestion a few years ago to give some time to ethnological realities. There has never been any Great Race, but a continual integration, dispersal, and even reintegration of active peoples drawn from the most diverse sources, and there is hardly a people which has not contributed some important release or achievement to the common progress.

Race trouble there is no doubt in very many regions of the world, but it may be questioned whether anywhere it is a trouble that arises entirely out of differences of race. Let us examine the conditions under which these conflicts have arisen. In no cases do racial stresses appear to be more powerful than the economic with which they are mingled.

The immediate result of the change of range and scale that has been going on since the ocean-going ship appeared, has been to bring together or to bring into vigorous reaction peoples once widely and securely separated, and almost always there have been profound differences in the culture and in the phase of social development of the peoples thus flung together. The western Europeans had the leadership in the new phase, a leadership given to them quite as much by geographical accident as by blood – for so level were east and west in material attainments five hundred years ago that it was practically a toss-up whether America should be discovered and settled by Chinese and Japanese junks or by European ships. The lead fell to the Europeans, and in America and Africa and the East Indies they blundered both upon vast regions for material exploitation and also upon populations sufficiently backward and helpless to be exploited in that work. The negro, as the extreme example, was needed as a slave and he was taken as a slave, and the interests of the whites came to help their prejudice in damning him to a natural inferiority. There have been the most powerful inducements for the spreading European to believe and to behave in accordance with the belief that the brown, yellow and black peoples upon whom his good fortune had thrust him were unteachable or weak-willed or ill-disposed or perverse, and fit only for a servile relationship to a profit-making master. The disadvantages that came from illiteracy and inexperience and inferior and antiquated traditions, are so indistinguishable from innate disadvantages, that the testimony against the exotic peoples was as ease to produce as it is difficult to confute.

Today we are still in the midst of this unequal struggle. The means of getting at the backward populations are still increasing their efficiency, the large scale handling of things, mass and plantation production, are still spreading, and the scientifically constructed state still lags in its attempts to overtake the headlong rapacity of its Crests, to whom its science has given weapons and wings. The methods of the modern order develop too slowly for the old traditions that possess men's imaginations. The Crests are for unskilled mass labour today, for serfdom and for slavery, just as firmly as the first Pharaohs, and as they once grabbed our coal and ore and turned our factories into hells for children and our industrial regions into slums, so now – as our own people have developed resistance and our industries have modernised their methods – they have spread their grasp wherever a less recalcitrant population seemed accessible to them.

Through all this picture I have been giving of my world as a developing economic and social system, runs the idea that in the process of change of scale that is going on now, there are two almost distinct strands, one unprecedented and one a repetition of a former human experience. The latter repeats the expropriation of small freemen and the concentration of wealth and economic power that made and then destroyed Imperial Rome. The former is something that men have never known before, it is the progressive organisation of a scientific conservation and exploitation of natural resources on a world scale, for the common ends of mankind. This is Brahma taking the sceptre from Vishnu. It means a new type of industry; a supersession of human toil by machinery whenever it is merely toil, the progressive abolition of the ignorant and unskilled human being and the progressive development of skilled and mentally participating workers. Wherever it goes, it seeks to sanitate, train, educate and reform. Its dearest, most cherished factor, is its labour. In the old system, labour was the cheapest, universal driving power under hunger and the whip. I have already drawn a contrast between our works at Downs-Peabody and the Crest Collieries. You may find that contrast running through all the industrial and agricultural developments of the world today and see the two systems everywhere fighting a still very uncertain battle.

The earlier system which arose from the first exploitation of the change of scale under the burthen of the old traditions, obsessed with the idea that an unlimited supply of labour, as nearly animal as possible, was a necessary condition to its progress, resisted education, resisted all organisation of its workers, underpaid them and did not protect them from the rapacity of adulterating retailers, sub-landlords and every sort of middlemen; it produced slums at every industrial centre, and it created swamps of agricultural labourers at the pauper level, slaves or peons, wherever it set up its plantations. The creative industrialism of today, demanding as it does a high type of labour and as much participation as possible, has no more use for slums and a reserve of unemployed than it has for ghettos or slave ships. It is not that it is humanitarian but that it looks further and works cleaner. But it is only winning its way slowly to the control of the world's economic life, and what is effectively ascendant in the processes of production and distribution today remains the scrambling, crowding, profit-seeking, unorganised competitive tradition that was developed in the eighteenth and nineteenth centuries. Its methods were evolved in western Europe, and they have extended throughout the world.

Now these broad facts need to be borne in mind when the question of contemporary race conflicts is considered. There has been modernisation everywhere, but it has not brought up the regions that were backward a century ago to a level with the still rapidly changing modern states. While in the Atlantic countries the slum phase is past its maximum, the once autonomous life of Asiatic and African countries is, with improving communications, being invaded and drawn into world-trading relationships and repeating the story of western Europe.

A large part of the brown, yellow and black population of the world is arriving now at a phase of economic development from which our Anglo-Saxon worker is gradually and with intermittent set-backs emerging. The baser factory industries emigrate to Asia. The east end of the world wins the empire of cheap and nasty from the east and of London. A universal characteristic of every population as it parts from its old economic and social balances and begins to eat bought and imported food and work regularly and uninterestingly for remote and unknown customers, is a vast, dingy proliferation. That happened in England. But it has ceased there. It is happening now over great areas of the world.

Not only do real and dreadful slums of the same type as those of middle nineteenth-century England appear in the great Indian and Chinese towns, but there is – what one might call a general "slumification" of entire populations. Their original economic and social balances are destroyed by an influx of new commodities and new employments. They become politically protected from warfare and raids. They lose native control over their best lands. The essence of a "slum" it seems to me is this; that it is a portion of population dependent on economic processes over which it has no control, fed so that it proliferates; it is the breeding of low-grade, uneducated employed. A Kaffir kraal, an Egyptian cotton-growing village, the Chinese quarter of a treaty town, an Italian township near some workable deposit of chemicals, may be as much of a slum now as a Lancashire cotton town or a black country district was in 1840.

The statistical aspects of this slum phase are extremely terrifying to all that sort of people who can be terrified by statistics. But indeed there is no reason for their terrors. Their "rising tide of colour," and so forth, is this natural and inevitable concomitant of the delocalisation of the economic life of the lands of "colour." Populations that have been at a kind of balance for centuries, multiply, add ten or fifteen per cent at every census. This does not mean any sort of biological success for the new peoples it is affecting. The new base population masses are at too low a grade of adaptability for effective settlement abroad. At the utmost they may transfer to congenial slums elsewhere where the sweating is a little better. Only in alarmist computations can they be considered capable of war. This "tide of colour" may rise in its own tanks to even tormenting pressures, but it will never overflow very extensively. And it is a tide that will ebb as the economic planet passes on to its next phase.

It is remarkable what intelligent people can be infected by these suggestions that we are all going to be turned black presently – or at any rate a dark chocolate – by these adverse birth-rates in the oriental and semi-tropical slums. They begin to fret about number and fret more and more. They are seized with a passionate advocacy of counter procreation. They write of books exhorting the "white" peoples to up and have a fearful lot of children. Nothing else they feel and declare will save us from colouring up like so many meerschaum pipes. We are to launch babe against babe. We are to smite the foeman with our loins and smite and smite again. I shall not be surprised to hear of exhortations to the quiet folk who listen in to the broadcasters. "*Think!* Seven little negroes and ten Chinese have been born in the last quarter of an hour. We are able to transmit the squeals of the last. Wa-a-a-a. A warning! Oh, good! Good news to hand! – Triplets in Bermondsey, *all* white, and twins at Salisbury. Good women! England expects – "

I cannot respond to this clamour for children.

It does not alarm me in the least that the English birth-rate for 1925 is the lowest on record. With a million and a half unemployed in England, I wish it could be lower. I hope it will be. I hope the time is not far off when every child born in England will be born because its parents fully meant it to be born and because they wanted it and meant to rear it. A time will come when all the world will have passed through and out of this slum phase in the development of a large scale economic life, and when birth control will be universal.

Birth control is indeed essential – nay, more, it is fundamental – to the conception of a new phase of human life that the world republic will inaugurate. I would make birth control my test of orthodoxy between liberalism and reaction. All who are for birth control are with me and essentially for the new world; all who are against it are against the progressive revolution.

Birth control embodies in the most intimate and vivid form, the essential differentiation of the newer conception of life from the old. The old was based upon the idea of a meticulous Providence. It not only took chances at every turn, but it found a kind of superstitious delight in taking chances. It was always expecting Providence to rig the game in favour of good intentions. It retained this childish attitude throughout life. Do what you are told to do, submit, make no attempts to control consequences; its spirit lay in such injunctions, and if it was so far inconsistent and illogical as to struggle against competitors and rivals, to promote wars and grip possessions, it always defended its inconsistency by a surprised assertion that in these things it obeyed the way of Nature and the Will of God. But the new idea of life admits no limit to man's attempt to control his destinies. It plans as largely as it can; it would plan more largely if it could; it gathers together every available force to free man from accident and necessity and make him master of the universe in which he finds himself.

I cannot conceive a world republic existing and continuing unless that automatic increase of population which follows every increment in the food supply is restrained, and it can only be restrained by a worldwide knowledge and universal acceptability of the methods and means of birth control. The material gains of the nineteenth century were largely swallowed up by the disorganised increase in population. Given sufficient wisdom to control that, and these nightmares of civilisation suffocating under the multiplicity of its darker and baser offspring, dissolve into nothingness.

No variety of the human species has any overwhelming and uncontrollable desire for offspring as such; that old Crone Nature has never yet given the desires of sex so long a range of vision; and as the standard of living and the multiplicity of interests increase, there are no sort of people anywhere who will not welcome the freedoms and the relief from burthensome families that birth control affords. The love and pride of children will ensure the sufficient continuation of the race. But that very love and pride is opposed to the swarming ill-conducted household under an exhausted mother that is the characteristic slum home. The most philoprogenitive would surely rather breed three masters than a dozen slaves.

When we find a race or a people alleged to have an overwhelming desire for children as children, it will be found almost always that they are living under conditions which render possible the early utilisation of these children, who are sent into the fields or sent out to work or sold for servitude and outrage – before childhood is fairly at an end. These simple-hearted folk, you will find, are breeding themselves, as well as their chickens and pigs, for profit. It is easy to cite the Bombay Hindu as a man who will recoil from birth control with a noble, a religious, an instinctive horror, but he is easier to understand when one learns that he may have two or three wives, get children by all of them, send wives and all the children as soon as they are toddling into the cotton mills and fill his paunch with their combined pay. But shut these mills to little children and married women, brace up his social and educational responsibilities, and you will find his ideas about the family westernising at a headlong pace. In a little while he will be another Hindu gone over, as they say, to "western materialism," and you will find him studying birth control advertisements in his native press as eagerly as he studies the offers of nerve tonics and cures for impotence that now adorn these publications.

I do not want to minimise the grave dangers of the slum strata, these pockets and mines and veins of slum matter, that are so widespread now on our changing planet. But they do not threaten us with great racial conflicts, wars of white against yellow, gigantic all-black insurrections or the like. And they are not to be cured by countervailing domestic activity that will distend every respectable "white" home with babies and send back the whites to insanitary medievalism. What these great "slumifications" my engender is a delaying and destructive malaria of ignorance and misconception, a fever of violent politics.

The remedy is not more white babies, but more civilisation. It lies in the hands of the men of worldwide business interests and great financial power. They and they alone can exercise a sufficient directive force to hurry the economic development of the more dangerous lands past the festering phase. It is they alone who can arm or disarm, corrupt or control. With them resides the possibility of a concerted breaking down of the fantastic barriers to trade, transport and intercommunication that now protect backward, wasteful, misplaced and slum-creating forms of employment. No other sort of men can do that, but only big business men. They can strengthen the hands of the labour intellectuals and enforce their demand for a rising minimum standard of living throughout the planet. With a rising standard of comfort the springs that feed these dank dangerous marshes of low-grade breeding will dry up, because whenever comfort rises, the birth-rate falls. And it is the big business men who can and who should subsidise and stimulate liberal education everywhere. They can loosen restrictions on press and publication in these matters, with an effectiveness peculiar to their position of advantage. Everywhere they can make aids and assistance conditional upon open windows and unrestricted light. Their moral influence can be enormous. Even now it can be enormous, and as their recognition of their responsibilities grows, as the Open Conspiracy realises itself, it will become the guiding power in world affairs.

And as the world republic dawns into economic being, this literature of race panic and breeding scares that now gives such grave concern to so many unsoundly informed people, will seem more and more preposterous and curious.

## 13 – *Antiquity of Youth*

There has been a fashion lately of flattering the young. The young have been told that they are the hope of the earth and that their naïve instincts are better than all the painfully acquired wisdom of mankind. But to be young is not necessarily to be new. All immaturity is by its very nature a throw-back. The gill arches of a human embryo recall the Cambrian period and are the roundabout way of nature to a jawbone that one would be glad to have developed more directly, and to earbones one could have wished better designed. The infantile mind recapitulates the successive suppressions of the ape and the savage. The adolescent young man or woman is a barbarian by nature, ready to revive, eager to revive, all the tawdry romanticism that we adults are clearing away. Young people are not conservative perhaps, but they are instinctively reactionary.

Since the war we have been much oppressed by the generation that grew up and missed it. They grew up while their fathers and elder brothers were away and for many of them the spanking hand, the reproving voice, never returned. It has seemed to many of this raw stratum that it was their business to take control of the earth. But their proper business is to learn something about the earth.

Adolescent mentality has had an opportunity to display itself since the war, as it has never had before in the whole history of mankind, and everywhere it has shown itself the same thing, violent, intolerant, emotional, dramatic, stupid and blind to all the vaster intimations of the catastrophe. Everywhere it has rushed to follow extremist leaders and to follow them with a fierce devotion. The Communist Party in Moscow is substantially youthful, and its devotees in Europe and America are rarely over thirty. The fascist nuisance is its natural counterpart.

The mind of youth is a medieval mind. It takes us back to the age of persecution, to the age of theology and urgent fear. Life crowds upon the young with an effect of intense impatience; all the decisions youth makes seem to its inexperience to be conclusive decisions. It snatches at guiding principles and defends them dogmatically. Youth like an undisciplined army dare not risk manoeuvre or retreat for fear of a panic. It seeks to silence and kill criticisms – not because it believes intensely but because it fears that it will not believe. Its violence veils a profound intellectual cowardice, the dread of a phase of indecision, the horror of being left at loose ends.

Few minds are mature enough and stout enough before thirty to achieve a genuine originality. The originality of the young is for the most part merely a childish reversal of established things. The independence of the young is commonly no more than a primitive resistance to instruction. The youthful revolutionary is merely insubordinate and his extremist radicalism an attempt to return to archaic conditions, to naturalism, indiscipline, waste and dirt. The youthful anti-revolutionary turns back to mystical loyalties and romance.

### 14 – *Supersession of Schoolmasters*

It is necessary to educate the young for the new order. But that everyone should be educated does not mean that everyone is to go to school or that schools are to be enlarged and multiplied. People are too apt to identify schools and education. Never was there a more mischievous error. Schools may merely fix and intensify those adolescent qualities it is the business of education to correct.

My distant cousin Wells has written frequently and abundantly of the supreme necessity of education, of that race he detects in human affairs between "education and catastrophe." I agree about the urgency of the need for education, but I doubt if he has sufficiently separated the idea of education from the idea of schoolmastering. He was, I believe, for some years at an impressionable age, a schoolmaster, and he had shown a pathetic disposition during a large part of his life to follow schoolmasters about and ask them to be more so, but different. His actions have belied his words. He was indeed so much of an educator that quite early he found it imperative to abandon schoolmastering. He produced encyclopaedic schemes and curricula that no schoolmaster would or could undertake. He wrote a text-book of history that shocked the scholastic mind beyond measure. Finally he settle down to a sort of propaganda of Sanderson of Oundle, whose chief claim to immortality is that there never was a man in control of a public school so little like a schoolmaster.

Dickon discovered Oundle, and both Dick and William spent their school years there, and in my capacity of uncle I met Sanderson quite a number of times. We two had just missed meeting him thirty odd years before. He must have come to Dulwich as science master a year or so after we had gone on to South Kensington. But what a schoolmaster! His methods were passionately anti-scholastic. The answer to the riddle, "When is a school not a school?" used to be, "When it is Oundle." He was trying to make his school a factory, a laboratory for agricultural biology, a museum, an institute for the preparation of reports upon everything under the sun, a musical and dramatic society. He would get explorers, investigators, industrial leaders, to come and freshen the scholastic air by talking to his boys. His enemies said he let down the games, let down the scholarship of the place. I believe he did. It is not least among his claims to honour. He made it as nearly an educational institution as any English public school has ever been. The games and grammar prig was at a discount at Oundle all through Sanderson's time.

Dickon was greatly taken by Sanderson; even physically they had something in common. They were both ruddy ample men with a spice of rhetoric in their composition. But Sanderson was always rather out of condition, fattish, with a shortness of breath that should have warned his friends of the heart weakness that snapped him off from life in mid-activity. He spoke with a pant in his voice and in broken sentences, and there was a faint remote echo of Northumbria in his intonations.

The school, he said, should be a model of the world – not of the world as it is but of the world as it ought to be. It had to send out boys prepared for adult life, ready to take hold of affairs. So he did his utmost to bring reality to them; he filled his place with machines and models of mines, with charts of trade and production. He sent batches of boys to factories and collieries, to live among the workers for a week or so. He put up a building which he called the Temple of Vision with money he got from Sir Alfred Yarrow, and he was going to fill it, he told me, with charts and exhibits to display the whole story of human achievement from its very beginnings to the present time. It was quite empty when I saw it, a little while before his death, and I believe it is empty still, but as he stood amidst its echoing bareness and expounded it to me, I saw plainly a vision of that soul of creative industrialism he was trying to evoke. He died before any of his wider plans materialised. His greater Oundle was never more than a project, and the big, prosperous and liberal school he left behind him reverts to the normal conditions of an English public school. The games and the "scholarship" have been restored; the novelties cut out; the Yarrow Memorial has never become a Temple of Vision. My nephews, I think, were lucky indeed to have fallen into Sanderson's time and have him as their master; they liked him enormously, not with awe but with a great affection; William particularly was his loyal friend.

When one met and talked with Sanderson it was possible to believe, as my cousin Wells believed, that there could be a mighty reconstruction of the life of England and the world, through schools, through an expansion and glorification of public schools. One saw for a dazzling interlude, England all dotted with Oundles, each with its biological laboratory in contact with agriculture, its workshops in contact with industry, its youngsters alive to the realities of the life of the community. One saw a new generation of young Englishmen, broad-minded, helpful, generous-spirited, capable, technically equipped, going out into the world, servants and masters of the republic of mankind. The fallacy of that hope lay in the fact that from the scholastic point of view Sanderson was a complete abnormality. There were no other schoolmasters like him, and there are not likely to be any. He was the antithesis of a public schoolmaster; a complete "outsider," in the opinion of most of his fellow heads, a lamentable, scandalous incident that had happened to a small, respectable grammar school.

You need only consult the nearest secondary schoolmaster to verify the statement. To ask such a one about Sanderson is like asking a "fully qualified," dull and dangerous general practitioner about that famous osteopath, Sir Herbert Barker, and his forty thousand forbidden cures. "*Oow!* – Sanderson? That Oundle fellow!" The man goes green. His nostrils twitch into a sneer. He intimates with an unreal gentleness that you know very little of schoolmastering if you think Sanderson is a schoolmaster; "very very little." And under encouragement he develops his case.

Sanderson was originally an *elementary* teacher, not a real schoolmaster at all. He went to Cambridge on a special scholarship – *late*. His religious orthodoxy was more than doubtful. He had radical views. His patriotism was uncertain. His mathematical teaching was eccentric. Moreover, he did nothing new, and whatever he did new was done better, elsewhere. "By men who don't advertise, y'know." And – "he let down the games and all that!" He was good at squeezing money out of his governors, of course. Had his points, no doubt.

So the secondary schoolmaster.

This idea that Sanderson in his later years entertained and expanded to the Rotary Clubs and to Weir and Yarrow and Bledisole and my cousin and all and sundry, this idea that we might start a new way for life, a new phase of civilisation in the schools, that we might make them models of the world as it ought to be, forecasts of and training places for new achievements in civilisation, is vitiated by just this one little flaw: that the last human beings in the world in whom you are likely to find a spark of creative energy or a touch of imaginative vigour are the masters and mistresses of upper middle-class schools. I say of upper-class schools because the origins and quality of the teachers in the popular schools of Europe make them psychologically an entirely different species. But these schoolmasters and schoolmistresses, as distinguished from teachers, to whom we entrust the sons and daughters of nearly all the owning and directing people of our world, are by necessity orthodox, conformist, genteel people of an infinite discretion and an invincible formality. Essentially they are a class of refugees from the novelties and strains and adventures of life. I do not see how as a class they can ever be anything else.

In the past there was nothing paradoxical in the fact that schools were conservative social organs. They were established not to innovate but restrain, to transmit a rule, a ritual, conventions of writing, speech and computation, to priestly neophytes, to prospective rulers. The less they changed, the better they observed the spirit of their foundation. So far as my casual knowledge goes, the idea of a *progressive* school dawned only after the onset of the New Learning at the Renaissance. Even then I doubt if the idea of the idea of progress actually entering the schools can be traced. The new schools were to teach Greek and open the world of liberal thought as the man left the school and went on into life. Greek was the key to a liberal and creative culture; but the school handed over the key rather than opened the door. The highest virtue of the school was still precision; with blows and exhortations it handed on a correct tradition of languages and calculation, and presumed but little beyond.

Larger pretensions on the part of the schoolmaster grew with the development of boarding-schools in the past three centuries. The Jesuit schools, which in accordance with Bacon's counsels, provided the pattern even in the most Protestant countries for the new schools of Europe, took boys right out of their homes for the most formative years in life. This no doubt did very much to break up the solidarity, the clannishness of families; but it substituted a new clannishness, loyalty to the school. Men became prouder of their schools than of their fathers. The pedagogue added the duties of a delegated parentage to his teaching. He set himself to character-building. The English public schools ran away with this pattern and became the extreme instance of the new development. In the nineteenth century their influence reached its zenith. By the middle of that century the prevalent Englishman abroad and in public affairs had become a type noticeably different from any other nationality. He had become stiff, arrogant, profoundly ignorant, technically honourable and utterly incomprehensible to the uninitiated rest of mankind. He was no longer the Englishman of the Elizabethan and Cromwellian model, half Kelt, half Viking; he was no longer any sort of man; he was a public schoolboy, the finished product. Amid the harsh realities of business he did not so much abound, and there and in art and literature one may still find the native Englishman, comparatively unwarped by schoolmastering. But the clue to the manifest change in character that Britain and its Empire have displayed during the last hundred years, the gradual lapses from a subtle and very real greatness and generosity, to imitative imperialism and solemn puerility is to be found, if not precisely upon the playing fields of Eton, in the mental and moral quality of the men who staff the public schools.

It was manifest to a man like Sanderson that the ruling and directive English of today had been *made* politically and socially by the public school. It seemed logical to him that if you turned the public school about towards creative things, you would in the same measure turn about the Empire and the drama of the world in which it still plays so large a part. But since he was a complete "outsider," as they said, to public-school life, since he picked his assistants very forcibly to suit himself and his own methods, it was natural for him to remain to the last blind to the inevitable characteristics of the men who would in general staff the boarding-schools of an upper class, wherever such boarding-schools came into existence, and their fantastic incompatibility with any such salvation of the world by schools as he projected.

The last time I was in England I had occasion to go to Dimbourne to put in a friendly word for my eldest grandson who is on the waiting list for that ancient foundation. It is not my wish that has sent him there. He has to go there because his father was a Dimbourne boy before him, and I am supposed to be influential because Walpole Stent, the next master under the Head – I forget for a moment his exact title – is my half-brother. He did not follow Dickon and myself to Dulwich and so come into the Sanderson orbit, because the Walpole Stents also had a Dimbourne tradition. He went to Dimbourne on some special terms reserved for the children of old Dimbournians and got a school scholarship for Oxford, achieved a moderate degree in Greats, and after various assistantships returned to the old place. There I found him and walked about the scattered school buildings with him, inspected the dormitories of his house, looked at some cricket, visited the wonderful old cloisters and the dreadful new War Memorial, all of white marble, and the arms of our allies and colonies and dependencies in gilt and colour, met his various colleagues and dined with the Head and refreshed my impressions of the directive forces at the heart of representative English manhood.

I had not seen him for a dozen years or more, and I was struck by his increasing resemblance to my departed stepfather. He bends his forehead forward now with just the same effect of pointless preoccupation that failed to win the respect of Dickon and myself forty odd years ago. I must be twelve or thirteen years older than he is; but I felt that of the two of us he was rather the senior. He seemed to realise that too. It came into my head suddenly when he greeted me that my father was a convicted felon and a suicide – a thing that had not troubled me in the least for a score of years. He seemed to feel that I was not quite worthy of Dimbourne, but that he would do his best to overlook that and be kind to me and make me understand the place. His voice is quite different from his father's. It is an acquired voice. At times it brays rather querulously. He pitches it up in the air and keeps it there, dominating you as no doubt it dominates a classroom. It seems to tire him. I do not remember my stepfather ever betraying fatigue in the use of his voice.

We sat in his study at night after I had been through the staff and the Head, and before I departed to sleep in the horrible parents' Inn, in the town. We talked as much like blood relations as possible. He has some traits of my mother in his chin and jaw and about his eyes. He tried to condescend but he had no courage. He speedily fell back upon the defensive offensive. At times sheer propitiation came to the surface. He knew I was the stronger animal and he left the conversational leads to me.

The room, like all scholastic studies I have ever seen, was lined with bookshelves. They reached up to about two-thirds of the height of the room, and above that against a dingy green wallpaper were various of those extraordinary violent black and white prints in which Piranesi guyed the monuments of Rome. All schoolmasters admire them. They exaggerate so heroically. There must be a perpetual copying and reprinting of these things to replenish the scholastic market. There were also two very large photographs of the Matterhorn which my intrepid half-brother has twice ascended, an ice-axe and some skis. And there was a cast, a very cheap cast, of the head of that statue of Antinous which is in a niche in the Vatican Museum. For some reason that is not perfectly clear to me it is associated with a memory of marshmallows growing in a marble basin. It is, I think, called the Belvedere Antinous, the one I mean with the downcast face. I remember the head as a very beautiful one, and I have seen many photographs and even copies of it that have recalled much of its loveliness, but this cast was a half-size cast, made from the work of some poor copyist, and it had, I reflected as the evening went on, much the same relationship to its fresh and gracious original that the erudition of a Greats scholar has to philosophy and the Greek spirit. That dulled reminiscence, that false claim to an intimacy never achieved, was so placed that it looked down on my half-brother as he sat and talked to me of the richness and wonder of the Dimbourne tradition. On the table was an untidy litter of papers, various books, a tobacco jar and pipes. My half-brother is a conscientious and systematic smoker, with a pipe for every day in the week. It is by his smoking and the mightiness of his pipes, by his cricket and by his feats among the classical mountains, that one knows him for a man.

I do not recall and I could not imitate our dialogue. I have already quoted him once, for it was he who called Sanderson "that Oundle fellow." I became curious to know how far he was still alive. I tried him over modern writers a little, rather carefully so as not to scare him. Shaw was "that crank who runs down Shakespeare"; Nietzsche was a madman of whom he could not "make head or tail"; Samuel Butler, William James, Maurice Baring, Philip Guedalla, Cunninghame Graham, James Joyce, James Branch Cabell, Christopher Morley, Sherwood Anderson, Mencken, Tchehov, Julian Huxley, Fairfield Osborne, Sir Arthur Evans, Jung, were among the names he had either never heard of or forgotten, but Freud, he knew, was "pigs' stuff." His phrase. He had caught two boys talking about Freud and "pulled them up pretty sharply." Anatole France he had heard of, but not read. That took my breath away.

"One can't keep pace with it all," he said wearily. "Luckily I don't have to buy for the school library. That falls to Gunbridge, and he tells me the difficulty of getting any modern books that a clean healthy boy may open without danger is – frightful."

W H Hudson, for some inexplicable reason, he supposed to have written a text-book of English literature. Sinclair Lewis, he thought, had "seduced poor George Eliot." Perhaps I was a little exacting about American writers, but I wanted to know what the young lions of a ruling class were likely to get from him about that really rather important country. So I tried him up and down the list. He knew absolutely nothing of any living American writer at all unless Professor Nicholas Murray Butler can be considered one; him he had met at some academic treat at Oxford. He spoke of the "poverty" of contemporary letters. "What wouldn't they give for our Newbolt or our Kipling?" he asked.

"You think there is no promise at all there?" I put in.

He shrugged his shoulders and grimaced. I pretended to understand.

I turned back to science and philosophy. Charles Darwin, he thought "rather blown upon nowadays." He had been "exposed a good deal," he understood, by the Abbé Mendl. Einstein for some occult reason, he said, "chopped logic." I would like to have pursued that, but I felt it might be unwise to press him too closely. Even as it was, he had become a little restive under my rather persistent soundings. "You have more time for reading than I have, I see," he expostulated suddenly. "Here the work is incessant – incessant. And when I have a holiday – well, I put a little worn volume of Catullus into my pocket. That suffices. Old-fashioned stuff, you will say. Old, old stuff. Yes, I admit it."

I note in passing that these rare holidays of his amount to almost three months in the year.

I felt he had managed his "get away" rather creditably. I did not pursue him further in that direction.

I got him to talk about the boys in the school. And the fathers and uncles – "and the mothers!" said my half-brother – who came respectfully and intermittently when the disciplines of the school permitted it. "Odd people we have now," he said. The waiting-list had never been longer. Business people from the Midlands were discovering Dimbourne, people with factories and so forth. "It's a good omen for the country," he said.

He had an air of forgetting that Dickon and I belonged to this lowly but opulent stratum. "We do what we can to civilise them," he said. "Some of the boys are quite jolly. But the fathers ask the most impossible things. Oh! One of them wanted us to take up Russian, and another was here only yesterday demanding a German master. I don't mean a man to teach German *inter alia*, I mean a real live Hun. Modern German. German without literature or history. So that they might *speak* it – like commercial travellers. And there's a working model of an ore crusher one of them has given us. It's in one of the corridors. A frightful thing for getting in the way. Near the Roman galley and the restoration of Jerusalem. One has to tide over that sort of thing. One has to parry. The mothers are fussy about health and warm baths and flowers on the dinner table, dreadfully fussy at times, but most of that falls on the matrons, thank Heaven! They are much more amenable about the curriculum – much more amenable. They seem to feel what we are really driving at, more than the men."

He was under way now and I found it less necessary to follow him up closely. I abstained from asking what he was really driving at. My eyes wandered to the bookshelves. There were hardly any real books at all. There were school books, dictionaries, Macaulay's History, Green's History of the English People, classical and Bible Encyclopaedias, Murray's Guide to Switzerland, school editions of the classics with notes, informative books on mountaineering and ski-ing and flyfishing and cricket. There was an annotated Shakespeare, the "Works" of Sir Walter Scott, the Valima Stevenson, various Kiplings, an odd volume of *Picturesque Europe*, something called *Rab and his Friends*, a book called *Friends in Council* – what could that have been? A stray Quaker volume? – a lot of dingy leather-bound books that looked like sermons and may have been bought to fill up. What on earth is the Badminton Library? There was a lot of it...

My attention reverted for a time to my half-brother. "I can say with a good deal of confidence, with considerable confidence in fact, that Dimbourne is one of the *cleanest* schools in England. It needs constant watchfulness...

"Send them to bed tired," said my half-brother thoughtfully, as he knocked out the ashes of his pipe upon the top bar of the grate. "Send them to bed tired."

So that was what he had got to. It was time I too was sent to bed tired.

I roused myself from a private meditation upon heredity. I had been thinking of the beach near Saint Raphaël – how many years was it ago? – and of a longer, leaner, but extremely similar Walpole Stent in knickerbockers, bowling and bowling to Dickon's hefty smacks, never by any chance getting him out, and all the while lecturing, helpfully, improvingly, confidently, on Dickon's way of holding his bat, which was wrong, which was all wrong. *Plonk*, and away went the ball for four. "You have a good eye," said my stepfather, "but it's all wrong; the knuckles of the left hand ought to be much more forward."

And from these memories I had strayed to questionings that touched my suppressed but incurable patriotic pride. Which of us represents "God's Englishman" – as Mr John Milton put it – most nearly? We Clissolds or these Walpole Stents – the wild English or the tame?

Whatever the answer to that may be, there is little doubt in my mind which of the two, Sanderson or Walpole Stent, is the representative schoolmaster, the schoolmaster with whom we creative people have to reckon. I do not see how it is possible in any country where there are great differences in class and where the schoolmasters are drawn from the middle and upper classes, that the average schoolmaster should ever be a much better thing than my half-brother. The whole crowd of upper-class youth has been picked over again and again before the schoolmasters come; the most vigorous and innovating men have gone in for diplomacy, the law, politics, the public services, science, literature, art, business, the hard adventure of life; and at last comes the residue. "Poor devil!" I once heard my nephew Dick say of a friend of his. "He's got a second-class. His people have no money. His games are pretty fair. He'll have to go into a school." A few public schoolmasters may have a vocation; the body of them, the substance of the profession, is that sort of residue. Its mentality is the mentality of residual men.

That is a neglected factor which has to be reckoned with in the history of the British Empire during the last hundred years. That is something the foreign observer has still to realise. A larger and larger proportion of its influential and directive men throughout this period have spent the most plastic years of their live under the influence of the least lively, least enterprising, most restrictive, most conservative and intricately self-protective types it was possible to find. We have bred our governing class mentally, as the backward Essex farmer bred his pigs, from the individuals that were no good for the open market. The intelligent foreigner complains that the Englishman abroad has been growing duller and stiffer in every generation. I offer up my half-brother, Walpole Stent, as the clue.

From quite early years this scholastic type has to develop a private system of compensatory false values. Life would be unendurable without it. These men of a secondary grade of vitality whose lot it is to figure in the rump of the first or second class in every examination and to go in to bat in the tail of the eleven, find their refuge in an ideal of modest worth, something richer, better and truer than flaunting success, something which is the real opposite of failure. Walpole Stent's phrase about Dimbourne cricket returns to me. "We always manage to put up a decent show." And he used another phrase, "We don't pretend to be miracle workers." It was an intimation that "miracle working" wasn't really in quite the best form. It was something you "pretended" to. The mathematical teaching at Dimbourne "does not claim to turn out calculating boys." But Dimbourne used to "cut a good figure" in the old Mathematical Tripos, and had a "decent" list of First, Second and Third Wranglers in that perverted test of unphilosophical discipline. Style, good form, is a great consolation for the impotent. Mr Shandy's bull, one remembers, was a master of style.

And another powerful word with Walpole Stent was "scholarly." The substance might be platitudinous, the argument inconclusive, the deductions wrong; those things were upon the knees of the gods; but one could at any rate be accurate upon minor points and polished, stylish, careful and allusive about the irrelevant. No examination ever discovered genius, intellectual power, and "all that sort of thing"; no examination is or can be a test for poverty of the imagination; and so the worthy man gets through "quite decently" and presently finds himself, in his armour of compensatory values, less thrust, it seems to him, than called, to domination over schoolboy minds. He has never been first before, but now in this world of school he is master, and he can make his compensations his standards. It is inevitable, it is without malice or compunction that he does so.

Inevitable he is conservative. He has abandoned free, novel and powerful things to bow himself to the existing state of affairs, and he resents the freedoms, enterprises and novel successes that reflect upon his own retractions. He becomes the quiet, inaggressive but obstinate champion of the old order against his bolder contemporaries. He desires their defeat because it involves his own justification. He will thwart where he can and deprecate always. But he loves to exalt the past, the classic, magnified past, the glory of the splendid dead – who are deader even than he. How can it be otherwise with him?

That is the stuff that must be in general control of the development of our youngsters so long as we are content to send them off to these boarding schools. No other stuff is available for such places, which by their very existence insist upon class distinctions and class traditions. And just as it is unavoidable that nine out of ten schoolmasters will be of this type, so also are certain reactions unavoidable upon the minds of the generations they will influence. They will not inspire, they will not compel, they will not stimulate nor evoke. If they had the quality to do that they would not be public schoolmasters. Catholic schoolmasters with the immense traditions of the Church behind them may try to shape boys to a preconceived pattern, but not the English public schoolmaster. His boys are too strong and well-connected for him to impose a type. His action is negative. He lets a type happen. His results lie not in what he imposes but in what he permits. He surrounds his boys with an atmosphere in which "good form" is better than great achievement. He infects with his habitual, his tacit, disparagement of exhaustive performance. Intensity or concentration of interest he marks as priggishness, as unhealthy, as presumption. New and stirring things are belittled – because if they are not belittled the humiliating question arises, "Why then are you not taking part in them?" Persistently the suggestion is conveyed to the boys that the great things of life are shams and only the little things are real. There is a fatal responsiveness in boys to such treatment.

Boys who will resist commands and prohibitions with the utmost vigour and persistence yield with extraordinary ease to a sneer. So he restrains the criticism of life; deflects attention from all strenuous issues towards formality and convention, in politics, in economic assumptions, in religion. For religion, the hushed voice, the averted mind. For sex, darkness. "Pigs' stuff." The world is full of things one does not do, one does not speak about.

And his teaching! The public schoolmaster is in temperamental sympathy with just that intractability, that hatred to being taught and changed which is natural to recalcitrant youth. He is the natural ally of the unenterprising boy against the boy who may make the pace too hard for the two of them. None of that at Dimbourne. He is doing nothing in the world but teaching, but how can one teach with any vigour unless one also does the thing one teaches and does it well? Who can teach mathematics who never deals with forms and quantities in real earnest, or a language if there is no attempt at expression? So he does not teach with vigour. He is bored and he bores. He bores apologetically. "You fellows do not like this stuff, nor do I. But it's the Right Thing to do it – in a certain fashion. It doesn't *mean* anything, of course, but the grind" – the *grind*, he calls it, "is good for you."

He flies from the classroom to the playing fields. There he has his strength as a man to exact a kind of respect for himself, from himself and the rest of them. "Well hit, Sir! *Oh! Well* hit!" One can forget one's contemporaries then who are struggling up to economic and political power, who are going about the great world outside, doing considerable things. There are some splendid moments after all for the schoolmaster. When his heart swells near to bursting for the dear old school. When he is popular about some petty issue, the Tuck Shop question or the Summer Camp, and the boys stand up and cheer. He composes himself to look modest and even a little ruffled. But how fresh, how honest is that schoolboy approval, bass and tenor and alto altogether! "Three cheers for Mr Walpole Stent. Hip. Hip. Hooray!"

These boys have an instinct. Many of these "painter fellows," these "much-belauded writers," these old scientific moles, never get such a cheer throughout their entire lives. Unless they come down to us for Speech Day and we incite the boys about them.

There is the real schoolmaster. I do not blame the man for being what he is, a retarding shadow upon the best youth of our country; he achieves his self-respect against great difficulties, and I would gladly leave him alone in his self-satisfaction if it were not for the manhood he arrests. But I do not see how we of the new order of things can be content to see our sons, our nephews, bright boys of every origin, every sort of boy who is to be given opportunity, the majority of our successors, left to his dwarfing restrictions for want of a better routine. So long as we pass our youth through the sieve of the public schools, we shall find them triturated down to his dimensions, and the "rank outsider" will still be needed to save us by his unimpaired initiatives. Dickon and I, like so many men in business and public affairs in England, are outsiders, but I do not hold a brief for the outsider as a class. They have faults all of their own, a huge carelessness, wastefulness, inco-ordination. Is not all this book about their faults? But at least they were not partially paralysed by growing up under the shadow of subconsciously futile men.

So there appears a third integral part of a creative revolution in my world, parallel with the gradual creation of a liberal world press, and equal in importance to the systematic replacement of militant ideals by police ideals: the development of a boldly conceived new education and a release of the main supply of our directive and progressive youth from the cramping influence of these establishments. All this sending apart of young people, out of our homes and affairs, to acquire an attitude of supercilious evasiveness towards living and progressive things, makes directly for stagnation and reaction. The best education for reality is contact with reality.

I can understand parents who live in an evil climate or lead disorderly lives or ply some disgraceful trade, sending their sons and daughters out of their surroundings into a better atmosphere, but not men and women pursuing active and influential careers, directing interesting industries, promoting important economic and social developments. I do not see how we can at one and the same time believe in ourselves and in the public schoolmasters. If our homes and business are not fit for our children to live through, it seems to me that a change in the spirit and direction of our home and business life is indicated. We should in that case mend our manners or our morals. If I had had sons I would have seen to it that they were first and foremost Clissolds and not "Dimbournians." I might have entrusted them to Sanderson at Oundle, but I know of no other school to which I would have delegated my paternity.

I would have us recover all this "formation of character" work, all the cultivation of taste, the interpretation of history and the establishment of standards of conduct and aim, out of the hands of these "upper-class" schoolmasters into which they have so largely drifted in Britain and western Europe and into which they seem to be drifting in America. And reduce these all too influential pedagogues to their original and proper function of the skilled teaching of specific things. If they proved – which is by no means certain – to be equal to the skilled teaching of specific things. We want skilled teachers badly, but the fewer schoolmasters we have the better. The world, and the social atmosphere it throws around us, is the final maker of all of us. When it was barbaric and dangerous, then there was some excuse for making little refuges and fostering places for civilised traditions and learning, under monastic sanctions. They gave a narrow and cramping education but it was better than none. Men like Saint Benedict and Cassiodorus, indeed, saved European learning, but that is no reason why we should go to Subiaco or the fastnesses of Monte Cassino now to learn to read and do sums. Now that the world grows safe and orderly and decent there is less and less justification for withdrawing young people from the general life in order to prepare them for that general life.

A good case is to be made out for the well-equipped, skilfully conducted, sociable kindergarten for a dozen or a score of children, against the home with only one or two. I do not think that childhood is the period when close contact between parent and child is most advisable. And since many of us now move about the world very freely and since social life increases in the variety of its relationship, there may be excellent reason for a great use and extension of schools of the "preparatory" type, as they call them in England, schools, often largely staffed by women, and not very big, where little fellows between seven and fifteen live a quasi-family life. But from fifteen onward the more directly a boy lives in contact with the real world the better alike for the real world and himself.

Then it is that the tradition of his family or the achievements of his parents may become of interest to him, and he may benefit by learning what these beings, so exceptionally like himself, think of life, and how they have dealt with it before him. By fourteen or fifteen special aptitudes should be apparent, and a boy should begin to work hard in some technical school according to his intentions and interests and quality. But if possible he should live at home. He should begin to see something of his father's life and his family business. There is a tremendous leap forward in the capacity of a boy's mind between fourteen and sixteen which the English public schools, retaining boys to eighteen or nineteen, do not recognise and help powerfully to arrest.

The boy's sister should be active upon parallel lines. They should both be reading widely, listening and talking freely in a community in which the boy will habitually encounter adult minds and girls and women, and the girl, men. They should go to special schools for special ends. Not even in these special schools should the boy meet Walpole Stent or sniff the wind of his frowsy study.

What will happen to Walpole Stent in a modernised world I do not know and I do not care. He might make a good timekeeper in a factory. The teachers of the modern specialist schools will not be the residuum of a social class, but specially equipped men of any social origin, and they will actually teach what they profess to teach. Their business will be what Sanderson called "tool sharpening"; mathematics, scientific processes, languages, and the only moral influence they will exert in their classrooms will be the best moral influence of all, the one our public schools most frequently omit, the example of work seriously and vigorously done.

When one turns either in England or in France from the old schools, the upper class schools with a long tradition, to the new popular schools for elementary instruction, sustained by the state, that have become numerous in the last century, one comes upon entirely different psychological processes. The two sorts of schools are different worlds. These latter schools were carefully planned to supply a certain necessary minimum of education to the working-classes without any disturbance of class relationships. They made no pretence of character forming; that they were given to understand from the first would be presumption; their business was to supply a carefully limited amount of instruction. They were designed to preserve a sense of inferiority in their pupils. Not even the residuum of the universities was cheap enough to staff them and a special sort of teacher was evolved, trained in a specially cheap and inferior college, or trained only by service under a trained assistant. These elementary teachers also were to be humble and industrious. They were to be pursued in their work by inspectors of a higher social class, and docked in their pay at any signs of slackening. So, without any serious rise in wages or loss of social discipline, it was hoped that a more intelligent type of workers would be bred. Even then, the dear old Victorians were astounded at their generosity in supplying these schools, and there was considerable repining at the idea of educating "other people's children."

But a better knowledge of psychology might have made our Victorians doubt the sustained subservience of these elementary teachers. In the main they were drawn from the working-class; they were the clever boys and girls who were not quite strong enough to be put to wages-earning early. They saw in the educational service a door to the life of an educated human being, and when they found themselves confronted by bars and barring prejudices to any ascent from the elementary schoolroom, when they realised the insufficiency of their pay for any cultivated way of living and the insulting cheapness of their educational opportunities, they displayed a certain resentment at the blessings conferred upon them. They were often individuals of considerable energy. While the secondary and upper-class teachers were essentially a residuum, these were essentially an élite. And drawn from a very numerous and hitherto untapped stratum. They had a vulgar energy. They refused to be suppressed. An expanding number struggled up to degrees in the new universities as external students. Many of them became, and many of them are, better teachers than the upper-class masters and mistresses. Many have clambered off into journalism, literature and all sorts of quasi-intellectual occupations. Many pass on into the upper-class schools, and infuse a new vigour into their classrooms. Sanderson for example. Few are as gracefully subservient as those who evoked them hoped they would be.

A lively social insubordination is as characteristic of the more intelligent trained elementary teacher as a discouraging conservatism is of his unskilled social superior. In England the elementary teachers supply a contingent to the Labour Party which brings in a disciplined mental vigour it might otherwise lack, and in France there would hardly be such a thing as a Communist party if it were not for the teachers. But in Britain elementary schoolmasters are to be found in all sorts of positions. There is quite a bunch of ex-elementary teachers in the House, and for example, G E Morgan, who practically runs our labour affairs at Downs-Peabody, was one. They constitute a very miscellaneous body in Great Britain; there is, I am told, a frightful fringe of barely qualified cheap teachers in the backward rural districts, but on the whole they are a new and increasingly important force in public life, and I am all for making them, and not the Walpole Stents, the backbone of the teaching profession of the future.

Above the elementary schools – which will run parallel for a time with our kindergartens and our excellent preparatory schools until these become good enough for us to dispense with any educational differences of class – we who possess the power of financial initiative can do much to develop the new system of special schools, studios and laboratories, for arts, sciences, languages and every sort of technical work. The style of work will be new. We want nothing of the classroom methods, the "prep," the recitations and all the other monkish devices the old schools have preserved. And it is to the sources that have given us the elementary teacher and not to the exhausted cadres of the universities that we must look for the staffing of these modern institutions with modern-spirited teachers. Even then it will be a teaching profession much more limited in its pretensions and much sounder in its work than is the schoolmaster, as prosperous English people know him today.

The reality of education for everyone over fourteen in a modern state lies more and more outside any classroom. The world grows more explicit every year. The finest minds in the world can speak now almost directly to everyone. A copious and growing literature about life and the direction of life makes the personal director unnecessary. The fewer the school-made values a boy has, the juster will be his apprehension of reality. So far as the general business of education goes, beyond mere special drillings and instructions, the need for schools dwindles to the vanishing point. So that I am rather an educational gaol-deliverer than a school reformer. I do not so much want to alter and improve the schoolmaster as induce him as gently as possible, and with the fullest recognition of his past services to mankind, to get out of the path of civilisation.

## 15 – *An Inquest on Universities*

I extend my scepticism about schools to universities, and particularly to what one might call the universities for juveniles like Oxford, Cambridge, Harvard and Yale, the annual cricket, boat-race, baseball and football universities, where every sort of intellectual activity is subordinated to a main business of attracting, boarding and amusing our adolescents. I think that we who deal with the world's affairs have been very negligent about the things that have been done to our sons and daughters in these institutions, and that we need to give them more attention than we have shown hitherto. In England they are not giving value for the money and respect they get – less even than public schools – and in America I have a suspicion they are worse even than in England.

My observations of these places are necessarily external. Dickon and I were under no sort of discipline during our student days in London; London University knows no proctors, and its undergraduates are as free in their private lives as errand boys. No tutors brood over their intellectual development; the London crowd scatters and absorbs them before they can develop consciousness of themselves as a class and a type. They never become aware of themselves as local colour and feel no consequent obligation to be sprightly and entertaining and characteristic. We took our university on the way to other things; we scarcely thought of it as a university; it stamped no pattern upon us.

My nephew Dick had two years at Oxford, and his career there was cut short by the war, so he too is no more than a partial witness. William refused stoutly to go either to Oxford or Cambridge. He said that he wanted to paint like a man from the start, and that at either place he would have to think and talk about painting and paint like a clever boy. When he was told that one went to a university to rub shoulders with one's fellows and exchange ideas, he said one exchanged nothing better than shibboleths. He thought he was quick-witted enough to pick up shibboleths as he went along without wasting three years upon their acquisition. When the advantages of meeting distinguished men were pointed out to him, he said first of all that dons were not as a class distinguished men, they were only men who had conferred distinctions upon one another, and secondly that in practice one never met them but only their "damned wives" at tea parties. The really distinguished men at Oxford and Cambridge were always "cutting up to London" at every possible opportunity, to get out of the "dried boy" atmosphere. One was much more likely to get talks with them in London. "Dried boys?" Interrogated on this remarkable phrase, William asked what else one could call them?

"And I shouldn't be able to stand the Rags," said William. "The Rags that are such a Delightful Feature of undergraduate life. The dressing-up and the oh! such fun! When the little bleaters started a rag I should want to go out and kill some of them."

So William, in accordance with the dictates of his savage Clissold heart, took up his abode in Chelsea, to prowl in studios and see men at work, to argue in the 1917 Club with all sorts of queer people, to write, to paint, to see all the new plays and pictures and dances so soon as they came out, to brood in museums and read voraciously, and to paint and again to paint.

I'm all on William's side. I believe that the day of Oxford and Cambridge as the main nuclei of the general education of a great empire, draws to an end. Since the war this has become very evident. These universities fail to do any adequate educational work upon the larger part of the youngsters who spend what are perhaps the cardinal years of their lives in their colleges. Only a minority do sound work. They do it against the current of opinion. Much of it they could do far better in closer touch with London or in any other habitable town. Both Oxford and Cambridge lie in low river valleys, the heavy air demands much time out of every day for exercise, and a vast industry of games has grown up to overshadow all intellectual activities. In spite of such exertions, there is a prevailing slackness. There is a tradition of irrelevance, which only the most resolute workers escape. Much time is given to "Rags," those industriously organised, toilsomely humorous interruptions of the leisurely routines of study. There is no effective supervision by the tutors who are supposed to guide the mental growth of the undergraduates, and a considerable number of these youngsters waste their time in little musical and dramatic societies that lead neither to musical nor to dramatic achievement, and in similar forms of amateurism. Such opportunities for frittering away time are endless.

Few of the dons are of a quality to grip the undergraduate imagination. Many of the most conspicuous seem to be wilful "Freaks" who set out to be talked about. Nowadays these dons seem more disposed to carry on the traditions of discouragement and suppression that dominate the great English public schools than to excite a new generation to vigorous thought and effort. Cambridge University earned an unenviable notoriety during the war by its treatment of Bertrand Russell, and it has recently done its best to dismiss a great biological teacher because he was co-respondent in a divorce suit. Oxford I see proposes to send down all youthful communists. By such tokens these places put the repressive training of the young above knowledge and freedom of thought.

I encounter a growing discontent with Oxford and Cambridge among many of my friends who have had undergraduate sons. I know three or four who have been bitterly disappointed in reasonable hopes. They send their boys trustfully and hopefully to these overrated centres. They find themselves confronted with pleasant, easy-going, evasive young men, up to nothing in particular and schooled out of faith, passion or ambition.

I think we must be prepared to cut out this three or four years holiday at Oxford or Cambridge, and their American compeers, from the lives of young men we hope to see playing leading parts in the affairs of the world. It is too grave a loss of time at a critical period; it establishes the defensive attitude too firmly in the face of the forcible needs of life. I offer no suggestions about the education of girls because I know very little about it, but the conviction has grown upon me in the last few years that as early as fifteen or sixteen a youth should be brought into contact with realities and kept in contact with realities from that age on. That does not mean that he will make an end of learning then, but only that henceforth he will go on learning – and continue learning for the rest of his life – in relation not to the "subjects" of a curriculum, but to the realities he is attacking. We are parting from the old delusion that learning is a mere phase in life. And all the antiquated nonsense of calling people bachelors and masters and doctors of arts and science, might very well go, with the gowns and hoods that recall some medical alchemist or inquisitor, to limbo. They mean nothing. There is no presumption that a man who has the diploma, or whatever they call it, of MA, is even a moderately educated man. The only good thing I have ever heard in defence of a university gown is that it is better than a tail coat for cleaning chalk off a blackboard. And even for that a pad of velvet is preferable.

One may argue that to clear out the colleges and disperse the crowds of spoilt and motiveless youth that now, under a pretence of some high and conclusive educational benefit, constitute the physical bulk of Oxford, Cambridge, Yale and Harvard, is not to put an end to universities; but the value of that argument depends upon the meaning we assign to the world university. No doubt the modern world requires an increasing number of institutions conducting research, gathering and presenting knowledge, affording opportunities for discussions and decisions between keenly interested men, working perpetually upon the perpetually renewed myriads of interrogations with which the intelligent adult faces existence; but are such institutions, without teaching pretensions, really universities in the commonly accepted sense of the world at all? A whole book might be written about the varying uses of that word. In one sense the Royal Society of London might be called a university, but it seems to me that in ordinary speech "university" conjures up first and foremost a vision of undergraduates engaged in graduation, a scene of caps and gowns, brightly coloured hoods and scarlet robes, of learned doctors who are supposed to have imparted their precious accumulations to the receptive youth at their feet, and of candidates, shaken and examined when full, certified to

"know all that there is to be knowed"

and sent into the world, in need of no further intellectual process for the rest of their lives except perhaps a little caulking. That is the current idea of a university, embalming the artless assumptions of an age that passes. It seems to me that age may very well take its universities with it – into history.

The new institutions, the research and post-graduate colleges if you cling to the word, will offer no general education at all, no graduation in arts or science or wisdom. The only students who will come to them will be young people who are specially attracted and who want to work in close relation as assistants, secretaries, special pupils, collateral investigators, with the devoted and distinguished men whose results are teaching all the world. These men will teach when they feel disposed to teach. They will write, they will communicate what they have to say by means of conferences and special demonstrations, and their utterance will be worldwide. There is no need whatever now for anyone to suffer and inflict an ordinary course of lectures again. The new institutions for the increase of knowledge will become the constituent ganglia of one single world university, and a special press and a literature of explanation and summary will make the general consequences of their activities accessible everywhere. The modern university, as Carlyle said long ago, is a university of books. So far as general education is concerned I agree entirely with that.

There it is that we to whom power is happening are still most negligent. It is not merely that we have great possibilities of endowment, we have also great opportunities of organisation. As the prestige of tradition and traditional institutions fades, an immense desire for knowledge and for new sustaining ideas spreads through the world. There are millions of people, half educated and uneducated, vividly aware that they are ill-informed and undirected, passionately eager to learn and to acquire a sense of purpose and validity. This new demand for information, for suggestion and inspiration, is perceptible now not only in the Atlantic communities but increasingly in India, in China, in Russia and in the Near East. We make no concerted effort to cope with it. We allow it to be exploited meanly for immediate profits, much absolute rubbish is fed to this great hunger, and still more adulterated food. This appetite, which should grow with what it feeds on, is thwarted and perverted.

It rests with us, the people with capital and enterprise, to treat this phase of opportunity with a better respect, to show a larger generosity in the promotion and distribution of publications, to use the great new possibilities of intellectual dissemination that arise worthily and fruitfully. The world university must be a great literature. We cannot have our able teachers wasting and wearying their voices any longer in the lecture theatres of provincial towns; we want them to speak to all the world. And it must be a literature made accessible by translation into every prevalent language. Each language and people will still produce its own literature, expressive of its own aesthetic spirit and developing its own distinctive possibilities, but the literature of ideas must be a worldwide literature sustaining one worldwide civilisation.

To this sustaining contemporary literature in its variety and abundance our young people of all classes must go for their general conception of life, and throughout all their subsequent lives they will follow it and react to it and develop mentally in relation to it. Such personal teaching of adolescents as will remain in the world will direct their attention to what is being written and said, and will advise and assist in study and selection. That in effect is the real upper education of today, that is how we are being kept alive as a thinking community now. Apart from the modicum of technical instruction they impart, the upper schools and universities of our world already betray themselves for an imposture, rather delaying, wasting and misleading good intentions, rather using their great prestige and influence in sustaining prejudice in favour of outworn institutions and traditions that endanger and dwarf human life, than in any real sense educating. They are the most powerful bulwarks necessarily and inseparably a part, a most vital and combative part, of that declining order which our revolution seeks to replace from the foundations upward.

Here as with monarchy and militant nationalism we do not need so much to attack as to disregard and neglect, to supersede and efface, through the steadfast development of a new world-wide organism of education and intercourse, press, books, encyclopaedias, organised translations, conferences, research institutions.

A time must come when Oxford and Cambridge will signify no more in the current intellectual life of the world than the monastery of Mount Athos or the lamaseries of Tibet do now, when their colleges will stand empty and clean for the amateur of architecture and the sight-seeing tourist.

Perhaps effigies wearing gowns and robes will be arranged in the Senate House to recall the quaint formalities of the ancient days. Or perhaps a residue of undivorced soundly orthodox and conservative dons will by that time have ossified into suitable effigies.

## 16 – *Liberalism as Simplification*

I have now sketched out the main lines of my hopes and sympathies in relation to the economic, social and political processes of my time. This book is primarily autobiographical and not a dissertation upon politics, and I tell of these things without detachment because they are a part of me, because they are the subject of a large proportion of my waking thoughts and determine my acts and the lay-out of my days more and more. This conception of an open conspiracy to realise the World Republic is the outline into which I fit most of my social activities. It is as much a part of me as my eyesight or my weight. I have tried to show not only the character of this outline, but how it has grown up in my mind.

This Fifth Book which now draws to its close – though I feel there is much that needs expansion in what I have set down – may be taken, I suggest, as a statement of twentieth-century liberalism. The statements of liberalism made in recent years, because of its entanglements with political factions and their transitory accommodations, have been formless and rhetorical, but liberalism is quite a definable thing, and I am by any possible definition a liberal type. I am as much a liberal as I am a Londoner or an industrialist or a Fellow of the Royal Society. It is a fundamental fact in any description of me.

Liberalism is essentially a product of the last two centuries and mainly of the last hundred years. It is an attempt to express in thought and social and political activities, the apprehension of urgent readjustments produced by the change in scale. It began therefore largely as a system of denials, as a repudiation of existing authority, of privilege, of dogma, of tradition. Its first profession was freedom; its first fruits upheaval. It found its natural exponents in the new social types in business men, in lawyers, in shipping people, in western industrialism. It talked republicanism. It sought help against established things among the excluded; it emancipated, it enfranchised. It stirred up subject peoples by "sympathising with their aspirations." From the first it was in conflict with national as well as social restrictions. It allied itself with the internationalism of Jewish finance. It evolved the idea of free trade.

In contact with things political it lost its way here and there. In Britain it was exploited by the Tory-spirited Gladstone, in France by Napoleon the Third. It was baffled by Trades Unionism. It could make nothing of, and it ought to have made a great deal of, this collateral synthetic process that was substituting a collective bargain for a chaotic scramble for work. Its advocacy of insurgent peoples made it presently a champion of nationalities and the instigator of pseudo-liberal nationalism in Germany and Italy. That pseudo-liberal nationalism has brought forward thorns of swords and bayonets and bitterly unattractive fruits. Moreover British liberalism became curiously imperialist at the end of its shipping lines, though even in India for a time it sought to educate and modernise, and promised to release. It got on in the world and made compromises with the Crests.

Already by the days of the Franco–German war of 1870, it had assumed something of its present loose amiable indeterminate cast of countenance; it was getting its Asquith face. But it still held stoutly to free trade, to popular education, to free speech, to the open mind in religion. It had unhappily pinned itself prematurely to an extreme freedom of private property, to the philosophy of Individualism, and it was perplexed when the socialists appeared with their idea of a large-scale non-competitive business organisation of society. They had got in front upon the constructive path by another route. In the subsequent controversies neither liberalism nor socialism succeeded in keeping more than a one-sided grasp upon the processes of economic and social developments. I have told how Dickon and I, typical adventurers of the new sort, typical cadets of the new scale, were puzzled in our student days by these conflicting statements. The history of our experiences and ideas, as I have spread it before the reader, is the history not merely of the struggle of our two minds but, in our two selves as samples, of the general practical intelligence of our generation, to get a comprehensive grip upon the main issues of our time.

This new statement of liberalism I am making here is the outcome. What we think, many other men, in business and public affairs, are beginning to think also. As I have written in an earlier section, individualism and socialism have reached a phase of coalescence and rephrasing. Political liberalism dies to be born again with firmer features and a clearer will.

It is remarkable how much of the liberalism of the middle nineteenth century is still living in our minds, in a fuller and more co-ordinated form. We two at least have returned to its republicanism and its cosmopolitanism. We realise ever more fully the fundamental importance of free speech, freedom of belief, freedom from barriers of privilege and adverse presumption. We can be bolder now in our cosmopolitanism because we have before our eyes a whole series of successful international experiments. We have a firmer apprehension of the means and methods by which the progressive transformation of human affairs towards the World Republic may be achieved. Our faith in progress has seventy years of added justification.

Essentially the project of modern liberalism is an immense simplification. For a century liberalism has been like the spirit of a young giant striving against almost intolerable bonds, bonds in which he was born and which cripple and threaten his growth and existence. Its main purpose it to clear away an infinitude of complications that trouble and waste life. It is creative by release, like the chisel of a sculptor. It sets its face against, and in the long turn it will overcome and efface the boundaries, the flags, the enforced and exaggerated separations that keep men from wholesome and brotherly co-operation round and about the world. It would smooth out every kink and every dark place in which greed, suspicion, cruelty and evil disposition can now find a purchase and operate and do harm to the human commonweal. To that end it would sweep away all the custom houses, passport requirements and all the barriers that far beyond nature's limitations cramp and confine human activities and human commerce upon this little planet. It would make the money and credit system of the world one; it would put the land and sea transport of the world under one control; it would watch over the production and distribution of staple needs everywhere. It would rationalise the property-money complex that holds us all together by scientific analysis and systematic law-making in accordance with that analysis. It would bring all men under a common law. It would recrystallise the political life of the world as a single economic and police directorate. It would remove crowns and courts and all the residue of the warring states of the past as a discreet surgeon will remove an appendix, because mischief lodges in these thing. And in the place of our little ancient secluded learning-places, in the place of knowledge given almost furtively by word of mouth, there would be a released education, a great common literature and universally accessible information, bringing all mankind into one understanding and a broad unanimity of will.

I have told how the conception of this simplification of human affairs grew up in my own mind, and what forces seem to me to drive towards it, making it not only possible but probable and necessary. I have painted my own mental and moral portrait against its only appropriate background, which is two hundred years of change of scale and the dawn of human unity. Believing in that progressive simplification and in the progress of man's spirit that will accompany it, I can take life serenely, I can find a purpose in my activities outside myself. This simplification, this clearing of the ground for a new beginning in the human adventure, makes effort seem worth while. But if now I lost the faith that has grown in me with my ripening, in the continuing power of these synthetic and creative processes, I confess that there would be little savour left for me in life. Without the idea of progress life is a corrupting marsh. If this present age is not an assembly for great beginnings, confused and crowded still but getting into order, then it is a fool's fair, noisy, tawdry, unsafe, dishonest, infectious. In spite of the strange light of beauty that falls at times upon it, in spite of incidental heroisms and relieving humours and the fun of first pushing one's way into it, it is a fool's fair, speedily wearying and at last repelling. The small insecure accumulations of science, the rare perfect art one finds in odd corners, unless they are to be recognised as mere intimations of greater things to come, are out of all measure insufficient to redeem so vast a futility. I should be glad to get out of the glare and turbulence of so unmeaning a spectacle, and I should not be particular what way I took back to nothingness and peace.

I have passed through deep moods of doubt and I am still not altogether immune to them. But these moods of doubt have always come in phases of fatigue, or when there was a great noise about me and when I was too close to things. It is disconcerting at times to read too many newspapers. They make life seem entirely a clamour of superficialities; they make it seem impossible that any men anywhere will ever think more than a week or so ahead in regard to public matters. There is only one newspaper that comforts my soul, and that is *Nature*. This place up here is good for retirement and thought, but there is a terrible infection of vacuity about the faces and bearing of all these well-to-do fellow countrymen who crowd Cannes and the front at Nice. When my business or some rare social occasion takes me down to these places, I have to resist the suggestion that within my brain I am perhaps a wild, fantastic, almost scandalous rebel, a "crank," a changeling, and that it would become me better as an Englishman of standing to put away Clementina privily and all these solicitudes for the republic of mankind, and to go down to Cannes and take up the quarters proper to my position, deport myself stiffly and carefully, talking about Suzanne and Miss Wills and polo and the fall of the franc and the severity of taxation in suitable terms, relaxing myself with bridge, and exercising myself with golf and elderly tennis until my time comes to an end. Instead of spending these days of sunshine and these nights of beauty in mental toil, in plotting, planning, writing and re-writing. Because, says the devil of that despondent mood, think I never so hard and work I never so well, these people will never understand, cannot understand; they will live and die, a mass against such solitary fretting sports as I, firmly sustaining all that I condemn and giving the lie to all my prophesying.

The other day I went to Marseilles, and as I sat with Clementina taking our coffee, after lunch, at a big café in the Cannebière and watched the active various crowd about me, each individually brighter than I, and all sanely intent upon little things, and all doing these little things so much better than I could do them, it came to me with overwhelming force that it was as reasonable to anticipate one planetary will from such beings as from a canful of small frogs in summer. I had some French newspaper in my hand telling me of the eighth or ninth failure of the petty inveterate political groups in Paris to pass a possible budget, and that the Treaty of Locarno, so recent, so hopeful, was already in effect moribund, poisoned by petty disputes about the entry of Germany into the League of Nations. That had set the key of my thoughts.

"Achieve!" said I. "They do not even desire. The republic of mankind is a dream."

But here in this secluded peaceful place and especially at night when everything is still, one can take a larger view, see things upon the scale of history, see the wide-sweeping radius of destiny tracing its onward path across the skies. Then change has a countenance of purpose, the World Republic like the stars seems close at hand, and it is the fashions of pose and occupation and the multifarious ends and conflicts of the hurrying eddying crowds that dissolve like the mists in the morning and take on the quality of a dream.

## 17 – *Fully Adult*

"But why should you care for a World Republic you will never see?" asks Clementina, who has set herself with a gathering tenacity to understand what I and this book are about.

"Why should the thought that men will never get to the World Republic make you unhappy when it does not seem to trouble you in the least that presently you must die?"

That is a fair question.

Why should I have become almost miserly with my days and hours in order to work for ends I can never live to see? Why do these things occupy and compel me so that I forget myself? Why do I not simply take the means of pleasure that I possess now so abundantly and "enjoy myself"?

The answer to that runs like a thread through all this complex fabric of observation and reasoning and suggestion that I have been weaving. It is that I have grown up.

I have become fully adult in a world in which as yet most human beings do not press on to a complete realisation of their adult possibilities. It has happened to me to do so not because there is anything very exceptional in my quality but because my circumstances and experiences have prevented my accepting and settling down to interpretations and routines that are satisfactory enough to delay and stop the development of the generality of people. I missed those public-school and university disciplines which arrest the development of so many of the fortunate minority at a puerile stage, I escaped from that employment by other people which robs the grater majority of its opportunities for full growth, I did not chance to marry happily and settle down to that family life which becomes as it were a plateau of cessation for those who live it. I was never so engaged and interested at any stage by the details of life as to forget my interest in life as a whole. I went on moving mentally when most other people, according to the customs and necessities of our world, were either sitting down of their own accord or being obliged to sit down. And thus left to the unchecked drive of the forces within me, I went on growing up.

I have grown at last altogether out of regarding myself as the prime concern of my life. I am no longer vitally impassioned by my own success or failure. I have done with my personal career as my chief occupation. That complete preoccupation with the feelings and deeds and pride and prospects of William Clissold with which I started has been modified by and has gradually given place to the wider demands of the racial adventure. That now grips me and possesses me. William Clissold dwindles to relative unimportance in my mind and "Man" arises and increases.

And though William Clissold, my narrow self, will surely die before any great portion of this present revolution can be achieved, yet just as surely will man, that greater self in which my narrow self is no more than a thought and a phase, survive. Insensibly I have come to think, to desire and act as Man, using the body and the powers of William Clissold that were once my whole self, as a medium. And while all that I do expressly and particularly for the pleasure, delight and profit of William Clissold ends, I perceive, and will presently to forgotten and its refuse put away in some grave, all that I think and attempt and do as man goes on towards a future that has no certain and definable end and that need not be defeated by death.

It is only by this conception of a slowly emergent fully adult phase of the human life cycle that I can explain the main facts of my own development, the gradual fading out of my childish intensities of hope and desire and fear, that were once as swift and fierce and transitory as the moods of an animal, the softening of my adolescent hardness of spirit, the wane of physical and worldly jealousies, the attainment of virtual indifference to happenings that once would have thrown me into furies of self-assertion, into despair of life or into the profoundest humiliation. And these things have fallen from me with no diminution of vitality but through the progressive establishment of a more disinterested system of passions that were at any earlier stage altogether outside the orbit of my concern. I have extended and become less self-centred, year by year. I care for myself less because I care more and more for the republic of mankind. There have been and are reversions to passion, to resentments and anger, to acute personal reference and spasmodic greed, but they become briefer, rarer and more completely amenable to the growing and releasing generosity of the wider reference. They become unreal and unimportant in relation to it.

And what has happened to me can happen to most people. It will begin to happen to many. My release from my excessive narrow self is not abnormal; it is only a little unusual at present to this extent. Most other people could be brought on past the stages of petty irrelevant occupations and habitual intense self-regard just as I have been. They all have occasional moods of larger interest. In a saner, juster, less meanly urgent world those moods would be sustained, multiplied, connected and made dominant.

In this present part of my book I have been stating this idea of a great revolution in the economics and politics and social relations of mankind, in the form of a project as wide as the earth. But it could also have been stated in another fashion, in an older fashion, in the form of a project as narrow and concentrated as a single heart. The attainment of the World Republic and the attainment of the fully adult life are the general and the particular aspects of one and the same reality. Each conditions the other. The former would release man from traditions, economic usages, social injustices, mental habits, encumbering institutions, needless subserviences and puerile interpretations, that dwarf, confuse and cripple his life upon this planet, that divide it, impoverish it, keep it in a continual danger from the wasting fever of war and threaten him with extinction. And the other would liberate the individual man from a servitude to instinctive motives, unreasonable obsessions and an embittering concentration upon personal ends that can have no other conclusion but age and enfeeblement, defeat, disappointment and death. In the service and salvation of the species lies the salvation of the individual. The individual forgets the doomed and defined personal story that possessed his immaturity, the story of mortality, and merges himself in the unending adventure of history and the deathless growth of the race.

That is my philosophy of conduct, my mysticism, if you will, my religion. That is my answer to Clementina's question. This is my final conception of my life as I live it, set in the frame of my world. To this fully adult state men and women are, I believe, finding their way through the glares and threats, the misstatements and absurdities, the violence, cruelties, tumults and perplexities of the present time. A few come to it now, doubtfully and each one alone, as I have done, but presently more will be coming to it. As they do, the path to the World Republic will open out and this new phase of human life become the common phase throughout our mounting race.

We shall put away childish things, childish extravagances of passion and nightmare fears. Our minds will live in a living world literature and exercise in living art; our science will grow incessantly and our power increase. Our planet will become like a workshop in a pleasant garden, and from it we shall look out with ever diminishing fear upon our heritage of space and time amidst the stars.

We shall be man in common and immortal in common, and each one of us will develop his individuality to the utmost, no longer as a separated and conflicting being but as a part and contribution to one continuing whole.

# Book Six

## Venus as Evening Star

## 1 – *Need of Adult Love*

This Sixth Book I shall dedicate to women, to the love and fellowship, distrusts and antagonisms of men and women. I have not yet done with my Fifth Book, but I shall leave that now for awhile until I can shape this Sixth Book out. A score of vast question have been started and left almost immediately in that Fifth Book; I must return to them later; but I am impatient, I do not know why, to see the completed form of my work before I deal with them further. The immense projection of a unified world civilisation is at any rate visible in Book Five as it stands. The great revolution is stated there.

But all such schemes are abstract and jejune until they are made real by the comprehension of women. Man comes from woman and returns to woman for confirmation and realisation. He may explore new worlds alone but he cannot settle, cannot establish himself, unless he bring his womankind.

My sense of the value of woman, my care for and interest in woman, has grown very greatly since I was a young man. I began with infantile dreams of abjection to women, these faded out in boyhood and gave place to indifference qualified by a hot unkindly lust. Desire tinged with antagonism was the quality of my adolescence. I had a considerable dread of losing my personal freedom. Imperceptibly a strongly suppressed craving for help and companionship escaped from its suppressions. Today, though I struggle against the admission, I find my mental serenity extraordinarily dependent upon the companionship of Clementina. If she were to vanish now this life here would collapse. I cannot estimate how great a tragedy that might not be for me.

I have known many women. I have known several of a masculine creativeness and vigour of self-assertion. Some of the main features of the modern view of life, the propaganda of the idea of birth control, for example, are largely woman's work. And yet I do not know how far this austere conception of life devoted to the establishment of a great deliberation in the place of the present impulsive confusions of the world, can count upon the support and service of women or how far they will be open antagonists or subtle opponents or passive, instinctive, or even unconscious obstructionists of the things we desire.

The revolutionary forces of today are at present operating through scattered individuals. It has been my argument that these forces cannot become efficient and consciously and securely dominant without the development of a social life to express and confirm them. What impresses me very greatly is that the active and creative men do not as a rule get into relationship with either actively creative women or with women who can be effective helpers and protectors and subordinates, and that, so far as I know, the much rarer women of creative and scientific quality remain single or are indifferently mated. They seem to think and speak in an idiom that is different and to have a different idiom of behaviour. This is not a complaint against the opposite sex – against either sex. It is rather a statement that these busy preoccupied men and women are careless in this relation, are taken unawares and do not know how to set about securing themselves against diversion and wastage. They are the critics and disturbers of the current world, and the current world, the habitual and accepted thing, protects itself and takes its unpremeditated revenge upon them by tying them up to demands, responses, exactions, obligations, conventions, recriminations, that distress, disorganise, disappoint, overstrain and help to defeat them.

I have much reason to be grateful to women, and I have a sense of ungraciousness in writing these doubts about them. But I cannot help but recognise the atmosphere of intensifying sexual antagonism in which we are living. One of the four women who have played large parts in my life sustains me loyally now; one would perhaps have become co-worker had she but had the strength left in her. But of the two others, one was a disloyal waster of my poor gifts, and the other a frank and open opponent, who in the end came to use her power over my emotions very ruthlessly. The story of my married life, brief, crude and vulgar, as I have told it, is yet very typical of the conflicts of the time. It is the common misunderstanding in gross and heavy detail.

I am dissatisfied with my sexual history and my dissatisfaction quickens my apprehension of the general uneasiness of the sexual world about me. A great majority of business men and active men of affairs I know are frittering their sexual interests away as I have done for most of my time, getting no use or companionship out of women in their essential lives, marrying wives elegantly aloof from their vital concerns, pedagogues and dons, practising small adulteries, having "affairs" with little dancers, chorus girls and a miscellany of such women. It is not what they want, if ever they stopped to ask themselves what they want on that side of life; it is what happens to them. No sort of woman is developed as yet to respect and look after them, and life has been too unexpected and crowded for them to be able to look after themselves.

I know that my insistence in this book upon a completely normal sexual life for an energetic man is a breach of literary decorum. I shall be called over-sexed, when indeed I am merely normally sexed and only abnormally outspoken. But our literary standards derive from schools and universities that have sheltered almost to the present day the dishonest and inwardly unclean chastity of medieval romanticism. We must, they rule it, either hide or titter. We must pretend we have no desires or only the very funniest desires, and that anyhow they do not matter in the least and have no significance whatever. I decline to follow these monkish usages and put a fig-leaf upon my account of myself, because once upon a time certain blushing prelates went round the Vatican Museum and started such wear for the classical statuary that had fallen into their hands. I do not believe that a normal man can go on living a full mental life in a state of sexual isolation. I refuse to entertain the idea that I should have accepted celibacy and devoted myself entirely to scientific work. On those questions our medical science is absurdly discreet and vague, and so I have to go upon observations that may be greatly deflected by my temperamental bias. My impression is that abstinence involves so large an amount of internal conflict, so urgent and continuous an effort of self-control, such moods and humiliations and compensatory adjustments, that the diversion of attention and the wastage of energy are far greater than the average disturbances and deflections of a normal life.

This is, I am convinced, as true for an ordinary woman as for an ordinary man. There may be exceptional types released from this issue altogether in some, to me, unimaginable fashion, and free to specialise vigorously in creative work. I know none, but it may be so. An unembarrassed abstinence is alleged to have been achieved by various religious mystics of great administrative power, Saint Theresa and Saint Dominic and Saint Ignatius Loyola for example. Such a release with unimpaired energy is against all biological presumptions, and the general tone of celibate priesthoods and devotional literature suggests not so much release to me as consuming negative obsession. For most of us sexual life is a necessity, and a necessity not merely as something urgent that has to be disposed of and got rid of by, for instance, incidental meretricious gratifications, but as a real source of energy, self-confidence and creative power. It is an essential and perhaps the fundamental substance of our existence. For me and my kind the house of ill-fame is of no more use than the monastery. My need is for the respect, friendship, sympathy and willing help of a woman or women just as much as for her sexual intimacies. And if you come to discuss this with a fully developed intelligent woman I believe she will say of herself exactly what I say of myself. Mate came before husband, wife or mistress in the story of life, and may outlast both of these relationships.

Most or all of the men and women who will constitute the main directive community of this modern world-state towards which human affairs are moving, must mate happily and live happily mated, if they are to do their work; and all the social institutions and moral codes that prevail today must continue or change in accordance with that primary condition. As they become aware of the distinctive difference of their aims and work, and as their own sexual life develops, they will evolve their own conception of restraints, imperatives and reasonable conditions, and fashion a new code. At present we live sexually in a world of mixed and broken codes, and irregular and extravagant experiments and defiances. Most people are doing or pretend to be doing what they believe to be right in the eyes of their friends and neighbours. Few people have the courage of their internal want of convictions. The larger part of the younger generation of educated and semi-educated people in Europe and America seems to me to have no sexual morals at all, but only cynical observances, the plain inevitable result of an atmosphere of manifest shams and insincerities.

It will be worth while to become historical again here and to go over the development of prohibitions, customs, traditions, codes and conventions that have contributed to our present welter. To discuss how one has got to a situation is often the way to discover how to get away from it again. Let us see to what extent this confusion can be analysed, and find out whether we are being reasonable or impossible in making this demand for a free society of mated and co-operative men and women.

It may be that we are asking for the moon, that an insoluble conflict of interests and instincts exists between men and women, and that to the end of the story our race must go on, as I have lived, as most of the people I know are living about me, now tormented, now delighted, now distracted, now wasted by the untamable and irreconcilable impulses of sex. Our creative work can never in that case amount to the sum of our lives, it will be only what we can rescue from this devouring inheritance of desires and gratifications that has arisen for us out of the struggle by which we were made.

## 2 – *Things Fundamental*

I write of men and women co-operating and mating on terms of equality. That is our modern idea. But have men and women ever met on terms of equality?

I am sceptical that there has ever been equality between them. The greater probability seems to me to be that from the ancestral ape upward the female of our line has been at much the same physical disadvantage as most other mammalian females. The sexual reactions of reptiles, fishes, insects, crustaceans, may follow lines entirely outside our sympathetic understanding, but the whole mammalian series has in common the devotion of the female to the young. The new creature hampers her before its birth, preys upon her, becomes her parasitic associate, clamours for her protection, and her instincts respond. The male, less preoccupied, grows to greater strength, is freer in his movements.

He is linked to the female primarily by desire. Nature in forming the mammal has never discriminated between the sexes so far as to deny the male and the female a touch of the acquisitions of the other; most male animals have a certain maternal tenderness for young things, and hardly any mammalian female is altogether a slave and sacrifice to breeding; but the broad distinction holds. I take it that primitive man as male desired, fought for, dominated and did his best to enslave his woman and have done with her. Most of us still do that. She complied or she evaded; she resisted or submitted. I doubt if she had much choice or much freedom of initiative. I do not suggest she was wholly passive, but on the whole the disadvantage was hers. When he and she were sexually attractive and active that was their relationship; that was and that is the primary sexual relationship.

But the life of the primitive men and the sub-men their ancestors were lives of struggle, and the sexual motive was not always uppermost. They hunted, and probably he hunted best. She was generally either immature or nursing or pregnant. She could not keep up with him, and so she stayed behind. She kept the fire and kept by the fire. As economic life began, the greater part of the work was not so much thrust upon her as fell upon her. It began naturally with minding the children and the fire, with tidying the lair and furnishing the lair. She probably had to gather fruits and little things. She cooked. She ground the seeds. He made his casual magnificent exertions, but the first toil was hers. Woman was the first drudge; the man sat about. But hers was the hearth and home. That must have been the primary economic relationship of the sexes. Put an ordinary man and woman together today in a hut or a cottage or a one-roomed tenement, and almost without discussion things adjust themselves in that spirit.

But there was a third primary relationship of a different sort. The man and woman were not always in a sexual relationship, male to female; sometimes he was son and junior, and she was mother and senior. Then she was his protector. She shielded him from the jealousy and injustice of his father; she was great and wise in his eyes, beautiful and kind and helpful. That wove a different strand of feeling into the complex of relationship. Most male animals seem to forget that phase, but the comparative helplessness of the human young last so long and memory is relatively so good in us, that in all our subsequent lives the appeal for feminine help and kindness lingers in our souls. I can trace that strand from quite infantile imaginings reappearing, vanishing, turning up again, throughout my life. And it interweaves with the two others, so that women at large are at once our seniors and our juniors. We do not classify them or they us; life is too entangled for that. They are this today and that tomorrow. When a woman takes a man in her arms she takes a duplex creature, a conqueror and a refugee. And he holds a queen and a slave. In the Egyptian mythology, Isis, the Star of Heaven, held the child Horus in her arms and Osiris was her lord and Horus was Osiris. This remembered dependence is the primary defence of women; the mitigation of the material inferiority to which their physical disadvantage subjects them. The woman resists, evades, submits, but also she aids and pities and mysteriously she commands respect.

In his intimate relations to a woman, without any planning or intention but of the necessity of his nature, a man is continually ringing the changes between these three primary colours of his emotional palette. And she flashes her own correlated variations. That much is in our natures. And in our natures also is something that I think transcends sex, though it is habitually turned to the uses of sex, and that is our personal abasement before some shining, lovely, admired and overwhelming person. The dog has this aptitude for personal worship extravagantly, but man now has it too.

All these things are natural inalterable factors that we must respect in perfecting the relations of modern men and women.

Another factor in our make-up that must come in for any sort of balance to exist between them is comradeship. Comradeship is a relationship that became emotional I think first between men and men, in the hunt, in the battle. It has still to enter into the ordinary tangle between the sexes. Whether it can do so is the most doubtful question of all. It is not in the established precedents of nature. Man, we must remember, is now the most social of animals, and the nearest approach to level mating has occurred hitherto among the more solitary beasts, lions and tigers and such great carnivores. Man is in the minority of social animals in his disposition to pair. None of the economic creatures pair. The social animals when they are undisturbed by rut, go off peaceably with their like, the hinds together, the young stags together. But man is not to be ruled by the practice of the beasts. He has to work out for himself his own distinctive methods. He is not subject to their seasons of rut and indifference.

In the past woman was the material and moral inferior of man mainly because she was so soon and so completely overtaken by the oppression of sex. Now that in the modern communities she is not so overtaken, since now she may carry that burthen as lightly as a man, it is interesting to see how rapidly she approximates to the freedoms and physical energy of a young man. The Western girl among the prosperous classes of today is far more different in physique and morale from the young lady of a hundred years ago, than she is from her brother. And one can think of her as a man's mate and comrade, as one could never do of the young lady. Perhaps now one exaggerates the resemblances as formerly one exaggerated the differences. But I find it possible to imagine a world in which a large proportion of the leading people will be mated colleagues. Assimilation can go further than it has gone. I doubt if it will ever obliterate the feminine disadvantage completely. Still more do I doubt if there will ever be any essential inversion of the rôles. Typically the man will produce the larger initiatives, and in their intimacy the pair will realise those balanced reactions of subjugation and tenderness that come to us from the past.

The world moves from uniformity to diversity, and there will be, no doubt, a multitude of exceptional cases, and there will be freedom and tolerance for such exceptions. What I am writing of here is the prevailing fashion in which the men and women of a creative energetic type would probably group themselves. And so far I have been discussing only the natural inherent reactions of men and women and the common-sense necessities of people whose lives are shaped by the desire for a maximum of creative work in a world at peace. Directly one turns outward from such speculations, one faces a world entirely antagonistic to them, a crowded gregarious world of feverish entertainment, of decoration and displays and general extravagance, excitements, provocations, pursuits, jealousies. One finds the companion-mate as a dream in the hearts of a few people here and there, as an experiment, an almost hopeless experiment, like a match lit in a high wind or a swimmer borne away by a stream.

Is it no more than a dream, this conception of an active austere social life, not crowded with persons, lived much in the company of a dear associate or so, but generous and free in spirit, and with interests and activities wide as the world? I do not think it is a dream. But how can I reconcile this project, this expectation, with the manifest realities of life today? Where, you ask, are there women, these mates, these men happily mated? Where are these fully emerged adults?

I cannot point to them; I have never met them; that is indeed my personal story. I can only foretell them. But I foretell them as I foretell a coming world control by sane and powerful people. This world control, gradually becoming evident, will make the flags and the armies, the rulers and governments, which seem to monopolise all the concrete realities of our collective life today, weaken, become thin and manifestly unreal, and presently fade very swiftly out of existence. So too I believe the current social life today will grow transparent and palpably flimsy and suddenly fade in a few decades out of its present compelling predominance. Our ways of living are even more provisional now than our governments. Everybody does this or that today which nobody will do tomorrow. The change in manners and morals, in customs and conventions during the last half-century has been tremendous, but it may seem nothing before the changes of the next half-century. We are living in the hectic last phase of a dying order.

## 3 – *Ruling Traditions*

The manners and morals, the laws and arrangements between the sexes today, the expectations people have and the rights they claim in love and marriage constitute now a vast, dangerous, unhappy conflict and confusion. It has ceased to follow a code or a system. It is like a panic, like a débâcle. In the past there had been stress, suppression and sorrow in sexual life, but never so chancy, unjust and wasteful a time as this one. It is a state of affairs in which no one is safe for happiness, and no conduct sure of success. For most of us there is an obligation to blunder.

I have tried to make out of my observations and experiences some sort of classification of the medley of traditions and guiding ideas which determine men's and women's treatment of one another. That is a necessary preliminary to any attempt to reach conclusions in the universal problem. We start complex in these affairs as I have shown, but that complexity is nothing to the complexity of our traditions and suggestions. We are always shifting about among these without realising what we are doing; now we behave in obedience to one set of values and before we know it we have changed our course because of a new wind from quite another quarter. To give the next generation some help in referring their motive ideas in sexual matters to their source is one of the main educational tasks before those who seek to realise a new and better phase of human life.

I have not seen much sexual happiness either in my own life or in the lives of those about me. I have seen much pleasant coming together and much bright hope, but the usual fate of the contemporary love-story is that it tarnishes and the colours fade. I do not believe there is any such natural antagonism of man and woman as to make disappointment necessary in this, the main affair of most people's lives. I believe nearly all the jangles and disappointments of contemporary life can be traced to a confused unpreparedness of mind, to a profound ignorance of physical and psychic fact, to fluctuating and impossible expectations and unjustifiable assumptions about what is right and reasonable and graceful and honourable in sexual conduct. Out of disappointments arise resentments, estrangement, malice, cruelty. The contemporary love-story begins in illusions and goes on by way of misunderstandings to conflict. It opens cheaply and ends in dispute or dull resignation.

Certain main classes may be distinguished into which all these codes, fragments of codes and traditions of sentiment and expectation which we find determining people's activities, fall. These classes differ in their fundamental nature, arise from different strata in our being, are not equivalent dimensions but things of diverse categories. First one may distinguish and set on one side all those motives, judgements, ways of taking sexual things, into which the idea of Sin enters. There is a factor of fear and repulsion. Of this one can make a first whole class of ideas. They give us what may be called the Woman of the Sinful Man. Desire drags against shame and a terrified predisposition to abstinence. There is an immense exaggeration of chastity. The ideal woman is a sexless female, helpful, serviceable, but perpetually virgin and even so a temptation; marriage, though it be consummated with extreme infrequency after prayer and fasting, amidst austerely unpleasant details, remains an unclean affair, a lapse from the better life. These ideals embody fundamentally masculine conceptions; the man of the sin-conscious woman is a secret that has never been betrayed in sane literature. But women, with their extraordinary facility for adapting themselves to expectation, have produced in response the rôle of the woman wholly chaste and unapproachable, have protected themselves enormously from unwelcome attentions by that impersonation, and have established an almost inestimable value for such shameful concessions as they may at last consent to make to the hysterical importunity of the sinful man in his phases of moral débâcle.

Within a lifetime the codes, manners, sentimental systems centering upon this conception of the sinfulness of sex, prevailed widely throughout the world. They gave women artificial value and dignity at the price of incessant restraint. But the great gales of controversy that have cleared away so much fear and moral fog from mankind, have left but little sense of sexual sin in the modern mind. The covered inaccessible woman, that veiled mysterious indulgence, is passing out of the general life. The protective shamming of indifference ceases to be a part of feminine tradition and training.

Less a code than a body of practice is a second great system of methods of treatment, the way of the vulgar sensible man and woman, the secular sexual life of the peasant, the farmer, the little shopkeeper, the man with a living need for a helper and confederate. In the settled communities of mankind throughout the ages, the multitude has lived in a roughly but rationally adjusted manner, poised in a not unequal fashion, and with the woman as near self-respect as women have ever got in the whole experience of the race. She was necessary, she was consulted, she need make no great attempt either to withhold herself or charm an exacting male. She could be mother to the full extent of her desires. At times her wishes in that direction were outrun, but the friendly germs of infant mortality kept the balance down. No doubt the priest troubled the couple at times with strange hints of sin and damnation, troubled but did not disturb profoundly, and no doubt, too, the law held the woman was man's chattel and would duck or chastise her spasmodically for small misbehaviours and disloyalties. But she knew her place and power better than the law; did she not cook the man's dinner, make his bed, and keep or shatter his peace and his pride?

For a hundred centuries from China to Peru this common life has gone on, in which the woman was as necessary and as respected upon all practical issues as the man. Its real practice – for like the English common law it had no code – was handed down from woman to woman and imparted by mother to son. Religions may permit polygamy to the prosperous, as Islam does, or Court or Town practise the most fantastic tricks; the common life has varied little from the common formula. The Anatolian peasant is as mated to his one woman as the Irish farmer. In this country about me the tradition of the vulgar sensible folk is to be found strained by new forces, but still vigorous among the jasmine and olive terraces, in every other *mas* that the rich Americans and economising artists and suchlike invaders as Clementina and I have left intact. It has been so much the life of our species since man became man, that for anyone without historical perspective it is easy to call it the immemorial natural life of mankind.

It is nothing of the sort. *Παντα ῥει.* That change of scale which is the present form of human experience as a whole, invades the vulgar sensible way of living in every practical detail and in every imagination. The niggling cultivation of the soil in small patches that was once the only possible basis of the social structure is becoming economically unsound, and even more is the toil of the woman being robbed of the dignity of necessity. The change is visible even here, in neglected olive-trees, in crumbling terrace walls and in the cyclist figures flitting along the paths at dusk to betray the fact that our typical neighbour is no longer a cultivator of the soil but a worker in a Grasse factory. These are new developments here. It is in the suburban homes of the great towns of our typical England and the United States – and England now for the half of its area is no better than a scattered suburb – that the change is most fully displayed. The man is still a worker and even more of a toiler than he used to be, but he works away. It needs a liberal education for him if he is to realise the significance and scope of the economic machine in which he is a cogwheel. And the woman at home has been stripped more and more of her fundamental economic importance and reduced to the position of a sexual complement. She knows little or nothing of her husband's affairs; they are too far off. She does not brew, she does not bake. She does not so much cook as "warm up." She does not make her linen or control her house, she merely "shops" for it. The gas company is her hewer of wood and the municipality her drawer of water. She touches a button to light her home. To her own relief and her husband's and the community's, she ceases to breed, and such children as she bears are far better educated for her by trained teachers in properly equipped schools. Change has robbed her of her normal employments just as it has released her and her man from the sense of sin. There she is.

What is she to do with herself – with herself and her immensely empty afternoons? What are we to do with her? The percentage of these Claras increases in all the modern communities. I am for making boys of them and breaking up these mere empty shells and shams of suburban households. Let them live in flats and chambers and have their men come and go until they find a proper mate and a task they can share with him.

Let them be educated and trained as well as their brothers and put to research and business and productive work. Let them cease to regard their sex – I will not say as a marketable commodity, but as a negotiable right for which they may secure a comfortable living. And as I think of some of the girls one sees today, short-cropped like handsome youths, as tall, as energetic and bold as their brothers and often franker in thought and act, it seems to me that in writing these things I write with the spirit of the time, of a not impossible transformation.

### 4 – *Romanticism in Flood*

But there is still another main class of ideas and traditions that have to be taken into account before this survey of the moral field of force in which women are living is complete. These are the various romantic and chivalrous traditions that complicate its issues and confuse most women's minds irreparably with the suggestion that woman is the queen of beauty, the chief object of men's lives, the sufficient reward for every conceivable service and devotion. She is not, she never had been, she never will be. But these traditions saturate poetic literature; their roots entangle with the whole history of our race.

The two groups of standards and values we have considered hitherto correspond to two main ways of living, to the way of living when misery is abroad and when religious fear predominates, and to a way of living of the cheerful, laborious, sensible, settled folk in normal times. For thousands of years the huge majority of ordinary men have lived with women continually, worked side by side with them, joked and planned with them, beaten and caressed them, and regarded them for most practical purposes as equals and responsible mates. But there has always been a third sort of man who went apart from women not to brood but to do. This was the herdsman, the hunter, the warrior, the knight-errant, the raiding nomad, the desert merchant, the seaman. In his phases of hardy abstinence came dreams of desire, but they came not with the quality of sin but with the quality of reward. No more than the God-fearing saint did he need woman as a companion. She and her possible litter would cumber the ship and lag upon the trail. But she was neither on the sea nor in the desert to distract him, and he did not see her as the saint saw her in the light of an incessant allurement, defeating his ends. He came back to her, alive with desire, excitable, with his hands full of spoil and pay.

There ensues from these lives of departure and return systems of relationship widely divergent either from those of the sin-haunted abstainer or the gross habitual familiarities of the accustomed man. This third type of system may be in its essence far more ancient than those of the normal settled life. The men of the Old Stone Age were hunters, and they have left paintings on the Spanish rocks showing the firelit feasting of a return or a tribal gathering – the hunters dancing and showing off, the women dancing too in poses that exaggerate the contours of their figures provokingly. The Spanish rock-paintings reflect the self-same spirit that one would find today in a party of Spanish-American or Anglo-Saxon cowboys come down after a spell of adventure to scatter their dollars among the women of the town. The men and women meet excited. The women allure, the man show off, they compete, fight perhaps for the women, pay and give. Even the gestures of the Spanish-American dancing are similar to those in the rock-paintings, the arms akimbo, the protruded breasts. There is much perplexing and wounding with jealousy. The men are in their brightest garments. The women paint and dress themselves for vividness and swift effect.

This third great class of sexual relationship in which the man comes along, goes far away, returns, is, with local variations, spread over all the world. It is an open-life way since first the plough began, and probably it has never been the way of more than a minority of humanity. But it has been a potent minority. The cowboy tradition prevails over the whole Spanish-speaking world. There it produces its typical beauty, its typical costume. Love is vivid and jealous in this life because of the pent-up period of separation. When the man has won his woman he is apt to demand her seclusion. The supreme virtue of woman becomes sexual loyalty to the absent man. Hardly any other is asked of her. "Can she brew or can she bake?" It matters little. Better a red carnation in her bright black hair and a shawl drawn lightly over the curves of breast and hip.

A parallel world of romance, dances, provocations, pursuits, seclusions, is that of the desert Arab. The Arab keeps his womankind veiled and in tents. They see nothing. Their housekeeping is despicable. They do not even sew. A little stenographer with her bicycle and her tennis in a crowded country like England knows far more of exercise and the open air than many a young woman in the vast spaces of the desert. The Arab woman reclines in the sultry shadows of the tent, planning her captivating allurements against her one great event, the man's return, his return and his choice. She brightens her eyes and paints her face and puts on her jewels and keeps herself supple for the secret dance. If she goes abroad she must go in state, protected, watched, bedizened with all the evidences of the man's appreciation. She is his supreme exploit; the symbol of his success. And this triumphant seclusion from dust and exertion, this life of honour in a place apart, is given her upon two simple conditions. She must keep faith with her man while he is away, and she must remain young and attractive. The romantic code takes little or no cognisance of old, worn, or ailing women.

This third group of codes is begotten of the life of wanderers and waste places, but its influence reaches far beyond those limits. It has gone with the sword of the rider – everywhere.

Since social history began there is a story of conquest and conquest and again conquest of the settled lands, the cultivated regions, the towns and cities, by men out of the wastes, out of the deserts or from overseas. The wanderer has the habit of the upper hand. He has supplied the rulers, the aristocracies, the tax-collectors, the landowners, the lordly ones of nearly every country in the world, and they have kept his standards. The conquered womenfolk have been quick to mitigate their first abasement. His assumptions about women have been inevitably romantic. He cannot play his distinctive rôle tied to a woman's apron strings. In the mood of going forth he finds them encumbrances, and after a phase of solitude they become magically attractive. They become objects of cupidity and then possession, animated possessions, richly decorated and pampered possessions, with hidden souls, whom one must watch jealously. Nobody planned the codes he follows; he brought the seeds of them with him into the settled lands; they are his natural reaction to his conditions. This is his way with women, just as a senior partnership is the peasant's way and avoidance the way of the sin-haunted soul.

The romantic codes, the codes of the adventurers, have had a disproportionate influence upon the life of today because they were associated naturally with ruling and powerful people, and so the poets and singers, the romancers and playwrights found their interest in observing them. They yielded better stories, with more colour in them. They carried more decoration. The common life is uneventful by nature; its good faith and sober industry yield no such strikingly recordable and transmissible impulses, have no such epic nor dramatic quality. Yet it is not from the conquerors and aristocrats and romantic, generous, wasteful figures of the past that the modern order arises, but from men addicted to creative toil, from sublimated artisans and skilful makers; and the mates they need if they are to round off their revolutionary activities into a new world system, are far more like the free-going, kindly, smiling, assisting womankind of the peasant and the artificer than the fascinating houri of the excited cowboy or her exaltation, the fine lady of the chivalrous tradition.

What has happened in the sexual life of our western communities during the last two centuries, and which is now becoming worldwide, can be represented by certain very broad statements about these three great systems of promise and sentiment. Firstly the economic revolution, the change of scale in economic operations, has done much to break up the homely practical equality of commonplace men and women, by taking one domestic task after another out of the woman's hands, taking economic realities out of her sight and understanding, gathering men workers into offices, office districts, factories and warehouses, and so reducing the link between husband and wife down at last to its sexual core. The increase of knowledge has also lifted the burthen of child-bearing from the woman. The circumstances of stratum after stratum of woman have approximated more and more to a low-grade, impoverished reproduction of the leisure and expectancy of the lady of the world of chivalry.

Meanwhile there had been a vast extension of reading and a cheapening of books. The literary methods have naturally followed the romantic tradition of the ruling class; for some generations women of the poorer sort were reading nothing but the cheap editions and worn library copies originally written and published at a high price for the gentlefolk, and this amounted in effect to a most subtle and effectual propaganda of the romantic attitude to sexual life. There has been a tremendous flooding of the thoughts and motives of the entire community with these cowboy-chevalier ideals. Hitherto these ideals had carried little weight in the main illiterate mass of the community; even in the upper classes they had been much restrained and modified by the sin idea and the defensive dignity that idea enabled many women to assume. But now the sense of sin was being lifted from the world with the decline in confidence of those old religious teachings. The theatre, and today with enormous force the cinema, are confirming the teachings of the reverie and the novelette. An increasing multitude of girls, probably a huge majority of them now, in America and western Europe, is growing up to womanhood with no idea of any sort of worth-while career except that of the heroine of a love-story with a powerful, patient, constantly excited and always devoted man.

Unhappily there has been no corresponding increase in the supply of cowboy-chevaliers and successful sailor adventurers. The young man who sits beside the thrilling girl in the cinema theatre is already, in ninety-nine cases out of the hundred, a subordinated young man; he is always going to be rather preoccupied with the interest and difficulties of the work he has to do, and he is never going far away to execute wonderful deeds. Still less is he ever coming back with his hands full of gifts and his eyes full of crystalline desire. He is doomed, therefore, to be treated as a second-best thing by a young woman who would, if she were put to the equivalent test as a heroine, fail to prove herself even second-rate. He is going to be judged by false standards and treated upon false assumptions. He may be goaded to spirited acts that will bring defeat upon him, and to a swagger that will fail to deceive her trained judgment. Humiliation awaits him, and for her wait the scurvy reactions of a humiliated man.

It is extraordinary how the whole aspect of social life has been changed since I was a child, by the flooding out of all other traditions by the traditions of romance. It is visible in the streets, where once the best part of the women were dowdy and uneventful. Now every two women out of three call for the man of spirit, in their provocative clothing, in their conscious assertion of a cared-for beauty, in their challenging bearing.

There have been times in London, in Paris, when I have wanted to go along the gallant streets apologising for myself and my sex. This change of attitude is evident even in our murders. England has few murders; it is not a murdering country, but such murders as there were in my boyhood were sordid, practical, business-like affairs, the realisation of an insurance, the removal of some encumbering person. Now three-fourths of our murders are romantic. In England, in the last eight or ten years, there have been hung some score of romantic lovers, for jealousy – lovers usually of the middle and lower middle class. They have done things, high tragic things, that seem to have been inspired by the aristocratic Elizabethan drama.

It is impossible to believe that this pervasion of the contemporary world by sexual romanticism is anything but a passing phase in the huge social readjustments now in progress. It is like a summer cloud-burst that leaves the crops flat for three or four days and scarcely hurts them. There is no substantial support for these new attitudes; the thrust of economic necessity is against them. The harsh truth is that there is now an over-production of willing beauties and heroines; the market is more than glutted. Every prosperous man, every successful adventurer, finds there are charming, cultivated, unscrupulous young women alert for him at every turn. A lot of us have our returned cowboy phases, no doubt, times when the easy dollars fly, but most of us are much too busy and preoccupied to give these delightful creatures the full attention they expect and demand. The comparatively successful ones who get a hold on a man, go off presently with dresses and furniture and precarious settlements. A few struggle to an unstable and mortified married state. Many never get anything at all but passing attentions, and hang on until the revealing dresses reveal beauty no longer but defeat. Our fiction is still romantic, and no one has yet written the true story of lovely women among modern rich men. They do better with the heirs, perhaps, which is one reason why most of us are prepared to put great restrictions upon inheritance. We prefer the survival of our business to the seduction of our sons.

The winding-up of this phase of over-competition among heroines lies with women themselves. The warnings of the disillusioned had already started off to overtake the romantic novel twenty-five years ago. The pursuit continues. It was inevitable that to begin with women should awake to a sense that they had been cheated and rail against the men for cheats. But men are not to blame for the comparative rarity of Douglas Fairbanks and Rudolph Valentino. It was in the nature of things, and not out of the blackness of the male heart, that these generations of the women should be led to expect too much and receive so little. The flow of romance still runs high and strong, but gradually the less agreeable truths about men and women will invade the consciousness of the young girl in time to save her from the current disappointment. She will be brought back to the fact that her equivalent man is neither a god nor a cheat but a human being very like herself, and that for all practical purposes there are neither gods nor villains after the fashion of the romancers.

She must realise that though she can be violently attractive to a man she is only spasmodically attractive, and that on the whole her need for him is greater than his need for her. The fatal delusion that a woman can be the crown of a man's life, his incentive to action, his inspiration, has to be cleaned out of her mind altogether. Women may have been an incentive to action for certain types of men, but that is a different statement. The desire for women has indeed driven men to robberies, piracies, gambling, insurrections, conquests, gripping possessiveness, waylaying and forestalling. Woman has been able to make a price and forced men to find it – and so brought herself under the obligations of a purchased article. But no man has ever done any great creative thing, painted splendidly, followed up subtle curiosities as a philosopher or explorer, organised an industry, set a land in order, invented machines, built lovely buildings, primarily for the sake of a woman. These things can only be done well and fully for their own sakes, because of a distinctive drive from within; they arise from that sublimated egotism we call self-realisation. Some women have prevented and thwarted the self-realisation of men, and others have protected and aided men, but from first to last they have been accessory. Man is and will remain incurably egotist. To cease to be an egotist is to cease in that measure to be individual. Even when he devotes himself wholly to the service of the species, it is that he seeks to realise his individual difference to the full in order to add it to the undying experience of his kind. Even religion has exaggerated rather than suppressed the egotist by its horrible lure of egoistic immortality. The devotee, prostrate with adoration in his cell, wants to make his service to his Lord exceptional and distinctive. "Lord," he prays, "remember ME."

It is the fundamental falsity of the romantic tradition that man should subordinate himself to the egotism of a woman. Let her not dream of it. It lures her on to the development of an enhanced exaggerated ego, pitifully painted, scented and adorned for worship. In that she sinks her actual personality and only perceives the cheat when she finds the slave become owner and bully, imprisoning his mistress in the jealousy that is his instinctive, unpremeditated revenge for the unnatural subordination that has been imposed upon him.

On the whole women are not so highly individualised nor so strongly egotistical as men. The romantic tradition suggests that they are more so. The first lesson the modern young woman has to learn is to reject that suggestion and accept the facts of the case. The greater part of the life of a modern woman – and it is astonishing now to see how far down these influences have extended – is the sedulous pursuit of an enforced and superposed individuality. In that pursuit goes all the vigour that might have enabled her to develop her more essential qualities. Her hair, her skin, her figure, her behaviour, her emotions, must be, in the same way, tortured to "distinction." Her very scent must be distinctive; her entry into a room must have "style"; she must wrap strange and striking effects of colour and texture round her mediocrity. Failing any inner radiance, she must secure the limelight. The manufacture of individuality for women is a vast industry; in Paris, in New York, in London it is dominant; it is perhaps the most skilful and wonderful industry in our world. Men and women of fine intelligence exert their utmost gifts to produce "creations"; those must be sold in secret and with passionate asseverations that they are exclusive, to the happy, rich, ordinary women who are lifted by such efforts for a few days or a few weeks out of that undistinguished chorus of female minds and bodies to which naturally they belong. A title, some historical pearls, a collection of jewels, a few anecdotes can be added with advantage. Then with a certain enterprise, and a setting and a retinue, titled attentions perhaps, and the press and the press photographers, the goddess is built up. And you take it home with you out of the clamour, and you take its marvellous clothes off it and you wash off what you can of its grease and paint and powder, and you find a poor little human body of no remarkable quality and a mind and a character of no quality at all.

The flower of the romantic tradition has been the fine lady, who disappears, who becomes already a little ghostly and incredible. Its practical outcome has been that curious code of claims and behaviour by which multitudes of women are living today, here in dear, lucid, logical, impatient, shallow-minded France particularly, and the code is embodied in the phrase "*La Femme.*" By it men and women cease altogether to be fellow-creatures. The first convention in the cult, *La Femme*, is that every woman, except such women as are to be altogether swept aside as *stupides* and *laides*, is delightful, desirable, exceptional and rare. The second is that without her life is intolerable to a man, that she is his comprehensive objective, that all he is and does is for her sake – her sake or her rival's. That is the one thorn in the paradise of *La Femme* – the other woman. The man appears in her life, seeking, seeking, sometimes rather blindly and requiring assistance, but always seeking his end, his completion. After suitable inquiries and an exchange of references between the parents, she allows herself to love. She "gives" herself. The male, faint with gratitude and amazement, becomes her slave. Her lifework is over; the rest is harvest. In return for this stupendous, this almost unheard-of beneficence she is entitled to dress, leisure, amusement, servants and an establishment considerably above her or her husband's station. The male is rewarded or admonished by repetitions or refusals of the supreme gift. It is adorned for his birthday and reserved during Lent.

*La Femme*, particularly in phases of doubt and disillusionment, is apt to become gregarious and voluble. She gathers in flats at tea-time and talks her fears and angers down and out. She asserts her inflexible principles, her unflinching claims. She exchanges views upon what may be borne and what justifies deceit and rebellion. Almost everything justifies deceit and rebellion. And at the back of her talk, most sacred of conventional beliefs, pretension no tea-party would ever dare to question or qualify, is the doctrine of the eager, accessible *amant*. An enormous number of prowling rich men are supposed to exist, men in reserve, the ultimate stabilisers of all the troubles of *La Femme*. If the husband prove intolerable, if his meanness and incapacity sink below the needs and pride of his impatient priceless one, she will, she declares, fall back at last upon that one certain resource. There it is. *Que voulez-vous?* She will just go out of the home, somewhere, and – a mere movement of prehension – "prendre un amant, un riche amant."

"Je les vois prenant ce riche amant," says Clementina, the wise, the disillusioned.

## 5 – *Sexual Integrity*

This phase of social life, this submergence of upper and middle class and even artisan life by a flood of sexual romanticism must be a transitory one. There are too many women and not enough men seeking to realise these dreams, and such romantic men as are to be found are discovering the increasing cheapness of their charmers. They become arrogant beyond enduring. The sense of sin was the last restrictive force upon the abundance of women, and it has gone. There is to much humiliation and disappointment in this interplay for girls and women and normally circumstanced men. The situation eases itself by young women taking up work with increasing sincerity and ability. It can be profoundly modified by the social atmosphere able women may create. But it will never ease itself completely until there is a great reduction in the prizes that can still fall to an impudent and lucky adventuress.

That rests with the men who have the power to change economic conditions. The final cure for the vulgarisation and suffusion of life by the extravagances of the romantic lady, in action or in magnificent retirement, and of her myriads of unsuccessful or partially successful imitators and competitors, is the abolition of the cowboy type, the lucky lad, the gambler. As we regularise business and the exploitation of staple productions, clip adventurous finance to economic subservience, destroy restrictive monopolies, mitigate the pressure of the mere creditor and restrain inheritance, the resources of the spendthrift male will dwindle and the ground vanish from under the feet of the heroine. As the sanitation of the world's economic life progresses, the romantic tradition will fade in the measure of that reorganisation. For some generations yet the romantic tradition will be fighting after its gorgeous fashion, in novel and play, in the press, upon the screen and in custom, costume, manners and conversation, in every daily affair, against the conception of a graver, non-parastic womanhood.

I know very little about the younger women of today. They say that quite new types have appeared since the war, but they have been outside my explicit experience. I find I am too old now to get any exchange of ideas with a woman under thirty. William Clissold the Second might be able to add much to what I am writing here. But I am neither deaf nor blind; I have a certain aptitude for seeing things with my left shoulder or the back of my head where girls and women are concerned. The romantic tradition is not altogether outside the imagination of these types, but a new code is pushing it aside. One sees the struggle in the dress they wear. The short hair, the kilts, spell freedom, but many of them – even the very young ones – paint like whores. Some of the leaders must know their own minds, but most of the rank and file seem quite uncertain whether it is heroine or comrade they mean to be. Chance may determine. Maybe Angelina is a comrade on Monday and reverts to the rôle of heroine after the excitement of the cinema on Tuesday evening. That must make very uncertain going for Edwin.

Chastity, by which I mean an invincible power of abstinence, has long been falling down the scale of feminine virtue from the days when it was not only the supreme but practically the only adornment needed by a good woman. She could be mendacious, cowardly and indolent; these things merely added an agreeable piquancy to the charm of her essential goodness. But if the new types no longer esteem virginity as a glory and chastity as an obligation, it does not follow that their code will tolerate a careless promiscuity and still less the mercenary exploitation of men's sexual desires. On that modern women join issue openly with the romantic tradition, which shelters under its ample pretences both the successful prostitute and the parasitic wife. At present I believe these recalcitrant women are working out their own conception of sexual integrity. They are in a phase of experiment, and for many of the weaker sisters experiment degenerates into aimless and undignified laxity. They do not so much follow the desires of their hearts as do what they are asked. The task of developing the new ideals is intricate and complex. The general proposition is an easy one: it is that women should make love only for love. But like most easy general propositions, it says very little because it is open for anything whatever to shelter under that word "love."

There is a Mediterranean lucidity about Clementina in these matters. There is a Mediterranean disregard of intentions that do not immediately clothe themselves in terms of explicit reality. She examined this repudiation of any mercenary element in love.

"You say a woman must not give herself for what she gets – only for love. Yes; very good. And what makes her love a man at first? In nine cases out of ten, what makes her begin to love him? The effect of kindness, the effect of power, the quality of the givah. Because she feels he can give. She gives herself for love – yes. But she loves because she feels something stronger, safer, protective in the man. Is that being mercenary?"

I considered the proposition.

"Do I love you?" she went on. "Do you doubt of it? You know I love you. You know. I would die for you. But what made me love you first? Desiah for your beauty, Clissoldaki mou? It was because you suddenly came to me, strong and kind and helping. Because you had powah over all the things that defeated me. You came to me. Confident you were. I was afraid. I was hungry – I was hungry that night. You said: 'If you want to go to Provence, my deah, go. I let you.' It was so wonderful. You can open roads, give freedoms, make houses and gardens submit to you, put safety round my life."

"Is it only that?"

"Not at all. You know. My deah, you know. But does a woman fall in love with a man if a man isn't that? If he fails. If he lets himself be frustrated. If he cannot protect and give. All the new ideahs in the world can't alter that. Women will turn to the strong man, the capable man, the man who has mastery. Their *hearts* will turn. Their honest love. As yours turn to beauty. When the love is won, ah! *Then* you can be weak. *Then* you can cruel. But to the end of time, my deah, you will never be able to tell whether this woman or that sold herself for the powah a man had or gave herself for the love he commanded."

Gestures from the isles of Greece came to reinforce her asseverations. "Many don't *know*," she drove it home. "Many never know."

Then with an extended finger: "I have seen girls sell themselves, and come to love their husbands, and come to despise the pooah lover who could do no better than a serenade – and make eyes at her. Could not even take her away. Failed."

This, I admit, is an important gloss on that definition of sexual integrity, but I do not see that it destroys it. The free-spirited woman who seeks to attract and welcomes as a mate a man with some sort of power is quite a distinguishable type from the one who cultivates her charms for the market. The superficial effect may be the same, but the direction of the attention is different. *Senena Blandish*, that pathetic novel, tells how the old-fashioned trade declines.

"Sexual integrity," said Clementina, "is not to be independent or dependent. Sexual integrity is to keep faith with your lovah."

"But if there is no lover?"

"To keep faith with the lovah that is to be."

"But in your own case – ?"

"I was finding my way to you."

There is at times a magnificence about Clementina that takes my breath away.

"I was talking," I said after a pause for recovery, "of the morals of the free and equal woman. I was not thinking of the woman who accepts her need of dependence on me. I was thinking of the sort of woman who has turned her back on the romantic tradition and sets out to be a self-subsisting citizen. She claims all the freedoms of a man. But since you took hold of the question this free and equal woman of mine has disappeared."

"Was she ever there?" said Clementina.

"She was materialising," I asserted.

"I can only speak of woman as I know them," said Clementina. "We have to love and we are not as strong as men."

But if Clementina has not met this new sort of woman, I at least have had glimpses of her and the sexual integrity she has in mind is something more and perhaps something less than sexual faithfulness to a lover actual or foreseen. In limiting it to that Clementina goes right back to the sentimental emotional view of woman's position. She is obsessed by the idea that love is the cardinal thing in life. That is just what the newer type is struggling away from – at any cost. They are in profound reaction against that idea because in it they find the clue to their general cheapness and subjection. Some repudiate it, by treating sex as something as trivial as chocolate. But there are others who appreciate it for the enormous and far-reaching thing it is in life, and yet are resolved not to be subordinated and enslaved through it. They want to reserve, it to keep it private, outside all negotiations, detached from all ambitions and all other activities. They want to do their work and establish their status in despite of it. As a man does. Freedom and dignity are the good things that it seems most to attack and endanger. For the sake of them they realise woman must cease to be beauty, heroine, temptress, darling, and become – a citizen. For the sake of them she must abandon the artificial advantages and refuse the restrictions of a wife. So they see it.

It is interesting to find in Clementina a vigorous antagonist to this conception of the modern woman's rôle, because it is one I seem to have held always. I do not remember that I ever scrutinised it very closely. Instinctively I have been in sympathy with it. As a student I was already talking to Clara about our being perfectly equal and perfectly free. I do not remember that I ever questioned the moral assumptions of Godwin and Shelley. I have taken this attitude with women all my life. It is only recently that I have come to realise the passion in Clementina's repudiation.

### 6 – *The Three Chief Failings of Women*

This sexual integrity towards which women seem to be moving from that conception of status entirely sexual which the romantic tradition imposed upon them is entangled with certain other moral dispositions. I have been trying to state them, not very successfully, because they are so interwoven. They are to be found already in the code of a man; it is just because they have been and are so disregarded by women that it is necessary to emphasise them in that relation. I had written yesterday a list beginning "(1) a greater hardness towards facts, a refusal to be accommodating towards a falsehood." Then came "(2) an acceptance of a natural personality in the place of the dressmaker's substitute." But I will not give the rest of that list. After lunch I invoked Clementina.

"Think for me a little," I said. "There are some things a woman ought never to do. What are they?"

Clementina made a false start. "If a woman loves a man," she began, "there is nothing – "

"I mean, whether she loves or not," I said, and pulled her back to the question again. "Clementina, tell me, what are the common faults of women? What are the chief weaknesses against which they ought to set rules and prohibitions for themselves if they are to look men in the face?"

"We are liahs," said Clementina unhesitatingly, and then fell into a meditation while I gave Titza crumbs of sugar from my coffee-cup.

"Listen," she said, and paused for my full attention. "There are three things wrong with us – three. There are three chief faults of women. They are all forms of weakness. We are liahs, we are vain, and we give no fair play in our dealings with men."

"*You* are different," I said.

"At the bottom of her heart," said Clementina, "a woman knows – knows she cannot accomplish fairly. She is afraid. She is afraid of herself. She is afraid she will go to pieces if she is left to do a thing alone. She has no confidence. She has no confidence she can do fairly."

"She has no confidence she will be treated fairly," I said.

"Anyhow, she has no confidence. So that as soon as things seem likely to go wrong she cheats. She lies, she shirks, she betrays. Feah."

"It is right," I interrupted, "that women should be fearful. It was – it still is – necessary for herself and her children. Always that has been so. She was afraid of the dark thing round the corner and of the quick violence of her offended mate. Hiding is instinctive. And so is lying. For a woman. She has had to ease off the truth so often. Diplomatic. Evasive. It wasn't her job to face the dark thing round the corner. And she had to keep the peace with the dark thing in the cave."

"It will be long before fear goes out of women's lives," said Clementina. "It isn't all upbringing; it isn't all circumstances. It is *in* us. We have clear minds even if we have weak bodies, and we know things, we *know*, which either you don't know or you are too polite to say. We have to judge men. We have to judge what goes to make success. We know the qualities. And we know we haven't got them. Little knowledge, little or no training, and something more. Not such power of concentration. Not able to keep on and keep on gripping. Women get quicklier tired and more muddled in their brains when they have to think out difficult things. They learn quickly – oh! we can be wonderfully clever, give us rules, details, words, but when it comes to big general things we *flinch*."

"Training," I said. "Tradition."

"I wonder."

"And the willing, convenient man ready to say: 'Leave it all to me'!"

"But no man will leave it all to someone else, even when you say it to him. But we are glad to leave it. We are afraid, even when we could."

"A traditional want of pride," said I.

"Pride," she said, and reflected.

"Women are not proud enough," said Clementina, thinking aloud. "Telling the truth is a sort of pride."

"This is how I see it, and be damned to you," I tried it over. "That's all right."

"And they are vain also because they have no pride. Their vanity. Their industrious vanity. They fly from their own real selves. They snatch at any flattery, they stick on any trimming, any colour, any ornament, because they feel they are nothing in themselves. It's not only food and shelter they want from men. They want, always they want, to be reassured. We say: 'Do you love me? Say that you love me!' Until you wave your arms at us as if we were flies and you say 'Shuddub' to us and 'Go away!' Pitiful it is. And we are greedy for the least bit of praise. Praise is the food of love. A wise man – a kind man – makes his woman feel that she is pretty – every day. And the less she is the more he ought to."

"I have seen men greedy for robes," I said. "I have known men find flattery sustaining."

"And their ungenerosity," said Clementina, pursuing her own thoughts. "Their absolute disregard of give and take. The way they will take from men they despise! The way they will let a worried, overworked husband they pretend to love pay and pay! The way they will take dependence as their privilege! The way they accept being put first, shirk little tasks, are lazy, and do not try! Until they are positively driven to try. And then – they drudge. Inattentively – not trying to do it. Protesting. All of it, all of it is want of pride. All of it. But you are right. We have no pride."

Then with a swift transition, with a lift of her eyebrows and a change of voice:

"Where is my pride with you, Clissoulaki? Where is my pride with you?"

She reverted to a philosophical attitude. "Can women have pride? Will they ever have pride?"

It would be impossible for a voice to express completer resignation.

"Clementina," I said, "women now are struggling towards pride out of conditions that have become increasingly humiliating for them. They have been trivialised and cheapened by economic forces, and demoralised and cheated by traditions that require them to be rare and sought after when in reality they are abundant and omnipresent. They can only get back to dignity by being proud, by refusing all differential treatment and insisting upon all the masculine virtues – whether the men like it or no. Courage. Truth. Fair play."

Clementina made no answer.

"That," I said, "is the quintessence of feminism. That is what the vote symbolised for them, and all the agitations of the last five-and-twenty years. A struggle back to pride."

But Clementina was away upon a trail of her own. Suddenly she looked up at me.

"In some things, Clissoulaki, you are very clever, and in some you are very dense. I do not think it has ever dawned on you in all your life how unfair and how cruel a thing it can be to take a woman into your life and treat her as your equal."

"How can it be unfair to play on equal terms?"

"Equal terms! When we love with all our beings! And you love – ! I love little Titza here, more than you have ever loved me."

### 7 – *Return to Morality*

Evidently I must come to a discussion of this love which Clementina, in spite of all my resistances, forces into the foreground of my mind. Yet still for a section I shall cling to my analysis of the forms of sexual relationship, if only because it is within these forms that love as she conceives it goes on. One cannot love in the air, painted ceilings notwithstanding. I will disentangle all I can of the general forces that interweave to make our individual cases before I come down to these last intimate realities. I will complete my bird's-eye view of the changes that are going on between men and women by a forecast of the coming state of affairs.

In spite of all the romanticism, extravagance, excitement, and waste in the life of women today, in spite of its almost universal levity and triviality, I do not believe that these conditions have any real permanence. Though the flood is nearly universal, the ground is near below. I do not believe this era of triviality will endure, because I perceive that there is too much disappointment and mortification in it for women. That the vast majority of women today shows no signs of any disposition to change the present state of affairs does not trouble me in the least. Women can adopt new attitudes *en masse* much more readily even than men. Feminine values are and always have been very unstable, and the zephyr of the afternoon may become the hurricane of tomorrow. I am prepared to find much promise therefore in very unsubstantial intimations.

Women in the past have shown the extremest plasticity in their ideals of life. We have seen the homely, sheltered woman swept away by the romantic inundation; we have had an epidemic of heroines; for a time it seemed as though woman had no other end but dancing. We have encountered the rebel woman, the frantic sex-antagonist. There are forces now that make for pride and reservation in women, and there is a great need for pride. As the creative and directive men who are building up a new world order in the living body of the old become aware of the full significance of the work they do and of their full possibilities, inevitably there will be women awakening also, to share in the new understandings and the new ambitions. They will be interested in these things not only directly, but because they interest the men. Nothing that men have nowadays is altogether kept from women. I do not see how these new women can be other than women practically active, soberly beautiful in dress and bearing, a little hidden in their love, and friendly to men.

Their standards and habits, more than any other single influence, will determine the tone of social life in that emerging world-community with its wider outlooks, its longer rhythms, its more sustained vitality I have anticipated. To these first adapted women will come influence and power and prestige as the active men will disentangled themselves and their time and energy from the worn-out nets of the meretricious women. When paint and scent go they will go very fast because they will be aware of their own conspicuousness. They are not inadvertent things. They came because there was a premium upon over-emphasis; they have no intrinsic beauty or charm. The new types will set the fashion and provide the models for their weaker, more imitative sisters. The swing back will pass far beyond the types it first expressed. Gravity, capacity, independence will become the common wear.

Nevertheless, I do not apprehend a wave of Quaker drab submerging the ten thousand standard advertisements of sex that now animate our streets. Women in desperation will no longer make a flagrant appeal to all and sundry, but that does not mean they will become indifferent to their effect. Within the code of pride I have foreshadowed for women the life of the new community will have much variety, and that will display itself in costume and bearing. The new community will be one of more freely developed personalities than ours, and upon the basis of its common standards there will be a far greater diversity of personal experiences. We shall not all be boxed up by twos and twos and relaxed in crowds. The new variety will be due, not to a tangled confusion of traditions and accidents, but to an open development of personal idiosyncrasies. Our lives today will seem as limited, uniform and stereotyped to the larger living, fuller living, wider living people of the days to come as a crowd of Central African negroes in an explorer's photograph – all alike in paint and feathers and armed alike and nearly all in the same attitude – looks to our eyes today.

The institution of marriage as we know it has a false air of having lasted unimpaired throughout the ages. It has, as a matter of fact, varied enormously, and it continues to vary, in its obligations, its restrictions its availability and solubility, its duration. People are constantly discussing, "Are you for or against marriage? Would you abolish it?" We are all for and against marriage, and we abolish it piecemeal continually. We vary the implications of the bond by fresh legislation every few years; we have in my lifetime reduced the former headship and proprietorship of the husband to a shadow, robbed him of rights of assault upon his wife, taken away his privilege of not educating his children, and relaxed the conditions of divorce. The marriage of today is not the marriage of yesterday, and still less is it likely to be the marriage of tomorrow. When you rule out of consideration all the points upon which marriage varies in the civilised communities today and consider what remains after the stripping, you will find it amounts to very little more than the legal recognition and enforcement of that natural tendency of the human animal to mate and to sustain a joint establishment for the protection of the resultant offspring.

The force of reason is in alliance with the forces of social convenience in narrowing down marriage to a child-protecting bond. Until that is done it is clear that the state will be depriving adults, needlessly, of their legitimate sexual freedom, to the grave demoralisation of such law and police organisations as may be required to enforce these all too intimate restrictions. The community only becomes concerned with sexual affairs when the public health is affected or a child is begotten and born. Then public responsibilities are incurred, obligations must be acknowledged, and home life and upbringing ensured for the new citizen of the world.

At present legal marriage is more than such a public bond, partly out of regard for the dwindling social necessity of a rule of inheritance and partly because of the impudent intolerance of our intellectually and morally discredited religious organisations. In every generation now we humiliate and injure scores of thousands of lives under the discrimination of bastardy, in deference to the imaginary needs of keeping together estates that our death duties are busily breaking up, and because the endowments of religion are still sufficient to maintain strenuously orthodox parsons and priests. These are things of the old order, and the forces of progress thrust them aside, slowly but steadily. As the bastard is equalised with the legitimate son, and the proprietorship of the husband and wife attenuated to the privileges of lover and mistress, the world will cease to inquire for a wife's "marriage lines" and marriage signify little more than habitual association.

Already some people are dropping the change of a woman's name at marriage, and that may extend until it is the general practice. When women write, or act, or paint, it is becoming common. Dr Marie Stopes is really Mrs Roe, Viola Tree is really Mrs Parsons, and there are hundreds of such cases. Hotel proprietors all over the world, and experienced butlers in the best houses, behave as though there were millions. The time may come when the ministrations of the clergyman, the orange blossoms and the robe of white, "The Voice that Breathed O'er Eden," the hired carriage and the white favours will be the quaint social survival of the backward suburbs and the provincial towns.

Such a fading out of marriage from its present stereotyped rigidity will put no end to mating. The men and women of the wider life and the larger views will still feel our common necessity to go in couples for longer or shorter periods. But there may be much diversity in the character of their coupling. The standardised relations of man and wife and of man and mistress – which latter are at present a sort of left-handed reflection of marriage – will have given place to many variations of association. In the ampler, easier, less crowed, less ceremonious social life of tomorrow, a life of more adult, more individualised people, the consorts will not always be upon a convention of equality. Perhaps they will rarely be upon terms of equality. As we begin to take off the stays, blinkers, traces, hoods, masks, fetters, gags we have put upon the sexual imaginations of human beings, and examine into the living realities below, we may realise that we have been trying to adapt an immensely various collection of types to one standard bilateral arrangement. We may find they are not only diverse in temperament, but that they go through diverse phases of development, so that what is reasonable and desirable for a man of five-and-twenty may be cruel nonsense if it is applied to a man of five-and-fifty. Our moral judgments may need to vary not only with temperament but with the stage of development of the individual we judge. Human growth goes on throughout life; we do not "grow up" and have done with it, as our forefathers supposed.

The Christian marriage, like most marriage institutions in the world, met the needs of a peasant life with a passable success. It happened normally about the early twenties, or a little later for a man, and it carried the couple on for twenty years, by which time toil and exposure had aged them, their children were growing up, and there was little more to be done for them. It is extraordinary how young in years some of the old women and bent ancients about here are. The romantic tradition of the nomad and his descendant, the aristocrat, was even nearer adolescence. One day came love and another death. I have already pointed out the youthfulness of Shakespearean romance. But nowadays we live much longer, we do not age so fast, we learn quicklier and mature more rapidly, and a new stage opens and widens in life between the thirties and the seventies, for which the institutions, traditions, sentiment and poetry of the past cannot be expected to provide a complete outline. This is the stage, the new adult stage, upon which the coming order will be built and which is being cleared of its encumbrances of childish, youthful and adolescent habits and feelings, and short and narrow views. Mating and marriage and the rearing of a family must still be a part of this new life, but only a phase of it. It was George Meredith, I think, who set the world talking twenty years ago by suggesting ten-year marriages. That is surely too short. The practical endurance of a marriage is determined by the need of children for a home. The home now does not last a lifetime. England now is full of houses left like a last year's nest. At best the old home, like Lambs Courts, becomes a meeting-place and club-house for the growing clan. Commonly it dissolves. The Riviera here swarms with people those homes have come to pieces.

Probably Darby and Joan will still be found in the new world, but it may be that the common practice will be an exchange between different ages. I have an impression that at the present time the very young people do not, in the majority of cases, hit it off together very easily. Youth is too egotistically preoccupied to show much consideration for the egotistical preoccupations of another undeveloped personality. Perhaps it is more natural to have one partner rather protective and stronger, and one fresher and more spontaneous.

Or it may be that the common human life passes through phases that begin with love for a strong adult type, go on to a love of equals, to partnership and the home and children, and give place to a keener interest in and a finer understanding for the young. Some of my contemporaries have gone through such phases, and I can find traces of them in my own rather aberrant experiences. But though this may be true of men, it may not be so true of women. I do not know. They are disguised from me, and I have not been so closely interested as I might have been in the feelings and reactions of women older than myself. Just as the young man, from the age of eighteen onward, under the pressure of the romantic tradition, is forced to imagine himself a virile adult, and stronger and coarser and wiser and more wilful than any woman at all, so every woman, unless she has turned her back upon all thoughts of attraction, must go on playing the tender juvenile part. Women pretend even to themselves, so that they can tell you nothing real; and it defeats my poor powers of psychic analysis altogether to guess at the suppressed and distorted might-bes of their imaginations. Venus Absoluta is, for all practical judgments, the unknown goddess.

Perhaps Catherine the Great of Russia and Ninon de Lenclos were intimations of the quality of Venus Absoluta. Or perhaps they were merely energetic and versatile men who happened to be of the female sex.

For many in the reconstituted human community matters may come full round to the ancient balance of the peasant life again when men and women alike were workers. At a higher level and in a more lucid co-operation. In just the measure that men are able to get rid of the predatory and gambling and merely acquisitive process in the new world society, in just that measure may the old intimate fellowship of man and woman return. And there, I think, comes a possible reconciliation of Clementina's assertion of ineradicable differences and dependences with the new spirit of freedom and pride. It becomes possible, when a man works not for himself but for the race, that a woman should at once remain equal and proud of herself and yet work in subordination to him. It may be that by nature his initiatives are more resolute and less hesitating than hers.

The humiliations of women in recent times have been very largely due to their realisation that their lives were subordinated to men's merely personal ends. That, they feel, is shameful, half-way to the common prostitute. Their recalcitrance was of a piece with the recalcitrance of a worker who finds his life limited, used and exhausted for the mere individual gratifications of a profit-hunting employer. There is no share nor pride in the end for the subordinate in either case. The forces of revolution work to abolish that sort of employment and any sort of dependence on individual whim. But subordination takes on an altogether different quality when it is subordination to a captain, who himself is subordinate. He also serves, and if manifestly he serves in good faith there is no loss of honour in following his leads. No social state has ever been conceived, nor can I conceive any, in which most of the men and women will not be living subordinated lives. I see no great hardship if in the future as in the past the rôle of a large proportion of women remains in reality ancillary. That need not prevent them from living happily and beautifully, proud of what they are and of what they do.

But I grow more and more speculative; and these women of the days to come, for all their pride and graciousness, remain conspicuously featureless. My reason evokes them, fine-spirited and wise, but they are aloof from me. Their faces remain blank ovals that have not so much as eyes to look towards me.

The night is late, and early tomorrow Clementina is coming down for a great walk we have long promised ourselves into those grey wildernesses of stone and scrub above Gourdon. It will be too far and too stony for Titza's incessant little feet. I shall carry food and drink in my rücksac, and we shall sit among the rocks in the sunlight under the blue sky and wrangle and discourse about these endless riddles.

## 8 – *Trouble in the Night*

I have been reading over the sections I have written in the past two months. Many of them impress me as bare and abstract. I have written of the change of scale in economic life, of the supersession of schools and colleges and methods and institutions and forms of government, of the conflict between traditions of relationship. It has been necessary to reason close and hard and stick to general terms.

"Tradition of relationship" is, I admit, an arid term to cover people's love troubles. I have been attempting a diagram of the whole of human life as I see it passing before me, and perhaps it is absurd of me to regret now that it is diagrammatic. Both the telescope and the microscope take us at last to the inhuman. But it is upon the gaunt loom of these economic processes, educational influences, guiding traditions, that all our lives are woven.

I return from this long flight, this bird's-eye view of human affairs in the sluices of change, to the hangar, so to speak, of this room. I clamber out of my framework of generalisations. I come back from map scale to life-size again. And I find many things in the story I have told of myself and my brother, and many other things I have seen in life that had seemed irrational and perverse and adventitious, falling into a kind of reasonableness in accord with the broad lines that outline inspection has revealed.

It is possible now to distinguish, if not to separate, the essential living matter of these experiences from the streams of suggested ideas, imitations, subconscious responses, imposed habits, uncritical acquiescences that flowed through that living matter into acts. I discover the compulsions in what seemed wilful actions, the mechanical quality of many inconsistencies and much misbehaviour.

Hitherto I have thought that Clara's offence against me was that she was unfaithful to me; but now I perceive that the essential trouble was this, that she married me and I her without lucidity or sincerity. I must have disappointed her acutely in many things; but most, and most disastrously, by my unconscious self-betrayals of my belief that I had bought her, that I had bought her at no great price, chiefly to relieve my cloddish sensuality – in relieving hers. The shams we had accepted to clothe our transaction were thin enough for at least a subconscious apprehension of the truth. Only now do I realise how much of our relationship stripped down to that. We phrased it differently, in phrases that I have largely forgotten. But by nearly all the standards that mingled in her mind she had, I see, a case against me, and though I might have pleaded that she misled me in what she promised me and in what she meant to give me, far more had I misled myself. She and her sisters were saturated in that degeneration of the romantic tradition which has turned the haughty and pampered beauty into a needy and pursuing beauty. It seemed normal and proper for them to cheat in the face of such marriages as confronted them. They were already primed to cheat and snatch before I knew them. At times she must have been amazed by the realisation of her own turpitude, at the net into which her temptations and prevarications and justifications had entangled her. She must have wondered, like a beast in a cage, how it had come about that she was in such a tangle.

It is easy to condemn Clara as a bad woman, and so dispose of her. That in effect is how I treated her. But there is another side to her offences that I am only now beginning to appreciate at its full significance. I have thought often enough how they hurt me, but for the first time I am coming to think how they hurt her. What devastating hours of dismay and perplexity must Clara have lived through – even before our rupture! When she thought of what she had done and how and when I might find out, and what would happen then, and why, why in Heaven's name she had done it! Because life had not been made plain to her, because she had been lured and shouted at by a confusion of impulses and voices bidding her to go hither and thither. For every impulse, for every suggestion there had been some sort of formula and a quality, however flimsy, of excuse. If it was only the excuse of saying I deserved it. She must have lain awake at nights by my side, trying to persuade herself she was safe and all was well with the outlook, while the gathering dangers marched round about her and threatened her. Or that by some feat of rhetoric and ratiocination she would be able to "explain." And afterwards, through the tangle of adventures and misrepresentations that ended in Weston dropping her and through her subsequent difficulties, what fresh series of unsolvable perplexities must have assailed her unprotected sleepless hours.

Some years ago the sort of people who find life too ample for them used up their surplus time in putting together again extremely dissected and dispersed pictures called jig-saw puzzles. Humorists would make the difficult impossible by mixing two or three of these puzzles and presenting a selection of the *mélange* to the unwary solver. The fact beneath poor Clara's indulgences, evasions and artificialities was a mixed jig-saw puzzle of problems of conduct. I doubt if she ever had a suspicion of the trick Mr G had played upon her life. She never saw anything of the joke – and now I see it too late to mitigate the harshness there was even in my belated kindness to her.

She had a capacity for suffering as great as mine. She never had any successes at all; life battered at her; she felt it all more than I should ever have done because she had nothing of my ultimate power of stoical self-detachment from pleasant or harmful things. She was altogether submerged in life and had no such escape. Perhaps she had her consolations, a run of luck at boule or roulette, a passing conquest, an assignation, and she may have got a fullness of gratification out of such things that I cannot imagine. They could not have balanced the account. Luck treated her badly, and I cannot jest with Mr G about her life as I can about my own.

I turn now to the memories of my other love adventures, the casual encounters, the passades, the brief passions of pursuit and success. I have told the reader little about them except that they occurred. What else was there to tell? Surveyed again now in this geographical, this historical fashion, they look less bright and smaller than they did before. They happened, they entertained me, some of them delighted me; I make no apology for them, and I do not repent. But there was little beauty in them, and a sort of pettiness pervaded them. I find the condemning quality about them an idleness, a pointlessness. Such things may happen with a certain grace and brightness in the heats and curiosities of youth, but not in the habitual life of a grown man. They have their value and justification in assuagement or in reassurance. But they were mere apologies to love. We were frittering away something precious for which our world provided no better use.

My life with Sirrie arose out of one of these passades and make an end to them. Few people, even among my nearest friends, seem to understand how good a thing for me were those years I spent with her. Why will they not accept my judgement of her? They have newspaper reports, scandalous stories, the false knowledge of a few hours. I lived with her for some years. Never was the bare truth about a woman so false a libel as it was on Sirrie. Never did facts make so cruel a caricature. I was the first friend she had ever met among men, and she was the first close friend I had ever known among women. When I think of the beauty and spirit she had, her mental and physical fineness and hardihood, I am grieved, even now I feel real grief, at the wastage of her and the suffering and desolation that brooded behind the drugs and drink and misdeeds to which she had resorted. I had no hand in that, and it is only now that I can consent to look squarely at all these poor flounderings and follies that dropped her at last, a coughing refugee, into my care.

But the solitary side of life! The sleepless nights when all our mental restraints have been put off with our daytime clothes, and our stark, defenceless selves face the immensities of remorse, of self-accusation and fear! I think of that eager, slender girl at seventeen, hopefully triumphant – I have a picture of her then, and she is adorable – and then of the woman who would come from her room to mine in our early days at Richmond, whispering shamefacedly in the darkness: "Pity me! Pity me! Take me in your arms. I can't *sleep*, Billy; I keep on thinking. I can't *sleep*."

It was a phase that came to an end with her, so that latterly she slept like a child and ceased to trouble, but it was a dreadful phase. Before she was twenty life was already staring and grimacing at her.

With her, just as with Clara, the impulses and voices in the confusion had urged her this way and that. How was she to judge?

How was she to know? The traps looked like fun. The base marriage looked like wisdom and help for all her family. These two unhappy brains are just glimpses of what a "conflict of traditions," what "variable standards of sexual conduct," what "obsolete marriage laws and insincere observances" mean when they are translate into individual sensations. The jig-saw puzzles have no solution. The baffled creatures struggle over the verge of despair.

Helen, too, suffered from life, though I knew far less of her inner world than I did of Sirrie's. She had the gifts of pride and anger, and they are powerful talismans against the powers of darkness. But was wept at nights, and I was an immense disappointment of her expectations. I still wish I could atone for that to her, though indeed it was not I, but the heroic standards she had chosen for her lover and the wide divergence of our ambitions, that tore up our romance. But if she wept with rage and chagrin, I also had my share of these wakeful torments. I have told already of a journey from Geneva to Paris, when my own mixed jig-saw had the upper hand with me. I must have spent scores of hours in my tortured endeavours to fit Helen and myself into one happy and hopeful scheme of life.

I have been writing of the equal, proud woman as an ideal. In Helen I met her. In the early days we were equal and proud to the swaggering pitch. But unless the proud and equal woman travels an identical road, how is one to keep her?

Neither Helen nor I need to be pitied as those others who are weaker and less coherent are to be pitied; both of us have something in us that sustains us and at last takes us out of all such distresses. At an early limit we grow exasperated, damn the jig-saw puzzle, and sweep it out of the way. The jig-saw puzzle is not a primary thing with us. We are more wilful and more strongly individualised than the common run of people. I have my philosophy of life, my faith, my religion, and she has the compelling impulse of her art.

A great actress is not the feminine equivalent of a great actor; being a great actress is not the same thing as acting; it is a thing peculiar to womankind. It is the sedulous development of a personality to superb proportions. The actress can lie and think of that effect she creates, that legend which grows, as I lie and think of the great revolution that began before I was born, that will continue after my death, to which I have given myself. We have these preoccupations in which our egotisms are chambered and protected; we know what we mean to do, we have banished all essential confusions of purpose; the gnawing desires for some particular but incompatible recognition, the hopes that are dependent on others, remorse for things that seemed right and yet became morally dislocated, the fluctuations of decision as one standard gives place to another; these things wait disregarded for the most part in the antechambers of our minds with little chance of snatching a passing audience and none of invading the inner places.

The schemes I entertain of a world republic, of a simplified economic system, of a cleansing and illumination of the individual and social and sexual relationships, may seem to aim only at the outer forms of life. I may seem to be harsh and merciless towards the dear old dignities and loyalties, the time-honoured social inequalities, the quaint moral prejudices, the romantic interpretations, the subtle, intricate, well-meaning religious dogmatisms, amidst which the great mass of human beings struggles up toward the light; but the brakes and thorns of this picturesque jungle are not simply outward things. They penetrate to the nerve centres and torture there.

The inner aspect of these things is hundreds of millions of baffled, perplexed, frustrated brains. The inner aspect is suppression and humiliation, the prowling onslaughts of thwarted desires and discharges of unreasoning hate that never come to the surface because of fear. We are all at sixes and sevens;

those we love disappoint our dearest expectations, and our acts recoil upon us amazingly, disconcertingly, embitteringly. The great herd of mankind wanders in strange and difficult and dangerous places; it has no clear guidance towards the open lands, and its insecurity and uncertainty determine the drama in well-nigh every brain that is born into it. These things belong together, the outward maladjustment of the race and its reflection in the individual mind.

The peace of the world, the just and creative society, and the common peace of the human soul can only come, each with and through the other. Some may escape the common lot by the vigour of their egotisms or the strength of their philosophy; some may reach forward in creative work from the incompatibilities of the present. Some find a drug or a religious dogma sufficient for stupefaction. The ordinary personal life is still a sensitised meeting-place of conflicting forces that rather imagines itself to be, than is as yet, an individual. These political, economic, social, historical discussions, so far from being unreal, touch the very core of reality; they are a sorting-out of the mixture of moral jig-saw puzzles in which every individual is entangled – a sorting-out that may at last leave the individual man or woman with a consistent problem that is capable of solution.

Biologists say that the greater part of our bodies is dead matter or mere nutrition, our hair, our skins, our bones and teeth, our blood. The only fully living reality is the protoplasmic thread hidden away in nerves and fibres and cells. And of the whole display of human life, the houses and cities and cultivations, the markets and crowds and factories and schools, the only vital part is really this struggle with the jig-saw puzzle of "What am I to do?"

I return to this inner and hidden life. This is what feels, this is what responds, this is what matters, this is what is. This is the life that in the daytime and commonly we hide even from ourselves. The night is its time for revelation. Then for all our resistances we find ourselves taken and stripped and put upon the rack of these blundering contradictions of standard and desire. Then come writhings and cries. The angel and the ape appear. The morning finds us already most sedulously forgetting that dreadful interview with our bare selves. We dress, we examine our faces in the glass to be sure that we are masked before we risk the observation of our fellow masqueraders.

The streets are alive with people, grave, decorous-looking people. They pass intent upon their various business, with an air of knowing exactly what they are and exactly what they are doing. And last night this self-possessed young woman bit her pillow and beat the air with clenched hands and cried, "Oh God! Oh God! Shall I never escape?" and that grave and respectable gentleman with the gold-tipped cane stared out of his bedroom window at the dawn and wished and came near contriving another man dead.

It is Clementina who has brought me down from my bird's-eye survey of humanity to these troubles of the innermost. She has been telling me things about herself that hitherto she has hidden. She has been so gay and happy a companion that I did not realise she could also be full of unspoken distresses. How blind and stupid we can be even to those whom we meet continuously and love dearly!

We walked up into those hills to the west of the Gourdon road as we had arranged, and Mr G gave us one of the best of his days. How few of the thousands who pass in their automobiles along that starred and recommended track and stop at the celebrated viewpoints and crane their necks over the grey battlements to look down into the gorge below, suspect the sweet desolations, the clean cool loveliness of the uplands they skirt! It is as if God had run short of matter when he made the rocks and turf and little flowers up there, and had woven in warm sunlight to complete the job. I lay on a patch of turf beside her and talked of these traditions of relationship about which I had been writing. No one, I said, has fully measured the cruelties that could happen within the bonds of marriage. When poorish respectable people were tied together and had no means of escape. The secret hatred, the ingenuities of vexation and humiliation that might occur.

"And if people are free," Clementina demanded, "they cannot be cruel?"

"Why need they be cruel? They can go away."

Clementina made no answer.

Presently I glanced up at her and she was sitting, chin in hand, with that long beautiful back of hers drooping, so that all her figure was a note of interrogation. She was not looking at me; she was brooding on what she wanted to say to me.

"Clissoulaki," she said. "Do you think – Do you think you have never tormented me?"

I considered it. "No."

"I want to tell you some things. You have been writing this great book of yours about everything in earth – and whatever used to be heaven, and you have come at last to women. You have been all over the world and seen and done all sorts of things. You know nearly everything, my dear. But do you know anything at all about love?"

"I know you," I said.

She shook her head. "I wish you did."

She had something prepared for me and so I waited for her to go on. "I want to tell you things. Some of them seem ungracious. Some of them are unfair. But I want to tell you them. I've hidden them…

"You took me when I was an utter failure. I had gone down. Heaven knows how far a woman can sink, or how long her natural cowardice will force her to endure things, but anyhow I was very low. I did not know how to set about killing myself. But my heart had gone. I should have been glad to die. And then you came, the friendly thing you are. Surely whatever you give I ought to take. Life began again. Hope! How happy you have made me! What happy times I have had here! And all the same you torment me. You give me heart-aches. I love you. I love you altogether. I give myself to you with both hands. And you smile. And put me aside as if all that was nothing."

She paused. "If you had not met me in the streets of Paris you would not put me aside.

"No, don't interrupt me, my dear. I shouldn't have said that. I want to tell you what I am telling you now while it is clear in my mind. Perhaps that was not true. At least you need not notice it. But I think it sometimes in the night. You should know I think it. When a women loves a man she forgets what she was or what he is. She is not even grateful to him if she loves him. She just wants him, and wants him with all her being. No other woman has ever loved you as I love you, and no other woman ever will. The more you give me, the happier and healthier I am here, the sweeter life is with you, the more I am tormented by the thought that this is just a holiday for you, a rest, and presently you will go away. All this year I have been hiding that. I have been thinking it and hiding it. It seemed so ungracious, so unfair. Why should you not do so if you chose to do so?

"Don't touch me, dear. Now I have begun, let me show you my heart…

"Night after night I have lain awake in my little bedroom – the bedroom that is so pretty and gay with the things you made me buy – and I have been tormented!… If I was to lose you, then I think it were better I had died in Paris, before I knew what happiness was. I am haunted perpetually by the fear of losing you. And particularly when you have been away in England, doing I don't know what. Always then I was sure you would never come back to me. Something would happen. You would be killed. You would be snatched away. Or simply – why should you come back to me? You used to send me those little off-hand cards, telling me nothing. Sometimes you missed three days. You were busy, I know. But down here I was not busy. Three days here can be eternity.

"I used to come for great walks up over these hills. I have been here sometimes, stumbling over the stones, belated, in the twilight, afraid of sheep-dogs. Because I was still more afraid of that little bedroom down below there.

"Misery! Misery beyond reason! I have stuffed the corner of my sheet into my mouth to prevent myself crying out and waking those English old maids in the next room."

"But had you no faith in me?"

"Faith! In the night! With you away!"

She turned upon me the eyes of an elf in despair. "You take love so lightly! You take it so easily! Love has come to you. Women have loved you. And you know nothing of love."

## 9 – *Change Hangs over the Villa Jasmin*

This situation at the Villa Jasmin is, I perceive, coming to an end. I return to earth again after my flight over past and present and future, and find the securities and tranquillities about this familiar writing-table dissolving and passing away. It has pleased me so well to come and write here that I watch the end approaching with a selfish pang. But always there has been a certain unreality in this happy refuge; from the beginning it had a touch of dream stuff in its composition.

It is a dream that seemed to have materialised more completely than it has done. I dreamt it first in that train journey from Geneva to Paris, and I wanted it and needed it so much that in some way it was bound to exist. It was easy to take the happy chance of Clementina and incorporate her and make her the priestess and divinity of the place. True, it should have been a little low white house and not pink as this one is, but I forgave it that for all the other pretty details with which it surprised me.

I have always maintained that this place and this seclusion could not last, that it was too serene and beautiful a setting to be permanent. Παντα ῥει; its little fountain greeted me with that remainder when first I came to it. But it was my belief that it would be Clementina who would shatter it all, by confessing herself bored, finding a more amusing and less preoccupied lover and departing. I had always prepared myself to let her go, and everything was in readiness to secure her going from the anxieties and indignities of material need. I should not have stayed long alone here. Each time I returned it was a delight to find her still eager for my coming.

But it is I and not she from whom the decree of conclusion must come. This freakish and fantastic ménage has been founded on distresses and hopes deferred, of which I had no inkling, and now that this has been brought home to me, the dream fades.

It was Helen who used to talk of "coming through" a part. Clementina has come through her part. She was the whimsical, delightful, elfin visitant of the Villa Jasmin. That was the rôle I thrust upon her. She chose to play at being utterly in love with me, and I to be cold and preoccupied. We talked of the siege of the Villa Jasmin. The siege is over and the play is done, and we find ourselves man and woman face to face. She has come through her part and it seems I am coming through mine.

While I was soaring up there in the air surveying "traditions of relationship" and men and woman in "general terms," I remarked, among other memorable things, that much of the present unhappiness of men and women was due to a reference to different standards; that people imposed their own codes and expectations upon one another and so almost unwittingly arranged conflicts and cruelties. But this is exactly what I have been doing to Clementina. I have assumed an extreme modernity in this antique mind of her, held her to the practice of it and treated her struggle against it as an entertaining pose. I have made her angry and baffled her and laughed at her a score of times and thought no more of it, and only now do I apprehend that I have also made her and may still be making her exceedingly unhappy.

I do not blame myself nor her for the creation of these stresses. They have happened. They might have been foreseen, but I did not foresee them. It was my impulse to make her free of me, to refuse to buy her, to give her a position and a salary and a light agreeable task beside me. That was well enough in its way. That she chose to make me her lover was my good fortune. I did not ask it or refuse it. The convention was that that might cease at any time, that she was free to take another lover or do whatever might please her. Her duties were to supervise my little house, stand between me and servants, buy and arrange furniture for me as she thought proper, lunch with me and companion me for the afternoon. Then with a liberal gesture I dismissed her to her excellent pension, she a free woman and I a free man. Here in Provence she could rest for a time, here was peace and healing and self-respect for her, and when she saw her way to a more attractive life I would help her to achieve it. These were the handsome pretences of our bargain.

At the pension, people came and went, quite possibly interesting people. I did not see them. She had two pleasant rooms, and we had obliterated the bleak furnishing with oriental rugs and hangings and a multitude of books. She could read, write poetry – if she chose to write poetry – readjust her perplexed and broken life. Down here in my gently modernised *mas* I could think and work, come and go as my mood or my business interests required. If I went away for long months or a year or so, that was my affair. She could draw her salary, keep an occasional eye on the place, travel if she felt disposed to do so – she had the means for that. Jeanne could be trusted to mind the house. There was no need that Clementina should fall in love with me, none that she should fall so extravagantly in love with me and charge all our reactions with passion.

But she has done so. She has gone beyond all the obligations of our agreement. She has worked for me as no one has ever worked for pay since time began. She has enveloped me with a tender personal devotion. I too, quiet insensibly, have lapsed from the hard rationalism of my first intentions. She is the most to blame, but I have been unwary. While I have been building up a conception of a finer, freer mating in the future, the passing days have betrayed me. A great affection has grown up between us now.

I do not know how necessary she has become to me, but it is plain she has become very necessary. Her company, her conversation, her ways, delight me as the warm sunshine delight me. I like the sound of her now and the sight of her; I find myself watching her unawares; her tastes please me; she pleases me wonderfully. But what is more than any of these things, her happiness and her unhappiness have taken hold of me so that I can no longer hurt her and be at peace.

But though there has been all this change and growth of feeling between us, the forms and customs of our life here still follow the light-hearted artificiality of our original treaty. Clementina is still the domestic secretary who walks down at lunch-time from her rooms at the pension to see that all is in order here, hushes the barking of Titza if I am still writing or thinking, interviews the gardener and the plumber and buys the material to re-cover the chairs. And I come and go upon my mighty businesses and make it plain that I am scandalised when she tempers her services with endearments and caresses. There is a convention which even Jeanne affects to observe that we are not lovers. But all this, which was so bright and entertaining a year ago, rings hollow now and more hollow every day. She wants to be more easily with me, and I want her more at hand.

Yet Villa Jasmin is a little house, and the silence of this study was very vital to me. In this place I can conceive no other way of life than the one we have led here.

This is the situation Clementina, with her face of involuntary distress, brings to a crisis. Her fears and instincts run ahead and confront her with the riddle of what is to come. "I love you wholly," she says. "I have put my life in your hands. I have no other life now but the life you made for me here. Do you mean to go away from me? What are you going to do with me now that the book you set out to write here is coming to an end?"

She may count upon it that I shall not go away from her. We shall go away together when the good days of the Villa Jasmin have reached their allotted term.

But I do not yet know how we shall go away nor whither we shall go. I have been so intent upon the diagrams of my world that this problem takes me by surprise. Until I have some inkling of the solution I do not know what to tell her.

## 10 – *Clementina's Idea of Love*

We began our life here in a vein of genial make-believe, and the play still goes on and masks the forms of the very deep and very far-reaching relationships that have come into being between us. Clementina has thrown a passionate love into our sunny comedy, and I have pretended not to see. We two love each other very greatly now, but each after his and her own fashion. The fashions are very different. I am not sure what we shall find when we cease to pretend, and come face to face with each other.

Clementina professes love. She is my instructress in this great science, this great art. It is her occupation, her subject. For her, love is an absolute; for me it is a thing to examine and question.

She speaks of love as of something that women understand by nature and that men do not; they have to learn. It is a difference between us as fundamental as the difference of sex, a matter that affects every possible view about the position and rights and wrongs and all the standards of women. Love, she maintains, is created and imparted by women.

This is frankly opposed to my treatment of love, throughout this book, throughout my life. I have dealt with it is as something as incidental as beautiful, as something that may come into a "sexual relationship" like the fires of red and gold that come suddenly from windows when the sunlight is reflected by them. And I have supposed it always to be a thing as much masculine as feminine.

I have told something of Clementina's mixed origins and varied misadventures. I do not know whether these things make her the most unique or the most representative of women, a freak or a compendium. I do not know whether we two are as Adam and Eve in a new world of men and women, or whether we are queer accidents of our time and of no significance to anyone except ourselves. Clementina has no doubt in the matter. She is Eve. Rarely it is "I and you" with her. "A woman feels," she says, or, "That is the way with a man."

I have argued with her that this love of hers, in its abundance and completeness, is not really a natural nor a fundamental thing at all. I declare it is an artificial thing, a disposition, and not a necessity. It does not come by instinct. It is developed, it is secondary; it is a thing of culture. It is a dogmatic thing, and she has wilfully given herself to its exaggeration and glorification. She has given herself to personal love exactly as some women give themselves to love in religion. Her love has the sedulous quality of a religious devotion. She searches her conscience for imperfections and disloyalties in her love in order to cast them out.

"But that is the nature of women," she pleads. "It is religion. It is same thing. Or rather – religion is love. One sort of love. My love for you is exactly like religion. If – I cannot imagine it – but if I thought of any man but you, it would be a sin. That is the great commandment. Thou shalt have no other love but me."

She argues very subtly about this specialisation of hers.

We all want to be held together within ourselves, she asserts, echoing my own thoughts in that. We all need interior unification for our peace of mind. I have this strange conception of world revolution, of the great creative work of setting up a World Republic, to which I give myself. By that I unify my aims and my life. She cannot unify upon that. "A woman" cannot unify on such great abstractions. But her personal love holds her together in just the same fashion. If she were to lose it, she would "go to pieces," just as I should go to pieces if I lost belief in my revolutionary idea.

"But why not religion?" I ask.

"A woman must see and touch," she says. "Women are more immediate. In convents now there are thousands of women praying, longing, desiring for what they call a vision. They call it a vision because they are taught to do so, but what they want is a tangible reality. For them images are a necessity. I tell you it is exactly that which holds me to love. You are my image. Have you noted the *life* they put into Catholic images – the blood, the distresses, the tears? Mortifications, inflictions, pain, these things comfort religious women because they are contact. Sacrifices, new refinements of material devotion, fill their minds. But even then one must have faith. Without that the images will not even sigh or turn their eyes. That is why I failed to be religious. At one time, almost, I had faith."

"You were a Catholic?"

"But things my father had said about the Catholics kept on seeming true. When he was not quite sober my father could be a wonderful theologian. He undermined me with things I hardly knew I was hearing at the time. But I found I could not believe. When I prayed, something he had woven into me said: 'You're not believing all that. 'You're just thinkin' you believe it!' And it was a live thing I wanted and not a spirit, a thing with a body, a man to respond and answer – *you.*"

But then, I said, bringing in St Augustine against her, she was not in love with me, she was in love with love.

"You complain that you are all directed to me and that I am directed away from you," I said. "But that is not true. You are no more turned to me than I to you. You are turned to love, and you are trying continually to make me also centre my life on love."

She can meet that with no rational argument. "It is you I love," she says.

There she stops with an absolute statement. No analysis avails here. This love, which has embodied itself in me, has become an inseparable, organic part of herself. It is exorbitant, but she has loved so plainly and consistently that I can no more deny the reality of this love of hers than the reality of her soft brown neck or her shining eyes.

It is intensively possessive love. It impels her to invade my liberties. I like flying, and at times when the skies are clear the plutocrat in me asserts himself, and I scrap my railway ticket hither and character an aeroplane from London to Antibes. A little while ago I flew from here to Geneva. But she has a fantastic dread of flying accidents; she will not distinguish between the many deaths that happen during training and experiments, and the rare casualties of passenger flights. Her discipline is not good enough to prevent her making appeals to me to promise, promise never to fly. I am in a quandary. I argue the matter because it goes right to the roots of our relationship. All my disposition is against such restrictions, but her despair is real. I make no promise, but my last two journeys here have been by boat and train, under protest.

"If you loved me," I say, "you would let me do what pleases me best."

"But if you should be killed!"

"It is part of man's job to be killed now and then."

Her tenderness entangles me. I cannot have the swift, sweet delight of the high air because she has infected me with a vision of herself intolerably alone, left desolate because I have seen fit to crash and burn myself to death. That thought pursues me now up among the clouds. I should feel the meanest thing in creation if I found myself rushing down to a disaster. I could not die with self-respect. Her tearful "told-you-so" would reproach my last moments. But if men are to be afraid with the fears of loving women, how can they ever be anything but afraid?

Yet also this possessiveness flows into a hundred gracious thoughts and services. It is a very captivating thing to know oneself cared for, thought for, and sure of willing agreement. I cannot tell of the absurd little attentions she shows me. They are too humble and too touching. Always when I need her no other thing may intervene, she is ready for walk or expedition and any help I wish from her. How often she effaces herself! How often has she kept a smiling face when she was faint with fatigue, until some little thing betrayed the hidden trouble!

She disciplines herself on account of love. I discover her suppressing her impulses, developing a tremendous self-control she did not possess a year ago. We are both extremely hot-tempered, but years have made me quick to arrest and recall and repair what I can of the evil of an angry act. But her instinct for expression is vigorous. Not for nothing are the Greek said to be the first people in history to make a rich and abundant use of language. And she has an over-sensitive vindictiveness begotten by her years of imposed inferiorities and humiliations. She used to watch for petty injustices from me and examine every careless criticism as an attack.

I should find it hard to describe one of our storms in detail. They sprang from minute wants of consideration on my part, from impalpable nothings, from a clumsy French phrase of mine or an English expression misunderstood. Then suddenly, in the course of a walk, at our lunch table, my sunny, happy companion would vanish, give place to a white-faced creature with wicked eyes, suffering unendurably, full of a wild passion to humiliate and wound.

Very deep in Clementina's heart is resentment at life. She was defrauded, ill-treated. Hers is more than the common resentment of those who start at a disadvantage; it has been embittered. Then at last she found me, and she has been building up and reconstructing her life upon me. She has turned once more, after defeat, defilement and disaster, to love. But she has to hold on hard to love. Sometimes she seems to find it quite easy to love me. But her grip is only now beginning to be sure. At first trivial accidents could loosen it. She would find herself slipping from the position she wanted so desperately to maintain.

It has always been some quite little thing that seemed to reveal to her the earthen substance of her god, a casual selfishness, a chance assumption. Then for a time I became just another of those men who had trampled on her life, one of those beings who trample over all life, taking, exacting, disregarding, making the world despair.

I did not understand at first. I would shrug my shoulders and meet her "temper" with a flinty face.

But these quarrels that came out of nothingness are disappearing. They would last in the beginning for a day or so – when she would not come down to the Villa Jasmin, when she gave me to understand she was packing for some unknown destination in this world or the next. How stonily I treated her then! How little I tried to find a way back for her! Later on these outbursts diminished in their violence and persistence. They came down to hours. Recently they have been mere jars of ten minutes or so, and, now I come to think of it, there have been hardly any for some time.

This change from fitful conflicts to serenity has been all her doing. She has taken that disposition to swift resentment in hand, just as a religious novice is trained to deal with a besetting sin. She has fortified her faith in me, until at last that jealous questioning of my quality has been almost overcome. So, deliberately and wonderfully. She has built up such a relationship with me as I had never known before, as I have never before believed could exist between two human beings. It is her work.

When last I came back here from England I discovered a portable typewriter in her sitting-room. She had not expected me, and she had thrown a piece of Indian silk over it. "I did not mean you to see that until I had had all my lessons," she said. She had bought the thing and gone to the school in Grasse and was already reasonably competent – and she taken all that trouble simply because I had been sometimes put out by waiting for the typist who clears up these writings for me in Cannes.

"After all, why should you send your typing away? I can do it."

"Why should you? It is toilsome and dull."

"I want to share in what you are doing. I want to take trouble for you."

"But you were to study for yourself. You were to read here. You were to write poetry. You were to find yourself."

"I've lost my interest in poetry. It was always poor stuff I wrote. Always. Since I have been here it has got more and more like the devotional books they used to give me in my Catholic days. I can't bear it. Love can be made ridiculous if you write it down – the more you love, the more strained and exaggerated it seems, and yet it is all true. And I want to know about this book of yours."

"You said once it was just about Marx and politics."

"I know better now."

Then with a change to vexation:

"Don't you see that I want to be useful? Don't you want me to be useful? Don't you see that I want to make myself necessary to you? Is it nothing to you that I want to necessary? I'm reading English. To get back my English perfectly. To cure my spelling. Every day when you are away from here I go into Grasse. I study. What else is there to do? Commercial stuff. *Comptabilité*. Sums, you call it! It isn't sums. It's business. I was always bad at calculation. Now I want to know about these business things. Oh! You think it's absurd. You *laugh!"*

"My dear!" I said. "No need for you to cry. But why do you not do work of your own? Why do you cast away and destroy everything that gives you a life outside mine? I'm writing out my own faith here, getting my ideas into order for the last spell of work that is left to me. Why don't you do the same thing for yourself, beside me? I am such a preposterous thing to worship – old, egotistical, slow in all sorts of ways – and the world we can serve is so complex, so full of splendid possibilities! I am ashamed to have such a slave. It makes me ridiculous. It confronts me with what I am. It makes me feel my hundred limitations. I love you. Don't I tell you so? Be my ally."

"An ally, yes – if I am always at your side?"

"After the same ends, my dear, wherever they lead us."

"No. At your side. The world means nothing to me unless I am with you. It can be cruel. It can be crowded and unjust and ugly. I do not care what becomes of it, as you do. After I have lost you I do not care if it is all burnt with fire. I do not want the world or life or anything except with you."

That is where Clementina stands.

She is certainly not acting or lying; if this was not her inevitable self, it is now her unalterable self. Is this indeed womanhood? Or is there some difference in race and quality between Clementina and the other women I have known? It was a woman speaking to another woman, who said: "Thy people shall be my people and thy God my God." Milton may have known more than we moderns give him credit for when he wrote of the devotion of Adam and Eve: "He for God only; she for God in him."

Clementina is unabashed at my argument that she has made a culture of love. "Every woman," she says, "who is properly a woman wants to make a culture of love. That does not mean that love is artificial because we cherish and protect it and make much of it. You might as well say a baby was artificial and not in the nature of women."

Still I doubt if this splendour of self-abandon is either wholly or permanently Clementina. For a time it is her self-expression. It seems to her to be her complete being. But I have known her for less than two years, and I have no data yet for the full cycle of her life. This may be a season, the high summer of love. This may be a phase in which many needs and desires converge and fuse. It may be Clementina's life will not always pour along this narrow channel of personal obsession. I am, I reflect, not merely Clementina's man, her mate and her lover; I am as yet her whole family, I am her children unborn. She is not only my companion and mistress; towards me she is also an arrested and perverted mother. I have monopolised the love of a household.

There, it seems, lies the clue not only to the inequalities of our passion, but to the nature of the new life to which we have to turn now that the routines of the Villa Jasmin are drawing to an end. For my own part, I confess, it has troubled me and restrained me and also made the daily substance of my life unprecedentedly happy to monopolise for these months of sunshine I have spent here the love of a household.

## 11 – *What is this Love?*

If this insatiable craving, this tender prostration that possesses Clementina is love, then it is true what she says: I have never loved, and I do not know what love is.

Perhaps what is true of me is true of all normal men.

There may seem to have been some moonlight resemblance to this radiant warmth in my desire for Helen and in my distress at her loss, but the resemblance goes no further than the desire and the distress. I wanted with an equal vigour indeed, but in an altogether different fashion. There was no devotion, no trace of self-subjugation; I did not change at all, I wanted Helen to change; though I demanded much I gave nothing, and our last two years of association were years of antagonism as strong almost as the necessity we felt for each other. I have never given myself to anyone. I have never wanted to given myself to anyone. Either, then, I am abnormal, or Clementina is abnormal, or here is a profound spiritual difference between the sexes that I am only now beginning to apprehend.

Here am I, very much in love. I am thinking now for a large part of my time of how I am to adjust my life so as to take Clementina wholly into it and to make her as completely happy as I can. I do this because in my fashion I love her, her happiness is my happiness. But let me tell the truth about myself plainly. Even now she is not necessary to me. I could and I should go on without her. I should suffer but I should go on. She is not necessary and no one had ever been necessary to me. I cannot conceive that anyone could ever be necessary to me. And what is more, I am not even necessary to myself. That is to say, I am not afraid to die. I am not distressed that presently I shall be completely dead, nor to think that in a little while I shall be altogether forgotten. Ultimately these things do not matter to me in the least.

Now Clementina is in life, inextricably in life. Life means so much to her that she could even, if it disappointed her dreadfully, commit suicide. It matters to her like that, and her suicide would be a real tragedy. But I do not believe that it would be possible for me to commit suicide. Or to make any very incredible exertions to escape death. Only by over-statement can I express what I am feeling after in these sentences. Let me say, then, that fundamentally I am outside life, receiving experiences. I like and want to do things with life; but I am not of the substance of life, any more than I am of the substance of matter.

It may be that here I am over-defining a difference between myself and Clementina. No doubt there are less than fundamental contrasts here. I have the resignation of sixty and she has the vitality of thirty, and I am Northern and metaphysical and she has all the positive realism of her Mediterranean blood. But after all deductions have been made on these scores I am still disposed to think that the fundamental difference that remains is one that holds good between the masculine and the feminine all up and down the scale of being. Masculine and feminine, I write, and not men and women, because in all men there is something of the woman, and in all women a touch of virility. Nature had never completely sorted out the sexes in any mammalian species. Nevertheless, the biological distinction of masculine and feminine is as plain as east and west. The female is the life itself, the continuation; the male is an experimental projection from life. It is in our nature as males to try and to do, to create and to pass away; it is in the nature of the women as feminine to seize upon our distinctive selves and to seek to preserve and perpetuate them. So it has been between the sexes since the beginnings of life; so it must continue to be for the race to survive. And how in any other fashion can the race go forward and endure?

## 12 – *Shadows of the End*

I do not see how I can ever part from the Villa Jasmin or let the simple peace of this room be disarranged. I shall try to buy this little house or get a lease that will at least make it ours for all our lives. And we will come back here ever and again. But from this time forth it ceases to be what it has been to me hitherto. For a time it was necessary for me to be alone, and here in the mornings and evenings and nights I have been alone, and I have been able to assemble my ideas and view my world simply. The outline and substance of my book exist; this end is incomplete, and Book Three still reads like chunks of a prospectus, but the thing is shaped. This may be the last evening for a long time that I shall spend in solitude at this table.

I have thought for a year and a half that, so far as Provence went, I was resting and reviewing life; but I discover that it is here, and neither in London nor at Downs-Peabody that I have been most actively living. That casual young man of the Parisian sunset has become by imperceptible degrees the dominant figure in my thoughts and life.

There is only one way to deal with our situation, and that is for me to marry her. That has been plain to me for some days. She has never betrayed a thought of marriage; she has had so extraordinary a training in social abasement from the days of Dou-Dou onward; and at first I believe it will dismay and terrify her to think of herself as a wife. She will imagine immense establishments, mysterious social duties, crowded functions, a stupendous strain, and it will take some time to dispel these terrors. They will be dispelled and she will have to marry me, even though she is carried squealing and protesting to the altar. I shall have to work out some way of living – a house near Paris, or in Touraine or Normandy or Brittany perhaps – in which methods of housekeeping and social procedures will not be too strange and difficult for her; and there she will gradually realise, what I have realised long ago, that she has considerable administrative ability, and will rapidly become a house-proud woman. There I can build her up socially.

She shall be slowly accustomed to the austere and dreadful manners of the English, and when by carefully selected sample visitors she is sufficiently indurated, I will take her to London.

It will amuse no end of people to find me at last a married man. I would like to take her to London in early June, and walk with her through St James's Park in the morning when Lu-Lu Harcourt's herbaceous perennials are at their best. We will feed the water-fowl and turn back to look at the towers and pinnacles of Westminster. Then we will taxi to Hyde Park Corner and walk on by way of the rhododendra paths to the Serpentine and lunch in the pavilion in the open air. Or, perhaps better, we will go by the trees in blossom and the flower-beds right through Kensington Gardens to the High Street and lunch in that grill-room in the big hotel where Orpen's Chef was once wont to preside. Afterwards we will visit that little sunk garden by Kensington Palace. She thinks London is a cramped, sombre, unbeautiful place, not to be compared with the artistic eloquence of Paris, and this may put her in a better frame of mind.

In that house we shall get I want her to have children. I see no reason why we should not have a son or so, and it is very important that we should. It is very important that Clementina's affections should come out of the cañon in which they flow at present and spread themselves. She will have great scope in a nursery. The sooner that comes the better.

It did not seem to matter so much when I chanced upon Clementina in Paris that I was a man close upon fifty-nine and she was under thirty. It has not been a very troublesome fact here. But now that things have become thus serious and practical between us, it is a fact I have to take into very careful consideration. I have to think of her whole life. It is a result of Clememtina's disastrous upbringing that she has never troubled to think so far on as to see me aged or dead; her mind had been filled by the ambition to become my assured and inseparable mistress, and after that – suicide or endurance. That was her training.

There are moments when I can find satisfaction in the thought of kicking Monsieur Dou-Dou, that Catholic young gentleman, her first and chief trainer, hard and continuously. She has accepted from everyone the rôle of a scrap of social wastage. Her mind even now does not go beyond a vision of that scrap in love and in luck. But indeed she is as good a woman as any woman, and it shall not be my fault if she does not, after all, get the full measure of life. She will not do that unless she is able to grow out of me before some hitch of health or accident brings out the disparity of our years. When our children come she will be a little distracted from me. She will love me just as much but not so actively and consciously. She will be more in the nursery and I shall be away in the study. Quite unawares she will acquire new habits, new interests; she is still a growing creature. Even down here I have marked how she has read and thought and extended her curiosities. I shall go on with this work I have plotted out for myself, always a little detached from her. She will be less eager to participate when she is more fully employed.

It has never been my habit to think about death, but latterly, once or twice, it has occurred to me that there were limits to one's right to behave as though one was immortal. One should begin to think of the delicate sensitive tentacles of affection and dependence that tie other people to oneself, as the final interruption becomes nearer and more probable. One has failed to live completely well if too large and painful a gap is left by one's going. The ripe fruit should fall off without tearing. The successors should be ready, the plan of campaign imparted, and no one should be monopolised, as in our youth we may monopolise those we love.

It is no ungraciousness to Clementina if I plan, not so much to break as to divert some of the threads in this matted web of feeling which she, dear spider of the heart that she is, has woven out of her living self about me. I see myself as a man of seventy-five or so, I hope not senile, I dread that, but going easy, working and handing the work on as York is doing now, and she a woman of four-and-forty, full of life, busy with many activities, our sons about her; making a domestic deity of me no doubt, a position I shall be well content to fill in her world, subject to the emendations of my sons, but no longer living as she does now, on my direct reactions. More and more I shall be accepted and taken for granted by her. I shall be less looked to for initiatives and interests. And at last a death may be achieved that will be ceremonial rather than tragic.

That is how I plan our life. I am a little amused to find myself making this plan, for plainly it is a retrogression. This is the old-fashioned marriage in which I have never believed, and I am linking myself to a woman of an ancient type according to ideas that are to be found in their full explicitness rather in the immemorial traditions of Hindu family than in our modern world. But for that Clementina and accident are to blame. She has said many acute and some very profound things to me, but none more memorable than her outcry that it was not fair to treat women on terms of equality unless they were prepared for it.

Never was a woman less prepared for it than Clementina.

I do not think I have gone back upon my old opinions materially, but I have – for my own case, anyhow – suspended them. I still think that in the progressive society of the future, sex will be a controlled and used and subordinate thing, that love will defer to and mingle with creative passion, and that there will be a very considerable assimilation of the sexes. They will become more alike in costume, bearing and behaviour. That is already going on, and it is most manifest in the new and northern societies. But it has a long way to go, it has to disentangle itself from a jungle of complex inheritances, and it has to evolve its proper social conventions before men and women can meet on terms of real quality. By all means let us help this development forward, but do not let men fall into the error of anticipating it to the hurt of women.

For nearly a couple of centuries advanced people have been making premature attempts at an unchartered freedom of relationship, without a proper regard for the handicaps of women. Shelley is a typical instance of this logically fair freedom which works out in practice as facile abandonment, cruelty and atrocious injustice. Shelley did all he did to women, I fully realise, in good faith, but all the Shelley-like adventures that go on about us are not in good faith. By all means let us treat women openly on equalitarian terms, but not in our secret thoughts. In truth they have not our weight of egotism, they have not our disregardfulness in aim. Commonly as it comes about, they are younger than we are. A man must hold himself responsible for the woman he deals with. The last concomitant of freedom she should have is the one that is first thrust upon her, responsibility. Let women hold women responsible for all they do; that is their affair, not ours. We have not the right.

And, anyhow, whatever progress the world has made towards free and equal womanhood, Clementina and I are, as a couple, far behind. She accepts, welcomes and cultivates the subordinate rôle. She puts herself defenceless in my hands, and she would always have put herself defenceless into somebody's hands. I have to protect her and foresee for her. I have to take care of her life.

That is why I shall insist upon marrying her. So far as I can read history the wife has always been something inferior to the free princess. She has been private property. I will not flood the reader with archaeological lore and quote from the Spartans to the Zulus and from Atkinson and Weismann upon the point. I shall marry her to direct and take care of her, because I am older, stronger and better placed than she. I will not continue with her as my mistress after our éclaircissements. To the best of my ability in my own poor practice in life I have made love to my mistresses on free and equal terms. But a woman who is in Clementina's position must be covenanted and ensured.

This is the logic of our situation. The reality is that I am filled with tenderness and solicitude for Clementina, that I mean to do all I can for her life, and that if the logic were all the other way round it would not make the least difference to what I am resolved we are to do.

I do not know where we shall go from this place nor what our next arrangements will be. I shall marry her soon. The particular dispositions to make will probably rest with her. What she asks for she can have. We may take our car on a sort of house-hunting honeymoon, westward toward the heart of France. My work will no longer be her rival and her danger, and she will, I know, do everything in her power to forward it in our reconstructed life.

In this dear peace and sunshine I have put my mind in order, and I have a far clearer idea than ever I had before of what I want to do with my world. Meditation is a good thing in so far as it contemplates an ultimate translation into action. For long spells of time out of the better part of two years I have pursued this meditation here, surveyed and questioned my world, until the great revolution has come out plain and sure, as the inevitable form and subject of all I shall henceforth do. It has been, all things considered, not so very unlike a piece of industrial research, leading to a reorganisation in method. I must go on now to the practical application of what this scrutiny of my will and experience has taught me. I must take this set of ideas to a number of people, and if they are sympathetic, consult them about its flotation.

Flotation is the word I choose deliberately. I contemplate the promotion of a new scheme for doing the business of mankind. I want to try over his conception of a World Republic, as something now ripe and seeking realisation, with variety of minds. If it seems to stand the test, or if it requires only partial amendment, then the rest of my life must be occupied in activities that will contribute to it. That is the logical development of situation. This germinating World Republic needs a literature; it has to invade the press; it must develop a propaganda for the young and youthful-minded. It has to discover, educate and organise its adherents, and find and try out every form of persuasion and publicity. It must develop a multitude of subsidiary schemes and define their relations one to another. There must be a discrimination between business, organisations, institutions, that with more or less modification are capable of incorporation in a world scheme of human activities, and those which are essentially useless, obstructive, or antagonistic. It has to pervade the minds and discourse f publicists and leading men and outstanding figures with a realisation of this creative process, the developing plot of a drama in which their activities go on. Just as they apprehend and secure it, are they significant and fit for history. Just as they disregard it are they trivial, mere nuisances and obstructions, supernumeraries, voices and figures in the crowd.

Things seem clear in the Villa Jasmin with a clearness that may be delusive. I want to try over all this that I have thought and written down here, on other active men, to discover why they are not already exactly of my way of thinking. I have to test my ideas by this question: how far has this man or that man whom I have sound reason to respect, got towards my positions? How far is he, within himself and less explicitly, of my way of thinking? I want to try it out on Roderick for example, and on one or two others of our directors who have imaginative breadth. I want to see what resistances Dickon will put up to my creed of creative action. And there are a number of other men against whom I would like to put it. A man who rouses my curiosity greatly is Sir Alfred Mond of Brunner Mond and Co., that kindred octopus which runs so parallel and interdigitates so frequently with our great network. He is difficult to talk to, nervous, and either aggressive or defensive. He flounders about in politics, and goes from party to party rather absurdly. I would give much to know what is his real philosophy, and if fundamentally he is anything coherent and determined. What at the bottom of his heart, if he has ever gone to such depths, does he think of parliamentary methods, of crown, of empire, of the war and the rule of the world? Or does he just accept it all as a cat accepts house and master? Some of his kind do, but not I think he. I must seek him out and a score of other men, Lord Weir, for example, and Sir Robert Hadfield, who have manifestly very active minds which range far beyond merely business activities. What is clear in them? What is implicit in them? And then I come to the financial side of human activities. Keynes I must certainly know more of, and such a man in and out of politics and finance as McKenna. I have never yet got to grips with a banker largely because my ideas hitherto have been too unformed to give him a definite hold in return for my own. Dickon declares that the minds of all financial people run about between fences, and that if they were not trained to respect their fences they would become too original and embezzle, but I believe that even now a number of them do look over their fences without such serious results, and that if they were encouraged they would look over quite a lot, and make all sorts of illuminating remarks about the ways of the economic process.

One sort of man is shall pursue with my inquiries will be the type of Lord Buckmaster, with whom the Rettinger-Dunton process has recently brought me into contact. He is a business man – in oil. Before he came into oil, he was a lawyer and a statesman; he was Lord Chancellor, if I remember rightly, under Mr Asquith. I have met him socially several times, and always he has pleased me. He talks well, thinks finely and powerfully, and he must have a very wide knowledge of both the political and economic worlds. Now how far is the present system, the parades of the royalties, the tedious humbug of parliamentary proceedings, the manoeuvres of the political groups, the social round, "patriotism" and our international rivalries, all this life that is so unreal and unsatisfactory to me, how far is it real and sufficient and final to him? How far does such a man merely go upon the surface of it, and how far does he penetrate? I cannot but believe he penetrates. And if he penetrate, how far does he see the revolution as I see it, and shape his thoughts and acts and conscience in relation to it? Has he an established sense of it as a coherent process? As I have? I am immensely curious about his sort of man. I name Buckmaster because he comes into my head as a convenient representative, but I could name a score of such men, able, prominent, successful, who seem to me manifestly too fine-minded to be satisfied with the play of human affairs as it is staged today, and yet who go about as if they were. Why are they not more explicitly restless and revolutionary?

Then I want to explore the socialists. The Labour Party – or it may be the Independent Labour Party, for I made no note at the time – has recently come out with a scheme for dealing with the coal mines. It is in many ways an excellent scheme, a large scale scheme of scrapping and reorganisation for exhaustive production that would make all British coal one business. It would override many of the arrangements of Romer, Crest and Co., but such things could be readjusted. It could be bolder upon the possibilities of civilising the miner than it is, and of changing his methods of work. Of course the Labour politicians the world knows best, those men who make speeches with their fists and monkey about in court suits, are as capable of carrying out such a scheme as Jeanne here, my excellent cook, is of taking a modern battleship into action. But I find in this report the hands of at least two men, Tawney and Greenwood, who are manifestly both men of wide knowledge and evident power. They must know as well as I do what their party, as a party, amounts to, what a mere cave in liberalism, what a dreary haggle for office it is. Their imaginations are certainly as broadly constructive as mine. Tawney is a man I would welcome upon the board of Romer, Steinhart, Crest and Co. almost as warmly as I would rejoice at the departure of Crest. He would be better occupied with us than in making schemes that can never be realised by the associates he has chosen. Why is he in one camp and Keynes in another and I in a third, while the Crests and the Percies and their kind in massive unity, with nothing but their instincts and traditions to hold them together, can impede progress for whole lifetime?

I mention Tawney and Greenwood as I have mentioned Buckmaster and the others, casually. They have happened to come first into my mind. They are types, not abnormalities. If I set about it I could make a list of some hundreds of Englishmen alone dispersed through the worlds of finance and industry and public affairs who are of a quality that makes their collective futility and their acquiescence in existing things amazing.

Now either my conception of a World Republic as the proper form of life presented to my intelligent and active contemporaries is false, or else it is latent, or it exists in some similar form, but perhaps under disguising terms, not as yet completely assembled, in the minds of all such men as those I have cited. They are all of them men at least as able and intelligent as myself; most of them are much abler and more intelligent; our brains must be all similarly constituted, and, with a few variations of proportion and angle, they know the facts as I know them. Of course, they are where they are, as I am where I am, without premeditation. They are got in and come though to it and found themselves at forty-five or fifty-five or sixty-five before they could make an extensive survey of things about them. But now? After the war, in the midst of the most illuminating stresses and troubles, with the needs of the world growing plain? Surely they must be awakening, as I have awakened, to possibilities that transcend all accidents of association with nation, caste, party, office or firm.

There are times when it seems to me that these men must be indeed far cleverer and far more subtle than myself, and that they see all that I do and far beyond. But that through some further subtlety they go on being scattered and divided one against another. At any rate, I have to come out of this retirement now in which I have been able to spin the web of my world state so happily, and I have to find just what it is, in my scheme or in my fellows, that bars its conscious use as a guide in public affairs. Then, with such adaptations as may be needed, I have to set about the work of getting them together in relation to it, first in groups and then through literary, journalistic and suchlike activities, and then with a conscious creative direction of monetary and industrial developments.

It is not a task I shall do well. I know that quite plainly. I have no such powers of persuasion and combination and arrangement as old Roderick, for instance. I am a sociable man, but not associative. I am by nature a solitary worker, and almost all my best results have been got with inanimate material, free of all malice or vexatious feelings, in the laboratory, in the open, or in the works' apparatus and routines. But the logic of my faith requires me to go on to this work until at least some abler person takes it on from me and does it better. As old Lubin would have put it, the word of the Lord is upon me and I have now to leave this pleasant wilderness and go down to London, that mighty Babylon, and prophesy. The trouble is that nowadays prophesying is a skilled occupation. The happy days when all that was wanted in a prophet was a large staff, some simple slogan, and a goatskin over his shoulders, and all that he had to do was to go down to the king and make himself unpleasant by repeating his slogan harshly and inexorably, have gone. I conceive that I have to contribute to the early stages of a very intricate, difficult, and enormous creative propaganda that will end in the world state, and it is a task in which I realise I may easily do more harm than good.

I shall begin in the world of English affairs, because there I best know my way about. Here on the Continent I cannot speak to people unless they know English well. I have come to speak French, German, Italian and Spanish fairly well, which means just not well enough for any really satisfactory conversation. I can talk to men like Caillaux and Citroën here in France enough to know they are upon the same line of thought, but not enough for any hand-and-glove relationship. In Germany there are the same difficulties. The next field for me after the English field, therefore, is the American field. Into that I must carry my inquiries and tentatives as soon as I have something started in England. American intellectual life has always been a riddle to me. It is not easy to get at, because it has no central meeting-place, and because it has not as yet developed any such periodical literature and methods of exchange as are needed for mental co-operation at a distance. Elementary ideas pass across the face of America like the sound of a trumpet-blast through a crowd, but you cannot find out what the exceptional and influential men are thinking. They do not converse. They have not the habit. Some talk, but with little give and take.

But I cling to the persuasion that the idea of an economic world republic and a single world civilisation, as an objective, must be developing in many more American brains, and developing further, than over here. That sententious emptiness of outlook, that resonant vacuity affected by so many American business men in their talk and speeches, cannot be anything but a mask and a shyness. I can no more accept the idea that they regard their blessed Constitution, the bragging nationalism that is taught in their common schools, the cold-blooded, jealous and selfish "patriotism" affected by their press as more than temporary conditions on the way to great destiny, than I can imagine my Lords Birkenhead and Buckmaster and Beaverbrook dying together romantically on the stricken field for a rightful king. They know, even more than we know, that these things are provisional. But what is wanted now is something more than knowledge and tacit assumptions; it is recognition, it is admission. The propaganda to which I have to give myself is not a propaganda for acceptance but a propaganda for open acknowledgment.

That is the nature of the work to which, it seems, my energies must be directed. I have just compared myself with a prophet, but, after all, that is not quite what I have to be. That is too grandiose a rôle. I can be neither the prophet nor the leader nor the organiser of a world revolution. I observe it advancing and seek to point it out. It is not the sort of revolution that has leaders and organisers. My work is to be a rather a ferment, a catalytic agent, a provocation. It is a difficult and subtle task, vague and inconclusive in its responses. Never shall I know what I have achieved nor what I have failed to achieve. It is a task to which I am quite unaccustomed and for which I am temperamentally unfitted. But here it is, at hand; I have, so to speak, thrust it into my own hand, and I must do it. I must find out how to do it and train myself where training is needed.

I wish I was not sixty; I wish I had more of Dickon's geniality; I wish there was an inexhaustible supply of nervous energy between myself and the phase of irritation. Sixty. Perhaps I have fifteen years still left, or it may be twenty. Much may be done in such a ration of time, with a flying start and good fortune. But it leaves little margin for delays and setbacks. When I began this book, a year and a half ago, I wrote that life was too short. More and more do I realise that. It is too short, much too short by the scale of modern things. I feel tonight that all my sixty years have been no more than a prelude and that it is now that life and work begin.

I must go warily in what I have to do. For all I know, I may find dozens of men presently attempting the same or kindred things. I have to keep my faith and yet remember that the scheme I profound is provisional and experimental in frame and detail. I have to be patient if presently I find men working upon schemes akin to mine and yet in some respects vexatiously askew to it. I have not been a patient man in such cases hitherto. Hard it is to do one's utmost in contentious things and yet keep one's place; to know that everything is exacted from one and yet that one is nothing, that no cause is great or worthy of service unless it calls indifferently on others and depends on no single person.

I have changed greatly since first I came here. My will was very exhausted then, and now it is renewed. I have rested and rallied myself, and ahead of me I see years of work and a home. I was a very homeless creature, an exile from nearly everything in life, in Paris a year and a half ago. None of this would have happened as it has done without Clementina. How much do I not owe to Clementina – or to the gods of Chance that gave me her!

My thoughts come back to her, to the almost new Clementina, the ultimately real Clementina, who has been growing upon my consciousness during the last few weeks. In November last year I wrote my account of our first meeting in Paris, and it is well I did it then, for now I do not think I could have recalled the brightly adventitious Clementina, the amusing Clementina, I have set down in the passage. The Clementina of the long siege of this *mas* is also beginning to fade, the intermittent Clementina of raids and starling incidents. The new Clementina is near and warm and larger; she fills more of the landscape and sky. She is still a lean, long, red-haired, clear-skinned woman, and she has kept her amber-brown eyes and that sweet oddity of brow and lip and nostril which betrays gnome blood. Her voice is the accustomed thread of bright silver in the world's fabric of sounds. But now she takes possession here and reaches past me into the future, and my future also is hers.

For her, just as for me, the future means much work and effort and little easy-going. She will have many disappointments, for it is her quality to expect vividly; she will often find things intractable and be tried to the limit of her patience. She will have to face endless difficulties in her home-making. She has been so long a nomad, adrift. And often I shall fail her. Just when she will want me to be patient and comforting, I shall be away in body or spirit, irritated by the effort of my own affairs, perplexed and totally absorbed by my perplexities, unwilling to fret a sore situation in my mind by talking about it even to her, by even telling her it is there. It has always been my habit when I work to work to the very limit of my capacity and good temper. We are both going back to activity, to effort and strain. Neither of us is completely and surely sugar-coated. She has not done with tears and resentments, nor I with fits of anger.

But these will be transitory things for us, the wind on the heath of live. This love, which she has invented and made and developed and wrapped about us, will temper and outlast all those storms. She can turn even her exasperations suddenly in mid-explosion into acts of beauty.

I come back to the point from which I started tonight. In some manner I must keep this *mas* in our lives and have it available for us. We must be able to come back at times to our memories of this good interlude and these simplicities. This must be our retreat from angers and peevishness and the incessancy of the world's demands.

My little grey room is a still as death, my papers seem to have fallen asleep in the circle of the lamplight, and outside the night is very still. It is late. I do not know how late, for my wrist-watch has stopped.

This may be the last of some two hundred or more of quiet nights I have spent before this window thinking my world into order. Never has the scene been quite the same. There is an unexampled loveliness at this moment, like nothing I have ever observed before. Everything is silent; there is not a whisper in the fronds of the palm. There are a few stars in the sky, dots upon a vast expanse of silky moonshine. All the hillside of Peyloubet is dreaming; very faint and yet very clear. I can distinguish the pale houses, the terraces, the patches of trees. The moon I cannot see.

It must be setting over the hill behind this house, and everything in the foreground is submerged in shadow and intensely, impenetrably black. The palm-tree, the olive-trees, the medlar rooted in the darkness of my terrace, come out against those luminous phantom slopes in exquisitely sharp silhouettes.

## 13 – *Spring Morning at the Villa Jasmin*

It was a grave, foreseeing man who wrote at this table last night and into the small hours of today. I read over what he has written with a sympathy that is already detached. I was *that*, ten, eight hours ago? The writing runs on with few hesitations, most reasonably. This is to be done, then that. There is a first list of names of people to be interviewed. I like the idea of the World Republic in hot pursuit of Sir Alfred Mond. And the treatment of Clementina is – to put it mildly – rational...

That methodical, anxious, planning fellow is, I admit, my better self. I am still so far identical with him that I can correct some slips of the pen and alter a sentence or so that has gone askew from its intention. But I can write nothing more in the vein.

Nor, it seems, in any vein. For an hour now I have not written a word. I sit at my table, according to the inflexible laws that have ruled the Villa Jasmin since first we came here, but my mind wanders away from me. I can think of nothing but Clementina.

What a queer, chance-begotten, whim-borne history ours has been! At the end, as the beginning of every individual thing, stands careless, irresponsible Chance, smiling at our rules and foresight and previsions. The great life of the species has, it may be, some other law – I more than half believe it has some other law – but this is the quality of its atoms, our individual lives.

Last night I was on terms with the stars. I was not simply historical and geographical; it was astronomical. I was immense. I sat and wrote of the great revolution of mankind, of growing old and of the grave responsibilities of growing old, and of death. This morning I am any age or none. I am a man, and presently my woman is coming down to me, and I have gifts for her and happiness I can bestow upon her.

I wish she were here with me now, but it is my own will that set these rules between us. I have kept her waiting a year and a half and now I am impatient over minutes. I want to tell her all I have decided upon.

Last night I see that I was not even sure when we would change things and doubted whether I would take her at once into this *mas*. Today I am consumed with eagerness to see her and sweep the last cloud from the sunshine of her mind. She will do as I wish. She shall do as I wish. And now. It would be intolerable to think that this afternoon we shall not be bringing down her possessions from the pension to install her here, her dear carpets, her little typewriter, her chosen books and her pots and bowls, and that she and I will not be talking together tonight of the united life that we have now to make for ourselves.

This day is full of sunshine, and only the habits of a year and the fact that Clementina is late in coming to lunch today keep me within hail of this writing-table. I sit, scribble a little, get up again. Thrice have I been downstairs and walked to the end of the terrasse to look up the straight green path down which she will come.

I know exactly how she will come, chin up, striding with that dancing step of hers – she is very light on her feet – her short skirts fluttering, her sweet face grave but charged with a smile – that suddenly flashes out at the sight of me. It is a most ungrudging smile. How often has it not delighted me!

I have been downstairs three times, but I do not know how many times I have looked out of the open window upon the bright array of the waiting lunch-table beside the palm under the Japanese medlar.

There is a quality of fête about the day; the sunlight is as if it had been burnished afresh this morning, and the shadows are still with expectation. Everything is quiet – a holiday quiet. Even my cat motionless upon the parapet might be the soft grey image of a cat. The flower-beds are blazing with colour. The roses are wonderful, and I have never seen such irises and such carnations.

I have felt just this pleasant torment of waiting for a dear event in my childhood at Mowbray, the same restlessness, the same going to look again and again when my father was coming home.

Something must have delayed her, something unimportant, and since there are ways down the hillside and she may come by either, I must needs stay here now and fiddle with these writing things until she comes.

I will wait for her in this room. Here we shall certainly be alone. Down there Jeanne may be hovering interested, and up the slope there may be some peasants at work ready to observe. The few words I have to say are for us alone. That moment must be particularly ours. Here it is I will say these words, here in this room which in theory has always been forbidden her.

I fancy I hear a distant yap, which may be Titza in attendance.

This April day is full of life and stir, full of the warmth and urgency of spring. I trembling, which is absurd.

Titza's little yelp again. And now I know that she is coming. I hear her voice quite close now, her clear, sharp voice, that makes me think of bright cold water. "Titza!" she cries. "Come. Come."

In a few moments now she will be standing in my doorway, doubtful of her reception. She will look gravely at me for an instant and then smile softly when she sees I have turned my chair away from my table. For that means the morning's writing is over.

There will be a moment of mutual scrutiny, for she will realise immediately that something has changed, and as for me, I shall be diffident, I know not why.

"Do I interrupt?" she will ask according to our custom.

And I shall say – My dear! My dear! What shall I say to you?

# The Epilogue

## Note by Sir Richard Clissold

## 1 – *The Death of William Clissold*

And there my brother ceased to write and never wrote again. None of these expectations was to be realised, none of these plans was to be carried out. No more work was required of him, beyond this strange book he had so nearly finished. I cannot guess what more he may have intended to say. There are not even notes for any later sections. It is manifest that as he wrote about her, Miss Campbell, his Clementina, came into the room. He ceased to write. And never returned again to his writing-table before the window.

He was killed in an automobile accident upon the narrow road leading from the gorge of the Loup to Thorenc on April 24th, 1926. Miss Campbell, who was with him in his car, was killed at the same time. This was perhaps only a day, or a day or two, after the unfinished passage was left. He was a skilful, careful driver, careful as every man with a quick imagination must needs be, but the chances were against him. The automobile of Dr Pierre Lot of Haut Thorenc was drawn up as much off that slender track as possible in a place where there was room to pass, and the doctor himself was up at the house of a shepherd which faces the ravine at this spot. My brother was passing the doctor's car when suddenly – so far as we could gather – one of the shepherd's children ran out from behind it and stopped dismayed in mid-road a metre or so from my brother's radiator. No doubt he clapped on his brakes, but also he swerved so as to miss the paralysed child. It was a matter of inches, the doctor told me.

The wheel tracks showed that his left wheels went over the turf edge of the road and that three or four stones loosely embedded in the turf gave way.

The car turned right over sideways, dropped a sheer score of yards, crushed its two passengers, rolled over them completely, and went smashing down for nearly thirty yards more. I have never seen a car so knocked to pieces. It had left a wheel and its seats and two mudguards behind it, and the radiator was pierced by a fir sapling. The doctor was called out to discover what had happened by the terrified child.

Miss Campbell was quite dead. Her head was dreadfully crushed. She must have died instantly. My brother was still alive. His back was broken, and he was mortally injured, but he lived, pointlessly and irrationally, for some time. The doctor seems to have acted with excellent sense and decision. He had straw and sacking and a mattress brought down to him from the shepherd's house, he made my brother as comfortable as he could on the slope where he lay, he had morphia available for an injection, and so without excessive suffering my brother lay in the sunlight for two hours and at last died. The doctor stayed beside him all that time.

The doctor speaks very passable English, and he was at some pains to tell me all that happened.

Billy became conscious after awhile. His eyes questioned the doctor. He said: "Une dame?"

The doctor told him not to trouble his mind, but he attempted to lift his head and look about him. The doctor restrained him.

"Is she badly hurt?" my brother asked, and appeared to have some difficult in recalling his French. "Elle est mal blessée?" The doctor with his instinct for documentation had written the exact words down.

The doctor assured him that she was not suffering. My brother did not hear that. "Testaments," he muttered. "Non. Non. My will. Depositions." He fretted. "Hell! What does one *do?*"

"I realised," said the doctor, "what it was that troubled him. 'Elle est morte,' I said."

"Morte?" He did not recognise the word for a moment, and then his expression became thoughtful and presently quite tranquil, as though a vexatious task had been lifted from his mind. "Good," he said.

Then: "Vraiment? She did not suffer?"

He also said something about "marriage."

The doctor reassured him, speaking slowly and in English. "Killed instantaneament. Never knew that she was dead. Before she could feel."

But after these exchanges the anaesthesia of shock wore off and pain surged up from his injuries. He was dreadfully broken; there was a possibility of frightful suffering. I thank God for the happy chance of the doctor and his morphia. He might have had to bear all that alone or with some peasant staring at him unhelpfully.

Towards the end the pain abated and for a little while his mind came back to the world again; it returned indistinctly and blindly through the drug, like someone who returns to his home in a fog and never quite gets to the door. He talked, but in English and disconnectedly; the doctor made a phonetic note of all that he could not understand. "Il a parlé de Monsieur Dji. Qui est ce Monsieur Dji?"

For a moment I could not recall.

The doctor consulted his notes. At once time my brother had seemed to smile. He has said something which the doctor had written down and could not interpret. "Il a dit quelque chose – '*neeta you Mister Dji.*' Un sourire."

I reflected. "Neat of you, Mr G!" I said.

"I do not understand," said the doctor.

I did not enlighten him. But the reader who has read my brother's book will be in a better position to guess what was going on in his fading brain. These were, I believe, his last words. The mind that came back to say them and smile – I can almost see that wry smile of his – receded into the fog, sank deep into the darkness, vanished from eyes and lips, and was swallowed up altogether in the night. That mind had meant, no doubt, to reach Thorenc and rest there and return to continue this truncated book, and carry out the schemes he had developed in it, but it had swerved just a few inches to the left and got into quite another direction, *sens unique*, from which there was no recall. Just this ineffective backing, this half return, this smile over the shoulder, before the decisive parting of the ways.

In that fashion did my brother leave the world.

Doctor Lot and the two or three peasants and their children who assisted at this scene were presently alone with the twisted and overturned car and with two stiff, broken bodies covered and quiet among the flowers and grey stones and turf upon the afternoon hillside.

## 2 – *Titza Sole Mourner*

There was some delay in communicating with me, and when I reached Provence the remains of my brother and his Clementina had already been brought back to the Villa Jasmin, and two graves had been made for them side by side below the wall of the cemetery of that church of Magagnosc which stands out so boldly to the right of the Nice road. I saw no reason for altering these arrangements. I could not have found a better or more suitable place. The people of Magagnosc are pleasant people and spoke of them both in a very kindly fashion. The two of them lie out on the headland, commanding a wide view of gorge and hill and valley and sea. The sea appears high and far and through a great gap, a broad and broken and flattened V in the hills. The olive terraces and wooded crests of Provence, that beautiful, kindly, slovenly land they both loved so well, spread unheeded before their feet. But old habits of imagination are strong in us all, and it seems to me that my brother must still be seeing and thinking up there, still surveying and planning the future of his world, still considering yet further additions to this book of books he had so spaciously conceived.

I was quite unable to trace any relations of Miss Campbell. I have never heard of anyone so completely alone in the world. Her little "brown muff" of a loulou, Titza, is in quarantine on its way to a kindly English home. It is a little oldish, sharp-nosed bitch, and for a time I feared it would be inconsolable. It wanted to follow its mistress' coffin to the grave, and then decided that she could not possibly be in that queer thing and returned to wander about the Villa Jasmin looking for her and whining. It set off once to find her at her boarding-house and was nearly run over by an automobile as it crossed the high-road, so distraught was it. Jeanne, the servant, who has a great affection for the dog, missed it and followed it and brought it back. It would touch no food for a day or so, and then it ate slinkingly and shamefacedly. But it ate and lived.

For a time I thought of leaving it with Jeanne, but Jeanne herself wants to take another situation; she knows no other way of living, and it is uncertain whether she will be able to carry a pet about with her. I did not care to leave the poor little thing to the chapter of accidents in Provence when I could be sure of kindness and bones and a not too austerely kept garden for it in England. So it broods and frets in quarantine on its way, I hope, to contentment.

They grey Persian cat my brother mentions once or twice, the philosopher of the mirror, betrayed no corresponding depth of feeling, and is quite comfortably housed and satisfied with a widowed lady in Cannes.

### 3 – *Editorial, Fraternal*

So it was my brother never completed his manuscript, and his dream of a vast conspiracy in London and America and throughout the world, to bring order into the dangerous chaos of human affairs, remains an unfinished scheme, a suggestion, a plan waiting to be worked out. I have given it to the reader as he left it, a thing begun, unproved, a project that is still half an interrogation.

He has played so large a part in my life, he has done so much to influence my ideas, that I cannot pretend to be anything but a partisan in the editorial task which falls naturally to me. I, too, am one of these discontented monetarily successful men who find this world unsatisfying. I adhere to his revolution. The show, I agree, is not good enough. It can and it must be made a better show. In all sorts of details I may differ from him, but in the main outlines of his world I am at one with him. If I could have written this book of his I should have written it much as he has done. I have secured suitable help and sought to give these writings as good a text and as advantageous a publication as possible. I have altered nothing and set nothing aside, although in our or two places I am moved – shall I say to demur? – to qualify some strokes that touch me rather nearly.

I do not mean in regard to myself. Occasionally it is manifest he makes fun of me, and I do not see why he should not make fun of me. Maybe it is easier to take me seriously if I am made fun of. There is no malice in what he writes of me, and in places his swift and fitful affectionateness comes darting through in a way that was wholly his own. He has, if I may so put it, been dramatising his economics, and he has seen fit to magnify me a little, magnify me in several ways and make me a representative of the democratic side of big business – the retailing and advertising side, business over the counter and in the newspaper. For this purpose he has even exaggerated my size and weight a little – I was hardly two inches taller than he, and I doubt if I was ever much more than a stone heavier, certainly not two – and, as he admits in one place, he has trimmed and dressed up my talk. But that, I think, is quite fairly done. I do not see why I should refuse to become a type. What I find impossible to leave without a word or so is his discussion of my wife.

And yet that is a very difficult word or so to write.

I understand the necessity he felt for that discussion. It has been one of the things in my life to which I can never be reconciled that my brother and my wife never quite hit it off together. I do not know what it was between them; I have not the gift to fathom that sort of misunderstanding. But he did not understand her, and though she never told me plainly what she thought of him I know she was always a little uneasy in his company. Perhaps she felt he criticised her and it made her self-conscious. And perhaps he felt she criticised him. Here in this book he discusses her, he *puzzles over her*.

It was just that puzzling over which made it impossible for him to be anything but puzzled by her. In life as I have found it, it is better to live first and think people over afterwards. Affection can only be invested with big risks. There are no gilt-edged securities in that world. You must put your heart down and take your chance. But both he and she, who differed in so many other things, had this in common that they thought first. He did not take her for granted so to speak at the beginning as I think one has to take people for granted from the first if affection, real affection, is to have fair play. He took me for granted, and he took our father for granted because we were in his world from the beginning, but the difficulty he had about other people, and the reason why he, who was one of the most interesting and attractive of men, had very few friends and hardly any intimates in the world, was due to this priority of the critical faculty in his mind that forbade provisional acceptance. Two people indeed he loved at last unreservedly, Mrs Evans and, as I now realise here for the first time from his manuscript, Miss Campbell, his Clementina, and in both cases it was because accident and his anger with the injustice of the world towards them, brought them close to him before he could institute that preliminary examination of his that was so hard to pass. Closeness and mutual trust was forced upon him. And so they got their chance.

It is with no little pain that I analyse his analysis of my wife. Pain on his account and on hers. What he says of her is so close to the reality and so far from being true. He too was troubled and dissatisfied by these impalpables that made an easy happy triple friendship impossible. Troubled and unable to recover them. He wanted that triple friendship, I can see, as Minnie wanted it, as we all wanted it. And then that streak of ruthless criticism came in between us, the analyst with his pitiless acids. His merciless intelligence seizes upon the fact that my wife was a little lacking in physical exuberance, that she was deliberate rather than quick in her responses, that it makes out a sort of case against her as a cold and cynical woman. His intelligence seems to oblige him to do this in spite of his disposition to think well of her. He carries her physical quality into his moral estimate of her. Cynicism is the word he weighs and uses. He tones it by a flattering adjective or so but it remains cynicism, albeit of the highest quality, carved ivory cynicism, as he explains. It is so wrong a judgement and yet so close a judegment that it baffles me. There was nothing at all cynical about my wife. It was the last word to use about her. Somehow – for reasons that still defeat me – he could not find the way to her gentle, finely sensitive nature. He saw her delicacies and difficulties as timidity or evasion or indifference. He did not know what things could hurt her, and not to know that much about a human being is to know very little… I have nothing of his aptitude for the suggestion or delineation of character or I would correct his story here, I would tell how beneath the pride and loyalty and honour that he recognised so plainly, lived such a deep sweetness and tenderness, a fragility and withal a courage so humanly appealing, that I have never in truth thought of any other woman as of quite the same species as my Minnie.

I fully realise that she too was difficult with him. I lament it. I cannot understand it. If I justify her against my brother, so equally do I justify him against her unspoken injustice. On both sides it was injustice. They were my nearest and my dearest human beings. I can find no fault with either. They were gold; they were the best of my life. I cannot express what they were to me. And they were opposed. There are, I think, a great multitude of such faint ineluctable estrangements between fine people in this world. Conceivably I am unreasonable. I may be greedy for perfect harmonies in a world in which there must needs be differences of key. But the waste through these fine differences!

There I must leave this. I would have given – I do not know what I would not have given – I would have given extravagantly to have what is told here about Minnie told differently – told with a touch of retrospective affection. It need not have been so very differently. I once showed him a letter of hers – he tells of it – because I thought it was a letter that would make him understand. After her death. But that too, I learn now for the first time, he found artificial. And it was so tender a letter!

I leave things as he wrote them. I cannot mutilate his book.

His loss is still very fresh with me. It has carried me back to our boyhood, to our years as step-sons in close alliance against rather suffocating suppressions, to our hard and strenuous life as students together. I feel there is little to add. Knowing him so well it is easy for me to find his personality quite sufficiently displayed in what he himself has given. I may however say here that he has a far kindlier disposition than is apparent in his manuscript, and that there is a tone of irritation in his attitude to many things in contemporary life that was not a part of his everyday self.

Always, you must remember, he intensifies. He found a sort of fun in overemphasis. He laughed in everyday affairs much more than this book conveys. Print cannot give his eyes, his intonations. Here he sweeps in his picture with bold strokes, in his third book more particularly; he does not trouble to niggle or accommodate his line. It may be that that was unavoidable. It may be there was no other way of telling things forcibly. One must state before one can qualify. He lays bare very great ideas that are coming into men's minds, that are necessarily antagonistic to established institutions, he wants to emphasise their contrast and antagonism, and in doing so his argument takes on a militant quality by the mere force of its direction; his tone becomes aggressive.

He could be very kind, indeed he was habitually kind to individuals, but he was impatient with humanity generally, and particularly so with certain classes and professions that seemed to him to embody the old order. Politicians, royalties, schoolmasters, dons, professional soldiers, professional literary men; he can hardly mention them without a cuff. I do not think he ever once names the unfortunate Ramsay MacDonald without an opprobrious epithet. Yet MacDonald is a man of conscious distinction, refined, high-principled and exceptionally cultivated. And how rough he is with our poor dear half-brother, Walpole Stent!

There was an evident change in my brother as his book progressed, due to the increasing reality of this vision he was evoking of a greater world, close at hand and within our reach. The more he believed in it – if I may be paradoxical – the more massive it became, the greater was the effort needed to believe, the greater the nervous stress. His expressed disrespect for contemporary conditions became more and more resentful. He was always a mocker at the vapid assurance of the established thing, even as a student he was a great mocker; he tells a little of that; but as his conviction that much that he mocked at was already superannuated and unnecessary, that here and now it could be replaced by better things and was not being so replaced, gathered power in him, his mockery betrayed with ever increasing plainness the anger surging up beneath. "Don't they mean to move it after all?" he asked himself. "Is all this still going on?" The effort for self-control is not always sustained. "Oh! stop this damned foolery! An end to this life-wasting foolery!" writhes and mutters beneath many a passage of this book.

His book in this regard does but parallel his life. His disposition to fly in the face of mass opinion was evident even in our student days. He recoiled from all crowds and not simply from "oafish" royalist crowds. With every year he seemed to trouble himself less about the standards and approval of his community. He became more and more estranged from the normal man. His disregard of minor social obligations became conspicuous after the war. He ignored people, neglected invitations, dropped all irksome civilities. He no longer kept up with current books and plays and the interests of the day. He was "leaving the show." If he dressed and behaved in the usual fashion it was simply to save himself the bother of being eccentric. He cared too little for everyday usage in such superficial things even to seem to challenge it.

There was indeed always something isolated about him. From the beginning he had an exceptional quality. Even as a boy he was rather alone. He was precocious and he had a marked individuality, and he went directly for the things that appealed to him. Cricket bored him as it bores most clever boys, because of the amount of time it demands if it is to be played well. He rebelled against that priggishness in games which is so sedulously forced upon English schoolboys, and on the other hand a laboratory drew him magnetically. But he was never aloof nor outcast. He could make himself very agreeable to other boys, and despite the harsh things he says about their profession his masters not only did not persecute him but one or two of them took a vivid interest in him. He did not sulk nor shirk; at times he could be delightfully facetious. But his inner isolation grew as his life went on out of his circumstances and with his convictions. Gradually he found out that he did not like the general tenor of existence, prevalent ideas, prevalent ways of behaving about things. People seemed to be wasting their lives in dull and stupid activities, and he felt that the best of his own possibilities were being wasted in the general waste. His belief in man's possibilities made him at times inhuman. He was harsh with our kind because he expected so much from it. His flight to the simple life of Provence, which he tells of so appreciatively, his increasing disposition to return thither and think of the world from that perspective, was only the coming to the surface of an innate tendency to free himself from immediate and distracting things.

Yet for all his isolation he was in no sense self-sufficient, and there I think lies the clue both to the religiosity of his attitude towards the Being of the Species and to the deeper element in the love affairs he describes. If he left his ordinary world it was not because he did not want a world, but because he wanted one more helpful and akin. Ours in London gave him too little that was worth having and encumbered him too much. The love affairs he tells about so frankly betray far more than a temperamental proclivity. It was as true of him as it can be of anyone that he was born out of his time. In the more "adult" days of 2026 AD he might have found an easy circle of understanding friends, and lovers after his own heart. He was by no means an unhappy man; he was temperamentally sanguine; unpleasant things made him combative rather than miserable; but the progressive detachment of his ideas, his undervaluation of things still widely accepted, the fear he seemed always to be fighting down that the crowd with its gregarious instincts might at last defeat him and his kind and all his dreams and go its own road to extinction, threw the shadow of a great loneliness on him, and he would set about exorcising it in ways which displayed only too plainly his almost unconscious contempt for established conventions.

His life with the notorious Mrs Evans, which did for a time estrange him from us, was more than an unconscious defiance. She was a banner for him. He would believe no ill of her. He would not listen to a word against her. He would see no harm in what she had done. She was his way of damning "all this chastity nonsense," as he would have called it at that time, and much else besides. He had acquired already in those days a real prejudice against women who were socially correct. That submission and acquiescence should count as possible virtues, roused him to fierce and practical denials. As hard was it for him to condemn rebellious courage, even such rebellious courage as that of Mrs Evans.

There must have been the same element of defiance in the beginning of the last affair with Clementina Campbell. He does not admit it but it peeps between the lines. He never told me of her, but that may have been because the apt occasion never came to us. We were both busy men, we did not meet very much in 1925, and he never wrote a letter if he could help it. I did not even know she existed until I went down to Provence after his death. I am extremely sorry that I never saw her; that except for a few snapshots I found of her in a drawer, I do not even know what she was like. Whatever his state of mind about her at first, whatever the quality of their earlier relationship, there can be no doubt of the depth and sincerity of their affection at the end. Mutual affection I think of a better quality than he had ever had before. His tenderness for her is manifest every time he mentions her. But it is not all tenderness towards her. He pulls at his cord. It does not need close reading between the lines to detect his disposition to symbolise her as he symbolised Mrs Evans before her, and turn her to his own rebellious uses. With her he might have succeeded. The way the people spoke of her round Magagnosc and Grasse suggested a very charming person indeed, and it may be that in there laxer times and married to her, he would have been able to reinstate her completely in the world that had cast her out. He loved her very much it is plain, more I should think than he had ever loved any other woman, but I am sure that the spectacle of the old order eating its own judgement upon her would have played no small part in his satisfaction at her happiness.

He was coming back into the world with her and he was coming back for a last great fight, a completer, more systematic fight than he had ever essayed before, against most established things. He was still full of life.

I wish he could have fought that fight. I wish he could have fought that fight and that I could have been beside him. It is not natural that he should have gone before me. He has been a great thing in my world, from those early days of brooding and brilliance when with a disadvantage of two years he could beat me in my school work almost as a matter of course. He has refreshed me and stimulated me all my life; I cannot imagine what I should have become if it had not been for his corrections. Circumstances threw us very closely together. Never at any time were we more than half estranged. And beyond habit and companionship there was something in him, strong yet weak, defiant yet dependent, free and obstinate in thought and action and yet cravingly affectionate, that leaves a heartache for him I must carry now to the end.

It is a curious thing to say, but I do not realise yet that he is dead. He had been so much in my life since its conscious beginnings that it is difficult to feel that he has gone right out of the world, that he is not away in America or Siberia or South Africa and presently coming back. I had a sense of his possible comments whenever I wrote. I have that still. If tomorrow I found a laconic postcard from him among my letters I should not be surprised. It would be only after a minute or so that I should begin to perceive it strange.

And it is all over. I think of an eager little chap in knickerbockers, with bright eyes and a quick colour – guying his governess or bolting from me with a squeak between delight and dismay after some outrageous unexpected attack. I remember him standing naked in the sunshine on a beach somewhere in France and how it dawned upon me that he was beautifully built. I fight again in a great scrap we had with some French boys at Montpellier. And there is the keen face of the young socialist, too intent upon his argument to note the spring flowers in Kensington Gardens, and the student gone clean over my head out of the common laboratory through the dark-green door that shut off research from the rank and file of learners. And so the memories come crowding one after the other, the better half before the twenties were reached. As it comes nearer the figure is large but less bright. I see him in tennis flannels at Lambs Court, now wary, now wild as a cat in thundery weather, a most uncertain player always; I see him smiling recognition at me on the gangway of a big liner or threading his way to my corner through the groups in the club smoking-room. And at the end comes the picture, so irrelevant and so dreadful, of that crumpled automobile I saw amidst torn turf and snapped-off saplings.

My dear brother!

*Παντα ῥει.* He too has passed. These words, and they are wonderful words and come like a refrain throughout his book, shall be put as his sole epitaph upon his grave.

# H G Wells

## The History of Mr Polly

Mr Polly is one of literature's most enduring and universal creations. An ordinary man, trapped in an ordinary life, Mr Polly makes a series of ill-advised choices that bring him to the very brink of financial ruin. Determined not to become the latest victim of the economic retrenchment of the Edwardian age, he rebels in magnificent style and takes control of his life once and for all.

ISBN 0-7551-0404-8

# H G Wells

## In the Days of the Comet

Revenge was all Leadford could think of as he set out to find the unfaithful Nettie and her adulterous lover. But this was all to change when a new comet entered the earth's orbit and totally reversed the natural order of things. The Great Change had occurred and any previous emotions, thoughts, ambitions, hopes and fears had all been removed. Free love, pacifism and equality were now the name of the game. But how would Leadford fare in this most utopian of societies?

ISBN 0-7551-0406-4

# H G WELLS

## THE INVISIBLE MAN

On a cold wintry day in the depths of February a stranger appeared in The Coach and Horses requesting a room. So strange was this man's appearance, dressed from head to foot with layer upon layer of clothing, bandages and the most enormous glasses, that the owner, Mrs Hall, quite wondered what accident could have befallen him. She didn't know then that he was invisible – but the rumours soon began to spread…

H G Wells' masterpiece *The Invisible Man* is a classic science-fiction thriller showing the perils of scientific advancement.

ISBN 0-7551-0407-2

# H G Wells

## The Island of Dr Moreau

A shipwreck in the South Seas brings a doctor to an island paradise. Far from seeing this as the end of his life, Dr Moreau seizes the opportunity to play God and infiltrate a reign of terror in this new kingdom. Endless cruel and perverse experiments ensue and see a series of new creations – the 'Beast People' – all of which must bow before the deified doctor.

Originally a Swiftian satire on the dangers of authority and submission, Wells' *The Island of Dr Moreau* can now just as well be read as a prophetic tale of genetic modification and mutability.

ISBN 0-7551-0408-0

# H G Wells

## Men Like Gods

Mr Barnstaple was ever such a careful driver, careful to indicate before every manoeuvre and very much in favour of slowing down at the slightest hint of difficulty. So however could he have got the car into a skid on a bend on the Maidenhead road?

When he recovered himself he was more than a little relieved to see the two cars that he had been following still merrily motoring along in front of him. It seemed that all was well – except that the scenery had changed, rather a lot. It was then that the awful truth dawned: Mr Barnstaple had been hurled into another world altogether.

How would he ever survive in this supposed Utopia, and more importantly, how would he ever get back?

ISBN 0-7551-0413-7

# H G Wells

## The War of the Worlds

'No one would have believed in the last years of the nineteenth century that this world was being watched keenly and closely by intelligences greater than man's...'

A series of strange atmospheric disturbances on the planet Mars may raise concern on Earth but it does little to prepare the inhabitants for imminent invasion. At first the odd-looking Martians seem to pose no threat for the intellectual powers of Victorian London, but it seems man's superior confidence is disastrously misplaced. For the Martians are heading towards victory with terrifying velocity.

*The War of the Worlds* is an expertly crafted invasion story that can be read as a frenzied satire on the dangers of imperialism and occupation.

ISBN 0-7551-0426-9

## OTHER TITLES BY H G WELLS AVAILABLE DIRECT FROM HOUSE OF STRATUS

| Quantity | £ | $(US) | $(CAN) | € |
|---|---|---|---|---|
| FICTION | | | | |
| ANN VERONICA | 9.99 | 14.95 | 22.95 | 16.50 |
| APROPOS OF DOLORES | 9.99 | 14.95 | 22.95 | 16.50 |
| THE AUTOCRACY OF MR PARHAM | 9.99 | 14.95 | 22.95 | 16.50 |
| BABES IN THE DARKLING WOOD | 9.99 | 14.95 | 22.95 | 16.50 |
| BEALBY | 9.99 | 14.95 | 22.95 | 16.50 |
| THE BROTHERS *AND* THE CROQUET PLAYER | 7.99 | 12.95 | 19.95 | 14.50 |
| BRYNHILD | 9.99 | 14.95 | 22.95 | 16.50 |
| THE BULPINGTON OF BLUP | 9.99 | 14.95 | 22.95 | 16.50 |
| THE DREAM | 9.99 | 14.95 | 22.95 | 16.50 |
| THE FIRST MEN IN THE MOON | 9.99 | 14.95 | 22.95 | 16.50 |
| THE FOOD OF THE GODS | 9.99 | 14.95 | 22.95 | 16.50 |
| THE HISTORY OF MR POLLY | 9.99 | 14.95 | 22.95 | 16.50 |
| THE HOLY TERROR | 9.99 | 14.95 | 22.95 | 16.50 |
| IN THE DAYS OF THE COMET | 9.99 | 14.95 | 22.95 | 16.50 |
| THE INVISIBLE MAN | 7.99 | 12.95 | 19.95 | 14.50 |
| THE ISLAND OF DR MOREAU | 7.99 | 12.95 | 19.95 | 14.50 |
| KIPPS: THE STORY OF A SIMPLE SOUL | 9.99 | 14.95 | 22.95 | 16.50 |
| LOVE AND MR LEWISHAM | 9.99 | 14.95 | 22.95 | 16.50 |
| MARRIAGE | 9.99 | 14.95 | 22.95 | 16.50 |
| MEANWHILE | 9.99 | 14.95 | 22.95 | 16.50 |
| MEN LIKE GODS | 9.99 | 14.95 | 22.95 | 16.50 |
| A MODERN UTOPIA | 9.99 | 14.95 | 22.95 | 16.50 |
| MR BRITLING SEES IT THROUGH | 9.99 | 14.95 | 22.95 | 16.50 |

ALL HOUSE OF STRATUS BOOKS ARE AVAILABLE FROM GOOD BOOKSHOPS OR DIRECT FROM THE PUBLISHER:

**Internet:** **www.houseofstratus.com** including synopses and features.

**Email:** **sales@houseofstratus.com**
**info@houseofstratus.com**
(please quote author, title and credit card details.)

## OTHER TITLES BY H G WELLS AVAILABLE DIRECT FROM HOUSE OF STRATUS

| Quantity | £ | $(US) | $(CAN) | € |
|---|---|---|---|---|
| **FICTION** | | | | |
| ☐ THE NEW MACHIAVELLI | 9.99 | 14.95 | 22.95 | 16.50 |
| ☐ THE PASSIONATE FRIENDS | 9.99 | 14.95 | 22.95 | 16.50 |
| ☐ THE SEA LADY | 7.99 | 12.95 | 19.95 | 14.50 |
| ☐ THE SHAPE OF THINGS TO COME | 9.99 | 14.95 | 22.95 | 16.50 |
| ☐ THE TIME MACHINE | 7.99 | 12.95 | 19.95 | 14.50 |
| ☐ TONO-BUNGAY | 9.99 | 14.95 | 22.95 | 16.50 |
| ☐ THE UNDYING FIRE | 7.99 | 12.95 | 19.95 | 14.50 |
| ☐ THE WAR IN THE AIR | 9.99 | 14.95 | 22.95 | 16.50 |
| ☐ THE WAR OF THE WORLDS | 7.99 | 12.95 | 19.95 | 14.50 |
| ☐ THE WHEELS OF CHANCE | 7.99 | 12.95 | 19.95 | 14.50 |
| ☐ WHEN THE SLEEPER WAKES | 9.99 | 14.95 | 22.95 | 16.50 |
| ☐ THE WIFE OF SIR ISAAC HARMAN | 9.99 | 14.95 | 22.95 | 16.50 |
| ☐ THE WONDERFUL VISIT | 7.99 | 12.95 | 19.95 | 14.50 |
| **NON-FICTION** | | | | |
| ☐ THE CONQUEST OF TIME *AND* THE HAPPY TURNING | 7.99 | 12.95 | 19.95 | 14.50 |
| ☐ EXPERIMENT IN AUTOBIOGRAPHY VOLUMES 1,2 | 12.99 | 19.95 | 29.95 | 22.00 |
| ☐ H G WELLS IN LOVE | 9.99 | 14.95 | 22.95 | 16.50 |
| ☐ THE OPEN CONSPIRACY AND OTHER WRITINGS | 9.99 | 14.95 | 22.95 | 16.50 |

**PAYMENT** (Please tick currency you wish to use):

☐ £ (Sterling) ☐ $ (US) ☐ $ (CAN) ☐ € (Euros)

Allow for shipping costs charged per order plus an amount per book as set out in the tables below:

CURRENCY/DESTINATION

| | £(Sterling) | $(US) | $(CAN) | €(Euros) |
|---|---|---|---|---|
| **Cost per order** | | | | |
| UK | 1.50 | 2.25 | 3.50 | 2.50 |
| Europe | 3.00 | 4.50 | 6.75 | 5.00 |
| North America | 3.00 | 3.50 | 5.25 | 5.00 |
| Rest of World | 3.00 | 4.50 | 6.75 | 5.00 |
| **Additional cost per book** | | | | |
| UK | 0.50 | 0.75 | 1.15 | 0.85 |
| Europe | 1.00 | 1.50 | 2.25 | 1.70 |
| North America | 1.00 | 1.00 | 1.50 | 1.70 |
| Rest of World | 1.50 | 2.25 | 3.50 | 3.00 |

PLEASE SEND CHEQUE OR INTERNATIONAL MONEY ORDER
payable to: HOUSE OF STRATUS LTD or HOUSE OF STRATUS INC. or card payment as indicated

STERLING EXAMPLE

**Cost of book(s):**...................... Example: 3 x books at £6.99 each: £20.97

**Cost of order:**...................... Example: £1.50 (Delivery to UK address)

**Additional cost per book:**............... Example: 3 x £0.50: £1.50

**Order total including shipping:**........... Example: £23.97

VISA, MASTERCARD, SWITCH, AMEX:

☐☐☐☐☐☐☐☐☐☐☐☐☐☐☐☐☐☐☐☐

**Issue number (Switch only):** ☐☐☐

**Start Date:** ☐☐/☐☐

**Expiry Date:** ☐☐/☐☐

**Signature:** ____________________

**NAME:** ____________________

**ADDRESS:** ____________________

**COUNTRY:** ____________________

**ZIP/POSTCODE:** ____________________

Please allow 28 days for delivery. Despatch normally within 48 hours.
Prices subject to change without notice.
Please tick box if you do not wish to receive any additional information. ☐

House of Stratus publishes many other titles in this genre; please check our website (**www.houseofstratus.com**) for more details.